KU-580-301

Summer Loving

JoAnn Ross

Tiffany White

Marie Ferrarella

Diane Pershing

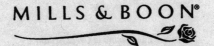

MILLS & BOON®

*First published in Great Britain 1998
by Harlequin Mills & Boon Limited,
Eton House, 18-24 Paradise Road,
Richmond, Surrey, TW9 1SR*

SUMMER LOVING © Harlequin Books S.A. 1998

*The publisher acknowledges the copyright holders of the
individual work as follows:*

IT HAPPENED ONE WEEK © JoAnn Ross 1996
MALE FOR SALE © Anna Eberhardt 1995
TRACI ON THE SPOT © Marie Rydzynski-Ferrarella 1997
Illustrations © Kim Barnes 1997
FIRST DATE: HONEYMOON © Diane Pershing 1997

ISBN 0 263 81184 0

49-9806

*Printed and bound in Great Britain
by Caledonian Book Manufacturing Ltd, Glasgow*

Bachelor Auction

There was no way she was going home to St. Louis without a male in tow. She picked up a 'Male for Sale' catalogue from the stack by the door. Unfortunately, there were no pictures to go with the profiles. She looked at each of the bachelors in turn, trying to guess which one went with the description that had caught her fancy.

At least she was sure it wasn't the bachelor at the end of the row. He certainly wasn't her idea of an escort for a formal wedding. He leaned back with his legs sprawled apart. His body was lanky and lean and she would have had to be dead not to notice it. He had a certain arrogance that would never do.

With her eyes glued to the man in the suit she'd decided on, Noelle placed the highest bid and won her bachelor. Her worries were over.

But the guy in the business suit didn't stand.

Noelle tried not to faint when the gorgeous, tousled blond outlaw stood and started to move towards her.

She'd really gone and done it this time!

Dear Reader,

Welcome to Mills & Boon's® *Summer Loving*, our really great value bumper offering for holiday reading this year. Four wonderfully talented authors bring you four complete, fun-filled sexy romances. JoAnn Ross and Tiffany White are stars from our Temptation® line, Marie Ferrarella has over fifty romances to her credit and Diane Pershing's writing just sparkles with love and laughter.

JoAnn Ross married her first love—twice!—so in *It Happened One Week* she knows exactly what she's talking about—the joy, the heartbreak and the final ecstasy! On the other hand, Tiffany White brings strangers together, a man and a woman who would never have met if she hadn't decided to *buy* a date for her *younger* sister's wedding. She certainly got more than she bargained for!

In *First Date: Honeymoon*, spend June in Europe's most romantic locations, pretend to be married to a tall, handsome hunk, and wait and see what happens...

Finally, in our fourth story, Marie Ferrarella's Morgan Brigham knew his summer playmate was about to marry Mr Wrong, but how to stop her?

Enjoy them all and have a wonderful summer!

The Editors

♥ First Love Quiz ♥

When you think of your first love, you

A) smile at the memories
B) wonder what you ever saw in him
C) wonder if he's single and available

If you came face-to-face with your first love, you would

A) give him a friendly hug
B) pray he doesn't recognize you
C) dream of being his bride

If your first love offered you a second chance, you would

A) fix him up on a blind date with a great girl
B) fix him up on a blind date from hell
C) elope

JOANN ROSS

It Happened One Week

About the author

I'm often asked, 'Where do you get your ideas?' At such times, writers are tempted to invent some lofty, literary answer. I've decided to tell you the truth.

This story was conceived late one summer night in a Karaoke bar, where I was having an after-dinner drink with a few of my foreign editors and Dianne Moggy, a senior editor based in Canada. When the man behind the keyboard began playing 'Love Letters in the Sand', Dianne looked up at the oversized screen and said, 'JoAnn, look, there's a great book idea!'

My first thought was that I didn't have time to write another book. I was, after all, already committed to several novels for Temptation® and another mainstream novel for MIRA®. But watching the video of the waves rolling up on the sparkling sand started my imagination stirring. By breakfast, I knew I had to write *It Happened One Week*.

This is one of my more autobiographical stories, drawing from my teenage days in Oregon and my own bittersweet summer romance. Fortunately, like my hero and heroine, Jay and I eventually got back together and went on to live mostly happily ever after.

Happy Reading!

JoAnn Ross

To Dianne Moggy—who provided the inspiration

Prologue

➤➤ ➤➤

Satan's Cove

The letters had been painstakingly carved into the shifting silver sands. Although she could see them from the top of the jagged cliff overlooking the Pacific Ocean, fifteen-year-old Amanda Stockenberg could not make out the message.

As she descended the stone steps to the beach, slowly at first, then faster, until she was nearly running, the words became clearer.

Dane loves Amanda.

Despite the fact that she'd spent most of last night crying, Amanda began to weep.

He was waiting for her in their secret, private place. Just as he'd promised. Just as she'd hoped.

Smugglers' Cave, carved by aeons of wind and ocean out of the rocky seaside cliffs, had long been rumored to be one of the local sites where pirates had once hidden stolen booty before moving it inland.

Amanda wasn't interested in the legends about the pirates' nefarious behavior. And despite the violence that supposedly occurred here, to her, Smugglers' Cave was the most romantic place on earth.

It was here, on a star-spangled July Fourth night, while the glare of fireworks lit up the night sky, that Dane first kissed her. Then kissed her again. And again. Until she thought she'd literally melt from ecstasy.

"I thought you wouldn't come," she cried, flinging herself dramatically into his strong dark arms. Her avid mouth captured his. The kiss was hot and long and bittersweet.

"I told you I would," he reminded her, after they finally came up for air.

"I know." Her hands were linked together around his neck. Her young, lithe body was pressed against his so tightly that it would have been impossible for the morning ocean breeze to come between them. "But I was so afraid you'd be mad at me."

"Mad?" Dane looked honestly surprised by the idea. "Why would I be mad at you?"

"For leaving." Just thinking about her imminent departure caused the moisture in Amanda's sea blue eyes to overflow.

"You don't have any choice, sweetheart." With more tenderness than she would have imagined possible, he brushed her tears away with his fingertips. "We've both known that from the beginning."

"That doesn't make it any less awful!" she wailed.

"No." Despite his brave words, Dane's dark eyes were every bit as bleak as hers as he traced her trembling, downturned pink lips with a tear-dampened finger. "It doesn't."

The tender touch left behind a taste of salt born of her overwhelming sorrow. "We could run away," she said desperately, grabbing his hand and holding it tightly between both of hers. "Just you and I. Somewhere no one could ever find us. To Wyoming. Or Florida."

"Don't think I haven't been tempted." His lips curved at the idea, but even as distressed as she was, Amanda noticed that the smile didn't reach his eyes. "But running away is never the answer, princess."

She was too desperate, too unhappy, to listen to reason. "But—"

"We can't." His tone, while gentle, was firm. "As attractive as the idea admittedly is, it's wrong."

"How can love be wrong?"

Dane sighed, looking far older, far more world-weary than his nineteen years. "You're only fifteen years old—"

"I'll be sixteen next week."

"I know." This time the reluctant smile turned his eyes to the hue of rich, warm chocolate. "But you still have your entire life ahead of you, honey. I'm not going to be responsible for ruining it."

"But you wouldn't!" she cried on a wail that scattered a trio of sea gulls. "You'd make it better. Perfect, even."

As much as she'd first resisted joining her family for this annual summer vacation on the Oregon coast, the moment she'd first seen Smugglers' Inn's sexy young bellhop, lifeguard, and all-around handyman, Amanda had changed her mind.

Over the past four glorious weeks, her life had been focused on Dane Cutter. He was all she wanted. All she would ever want. She'd love him, Amanda vowed, forever.

But now, she didn't want to waste time talking. Not when their time together was coming to an end, like sands falling through some hateful hourglass. Rising on her toes, she pressed her lips against his once more.

The morning mist swirled around them; overhead, sea gulls squawked stridently as they circled, searching for mussels in the foaming surge. Caught up in emotions every bit as strong—and as old—as the forces that had formed the craggy coastline, neither Dane nor Amanda heard them.

The ocean's roar became a distant buzz in Amanda's ears. For this glorious suspended moment, time ceased to have meaning. The hungry kiss could have lasted a minute, an hour, an eternity.

Finally, the blare of a car horn managed to infiltrate its way into Amanda's consciousness. She tried to ignore it, but it was soon followed by the sound of an irritated male voice cutting through the fog.

Dane dragged his mouth from hers. "Your father's calling." He skimmed his lips up her cheeks, which were damp again from the cold ocean mist and her tears.

"I know." She swiped at the tears with the backs of her trembling hands, looking, Dane thought, more like an injured child than the almost-grown-up woman she insisted that she was. Unwilling, unable to leave, she twined her arms around his neck again and clung.

For not the first time since her arrival in Satan's Cove, Dane found himself sorely tested. For not the first time, he reminded himself that she was far too young for the thoughts he kept having, the feelings he kept experiencing. But even as his mind struggled to hold on to that crucial fact—like a drowning man clinging to a piece of driftwood in a storm-tossed sea—his body was literally aching for fulfillment.

Dane was not inexperienced. He'd discovered, since losing his virginity to a sexy blond Miss Depoe Bay the summer of his sixteenth year, that sex was easy to come by. Especially during vacation season, when the beaches were filled with beautiful girls looking for a summer fling.

But he'd never wanted a girl as he wanted Amanda. What was worse, he'd never *needed* a girl as he needed Amanda. Accustomed to keeping a tight rein on his emotions, Dane wasn't at all comfortable with the effect Amanda Stockenberg had had on him from the beginning.

Finally, although it was nearly the hardest thing he'd ever had to do—second only to refusing her ongoing, seductive pleas to make love these past weeks—Dane gently, patiently, unfastened Amanda's hold on him.

"You have to go," he said again, prying her hands from around his neck. He kissed her fingers one at a time. "But it's not over, princess. Not unless you want it to be."

Distraught as she was, Amanda failed to hear the question—and the uncharacteristic lack of assurance—in his guarded tone.

"Never!" she swore with all the fervor of a young woman in the throes of her first grand love. "I promise."

Her father called out again. The Volvo station wagon's horn blared. Once. Twice. A third time.

Giving Dane one last desperate kiss, Amanda spun around, sobbing loudly as she ran up the rock stairs. She did not—could not—look back.

He stood there all alone, hands shoved deep into the pockets of his jeans, and watched her leave, resisting the urge to call out to her. He heard the car drive off, taking her far away from Satan's Cove. Away from him.

Dane stayed on the windswept beach for a long, silent time, watching as the relentless ebb and flow of the tide slowly, inexorably, washed away the love letter he'd written in the drifting silver sand.

1

Portland, Oregon
Ten years later

"This can't be happening. Not to me. Not now!"

Amanda Stockenberg stared in disbelief at the television screen where towering red-and-orange flames were engulfing the Mariner Seaside Golf Resort and Conference Center located on the Oregon coast.

"It *is* lousy timing," her administrative assistant, Susan Chin, agreed glumly. It had been Susan who'd alerted Amanda to the disaster, after hearing a news bulletin on the radio.

"That has to be the understatement of the millennium," Amanda muttered as she opened a new roll of antacids.

Hoping for the best, but fearing the worst, she'd left a meeting and run down the hall to the conference room.

Now, as the two women stood transfixed in front of the television, watching the thick streams of water prove ineffectual at combating the massive blaze, Amanda could see her entire career going up in smoke right along with the five-star resort.

She groaned as the hungry flames devoured the lovely cedar-shake shingled roof. The scene shifted as the cameras cut away to show the crews of helmeted firemen valiantly fighting the fire. From the grim expressions on their soot-stained faces, she sensed that they knew their efforts to be a lost cause.

And speaking of lost causes...

"It's obvious we're going to have to find a new site for the corporate challenge," she said, cringing when what was left of the wooden roof caved in with a deafening roar. Water from the fire hoses hit the flames, turned to steam and mixed with the clouds of thick gray smoke.

"I'd say that's a given," Susan agreed glumly. "Unless you want to have the group camping out on the beach. Which, now that I think about it, isn't such a bad idea. After all, the entire idea of this coming week is to present the creative teams with challenges to overcome."

"Getting any of the managers of *this* company to work together as a team is going to be challenge enough." Amanda sank into a chair, put her elbows on the long rectangular mahogany conference table and began rubbing at her temples, where a headache had begun to pound. "Without tossing in sleeping in tents on wet sand and bathing out of buckets."

Advertising had been a cutthroat, shark-eat-shark business since the first Babylonian entrepreneur had gotten the bright idea to chisel the name of his company onto a stone tablet. Competition was always fierce, and everyone knew that the battle went not only to the most creative, but to the most ruthless.

Even so, Amanda felt the employees of Janzen, Lawton and Young took the idea of healthy competition to unattractive and often unprofitable extremes. Apparently, Ernst Janzen, senior partner of the company that had recently purchased Amanda's advertising agency, seemed to share her feelings. Which was why the idea of corporate-management teams was born in the first place.

In theory, the concept of art, copy, and marketing working together on each step of a project seemed ideal. With everyone marching in unison toward the same finish line, the firm would undoubtedly regain superiority over its competitors.

That was the plan. It was, Amanda had agreed, when she'd first heard of it, extremely logical. Unfortunately, there was little about advertising that was the least bit logical.

The agency that had hired her directly after her graduation from UCLA, Connally Creative Concepts, or C.C.C., had made a name for itself by creating witty, appealing and totally original advertising that persuaded and made the sale through its ability to charm the prospect.

Although its location in Portland, Oregon, was admittedly a long way from Madison Avenue, some of the best copywriters and art directors in the country had been more than willing to leave Manhattan and take pay cuts in order to work long hours under the tutelage of Patrick Connally. C.C.C. had been like a family, Patrick Connally playing the role of father to whom everyone came for inspiration and guidance.

Unfortunately, two years ago Patrick Connally had died of a heart attack at the age of seventy-five, after a heated game of tennis. His widow, eager to retire to Sun City, Arizona, had sold the agency to another company. Eight months after that, the new owner merged the united agencies with yet a third creative shop.

Unsurprisingly, such multiple mergers in such a short span of time resulted in the dismissal of several longtime employees as executives trimmed excess staff. A mood of anxiety settled over the offices and morale plummeted as everyone held their collective breath, waiting to see who was going to be "downsized" next.

After the initial purge, things had seemed to be settling down until the advertising wars kicked up again. A six-month battle that played out daily on the pages of *The Wall Street Journal* had resulted in an unfriendly takeover by the international mega-agency of Janzen, Lawton and Young, and those employees who'd been breathing at last, found their livelihoods once again in jeopardy.

Janzen, Lawton and Young had long had a reputation for the most artless and offensive commercials to run on American airwaves. But it also boasted the highest profits in the business. In order to keep profits up to the promised levels, a new wave of massive staff cuts had hit the agency.

Morale plummeted to new lows.

Unsurprisingly, the same creative people who had once been responsible for some of the most innovative—and effective—advertising in the business, turned on one another.

A recent case in point was today's client meeting. The creative group had been assigned to propose a new concept for a popular line of gourmet ice cream. From day one, the members of the recently established team had been at each other's throats like a pack of out-of-control pit bulls.

"I can't believe you seriously expect me to be a part of this presentation," Marvin Kenyon, the head copywriter, had complained after viewing the animated sequence proposed by award-winning art director Julian Palmer.

"It's a team effort," Amanda reminded him mildly. "And you *are* a valuable member of the team."

The copywriter, who'd won his share of awards himself, folded his arms over the front of his blue oxford-cloth shirt and said, "I categorically refuse to share blame for something as sophomoric and static as that animation sequence."

"Sophomoric?" Julian Palmer rose to his full height of five feet five inches tall. What he lacked in stature, he more than made up for in ego. "Static? Since when are you an expert on visuals?"

"I know enough to see that if we present your idea, we'll blow the account for sure," Marvin retorted. "Hell, a baboon with a fistful of crayons could undoubtedly create a more visually appealing storyboard."

Julian arched an eyebrow as he adjusted the already perfect Windsor knot in his Italian-silk tie. "This from a man who creates—" he waved the printed sheets Marvin had handed out when he'd first arrived in the presentation room like a battle flag "—mindless drivel?"

"Drivel?" Marvin was on his feet in a shot, hands folded into fists as he came around the long, polished mahogany table.

"Marvin," Amanda protested, "please sit down. Julian didn't mean it, did you, Julian?"

"I never say anything I don't mean," the artistic director replied. "But in this case, I may have been mistaken."

"There, see?" Amanda soothed, feeling as if she were refereeing a fight between two toddlers in a kindergarten sandbox. "Julian admits he was mistaken, Marvin. Perhaps you can amend your comment about his work."

"I *was* wrong to call it drivel," Julian agreed. "That's too kind a description for such cliché-ridden rubbish."

"That does it!" Marvin, infamous for his quicksilver temper, was around the table like a shot. He'd grabbed hold of his team member's chalk-gray vest and for a moment Amanda feared that the two men were actually going to come to blows, when the conference-room door opened and the client arrived with Don Patterson, the marketing manager, on his heels.

"Am I interrupting something?" the longtime client, a man in his mid-fifties whose addiction to ice cream had made him a very wealthy man, asked.

"Only a momentary creative difference of opinion," Amanda said quickly. "Good afternoon, Mr. Carpenter. It's nice to see you again."

"It's always a pleasure to see you again, Ms. Stockenberg." The portly entrepreneur took her outstretched hand in his. His blue eyes warmed momentarily as they swept over her appreciatively. "I'm looking forward to today's presentation," he said as his gaze moved to the uncovered storyboard.

Wide brow furrowed, he crossed the room and began studying it for a long silent time. Since it was too late to begin the presentation as planned, the team members refrained from speaking as he took in the proposed campaign. Amanda didn't know about the others, but she would have found it impossible to say a word, holding her breath as she was.

When Fred Carpenter finally did speak, his words were not encouraging. "You people have serviced my account for five years. I've dropped a bundle into your coffers. And this is as good as you can come up with? A cow wearing a beret?"

"Let me explain the animation," Julian said quickly. Too quickly, Amanda thought with an inner sigh. He was making the fatal mistake of any presenter: appearing desperate.

"Don't worry, the art can be rethought," Marvin interjected as Julian picked up the laser pen to better illustrate the sequence. "Besides, it's the words that'll sell your new, improved, French vanilla flavor, anyway." He paused, as if half expecting a drumroll to announce his message. "A taste of Paris in every spoonful."

"That's it?" the snack-food executive asked.

"Well, it's just the beginning," Marvin assured him. Moisture was beading up on his upper lip, his forehead. Another rule broken, Amanda thought, remembering what Patrick Connally had taught her about never letting the client—or the competition—see you sweat. "See, the way I envision the concept—"

"It's drivel," Julian said again. "But the team can fix that, Fred. Now, if we could just get back to the art."

"It's not drivel," Marvin exploded.

"Marvin," Amanda warned softly.

"I've seen cleverer copy written on rolls of novelty toilet paper," the art director sniffed.

"And I've seen better art scrawled on the sides of buildings down at the docks!"

Amanda turned toward the client who appeared less than amused by the escalating argument. "As you can see, Mr. Carpenter, your campaign has created a lot of in-house excitement," she said, trying desperately to salvage the multimillion-dollar account.

"Obviously the wrong kind," Carpenter said. "Look, I haven't liked how all these mergers resulted in my account being put into the hands of the same agency that handles my competitors. It looks to me as if you guys have been instructed by your new bosses to soften your approach—"

"The hell we have," both Julian and Marvin protested in unison, agreeing for once. Amanda tried telling herself she should be grateful for small favors.

"Then you've lost your edge," the self-proclaimed king of ice cream decided.

"That's really not the case, Fred," Don Patterson, the marketing member of the team, finally interjected. A man prone to wearing loud ties and plaid sport jackets, he was nevertheless very good at his job. "Perhaps if Julian and Marvin went back to the drawing board—"

"There's no point. We've had five great years working together, you fellows have helped make Sweet Indulgence the second-bestselling ice cream in the country. But, the team over at Chiat/Day assures me that they can get me to number one. So, I think I'm going to give them a try."

He turned toward Amanda, who could literally feel the color draining from her face. "I'm sorry, Ms. Stockenberg. You're a nice, pretty lady and I'd like to keep my account here if for no other reason than to have an excuse to keep seeing you. But business is business."

"I understand." With effort, Amanda managed a smile and refrained from strangling the two ego-driven creative members of the ill-suited team. "But Don does have a point. Perhaps if you'd allow us a few days to come up with another concept—"

"Sorry." He shook his head. "But things haven't been the same around here since all the mergers." His round face looked as unhappy as hers. "But if you'd like," he said, brightening somewhat, "I'll mention you to the fellows at Chiat/Day. Perhaps there's a spot opening up over there."

"That's very kind of you. But I'm quite happy where I am."

It was what she'd been telling herself over and over again lately, Amanda thought now, as she dragged her mind from the disastrous meeting to the disaster currently being played out on the television screen.

"You know," Susan said, "this entire challenge week isn't really your problem. Officially, it's Greg's."

"I know." Amanda sighed and began chewing on another Tums.

Greg Parsons was her immediate supervisor and, as creative director, he was the man Ernst Janzen had hand-selected for the job of instituting the team concept. The man who had moved into the executive suite was as different from Patrick Connally as night from day. Rather than encouraging the cooperative atmosphere that had once thrived under the founder of C.C.C., Greg ruled the agency by intimidation and fear.

From his first day on the job, he'd set unrealistic profit targets. This focus on profits diverted attention from what had always been the agency's forte—making clients feel they were getting superior service.

Apparently believing that internal competition was the lifeblood of success, he instigated political maneuvering among his top people, pitting one against the other as they jockeyed for key appointments.

Although such intrigue usually occurred behind the scenes, one of the more visible changes in policy was the conference table at which Amanda was sitting. When she'd first come to work here, the room had boasted a giant round table, the better, her former boss had declared, to create the feeling of democracy. Now, five days a week, the staff sat around this oblong table while Parsons claimed the power position at the head.

Although it might not seem like such a big thing, along with all the other changes that had taken place, it was additional proof that C.C.C. had lost the family feeling that had been so comfortable and inspirational to both employees and clients.

Desperate to salvage his foundering career, Parsons had come up with the idea of taking the teams to a resort, where, utilizing a number of outward-bound-type game-playing procedures he'd gleaned from his latest management-training tape, the various independent-minded individuals would meld into one forceful creative entity.

"The problem is," Amanda said, "like it or not, my fortunes are tied to Greg."

"Lucky him. Since without you to run interference and do all his detail work, he'd undoubtedly have been out on his Armani rear a very long time ago," Susan said.

"That's not very nice."

"Granted. But it's true."

Amanda couldn't argue with her assistant's pithy analysis. From the time of Greg's arrival from the Dallas office three months ago, she'd wondered, on more than one occasion, exactly how the man had managed to win the corporate plum of creative director. It certainly hadn't been on merit.

Then, six weeks after he'd moved into the expensively redecorated executive office, the question was answered when Susan returned from a long lunch with the other administrative assistants where she'd learned that Greg just happened to be married to Ernst Janzen's granddaughter. Which, Amanda had agreed, explained everything.

It was bad enough that Greg was frightfully incompetent. Even worse was the way he saw himself as a modern-day Napoleon—part dictator, part Don Juan. And although she'd deftly dealt with his less-than-subtle passes, her refusal had earned Amanda her superior's antipathy. He rode her constantly, belittling her work even as he routinely took credit for her ideas in upper-level corporate meetings.

It was no secret that the man was unhappy in Portland. He constantly berated the entire West Coast as hopelessly provincial. It was also common knowledge that he had his eye on a superior prize—that of national creative director and vice president. Along with the requisite increase in salary and numerous perks, the coveted slot also came with a corner-window penthouse office on Manhattan's famed Madison Avenue.

"I still don't see why you put up with the man," Susan said, her acid tone breaking into Amanda's thoughts.

"It's simple. I want his job."

"It should have been yours in the first place."

Once again, Amanda couldn't argue with the truth. While she hadn't specifically been promised the creative director's spot when she was first hired, there'd been every indication that Patrick Connally considered her on the fast track to success.

She'd worked hard for the past four years, forgoing any social life, giving most of her time and energy to the company.

The sacrifices had paid off; there had been a time, not so long ago, when the job of creative director had looked like a lock. Until Greg Parsons arrived on the scene.

"Blood's thicker than water. And unfortunately, Greg happens to be married to Mr. Janzen's granddaughter."

"Talk about sleeping your way to the top," Susan muttered.

"Unfortunately, family ties seem to have gotten Greg this far." Amanda frowned up at the oil portrait of the new creative director hanging on the wall. The ornate, gilt-framed painting featured Parsons in one of his dress-for-success chalk-striped suits, holding the cigar he was never without. The same cigar he took pleasure in lighting during meetings, never mind that it caused everyone there discomfort.

"But," she continued, "after the problems he's had instituting the team concept, he's stalled in the water."

Susan arched a jet eyebrow. "Are you saying you think he's on the way out?"

"Unfortunately, I don't think—unless Jessica Janzen Parsons wises up and divorces him—there's any chance of that. So, I've come up with a plan to get the guy out of my life—and out of town—once and for all."

"Please tell me it involves tar and feathers."

"Not quite." Actually, although she'd never admit it, Amanda found the idea of running Parsons out of town on a rail—like in the good old days of the Wild West—eminently appealing.

"Actually, it's simple. Or at least it was," she amended with another bleak glance toward the television screen. "Until the resort went up in smoke."

"Let me guess. You were going to lure the bastard out onto the cliff behind the resort late one night, hit him in the head with his precious new PING nine iron, then shove him into the ocean. Where, with any luck, he'd be eaten by killer sharks."

Despite all her problems, Amanda smiled. "As attractive as that scenario may be, the sharks would probably spare him because of professional courtesy. Besides, I've come to the conclusion that the easiest way to get Greg out of my hair is to give him what he most wants."

"Don't tell me that you're going to go to bed with him?"

"Of course not." Amanda literally shuddered at the unpalatable idea. "Actually, I've decided to get him promoted."

A slow, understanding grin had Susan's crimson lips curving. "To Manhattan."

Amanda returned the smile with a cocky, confident grin of her own. "To Manhattan."

Amanda couldn't deny that losing the conference-center resort to fire was a setback. After all, without someplace to hold the corporate challenge, Greg couldn't prove that his idea had merit. Which in turn would keep him here in Portland indefinitely.

But it wasn't the first challenge she'd overcome in her rise up the advertising corporate ladder. Amanda doubted it would be her last.

A part of her hated the idea of Greg Parsons getting any more credit, when in reality, if the upcoming week proved a success, it would be her doing. A stronger part of her just wanted him gone. She would swallow her pride, along with her ego, if it meant getting the obnoxious man out of her life.

Now all she had to do was find some other location for the challenge. Which wasn't going to be easy, considering this was the high tourist season on the Oregon coast.

Could she do it? Amanda asked herself as she pointed the remote toward the television and darkened the screen.

You bet.

Satan's Cove

"We've got a problem."

Dane Cutter stopped in the act of nailing down cedar shingles and glanced over the steep edge of the roof. "So why don't you tell me something I don't know?"

He'd been the proud owner of Smugglers' Inn for two months. Well, if you wanted to get technical, he and the bank actually owned the century-old landmark building. Since he'd signed the final papers, Dane doubted a single day had gone by that he hadn't had to overcome some new catastrophe.

Having paid for an extensive professional inspection of the building that, because of competition from larger, fancier resorts catering to the corporate trade, had fallen into disrepair during his time away from Satan's Cove, Dane knew the problems he was taking on. And although they were considerable, he'd foolishly expected to have some time to do all the necessary renovations.

Thus far, he'd tackled the inn's ancient plumbing and electrical systems, evicted countless field mice and killed more spiders than he cared to think about.

He'd also replaced the ancient gas oven, replastered the algae-filled swimming pool, and was in the process of replacing the shingles that had blown away during last night's storm.

The next thing on his lengthy list—barring any further emergencies—was replacing the ancient gas heater, after which he planned to resand and seal the oak parquet floors in the public rooms, then resurface the tennis court.

Since reopening last week, he'd reassured himself at least daily that it was just as well potential guests weren't exactly beating down his door. Although he admittedly needed all the bookings he could get to make the hefty mortgage payments, he also needed time to restore the inn to its former glory.

Reva Carlson grinned up at him. "Technically it's a bit of good news and some bad news. I suppose it's all in how you look at it."

"Why don't you give me the good news first?"

The way things had been going, after the storm and the burst pipe that had left the inn without water for twenty-four hours, Dane figured he could use a little boost. Hell, what he needed was a miracle. But he was willing to settle for whatever he could get.

"Okay." Reva's grin widened. "It looks as if we're going to meet this month's mortgage payment, after all."

"We got a booking?" If he'd had his choice, he would have kept the inn closed until all the needed repairs could be done. Unfortunately, his cash flow being what it was, he'd been forced to open for limited occupancy.

"We've sold out the entire place," Reva revealed proudly.

She was right. This was definitely a case of good and bad news. "Not including the tower room?" The last he'd looked into the hexagonal-shaped room that boasted a bird's-eye view of the Pacific Ocean, the wallpaper had been peeling off the walls.

"Of course not. You're good, boss, but you're not exactly a miracle worker. However, every other room, every bed, every last nook and cranny of Smugglers' Inn is going to be taken over by some Portland ad agency for an entire week.''

Dane rapidly went over a mental list of repairs he'd have to accomplish in order to accommodate such a crowd.

"So, when are these ad people scheduled to arrive, anyway?"

"You could at least pretend to be pleased," she complained. "Besides, it's not that bad. We've plenty of time to get ready."

"What, exactly, do you consider plenty of time?"

"Three days."

"Three days?" He dragged his hand through his hair.

"Well, technically four. Including this one."

It was already four in the afternoon. "Damn it, Reva—"

"You're the one who's been bitching about needing bookings," she reminded Dane. "Well, now you've got some. Or would you rather me call the woman back and tell her that we're full?"

Reminding himself that the difficult could be accomplished immediately, while the impossible might take a bit longer, he said, "You did good, lady."

Another thought, beyond the necessary repairs, occurred to him. "You'd better warn Mom." He'd taken his mother out of a forced retirement and put her back in the remodeled kitchen, where she had happily begun stocking the pantry and whipping up recipes that rivaled those of any five-star resort in the country.

"I already did," she assured him, reminding him why he'd hired the former night manager away from the world-famous Whitfield Palace hotel chain. "Which reminds me, she told me to tell you that you'll have to drive into town for supplies."

"Tell her to make out a list and I'll do it as soon as I finish with the roof."

Dane returned to his hammering. And even as he wondered exactly how he was going to get everything done in time for the arrival of all those guests, he allowed himself to believe that things around Smugglers' Inn were definitely beginning to look up.

2

Portland

"**Y**ou were right about every motel, hotel, resort and cottage up and down the coast being booked to the rafters," Susan reported to Amanda. "Every place with the exception of Smugglers' Inn, which, I'll have to admit, made me a little nervous. But the woman from the Satan's Cove visitors' bureau assured me that it's listed on the historical register."

"It is," Amanda murmured, thinking back to that wonderful summer she'd spent at Satan's Cove.

The memory was, as always, bittersweet—part pleasure and part pain. She'd never been happier than she'd been that summer of her first love. Nor more heartbroken than on the day she'd driven away from Smugglers' Inn—and Dane Cutter—back to Los Angeles with her family.

He'd promised to write; and trusting him implicitly, Amanda had believed him. For the first two weeks after arriving home, she'd waited for a letter assuring her that she was not alone in her feelings—that the kisses they'd shared, along with the desperate promises, had been more than just a summer romance.

When three weeks passed without so much as a single postcard, Amanda had screwed up enough nerve to telephone Dane at the inn. But the woman working the desk informed her that he'd left Satan's Cove to return to college. No, the woman had insisted, in a bored tone, he hadn't left any forwarding address.

She'd thought about asking to talk to his mother, who'd been the inn's cook. But youthful pride kept her from inquiring further. So, believing she'd simply been one more conquest for a drop-dead-gorgeous college boy who already had more than his share of girls throwing themselves at him, Amanda tried to write the intense, short-lived romance off to experience.

And mostly, she'd been successful. But there were still times, when she would least expect it, that she'd think back on that summer with a mixture of wistfulness and embarrassment.

"I'm surprised they could take us," she said now, recalling the inn's popularity. Her father had had to book their rooms six months in advance. "They must have had a huge cancellation."

"According to the reservations clerk, the place has been closed for several years," Susan revealed. "Apparently it's recently changed hands. This is the new owner's first season."

"I'm not sure I like the sound of that," Amanda muttered. Even in an industry built on ego and turf, the agency had become a nest of political intrigue and backbiting. The corporate team challenge week was going to be tough enough without them having to serve as some novice innkeeper's shakedown summer season.

"You can always call Popular Surplus and order up the tents."

Despite her concerns, Amanda laughed. The truth was, she really didn't have any other choice. She could put twenty people—none of whom got along very well in the best of circumstances—into tents on the beach, eating hot dogs cooked over an open fire, or she could trust the new owner of Smugglers' Inn to know what he or she was doing.

After all, how bad could it be? The landmark inn, located on one of the most scenic stretches of Pacific Coast, was pretty and cozy and wonderfully comfortable. She thought back on the lovely flower-sprigged wallpaper in the tower room she'd slept in that long-ago summer, remembered the dazzling sunsets from the high arched windows, recalled in vivid detail the romance of the crackling fires the staff built each evening in the stone fireplace large enough for a grown man to stand in.

"Smugglers' Inn will be perfect," she said firmly, as if saying the words out loud could make them true. "I don't know why I didn't think of it in the first place."

"Probably because you've had a few other things on your mind," Susan said, proving herself to be a master of understatement. "And although I have no doubt you can pull this thing off, I'm glad I'll be holding down the fort here while you lead the troops in their wilderness experience."

That said, she left Amanda to worry that this time she'd actually bitten off more than she could chew.

Never having been one to limit herself to a normal, eight-hour work schedule, Amanda remained at her desk long into the night, fine-tuning all the minuscule details that would ensure the challenge week would be a success.

But as hard as she tried to keep her mind on business, she could not keep her unruly thoughts from drifting back to the summer of her fifteenth year.

She'd fallen in love with Dane the first time she'd seen him. And although her parents had tried to convince her otherwise, she knew now, as she'd known then, that her feelings had been more than mere puppy love.

It had, admittedly, taken Dane time to realize they were a perfect match. But Amanda had steadfastly refused to give up her quest. She pursued him incessantly, with all the fervor of a teenager in the throes of a first grand love.

Everywhere Dane went, Amanda went there as well, smiling up at him with a coy Lolita smile overbrimming with sensual invitation. After discovering that one of his duties was teaching a class in kayaking, despite her distaste for early-morning awakenings, she showed up on the beach at six-thirty for lessons. Although the rest of the class was sensibly attired for the foggy sea air in jeans and sweatshirts, she'd chosen to wear a hot-pink bikini that barely covered the essentials.

And that was just the beginning. During Dane's lifeguarding stint each afternoon, she lounged poolside, wearing another impossibly scant bikini, her golden skin glowing with fragrant coconut oil. Grateful for childhood diving lessons, she would occasionally lithely rise from the lounge to treat him to swan dives designed to show off her budding female figure.

She tormented him endlessly, pretending to need his assistance on everything from a flat bicycle tire to fastening her life jacket before going out on a sight-seeing boat excursion.

Adding local color to the inn's reputation had been the legend—invented by a former owner—that it was haunted by a woman who'd thrown herself off the widow's walk after her fiancé's ship was sunk by pirates off the rocky shoals. One night, Amanda showed up at Dane's room, insisting that she'd seen the ghost.

It would have taken a male with inhuman strength to resist her continual seduction attempts. And, as Dane later confessed, he was, after all, only human.

Which was why, seven days after Amanda Stockenberg's arrival at Smugglers' Inn, Dane Cutter succumbed to the inevitable. However, even as they spent the star-spangled nights driving each other insane, Dane had steadfastly refused to make love to her.

"I may be too damn weak where you're concerned, princess," he'd groaned during one excruciatingly long petting session, "but I'm not reckless enough to have sex with a minor girl."

She'd sworn that no one would ever know, promised that she'd never—ever—do anything to get him in trouble. But on this point, Dane had proved frustratingly intractable.

And although, as the years passed, Amanda begrudgingly admitted that he'd done the right and noble thing, there were still times, such as tonight, when she was sitting all alone in the dark, that she'd think back over the bliss she'd experienced in Dane Cutter's strong young arms and wish, with all her heart, that he hadn't proved so strong.

Satan's Cove

The day before the group was due to arrive at Smugglers' Inn, Dane was beginning to think they just might make it.

The roof was now rainproof, the windows sparkled like diamonds, and every room in the place—with the exception of the tower room, which he'd written off as impossible to prepare in such short time—was white-glove clean. And although the aroma of fresh paint lingered, leaving the windows open another twenty-four hours should take care of that little problem.

His mother had definitely gone all out in the kitchen. The huge commercial refrigerator was stuffed with food and every shelf in the pantry was full. Kettles had been bubbling away on the new eight-burner stove nearly around the clock for the past two and a half days, creating mouthwatering scents.

Using the hefty deposit Reva had insisted upon, he'd hired additional staff and although the kids were as green as spring grass, they were bright, seemingly hardworking and unrelentingly cheerful.

He was passing the antique registration desk on his way to the parlor, planning to clean the oversize chandelier, when the sound of a stressed-out voice garnered his instant attention.

"I'm sorry, ma'am," Mindy Taylor, the nineteen-year-old cheerleader, premed student and local beauty queen he'd hired, said in an obviously frustrated voice. "But—"

She sighed and held the receiver a little away from her ear, indicating that it was not the first time she'd heard the argument being offered on the other end of the line.

"Yes, I can appreciate that," Mindy agreed, rolling her expressive eyes toward the knotty-pine ceiling. "But I'm afraid it's impossible. No, it's not booked, but—"

Dane heard the renewed argument, although he couldn't make out the words.

"It's a woman from that Portland advertising agency." Mindy covered the mouthpiece with her hand to talk to Dane. "She's insisting on the tower room, even though I told her that it wasn't available."

Dane held out his hand. "Let me talk to her."

"That's okay." Perfect white teeth that Dane knew had cost her parents a fortune in orthodontia flashed in the dazzling smile that had earned Mindy the Miss Satan's Cove title two years running. As this year's Miss Oregon, she'd be competing in the national pageant, which made her a local celebrity.

"It'll be good practice for Atlantic City. I need to work on my patience," she admitted. "Sometimes I think if I'm asked one more stupid question by one more judge I'm going to scream.

"I understand your feelings," Mindy soothed into the receiver as she tried yet again. "But you see, Ms. Stockenberg, Smugglers' Inn has been closed for the past few years, and—"

"Wait a minute," Dane interrupted. "Did you say Stockenberg?"

The name hit him directly in the gut, reminding him of the time he'd been standing behind the plate and his cousin Danny had accidentally slammed a baseball bat into his solar plexus.

"Excuse me, but could you hold a moment, please?" Mindy put her hand over the mouthpiece again and nodded. "That's right."

"Not Amanda Stockenberg?" It couldn't be, Dane told himself, even as a nagging intuition told him it was true.

"That's her." Mindy appeared surprised Dane knew the name. "The guest list the agency sent along with their deposit lists her as an assistant creative director.

"I put her in the cliff room, but she's insisting on being moved to the tower. Something about it having sentimental meaning. I explained that it was impossible, but—"

"Let her have it."

"What?" Eyes the color of a sun-brightened sea widened to the size of sand dollars.

"I said, book Ms. Stockenberg into the tower room." His tone was uncharacteristically sharp and impatient.

Mindy was not easily cowed. Especially by a man she'd been able to talk into playing Barbie dolls back in his teenage baby-sitting days, when their mothers had worked together at this very same inn. "But, Dane, it's a terrible mess."

She wasn't telling him anything he didn't already know. "Don't worry," he said, softening his voice and his expression. "I'll take care of it."

Mindy eyed him with overt curiosity. Then, as the voice on the other end of the phone began talking again, she returned her attention to the conversation.

"It seems I was mistaken, Ms. Stockenberg," she said cheerfully, switching gears with a dexterity that had Dane thinking she'd ace her Miss America interview. "As it happens, the tower room is available after all. Yes, that is fortunate, isn't it?"

She turned to the computer Dane was still paying for. Her rosy fingernails tapped on the keys, changing Amanda Stockenberg from the cliff room to the tower suite.

"It's all taken care of," she assured Dane after she'd hung up. Her expressive eyes held little seeds of worry. "It's none of my business, but I sure hope you know what you're doing."

"If I knew what I was doing, I wouldn't have bought the inn in the first place." His crooked grin belied his complaint. After years of traveling the world for the Whitfield Palace hotel chain, there was no place he'd rather be. And nothing he'd rather be doing. "If you see Reva, tell her I had to run into town for some wallpaper."

"Ms. Stockenberg mentioned little blue flowers," Mindy said helpfully.

"I remember."

And damn it, that was precisely the problem, Dane told himself two hours later as he drove back to Smugglers' Inn from the hardware store in Satan's Cove with the newly purchased wallpaper. He remembered too much about Amanda Stockenberg's long-ago visit to Satan's Cove.

The only daughter of a wealthy Los Angeles attorney and his socialite wife, Amanda had come to the Oregon coast with her family for a month-long vacation.

Pampered and amazingly sheltered for a teenager growing up in the 1980s, she'd obviously never met anyone like him. Unfortunately, during his years working at Smugglers' Inn—part-time while in high school, then summers and vacations to put himself through college—Dane had run across too many rich girls who considered him along the same lines as a summer trophy.

Dane's own father, scion of a famous Southern department-store family, had been a masculine version of those girls. Rich and spoiled, he'd had no qualms about taking what he wanted, then moving on after the annual Labor Day clambake, leaving behind a young, pregnant waitress.

Although Mary Cutter—a quiet, gentle woman who'd gone on to be a cook at the inn—had brought Dane up not to be bitter about his father's abandonment, he'd decided early on that it was better to stick with your own kind.

Which was why he'd always avoided the temptation of shiny blond hair and long, tanned legs. Until Amanda Stockenberg arrived on the scene.

She pursued him endlessly, with the single-mindedness of a rich, pretty girl accustomed to getting her own way. She was part siren, part innocent; he found both fascinating.

When she showed up at his door in the middle of the night during a thunderstorm, swearing she'd seen the ghost reputed to haunt the inn, Dane took one look at her—backlit by flashes of lightning, clad in a shorty nightgown—and all his intentions to resist temptation flew right out the window.

Being male and all too human, he allowed her into his room.

"That was your first mistake," he muttered now, at the memory of the sweet lips that had kissed him senseless. His second mistake, and the one that had cost him dearly, had been letting Amanda Stockenberg into his heart.

They did not make love—she was, after all, too young. And even if he'd wanted to—which, Lord help him, he did—he knew that by legal standards Amanda was jailbait. And from the no-holds-barred conversation Stockenberg had with Dane when even he could no longer ignore his daughter's outrageously flirtatious behavior, Dane knew the attorney would not be averse to filing statutory rape charges on any boy who dared take Amanda to bed.

Dane's mother, remembering her own youthful summer romance, had worried about his succumbing to his raging hormones and blowing his chances at finishing college.

"Don't worry, Mom," he'd assured her with the cocky grin that had coaxed more than one local beauty into intimacy. "I won't risk prison for a roll in the hay with a summer girl."

With that intent firmly stated, he'd managed to resist Amanda's pleas to consummate their young love. But drawn to her in ways he could not understand, Dane had spent the next three weeks sneaking off to clandestine trysts.

Dane and Amanda exchanged long slow kisses in the cave on the beach, forbidden caresses in the boathouse, passionate promises in the woods at the top of the cliff overlooking the sea, and on one memorable, thrilling, and terrifying occasion, while her parents slept in the room below them, they'd made out in Amanda's beloved tower room with its canopied bed and flower-sprigged walls.

Although he'd tried like hell to forget her, on more than one occasion over the past years, Dane had been annoyed to discover that her image had remained emblazoned on his mind, as bright and vivid—and, damn it, as seductive—as it had been a decade ago.

"It's been ten years," he reminded himself gruffly as he carried the rolls of paper and buckets of paste up the narrow, curving staircase to the tower room.

And, damn it, he'd dreamed about her over each of those ten years. More times than he could count, more than he'd admit. Even to himself.

"Hell, she's probably married."

It took no imagination at all to envision some man—a rich, suave guy with manicured fingernails and smooth palms that had never known the handle of a hammer, a man from her own social set—snapping Amanda up right after her debut.

Did girls still have formal debuts? Dane wondered, remembering a few he'd worked as a waiter during college—formal affairs in gilded hotel ballrooms where lovely rich girls donned long elbow-length gloves, their grandmothers' pearls and fancy white dresses that cost nearly as much as a semester's tuition, and waltzed with their fathers. He'd have to ask Mindy. The daughter of a local fisherman, she'd certainly met her share of society girls at various beauty pageants. On more than one occasion she'd complained to Dane that those rich girls only entered as a lark. Their futures, unlike hers, didn't depend on their winning the scholarship money. The fact that Amanda still had the same name as she had that long-ago summer meant nothing, Dane considered, returning his thoughts to Amanda Stockenberg's marital status. Married women often kept their maiden names for professional reasons.

His jaw clenched at the idea of Amanda married to some Yuppie who drove a BMW, preferred estate-bottled wine to beer, bought his clothes from Brooks Brothers, golfed eighteen holes on Saturday and sailed in yachting regattas on Sundays.

As he'd shopped for the damn wallpaper, Dane had hoped that he'd exaggerated the condition of the tower room when he'd measured the walls after Amanda's telephone call. Unfortunately, as he entered it now, he realized that it was even worse.

He wasn't fixing it up for sentimental reasons, Dane assured himself firmly. He was only going to the extra trouble because he didn't want Amanda to think him unsuccessful.

He pulled the peeling paper from the walls, revealing wallboard stained from the formerly leaky roof. Water stains also blotched the ceiling, like brown inkblots in a

Rorschach test. The pine-plank floor was badly in need of refinishing, but a coat of paste wax and some judiciously placed rugs would cover the worst of the damage.

A sensible man would simply turn around and walk out, close the door behind him and tell the lady, when she arrived, that the clerk had made a mistake; the tower room wasn't available.

For not the first time since he'd gotten the idea to buy Smugglers' Inn, Dane reminded himself that a sensible man would have stayed in his executive suite at the New Orleans home office of the Whitfield Palace hotel chain and continued to collect his six-figure salary and requisite perks.

I'll bet the husband plays polo. The thought had him snapping the plumb line with more force than necessary, sending blue chalk flying. Dane had not forgotten Amanda's father's boastful remarks about the polo ponies he kept stabled at his weekend house in Santa Barbara.

What the hell was he doing? Dane asked himself as he rolled the paper out onto a board placed atop a pair of sawhorses and cut the first piece. Why torture himself with old memories?

He slapped the paste onto the back of the flowered paper and tried not to remember a time when this room had smelled like the gardenia cologne Amanda had worn that summer.

When something was over and done with, you forgot it and moved on.

Wasn't that exactly what she had done?

After promising him "forever," Amanda Stockenberg had walked out of his life without so much as a backward glance.

And ten years later, as he climbed the ladder and positioned the strip of paper against the too-heavy blue chalk line, Dane was still trying to convince himself that it was only his pride—not his heart—that had been wounded.

*   *   *

Although many things in Amanda's life had changed over the past ten years, Smugglers' Inn was not one of them. Perched on the edge of the cliff overlooking the Pacific Ocean, the building's lit windows glowed a warm welcome.

"Well, we're here, folks," the driver of the American Charter bus announced with a vast amount of cheer, considering the less-than-ideal circumstances of the trip. A halfhearted round of applause rippled down the rows.

"It's about time," Greg Parsons complained. He speared Amanda a sharp look. "You realize that we've already lost the entire first day of the challenge."

Having been forced to put up with her supervisor's sarcasm for the past hour, Amanda was in no mood to turn the other cheek.

"That landslide wasn't my fault, Greg." They'd been stuck on the bus in the pouring rain for five long, frustrating hours while highway crews cleared away the rock and mud from the road.

"If we'd only left thirty minutes earlier—"

"We could have ended up beneath all that mud."

Deciding that discretion was the better part of valor, Amanda did not point out that the original delay had been caused by Kelli Kyle. The auburn-haired public-relations manager had arrived at the company parking lot twenty-five minutes after the time the bus had been scheduled to depart.

Watercooler rumors had Kelli doing a lot more for Greg than plotting PR strategy; but Amanda's working relationship with Greg was bad enough without her attacking his girlfriend.

She reached into her purse, took out a half-empty roll of antacids and popped two of the tablets into her mouth. Her stomach had been churning for the past twenty miles and a headache was threatening.

Which wasn't unusual when she was forced to spend the entire day with Greg Parsons. Amanda couldn't think of a single person—with the possible exception of Kelli Kyle— who liked the man.

The first thing he'd done upon his arrival in Portland was to prohibit staffers from decorating their office walls and cubicles with the crazy posters and wacky decorations that were a commonplace part of the creative environment at other agencies. When a memo had been sent out two months ago, forbidding employees even to drink coffee at their desks, Amanda had feared an out-and-out rebellion.

The hand grenade he kept on his desk and daily memos from *The Art of War* also had not endeared him to his fellow workers.

"Let's just hope we have better luck with this inn you've booked us into," he muttered, scooping up his crocodile attaché case and marching down the aisle. "Because so far, the corporate challenge is turning out to be an unmitigated disaster."

Unwilling to agree, Amanda didn't answer. The welcoming warmth of the fire crackling in the large stone fireplace soothed the jangled nerves of the challenge-week participants, as did the glasses of hot coffee, cider and wine served on a myrtle-wood tray by a handsome young man who vaguely reminded Amanda of Dane Cutter.

The young girl working behind the front desk was as pretty as the waiter was handsome. She was also, Amanda noticed, amazingly efficient. Within minutes, and without the Miss America smile fading for a moment, Mindy Taylor had registered the cranky chilled guests into their rooms, handed out the keys and assigned bellmen to carry the luggage upstairs.

Finally it was Amanda's turn. "Good evening, Ms. Stockenberg," Mindy greeted Amanda with the same unfailing cheer she had the others. "Welcome to Smugglers' Inn."

"It's a relief to be here."

The smile warmed. "I heard about your troubles getting here from Portland." She tapped briskly on the computer as she talked. "I'm sure the rest of your week will go more smoothly."

"I hope so." It sure couldn't get any worse.

"You're in the tower room as requested." Mindy handed her the antique brass key. "If you don't mind waiting just a moment, Kevin will be back and will take your suitcases up for you."

"That's not necessary," a male voice coming from behind Amanda said. "I'll take care of Ms. Stockenberg's luggage."

No, Amanda thought. *It couldn't be!*

She slowly turned around, taking time to school her expression to one of polite surprise. "Hello, Dane."

Although a decade had passed, he looked just the same. But better, she decided on second thought. Dark and rugged, and so very dangerous. The kind of boy—no, he was a man now, she reminded herself—that fathers of daughters stayed awake nights worrying about.

His shaggy dark hair was still in need of a haircut, and his eyes, nearly as dark as his hair, were far from calm, but the emotions swirling in their midnight depths were too complex for Amanda to decipher. A five-o'clock shadow did nothing to detract from his good looks; the dark stubble only added to his appeal.

His jeans, white T-shirt and black leather jacket were distractingly sexy. They also made her worry that standards might have slipped at the inn since the last time she'd visited.

"Hello, princess." His full, sensual mouth curved in a smile that let her know the intimacy implied by the long-ago nickname was intentional. "Welcome to Smugglers' Inn." His gaze swept over her. "You're looking more lovely than ever."

Actually, she looked like hell. To begin with, she was too damn thin. Her oval face was pale and drawn. Her beige linen slacks and ivory tunic top, which he suspected probably cost as much as the inn's new water heater, looked as if she'd slept in them; her hair was wet from her dash from the bus, there were blue shadows beneath her eyes, and sometime during the long trip from Portland, she'd chewed off her lipstick.

Dane knew he was in deep, deep trouble when he still found her the most desirable woman he'd ever seen.

Amanda struggled to keep Dane from realizing that he'd shaken her. All it had taken was his calling her that ridiculous name to cause a painful fluttering in her heart.

How could she have thought that she'd gotten over him? Dane Cutter was not a man women got over. Not in this lifetime. Her hand closed tightly around the key.

"Thank you. It's a relief to finally be here. Is the dining room closed yet? I know we're late, but—"

"We kept it open when it was obvious you'd gotten held up. Or, if you'd prefer, there's room service."

The idea of a long bath and a sandwich and cup of tea sent up to her room sounded delightful. "That's good news." The first in a very long and very trying day.

"We try to make our guests as comfortable as possible."

He scooped up both her cases, deftly tucked them under his arm and took her briefcase from her hand. It was biscuit-hued cowhide, as smooth as a baby's bottom, with her initials in gold near the handle. "Nice luggage."

She'd received the Louis Vuitton luggage from her parents as a graduation present. Her mother had been given a similar set from her parents when she'd married. And her mother before her. It was, in a way, a family tradition. So why did she suddenly feel a need to apologize?

"It's very functional."

His only response to her defensive tone was a shrug. "So I've heard." He did not mention that he'd bought a similar set for his mother, as a bon voyage gift for the Alaskan cruise he'd booked her on last summer. "If you're all checked in, I'll show you to your room."

"I remember the way." It had been enough of a shock to discover Dane still working at the inn. Amanda didn't believe she could handle being alone in the cozy confines of the tower room with him. Not with the memory of their last night together still painfully vivid in her mind.

"I've no doubt you do." Ignoring the clenching of his stomach, Dane flashed her a maddening grin, letting her know that they were both on the same wavelength. The devil could probably take smiling lessons from Dane Cutter. "But someone needs to carry your luggage up and Jimmy and Kevin are tied up with other guests."

"There's no hurry." Her answering smile was as polite as it was feigned. Although she'd never considered herself a violent person, after the way Dane had treated her, dumping her without a single word of explanation, like he undoubtedly did the rest of his summer girls, her hands practically itched with the need to slap his face. "I'll just go on up and they can bring my bags to the tower whenever they're free."

"I have a feeling that might be a while." He nodded his head toward the doorway, declaring the subject closed.

Not wanting to create a scene in front of the avidly interested young clerk, Amanda tossed her damp head and marched out of the room.

This was a mistake, she told herself as she stood beside Dane in the antique elevator slowly creaking its way up to the third floor. The next few days were the most important in her life. Her entire career, everything she'd worked so hard to achieve, depended on the corporate challenge week being a success. She couldn't allow herself to be distracted.

Unfortunately, Smugglers' Inn, she was discovering too late, held far too many distracting memories.

"I'm surprised to find you working here," she murmured, trying to ignore the familiar scent of soap emanating from his dark skin.

He chuckled—a low, rich tone that crept under her skin and caused her blood to thrum. "So am I." He put the bags on the floor, leaned against the back wall and stuck his hands in his pockets. "Continually."

Amanda thought about all the plans Dane had shared with her that summer. About how he was going to get out of this isolated small coastal town, how he planned to make his mark on the world, how he was going to be rich by his thirtieth birthday.

She did some rapid calculations and determined him to be twenty-nine. Obviously, if his unpretentious clothing and the fact that he was still carrying bags for guests at the inn were any indication, if Dane hoped to achieve even one of those goals, he'd have to win the lottery.

"Looks as if you've done all right for yourself." His measuring glance swept over her. "Assistant creative director for one of the top advertising firms in the country. I'm impressed."

"Thank you."

"Tell me, do you have a window office?"

"Actually, I do." Realizing that he was daring to mock her success, she tossed up her chin. "Overlooking the river."

"Must be nice. And a corporate credit card, too, I'll bet."

"Of course." She'd been thrilled the first time she'd flashed the green American Express card granted only to upper-level management personnel in an expensive Manhattan restaurant. It had seemed, at the time, an important rite of passage. Having been born into wealth, Amanda wanted—needed—to achieve success on her own.

"High-backed swivel desk chair?"

Two could play this game. "Italian cream leather."

She refused to admit she'd bought the extravagant piece of office furniture for herself with last year's Christmas bonus.

Of course, the minute Greg Parsons had caught sight of it, after returning from a holiday vacation to Barbados, he'd rushed out and bought himself a larger, higher model. In jet leather. With mahogany trim.

Dane whistled appreciatively. "Yes, sir, you've definitely come a long way. Especially for a lady who once professed a desire to raise five kids in a house surrounded by a white picket fence, and spend summers putting up berries and long dark winters making more babies in front of a crackling fire."

How dare he throw those youthful fantasies back into her face! Didn't he realize that it had been *him* she'd fantasized about making love to, *his* babies she'd wanted?

After she'd been forced to accept the fact that her dreams of marrying Dane Cutter were only that—stupid, romantic teenage daydreams—she'd gone on to find a new direction for her life. A direction that was, admittedly, heavily influenced by her father's lofty expectations for his only child.

"People grow up," she said. "Goals change."

"True enough," he agreed easily, thinking how his own life had taken a 180-degree turn lately. "Speaking of changes, you've changed your scent." It surrounded them in the enclosed space, more complex than the cologne that had haunted his dreams last night. More sensual.

"Have I?" she asked with feigned uninterest. "I don't remember."

"Your old cologne was sweet. And innocent." He leaned forward, drinking it in. "This makes a man think of deep, slow kisses." His breath was warm on her neck. "And hot sex on a steamy summer night."

His words, his deep voice, the closeness of his body to hers, all conspired to make her knees weak. Amanda considered backing away, then realized there was nowhere to go.

"I didn't come here to rehash the past, Dane." Her headache was building to monumental proportions. "This trip to Satan's Cove is strictly business."

"Yeah, I seem to recall Reva saying something about corporate game-playing stunts."

Her remarkable eyes were as blue as a sunlit sea. A careless man could drown in those wide eyes. Having succumbed to Amanda Stockenberg's siren call once before, Dane had no intention of making that mistake again. Although he knew that to touch her would be dangerous, he couldn't resist reaching out to rub the pads of his thumbs against her temples.

Amanda froze at his touch. "What do you think you're doing?"

Her voice might have turned as chilly as the rain falling outside, but her flesh was warming in a way he remembered all too well. "Helping you get rid of that headache before you rub a hole in your head."

He stroked small, concentric circles that did absolutely nothing to soothe. One hand roamed down the side of her face, her neck, before massaging her knotted shoulder muscle.

His hand was rough with calluses upon calluses, hinting at a life of hard, physical work rather than the one spent behind a wide executive desk he'd once yearned for. It crossed Amanda's mind that in a way, she was living the successful, high-powered life Dane had planned for himself. Which made her wonder if he was living out her old, discarded dreams.

Was he married? Did he have children? The idea of any other woman carrying Dane Cutter's baby caused a flicker of something deep inside Amanda that felt uncomfortably like envy.

"You sure are tense, princess." His clever fingers loosened the knot even as they tangled her nerves.

She knew she should insist he stop, but his touch *was* working wonders on her shoulder. "Knotted muscles and the occasional headache come with the territory. And don't call me *princess*."

Dane knew the truth of her first statement all too well. It was one of several reasons he'd bailed out of corporate life.

"How about the occasional ulcer?" He plucked the roll of antacids from her hand, forestalling her from popping another tablet into her mouth.

"I don't have an ulcer."

"I suppose you have a doctor's confirmation of that?"

She tossed her head, then wished she hadn't when the headache stabbed like a stiletto behind her eyes. "Of course."

She was a liar. But a lovely one. Dane suspected that it had been a very long time since Amanda had taken time to visit a doctor. Her clothes, her title, her luggage, the window office with the high-backed Italian-leather chair, all pointed to the fact that the lady was definitely on the fast track up the advertising corporate ladder.

Her too-thin face and the circles beneath her eyes were additional proof of too many hours spent hunkered over advertising copy and campaign jingles. He wondered if she realized she was approaching a very slippery slope.

He was looking at her that way again. Hard and deep. Just when Amanda thought Dane was going to say something profound, the elevator lurched to a sudden stop.

"Third floor, ladies' lingerie," he said cheerfully. "Do you still wear that sexy underwear?"

She wondered if he flirted like this with all the female guests, then wondered how, if he did, he managed to keep his job. Surely some women might complain to the management that the inn's sexy bellhop brought new meaning to the slogan Service With a Smile.

"My underwear is none of your business." Head high, she stepped out of the elevator and headed toward the stairway at the end of the hall, leaving him to follow with the bags.

"I seem to remember a time when you felt differently."

"I felt differently about a lot of things back then. After all, I was only fifteen." The censorious look she flashed back over her shoulder refused to acknowledge his steadfast refusal to carry their teenage affair to its natural conclusion.

"I recall mentioning your tender age on more than one occasion," he said mildly. "But you kept insisting that you were all grown-up."

Not grown-up enough to hold his attention, Amanda thought grimly. As she climbed the stairs to the tower room, she decided she'd made a major mistake in coming to Smugglers' Inn.

Her focus had been clear from the beginning. Pull off the corporate challenge week, get the obnoxious Greg Parsons promoted out of her life, then move upward into his position, which should have been hers in the first place.

Awakening old hurts and reliving old memories definitely hadn't been part of the plan.

And neither had Dane Cutter.

3

The first time Amanda had seen the tower room, she'd been entranced. Ten years hadn't lessened its appeal.

Delicate forget-me-nots bloomed on the walls, the high ceiling was a pale powder blue that had always reminded her of a clear summer sky. More blue flowers decorated the ribbon-edged curtains that were pulled back from the sparkling window and matched the thick comforter.

"The bed's different," she murmured.

"Unfortunately, during the time the inn was closed, it became a termite condo and had to go."

"That's too bad." She'd loved the romantic canopy. "But this is nice, too." She ran her hand over one of the pine-log posts that had been sanded to a satin finish.

"I'm glad you approve."

He'd taken the bed from his own room this morning. Now, watching her stroke the wooden post with her slender fingers, Dane felt a slow, deep ache stir inside him.

"I'd suggest not getting too near the woodwork," he warned. "The paint's still a bit sticky."

That explained the white specks on his jeans. A pang of sadness for lost opportunities and abandoned dreams sliced through Amanda.

"Well, thank you for carrying up my bags." Her smile was bright and impersonal as she reached into her purse.

An icy anger rose inside him at the sight of those folded green bills. "Keep your money."

All right, so this meeting was uncomfortable. But he didn't have to get so nasty about it. "Fine." Amanda met his strangely blistering look with a level one of her own. "You realize, I suppose, that I'm going to be here at the inn for a week."

"So?" His tone was as falsely indifferent as hers.

"So, it would seem inevitable that we'd run into each other from time to time."

"Makes sense to me."

It was obvious Dane had no intention of helping her out with this necessary conversation. "This is an important time for me," she said, trying again. "I can't afford any distractions."

"Are you saying I'm a distraction?" As if to underscore her words, he reached out and touched the ends of her hair. "You've dyed your hair," he murmured distractedly.

"Any man who touches me when I don't want him to is a distraction," she retorted, unnerved at how strongly the seemingly harmless touch affected her. "And I didn't dye it. It got darker all on its own."

"It was the color of corn silk that summer." He laced his fingers through the dark gold hair that curved beneath her chin. "Now it's the color of caramel." He held a few strands up to the light. "Laced with melted butter."

The way he was looking at her, the way he kept touching her, caused old seductive memories to come barreling back to batter at Amanda's emotions.

"Food analogies are always so romantic."

"You want romance, princess?" His eyes darkened to obsidian as he moved even closer to her.

As she tried to retreat, Amanda was blocked by the edge of the mattress pressing against the backs of her knees. Unwilling desire mingled with a long-smoldering resentment she'd thought she'd been able to put behind her.

"Damn it, Dane." She put both hands on his shoulders and shoved, but she might as well have been trying to move a mountain. He didn't budge. "I told you not to call me *princess*."

"Fine. Since it's obvious that you've grown up, how about *contessa?*"

It suited her, Dane decided. *Princess* had been her father's name for a spoiled young girl. *Contessa* brought to mind a regal woman very much in charge of her life, as Amanda appeared to be.

The temper she'd kept on a taut leash during a very vexing day, broke free. "You know, you really have a lot of nerve." Her voice trembled, which made her all the more angry. She did not want to reveal vulnerability where this man was concerned. "Behaving this way after what you did!"

"What I did?" His own temper, worn to a frazzle from overwork, lack of sleep, and the knowledge that Amanda was returning to Satan's Cove after all these years, rose to engulf hers. "What the hell did I do? Except spend an entire month taking cold showers after some teenage tease kept heating me up?"

"Tease?"

That did it! She struck out at him, aiming for his shoulder, but hitting his upper arm instead. When her fist impacted with a muscle that felt like a boulder, the shock ran all the way up her arm.

"I loved you, damn it! Which just goes to show how stupid a naive, fifteen-year-old girl can be."

What was even more stupid was having wasted so much time thinking about this man. And wondering what she might have done to make things turn out differently.

His answering curse was short and rude. "You were too self-centered that summer to even know the meaning of the word *love*." Impatience shimmered through him. "Face it, contessa, you thought you'd get your kicks practicing your feminine wiles on some small-town hick before taking your newly honed skills back to the big city."

He would have her, Dane decided recklessly. Before she left Smugglers' Inn. And this time, when she drove away from Satan's Cove, he'd keep something of Amanda for himself. And in turn, leave her with something to remember on lonely rainy nights.

"I loved you," she repeated through clenched teeth. She'd never spoken truer words. "But unfortunately, I was stupid enough to give my heart away to someone who only considered me a summer fling."

Thank heavens she'd only given her heart. Because if she'd given her body to this man, she feared she never would have gotten over him.

Which she had.

Absolutely. Completely.

The hell she had.

The way he was looking at her, as if he couldn't decide whether to strangle her or ravish her, made Amanda's heart pound.

"You were a lot more than a summer fling." His fingers tightened painfully on her shoulders. His rough voice vibrated through her, causing an ache only he had ever been able to instill. "When I went back to college, I couldn't stop thinking about you. I thought about you during the day, when I was supposed to be studying. I thought about you at night, after work, when I was supposed to be sleeping. And all the time in between."

It was the lie, more than anything, that hurt. All right, so she'd misinterpreted their romance that long-ago summer.

Amanda was willing to be honest with herself. Why couldn't he be equally truthful?

"It would have been nice," she suggested in a tone as icy as winter sleet, "if during all that time you were allegedly thinking of me, you thought to pick up a pen and write me a letter. A note. Hell, one of those postcards with the lighthouse on it they sell on the revolving rack downstairs next to the registration desk would have been better than nothing."

"I did write to you." He was leaning over her, his eyes so dark she could only see her reflection. "I wrote you a letter the day you left. And the next day. And for days after that. Until it finally got through my thick head that you weren't going to answer."

The accusation literally rocked her. The anger in his gritty voice and on his face told Amanda that Dane was telling the truth. "What letters? I didn't get any letters."

"That's impossible." His gaze raked over her snow-white face, seeking the truth. Comprehension, when it dawned, was staggering. "Hell. Your parents got to them first."

"Apparently so." She thought about what such well-meaning parental subterfuge had cost her. What it had, perhaps, cost Dane. Cost them both.

"You know, *you* could always have written to *me*," Dane said.

"I wanted to. But I couldn't get up the nerve."

He arched a challenging eyebrow. But as she watched reluctant amusement replace the fury in his eyes, Amanda was able to breathe again.

"This from a girl nervy enough to wear a polka-dot bikini horseback riding just to get my attention?" The ploy had worked. The memory of that cute little skimpily clad butt bouncing up and down in that leather saddle had tortured Dane's sleep.

The shared memory brought a reluctant smile from Amanda. She'd paid for that little stunt. If Dane's mother hadn't given her that soothing salve for the chafed skin on the insides of her legs, she wouldn't have been able to walk for a week.

"It was different once I got back home," she admitted now. "I kept thinking about all the older girls who worked at the inn, and went to college with you, and I couldn't imagine why you'd bother carrying a torch for a girl who'd only just gotten her braces off two weeks before coming to Satan's Cove."

Damn. He should have realized she might think that. But at the time, he'd been dazzled by the breezy self-confidence he'd assumed had been bred into Amanda from generations of family wealth.

Oh, he'd known she was too immature—her passionate suggestion that they run away together had been proof of that. But it had never occurred to him that she wasn't as self-assured as she'd seemed. She had, after all, captured the attention of every male in Satan's Cove between the ages of thirteen and ninety. She'd also succeeded in wrapping him—a guy with no intention of letting any woman sidetrack his plan for wealth and success—around her little finger.

Looking down at her now, Dane wondered how much of the girl remained beneath the slick professional veneer Amanda had acquired during the intervening years.

"I did work up my nerve to call you once," she said quietly. "But you'd already gone back to school and the woman who answered the phone here said she didn't have your forwarding address."

"You could have asked my mother."

Her weary shrug told him that she'd considered that idea and rejected it.

Dane wondered what would have happened if his letters had been delivered. Would his life have turned out differently if he'd gotten her call?

Never one to look back, Dane turned his thoughts to the future. The immediate future. Like the next week.

"It appears we have some unfinished business." His hand slipped beneath her hair to cup the back of her neck.

"Dane—" She pressed her palm against his shirt and encountered a wall of muscle every bit as hard as it had been when he was nineteen. There was, she decided recklessly, definitely something to be said for a life of physical work.

"All this heat can't be coming from me." His fingers massaged her neck in a way that was anything but soothing as his lips scorched a trail up her cheek. "The sparks are still there, contessa." His breath was warm against her skin. "You can't deny it."

No, she couldn't. Her entire body was becoming hot and quivery. "Please." Her voice was a throaty shimmer of sound. "I can't concentrate when you're doing that."

"Then don't concentrate." His mouth skimmed along her jaw; Amanda instinctively tilted her head back. "Just feel." When his tongue touched the hollow of her throat, her pulse jumped. "Go with the flow."

"I can't," she complained weakly, even as her rebellious fingers gathered up a handful of white cotton T-shirt. "This week is important to me."

"I remember a time when you said *I* was important to you." The light abrasion of his evening beard scraped seductively against her cheek as his hands skimmed down her sides.

"That was then." She drew in a sharp breath as his palms brushed against her breasts and set them to tingling. In all her twenty-five years Dane was the only man who could touch off the fires of passion smoldering deep inside her. He was the only man who could make her want. And, she reminded herself, he'd been the only man who'd ever made her cry. "This is now."

"It doesn't feel so different." He drew her to him. "*You* don't feel so different."

He wanted her. Too much for comfort. Too much for safety. The way she was literally melting against him made Dane ache in ways he'd forgotten he could ache.

"This has been a long time coming, Amanda." His hands settled low on her hips. "We need to get it out of our systems. Once and for all."

She could feel every hard male part of him through her clothes. He was fully, thrillingly aroused. Even as she tried to warn herself against succumbing to such blatant masculinity, Amanda linked her fingers around his neck and leaned into him.

"I don't know about *your* system," she said breathlessly, as his tongue skimmed up her neck, "but mine's doing just fine."

"Liar." His lips brushed against hers. Teasing, testing, tormenting.

Desire throbbed and pooled between her thighs. Flames were flicking hotly through her veins. She'd never wanted a man the way she wanted Dane Cutter right now. Worse yet, she'd never *needed* a man the way she needed him at this moment.

Which was why she had to back away from temptation. When, and if, she did make love to Dane, she wanted to make certain she knew exactly what she was doing. And why.

She needed to be certain that the desire coursing through her veins was not simply a knee-jerk response to the only man who'd ever made her burn. She had to convince herself that she wasn't succumbing to the seduction of the romantic setting, old memories, and sensual fantasies.

After suffering the resultant pain from her impulsive, teenage behavior, Amanda had acquired a need for an orderly, controlled life. Unfortunately, there was nothing orderly or controlled about the way Dane Cutter made her feel.

"I need to think," she protested weakly. "It's been a long and frustrating day and I'm exhausted, Dane."

"Fine." He'd give her that. There would, Dane told himself, be other times. "But before I go, let me give you something to think about."

Amanda knew what was coming. Knew she should resist. Even as she warned herself to back away now, before she got in over her head, another voice in the back of her mind pointed out that this was her chance to prove she was no longer a foolish young girl who could lose her heart over a simple kiss.

Since the second option seemed the more logical, Amanda went with it. She stood there, her palms pressed against his chest, as he slowly, deliberately, lowered his mouth to hers.

It was definitely not what she'd been expecting.

The first time he'd kissed her, that long-ago night when she'd come to his room, clad in her sexiest nightie, Dane had been frustrated and angry—angry at her for having teased him unmercifully, angry at himself for not being able to resist.

His mouth had swooped down, causing their teeth to clang painfully together as he ground his lips against hers. He'd used his mouth and his tongue as a weapon and she'd found it shocking and thrilling at the same time.

Later, as the days went by, Dane had grown more and more sexually frustrated, and it had showed. Although his kisses were no longer tinged with anger, they were riddled with a hot, desperate hunger that equaled her own.

Although the attraction was still there a decade later, it was more than apparent to Amanda that the years had mellowed Dane, taught him patience. And finesse.

He cupped her face in his hands and she trembled.

He touched his mouth to hers and she sighed.

With a rigid control that cost him dearly, Dane forced himself to take his time, coaxing her into the mists by skimming kisses from one side of her full, generous mouth to the other.

"Dane—"

Ignoring her faint protest, he caught her bottom lip in his teeth and tugged, causing a slow, almost-languid ache.

Prepared for passion, she had no defenses against this exquisite, dreamy pleasure. Amanda twined her arms tighter around his neck and allowed herself to sink into his kiss.

"Oh, Dane . . ."

"Lord, I like the way you say my name." His breath was like a summer breeze against her parted lips. "Say it again."

At this suspended moment in time, unable to deny Dane anything, Amanda softly obliged.

"Your voice reminds me of warm honey." He soothed the flesh his teeth had bruised with his tongue. "Sweet and thick and warm."

He angled his head and continued making love to her with his mouth. The tip of his tongue slipped silkily between her lips, then withdrew. Then dipped in again, deeper this time, only to withdraw once more.

Every sense was heightened. Every nerve ending in her body hummed.

His clever, wicked tongue repeated that glorious movement again and again, each time delving deeper, seducing hers into a slow, sensual dance. The rest of the world drifted away. Until there was only Dane. And the pure pleasure of his mouth.

Damn. This wasn't going the way he'd planned. The rich, warm taste of her was causing an ache in his loins far worse than the teenage horniness he'd suffered the last time he'd been with Amanda like this. Sweat broke out on his forehead as he felt the soft swell of her belly pressing against his erection.

Her throaty moans were driving him crazy and if she didn't stop grinding against him that way, stoking fires that were already close to burning out of control, he was going to throw her down on that bed and rip away those travel-rumpled clothes.

He imagined sliding his tongue down her throat, over her breasts, swirling around the hard little nipples that were pressing against his chest, before cutting a wet swath down her slick, quivering stomach, making her writhe with need; then lower still, until he was sliding it between her legs, gathering up the sweet taste—

"Hell."

Jerking his mind back from that perilous precipice, Dane literally pushed himself away from her. For his sake, not hers.

It had happened again! Ten minutes alone with Amanda and he'd nearly lost it. What was it about this woman? Even at nineteen he'd been far from inexperienced. Yet all it had taken then—and, apparently, all it took even now—was a taste of her succulent lips, the feel of her hot, feminine body pressed against his, to bring him to the brink of exploding.

Her head still spinning, her body pulsing, Amanda stared at Dane and watched as his rugged face closed up.

He jammed his hands into the pockets of his jeans with such force that her eyes were drawn to the brusque movement. Heaven help her, the sight of that bulge pressing against the faded denim caused something like an ocean swell to rise up from her most feminine core.

Realizing what she was staring at, Dane again cursed his lack of control. "I'm not going to apologize." His voice was distant, and amazingly cold for a man who, only moments earlier, had nearly caused them both to go up in flames.

"I wouldn't ask you to." She dragged her hair back from her temples, appalled by the discovery that her hands were shaking. "I'm no longer a teenager, Dane. You don't have to worry about my father showing up at the door with a shotgun."

Dane almost laughed. He wondered what she'd say if he told her that he found the idea of an irate father far less threatening than what he was currently feeling.

"You're tired." And she had been for some time, if the circles beneath her eyes were any indication. "We'll talk tomorrow. After you've had some rest."

"There's no need to—"

"I said, we'll talk tomorrow."

Amanda stiffened, unaccustomed to taking such sharp, direct orders from any man. Before she could argue, he said, "Just dial three for room service. The cook will fix anything you'd like. Within reason."

With that, he was gone. Leaving Amanda confused. And wanting.

As he descended the narrow, curving stairway, Dane assured himself that his only problem was he'd been taken by surprise. Initially, he hadn't expected Amanda to show up from the shadows of the past. Then, when she had arrived, he certainly hadn't expected such a knee-jerk, gut-wrenching physical reaction.

By tomorrow morning, Dane vowed, he'd have control of his body.

What was worrying the hell out of him was the problem he feared he was going to have gaining control over his heart.

4

─────►◄─────

Amanda was not in a good mood the following morning, as she went downstairs to prepare for the kickoff meeting. Her headache had returned with a vengeance and her stomach was tied up in knots. She'd spent the night tossing and turning, reliving old memories of her days—and nights—at Smugglers' Inn.

And then, when she had finally fallen asleep shortly before dawn, her dreams had been filled with the man who had, impossibly, become an even better kisser. The sensual dreams had resulted in her waking up with an unhealthy curiosity about all the women with whom Dane had spent the past ten years practicing his kissing technique.

After a false turn, she found the conference room Susan had reserved. Ten years ago, the room had been a sleeping porch. The oversize green screens had been replaced with glass, protecting occupants from the unpredictable coastal weather without taking away from the dazzling view, which, at the moment, was draped in a soft silver mist.

It was absolutely lovely. Greg would find nothing to complain about here. The only problem would be keeping people's minds off the scenery and focused on the challenge.

Drawn by the pull of the past, she walked over to the wall of windows and gazed out, trying to catch a glimpse of the cave where she and Dane had shared such bliss.

Both relieved and disappointed to see the fog blocked the view of that stretch of beach, she turned her back on the sea and crossed the room to a pine sideboard where urns of coffee and hot water for tea had been placed. Beside the urn were baskets of breakfast breads, and white platters of fresh fruit.

Amanda poured herself a cup of coffee and placed some strawberries onto a small plate. When the fragrant lure proved impossible to resist, she plucked a blueberry muffin from one of the baskets, then set to work unpacking the boxes of supplies.

As she separated T-shirts bearing the team challenge logo into red and blue stacks, Amanda wondered what Dane was doing.

Although she remembered him to have been an early riser, she doubted he'd have arrived at the inn. Not after the late hours he'd worked yesterday. Which was just as well, since she still hadn't sorted out her feelings. All the agonizing she'd done during the long and sleepless night had only confused her more.

Last night, alone with him in the tower room that had been filled with bittersweet memories, it had felt as if no time at all had passed since that night they'd lain in each other's arms, driving each other to painful distraction, whispering tender words of love, vowing desperate promises.

This morning, Amanda was trying to convince herself that stress, exhaustion and the surprise of seeing Dane again had been responsible for her having responded so quickly and so strongly to him. To his touch. His kiss.

Memories of that enticing kiss flooded back, warming her to the core. "You have to stop this," she scolded herself aloud.

It was imperative that she concentrate on the difficult week ahead. If she allowed her thoughts to drift constantly to Dane Cutter, she'd never pull off a successful challenge. And without a successful challenge, not only would she lose her chance for promotion, she could end up being stuck with Greg Parsons for a very long time.

"And that," she muttered, "is not an option."

"Excuse me?"

Having believed herself to be alone, Amanda spun around and saw a woman standing in the doorway. She was casually dressed in navy shorts, a white polo shirt and white sneakers. If it hadn't been for her name, written in red script above her breast, Amanda would have taken her for a guest.

"I was just talking to myself," she said with embarrassment.

"I do that all the time." The woman's smile was as warm and friendly as Mindy Taylor's had been last night. "Sometimes I even answer myself back, which was beginning to worry me, until Dane said that the time to worry was if I began ignoring myself."

She crossed the room and held out her hand. "I'm Reva Carlson. And you must be Amanda Stockenberg."

Having observed the frenzied activity that had gone into preparing the tower room, then hearing how Dane had insisted on carrying Amanda's bags last night, Reva was more than a little interested in this particular guest. As was every other employee of Smugglers' Inn.

"You're the conference manager Susan spoke with," Amanda remembered.

"Among other things. The management structure around this place tends to be a bit loose."

"Oh?" Amanda wasn't certain she liked the sound of that. One of the advantages of the Mariner Seaside Golf Resort and Conference Center had been an assistant manager whose sole function had been to tend to the group's every need.

"Everyone's trained to fill in wherever they're needed, to allow for optimum service," Reva revealed the management style Dane had introduced. "Although I'm embarrassed to admit that I've been barred from the kitchen after last week's fire."

"Fire?" After having watched her first choice of resort go up in flames, Amanda definitely didn't like hearing that.

"Oh, it wasn't really that big a deal." The shoulders of the white knit shirt rose and fell in a careless shrug. "I was merely trying my hand at pears flambé. When I poured just a smidgen too much brandy into the pans, things got a little hot for a time." Her smile widened. "By the time the fire department showed up, Dane had things under control."

When even the sound of his name caused a hitch in her breathing, Amanda knew she was in deep, deep trouble. "Dane was working in the kitchen?"

"Sure." Another shrug. "I told you, we're pretty loose around here. And Dane's amazingly handy at everything. He shot the pan with the fire extinguisher, and that was that. But in the meantime, I've been banned from any further cooking experiments, though Mary did promise to let me frost a birthday cake for one of our guests tomorrow."

"Mary?" At the familiar name, Amanda stopped trying to picture Dane in an apron, comfortable in a kitchen. "Mary Cutter?"

"That's right." Reva tilted her head. "Sounds as if you know her."

"I used to." Amanda couldn't quite stop the soft sigh. "I came here with my parents on a vacation ten years ago."

"Mindy mentioned something about that." Reva's friendly gaze turned speculative. "I guess Dane must have been working here at the time, too." Her voice went up on the end of the sentence, turning it into a question.

It was Amanda's turn to shrug. "I suppose. It was a long time ago, and there was quite a large staff, so it's hard to remember everyone."

From the knowing expression in the convention manager's eyes, Amanda had the feeling she wasn't fooling her for a moment. "I do remember his mother made the best peach pie I've ever tasted." She also, Amanda had discovered this morning, baked dynamite blueberry muffins.

"Mary's peach pie wins the blue ribbon at the county fair every year." Returning to her work mode, Reva glanced around the room. "Do you have everything you need?"

"I think so." Amanda's gaze took another slow sweep around the room, trying to seek out any lapses Greg might catch.

"If you think of anything—anything at all—don't hesitate to call on any of us. I have to run into town on some errands, but Dane's around here somewhere."

"I'm sure we'll be fine," Amanda said quickly. Too quickly, she realized, as Reva's gaze narrowed ever so slightly.

"Well, good luck." Reva turned to leave. "With everything."

Matters taken care of to her satisfaction, Reva Carlson returned to her own work, leaving Amanda with the feeling that the woman's parting comment had little to do with the upcoming challenge exercises.

After she finished unpacking the boxes, Amanda headed down the hall to the kitchen, to thank Mary Cutter for the superb Continental breakfast, when she heard her name being called.

Believing it to be someone from the agency, she turned, surprised to see two familiar faces.

"Miss Minnie? Miss Pearl?" The elderly sisters had been guests the last time Amanda had stayed at the inn.

"Hello, dear," one of them—Minnie or Pearl, Amanda couldn't remember which was which—said. Her rosy face was as round as a harvest moon and wreathed in a smile. "We heard you'd come back. It's lovely to see you again."

"It's nice to see you, too. It's also a surprise."

"I don't know why it should be," the other sister said. "With the exception of the three years the inn was closed—"

"A terrible shame," the other interrupted. "As I was telling Dane just yesterday—"

"Sister!" A scowl darkened a sharp, hatchet face. "I was speaking."

"I'm sorry, sister." There was a brief nod of a lavender head that had been permed into corkscrews; the pastel hue complemented the woman's pink complexion. "I was just pointing out to Amanda how sad it was that such a lovely inn had been allowed to fall into disrepair."

"You'd never know that to look at it now," Amanda said.

"That's because Dane has been working around the clock," the thinner of the two sisters huffed. It was more than a little obvious she resented having her story side-tracked. "As I was saying, with the exception of those three unfortunate years, we have been visiting Smugglers' Inn since 1932."

"I believe it was '33, sister."

A forceful chin thrust out. "It was 1932."

"Are you sure?"

"Of course. It was the year the Lindberg baby was kidnapped and all the guests were talking about the tragedy."

"I seem to remember everyone talking about those two bank robbers."

"That was two years later," the other snapped with the certainty of a woman who'd spent forty-five years as the research librarian for the Klamath County Library in southern Oregon. "Bonnie and Clyde were shot in 1934. That was also the year FBI agents killed John Dillinger outside that movie theater."

The term *sibling rivalry* could have been invented to define Minnie and Pearl Davenport. Recalling all too well how these arguments could go on all day, Amanda repeated how nice it was to see the women again and escaped into the kitchen.

This room, too, was as she remembered it—warm and cheerful and immensely inviting. Fragrant, mouth-watering steam rose from the pots bubbling away on the gleaming stove; more copper pots hung from a ceiling rack and the windowsill was home to a row of clay pots filled with fresh green herbs.

An enormous refrigerator that hadn't been there the last time Amanda had sneaked into the kitchen for a heart-to-heart talk with Mary Cutter was open.

"Hello?"

A dark head popped out from behind the stainless-steel door. "Amanda, hello!" Dane's mother's expression was warm and welcoming. She closed the refrigerator and opened her arms. "I was hoping you'd get a chance to escape those boring old business meetings and visit with an old friend."

As she hugged the woman, Amanda realized that Mary Cutter had, indeed, become a friend that summer. Even though, looking back on it, she realized how concerned Mary had been for Dane. As she would have been, Amanda admitted now, if some sex-crazed, underage teenage girl had been chasing after her son.

"They're not that bad." Amanda felt duty-bound to defend the group.

"Oh?" Releasing her, Mary went over to the stove and poured two cups of coffee. She put them on the table, and gestured for Amanda to sit down. "Then why do you have those dark circles beneath your eyes?"

Amanda unconsciously lifted her fingers to the blue shadows she thought she'd managed to conceal successfully this morning. It was bad enough having to deal with Dane and their past, which now seemed to be unsettled. By the time the corporate challenge week was over, she'd undoubtedly be buying Erase by the carton.

"I've been working long hours lately."

"You're not sleeping very well, either, I'd suspect. And you have a headache."

"It's not that bad," Amanda lied as Mary reached out and rubbed at the lines carving furrows between her eyes.

The older woman's touch was gentle and more maternal than any Amanda had ever received from her own mother. Then again, the Stockenbergs never had been touchers. The Cutters—mother and son—definitely were.

Mary's smile didn't fade, but the way she was looking at her, hard and deep, made Amanda want to change the subject. "I just ran into Miss Minnie and Miss Pearl," she said. "But I couldn't remember which was which."

"Minnie is the one with white hair and an attitude. Pearl has lavender hair and hides Hershey's Kisses all over the inn."

"Why would she do that?"

"Because the poor dear has an enormous sweet tooth. And Minnie has her on a diet that would starve a gerbil." Mary flashed a quick grin that was remarkably like her son's, although it didn't have the capability to affect Amanda in such a devastating manner. "I feel so sorry for Pearl. She's been sneaking in here for snacks ever since they arrived last week."

"Well, I can certainly understand that. I had a muffin that was just short of heaven."

"I'm so pleased you enjoyed it." Mary's eyes skimmed over Amanda judiciously. "You're a bit thin, dear. We'll have to see what we can do about fattening you up a little."

"A woman can never be too thin," Amanda said, quoting one of her sleek mother's favorite axioms.

"Want to bet?" a deep voice asked from the doorway.

Amanda tamped down the little burst of pleasure brought about by the sight of Dane, clad again in jeans. Today's shirt was faded chambray; his shoes were high-topped sneakers.

Mary greeted him with a smile. "Good morning, darling."

"Morning." He crossed the room on a long, easy stride and kissed his mother's cheek. "Do I smell sugar cookies?"

"It's my new cologne," Mary said with a laugh. "The saleswoman said it has vanilla in it." She shook her head in mock regret. "She also said men would find it impossible to resist. I'm afraid I was oversold."

"Never met a man yet who didn't like sugar cookies," Dane said agreeably. His grin slipped a notch as his attention turned to Amanda. "Good morning."

Amanda had watched the way he brushed his finger down his mother's cheek in a casual, intimate gesture that was as natural to him as breathing. Once again she was reminded how different the Cutters were from the Stockenbergs. It would be wise to keep those differences in mind over the next several days.

"Good morning." Her tone was friendly, but cool. She could have been speaking to a stranger at a bus stop.

"Sleep well?" His tone was as studiously casual as hers.

"Like a baby," she lied. She pushed herself up from the table. "Well, I really do have to get back to work. I just wanted to stop in and say hi," she told Mary. "And to thank you for the lovely breakfast."

"It's been lovely seeing you again, dear." Dane's mother took Amanda's hand in both of hers. "I realize you're going to be extremely busy, but I hope you can find time to visit again."

"I'd like that." It was the truth.

Without another word to Dane, Amanda placed her cup on the counter, then left the kitchen.

"Well, she certainly has grown up to be a lovely young lady," Mary said.

"Really?" Dane's answering shrug was forced. "I didn't really notice."

Mary poured another cup of coffee and placed it in front of him. "Reva says she has a very responsible position at that advertising agency."

This earned little more than a grunt.

"I couldn't help noticing she's not wearing any ring on her left hand."

Dane's face shuttered. "No offense, Mom, but I really don't want to talk about Amanda."

"Of course, dear," Mary replied smoothly. But as she turned to the stove and poured pancake batter into an iron skillet, Mary Cutter was smiling.

Despite instructions that they were to meet at eight o'clock sharp, the team members straggled into the conference room. By the time everyone had gotten coffee, fruit and pastries and taken their seats, it was twenty-eight minutes past the time the kickoff had been scheduled to begin.

"Well, this is certainly getting off to a dandy start," muttered Greg, who was sitting beside Amanda at the pine trestle table at the front of the room. "Didn't you send out my memo letting the troops know I expected them to be prompt?"

"Of course." Amanda refrained from pointing out that if one wanted troops to follow orders, it was helpful if they respected their commanding officer. "We arrived awfully late last night," she said, seeking some excuse for the tardy team members. "Everyone was probably a little tired this morning."

His only response to her efforts was a muttered curse that did not give Amanda a great deal of encouragement.

Greg stood and began to outline the week's activities, striding back and forth at the front of the room like General Patton addressing the soldiers of the Third Army. He was waving his laser pointer at the detailed flowchart as if it were Patton's famed riding crop. The troops seemed uniformly unimpressed by all the red, blue and yellow rectangles.

As he set about explaining the need for consistent process and implementation, even Amanda's mind began to wander, which was why she didn't hear the door open at the back of the room.

"I'm sorry to interrupt," one of last night's bellmen, who bore an amazing resemblance to Brad Pitt, said. "But Ms. Stockenberg has a phone call."

"Take a message," Greg snapped before Amanda could answer.

"He says it's urgent."

"I'd better take it," Amanda said.

"Just make it quick. I intend to get on schedule."

"I'll be right back." Amanda resisted the urge to salute.

The news was not good. "But you have to come," she insisted when the caller, the man she'd hired to conduct the physical adventure portion of the weekend, explained his predicament. "I understand you've broken your leg. But surely you can at least sit on the beach and instruct—"

She was cut off by a flurry of denial on the other end of the line. "Oh. In traction? I'm so sorry to hear that." She reached into her pocket, pulled out the antacids she was never without and popped one into her mouth.

"Well, of course you need to rest. And get well soon."
She dragged her hand through her hair. "There's no need to
apologize. You didn't fall off that motorcycle on purpose."

She hung up the phone with a bit more force than necessary. "Damn."

"Got a problem?"

Amanda spun around and glared up at Dane. "I'm getting a little tired of the way you have of sneaking up on
people."

"Sorry." The dancing light in his eyes said otherwise.

"No." She sighed and shook her head. "I'm the one who
should apologize for snapping at you. It's just that I really
need this week to go well, and before we can even get started
on the kayak race, my adventure expert ends up in the hospital."

"That *is* a tough break."

She could hear the amusement in his voice. "Don't you
dare laugh at me."

"I wouldn't think of it." He reached out and rubbed at
the parallel lines his mother had smoothed earlier. "I don't
suppose a hotshot businesswoman—with her own window
office and fancy Italian-leather chair—would need any advice?"

The soothing touch felt too good. Too right. Amanda
backed away. "At this point, I'd take advice from the devil
himself." Realizing how snippy she sounded, she felt obliged
to apologize yet again.

"Don't worry about it. People say things they don't mean
under stress." Which he knew only too well. Dane had
found it enlightening that the temper he'd developed while
working for the Whitfield Palace hotel chain seemed to have
vanished when he'd bought the inn, despite all the problems refurbishing it had entailed. "How about me?"

"How about you, what?"

"How about me subbing for your kayak guy?"

Remembering how he'd taught her to paddle that double kayak so many years ago, Amanda knew it was the perfect solution. Except for one thing.

"Don't you have work to do?"

Dane shrugged. "It'll keep."

"I wouldn't want you to get in trouble."

"Why don't you let me worry about that, contessa? Besides, we all kind of pitch in where needed around here."

That was exactly what Reva had told her. And Amanda was grateful enough not to contest that ridiculous name. "Thank you. I really appreciate your help."

"Hey, that's what we're here for." He grinned and skimmed a dark finger down the slope of her nose. "Service With a Smile, that's the motto at Smugglers' Inn."

The knot of tension in her stomach unwound. It was impossible to worry when he was smiling at her that way. It was nearly impossible to remember that the man represented a dangerous distraction.

Relieved that she'd overcome the first hurdle of the week, and putting aside the nagging little problem of what she was going to do about the rest of the scheduled adventure exercises, Amanda returned to the conference room and began handing out the challenge-team shirts.

"What the hell are these?" Don Patterson, the marketing manager, asked.

"They're to denote the different teams," Amanda explained. "Reds versus blues."

"Like shirts versus skins," Marvin Kenyon, who'd played some high school basketball, said.

"Exactly."

"I wouldn't mind playing shirts and skins with Kelli," Peter Wanger from the computer-support division said with a leer directed toward the public-relations manager, who was provocatively dressed in a pair of tight white jeans and a red jersey crop top. Her navy suspenders framed voluptuous breasts that, if they hadn't been surgically enhanced, could undoubtedly qualify as natural wonders of the world.

"Watch it, Peter," Amanda warned. "Or you'll have to watch that video on sexual harassment in the workplace again."

"Oh, Peter was just joking," Kelli said quickly, sending a perky cheerleader smile his way. "It doesn't bother me, Amanda."

That might be. But it did bother Greg. Amanda watched her superior's jaw clench. "Amanda's right," he growled. If looks could kill, Peter would be drawn and quartered, then buried six feet under the sand. "Just because we're not in the office doesn't mean that I'll stand for inappropriate behavior."

It sounded good. But everyone in the room knew that what was really happening was that Greg had just stamped his own personal No Trespassing sign on Kelli Kyle's wondrous chest.

"Talk about inappropriate," Laura Quinlan muttered as Amanda handed her a red T-shirt. "My kid's Barbie doll has tops larger than that bimbo's."

At thirty-six, Laura was a displaced homemaker who'd recently been hired as a junior copywriter. Amanda knew she was struggling to raise two children on her own after her physician husband had left her for his office assistant—a young woman who, if Laura could be believed, could be Kelli Kyle's evil twin.

Secretly agreeing about the inappropriateness of Kelli's attire, but not wanting to take sides, Amanda didn't answer.

"I can't wear this color," Nadine Roberts complained when Amanda handed her one of the red shirts. "I had my colors done and I'm a summer."

"This week you're an autumn." Amanda tossed a blue shirt to Julian Palmer.

"You certainly chose a graphically unsatisfying design," he complained.

"We should have come to you for help," she said, soothing the art director's easily ruffled feathers. Personally, she thought the white Team Challenge script just dandy. "But I knew how overworked you've been with the Uncle Paul's potato chip account, and didn't want to add any more pressure."

"The man's an idiot," Julian grumbled. "Insisting on those claymation dancing barbecue chips."

"It worked for the raisin growers," Kelli reminded everyone cheerfully. Despite all the rumors that had circulated since the woman's arrival two weeks ago, no one could accuse her of not being unrelentingly upbeat.

Amanda had been surprised to discover that beneath that bubbly-cheerleader personality and bimbo clothing, Kelli possessed a steel-trap mind when it came to her work. Which made it even more surprising that she'd stoop to having an affair with a man like Greg.

Not that there was actually any proof, other than gossip, that they were sleeping together, she reminded herself. However, given Greg's Lothario tendencies, along with all the time the pair spent together in his office with the door closed, Amanda certainly wouldn't have bet against the possibility.

Julian stiffened and shot Kelli a look that suggested her IQ was on a level with Uncle Paul's. "Potato chips," he said, "are not raisins."

No one in the room dared challenge that proclamation.

"Wait a damn minute," Marvin Kenyon complained when Amanda handed him a blue shirt. "I categorically refuse to be on *his* team." He jerked a thumb in Julian's direction.

Amanda opened her mouth to answer, but Greg beat her to the punch. "You'll be on whatever team I tell you you're on," he barked from the front of the room. "In case I haven't made myself clear, people, challenge week isn't about choice. It's about competition. Teamwork.

"And effective immediately, you are all going to work together as teams. Or at the end of the week, I'll start handing out pink slips. Do I make myself clear?"

He was answered by a low, obviously unhappy mumble.

Smooth move, Greg, Amanda thought.

The worst problem with mergers was their effect on the employees. Even more so in advertising, where people were the agency's only real assets.

The rash of changeovers had caused dislocation, disaffection, underperformance and just plain fear. Which explained why more and more accounts were leaving the agency with each passing day. It was, after all, difficult to be creative when you thought you were going to be fired.

There were times, and this was definitely one of them, when Amanda wished she'd stuck to her youthful dreams of creating a family rather than an ad for a new, improved detergent or a toothpaste that supposedly would make the high school football quarterback ask the class wallflower to the prom.

When the idea of home and children once again brought Dane to the forefront of her mind, she shook off the thought and led the group out of the room, down to the beach where the first challenge activity was scheduled to take place.

5

———◆———

"Oh, my God," Laura said as the group reached the beach and found Dane waiting. "I think I'm in love."

While Greg had been harassing the troops and Amanda had been handing out T-shirts, Dane had changed into a black neoprene body glove. The suit somehow seemed to reveal more of him than if he were stark-naked.

His arms, his powerful legs, his chest, looked as if they had been chiseled from marble. No, Amanda decided, marble was too cold. Dane could have been hewn from one of the centuries-old redwoods found in an old-growth forest.

"That man is, without a doubt, the most drop-dead-gorgeous male I've ever seen in my life." Kelli was staring at Dane the way a religious zealot might stare at her god. "Oh, I do believe I'm going to enjoy this week."

"We're not here to enjoy ourselves," Greg ground out. "It's not a damn holiday." He turned his sharp gaze on Amanda. "That's the guy you hired to lead the adventure exercises?"

Call her petty, but Amanda found watching Greg literally seething with masculine jealousy more than a little enjoyable. Less enjoyable was the realization that Kelli's and Laura's lustful looks and comments had triggered a bit of her own jealousy.

"Not exactly."

Blond brows came crashing down. "What does that mean?"

"I'll explain later." She cast a significant glance down at her watch. "You're the one who wanted to stay on schedule, Greg. Come with me and I'll introduce you."

The introductions were over quickly, neither man seeming to find much to like about the other.

"The plan," Amanda explained to Dane, "as it was originally laid out to me, works like a relay race. Team members pair up, two to a kayak, paddle out to the lighthouse, circle it, then return back to the beach where the next group takes their places in the kayak and follows the same course. The best combined times for the two out of three heats is declared the winner."

Dane nodded. "Sounds easy enough."

"Easy for you to say. You haven't seen this group in action."

Seeing her worried expression and remembering what she'd told him about this week being vastly important to her, Dane understood her concern.

"Don't worry, Ms. Stockenberg," he said in his best businesslike tone, the one that had served him well for all those years in the big city, "before the week's over, you'll have turned your group into a lean, mean, advertising machine."

"That's the point," Greg Parsons snapped.

Amanda, who'd detected the sarcasm in Dane's tone, didn't respond. Instead, she introduced Dane to the others, then stood back and ceded control to the man she hoped could pull it off.

He didn't raise his voice above his usual conversational tone, but as he began to explain the basics of kayaking, Amanda noticed that a hush settled over the suddenly attentive group. Even the men were hanging on every word.

It was more than the fact that he was a stunningly good-looking male specimen. As amazing as it seemed for a man who'd been content to stay in the same job he'd had in high school, Dane Cutter definitely displayed leadership potential, making Amanda wonder yet again what had happened to sidetrack all his lofty career goals.

Perhaps, she considered, once this week was over and she'd earned the position of Northwest creative director, she'd offer Dane a job in management. After all, if he actually managed to pull this disparate, backbiting group into cohesive teams, helping him escape a dead-end life in Satan's Cove would be the least she could do.

Then again, she reminded herself firmly when she realized she was thinking too much like her autocratic father, there was no reason for Dane to be ashamed of having chosen a life of manual labor. It was, she admitted reluctantly, more honest than advertising.

Dane gave the teams a brief spiel about the versatility of kayaks, demonstrated forward and bracing strokes, explaining how the foot-operated rudder would help steer in crosswinds or rough seas, and skimmed over the wood-paddles-versus-fiberglass argument.

Amanda was not surprised to discover that despite the introduction of high-tech Kevlar and carbon-fiber models, Dane remained an advocate of wood. The fact that he obviously felt strongly about a century-old inn proved he was a traditionalist at heart.

When he asked for questions, Kelli's hand shot up. "Shouldn't we be wearing wet suits like yours?" she asked.

"It's not really necessary," Dane assured her, making Amanda extremely relieved. She figured the sight of Kelli Kyle in a neoprene body glove could easily cause at least two heart attacks.

"But what if we get wet?"

"One can only hope," Peter murmured, earning laughter from several of the men and another sharp glare from Greg. At the same time, Amanda worried that Kelli in a wet T-shirt could be even more distracting than Kelli in a snug neoprene suit.

"Hopefully that won't prove a problem," Dane said with an answering smile.

"I've seen kayaking on the Discovery channel." This from Nadine Roberts. "And they always tip over."

"That technique is called an Eskimo roll. And you don't have to worry about learning it for this exercise," Dane told her.

"What if we don't intend to learn it? What if we roll anyway?" An auditor in the accounting department, Nadine was not accustomed to letting things slide.

"Never happen." Dane's grin was quick and reassuring. "You're thinking of the Inuit cruiser style, which is designed for speed and minimum wind interference. You'll be in double touring kayaks, which are extremely stable. Think of them as floating minivans."

"My minivan is a lot bigger," Laura argued.

"People," Greg interjected sharply, "we're wasting valuable time here." He turned toward Dane. "As fascinating as all this might be," he said, his sarcastic tone indicating otherwise, "we don't have all day. So, if you're through with the instructions, Cutter, it's time to get this show on the road."

"It's your show," Dane said agreeably. But Amanda could see a simmering irritation in his dark eyes. "I'll need a volunteer for a demonstration." His seemingly casual gaze moved over the group before landing on Amanda. "Ms. Stockenberg," he said, "how about helping me with a little show-and-tell?"

Every head on the beach had turned toward her. Knowing that refusal would garner unwanted interest, Amanda shrugged. "Fine."

She took the orange life jacket Dane held out to her and put it on over her challenge T-shirt.

"Need any help with that?" he asked, reminding her of the time she'd pretended to need him to fasten the ties for her.

"I'm fine, thank you."

"Actually," he murmured, for her ears only, "you're a helluva lot better than fine, contessa."

Her temper flared, predictably. Remembering where she was, Amanda tamped it down.

"You'll need this." He handed her a helmet not unlike the one she wore when rollerblading or biking. "There are a lot of rocks around the lighthouse."

"I thought you said there's no risk of capsizing," she argued as she nevertheless put the white fiberglass helmet on.

"Good point. But it never hurts to be prepared."

Good point, she echoed mentally as she watched him drag the kayak toward the water. If she'd been prepared to discover Dane still working here, she wouldn't be suffering from these unsettling feelings.

Within minutes of being afloat, she began to remember the rhythm he'd so patiently taught her that long-ago summer. Holding the blade of the wooden paddle close to her chest, her hands a bit more than shoulders' width apart, she plunged the blade in cleanly, close to the hull, pulling back with her lower hand, using torso rotation rather than arm strength, punching forward with her upper hand at the same time. When the blade of the paddle reached her hip, she snapped it out of the water and stroked on the other side.

Stab, pull, snap. Stab, pull, snap. Behind her, she could feel Dane moving in concert. *Stab, pull, snap.* "Not bad,"

Dane said. "For someone who probably considers the rowing machine at the gym roughing it."

Since his remark hit close to the truth, Amanda opted not to take offense. "I can't believe it's coming back so fast." *Stab, pull, snap. Left, right, left, right.* Although the touring kayak was built for stability, not speed, they were skimming through the surf toward the lighthouse. "I suppose it's like riding a bicycle."

"Or kissing," Dane suggested. *Stab, pull, snap.* The paddles continued to swish through the water. "We always did that well together, too. Ten years ago. And again, last night."

His words stopped her cold. "I don't want to talk about last night." Unnerved, she forgot to pull the paddle out until it had drifted beyond her hip. When she did, she caused the boat to veer off course.

The brisk professional ad executive was back. Dane was tempted to flip the kayak just to teach her a lesson. And to cool himself off. Didn't she know what she'd done to him last night? Didn't she realize how all it had taken was the taste of those succulent lips and the feel of that soft body against his to cause time to go spinning backward and make him feel like a horny, sex-starved teenager again?

"Tough," he deftly corrected, setting them straight again. Didn't she know that showing up this morning in that soft cotton T-shirt and those shorts that made her legs look as if they went all the way up to her neck was like waving a red flag in front of a very frustrated bull?

When he felt his hand tighten in a death grip on the smooth wooden shaft, he flexed his fingers, restraining the urge to put them around her shoulders to shake her.

"Because I have no intention of spending the next five nights lying awake, thinking about might-have-beens."

His tone was gruff, but Amanda was no longer an easily cowed fifteen-year-old girl. She began to shoot him a glare over her shoulder, but the lethal look in his eyes had her missing yet another stroke.

"You agreed to teach the kayaking just to get me alone with you, didn't you?"

"I could see from that schedule you and Mr. Slick have devised for the week that having you to myself for any decent length of time was going to be difficult, if not impossible," he agreed without displaying an iota of guilt about utilizing such subterfuge. "Fortunately, I've always prided myself on managing the impossible. Like resisting making love to a painfully desirable teenager."

"Dane..." Words deserted her as something far more dangerous than anger rose in those dark eyes.

They were behind the lighthouse now, out of view of the challenge-team members waiting for them back on the beach.

Dane stopped stroking and laid his paddle across the kayak. "I've thought about you, Amanda. I've remembered how you felt in my arms, how you tasted, how my body would ache all night after I'd have to send you back to your room."

"Don't blame me. *You're* the one who didn't want to make love."

"Wrong. What I wanted to do and what I knew I had to do were two entirely different things, contessa. But just because I was trying to do the honorable thing—not to mention staying out of jail—doesn't mean that I haven't imagined how things might have been different. If we'd met at another time."

"It wouldn't be the same." It was what she'd been telling herself for years. "That summer was something apart, Dane. Something that belongs in its own time and its own place. It doesn't even seem real anymore. And it certainly doesn't fit in our real lives."

She wasn't saying anything Dane hadn't told himself in-numerable times. The problem was, he hadn't bought the argument then. And he wasn't buying it now.

"Are you saying you haven't thought about me?"

"That's exactly what I'm saying." It was the first and only lie she'd ever told him.

"Never?"

"Never."

He considered that for a moment. "All right. Let's fast-forward to the present. Tell me you didn't feel anything last night, and I'll never mention it again."

"I didn't mean for that to..." She shook her head. "It just happened," she said weakly.

"Tell me."

She swallowed and looked away, pretending sudden in-terest in a trio of dolphins riding the surf on the horizon. There was a tug-of-war going on inside her. Pulling her emotionally toward Dane, pushing her away. Pulling and pushing. As it had done all during the long and lonely night.

"Tell me you haven't thought about how it could be," he continued in a low, deep voice that crept beneath her skin and warmed her blood. "Tell me you haven't imagined me touching you. You touching me. All over. Tell me that you don't want me."

Amanda knew that the easy thing, the safe thing, would be to assure him that the kiss they'd shared had been merely pleasant. But certainly nothing to lose sleep over. Unable to lie, she did the only thing she could think of. She hedged.

"You're certainly not lacking in ego." She tried a laugh that failed. Miserably.

"Tell me." His soft, gently insistent tone, touched with a subtle trace of male arrogance, was, in its own way, more forceful than the loudest shout. Once again Amanda won-dered why Dane was wasting such talents here, at a small inn in a small coastal town, miles from civilization.

"I can't." She closed her eyes and shook her head.

Dane let out a long relieved breath that Amanda, caught up in the grips of her own turmoiled emotions, did not hear. So he'd been right. She wanted him, even as she didn't want to want him. He knew the feeling all too well.

"Have dinner with me tonight."

Was there anyone in the world who could resist that deep velvet voice? She certainly couldn't.

"I can't." Her voice shimmered with very real regret. "Greg and I have to go over today's results at dinner. And try to come up with substitutes for the bike race, backpacking trip and rock climb, now that we've lost our adventure leader."

"That's no problem. I'll do it."

The part of her who was desperate for the challenge week to be a success wanted to jump at his offer. Another, even stronger part of her, the part she feared was still a little bit in love with Dane, could not put his job in jeopardy on her account.

"I can't let you do that."

"I told you, it's no big deal."

"You won't think so if you lose your job."

Dane shrugged. "Jobs are easy to come by." His smile, while warm, was unthreatening. "Now, dinner with a beautiful woman, that's well worth throwing caution to the wind for.

"I'm volunteering for purely selfish reasons, Amanda. If I help out with the rest of the challenge week, you won't have to spend so much of your evenings with that cretin you're working so hard to get promoted back East, so I can be with you."

Her eyes widened. "How did you know I was trying to get Greg promoted to Manhattan?"

Amanda desperately hoped that he hadn't overheard any of the team members discussing such a possibility. She hadn't wanted anyone but Susan to know about her plan to win Greg Parsons's job. The job, she reminded herself, that should have been hers.

He watched the fear leap into her eyes and wondered if she realized that the goal she was chasing was not only illusive, but not worth the struggle.

"Don't worry. It was just a wild shot in the dark." He wanted to touch her—not sexually, just a hand to her cheek, or her hair, to soothe her obviously jangled nerves. "It's you city folks who are big on corporate intrigue. Out here in the boonies, we tend to spend more time trying to decide whether to take our naps before dinner or afterward."

Amanda still hadn't gotten a handle on Dane. But she knew he wasn't the country bumpkin he was pretending to be.

"I'd love to have you take over leading the corporate challenge. Of course, the agency will insist on paying you."

The figure she offered would pay for the new furnace the inn needed if he wanted to stay open year-round. Pride had Dane momentarily tempted to turn it down. He remembered just in time that the money would not come out of Amanda's pocket, but from the corporate checkbook of a very profitable advertising agency.

"That sounds more than reasonable. It's a deal."

"Believe me, Dane, you're saving my life."

He watched the worry lines ease from her forehead and wished that all her problems could be so simple to solve. He also wondered how bad those headaches would become, and how many cases of antacids she'd have to chew her way through before she realized that advertising wasn't real life.

"So, now that we've solved that problem, what about dinner?"

"I honestly can't."

She paused, running through a mental schedule. Now that they didn't have to come up with new activities, she and

Greg didn't have all that much to cover. Besides, he'd undoubtedly want to get away early in order to sneak off to Kelli's room. Which, she'd noticed, conveniently adjoined his.

"How about dessert? We have to get together," he reminded, "so you can fill me in on the rest of the activities the leader you originally hired had planned for the week."

Telling herself that she'd just have to keep things on a strictly business level, Amanda said, "With your mother in the kitchen, how can I turn down dessert?"

"Terrific." His smile was quick and warmed her to the core. "I'll meet you down by the boathouse."

The boathouse had been one of their secret meeting places. Amanda knew that to be alone with Dane in a place that harbored so many romantic memories was both foolhardy and dangerous.

"Something wrong with the dining room?"

"It's too public."

"That's the idea."

"Ah, but I was under the impression that part of the corporate challenge agenda was to keep the teams off guard. So you can observe how they respond to unexpected trials."

Amanda vaguely wondered how Dane knew so much about corporate game-playing strategy. "So?"

"So, if we go over the events you have planned in any of the public rooms, some of the team members might overhear us."

He had, she admitted reluctantly, a good point.

"There's always my room," he suggested when she didn't immediately answer.

"No," she answered quickly. Too quickly, Dane thought with an inward smile. It was obvious that they were both thinking about the first time she'd shown up at his door.

"Okay, how about the tower room?"

Not on a bet. "The boathouse will be fine."

"It's a date."

"It's not a date." Amanda felt it important to clarify that point up front. "It's a business meeting."

Dane shrugged. "Whatever." Matters settled to his satisfaction, he resumed paddling.

As Amanda had suspected, other than complain about the outcome of the first challenge event, Greg was not inclined to linger over dinner. Forgoing appetizers, he got right to the point of their meeting as he bolted through the main course.

"Today was an unmitigated disaster." His tone was thick with accusation.

"It wasn't all that bad," she murmured, not quite truthfully. The race hadn't been as successful as she'd hoped.

Unsurprisingly, Julian and Marvin had not meshed. They never managed to get their stroking rhythm in sync, and although each continued to blame the other loudly, their kayak had gotten so out of control that it had rammed into the one piloted by Laura and Don at the far turn around the lighthouse. Fortunately, Dane was proved right about the stability of the craft. But although neither kayak overturned, once the four were back on the beach, the three men almost came to blows.

Needless to say, Greg's subsequent cursing and shouting only caused the friction level to rise even higher. The only thing that had stopped the altercation from turning into a full-fledged brawl was Dane's quiet intervention. Amanda had not been able to hear what he was saying, but his words, whatever they were, obviously did the trick. Although their boatmanship didn't improve much during the second heat, the combatants behaved like kittens for the remainder of the afternoon.

"It was a disaster," Greg repeated. He pushed his plate away and lit up one of the cigars he was never without. "I don't have to tell you that your career is on the line here, Amanda.''

She refused to let him see how desperately she wanted the week to be successful. If he knew how important it was to her, he might try to sabotage her participation.

She held back a cough as she was engulfed in a cloud of noxious blue cigar smoke. "If I remember correctly, this entire scheme was *your* idea.''

"True.'' He turned down a second cup of coffee from a hovering waitress, and declined dessert. "But my job's not in jeopardy so long as *I'm* the one who eats a family holiday dinner with Ernst Janzen every Christmas.'' He placed his napkin on the table and rose.

"Make it work, Amanda,'' he warned, jabbing the lit cigar toward her. "Or you'll be out on the street. And your assistant will be pounding the pavement, looking for a new job right along with you.''

She felt the blood literally drain from her face. It was just an idle threat. He couldn't mean it, she assured herself. But she *knew* he did.

It was one thing to blow her plans for advancement. She was also willing to risk her own career. But to be suddenly responsible for Susan's job, six months before her assistant's planned wedding, was more pressure than Amanda needed.

"I expect tomorrow's exercise to be a model of efficiency and collaboration,'' he said. "Or you can call Susan and instruct her to start packing both your things into boxes.''

With that threat ringing in her ears, he turned on his heel and left the dining room.

The long day, preceded by a sleepless night, had left Amanda exhausted. Her dinner with Greg had left her depressed. And although she'd been secretly looking forward to being with alone with Dane, now that the time had arrived, Amanda realized she was more than a little nervous.

Butterflies—no, make that giant condors—were flapping their wings in her stomach and she'd second-guessed her agreement to meet with him at least a dozen times during dinner.

Admittedly stalling, she was lingering over dinner when Mary appeared beside the table, a small pink bakery box in her hand.

"How was your meal?"

Amanda smiled, grateful for the interruption that would keep her from having to decide whether or not to stand Dane up again. Which would be difficult, since they were scheduled to spend the remainder of the week working on the challenge together.

"Absolutely delicious." The salmon pasta in white-wine sauce had practically melted in her mouth. "I'll probably gain ten pounds before the week is over."

"From what Dane tells me, with the week you have planned, you'll undoubtedly work off any extra calories." Mary held out the box. "I thought you and Dane might enjoy some carrot cake."

For ten years Amanda had been searching for a carrot cake as rich and sweet as Mary Cutter's. For ten years she'd been constantly disappointed.

"Make that twelve pounds," she complained weakly, eyeing the box with culinary lust.

Mary's look of satisfaction was a carbon copy of her son's. Although not as direct as Dane, in her own way, Mary Cutter could be a velvet bulldozer. "As I said before, a few extra pounds couldn't hurt, dear."

Running her hand down Amanda's hair in another of those maternal gestures Amanda had never received from her own mother, Mary returned to the kitchen, leaving

Amanda with two pieces of carrot cake and a date for which she was already late.

She was on her way across the front parlor when someone called her name. Turning, she viewed the gorgeous young woman who'd been on duty last night, standing behind the desk.

"Yes?"

"I hate to ask, especially since you're a paying guest and all, but would you mind doing me a favor?" Mindy Taylor asked.

"If I can."

"Could you tell Dane that the furnace guy promised to begin work on Friday?"

Two things crossed Amanda's mind at nearly the same time. The first being that her meeting with Dane seemed to be common knowledge. The second being the fact that along with his other duties, Dane appeared to be in charge of maintenance.

"If I see him," she hedged.

"Great." Mindy flashed her dazzling Miss Satan's Cove smile. "Isn't it great how things work out?"

"What things?"

"Well, if the Mariner resort hadn't burned down, your advertising agency wouldn't have come here in the first place. Then, if your adventure leader hadn't spun out on his Harley on that rain-slick curve, you wouldn't have needed to hire Dane to fill in, and the inn would have to close after Labor Day."

Last night, Amanda had been impressed with Mindy's seeming combination of intelligence and beauty. Tonight she wondered if she'd made a mistake in judgment.

"I don't understand what hiring Dane to lead the challenge week has to do with Smugglers' Inn being able to remain open after Labor Day."

''Without a new furnace, we would have had to shut down for the winter.''

''But what does that have to do with Dane?''

It was Mindy's turn to look at Amanda as if she was lacking in some necessary intelligence. ''Because he's using the check from your agency to buy the new furnace.''

''But why would Dane...'' Comprehension suddenly hit like a bolt of lightning from a clear blue summer sky. ''Dane's the new owner of Smugglers' Inn.''

''Lock, stock and brand-new gas furnace,'' Mindy cheerfully confirmed.

6

A full moon was floating in an unusually clear night sky, lighting Amanda's way to the boathouse. At any other time she might have paused to enjoy the silvery white path on the moon-gilded waters of the Pacific Ocean, or stopped to gaze up at the millions of stars sparkling overhead like loose diamonds scattered across a black velvet jeweler's cloth.

But her mind was not on the dazzling bright moon, nor the silvery water, nor the stars. Amanda was on her way to the boathouse to kill Dane Cutter.

He was waiting for her, just as he'd promised. Just as he had so many years ago. Unaware of the pique simmering through her, Dane greeted her with a smile that under any other conditions she would have found devastatingly attractive.

"I was getting worried about you."

She glared up at him, a slender, furious warrior with right on her side. "I got held up."

"So I see." Lines crinkled at the corners of his smiling eyes. "I hope that's Mom's carrot cake."

She'd forgotten she was still carrying the pink box. "It is." She handed it to him. Then reached back and slammed her fist into his stomach.

He doubled over with a grunt of surprise, dropping the cake box. "Damn it, Amanda!"

He gingerly straightened. She was standing, legs braced, as if intending to pound him again. He waited until he was sure his voice would be steady.

"You get one free shot, contessa. That's it. Try another cheap stunt like that and I'll have no choice but to slug you back."

"You wouldn't dare!" He might be a liar, but the man she'd fallen in love with ten years ago would never strike a woman. Then again, she reminded herself, apparently there was a lot she didn't know about the man Dane Cutter had become.

"I wouldn't risk putting it to the test." His dark eyes were hard. Implacable.

Dane saw her hand move to her stomach and damned himself for having caused another flare-up of her obviously touchy nerves.

But damn it, he hadn't started this. His plans for the evening had been to start out with some slow, deep kisses. After that, he'd intended to play things by ear, although if they ended up in bed, he certainly wasn't going to complain.

The worst-possible-case scenario was that they might waste valuable time together actually talking about her damn challenge-week events. One thing he hadn't planned on was having a fist slammed into his gut.

"You know, you really ought to see a doctor about that."

She frowned, momentarily thrown off track. "About what?"

"You could have an ulcer."

Following his gaze, she realized that the way her hand was pressed against the front of her blouse was a sure giveaway that she wasn't as much in control as she was trying to appear. "I don't have an ulcer."

"You sure? They can treat them with antibiotics, so—"

"I said, I don't have any damn ulcer."

Dane shrugged. "Fine. Then I'd suggest you work on your attitude."

"My attitude?" Her hands settled on her hips. "How dare you question *my* attitude. After what you've done!"

"What, exactly, have I done? Other than to offer to pull your fat out of the fire? Corporately speaking, that is."

Physically, she didn't appear to have an ounce of fat on her—one of the things he was hoping his mother's cooking could change. Amanda's society mother had been wrong; there was such a thing as a woman being too thin.

"That wasn't exactly the act of pure selflessness you made it out to be at the time," she countered with a toss of her head. "Not when you consider the new furnace for the inn. Which is scheduled to be installed Friday, by the way."

"Ah." It finally made sense. "Who told you?"

Amanda didn't know which made her more angry. That Dane had lied to her in the first place, or that he appeared so cavalier at having gotten caught.

"That doesn't matter," she said between clenched teeth. "What matters is that you lied to me."

Now that he knew what all the storm and fury was about, Dane found himself enjoying the murder in her eyes. It spoke of a passion he had every intention of experiencing before this week was over.

"I'd never lie to you, Amanda."

She folded her arms and shot him a disbelieving look. "I don't recall you telling me that you were the new owner of Smugglers' Inn."

"I don't recall you asking."

Frustrated and furious, Amanda let out a huff of breath. "It's not the sort of question one asks a person one believes to be a bellman."

Her words were dripping icicles. Although hauteur was not her usual style, having been on the receiving end of her mother's cool conceit for all of her twenty-five years,

Amanda had learned, on rare occasions, to wield the icy weapon herself. Tonight was one of those occasions.

Dane revealed no sign of having been fatally wounded. "You know, that snotty attitude doesn't suit you, contessa." Ignoring her warning glare, he reached out and stroked her hair. "It's too remote." Stroked her cheek. "Too passionless." Stroked the side of her neck. "Too untouchable."

That was precisely the point, damn it! Unfortunately, it wasn't working. Seemingly undeterred by her fury, he was jangling her nerves, weakening her defenses. Reminding herself that she was no longer a naive, hopelessly romantic young fifteen-year-old, Amanda moved away from his beguiling touch.

"You let me think you were still just an employee." Although his touch had regrettably cooled her ire, the thought that he might have been laughing at her still stung.

Just an employee. He wondered if she knew how much like her rich, snobbish mother those words sounded. "I suppose I did." Until now, Dane hadn't realized that he'd been testing her. But, he admitted, that was exactly what he'd been doing.

"Does it really make that much of a difference? Whether I work at the inn? Or own it?" Her answer was suddenly uncomfortably important.

Amanda had worked long enough in the advertising jungle to recognize a verbal trap when she spotted one. "That's not the point," she insisted, sidestepping the issue for the moment.

He lifted an eyebrow. "May I ask what the point is, then? As you see it?"

"You were pretending to be something you weren't."

"We all pretend to be something—or someone—we aren't from time to time."

Like that long-ago summer when she'd pretended to be the Lolita of Satan's Cove. She hadn't fooled Dane then. And she didn't now. Although he had no doubt that she was more than capable of doing her job, he also knew that she wasn't the brisk, efficient advertising automaton she tried so hard to appear.

"I don't." She jutted her chin forward in a way that inexplicably made Dane want to kiss her. Then again, he'd been wanting to kiss her all day long.

Thinking how ridiculous their entire situation was turning out to be, Dane threw back his head and laughed.

"I hadn't realized I'd said anything humorous," she said stiffly.

Her vulnerability, which she was trying so hard to conceal, made him want to take her into his arms. "I'm sorry." He wiped the grin from his face. "I guess you've spent so many years perfecting your Joan Crawford career-woman act that you've forgotten that it really isn't you."

His accusation hit like the sucker punch she'd slammed into his stomach. The familiar headache came crashing back. "It isn't an act."

"Of course, it is." As he watched the sheen of hurt, followed by a shadow of pain, move across her eyes, Dane damned himself for putting them there. Laying aside his romantic plans, he began massaging her throbbing temples, as he had last night.

"I don't want you to touch me," she complained.

"Sure you do. The problem is you don't want to *want* me to touch you." His fingertips were making circles against her skin. Igniting licks of fire, burning away the pain. "Would it make you feel any better if I promised not to seduce you tonight?"

"As if you could," she muttered, trying to ignore the delicious heat that his caresses were creating.

Dane didn't answer. They both knew there was no need.

He abandoned his sensual attack on her headache, sliding his hands down her neck, over her shoulders, and down her arms. Amanda did not resist as he linked their fingers together.

"For the record, I think you're intelligent, creative, and ambitious. You believe you think you know what you want—"

"I do know," she insisted.

"And you're not going to stop until you get it," he said, ignoring her firmly stated correction. "Whatever the cost."

"I have every intention of becoming Northwest regional creative director of Janzen, Lawton and Young." Determination burned in her eyes and had her unconsciously lifting her chin. "Once I get rid of Greg Parsons, just watch me go."

He smiled at that, because tonight, despite the change in plans, was not a night for arguing. "Believe me, I have no intention of taking my eyes off you."

Alerted by the huskiness in his tone, Amanda blew out a breath. "Am I going to have trouble with you?"

His answer was a slow masculine grin. "I certainly hope so." He moved closer. "Lots and lots of it."

She pulled a hand free and pressed it against his shoulder. "Damn it, Dane—"

He touched a finger against her mouth, cutting off her weak protest. "If you can forget what we had together, Amanda, you're a helluva lot stronger person than I am."

With effort, she resisted the urge to draw that long finger into her mouth. "It's over. And has been for years."

"That's what you think." He lifted the hand he was still holding and pressed his lips against her knuckles. Their eyes met over their linked hands—his, hot and determined; hers, soft and wary. "It's just beginning, Amanda. And we both know it."

Those words, so quietly spoken, could have been a promise or a threat. Needing time to think, not to mention space in which to breathe, Amanda tugged her hand free and backed away. Both physically and emotionally.

"I only came down here to discuss the challenge."

Frustration rose; Dane controlled it. For now. "You're the boss," he said agreeably.

"Not yet," Amanda corrected. "But I will be." Because her unpleasant conversation with Greg was still in her mind, her shoulders slumped. "If I'm not fired first."

He wondered if she had any idea how vulnerable she could appear and decided that bringing it up now, after what even he would have to admit had not been the most successful of days, would serve no purpose.

Dane wanted to put his arm around her, to soothe more than seduce, but knew that if he allowed himself to touch her again, all his good intentions would fly right out the window. That being the case, he slipped his hands into the pockets of his jeans to keep them out of trouble.

"I can't see that happening."

"Believe me, it's a distinct possibility." She hadn't thought so, before today. Oh, she'd considered herself so clever with her little plan to get Greg promoted. Caught up in the logistics of getting the horrid man out of Portland, she hadn't given enough thought to the inescapable fact that half the challenge team actively disliked the other half. "After what happened today."

She dragged her hand through her hair. "Speaking of which, I suppose I ought to thank you."

"And here I thought you wanted to knock my block off."

"I did. Still do," she admitted. "But, as angry as I am at you for not being entirely honest with me, I can't overlook the fact that you were probably the only thing standing between me and the unemployment line today."

She sighed and shook her head as she stared out over the gilded sea. "From the way Julian, Marvin, Don, and Greg were behaving, you'd think we'd all come here to play war games."

"Business is probably as close to war as most people get," Dane said. "Other than marriage."

His grim tone suggested he was speaking from experience. A thought suddenly occurred to her. "You're not married, are you?"

Dane swore. Annoyance flickered in his dark eyes, and drew his lips into a hard line. "Do you honestly believe that if I had a wife, I'd be planning to take you to bed?"

"Planning is a long way from doing." As she'd learned, only too well. She'd had such plans for this week!

"That may be true for some people. But I've developed a reputation for being tenacious." He cupped her chin between his fingers, holding her gaze to his. "I'm going to have you, contessa. And you're going to love it."

The last time she'd allowed him to bait her, she'd ended up kissing him as if there were no tomorrow. Afraid that the next time she wouldn't be able to stop with a mere kiss, Amanda jerked her head back, folded her arms across her chest and reminded herself that it was important at least to pretend to remain cool.

"You may be accustomed to women succumbing to your seduction techniques, Dane. But I have no intention of joining the hordes. I'm also a tougher case than you're obviously accustomed to."

"Victories are always more satisfying when they don't come easily. And you haven't answered my question."

Discounting his arrogant male statement about taking her to bed, despite the fact that he was also confusing, beguiling, and distracting her, Amanda sensed that Dane was a caring, compassionate individual. And although he had misled her, she knew, from past experiences, that he was also an honorable man. Most men would have taken what she was literally throwing at him ten years ago without a backward glance when the summer was over. But Dane was not most men.

"I suppose I can't imagine you committing adultery."

"Well, I suppose that's a start. Perhaps I ought to have someone write a reference letter. How about my mother? She'd love an opportunity to sing my praises."

"That's not the way I remember it."

"Ten years ago she was a single mother concerned her son was about to repeat her own romantic mistake." Because he could not continue to stand this close to Amanda without touching, he reached out and twined a strand of her hair around his finger.

"These days, she's a mother who's begun to worry that her son isn't ever going to provide her with the grandchildren she's so eager to spoil."

That was yet another difference between the Stockenbergs and the Cutters. Amanda's mother refused even to discuss the possibility of becoming a grandmother anytime in this century. While her father had warned her on more than one occasion of the dangers of falling prey to the infamous "baby track" that would hinder her success.

"How do you feel about that?" she asked.

"Actually, I think it's a pretty good idea. With the right woman, of course."

She couldn't help thinking of a time when she'd dreamed of having children with this man. She also had no intention of asking Dane what type of woman fit his criteria. Deciding that the conversation was drifting into dangerous territory, she opted to change the subject.

"May I ask a question?"

"Shoot."

"What did you say to Greg and the others today? To stop them from brawling on the beach?"

Dane shrugged. "Not that much. I merely pointed out to Parsons that he had too much riding on this week to risk getting into a fistfight with his employees."

That was why Greg had marched away, steam practically coming from his ears, Amanda decided. "But what about Julian and Marvin? They were at each other's throats after that disastrous first heat, but by the end of the day they were behaving as if they were candidates for the Kayaking Olympic Dream Team."

Dane knew he was treading in dangerous waters again. He didn't want to lie to Amanda. But if he told her the truth about his conversation with the art director and head copywriter, she'd undoubtedly want to slug him again.

She'd also be furious that he'd interfered, little mind the fact that she'd needed some help at the time. Especially since her egocentric supervisor was obviously not only a bully, but an incompetent idiot to boot.

"I said pretty much the same thing to them I did to Parsons." He forced himself to meet her lovely, serious eyes. "I suggested this week was going to be long and tough enough to get through without complicating things with useless feuds.

"I also mentioned that since management, in its own ignorance, tended to take things like this ridiculous corporate challenge week seriously, it made sense to save their differences for the creative arena where it mattered, bury their individual hatchets and cooperate by trying to win the thing together."

"I'm impressed."

"It's not that big a deal."

It was the truth, so far as it went. What he'd failed to mention was that he'd also told the two combatants that if they didn't shape up and do their best to make this week a success, he'd throw them both off the cliff. Then drown them.

Although they'd resorted to bluster, from the uneasiness in their eyes, he realized that they'd half believed he might actually do it. And, although he wasn't violent, such behavior was undeniably tempting. If it helped Amanda.

Watching her today, seeing how seriously she took her work, understanding how important it was to her that she pull off this week, Dane knew that in order to get what *he* wanted, he would have to see that Amanda got what *she* wanted. And what she wanted, it seemed, was Greg Parsons's job. That being the case, he intended to move heaven and earth—and a portion of the Oregon coast, if necessary—to ensure her success.

"Believe me, Dane, it was a very big deal." Thinking back on what he'd done for her—for no other reason than that he'd wanted to help—Amanda felt guilty. "I'm sorry I hit you."

Her hand was on his arm. Dane covered it with his. "You were right. I haven't exactly been the most forthright guy in the world the past couple of days. But I never meant to hurt you. Or to make you feel I was having fun at your expense."

His hand was darker than hers. Larger. And warmer. When she began imagining it moving over her body, touching her in places that were aching for just such a sensual touch, Amanda knew that no matter how hard she tried to deny it, Dane was right. Before this week was over, they would become lovers.

That idea was thrilling and terrifying at the same time.

"There's something I don't understand," she murmured.

"What's that?"

"What made you decide to buy the inn? After swearing that you couldn't wait to get away from Satan's Cove, I'm surprised to find you still here."

"Not still."

"Pardon me?"

"I said, I'm not still here. I'm back."

"Oh." That made a bit more sense, she supposed. "What did you do in between?"

Dane took encouragement from the fact that she cared about how he'd spent his life during those intervening years. "A little of this. A little of that."

"That's not very enlightening."

"I suppose not." He gave her a long look. "I guess I just can't figure out why you'd care. Since you've already said you haven't thought about me since that summer."

"I may have thought of you," she admitted, realizing that there was no way she'd be able to keep up the subterfuge. "From time to time."

Dane didn't answer. He just stood there, looking down at her, a frustratingly inscrutable look on his face, as the tension grew thicker and thicker between them.

"All right!" She threw up her hands in surrender. "I lied. I thought about you a lot, Dane. More than I should have. More than I wanted.

"Every man I've ever gone out with, I've ended up comparing to you. Once I dated a man for six months because, believe it or not, if I closed my eyes, his voice reminded me of yours.

"I go to work, and if I'm not careful, my mind will drift and I'll think of you and wonder where you are, and what you're doing. And at night—" On a roll now, she began to pace. "At night I'll lie in bed, and you'll be lying there beside me, kissing me, touching me, loving me.

"And then I'll wake up, and realize it was only a dream. But it doesn't seem like a dream, damn it. It seems real! And then, last night, I was tired and cranky, and worried, and all of a sudden I heard this voice I've dreamed about time and time again, and I turned around and there you were, and this time you weren't a dream.

"You were real. Wonderfully, marvelously real! And it was all I could do not to throw myself in your arms and beg you to make love to me—with me—for the rest of my life!

"So, there." She stopped in front of him, close enough that he could see the sheen of tears in her expressive blue eyes. "Now you know. Is that what you wanted to hear me say? Is your almighty male ego satisfied now?"

She was trembling. Once again the need to comfort warred with the desire to seduce. Once again comfort won out. "Yes. It's what I wanted to hear."

He put his hands on her shoulders and drew her to him. And although she remained stiff, she wasn't exactly resisting, either.

He cupped her chin again. "But only because it's a relief to know that I wasn't the only one feeling that way."

Amanda read the truth in his warm, loving gaze and felt even more like weeping. Her emotions were in a turmoil. She couldn't think straight. She could only feel. She wrapped her arms around his waist and clung. "Really?"

"Really." His smile was that crooked, boyish one that had once possessed the power to make her young heart turn somersaults. It still did.

"And if you think it's dumb dating a guy for six months because he sounds like someone else, how about marrying someone because she has the same laugh as a girl you once loved?"

"You didn't!"

"Guilty." His grin turned sheepish. "I was young and determined to get you out of my system when I met Denise."

Denise. Dane had been married to a woman named Denise. A woman with her laugh. Amanda hated her. "What happened?"

"It's a long story."

"I'm not in any hurry to be anywhere." On the contrary, a very strong part of Amanda wished she could stop time and make this night last forever.

There'd been a moment, during her passionate speech about how many times she'd thought of him over the intervening years, that Dane had thought perhaps tonight would turn out to be the night he finally made love to Amanda. Now that he'd made the mistake of bringing up his ex-wife, he knew he'd have to remain patient a bit longer.

Reminding himself that Amanda was worth waiting for, Dane took her hand and led her over to a rowboat tied to the pier.

"We may as well get reasonably comfortable," he said. "Because this is going to take a while."

7

Dane's fingers curved around her waist as he lifted her easily into the boat. Amanda sat down on the bench seat, leaned back against the bow and waited.

Dane sat down beside her. When he began talking, his words were slow and measured.

"I liked Denise from the moment I met her. Along with the all-important fact that she had your laugh, she was also beautiful and smart and sexy. And the only woman I'd ever met who was every bit as driven to succeed as I was."

"She sounds like an absolute paragon."

Dane would have had to be deaf not to hear the female jealousy in Amanda's dry tone. He chuckled as he put his arm around her shoulder, encouraged when she did not pull away.

"Unfortunately, except for our work, we didn't have a single solitary thing in common. Six months later, when neither of us had much to laugh about, we decided to call it quits before our disastrous marriage ruined a very good working relationship."

"I can't imagine working with an ex-husband."

Dane shrugged. "It hadn't been a typical marriage from the beginning. I'd married her to get over you and she married me on the rebound after her divorce from a miserable first marriage. Right before the split, I was promoted into a position that involved a lot of traveling. After a time, it was as if our marriage had never happened and we found we could be friends again. Two years ago, I introduced her to an old college friend of mine who's a stockbroker in San Francisco. They clicked right off the bat, got married, and I got a note from her last week announcing her pregnancy. So things worked out for the best.''

''You said you were young?''

Dane sighed. Although he'd overcome any regrets he'd once harbored over his marriage, revealing such irresponsible behavior to the one woman he wanted to impress was proving more than a little embarrassing.

''I graduated from University of Oregon the summer after I met you,'' he said. ''Mom was there, of course, along with Denise—who was my supervisor during my apprentice program at Whitfield. We went out to dinner, then after I took Mom back to her hotel, Denise invited me out for a drink to celebrate.

''One toast led to another, and another, and a few more, then we bought a bottle of champagne—a magnum—and the next thing I remember we were waking up in a motel room in Reno, Nevada.

''Denise couldn't remember much of anything, either, but the signed certificate from a justice of the peace on the dresser spoke for itself, so after several cups of strong coffee and a great many aspirin, we figured, since we'd always gotten along so well at the office, we might as well try to make a go of it.''

Amanda didn't know which part of the story—so unlike the Dane she'd known who'd driven her crazy with his self-control—she found most amazing. ''You actually married your boss?''

This time his grin was more than a little sheepish. ''Women aren't the only ones who can sleep their way to the top of the company.''

Since she knew he was joking, Amanda overlooked his blatantly chauvinistic remark. "She must have been older."

"About twelve years. But that didn't have anything to do with the breakup. We were just mismatched from the get-go."

In all his travels around the world, Dane had met a great many chic women, but none of them had oozed sophistication like his former wife. Denise preferred Placido Domingo to Garth Brooks, champagne cocktails at the symphony to hot dogs at the ballpark, and given the choice between spending an afternoon at a stuffy art museum with her uptown friends or fly-fishing on a crystal-clear Oregon river, she'd choose Jackson Pollack over rainbow trout any day.

Dane had often thought, over these past months since his return to Satan's Cove, that if he and Denise hadn't broken up that first year, they definitely would have divorced over his need to leave the city for this wildly beautiful, remote stretch of Oregon coast. Since there could have been children involved by this point, he was grateful they'd cut their losses early.

So stunned was Amanda by the story of Dane's marriage, it took a while for something else he'd said to sink in.

"You said she was your supervisor at Whitfield. Whitfield as in the Whitfield Palace hotel chain? 'When Deluxe Will No Longer Do'?" she asked, quoting the world-famous slogan. "*That's* where you were working?"

"I was in the intern program at Whitfield while I was in college and they hired me full-time after graduation."

This was more like it. This fit the burning need Dane had professed to escape Satan's Cove. This was the man, when she'd daydreamed about Dane, she'd imagined him to be. "What did you do there?"

"A bit of everything. Whitfield makes its managerial prospects start at the bottom and work in all the different departments. I was assigned to the custodial department my sophomore year at U of O, worked my way up to house-keeping my junior year, reservations my senior year, then spent the summer after graduation in the kitchen.''

"That's the summer you were married." Even knowing that it hadn't worked out, Amanda realized that she hated the idea of any other woman sharing Dane's life. Let alone his bed.

It should have been her, Amanda thought with a surpris-ingly furious burst of passion. It could have been her, if her parents hadn't manipulated things to keep them apart. Or if her feelings hadn't been so wounded and his pride so stiff.

Unaware of her thoughts, Dane nodded. "That's it. By Christmas I was on my way to being single again."

Denise's petition for divorce—they'd agreed she'd be the one to file—had arrived at his office on December 23. He'd spent the next two days in Satan's Cove with his mother.

The morning after Christmas, he was on a plane to Paris. And after that Milan. Then Zurich. And on and on until he was spending so much of his life at 30,000 feet, he'd often joked—not quite humorously—that he should just give the postal service his airline schedule.

"And then you began traveling." Amanda recalled the earlier condensed version. "Still for Whitfield?"

"When Denise and I split, I'd just gotten promoted to assistant director of guest relations, working out of the New Orleans headquarters. Essentially, it was my job to visit each hotel at least twice a year and pull a surprise inspection."

"You must have been popular," Amanda said dryly.

"I like to think I bent over backward to be fair. But I will admit to being tough. After all, guests pay big bucks to stay at a Whitfield Palace. It's important they feel they're get-ting their money's worth."

"I stayed at the Park Avenue Whitfield last month," Amanda revealed, "on a trip back to Manhattan. The New

York agency handles their advertising account." With luck and Dane's help, Greg Parsons would soon be transferring to those renowned Madison Avenue offices. "It really was like being in a palace."

Although she'd grown up with wealth, Amanda hadn't been able to keep from staring at the sea of marble underfoot or the gleaming crystal chandeliers overhead. She'd had the impression that at any minute, Princess Di would suddenly appear from behind one of the gilded pillars.

"That's the point," Dane said.

"True." Whoever had named the worldwide hotel chain had definitely hit the nail right on the head.

Amanda also remembered something else about her stay at the flagship hotel that Ivana Trump was rumored to have used as a model for her refurbishing work on the Plaza. Her room, furnished with genuine antiques and boasting a view of the leafy environs of Central Park, had been comfortably spacious. And the marble bathrooms had an amazing selection of French milled perfumed soaps, shampoos and lotions. In addition, the staff had been more than accommodating. Still, even with all that, Amanda had felt vaguely uncomfortable during her three-day stay.

"You know," she said thoughtfully, "as luxurious as the Park Avenue Whitfield is, I like what you've done with Smugglers' Inn better. It's more comfortable. Cozier."

His slow, devastating grin reached his eyes. "That's the point." Dane was undeniably pleased that she understood instinctively the mood he'd wanted to create. "I'm also glad you approve."

"I really do." He was looking at her as if he wanted to kiss her again. Her heart leaped into her throat. Then slowly settled again. "It's lovely, Dane. You should be very proud."

The sea breeze fanned her hair, causing it to waft across her cheek. Dane reached out to brush it away and ended up grabbing a handful. "Speaking of lovely..."

He pulled her closer with a gentle tug on her hair.

"It's too soon," she protested softly.

Personally, Dane thought it was about ten years too late. "Just a kiss." His mouth was a whisper from hers. "One simple kiss, Amanda. What could it hurt?"

She could feel herself succumbing to the temptation in his dark eyes, to the promise of his silky breath against her lips, to the magic in the fingers that had slipped beneath her hair to gently massage the nape of her neck.

A simple kiss. What could it hurt?

"Just a kiss," she whispered in a soft, unsteady breath. Her lips parted of their own volition, her eyes fluttered shut in anticipation of the feel of his mouth on hers. "You have to promise."

He slid the fingers of his free hand down the side of her face. "I promise." He bent his head and very slowly, very carefully, closed the distance.

The stirring started, slow and deep. And sweet. So achingly, wonderfully sweet.

There was moonlight, slanting over the sea, turning it to silver. And a breeze, feathering her hair, whispering over her skin, carrying with it the salt-tinged scent of the sea. Somewhere in the distance a foghorn sounded; the incoming tide flowed over the rocks and lapped against the sides of the boat that was rocking ever so gently on the soft swells.

His lips remained night-cool and firm while hers heated, then softened. Amanda's hand floated upward, to rest against the side of his face as Dane drew her deeper and deeper into a delicious languor that clouded her mind even as it warmed her body to a radiant glow.

Although sorely tempted, Dane proved himself a man of his word, touching only her hair and the back of her neck.

With scintillating slowness, and using only his mouth, he drew out every ounce of pleasure.

A soft moan slipped from between Amanda's heated lips. No man—no man except Dane—had ever been able to make her burn with only a kiss. He whispered words against her mouth and made her tremble. He murmured promises and made her ache.

Dane had spent most of the day hoping that he'd overreacted to last night's encounter. A man accustomed to thinking with his head, rather than his heart—or that other vital part of his anatomy that was now throbbing painfully—he'd attempted to make sense out of a situation he was discovering defied logic.

Despite all the intervening years, despite all the women he'd bedded since that bittersweet summer, Dane found himself as inexplicably drawn to Amanda as ever.

The first time they'd been together like this, his desire had been that of a boy. Last night, and even more so now, as he shaped her lips to his, forcing himself to sample their sweet taste slowly, tenderly, Dane knew that this desire was born from the age-old need of a man for his mate.

Because he could feel himself rapidly approaching that dangerous, razor-thin line between giving and taking, Dane lifted his head. Then waited for Amanda to open her eyes.

Those wide eyes he'd never been able to put out of his mind were clouded with unmistakable desire as she stared up at him in the moonlight.

He could have her, Dane knew. Right here, he could draw her into his arms and crush her mouth to his until she was senseless, until she couldn't speak, couldn't think, couldn't breathe. And couldn't run away.

Although he'd never considered himself a masochist, Dane fantasized about the way her body would feel next to his, beneath his, on top of his. He wanted her in every way possible.

The problem was, Dane realized with a stunned sense of awareness, he also wanted her forever.

She murmured a faint, inarticulate protest as he brushed one last quick kiss against her parted lips, then stood.

"Just a kiss," he reminded her, holding out his hand to help her to her feet.

Amanda needed all the assistance she could get. Her mind was still spinning from that devastating, heart-swelling kiss and she wasn't certain if her legs would hold her. She wanted Dane. Desperately. Worse yet, she needed him. Absolutely. For not the first time in her life, Amanda found herself damning his iron control.

"This is getting impossible," Amanda said.

Watching the myriad emotions storm in her eyes—desire, confusion, frustration—Dane vowed that there would be a time when he would take more. But for tonight, that kiss would have to be enough.

"What's that?" he asked mildly.

"You. Me. And what's happening between us. I had my life planned. I knew what I wanted. But ever since I arrived back in Satan's Cove, I can't understand what I'm feeling."

Sympathy stirred as the hair she'd ruffled with unsteady fingers fell back into place. "I think the problem is that you understand exactly what you're feeling."

"All right," she said on a frustrated sigh. "You're right. I do know. But you have to understand that I'm not that silly teenager who threw herself at you ten years ago, Dane. I've worked hard to get where I am. My entire life, from the day I chose a major in college, has revolved around advertising."

Personally, Dane thought that was about the saddest thing he'd ever heard, but not wanting to get into an argument over the art and artifice of the advertising marketplace, he kept silent.

"I've given up so many things, made so many sacrifices, not to mention plans—"

"They say life is what happens when you're making plans," he interjected quietly.

Amanda stared up at him and shook her head. "Yes. Well."

She, who'd always been so smug about her ease with words, could not think of a single thing to say. Still unnerved by the kiss they'd shared, and uneasy at the way he was looking down at her, so calm, so comfortable with who he was and where he was, Amanda dragged her gaze back out to sea. A boat drifted by on the horizon, the running lights looking like fallen stars on the gleaming black water.

They stood there, side by side, looking at the ocean, all too aware of the closeness of the other.

"Damn it," she said with a sudden burst of frustration. "You, of all people, should understand. You obviously didn't succeed at Whitfield because you married your supervisor. You had to have worked hard."

"Sixteen to eighteen hours a day," he agreed. "Which is one of the reasons I quit."

"Yet I'll bet there are still days when you put in that many hours."

"Sure." Dane thought about the hours he'd spent fixing up the tower room. Just for her. He'd told himself at the time that the work had been done out of ego, because he wanted her to see what a success he'd made of the place. But now Dane suspected that his motives had been far more personal.

"But I said long hours were *one* of the reasons I quit Whitfield," he reminded her. "There were others."

"Such as?" Amanda was genuinely interested in whatever roads Dane had taken that had led him all over the world before returning to Satan's Cove.

"I wasn't overly fond of corporate structure." That was the truth. "And corporate structure wasn't overly fond of me."

That was a major understatement. Fortunately, he'd been successful enough that the guys in the pin-striped suits in the executive towers had overlooked his independent streak. Most of the time.

Granted, he'd thoroughly enjoyed the work in the beginning. Especially the travel. For a young man who'd grown up in an isolated coastal town of less than two hundred people, his early years at the hotel chain had been an exhilarating, eye-opening experience.

But newness faded over time and the day he'd realized he was close to suffocating in the luxurious eighteenth-floor corner window suite of the glass tower that dominated New Orleans's central business district, he'd turned in his resignation.

Eve Whitfield Deveraux—who'd inherited control of the hotel chain from her father—had asked him to reconsider. Having married a maverick herself, the hotel CEO appreciated having someone she could always count on to tell her the truth. There were already too many sycophants around her, she'd told him on more than one occasion. What she needed was a few more rebels like Dane Cutter.

As much as he'd genuinely liked her, Dane couldn't stay. So he'd cashed in his stock options and his IRA, closed his money-market and checking accounts, and returned home.

Dane realized that while his mind had been drifting, Amanda had been quietly waiting for him to continue.

"Besides," he said, "working long hours these days is a helluva lot different. Because Smugglers' Inn is mine. It's not some trendy real-estate investment I plan to sell to some foreign development company in a few years for a quick profit.

"I've put more than money into the place, though to be truthful, it's just about cleaned out my bank account, which is the only reason I decided to take that money from your agency.

"But I don't really mind the broken heaters and clogged pipes and leaky roofs, because I'm building something here, Amanda. I'm building a home. For myself and my family.

"Because as much of a rush as it admittedly was at first, flying all over the world, staying in presidential suites, having everyone snap to attention the moment my car pulled up in front of a Whitfield Palace hotel, the novelty eventually wore off.

"That was when I realized that what I truly wanted, more than money, or power, or prestige, was someone to come home to at the end of the day.

"Someone to walk along the beach with in the twilight of our years. Someone who'll love me as much as I'll love her—and our children, if we're lucky enough to have them."

He'd definitely been on a roll. It was, Dane considered as he felt himself finally running down, probably the longest speech he'd ever given. And, he thought, perhaps his most important.

Amanda didn't speak for a long time. Dane's fervent declaration, while sounding well-thought-out, had definitely taken her by surprise. Since arriving at Smugglers' Inn, she'd been trying to make the various aspects of Dane mesh in her mind.

The young man she'd first fallen in love with had been the most driven individual she'd ever met. And that included her father, who was certainly no slouch when it came to workaholic, success-at-all-cost strategies.

Remembering all Dane's lofty dreams and plans and ambitions, when she'd mistakenly believed he'd never left Satan's Cove, she hadn't been able to understand how he could have failed so miserably in achieving his goals.

Then she'd discovered he actually owned the landmark inn. And, as lovely as it admittedly was, she couldn't help wondering how many people could so easily turn their back on power and prestige.

"That picture you're painting sounds lovely."

"You almost sound as if you mean that."

He wondered if she realized it was almost the exact same picture she'd painted for him so many years ago. It was, Dane considered, ironic that after all these years apart they were back here in Satan's Cove, still attracted to one another, but still at cross purposes. It was almost as if they'd entered a parallel universe, where everything—including their individual dreams and aspirations—was reversed.

"Of course I mean it. I also admire you for knowing yourself well enough to know what's right for you."

"I think I hear a *but* in there."

"No." She shook her head. "Perhaps a little envy."

"I don't know why. Seems to me you're in the catbird seat, contessa. All you have to do is get Parsons out of your way and you're definitely back on the fast track."

"So why does it feel as if the lights at the end of the tunnel belong to an oncoming train?" She was not accustomed to revealing weakness. Not to anyone. But tonight, alone at the edge of the world with Dane, it somehow seemed right.

"Because you're tired." Dane couldn't resist touching her. "Because change is always disruptive," he murmured as he began kneading her tense, rocklike shoulders. "And with the takeovers and mergers, you've been going through a lot of changes lately.

"Not to mention the fact that Parsons is the kind of jerk who'd stress out Mother Teresa. And along with trying to juggle this stupid corporate challenge week, you're being forced to confront feelings you thought you'd put behind you long ago."

His talented fingers massaged deeply, smoothing out the knots. "If I were a better man, I'd leave you alone and take a bit of the pressure off. But I don't think I'm going to be able to do that, Amanda."

She knew that. Just as she knew that deep down inside, she didn't really want Dane to give up on her.

"I just need a little more time." She was looking up at him, her eyes eloquently pleading her case. When she allowed her gaze to drift down to his mouth—which she could still taste—Amanda was hit with an arousal more primal and powerful than anything she'd ever known.

She imagined those firmly cut lips everywhere on her body, taking her to some dark and dangerous place she'd only ever dreamed about. "To think things through."

It wasn't the answer he wanted. Unfortunately, it *was* the answer he'd been expecting.

Dane's response was to cup the back of her head in his hand and hold her to a long, deep kiss that revealed both his hunger and his frustration. And, although she was too caught up in the fire of the moment to recognize it, his love.

"Think fast," he said after the heated kiss finally ended.

Still too aroused to speak, Amanda could only nod.

8

Amanda was more than a little relieved when the next day began a great deal more smoothly than the previous day's kayak races. When team members woke to a cool, drizzling rain streaming down the windows that necessitated putting off the bike race until afternoon, she was prepared to switch gears.

Taking the indoor equipment from her store of supplies, she divided the teams into subgroups and put everyone to work building a helicopter from pieces of scrap paper, cardboard, rubber bands and Popsicle sticks. Although speed was of the essence, it was also important that the constructed vehicle manage some form of brief flight.

"I still don't get the point of this," Laura complained as yet another attempt fatally spiraled nosefirst into the rug.

"You're blending science and art," Amanda explained patiently yet again. "Advertising is a subtle, ever-changing art that defies formularization."

"That's what it used to be," Luke Cahill muttered as he cut a tail rotor from a piece of scarlet construction paper. "Until the invasion of the M.B.A.'s." A rumpled, casual man in his mid-thirties, he possessed the unique ability to pen a catchy tune and link it with an appealing advertising idea.

Amanda had always considered Luke to be the most easygoing person working at the agency. She realized the recent stress had gotten to him as well, when he glared over at Don Patterson, the financially oriented marketing manager, who stopped remeasuring the length of the cardboard helicopter body to glare back.

"However much you artsy types would like to spend the day playing in your creative sandboxes, advertising is a business," Don countered. "I, for one, am glad to see this agency finally being run as a profit-making enterprise."

"You won't *have* any profits if the product suffers," Luke snapped back. "Advertising is more than numbers. It's our native form of American anthology."

"He's right," Marvin Kenyon said. "Advertising—and life—would be a helluva lot easier if it could be treated like science—A plus B equals C—but it can't.

"Life is about change, damn it. And advertising reflects that. The best advertising, the kind we *used* to do for C.C.C., can even act as an agent for change."

Greg, who was sitting off to the side, watching the group, applauded, somehow managing to make the sound of two hands coming together seem mocking.

"Nice little speech, Kenyon." He pulled out a cigar—his second of the morning—and lit it. "But if you're not part of the solution you're part of the problem. If you can't get with the program, perhaps you don't belong in advertising."

"Not belong?" This from Julian. "You *do* realize that you're talking to a man who has twenty-nine years' experience creating witty, appealing, and totally original advertising that makes the sale through its ability to charm prospective buyers?"

As she heard the art director stand up for the head copywriter, Amanda felt a surge of excitement. As foolish as these games had seemed at first, something was happening.

Until the pressures brought about by first the mergers, then the takeover, C.C.C. had been viewed throughout the advertising world as a flourishing shop.

Unfortunately, because of the political machinations that were part and parcel of becoming a bigger agency, Marvin and Julian had started sniping at each other, causing morale to tailspin as sharply and destructively as Laura's failed helicopter model.

But now, thanks to Greg's threat, Julian had just felt the need to stand up for his former creative partner. And although she wondered if they'd ever regain the sense of "family" that had been the hallmark of Connally Creative Concepts, Amanda hoped such behavior was a sign that the creative members of the agency would resume encouraging each other, spurring their colleagues to even greater achievements, as they'd done in the past.

"We can't ignore the fact that we're in a service business," she said. "Unfortunately, no matter how creative our advertising is, if we don't possess the organization to effectively service our clients, we'll fail."

"That's what I've been trying to say," Don insisted.

"On the other hand," Amanda said, seeking a middle ground, "we could have the best media buying and billing system in the world but if creativity suffers because everyone's getting mired down in details, we won't have any clients to bill. And no profits. Which, of course, eventually would mean no salaries."

She reached out and picked up the helicopter the blue team had just finished and held it above her head. When she had their undivided attention, she let it go. The copter took off on a sure, albeit short flight, ending atop a bookcase.

"That was teamwork, ladies and gentlemen," she said with a quick, pleased grin. "Science and creativity, meshing into one efficient, artistic entity."

Dane had slipped into the back of the room during the beginning of the argument. He'd convinced himself that Amanda wasn't really happy in her work; that deep down inside, where it really counted, she was still the young girl who wanted to have babies and make a comfortable home for her family.

Now, having observed the way she'd deftly turned the discussion around, he was forced to admit that perhaps Amanda really did belong exactly where she was.

It was not a very satisfying thought.

Her spirits buoyed by the successful helicopter project, Amanda found herself thoroughly enjoying the excellent lunch of grilled sockeye salmon on fettucini, black bean salad, and fresh-baked sourdough bread, the kind that always reminded her of San Francisco's famed Fisherman's Wharf. Dessert was a blackberry cobbler topped with ice cream. The berries, Mary told the appreciative guests, had been picked from the bushes growing behind the inn; the ice cream, which was almost unbearably rich with the unmistakable taste of real vanilla beans, was homemade.

"It's a good thing I'm only spending a week here," Amanda said when she stopped by the kitchen to thank Dane's mother again for helping make the week a success.

"Oh?" With lunch successfully behind her, Mary had moved on to preparing dinner and was slicing mushrooms with a blindingly fast, deft stroke that Amanda envied, even as she knew she'd undoubtedly cut her fingers off if she ever dared attempt to duplicate it. "And why is that, dear?"

"Because I'd probably gain a hundred pounds in the first month." She still couldn't believe she'd eaten that cobbler.

"Oh, you'd work it all off," Mary assured her easily. "There's enough to do around here that burning calories definitely isn't a problem."

"I suppose you're right." Amanda had awakened this morning to the sound of hammering. Although the sun was just barely up, when she'd looked out her window she'd seen Dane repairing the split-rail fence that framed the front lawn and gardens. "Dane certainly seems to be enjoying it, though."

"He's happy as a clam."

"It's nice he's found his niche."

"It's always nice to know what you want out of life," Mary agreed easily. "Even nicer if you can figure out a way to get it."

"You must have been proud of him, though. When he was working for the Whitfield Palace hotel chain."

Amanda had the feeling that if she'd made the life-style reversal Dane had chosen, her father would have accused her of dropping out. Amanda's father remained vigilant for any sign that his daughter might be inclined to waver from the straight-and-narrow path he'd chosen for her—the one that led directly to an executive suite in some Fortune 500 company.

Never having been granted a son, Gordon Stockenberg had put all his paternal dreams and ambitions onto Amanda's shoulders. And except for that one summer, when she'd fallen in love with a boy her father had found totally unsuitable, she'd never let him down.

"I'd be proud of Dane whatever he chose to do." Mary piled the mushrooms onto a platter and moved on to dicing shallots. "But I have to admit that I'm pleased he's come home. Not only do I enjoy working with my son, it was obvious that once he became a vice president at Whitfield, he began feeling horribly constrained, and—"

"Vice president?"

"Why, yes." Mary looked up, seeming surprised that Amanda hadn't known.

"Dane was actually a vice president at Whitfield Palace hotels?" After last night's conversation, she'd realized he'd been important. But a vice president?

"He was in charge of international operations," Mary divulged. "The youngest vice president in the history of the hotel chain. He was only in the job for a year, and Mrs. Deveraux—she's the CEO of Whitfield—wanted him to stay on, especially now that she and her husband have begun a family and she's cut back on her own travel, but Dane has always known his own mind."

Once again Amanda thought of her boastful words about her window office and her lovely, expensive Italian-leather chair. Unfortunately, as much as she wanted to be irritated at Dane for having let her make a fool of herself, she reluctantly admitted that it hadn't really been his doing. She'd been so eager to prove how important she was....

A vice president. Of International Operations, no less. She groaned.

"Are you all right, dear?"

Amanda blinked. "Fine," she said, not quite truthfully. She took out her roll of antacids. Then, on second thought, she shook two aspirin from the bottle she kept in her purse.

Mary was looking at Amanda with concern as she handed Amanda a glass of water for the aspirin. "You look pale."

"I'm just a little tired." And confused. Not only did she not really know Dane, Amanda was beginning to wonder if she even knew herself.

"You're working very hard." The stainless-steel blade resumed flashing in the stuttering coastal sunlight coming in through the kitchen windows. "Dane told me how important this week is to you."

"It is." Amanda reminded herself exactly how important. Her entire career—her life—depended on the challenge week's being a success.

"He also told me you're very good at motivating people."

"Dane said that?" Praise from Dane Cutter shouldn't mean so much to her. It shouldn't. But, it did.

"I believe his exact words were, barring plague or pestilence, you'll have your promotion by the end of the week."

"I hope he's right."

Mary's smile was warm and generous. "Oh, Dane is always right about these things, Amanda. He's got a sixth sense for business and if he says you're going to win your creative director's slot, you can count on it happening."

It was what she wanted, damn it. What she'd worked for. So why, Amanda wondered as she left the kitchen to meet the members of the team, who were gathering in the parking lot for their afternoon bicycle race, did the idea leave her feeling strangely depressed?

The mountain bikes, like the team-challenge T-shirts and accompanying slickers, were red and blue.

"At least they look sturdy," Julian decided, studying the knobby fat tires.

"And heavy," Kelli said skeptically. "What's wrong with a nice, lightweight ten-speed?"

"Kelli has a point, Amanda," Peter interjected with what Amanda supposed was another attempt to make points with the sexy public-relations manager. "Why can't we just use racing bikes?"

"In the first place, you're not going to be sticking to the asphalt." Amanda handed everyone a laminated map of the course. "You'll need a sturdy bike for all the detours over gravel and dirt roads and creekbeds."

When that description earned a collective groan, Amanda took some encouragement from the fact that everyone seemed to share the same reservations. That, in its own way, was progress.

"Think of it as touring new ground," she suggested optimistically.

"That's definitely pushing a metaphor," Marvin complained over the laughter of the others.

Amanda's grin was quick and confident. "That's why I leave the copywriting to you."

She went on to explain the rules, which involved the riders leaving the parking lot at timed intervals, following the trail marked on the maps, then returning to the inn, hopefully in time for dinner. She would ride along as an observer and, if necessary, a referee. Once everyone was back, the collective times would determine which team had won.

"Any questions?" she asked when she was finished.

"I have one." Laura was adjusting the chin strap on her helmet with the air of someone who'd done this before. "Since it's obvious you can't be at every checkpoint, how are you going to ensure some people don't skip a segment?"

"Are you accusing people of not being honest?" Don complained.

"You're in advertising marketing, Don," Luke reminded. "I'd say a lack of forthrightness goes with the territory."

When everyone laughed, Amanda experienced another surge of optimism. Only two days ago, such a comment would have started a fight. Things were definitely looking up!

"Not that I don't trust everyone implicitly," Amanda said, "but now that you bring it up, there will be referees at all the checkpoints to stamp the appropriate section of your map." She had arranged with Dane to hire some of his off-duty employees.

"Is Mindy going to be one of those referees?" Peter asked hopefully.

"Mindy Taylor will be working the second segment," Amanda revealed.

"There go our chances," Don grumbled as he pulled on a pair of leather bicycle gloves. "Because with Miss America working the second checkpoint, Peter will never get to number three.''

There was more laughter, and some good-natured teasing, along with the expected complaints from Peter, which only earned him hoots from his fellow teammates and the opposing team.

"Well," Amanda said, glancing down at her stopwatch, "if everyone's ready, we'll send off the first team."

"Oh, look!" Kelli exclaimed, pointing toward the inn. "Here comes Dane." Amanda found the public-relations manager's smile far too welcoming. "Hey, coach," Kelli called out, "any last advice?"

Since the course was easily followed and everyone knew how to ride a bike, Amanda had decided it wouldn't be necessary for Dane to be along. He was, however, scheduled to lead the upcoming backpacking trip and rock-climbing expedition.

"Just one." He rocked back on his heels and observed the assembled teams with mild amusement. "Watch out for logging trucks."

Marvin frowned. "I didn't realize they were logging this part of the coast."

"Well, they are. And those drivers aren't accustomed to sharing the back roads. Stay out of their way. Or die."

With that ominous warning ringing in everyone's ears, the teams pedaled out of the parking lot.

She was going to die. As she braked to a wobbly stop outside the inn, Amanda wondered if she'd ever recover the feeling in her bottom again.

"You made good time," Dane greeted her. He was up on a ladder, painting the rain gutter. He was wearing cutoff jeans and a white T-shirt. "Considering all the extra miles Kelli said you put in riding back and forth between teams."

"You'd think adults could conduct a simple bike race without trying to sabotage one another, wouldn't you?" Amanda frowned as she remembered the fishing line members of the blue team had strung across a particularly rocky stretch of path.

"You wanted them working together," he reminded her. "Sounds as if that's exactly what they were doing."

"I wanted them to cooperate," she muttered. "Not reenact the Desert Storm war." The red team had, naturally, sought to retaliate. "Thanks for the suggestion to take along the extra tire tubes. I still haven't figured out where they got those carpet tacks."

"I've got a pretty good guess." Dane had found evidence of someone having been in the workshop.

"Well, other than a few bumps and bruises, at least no one got hurt," Amanda said with a long-suffering sigh. "You were also right about those logging trucks, by the way. They're scary."

"Like bull elk on amphetamines." As he watched her gingerly climb off the bike, Dane wiped his hand over his mouth to hide his smile. "You look a little stiff."

How was it that she had no feeling at all in her rear, yet her legs were aching all the way to the bone? "That's an understatement." She glared at the now muddy mountain bike that had seemed such a nifty idea when the original challenge coach, who'd conveniently managed to avoid taking part in the week's activities, had first suggested it. "I swear that seat was invented by the Marquis de Sade."

"If you're sore, I can give you a massage. To get the kinks out," he said innocently when she shot him a stern look. "I've got pretty good hands. If I do say so myself." He flexed his fingers as he grinned down at her from his perch on the ladder.

Amanda had firsthand knowledge of exactly how good those hands were. Which was why there was absolutely no way she was going to take Dane up on his offer.

"Thanks, anyway. But I think I'll just take a long soak in a hot bath." Suddenly uncomfortably aware of how dirty and sweaty she must look, she was anxious to escape.

"Suit yourself." He flashed her another of those devastating smiles, then returned to his painting.

She was halfway up the steps when he called out to her.

"Yes?" She half turned and looked up at him. He was so damn sexy, with that tight, sweat-stained T-shirt and those snug jeans that cupped his sex so enticingly. He reminded her of the young Brando, in *A Streetcar Named Desire*. Rough and dangerous and ready as hell.

It crossed Amanda's mind that if Eve Deveraux had ever seen her vice president of international operations looking like this, she probably would have offered to triple his salary, just to keep him around to improve the scenery.

"If you change your mind, just let me know."

"Thank you." Her answering smile was falsely sweet. "But I believe that just might be pushing your hospitality to the limit."

"We aim to please." The devilish grin brightened his dark eyes. "Service With a Smile. That's our motto here at Smugglers' Inn."

She might be confused. But she wasn't foolish enough to even attempt to touch that line. Without another word, she escaped into the inn.

Enjoying the mental image of Amanda up to her neck in frothy white bubbles, Dane was whistling as he returned to work.

9

After a long soak and a brief nap, Amanda felt like a new woman. During her time in the claw-footed bathtub, she'd made an important decision. The next time Dane tried to seduce her, she was going to let him.

Having already spent too much time thinking of him, she'd come to the logical conclusion that part of her problem regarding Dane was the fact that they'd never made love.

Tonight, Amanda vowed as she rose from the perfumed water, toweled off and began dusting fragrant talcum powder over every inch of her body, she was going to remedy that nagging problem.

She dressed carefully for dinner, in an outfit she'd providentially thrown into her suitcase at the last minute—a broomstick gauze skirt that flowed fully to her calves in swirls the color of a summer sunrise, and a matching scoop-necked top with crisscross lacing up the front. The bright hues brought out the heightened color in her cheeks.

She paused in front of the mirror, studying her reflection judiciously. Her freshly washed hair curved beneath her chin, framing her face in gleaming dark gold. Anticipation brightened her eyes, while the fullness of the skirt and blouse suggested more curves than she currently possessed.

"You'll do," she decided with a slow smile ripe with feminine intent. Spritzing herself one last time with scent, she left the tower room, heading downstairs to dinner. And to Dane.

He wasn't there! Amanda forced a smile and attempted to make small talk with the other people at her table as the evening droned on and on. On some level she noted that her meal of shrimp Provençal and tomato, mushroom and basil salad was excellent, but the food Mary Cutter had obviously labored over tasted like ashes in Amanda's mouth.

She wasn't the only person inwardly seething. Greg, who was seated at the neighboring table, did not even bother to conceal his irritation at the fact that Kelli was also absent from the dining room. He snapped at his table companions, glared at the room in general, ordered one Scotch after another and puffed away on his infamous cigars until a thick layer of smoke hovered over the dining room.

Finally, obviously fed up, Miss Minnie marched up to the table and insisted that he display more consideration.

"This is, after all," she declared with all the haughty bearing of a forceful woman accustomed to controlling those around her, "supposed to be a nonsmoking dining room."

Greg looked up at her through increasingly bleary eyes. Noxious puffs of smoke rose between them. "In case it's escaped your notice," he said, the alcohol causing him to slur his words, "the firm of Janzen, Lawton and Young happens to have booked every room in this inn, with the exception of the suite occupied by you and your sister."

His jaw was jutted out; his red-veined eyes were narrowed and unpleasant. "That being the case, if you have a problem with my smoking, I would suggest that you just hustle your skinny rear end upstairs and order room service."

A hush fell over the dining room. Shocked to silence for what Amanda suspected was the first time in her life, Miss

Minnie clasped a blue-veined hand to the front of her dove-brown silk dress.

Out of the corner of her eye, Amanda saw Mary emerging from the kitchen at the same time Mindy was entering from the lobby. Feeling somehow to blame—she was responsible for the horrid man having come to Smugglers' Inn, after all—Amanda jumped to her feet and went over to Greg's table.

"You owe Miss Minnie an apology, Greg," she said sternly. She bestowed her most conciliatory smile upon the elderly woman. "It's been a long day. Everyone's tired. And out of sorts."

"Don't apologize for me, Amanda," Greg growled, continuing to eye the elderly woman with overt contempt.

"But—"

"He's right," Miss Minnie agreed in a voice that could have slashed through steel. "There's no point in trying to defend such uncouth behavior. It would be like putting a top hat and tails on an orangutan and attempting to teach him how to waltz." She lifted her white head and marched from the room.

A moment later, Miss Pearl, who'd been observing the altercation from across the room, hurried after her sister, pausing briefly to place a plump hand on Amanda's arm.

"Don't worry, dear," she said. "My sister actually enjoys these little tiffs." Dimples deepened in her pink cheeks. "She insists it keeps her blood flowing." With that encouragement ringing in Amanda's ears, she left the room.

Perhaps Miss Minnie found such altercations beneficial, but this one had sent Amanda's blood pressure soaring. "That was," she said, biting her words off one at a time, "unconscionable behavior."

"Don't take that holier-than-thou tone with me, Amanda," Greg warned. "Because, in case it's escaped that empty blond head of yours, I can fire you. Like that." He attempted to snap his fingers, but managed only a dull rubbing sound that still managed to get his point across. Loud and clear.

"You're representing the agency, Greg. It seems you could try not to be such a bastard. At least in public."

"It's not *me* you need to worry about, sweetheart," he drawled as he ground the cigar out into his dinner plate. "We both know that what's got you so uptight tonight is that our host is off providing personal service to the missing member of our challenge team."

No. As furious as she'd been at Dane, Amanda couldn't believe that the reason he hadn't come to dinner was because he preferred being with Kelli Kyle. Her eyes unwillingly whipped over to Laura—who was Kelli's roommate. When Laura blushed and pretended a sudden interest in the tablecloth, Amanda realized that about this, at least, Greg wasn't lying.

"You're wrong," she managed to say with a composure she was a very long way from feeling. "But there's nothing so unusual about that, is there? Since I can't think of a single thing you've been right about since you arrived in Portland.

"You're stupid, Greg. And mean-spirited. Not to mention lazy. And one of these days, Ernst Janzen is going to realize that nepotism isn't worth letting some incompetent bully destroy his empire."

Amazingly, the knot in her stomach loosened. She might have lost her job, but she'd finally gotten out feelings she'd been keeping bottled up inside her for too long.

When the other diners in the room broke out in a thundering ovation, she realized she'd been speaking for everyone. Everyone except, perhaps, the missing Kelli.

"And now, if you'll excuse me," she said, lifting her head, "I've another matter to take care of."

As fate would have it, Amanda passed Kelli coming into the inn as she was coming out.

"Hi, Amanda," Kelli said with her trademark perky smile. "Isn't it a lovely evening?"

Amanda was not inclined to bother with pleasantries. "Where's Dane?"

The smile faded and for a suspended moment, Kelli appeared tempted to lie. Then, with a shrug of her shoulders, she said, "On the beach."

Amanda nodded. "Thank you."

"Anytime."

Intent on getting some answers from Dane, as she marched away, Amanda didn't notice Kelli's intense, thoughtful look.

She found Dane at the cave. The place where those long-ago pirates had allegedly stashed their treasure. The place she'd always thought of as *their secret sanctuary*. He'd lit a fire and was sitting on a piece of driftwood beside it, drinking a beer. The lipstick on the mouth of the empty bottle beside the log told its own story.

"Hello, contessa." His smile was as warm as any he'd ever shared with her. "I've been waiting for you."

As confused as Amanda had been about everything else, the one thing she'd thought she could believe for certain was that Dane was an honorable man. To discover otherwise was proving terribly painful.

"Why don't you tell that to someone stupid enough to believe you." She'd tried for frost and ended up with heat. Instead of ice coating her words, a hot temper made them tremble.

Amanda's bright gauze skirt was almost transparent in the firelight. Dane found it difficult to concentrate on her anger when his attention was drawn to her long, firm legs.

He slowly stood. "I think I'm missing something here."

"I can't imagine what." Amanda sent him a searing look. "Unless it's your scorecard." When he gave her another blank look, she twined her fingers together to keep from hitting him as she'd done the other night. "To keep track of all your women."

"What women? I don't—"

"Don't lie to me!" When he reached out for her, she gave him a shove. "I passed Kelli on the way down here." Her voice rose, shaky but determined. "She told me where to find you."

"I see." He nodded.

She'd hoped he would explain. On her way down the steps to the beach, she'd prayed that he would have some logical reason for being alone on a moonlit beach, or worse yet, in this cozy cave, with a woman like Kelli Kyle.

Her imagination had tossed up scenario after scenario— perhaps the faucet was dripping in Kelli's bathroom, or perhaps her shutters had banged during last night's brief storm. Perhaps...

Perhaps she'd decided that Dane would make a better lover than Greg Parsons.

Ignoring the anger that was surrounding Amanda like a force field, Dane put his hands on her shoulders. "I can explain."

"That's not necessary." She shrugged off his touch and turned away. "Since it's all perfectly clear. 'Service With a Smile.' Isn't that what you said?"

He spun her around. "Don't push it, Amanda."

Threats glittered in his dark gaze, frightening her. Thrilling her. "And don't *you* touch *me.*"

She was still gorgeous. Still stubborn. And so damn wrong. "I'll touch you whenever I want."

"Not after you've been with her. But don't worry, Dane, I understand thoroughly. Kelli was just a fling for you. Like you would have been for me."

Temper, need, desire, surged through him. "You still know what buttons to push, don't you, sweetheart?"

Before she could answer, his head swooped down. Unlike the other times he'd kissed her over the past few days, this time Dane wasn't patient.

His mouth crushed hers with none of his usual tenderness. The hard, savage pressure of his lips and teeth grinding against hers was not a kiss at all, but a branding.

Fear battered, pleasure surged. She tried to shake her head, to deny both emotions, but his hand cupped the back of her head, holding her to the irresistible assault.

All the passions Amanda had suppressed, all the longings she'd locked away, burst free in a blazing explosion that turned her avid lips as hungry as his, had her tongue tangling with his, and had her grabbing handfuls of his silky hair as she gave herself up to the dark. To the heat. To Dane.

He pulled back, viewed himself in her passion-clouded eyes, then took her mouth again.

This time Amanda dived into the kiss, matching his speed, his power. She'd never known it was possible to feel so much from only a kiss. She'd never known it was possible to need so much from a man.

Having surrendered to the primitive urges coursing through her blood, she clung to Dane as she went under for the third time, dragging him down with her.

Somehow—later she would realize that she had no memory of it happening—they were on their knees on the blanket he'd laid on the sand when he'd first arrived at the cave, and his hand was beneath her skirt while she was fumbling desperately with the zipper at the front of his jeans.

Despite the danger of discovery—or perhaps, she would consider later, because of it—as those clever, wicked fingers slipped beneath the high-cut elastic leg of her panties, seeking out the moist warmth pooling between her legs, Amanda wanted Dane. Desperately.

There were no soft words. No tender touches. His hands were rough and greedy. And wonderful. As they moved over her body, creating enervating heat, Amanda gasped in painful pleasure, reveling in their strength, even as she demanded more.

A fever rose, rushing through her blood with a heat that had nothing to do with flames from the nearby fire. Her need was rich and ripe and deep, causing her to tear at his clothing as he was tearing at hers. She wanted—needed—the feel of flesh against flesh. Her skin was already hot and damp. And aching.

There was a wildness in Dane that thrilled her. A violence that staggered Amanda even as she strained for more. This was what she'd wanted. This mindless passion that she'd known, instinctively, only he could create.

She hadn't wanted gentle. Or tender. What she'd sought, what she'd been waiting for all of her life, was this heat. This madness. This glory.

Dane Cutter knew secrets—dark and dangerous secrets. Tonight, Amanda swore, he would teach them to her.

She was naked beneath him, her body bombarded by sensations her dazed mind could not fully comprehend. When his harshly curved lips closed over her breast, she locked her fists in his jet hair and pressed him even closer.

She said his name, over and over. Demands ripped from her throat. "Take me," she gasped, arching her hips upward as something dark and damning curled painfully inside her. "Now. Before I go mad."

She was wet and hot. Her flesh glowed in the flickering orange light from the flames. She looked utterly arousing.

She was not the only one about to go mad. His long fingers urgently stroked that aching, swollen bud between her quivering thighs with wicked expertise. Within seconds she was racked by a series of violent shudders that left her breathless.

Trembling, she stared up at Dane, momentarily stunned into silence, but before she could recover, his hands had grasped her hips, lifting her against his mouth. He feasted greedily on the still-tingling flesh. She was pulsing all over, inside and out. Amanda clung to Dane, unable to do anything else as he brought her to another hammering climax.

Her body was slick and pliant. His was furnace hot. Dane wanted Amanda with a desperation like nothing he'd ever known. There was no thought of control now. For either of them.

Hunger had them rolling off the blanket and onto the sand, hands grasping, legs entwined, control abandoned. As the blood fired in his veins and hammered in his head, Dane covered her mouth with his and plunged into her, swallowing her ragged cry.

For a suspended moment as he encountered the unexpected barrier, Dane turned rigid, his burning mind struggling to make sense of the stunning message riveting upward from his pounding loins. But before he could fully decode it, a red haze moved over his eyes and he was moving against her, burying himself deep within her heat.

Sensations crashed into passion, passion into love, with each driving stroke. It was more than Amanda could have imagined, more than she'd ever dreamed. The pain she'd expected never came. Instead, there was only glorious heat and dazzling pleasure.

She wrapped her legs around Dane's lean hips, pressed her mouth against his and hung on for dear life.

Just when she thought she couldn't take any more, he was flooding into her. Then entire worlds exploded.

Her mind was numb, her body spent. She lay in his arms, her hair splayed over his chest, her lips pressed over his heart, which seemed to be beating in rhythm with her own.

Although the stinging pulsating had begun to diminish, Amanda's entire body remained devastatingly sensitized. His hand, resting lightly at the base of her spine, seemed to be causing her body to glow from inside with a steady, radiant heat.

"Why the hell didn't you tell me?" Emotions churned uncomfortably inside Dane. Of all the stupid mistakes he'd made concerning this woman, this one definitely took the cake.

Amanda knew there was no point in pretending ignorance. She knew exactly what he was talking about. Besides, she'd made her decision and had no intention of apologizing for it.

"I didn't think it mattered." She closed her eyes and wished that this conversation could have waited until she was ready to return to the real world. And her real life.

"She didn't think it mattered." He grabbed hold of her hair—not gently—and lifted her composed gaze to his. "My God, Amanda, I practically raped you."

The fire was burning down, but there was still enough light for her to see the guilt in his dark eyes.

"It wasn't anything near rape." Amanda refused to let Dane take away what he'd given her. Refused to let him reject what she'd given him.

"I sure as hell didn't use any finesse."

"I know." She stretched, enjoying the feel of his muscular legs against her thighs. "And it was wonderful." Actually, it was better than wonderful. But there were not enough words in all the world to describe what she was feeling.

"I was too damn rough." His dark eyes, already laced with chagrin, turned bleak with self-disgust. He frowned as he viewed the bruises already beginning to form on her arms, her hips, her thighs.

He brushed his knuckles over the tops of her breasts, which were also marred with angry smudges. "A woman's first time should be special." He touched the tip of his tongue to a nipple and heard her sigh.

"It *was* special." She lifted her hands to comb them through his hair, but a lovely lethargy had settled over her, infusing her limbs, and she dropped them back to her sides. "The most special thing that ever happened to me."

Her softly spoken words could not quite expunge his feelings of guilt. "It was too fast."

She laughed at that. The rich, satisfied sound of a woman in love. "Don't worry," she murmured against his neck as she pressed her body against his, rekindling cooling sparks. "We can do it again." She ran her tongue in a provocative swath down his neck. "And this time, you can take all night."

It was an offer he was not about to refuse. But having already screwed up what should have been one of the most memorable occasions of her life, Dane intended to do things right.

Wanting to set a more romantic stage—and on a practical level, wanting to wash off the sand he feared was embedded in every pore—he suggested moving to the house. To his room.

Amanda immediately agreed. "But I'd rather we make love in the tower room." Her smile, as she refastened the lacy bra he'd ripped off her, was as warm as any a woman had ever shared with any man. "It already has warm memories for me. I love the idea of making more."

He suddenly realized that he definitely wasn't pleased by the thought that she'd soon be leaving Satan's Cove. Whatever they did together tonight in the refurbished tower room would simply become another memory that she'd look back on with fondness over the coming years.

"Dane?" She witnessed the shadow moving across his eyes, watched his lips pull into a taut line. "Did I say something wrong? If I'm pushing you—"

"No." Her hands had begun to flutter like frightened birds. He caught them by the wrists, lifted them to his mouth and kissed them. "I want you, Amanda. I have from the moment you walked in the door. The problem is, I don't know what you want."

"I want you." The answer was echoed in the sweet warmth of her smile.

Dane couldn't help himself. He had to ask. "For how long?"

He could not have said anything worse. Amanda flinched inwardly even as she vowed not to let him see he'd scored such a direct hit. Obviously, she considered, now that he'd discovered she'd been a virgin, he was concerned she'd take what had happened between them, what was about to happen again, too seriously.

He'd already professed the belief that he should have done more—as if such a thing was humanly possible—to make her first lovemaking experience special. Now, it appeared he was afraid of becoming trapped in a permanent relationship he hadn't initially bargained for.

"If you're asking if I'm going to call my father and have him show up in Satan's Cove with a shotgun, you don't have to worry, Dane." She withdrew her hands from his and backed away, just a little.

As he watched her trying to relace the blouse he'd torn open, Dane experienced another pang of regret for having treated her so roughly.

"Just because I chose to make love with you, doesn't mean that I'm foolish enough to get all misty-eyed and start smelling orange blossoms and hearing Lohengrin." Her voice was remarkably calm, given the fact that she was trembling inside.

Once again he found himself missing the young girl who wanted nothing more from life than to spend her days and nights making babies with him. On the heels of that thought came another.

"Hell." This time he dragged both hands through his hair. "I didn't use anything."

He'd put the condoms in his pocket before coming down here, but then he'd gotten sidetracked by Kelli Kyle. Then, when Amanda had arrived, she'd been so busy spitting fire at him and had made him so angry, he'd completely forgotten about protection.

Smooth move, Cutter, he blasted himself. Even in his horny, hormone-driven teenage days, he'd never behaved so irresponsibly.

He looked so furious at himself, so frustrated by the situation, that Amanda wrapped her arms around his waist and pressed a brief kiss against his scowling mouth. "It's okay. It's a safe time of the month for me."

He'd heard that one before. "You know what they call people who use the rhythm method of family planning, don't you?"

She tilted her head back and looked up at him. "What?"

"Parents." He shook his head again, thinking that tonight was turning out to be just one disaster after another. "I'm sorry."

"I do wish you'd stop saying that," she said on a soft sigh. "Truly, Dane, it would take a miracle to get me pregnant tonight. And besides, it was only one time."

Dane wondered how many pregnant women had ended up reciting that old lament. "Things aren't the same as they were that summer, Amanda. There's a lot more to be worried about than pregnancy, as serious as that is."

His expression was so somber, Amanda almost laughed. "I don't need a lecture, Dane. I know the risks. But I also know you. And trust you."

"Sure. That's why you went ballistic when you realized I'd been drinking beer out here with Parsons's PR manager."

She'd been hoping that wouldn't come up. She still couldn't believe that she'd behaved like a teenager who'd just caught her date necking with another girl in the parking lot outside the senior prom.

"I *was* jealous," she admitted reluctantly.

"Join the club." He smiled and ran the back of his hand down the side of her face in a slow, tender sweep. "When Jimmy was adjusting your bike pedals today, I just about saw red."

The Brad Pitt look-alike had been unusually attentive. At the time, Amanda had been flattered by his obvious admiration. Especially when the inn was overrun with young girls who could compete with Mindy for her Miss Satan's Cove crown.

"You're kidding."

"I'd already decided that if he touched your leg one more time, I'd fire him."

Amanda laughed at that, finding Dane's confession surprising and wonderful. "I suppose having a crush on an older woman is natural at nineteen."

"I wouldn't know." He gathered her close and kissed her smiling mouth. Lightly. Tenderly. Sweetly. As he'd planned to do all along. "When *I* was nineteen I was so bewitched by a sexy young siren, I wouldn't have thought of looking at anyone else."

It was exactly what she'd been hoping he'd say. Rising up on her toes, she twined her arms around his neck and clung.

"By the way," Dane said when the long, heartfelt kiss finally ended, "I had a life-insurance physical when I bought this place. You don't have to worry about any diseases."

"I wasn't worried." She watched him carefully put out the fire. When he crouched down, his jeans pulled tight against his thighs, making her all too aware of how wonderful those strong, firm legs had felt entwined with hers. "May I ask one question without sounding like a jealous bitch?"

"You could never sound like a bitch." Satisfied with his efforts, he stood again. "But shoot."

"What *was* Kelli doing down here?"

Dane shrugged. "Damned if I know." Seeing the disbelief on her face, he mistook it for another stab of feminine pique. "But if she was trying to lure me into her bed, she sure had a funny way of going about it."

"Oh?" Amanda believed that was exactly what Kelli had had in mind. Obviously she'd tired of Greg and was looking for some way to pass the time until returning to Portland. What better diversion than a man for whom the word *hunk* had been invented?

"She spent the entire time it took her to drink that beer talking about you," he revealed.

"Me?" That was a surprise. "Why on earth would she be interested in me? And what did she say?"

"It was more what she wanted me to say." He rubbed his chin thoughtfully. The conversation had seemed strange at the time. Looking back, it didn't make any more sense.

Unless, of course, Greg was using her to pump him to discover any flaws he might use against Amanda in their corporate warfare. "She asked a lot of questions about how I thought you were conducting the challenge week. If you'd mentioned your feelings about the value of the games. And whether or not you had discussed individual team members with me."

"That doesn't make any sense," Amanda mused. "Perhaps Greg's using her as a spy. To discover my weak points. And to find out if I'm trying to unseat him."

"That'd be my guess." Even as Dane agreed, he thought that although the explanation made sense, it hadn't seemed to fit Kelli Kyle's probing questions. Putting the nagging little problem away for now, he ran his hands through Amanda's tousled hair, dislodging silvery grains of sand.

"Are we through talking about business?"

"Absolutely." She beamed up at him. "Are you going to make love to me again?"

"Absolutely." And, after a long interlude spent beneath the shower in the bath adjoining the tower room, that's exactly what Dane did.

With a restraint that she never would have guessed possible, he kept the pace slow and this time when he took her, the ride was slow and long and heartbreakingly gentle. But no less dizzying.

Amanda had mistakenly believed that in that whirlwind mating in the cave, Dane had taught her everything he knew about love. Before the sun rose the following morning, she realized that she'd been wrong.

Her first heady experience, as dizzying as it had proved to be, had only been a prelude to the most glorious night any woman could have known.

A night she knew she would remember for the rest of her life.

10

━━━◆━━━

It was the coo of a pigeon sitting on her windowsill that woke her. Amanda stretched luxuriously and felt her lips curve into a slow, satisfied smile. For the first time in her life she knew exactly how Scarlett had felt the morning after Rhett had carried her up all those stairs.

Although she felt a pang of regret to find herself alone in bed, she decided that Dane must have slipped away to prevent gossip. Not that anyone would actually come all the way up here to the tower room. But it was thoughtful of him all the same.

It certainly wouldn't help matters to have the team members gossiping about her and Dane sleeping together. Not that either of them had gotten much sleep.

Besides, they both had a busy day today. Amanda was taking the team out on a deep-sea fishing trip, while Dane caught up on some much-needed grounds work.

She climbed out of the high log bed, aware of an unfamiliar stiffness. *To think you've wasted all that time on the stair stepper,* she scolded herself lightly. *When there are far better ways to work out.*

Perhaps, she considered with an inward grin, she should take Dane back to Portland with her at the end of the challenge. *Maybe, with the raise that comes with the creative director's slot, I could hire him to be my personal trainer.* And dear Lord, how *personal* he'd been!

Even as she found the idea more than a little appealing, it brought home, all too clearly, that their time together was coming to an end. If everything went according to plan, in two short days she'd be getting back on that bus and returning to Portland, where hopefully she'd move into Greg's office. While Dane would stay here, in Satan's Cove, living the bucolic life of a coastal innkeeper.

The thought of losing him, just when she'd found him again, was not a pleasant one. But unwilling to spoil what brief time they had left together, Amanda decided to take yet another page out of Scarlett O'Hara's story and think about that tomorrow.

She went into the adjoining bathroom, which was now overbrimming with memories of the long hot shower they'd taken together last night.

This morning, as she stood beneath the streaming water, she wondered if she'd ever be able to take a shower again without remembering the feel of Dane's strong, sure hands on her body, or the taste of his lips on hers, or the dazzling, dizzying way his mouth had felt when he'd knelt before her and treated her to lovemaking so sublime she'd actually wept.

When memories began flooding her mind and stimulating her body yet again, Amanda decided it was time to get to work. She turned off the water and slipped into the plush white robe—reminiscent of those favored by the Whitfield Palace hotels—hanging on the back of the door.

She found Dane pouring coffee. The scent of the rich dark brew, along with the aroma of Mary Cutter's freshly baked croissants, drew her like a magnet.

"You weren't kidding about special service."

"With a smile." He handed her a cup of steaming coffee, but before she could drink it, he bent his head and kissed her. "I knew it."

"What?" How was it that he could set her head spinning with a single kiss? Although she doubted they'd had more than three hours' sleep, Amanda had never felt more alive.

"That you'd be drop-dead gorgeous in the morning." His eyes took a slow tour of her, from her wet caramel-colored hair down to her toes, painted the soft pink of the inside of a seashell. Beads of water glistened on the flesh framed by the lapels of the bulky white robe. Dane was struck with an urge to lick them away.

"Flatterer." She laughed and dragged a hand through her damp hair. "And if you don't stop looking at me that way, I'll miss the fishing boat."

"If you've ever smelled a fishing boat, you'd know that would be no great loss." His own smile faded. "I've been thinking about the final challenge event."

Amanda nodded. It had been on her mind, as well. "The cliff climb."

"You realize there isn't much room for error in rock climbing."

"I know." She sat down at the skirted table and tore off a piece of croissant. It was as flaky as expected, layered with the sweet taste of butter. "I trust you to keep things safe."

"I'm not in the survival business." He sat down as well, close enough that their knees were touching.

"I know that, too." After last night, Amanda couldn't find it in her to worry about anything. "But so far, you've done a wonderful job."

"You haven't been so bad, yourself, sweetheart. The way you've kept those team members from going for one another's throats would probably earn you a top-level job in the diplomatic corps, if you ever decide to give up advertising."

She wondered what he'd say if he knew she thought about exactly that on an almost daily basis lately. One of the things that had drawn her to advertising in the first place was that it was a service business, a business that prospered or failed on how it served its clients.

With all the recent megamergers, there seemed to be very little benefit to clients. In fact, more than one old-time C.C.C. client had proclaimed to be upset by a supposed conflict of interest now that the same huge agency was also handling their competitors' advertising.

"You know," she murmured, "a lot of people—mostly those in New York—used to consider C.C.C. old-fashioned. And perhaps it was." Which was, she'd often thought lately, one of the things she'd loved about Connally Creative Concepts. "But it was still an agency where clients' desires were catered to.

"These days, it seems that if you can't win new accounts by being creative, you buy them by gobbling up other, more innovative shops. But the forced combination inevitably fails to create a stronger agency."

"Instead of getting the best of both worlds, you get the worst of each," Dane guessed.

"Exactly." Amanda nodded. "Creativity becomes the last item on the agenda. And, although I hate to admit it, the advertising coming out of Janzen, Lawton and Young these days shows it. In the pursuit of profits, our clients have become an afterthought. They're getting lost in the shuffle."

"It's not just happening in advertising," Dane observed. "The workplace, in general, has become increasingly impersonal."

Which was another of the reasons he'd left the world of big business. Although, under Eve Whitfield Deveraux's guidance, the Whitfield Palace hotel chain routinely topped all the Best 100 Corporations to Work For lists, it was, and always would be, a profit-driven business.

"Every day I arrive at my office, hoping to rediscover the business I used to work in." Amanda had been so busy trying to keep things on an even keel at work, she hadn't realized exactly how much she'd missed the often-frantic, always-stimulating atmosphere of C.C.C. "But I can't. Because it's disappeared beneath a flood of memos and dress codes and constantly changing managerial guidelines."

She sighed again. "Would you mind if we tabled this discussion for some other time?" The depressing topic was threatening to cast a pall over her previously blissful mood.

"Sure." It was none of his business anyway, Dane told himself again. What Amanda chose to do with her life was no one's concern but her own. Knowing that he was utterly hooked on this woman who'd stolen his heart so long ago, Dane only wished that were true.

"May I ask you something?"

There was something in his low tone that set off warnings inside Amanda. She slowly lowered her cup to the flowered tablecloth. "Of course."

"Why me? And why now?"

Good question. She wondered what he'd say if she just said it right out: *Because I think—no, I know—that I love you.*

She put her cup down and stared out at the tall windows at the sea, which was draped in its usual silvery cloak of early-morning mist.

"When I was a girl, I was a romantic."

"I remember." All too well.

"I believed that someday a handsome prince would come riding up on his white steed and carry me off to his palace, where we'd live happily ever after." Dane had had a Harley in those days instead of a white horse, but he'd fit the romantic fantasy as if it had been created with him in mind. He still did.

"Sounds nice," Dane agreed. "For a fairy tale." Speaking of fairy tales, he wondered what would happen if, now that he finally had her back again, he just kept Amanda locked away up here in the tower room, like Rapunzel.

"For a fairy tale," she agreed. "I also was brought up to believe that lovemaking was something to be saved for the man I married."

"A not-unreasonable expectation." Dane considered it ironic that he might have Gordon Stockenberg to thank for last night.

"No. But not entirely practical, either." She ran her fingernail around the rim of the coffee cup, uncomfortable with this discussion. Although they'd been as intimate as two people could be, she was discovering that revealing the secrets of her heart was a great deal more difficult than revealing her body.

"If we'd made love that summer, I probably would have found it easier to have casual sex with guys I dated in college. Like so many of my friends.

"But you'd made such a big deal of it, I guess I wanted to wait until I met someone I could at least believe myself to be in love with as much as I'd been in love with you."

Which had never happened.

"Then, after I graduated, I was so busy concentrating on my work, that whenever I did meet a man who seemed like he might be a candidate, he'd usually get tired of waiting around and find some more willing woman."

"Or a less choosy one."

She smiled at that suggestion. "Anyway, after a time, sex just didn't seem that important anymore."

"You *have* been working too hard."

Amanda laughed even as she considered that now that she'd experienced Dane's magnificent lovemaking, sex had taken on an entirely new perspective.

"Anyway," she said with a shrug designed to conceal her tumultuous feelings, "perhaps it was old unresolved feelings reasserting themselves, but being back here again with you, making love to you, just felt so natural. So right."

"I know the feeling." He covered her free hand with his, lacing their fingers together. "You realize, of course, that you could have saved me a great many cold showers if you'd just admitted to wanting me that first night?"

The way his thumb was brushing tantalizingly against the palm of her hand was creating another slow burn deep inside Amanda. "Better late than never."

"Speaking of being late..." He lifted her hand to his lips and pressed a kiss against the skin his thumb had left tingling. "How much time do we have before you're due at the dock?"

She glanced over at the clock on the pine bedside table and sighed. "Not enough."

"I was afraid of that." He ran the back of his hand down her cheek. "How would you like to go into town with me tonight?"

The opportunity to be alone with Dane, away from the prying eyes of the others, sounded sublime. "I'd love to."

"Great. Davey Jones's Locker probably isn't what you're used to—I mean, the tablecloths are white butcher paper instead of damask and the wine list isn't anything to boast about. But the food's pretty good. And the lighting's dark enough that we can neck in the back booth between courses."

Her smile lit her face. "It sounds absolutely perfect."

Other than the fact that the sea had turned rough and choppy by midafternoon, and Dane had been right about the smell of fish permeating every inch of the chartered fishing boat, the derby turned out better than Amanda had honestly expected.

The teams seemed to be meshing more with each passing day, and at the same time the competitive viciousness displayed on the bike race had abated somewhat. At least, she considered, as the boat chugged its way into the Satan's Cove harbor, no one had thrown anyone overboard.

As team members stood in line to have their catch weighed and measured, Amanda noticed that Kelli was missing. She found her in the rest room of the charter office, splashing water on her face. Her complexion was as green as the linoleum floor.

"Whoever thought up this stupid challenge week should be keelhauled," the public-relations manager moaned.

Since the week had been Greg's idea, Amanda didn't answer. "I guess the Dramamine didn't work." Prepared for seasickness among the group, Amanda had given Kelli the tablets shortly after the boat left the dock, when it became obvious that the woman was not a natural-born sailor.

"Actually, it helped a lot with the seasickness. I think it was the smell of the fish that finally got to me." She pressed a hand against her stomach. "I'm never going to be able to eat salmon or calamari again."

"I'm sorry," Amanda said, realizing she actually meant it. "Is there anything I can do?"

"No." Kelli shook her head, then cringed, as if wishing she hadn't done so. "I just want to get back to the inn, go to bed, pull the covers over my head and if not die, at least sleep until morning."

"That sounds like a good idea. I'll ask Mary Cutter to fix a tray for you to eat in your room."

If possible, Kelli's complexion turned an even sicklier hue of green. "I don't think I could keep down a thing."

"You need something in your stomach. Just something light. Some crackers. And a little broth, perhaps."

Although obviously quite ill, Kelli managed a smile. "You know, everything I've been told about you suggests you're a dynamite advertising executive. Yet, sometimes, like during that stupid helicopter session, you seem to be a born diplomat."

"Thank you." Amanda was surprised to receive praise from someone so close to her nemesis.

"You don't have to thank me for telling the truth," Kelli said. "But there's another side to you, as well. A softer, nurturing side. So, what about children?"

The question had come from left field. "What about them?"

"Do you intend to have any?"

"I suppose. Someday."

"But not anytime soon?"

"Getting pregnant certainly isn't on this week's agenda," Amanda said honestly.

For some reason she could not discern, Kelli seemed to be mulling that over. Amanda waited patiently to see what the woman was up to.

"You don't like me much, do you?" Kelli asked finally.

"I don't really know you."

"True. And spoken like a true diplomat. By the way, Dane was a perfect gentleman last night."

"I can't imagine Dane being anything but a gentleman."

"What I mean is—"

"I know what you mean." Amanda didn't want to talk about Dane. Not with this woman.

Kelli reached into her canvas tote, pulled out a compact and began applying rose blush to her too-pale cheeks. "You love Dane, don't you?"

"I really don't believe my feelings are anyone's business but my own."

"Of course not," Kelli said quickly. A bit too quickly, Amanda thought. "I was just thinking that advertising is a very unstable business, and if you were to get involved with our sexy innkeeper, then have to move back East—"

"I doubt there's much possibility of that. Besides, as exciting as New York admittedly is, I'm comfortable where I am."

Kelli dropped the blush back into the bag and pulled out a black-and-gold lipstick case. "Even with Greg as creative director?"

She'd definitely hit the bull's-eye with that question.

"Greg Parsons isn't Patrick Connally," Amanda said truthfully. "And his management style is a great deal different." Sort of like the difference between Genghis Khan and Ghandi. "But, as we've pointed out over these past days, advertising is all about change."

"Yes, it is, isn't it?" Kelli looked at Amanda in the mirror. Her gaze was long and deep. Finally, she returned to her primping. After applying a fuchsia lipstick that added much-needed color to her lips, she said, "I suppose we may as well join the others."

As they left the rest room together, Amanda couldn't help thinking that their brief conversation wasn't exactly like two women sharing confidences. It had strangely seemed more like an interview. Deciding that she was reading too much into the incident, she began anticipating the evening ahead.

Amanda hadn't been so nervous since the summer of her fifteenth year. She bathed in scented water that left her skin as smooth as silk, brushed her newly washed hair until it shone like gold and applied her makeup with unusual care. Then she stood in front of the closet, wondering what she could wear for what was, essentially, her first real date with Dane.

She'd only brought one dress, and she'd already worn it last night. Besides, somehow, the front ties had gotten torn in their frantic struggle to undress. And although she had no doubt that the patrons of Davey Jones's Locker wouldn't complain about her showing up with the front of her blouse slit down to her navel, she figured such sexy attire would be overkill for Satan's Cove.

Although she'd been underage, hence too young to go into the bar/restaurant the last time she'd visited the coastal town, from the outside, the building definitely did not seem to be the kind of place where one dressed for dinner.

With that in mind, she finally decided on a pair of black jeans and a long-sleeved white blouse cut in the classic style of a man's shirt. Some gold studs at her ears, a gold watch, and a pair of black cowboy boots completed her ensemble.

"Well, you're not exactly Cinderella," she murmured, observing her reflection in the antique full-length mirror. "But you'll do."

So as not to encourage unwanted gossip, she'd agreed to meet Dane in the former carriage house that had been turned into a garage. As she entered the wooden building, his eyes darkened with masculine approval.

"You look absolutely gorgeous, contessa."

She was vastly relieved he hadn't seen her when she'd arrived from the boat, smelling of fish, her face pink from the sun, her nose peeling like an eleven-year-old tomboy's and her hair a wild tangle.

"I hope this is appropriate." She ran her hands down the front of her jeans. "I thought I'd leave my tiara at home tonight."

"All the better to mingle with your subjects," he agreed, thinking that although she'd cleaned up beautifully, he still kind of liked the way she'd looked when she'd returned from the fishing derby today.

He'd been in the garden, tying up his mother's prized tomato plants, when he'd seen her trying to sneak into the lodge, her complexion kissed by the sun and her tangled hair reminding him of the way it looked when she first woke up this morning after a night of passionate lovemaking.

"I got to thinking," he said, "that perhaps, after a day on a fishing boat, taking you out for seafood wasn't the best idea I've ever had."

"Don't worry about me." Her smile was quick and warm and reminded him of the one he'd fallen for when he was nineteen. "I've got a stomach like a rock. And I adore seafood."

"Terrific. Iris has a way with fried oysters you won't believe."

"I love fried oysters." She batted her lashes in the way Scarlett O'Hara had made famous and a fifteen-year-old girl had once perfected. "They're rumored to be an aphrodisiac, you know."

"So I've heard. But with you providing the inspiration, contessa, the last thing I need is an aphrodisiac."

He drew her into his arms and gave her a long deep kiss that left her breathless. And even as he claimed her mouth with his, Dane knew that it was Amanda who was claiming him. Mind, heart and soul.

Satan's Cove was laid out in a crescent, following the curving shoreline. As Dane drove down the narrow main street, Amanda was surprised and pleased that the town hadn't changed during the decade she'd been away.

"It's as if it's frozen in time," she murmured as they drove past the cluster of buildings that billed themselves as the Sportsman's Lodge, and the white Cape Cod-style Gray Whale Mercantile. "Well, almost," she amended as she viewed a window sign on another building that advertised crystals and palm readings. A For Rent sign hung in a second-story window above the New Age shop.

"Nothing stays the same." Dane said what Amanda had already discovered the hard way at C.C.C. "But change has been slow to come to this part of the coast."

"I'm glad," she decided.

"Of course, there was a time when Satan's Cove was a boomtown. But that was before the fire."

"Fire?"

"Didn't you learn the town's history when you were here before?"

"I was a little preoccupied that summer," she reminded. "Trying to seduce the sexiest boy on the Pacific seaboard. Visiting dull old museums was not exactly high on my list of fun things to do."

Since he'd had far better places to escape with her than the town museum, Dane decided he was in no position to criticize.

"With the exception of Smugglers' Inn, which was located too far away, most of the town burned down sixty-some years ago. Including the old Victorian whorehouse down by the docks. Well, needless to say, without that brothel, the fishermen all moved to Tillamook, Seaside and Astoria."

"Amazing what the loss of entrepreneurs can do to a local economy," she drawled sapiently. "So what happened? Didn't the women come back after the town was rebuilt?"

"By the time the city fathers got around to rebuilding in the mid-thirties, the prohibitionists had joined forces with some radical religious reformers who passed an ordinance forbidding the rebuilding of any houses of ill repute.

"After World War II, alcohol returned without a battle. And so did sex. But these days it's free." He flashed her a grin. "Or so I'm told."

Even though she knew their time was coming to an end, his flippant statement caused a stab of purely feminine jealousy. Amanda hated the idea of Dane making love to any other woman. But short of tying him up and taking him back to Portland with her, she couldn't think of a way to keep the man all to herself.

She was wondering about the logistics of maintaining a commuter relationship—after all, Portland was only a few hours' drive from Satan's Cove—when he pulled up in front of Davey Jones's Locker.

From the outside, the weathered, silvery gray building did not look at all promising. Once inside, however, after her eyes adjusted to the dim light, Amanda found it rustically appealing.

Fish, caught in local waters, had been mounted on the knotty-pine-paneled walls, yellow sawdust had been sprinkled over the plank floor and behind an L-shaped bar was a smoky mirror and rows of bottles.

"Dane!" A woman who seemed vaguely familiar, wearing a striped cotton-knit top and a pair of cuffed white shorts, stopped on her way by with a tray of pilsner glasses filled with draft beer. Her voluptuous breasts turned the red and white stripes into wavy lines. "I was wondering what it would take to get you away from that work in progress."

She flashed Dane a smile that belonged in a toothpaste commercial and her emerald eyes gleamed with a feminine welcome Amanda found far too sexy for comfort. Then her eyes skimmed over Amanda with unconcealed interest.

"Just grab any old table, you two," she said with an airy wave of her hand. "As soon as I deliver these, I'll come take your drink order."

With that, she was dashing across the room to where a group of men were playing a game of pool on a green-felt-topped table. The seductive movement of her hips in those tight white shorts was nothing short of riveting.

"Old friend?" Amanda asked as she slipped into a booth at the back of the room.

"Iris and I dated a bit in high school," Dane revealed easily. "And when I first returned to town. But nothing ever came of it. We decided not to risk a great friendship by introducing romance into the relationship."

Relief was instantaneous. "She really is stunning." Now that she knew the woman wasn't a threat, Amanda could afford to be generous.

"She is that," Dane agreed easily. "I've seen grown men walk into walls when Iris walks by. But, of course, that could be because they've had too much to drink."

Or it could be because the woman had a body any *Playboy* centerfold would envy. That idea brought up Dane's contention that she was too thin, which in turn had Amanda comparing herself with the voluptuous Iris, who was headed back their way, order pad in hand. The outcome wasn't even close.

"Hi," she greeted Amanda with a smile every bit as warm as the one she'd bestowed upon Dane. "It's good to see you again."

Amanda looked at the stunning redhead in confusion. "I'm sorry, but—"

"That's okay," Iris interrupted good-naturedly. "It's been a long time. I was waiting tables at Smugglers' Inn the summer you came for a vacation with your parents."

Memories flooded back. "Of course, I remember you." She also recalled, all too clearly, how jealous she'd been of the sexy redheaded waitress who spent far too much time in the kitchen with Dane. "How are you?"

"I'm doing okay. Actually, since I bought this place with the settlement money from my divorce, I'm doing great." She laughed, pushing back a froth of copper hair. "I think I've found my place, which is kind of amazing when you think how badly I wanted to escape this town back in my wild teenage days."

She grinned over at Dane. "Can you believe it, sugar? Here we are, two hotshot kids who couldn't wait to get out of Satan's Cove, back home again, happy as a pair of clams."

"Iris was making a pretty good living acting in Hollywood," Dane revealed.

"Really?" Although she'd grown up in Los Angeles, the only actors she'd ever met were all the wanna-bes waiting tables at her favorite restaurants. "That must have been exciting."

"In the beginning, I felt just like Buddy Ebsen. You know—" she elaborated at Amanda's confused look "—'The Beverly Hillbillies.' Movie stars, swimming pools... Lord, I was in hog heaven. I married the first guy I met when I got off the bus—an out-of-work actor. That lasted until I caught him rehearsing bedroom scenes with a waitress from Hamburger Hamlet. In our bed.

"My second marriage was to a director, who promised to make me a star. And I'll have to admit, he was doing his best to keep his promise, but I was getting tired of being the girl who was always murdered by some crazed psycho. There's only so much you can do creatively with a bloodcurdling scream.

"Besides, after a time, a girl gets a little tired of her husband wearing her underwear, if you know what I mean."

"I can see where that might be a bit disconcerting," Amanda agreed. She'd never met anyone as open and outgoing as Iris. She decided it was no wonder the woman had chosen to leave the art and artifice of Hollywood.

"After my second divorce, I got fed up with the entire Hollywood scene and realized, just like Dorothy, that there's no place like home."

"I just realized," Amanda said, "I've seen one of your films."

"You're kidding!"

"No. I went to a Halloween party a few years ago and the host screened *Nightstalker.*"

"You've got a good eye," Iris said. "I think I lasted about three scenes in that one."

"But they were pivotal," Amanda said earnestly, remembering how Iris's character—a hooker with a heart of gold—had grabbed her killer's mask off, enabling a street person rifling through a nearby Dumpster to get a glimpse of his scarred face. Which in turn, eventually resulted in the man's capture.

"I knew I liked you." Iris flashed a grin Dane's way. "If I were you, I'd try to hold on to this one."

"Thanks for the advice." Dane didn't add that that was exactly what he intended to do.

11

Although the ambience was definitely not that of a five-star restaurant, and the food was not covered in velvety sauce or garnished with the trendy miniature vegetable-of-the-week, Amanda couldn't remember when she'd enjoyed a meal more.

There was one small glitch—when Julian, Marvin, and Luke Cahill had unexpectedly shown up. Fortunately, they appeared no more pleased to see her than she was to see them, and after a few stiltedly exchanged words, settled into a booth across the room.

Amanda wondered what the three were doing together. They could be plotting strategy, were it not for the fact that Marvin and Julian were on the blue team and Luke was on the red.

As much as she had riding on the corporate challenge, for this one night Amanda refused to think about her plan for success. After all, here she was, on her first real date with the man she'd always loved, and she wasn't going to spoil things trying to figure out this latest bit of corporate intrigue.

Instead, she took a sip of the house white wine, smiled enticingly over the heavy rim of the glass, and allowed herself to relax fully for the first time since arriving in Satan's Cove.

It was late when they returned to the inn. The moon and stars that had been so vivid the other night were hidden by a thick cloud of fog.

Someone—undoubtedly Mindy—had left a lamp in the downstairs reception parlor on; it glowed a warm welcome. The lights in the upstairs windows were off, revealing that the other guests had gone to bed.

Amanda didn't invite Dane up to her room. There was no need. Both of them knew how the night would end.

The elevator was cranking its way up to the third floor when Dane turned and took her in his arms. "I'd say tonight went pretty well," he murmured against her cheek. "For a first date."

"Better than well." She sighed her pleasure as she wrapped her arms around his waist. "I can't remember when I've enjoyed myself more."

"I'm glad." His lips skimmed up to create sparks at her temple. Dane didn't add that he'd worried she'd find Davey Jones's Locker too plebeian for her city tastes.

"And just think—" she leaned back a bit, sensual amusement gleaming in her eyes "—the night's still young."

Actually, that wasn't really the case. But Dane wasn't about to argue. After all the sleep he'd lost fixing up the inn, he wasn't about to complain about losing a bit more if it meant making love again to Amanda.

Lowering his head, he touched his lips to hers. At first briefly. Then, as he drew her closer, the kiss, while remaining tender, grew deeper. More intimate. More weakening.

Her limbs grew heavy, her head light. Amanda clung to him, wanting more. She'd never known an elevator ride to take so long.

The cage door finally opened. Hand in hand, they walked to the stairwell at the end of the hallway. It was like moving in a dream. A dream Amanda wished would never end.

They'd no sooner entered the tower room than Dane pulled her close and kissed her again. Not with the slow self-control of a man who knew how to draw out every last ounce of pleasure, but with the impatient demand of a lover who realized that this stolen time together was rapidly coming to an end.

With a strength and ease that once again bespoke the life of hard, physical work he'd chosen over shuffling papers, Dane scooped her up in his arms and carried her across the plank floor to the bed, which had been turned down during their absence. A mint, formed in the unmistakable shape of the inn, had been left on the pillow. Dane brushed it onto the floor with an impatient hand and began unbuttoning Amanda's blouse.

"No." It took an effort—her bones had turned to syrup—but she managed to lift her hands to his.

"No?" Disbelief sharpened his tone, darkened his eyes.

She laid a calming hand against his cheek and felt the tensed muscle beneath her fingertips. "It's my turn." Unconsciously, she skimmed her tongue over her lips, enjoying the clinging taste of him. "To make love to you."

It was at that moment, when every atom in his body was aching to take Amanda—and take her now—that Dane realized he could deny this woman nothing.

His answering smile was slow and warm and devilishly sexy. "I'm all yours, contessa." He'd never, in all his twenty-nine years, spoken truer words.

He rolled over onto his back, spread out his arms and waited.

Never having undressed a man—last night's frantic coupling in the cave didn't really count, since Amanda still couldn't remember how they'd ended up naked—she was more than a little nervous. But, remembering how his bare torso had gleamed like bronze in the firelight, she decided to begin with his shirt.

With hands that were not as steady as she would have liked, she tackled the buttons one by one. She'd known he was strong—his chest was rock hard and wonderfully muscled. But it was his inner strength that continued to arouse her. Just as it was his loyalty, integrity and steely self-confidence that Amanda had fallen in love with.

When she reached his belt, she had two choices—to unfasten his jeans or tug the shirt free. Unreasonably drawn to the enticing swell beneath the crisp indigo denim of the jeans that had become his dress slacks when he'd changed lifestyles, Amanda stuck to her vow to keep things slow.

Dane was moderately disappointed when she took the easy way out and pulled his shirt free of his waistband—until she folded back the plaid cotton and pressed her silky lips against his bare chest. Her mouth felt like a hot brand against his flesh, burning her claim on him, just as she'd done so many years ago.

"I'm not very experienced." Her lips skimmed down the narrow arrowing of ebony chest hair, leaving sparks. "You'll have to tell me what you like." Retracing the trail her mouth had blazed, she flicked her tongue over a dark nipple. The wet heat caused a smoldering deep in his loins, which threatened to burst into a wildfire.

"That's a dandy start," he managed in a husky voice roughened with hunger.

"How about this?" She bestowed light, lazy kisses back down his chest, over his stomach.

"Even better," he groaned, when she dipped her tongue into his navel. His erection stirred, pushing painfully against the hard denim barrier. Realizing that it was important to cede control to Amanda, Dane ignored the ache and concentrated on the pleasure.

He could have cursed when she suddenly abandoned her seduction efforts. Relief flooded through him as he realized she was only stopping long enough to take off his shoes and socks.

For a woman who a little more than twenty-four hours ago had been a virgin, Amanda was definitely making up for lost time.

"I've never noticed a man's feet before," she murmured, running her hands over his. "Who could have guessed that a foot could be so sexy?"

He began to laugh at that outrageous idea, but when she touched her lips to his arch, lightning forked through him, turning the laugh into a choked sound of need.

"Lord, Amanda—" He reached for her, but she deftly avoided his hands.

She touched her mouth to his ankle, felt the thundering of his pulse and imagined she could taste the heat of his blood beneath her lips.

Realizing that she was on the verge of losing control of her emotions, Amanda shifted positions, to lie beside him. She returned her mouth to his face, kissing her way along his rigid jaw as her hands explored his torso, exploiting weaknesses he'd never known he possessed.

She left him long enough to light the fire he'd laid while she'd been out on the fishing boat. Then she proceeded to undress. She took as much time with her buttons as she had with his. By the time the white shirt finally fluttered to the floor, Dane had to press his lips together to keep his tongue from hanging out. As he observed her creamy breasts, unbearably enticing beneath the ivory lace bra, Dane discovered that ten years hadn't lessened his reaction to the sexy lingerie that had driven a sex-crazed nineteen-year-old to distraction.

She sat down in the wing chair beside the bed, stuck out a leg and invited him to pull off the glove-soft cowboy boot. Dane obliged her willingly. The left boot, then the right, dropped to the floor.

The jeans were even tougher to get off than the boots. "I should have thought this through better," she muttered as she tugged the black denim over her hips, irritated she'd lost the sensual rhythm she'd tried so hard to maintain.

"You certainly don't have to apologize, contessa." The sexy way she was wiggling her hips as she struggled to pull the tight jeans down her legs had Dane feeling as if he was about to explode. "Because it definitely works for me."

Their gazes touched. His eyes were dark with desire, but tinged with a tender amusement that eased her embarrassment.

She had to sit down in the chair again to drag the jeans over her feet, but then she was standing beside the bed, clad only in the lacy bra and panties. The soft shadow beneath the skimpy lace triangle between her thighs had Dane literally biting the inside of his cheek.

"Don't stop now."

Thrilled by the heat flashing in his midnight-dark eyes, along with the hunger in his ragged tone, Amanda leaned forward, unfastened the back hooks of the bra, then held it against her chest for a suspended moment. With her eyes still on his, she smiled seductively.

As she raised her hands to comb them through her hair in a languid gesture, the lace bra fell away.

Unbearably aroused, Dane drank in the sight of her creamy breasts. While not voluptuous, they were smooth and firm. He remembered, all too well, how perfectly they had fit in his hands. In his mouth.

Watching him watch her, Amanda experienced a rush of power—followed by a wave of weakness. Although far more nervous now than when she'd begun the impromptu striptease, Amanda was determined to see it through. She hooked her fingers in the low-cut waistband, drawing the lace over her hips and down her legs.

"You are absolutely gorgeous." The truth of his words was echoed in his rough voice.

"And you're overdressed." Returning to the bed, she knelt over him, struggling with his belt buckle for a few frustrating seconds that seemed like an eternity.

Success! She dragged his jeans and white cotton briefs down his legs, then kissed her way up again.

"You're killing me," he moaned as her hand encircled his erection.

"Now you know how I felt." His sex was smooth and hot. "Last night." She lowered her head, and her hair fell over his hips like a gleaming antique-gold curtain as she swirled her seductive tongue over him.

Curses, pleas, or promises, Dane wasn't sure which, were torn from his throat. For the first time in his life, he understood what it was to be completely vulnerable.

She touched. He burned.

She tasted. He ached.

Amanda straddled Dane, taking him deep inside her, imprisoning him willingly, wonderfully, in her warmth.

Their eyes locked, exchanging erotic messages, intimate promises that neither had dared put into words.

Then, because they could wait no longer, she began to move, quickly and agilely, rocking against him, driving him—driving herself—toward that final glorious crest.

Although their time together was drawing to an end, neither Amanda nor Dane brought up the subject of what would happen once the challenge week ended. By unspoken mutual agreement, they ignored the inevitable, intent on capturing whatever pleasure they could. Whenever they could.

On the overnight backpacking trip, while the others tossed and turned, unaccustomed to sleeping on the ground, Dane slipped into Amanda's tent. Their lovemaking, while necessarily silent, was even more thrilling because of the risk of discovery. And when she couldn't remain quiet at the shattering moment of climax, Dane covered her mouth with his, smothering her ecstatic cry.

Time passed as if on wings. On the day before she was scheduled to leave, while Dane was on the beach, preparing for the final event of the challenge week—the cliff climb—Amanda was alone in her room, her eyes swollen from the tears she'd shed after he'd left her bed.

The knock on her door had her wiping her damp cheeks. "Yes?"

"Amanda?" It was Kelli. "May I speak with you?"

Although they hadn't exchanged more than a few words since the fishing-boat incident, Amanda had gotten the impression that Kelli had been watching her every move, which had only increased her suspicions that the public-relations manager was spying for Greg.

"Just a minute." She ran into the adjoining bathroom, splashed some cold water on her face and pulled a brush through her hair. Then she opened the door.

"I'm sorry to bother you, but..." Kelli's voice drifted off as she observed Amanda's red-rimmed eyes. "Is something wrong?"

"No." When Kelli arched an eyebrow at the obvious lie, Amanda said, "It's personal."

Kelli's expression revealed understanding. "Love can be a real bitch, can't it?"

"Is it that obvious?" Amanda thought she and Dane had been so careful.

"Not to everyone," Kelli assured her.

Amanda decided it was time to get their cards on the table. "That's probably because not everyone has been watching me as closely as you."

If she'd expected Kelli to be embarrassed, Amanda would have been disappointed.

"That's true. But none of the others were sent here from Manhattan to evaluate the office."

"So you *are* a company spy?"

"*Spy* is such a negative word, don't you think?" Kelli suggested mildly. "I prefer to think of myself as a trouble-shooter."

"Then you ought to shoot Greg Parsons," Amanda couldn't resist muttering.

"I've considered that. But my recommendation is going to be to fire him, instead."

"You're kidding!" Amanda could have been no more surprised than if Kelli had told her that Martians had just purchased the agency. "But he's family."

"Not for long," Kelli revealed. "It seems his wife has gotten tired of his philandering and is about to file for divorce. Obviously, Mr. Janzen isn't eager to employ the man who's broken his granddaughter's heart."

"It probably helps that he's incompetent to boot."

"That is a plus," Kelli agreed. "Which is, of course, where you come in." She paused a beat. For effect, Amanda thought. "You're the obvious choice to replace Greg as regional creative director."

"I'd hoped that was the case."

"I've already informed the partners that you'd be terrific at the job. But after receiving my daily faxes, they've instructed me to offer you another position.

"You also know that all the recent mergers and downsizing has created a great deal of anxiety."

"Of course."

"Your Portland office is not unique. Janzen, Lawton and Young has been experiencing the same problems with all its new worldwide acquisitions. Which is why the partners have come up with the idea of creating the post of ombudsman. Which is where you come in.

"If you decide to accept the position, you'll achieve upper-management status and be required to travel between offices, creating the same good feeling and teamsmanship you've managed with this group."

"I'd rather have a root canal than repeat this challenge week."

Kelli grinned. "After that fishing trip, I'm in your corner on that one. Actually, the partners think the challenge week was overrated and undereffective. They believe that you could achieve the same results simply by visiting each office and employing your diplomatic skills to assure the employees that the mergers are in everyone's best interests."

"Even if I don't believe they are?" Amanda dared to ask.

"You're in advertising," Kelli reminded her with one of her perky trademark smiles. "Surely you're not averse to putting a positive spin on things. As you've done to get Marvin and Julian working together this week. You weren't lying when you stressed how important it was for the creative people and the accounting people to work together, were you?"

"Of course not, but—"

"Take some time to think it over," Kelli suggested. She went on to offer a salary that was more than double what Amanda was currently making. "Of course, you'll have a very generous expense account. Since image is important in advertising, all upper-level employees travel first-class."

"It sounds tempting," Amanda admitted. She thought about what her father would say when she called him with the news.

"Believe me, you'll earn every penny."

"If I decide not to accept—"

"The job of creative director for the Northwest region is still yours."

"How much time do I have?"

''The partners would like your answer by the end of next week. Sooner if possible.''

With that, Kelli flashed another self-assured grin and turned to leave. She was in the doorway when she looked back. ''I'd appreciate you not saying anything about this to Greg.''

''Of course not,'' Amanda murmured, still a bit stunned by the out-of-the-blue offer. It was more than she'd dared hope for. More than she'd dreamed of. So why wasn't she ecstatic?

12

———▶◀———

The rock cliffs towered above the beach, looking cold and gray and forbidding.

"Who'll take care of my kids when I die?" Laura asked, her lack of enthusiasm obvious.

"No one's going to die," Dane assured her.

"This isn't fair to the women," Nadine complained. "I've seen rock climbers on the Discovery channel, and they're mostly all men."

"It's true that some climbing—like overhangs—requires strength in the shoulders and arms. But the fact that women aren't usually as strong in those areas isn't as important as you'd think," Dane said. "Since women tend to be smaller than men, they don't need as much strength. In fact, on the average, smaller people have a better strength-to-weight ratio, which is what's important in climbing."

"That's easy for you to say," Nadine muttered, casting a disparaging glance at Dane's muscular arms.

"It's true. Climbing is done primarily with the legs and feet because they're stronger. You can stand for hours at a time on your feet, but even the strongest man can only hang from his arms for a few minutes. The most essential element of climbing is balance."

While the group eyed the cliff with overt suspicion, Dane explained the basics of rock climbing. "One of the most important things to remember," he told the team members, "is that although the tendency is to look up for handholds, you should keep your hands below your shoulders and look down for footholds.

"Balance climbing, which is what you'll be doing, is like climbing stairs, although today you'll be climbing more sideways than vertically. You find a place for your foot, settle into a rest step, then make a shift of your hips and move on to the next step, always striving to keep your body poised over one foot.

"You can pause, or rest supported by both feet. You can also lift your body up with both legs, but never advance a foot to the next hold until you're in balance over the resting foot."

"What about ropes?" Laura, still unconvinced, asked.

"There's an old adage—'It's not the fall that hurts, it's the sudden stop.' If a rope stops a fall too fast, you can end up with a broken body. Or, a rope can pull loose and let you continue to fall. So, although you'll be equipped with a rope harness, since there are plenty of ledges and handholds, you shouldn't need to use the rope on this climb."

"We're not going to rappel?" Luke asked.

"Not today." Dane's assurance drew murmurs of relief.

After more explanation of terms and techniques, Dane climbed up the side of the cliff to set the woven climbing rope while the others watched.

"He makes it look so easy," Laura said.

"Michael Jordan makes hoops look easy, too," Luke added. "But I wouldn't be stupid enough to play one-on-one with the guy."

"It's tricky," Kelli allowed. "But this cliff is only a grade one."

"What does that mean?" Julian asked. "And how do you know so much about it?"

"I've been climbing since my teens," she answered the second question first. "As for the rating, climbs are divided into grades from one to six. A grade one, like this one, will only have one to two pitches. A grade six, like some of the routes on El Capitan, can have more than thirty pitches.''

''Terrific,'' Julian muttered. ''The red team's brought in a ringer.''

''I've already decided to take myself off the team,'' Kelli revealed, as Dane came back down the rocks with a deft skill that Amanda admired, even as her heart leaped to her throat.

''That's not necessary,'' Marvin said. ''I've been climbing since college. And while I haven't done El Capitan, I think I can do my bit for the blue team.''

With the competitive balance restored, the final challenge event began. To everyone's surprise, the climb went amazingly well. Even Laura, who'd sworn that she wouldn't be able to get past the first rest stop, managed to make her way to the top, then back down again.

The final participant was Julian, who was making record time when, eager to reach the top of the cliff, he leaned too far into the slope, pushing his feet outward, causing him to slip. Sensing he was about to slide, he grabbed for a handhold, causing a small avalanche of pebbles.

Everyone watching from below breathed a united sigh of relief as the rope looped around his waist held.

''There's a ledge six inches to the left of you,'' Dane called out. ''Just stay calm. You can reach it with no trouble.''

Dangling against the cliff, Julian managed to edge his left foot sideways until it was safely on the ledge.

''That's it,'' Dane said encouragingly. ''Now, put the heel of your right foot on that outcropping just below where it is now.''

Although he was trembling visibly, Julian did as instructed.

"It's going to be okay," Dane assured Amanda and the others. "He's not in any danger." He lifted his cupped hands again. "Now, all you have to do is come back down the way you went up and you're home free."

Later, Amanda would decide that the next moment was when Julian made his mistake. He looked down, viewed the gathered team members far below, realized exactly how close he'd come to falling—and literally froze.

Dane was the first to realize what had happened. He cursed.

"I'd better go bring him down."

"No," Marvin said. "He's my teammate. I can talk him the rest of the way up."

"It's just a game," Amanda protested. "Winning isn't worth risking anyone's life."

"I know that." Marvin gently pried her fingers off his arm. "But there's more at risk than winning, Amanda. Julian will never forgive himself if he gives up now."

That said, he repeated the ascent path he'd worked out the first time he'd scaled the cliff. Within minutes he was perched on a rock horn beside the art director and although it wasn't possible to hear what they were saying, it was obvious the two men were engaged in serious conversation.

When Julian looked down again, Amanda drew in a sharp breath, afraid that he'd panic and lose his balance again. But instead, he turned his attention back to the rock wall and began slowly but surely moving upward, with Marvin right behind him, offering words of encouragement and pointing out possible paths.

When Julian reached the top of the cliff, cheers rang out from the team members below.

"Talk about teamwork," Kelli murmured to Amanda. "You've definitely pulled it off, Amanda. I hope you're seriously considering the partners' offer."

"How could I not?" Amanda answered.

As Julian and Marvin made their way back down the cliff, Dane came over to stand beside Amanda. "I couldn't help overhearing Kelli. Congratulations. You'll be great."

She looked up at him with confusion. "You know?"

It was Dane's turn to be confused. "Know what? I assumed you'd been offered Parsons's job."

"I was." She glanced around, not wanting the others to hear. "But it's turned out to be a bit more complicated."

She didn't want to discuss the amazing offer with Dane until they were alone and she could attempt to discern how he felt about her possibly moving to New York.

If he asked her to stay, she would. Already having missed one opportunity with this man, she was not about to blow another.

Something was wrong. Dane felt it deep in his gut. He was going to lose her again.

The ride back to the inn was a boisterous one. Although the blue team had won the week's event on points, even their opponents were fired up by Julian and Marvin's cooperative team effort. By the time the van pulled into the parking lot of the inn, everyone had decided to go into Satan's Cove to celebrate having ended the week on such a high note.

"Are you sure you don't want to come with us?" Kelli asked an hour later, after the trophies had been handed out.

"It's been a long day," Amanda demurred. "I have a lot to think about. I think I'll just stay here."

"If you're sure."

"I'm sure."

Kelli glanced at Dane, who'd come into the room during the awards ceremony, then back at Amanda. "It's a fabulous offer, Amanda."

"I know."

"But then again, men like Dane Cutter don't come into a girl's life every day."

"I know that, too." She'd had two chances with Dane. How many more would she be lucky enough to be given?

"Well, I don't envy you your choice, but good luck." Kelli left the room to join the others, who were gathering in the reception foyer for their trip to town.

Unbearably nervous, Amanda stood rooted to the spot as Dane walked toward her.

"Your hands are cold," he said as he took both of them in his.

"It's the weather." Rain streaked down the windows, echoing her mood. "It'll be good when you get the new furnace installed."

"Yes." It wasn't the chill outside that had turned her fingers to ice, but a nervousness inside, Dane decided.

"Would you like to talk about it?" he asked quietly.

Amanda swallowed past the lump in her throat. "Actually," she said, her voice little more than a whisper, "I would. But first I'd like to make love with you."

Dane needed no second invitation.

Alone in the tower room, Dane and Amanda undressed each other slowly, drawing out this suspended time together with slow hands and tender touches.

The candles she'd lit when they'd first entered the room burned low as they moved together, flowing so effortlessly across the bed, they could have been making love in an enchanted world beneath the sea.

Whispered words of love mingled with the sound of rain falling on the slate roof; soft caresses grew more urgent, then turned gentle again as they moved from patience to urgency, returning to tenderness, before continuing on to madness. All night long.

The candles stuttered out. The rain stopped, the moon began to set. And despite their unspoken efforts to stop time, morning dawned. Gray and gloomy.

Amanda lay in Dane's arms, feeling more loved than she'd ever felt in her life. And more miserable.

"Are you ready to talk about it?" he asked quietly.

As his thumb brushed away the errant tear trailing down her cheek, she squeezed her eyes tight and helplessly shook her head.

"We have to, Amanda." His voice was as calm and self-controlled as it had been ten years ago, making her feel like a foolish, lovestruck fifteen-year-old all over again. "We can't put it off any longer."

"I know."

With a long sigh, she hitched herself up in bed. Dane wondered if she realized how beautiful she was, with her face, flushed from making love, framed by that tousled dark gold cloud of hair. Her eyes were wide and laced with more pain than a woman who'd spent the night making mad, passionate love should be feeling. She dragged her hand through her hair. "I don't know where to start."

He sat up as well and put his arm around her shoulder. "How about at the beginning?"

This wasn't going to be good. Dane's mind whirled with possibilities, trying to get ahead of the conversation so he could supply an argument to any reason she might try to give for leaving.

"Kelli *is* a company spy. But not for Greg."

"She works for the home office." All the pieces of the puzzle that had been nagging at him finally fell into place.

"Yes."

"When did you find out?"

"Right before the rock climb. She told me Greg was going to be fired. And that his job was mine, if I wanted it."

"Which you do." Dane decided there were worse things than commuter marriages. Portland wasn't that far away, and if her job made her happy...

"I thought I did." Her fingers, plucking at the sheets, revealed her nervousness. Dane waited.

"She offered me another position."

"Oh?" His heart pounded hard and painfully in his chest. "In Portland?"

Her words clogged her throat. Amanda could only shake her head.

"The job's in Manhattan," Dane guessed flatly.

"Yes." She shook her head again. "No."

"Which is it? Yes? Or no?" An impatience he'd tried to control made his tone gruff.

"My office would be in Manhattan. But I'd be traveling most of the time. In an ombudsman position."

It made sense. Having watched her in action, Dane knew she'd be a natural. And Lord knows, if the lack of morale the employees of the former C.C.C. agency had displayed when they'd first arrived at Smugglers' Inn was indicative of that of the international firm's other acquisitions, they were in desperate need of an effective ombudsman.

"That's quite an offer."

"Yes." Her voice lacked the enthusiasm he would have expected. "I think I could be good at it."

"I know you'd be great." It was, unfortunately, the absolute truth.

"And the salary and benefits are generous."

When she related them to Dane, he whistled. "That would definitely put you in the big leagues." Which was where her father had always intended her to be.

"I've dreamed of ending up on Madison Avenue, of course," Amanda admitted. "But I never thought my chance would come this soon. My parents would probably be proud of me," she murmured, echoing his thoughts.

"They'd undoubtedly be proud of you whatever you did." It wasn't exactly the truth. But it should be.

Her crooked, wobbly smile revealed they were thinking the same thing.

"When do you have to give the partners your answer?"

"By the end of next week." *Tell me not to go,* she begged him silently.

Dane wanted to tell her to turn the offer down. He wanted to insist she stay here, with him, to make a home during the day and babies at night, as they'd planned so many years ago.

But, just as he'd had to do what was right for him, Dane knew that Amanda could do no less for herself.

"It's a terrific opportunity," he forced himself to say now. "I'm sure you'll make the right choice."

Because he feared he was going to cry, Dane drew her back into his arms, covered her mouth with his, and took her one last time with a power and a glory that left them both breathless.

Not wanting to watch Amanda walk out of his life for a second time, later that morning Dane went down to the beach, seeking peace.

In the distance, he heard the bus taking the corporate team—and Amanda—away.

He knew that Eve Deveraux would be happy to give him a job at the Park Avenue Whitfield Palace. But, although it would allow him to be with Amanda, Dane was honest enough with himself to admit that there was no way he could return to the rat race of the city.

During his last years at Whitfield, he'd become driven and impatient. He hadn't liked that hard-edged individual, his mother definitely hadn't, and he knew damn well that Amanda wouldn't, either. Which made his choice to go to Manhattan no choice at all.

He saw the words written in the sand from the top of the cliff, but the mist kept him from being able to read them.

As he climbed down the stone steps, the words became clearer.

Amanda loves Dane.

"I love you." The soft, familiar voice echoed her written words. Dane turned and saw Amanda standing there, looking like his every dream come true.

"We found something together the other night in the cave, Dane. Something that's far more valuable to me than any alleged pirate's treasure. I want to stay. Here, in Satan's Cove with you." Her heart was shining in her eyes. "If you'll have me."

As much as he wanted to shout out *Yes!,* Dane knew they'd never be happy if she felt her decision was a sacrifice.

"What about New York?"

"It's a great place to visit."

"But you wouldn't want to live there."

"Not on a bet."

He felt a rush of relieved breath leave his lungs. "What about the job of creative director?"

"You're not going to make this easy for me, are you?" she asked with a soft smile.

"I don't think a decision this important *should* be easy."

"True." She sighed, not having wanted to get into the logistics of her decision right now. "The problem is, if I move into Greg's job, I'd still be working for a huge agency. Which wasn't why I got into advertising in the first place.

"After you left the room this morning, I had some visitors. Marvin, Julian, and Luke. They've been as unhappy as I have with the profit craze that's taken over the industry lately. They also decided Satan's Cove was a perfect place to open a shop.

"They've arranged to lease the offices above the crystal store and asked me to join them." Her smile was beatific, reminding Dane of how she looked after they'd made love.

"As much as I love the idea of you staying here, with me," Dane said, "I have to point out there aren't many prospective accounts in Satan's Cove, sweetheart."

"They've already contacted former clients who are unhappy with the way things have been going, and want to sign on. A lot of our business can be done by phone and fax, with the occasional trip into the city.... And speaking of local clients, I thought you might consider redoing your brochure."

"What's wrong with my brochure?"

"It's lovely. But it could use some fine-tuning. Why don't I give you a private presentation later?" She'd also come up with a nifty idea for Davey Jones's Locker she intended to run by Iris.

Putting advertising aside for now, Amanda twined her arms around Dane's neck and pressed her smiling lips to his.

As they sealed the deal with a kiss, the last of the fog burned off.

Amanda loves Dane.

The brilliant sun turned the love letter she'd written in the sand to a gleaming gold nearly as bright as Dane and Amanda's future.

* * * * *

A checklist of what Noelle wanted in a date for her sister's wedding:

❏ He had to look good in a suit.

❏ He had to be able to make social chitchat.

❏ Most importantly, he had to be completely forgettable so she could go back to her regular, work-filled, no-time-to-date life.

What she actually got:

✓ A devilishly handsome bad boy who preferred *un*dressing to dressing.

✓ Chitchat? The man was a certified flirt!

✓ Forgettable? Only if she was suddenly struck with amnesia. She'd *never* forget one hot second for the rest of her completely changed life...

TIFFANY WHITE

Male for Sale

Prologue

—————◄————

Noelle Perry was royally bummed out. She glared at the pristine white gold-lettered invitation to her baby sister Sophie's wedding. Frowning at the piece of parchment that had mocked her for the past five weeks, she cried out in exasperation, "Damn, Sophie—why did you have to go all traditional now? Why couldn't you have stayed true to character and eloped?"

Noelle had yet to come up with a man to attend Sophie's wedding as her escort. And there was *no way* she was going back home to St. Louis for the wedding without a male in tow. She wasn't up to enduring a barrage of grilling questions from relatives and smug looks from old boyfriends.

In frustration, she tossed the invitation onto a pile of papers on her desk. It landed on a bright blue sheet—an invitation to attend the "Male for Sale" bachelor auction at the Fairmont Hotel.

She picked up the blue paper, studied it, and made her decision.

1

Noelle stood outside the Moulin Rouge Room at the Fairmont Hotel, astonished that she'd actually gone through with her decision. Okay, she was pretty desperate and time was running out, but still... Half embarrassed she glanced around the corridor before picking up a "Male for Sale" catalogue from the stack on a table by the door.

She was certain she could afford the bidding. One of the reasons she'd relocated to Chicago from St. Louis was the higher salary she'd been offered.

Her only consolation for what she was about to do tonight was the fact that the money would go to charity. Soothed by that justification, she carefully read through the paragraph describing each of the bachelors up for auction. Each bachelor was to spend a weekend with the woman who bid the highest for him.

In Noelle's case, the lucky man would be spending the weekend as her date for Sophie's wedding. She could imagine just how *thrilled* the bachelor would be when he learned that little bit of news.

Unfortunately, there were no pictures to go with the bachelor profiles. Tonight's auction was unique in that the women were to bid on the bachelors "sight unseen" while the unidentified bachelors sat onstage. None of the women would learn the identity of the bachelor she'd bought until *after* she'd made her purchase.

Taking a deep breath, Noelle went inside the packed room and found a seat at one of the banquet tables. She looked around her and estimated that there were about two hundred chattering, excited women seated in the Moulin Rouge Room. Noelle sized up the crowd. There were a few women dressed as she was— in a business suit. But the majority were all glammed up as if they were trying to make an impression.

At least, in keeping with the discreet nature of the auction, no press or television cameras were allowed. Noelle's only fear was that one of the bachelors would turn out to be a member of the banking community. As a bank vice president, she'd be mortified if she ended up purchasing some banking professional who would spread the news that she was so hard up that she had to buy a date for her sister's wedding.

That thought alone kept her from swallowing any of the delicious desserts on the table.

She smiled nervously at the women around her as the bachelors paraded out to take their seats onstage. If there was a banker among them, she didn't recognize him—thank God!

Hunter Ashton sat onstage wondering what sort of descriptive paragraph his sister had written up for him. He looked out over the sea of women and a grin took up residence on his lips. Come on, ladies, step right up, his grin said, I aim to enjoy.

Noelle looked at each of the bachelors in turn, try-ing to guess which was the one who went with the de-scription that had caught her fancy. She was pretty sure it was the man in the gray double-breasted suit. He definitely would make a nice showing at the wed-ding.

At least she was sure it wasn't the bachelor at the end of the row. He certainly wasn't her idea of an es-cort for a formal wedding. The woman who bought him would be the type whose idea of paradise was a wild ride on a motorcycle.

The guy didn't even have the manners to sit up straight. Instead he leaned back with his legs sprawled apart. His tousled blond locks needed a trim. He'd left his long, slim-fitting navy jacket unbuttoned. Be-neath it he wore a slate-gray polo shirt paler than the jacket. His body was lanky and lean and she would have had to be dead not to notice it. He had a certain arrogance—or was it mischievousness?—that would never do.

As the female emcee stepped up to the microphone to begin the auction, Noelle scanned the catalog to see if she could guess which profile belonged to that born-to-raise-hell bachelor. Physical characteristics such as height, weight, hair and eye color couldn't be men-tioned, but she thought she had his description pegged anyway.

A good-looking stud. Adventurous and sensual. Interests include car races, windsurfing and rid-ing my motorcycle.

The auction began. The first bachelor to be auctioned off was a jock.

The next bachelor up was the one whom she'd decided to bid on.

Attractive, college-educated professional. Generous, romantic twenty-eight-year-old with a variety of interests, including music, art and reading.

With her eyes glued to the bachelor in the gray double-breasted suit, she placed the opening bid. The bidding was spirited. A woman at the table next to hers stayed with the bidding all the way to seven hundred dollars. Determined and frustrated, Noelle finally called out, "One thousand dollars."

The other woman dropped out.

Noelle had paid more than she'd planned to, but she'd placed the highest bid and won her bachelor. Her worries were over.

But the guy in the gray business suit didn't stand.

None of the bachelors did until the female emcee with the long blond hair went over to the man at the end of the row and whispered something to him.

He stood then, to acknowledge he was the bachelor she'd bought with her bid of one thousand dollars.

Noelle tried not to faint.

She'd really gone and done it this time.

No way would her parents forget this guy by her next visit. She was bringing one more child home to play.

She'd grown up the only adult in her family. Her own parents shared a joy for life that was beyond Noelle's understanding. They went in and out of businesses on a whim. As a result their fortunes were a roller coaster of ups and downs. They'd moved from mansions to shacks.

No one in her family was responsible.

Except her.

And look what she'd bought to escort her to the wedding.

Peter Pan lived!

Maybe she could sneak out quietly and no one would notice. Going to the wedding alone would be preferable to showing up with the gorgeous outlaw who was now—oh, no!—heading toward her.

It was too late to run.

Too late to hide.

But not too late to faint.

Which she did, with none of the aplomb of a Southern belle. It wasn't a swoon. It was more like a slump.

"Stand back, everyone. Give the girl some air," came a masculine command as Noelle's eyes fluttered open and she heard the excited murmuring swirling around.

"Poor little thing just fainted from all the excitement of winning me," the same voice continued, cocky as hell.

"Hunter, will you shut up and let me take care of—"

"Oh, Daphne, chill out. I just saw her pretty brown eyes open. There's no blood, so she doesn't need a nurse. I'll just lift her up in my arms and take her outside for some air."

"No!" Noelle couldn't understand why no one heeded her loud objection. She had screamed it, hadn't she? She moved her lips but no sound came out. She was helpless as the strong arms lifted her easily.

"All right, Hunter—but behave. I've got to finish up this auction. I'm counting on you to be a gentleman and take proper care of—"

"Noelle. Her name is Noelle," Hunter said. "Pretty name for a pretty lady. I thought so when she started bidding on me. I was hoping she could afford me. She's exactly my type: prim, proper and unapproachable with her dark hair pulled back in a tight knot, her blouse buttoned up to her throat. You know how I like a challenge. But truly I thought it would take more than five minutes to make her swoon."

"Don't be getting a swelled head, Hunter. Just take care of Noelle. I'll get back to you when I finish here."

"Yes, Daphne dear."

Noelle was wide-awake, but kept her eyes closed until Hunter began carrying her to the door.

"Would you please put me down, you... you..." she sputtered, unable to form a coherent word.

"Hunter. My name is Hunter," he said, whipping out that lethal grin of his.

"Okay, Hunter. Would you kindly put me down? I'm perfectly fine now."

"Oh, you won't get any argument from me on that score. You are a perfectly fine-looking woman."

But he still didn't put her down.

"I'll scream—"

"Now why would you want to do that?" he asked, genuinely puzzled.

"Because this was all a mistake. If you'll just put me down, I'll pay my bid and be gone. There is no need for you to honor your agreement for a weekend date. I'll consider the thousand dollars a charity donation for a good cause and be done with it."

"I don't understand," he said, putting her down. "Why did you bid on a date if you didn't want one? Weren't you planning on—"

"It was for a wedding, okay?" Noelle replied, figuring it would dissuade him. No man ever went willingly to a wedding—even the groom.

"A wedding! I love weddings."

"You do?" she responded, caught off guard by his exclamation of delight.

"Of course."

She didn't believe him—not for a minute. "You really love weddings?" she repeated.

"Are you kidding? All that virginal white, flowing champagne, and lust in the air. The only thing more explosive and exciting is the Fourth of July."

Noelle groaned. He was her worst nightmare. And she had the sinking feeling he was a nightmare that was going to be hard to banish. He was as persistent as a frisky puppy.

"It would be for the whole weekend with my family at their house," she began, in her effort to persuade him that escorting her to the wedding wasn't something he'd want to do. "You'd have to go to the rehearsal dinner. You'd have to attend the wedding

and the reception. And any other family obligations
involved—''

''Hell, I'll even go to the bachelor party,'' Hunter
offered, way too agreeably.

''You would.''

''What?'' he asked, bending down to catch what
she'd muttered under her breath.

''Nothing.'' She frowned. How on earth was she
going to discourage him? She couldn't believe she was
in the position of wanting to do so. All along she'd
been working on arguments to get her bachelor to
agree to escort her to Sophie's wedding. What a re-
volting development. It wasn't as if she'd had a lot of
experience beating men off with a stick. Her mother
and sister were the femmes fatales in the family.
Somehow she hadn't inherited the flirting gene. It was
probably for the best. No telling what sorts of trouble
she'd have gotten herself into if she had. She might
have married a wild man like her father or married at
the tender age of eighteen—as Sophie was just about
to do.

When *she* married, it would be a marriage of reason between two sensible adults.

''So...'' Hunter prompted.

''I'm sorry?'' Noelle said, not catching the drift of
what he was asking.

''Are you going to keep me or return me and embarrass me before all the curious women inside?''

She hadn't thought of *that*. It wasn't in her nature
to hurt anyone's feelings. Though she was fairly certain Hunter's pout was more for effect than real. She'd

bet it would be next to impossible to embarrass Hunter.

"If you keep me, you can just give me the check and I'll turn it in for you so you don't have to go back inside, if you feel funny about having fainted in front of everyone," he offered, nudging her to make the decision in his favor.

Heavens, she'd never seen a man so anxious to get dressed up in a monkey suit. Maybe he cleaned up real nice. Maybe he'd behave. Maybe it wouldn't be such a bad idea.

Maybe she was crazy.

But she wrote out a check and gave it to him anyway.

"Aren't you forgetting something?" he asked, pocketing the check she'd made out to the hospital for a thousand smackers.

"A thousand dollars, right? That was the sum I bid—"

"Yes, that's right. I'm talking about your address. If I'm going to escort you to this shindig, I'm going to have to know where to pick you up."

She gave him her address, which wasn't on her check. She used a post-office box number on her checks. A single woman couldn't be too careful. You never knew what kind of loony would take a liking to you.

One like Hunter.

Unfortunately, it was too late to reconsider and give him a fake address. Besides, for some strange reason, Hunter was determined to go to the wedding with her.

"You're smiling," Hunter observed. "You should do that more often. You're really pretty when you smile."

"I already said you could go," Noelle returned, not about to be taken in by a smooth talker.

"So you did. Just tell me where and what time you want me to bring the carriage 'round to pick you up and we'll call it a night. We don't want you getting faint on me again."

"I need to leave for St. Louis—did I mention the wedding is in St. Louis? Maybe you won't want to go out of town on such short notice. Your boss might object," she said, still snatching at straws to wiggle out of the deal.

"My boss won't object," he assured her.

"I'll want to get an early start—say, seven—so I'll have time to freshen up for the rehearsal dinner after the six-hour drive."

"No problem," he continued to assure her.

She played what she believed was her trump card with a flourish: "I need to leave this Thursday morning. The wedding is *this* weekend."

"Perfect."

"Perfect?"

"Right. I just finished a long project and my boss wants me to take some time off to recharge my batteries, so to speak."

"Your boss is . . ."

"Me," he supplied with a wicked wink.

"Tell me, Valerie, love . . . if you could date any superhero, whom would you date?" Hunter Ashton asked, looking at the disaster area his home office had become. He knew he ought to clean it, but he was too tired. The end of a project always left him feeling completely drained of energy. But he was never too tired for the mental conversations he held with the blond amazon cartoon character he'd created. With her swing of long blond hair, buxom curves, legs that went on forever and savvy attitude, Valerie seemed real to him.

"A superhero?" Valerie repeated, considering her options.

"Right." Hunter made a halfhearted attempt to pick up some of the clutter. "I know. I bet you'd choose Superman, wouldn't you? After all, he is the primo superhero."

"No, it wouldn't be Superman."

"Really?" Easily distracted, Hunter gave up on tidying and sprawled his length over the sofa to consider. "Why not?"

Valerie came over to the sofa and perched on the armrest. Swinging her long legs, she turned toward Hunter and gave him a disdainful look. "Are you kidding? What woman would want to date a man who's faster than a speeding bullet?"

"Valerie!"

"Well, you asked," she said, flicking back the mane of long, thick blond hair.

"Okay, then how about Spiderman? Do you think women like men with big feet?" he asked, straying from the subject as he kicked off his sneakers and stared at his own size twelves.

"Spiderman never blinks...too creepy. As for big feet— You know what they say about men with big feet...."

Hunter smiled, waving his toes. "Batman," he suggested.

"Pu-lease. He hangs out with Robin *all* the time. Three would be a crowd."

Hunter stretched and yawned. "Spawn, then. He's a moody, romantic superhero."

"Angst, but no angst. He's hung up forever on his first love."

Hunter shrugged in agreement and reached for the comics section of the newspaper scattered beneath the coffee table.

"How about the Green Hornet?"

"I'm not into insects."

"Plastic Man ..."

"Too artificial."

"Wait a minute." Hunter snapped his fingers and sat up. "I'm forgetting about the perfect alpha male superhero— Wolverine."

"No way. I don't want claw marks on my back." She stretched and arched her back. "Besides, haven't you seen the cover of *Mouth to Mouth?* Wolverine is into supermodel Claudia Schiffer."

"Who isn't?" Hunter said, picturing the supermodel in a sexy outfit, something racy red. After a brief erotic detour of the mind he returned to the subject at hand. "Okay, I'm out of guesses. You tell me."

Valerie snapped her fingers. "Captain Marvel, of course."

"Captain Marvel? Why would you choose Captain Marvel?"

"Because, silly, I'd want to find out what's so bloody marvelous about him."

"You're such a princess."

"You know, Hunter Ashton, you ought to get out more. See other women."

"But I like you, princess. You're so lush and full of life. You're always ready for adventure."

"You don't think maybe I'm a little too lush...?" she asked. Glancing down at her ample cleavage, she tugged her bustier up.

"Hey, lush works for Wolverine," he reminded her. "Besides, I like women who are bigger than life. You know. Big hair, big...ah...and a big cape."

"You're such a pervert, Hunter. Don't you think it's a little odd for a grown man like you to want to dress me up in thigh-high boots and skimpy outfits?"

"No. I think you look way cool."

"So why didn't you name me the Ice Princess?"

"Because Valerie Valor, the Viking Princess of Venus, is a proper name for a superheroine. Aren't you being a bit ungrateful? After all, I've turned you into the bestselling comic-book character you are."

"Maybe I'm tired of being good all the time."

"Don't tell me you want to be a bad girl—"

"What's wrong with that?"

"It involves a lot of erasing."

"Not the eraser! Please, Hunter, don't rub me out. I'll be good. I promise."

"I know."

* * *

"You need a keeper," Daphne Ashton chided her twin brother, Hunter. "This whole apartment looks like a frat house—after a keg party." She lifted a pair of socks gingerly and dropped them into the wicker basket with the rest of the clothing she'd collected.

Hunter looked up from the splash page he'd just added one final touch to, reluctant to let go of his latest project. Stretching his lanky frame, he rolled his neck from side to side, as it was still stiff from the long hours spent drawing. "I was on deadline, sister dear. You know I can't be creative and domestic at the same time. I'll clean now that I've finished Valerie Valor's latest adventure." He fiddled with his white leather-thong bracelet while Daphne sliced him a considering look that said they both knew there wasn't *any* time when Hunter wasn't being "creative."

"Why are you here, Daphne? We both know you didn't come over to clean my apartment."

"Can't a sister visit her brother—"

"She can, but you hardly ever do. You're always busy in the emergency room at Cook County."

"Northwestern," Daphne corrected.

"Whatever. Don't you have some patients at the hospital to torture? Or is it a slow day in the windy city? What, no political candidates shooting themselves in the foot today...?"

"It's my day off. You have heard of a day off? You should try giving the concept a try, you know. Never can tell, you might even like it. At least it would give you some perspective on the fantasy world you live in most of the time. I worry about you sometimes, Hunter.''

"Yeah, you *and* Valerie."

She arched an eyebrow. Startling blue eyes the same color as his censured him. "See what I mean?"

"Why are you here, Daphne?" Hunter asked again, refusing to bite on an old ongoing dialogue between them.

Daphne set the basket down. "Okay, you're right. I came over here to ask you a big favor."

"Sure, whatever you need," Hunter agreed, reaching for a cloth to wipe off his pen point.

"But you haven't even heard what the favor is."

"Does it matter? You know you'll only wheedle it out of me whatever it is, anyway, Daphne."

"But aren't you even a little bit curious?"

Hunter put down the cloth he was using and began paying attention. "You know the rules. As long as it doesn't involve any hospital-type stuff. You know how I am around blood."

Daphne slid down onto the sofa. "I can't believe you faint at the sight of blood and I'm a trauma nurse. Are you sure you weren't adopted?"

"We're twins," Hunter said, deliberately rubbing it in.

"If you're such a wuss, Hunter, how come you have Valerie Valor pummeling everyone in the comic series?"

"Hey, women love Valerie doing in the bad guys. That's a big part of why my series is such a success. Valerie is my strike at equality for women. My comic is more than just entertainment—Valerie is a role model for women."

Daphne choked out a laugh. "Yeah, in the comics. A status quo, long-legged, big-busted blonde who performs her job wearing a red bustier," she said, throwing her hands up in exasperation.

"Oh, like guys don't get off on seeing you coming with your blond hair, blue eyes and nurse whites. They probably think they're already dead and gone to heaven."

Daphne just shook her head and closed her eyes. When she opened them, her gaze fell on a catalog on the edge of the table beside his drawing board. She recognized the cover. "Dare I ask why you're reading a Victoria's Secret catalog, Hunter?"

Hunter shrugged. "I was thinking about updating Valerie's wardrobe."

"You've got to get out more, Hunter."

"I am. This weekend, as a matter of fact. I'm going to a wedding."

"Wedding?"

"The babe who bought me wants to take me."

"Which brings me to the favor. I want you to behave on this date, okay? I organized the bachelor auction benefit. It was my idea. I don't want the whole thing to blow up in my face because you . . ."

"Aw, come on, Daphne. . . ."

"Just behave."

"I'll make them love me, I promise."

"See that you do."

"Whatcha doing?"

Noelle looked over her shoulder at Barbara Ann, the chubby, brown-haired seven-year-old who lived across the hall in the apartment building. Barbara Ann's mother was a single parent and occasionally worked overtime. It was understood that Barbara Ann would wait in Noelle's apartment until her mother arrived home.

"Painting my toenails for the wedding."

"Oh. Did you find a dress? You said it had to be perfect."

"Yes, I found one," Noelle said, finished painting her toenails. She put the stopper back in the bottle. "Want to see it?"

"Can I?" Barbara Ann's dark brown eyes were saucer wide.

"Sure, come on, it's in my closet. You can see my shoes I had dyed to match, too." Noelle led the way to her peach bedroom. Like the rest of the apartment, the decor was soft and pretty, but not homey.

Barbara Ann crawled up on the floral-print bedspread and sat cross-legged with her chin cupped in her hands, waiting.

Noelle withdrew her dress for the wedding from the closet. It was the one thing about Sophie's wedding that had gone right for her so far. The dress was perfect.

Pale celery green, it had a high jewel neckline and long sleeves. From the wrist to about two inches from the elbow, a row of tiny silk-covered buttons decorated each sleeve.

"Well . . . what do you think?" Noelle asked.

"It's not very fancy, is it?"

"You don't like it?" Noelle asked, surprised.

"Well, I thought it might be red," Barbara Ann said, raising and lowering her shoulders.

"Red?"

"It's my favorite color," Barbara Ann announced. "Are your shoes red?"

"No, they match the dress."

"Oh."

Noelle picked up a pair of white dress gloves and held them up for Barbara Ann's approval. "Do you like my gloves?"

"They're all right." Tilting her head, the seven-year-old thought a moment, then asked, "Are you going to wear a hat to the wedding? Do you have a hat?"

"No, no hat."

"When I was a flower girl, I wore a ring of flowers in my hair. You could do that," she suggested. "They smelled real nice, and they had ribbon streamers."

"A garland."

"What?"

"The flowers you wore in your hair are called a garland. I bet you were a very pretty flower girl."

"I got sick."

"You did?"

"Uh-huh. I ate too much wedding cake and ice cream."

"Would you like some ice cream now?" Noelle asked, searching for something Barbara Ann might like.

She hated that the child she adored might find her boring. If only she could abandon herself enough to play.

She had a feeling her bachelor-auction date for Sophie's wedding was going to be just as bored with her dress as Barbara Ann was.

And worse, that she was going to be the most boring date of Hunter Ashton's life.

Noelle's week went smoothly until Wednesday, despite her constant misgivings about her escort for Sophie's wedding.

On Wednesday, however, things began to go awry.

First, the corporate account she'd been working to acquire requested a male vice-president. The patriarch of the wine company didn't cotton to a woman handling his money. There wasn't much she could do, because you could hardly sue the customer.

To counter the slant against women in banking, in all the public speaking she did, she encouraged women to get over their fear of math and money, and take charge of their finances.

She then returned to worrying about what could go wrong with the wedding, starting with the word *carriage,* which Hunter had used when he'd said he would pick her up.

A carriage could be anything from a low rider to a motorcycle.

Please, not the motorcycle, she prayed daily.

And again Thursday morning as she stood waiting for Hunter to arrive.

Her palms were sweaty and her imagination was racing when the doorbell rang.

But it wasn't Hunter who greeted her. Instead it was Barbara Ann.

"What are you doing home this time of the morning?" Noelle asked.

"I'm home from school 'cause I didn't feel so good this morning."

"Where's your mom?"

"She stayed home with me. She's on the computer with her office. She said I could come over and say hi to you before you left for work, but I wasn't to bother you. Am I bothering you?"

"No, of course not. Come on in. I'm waiting for my— Actually, I'm waiting for Prince Charming to arrive to take me to the wedding."

"But you're not dressed up in your pretty dress."

"I'm taking it with me. The wedding isn't until Saturday night. Tonight is the rehearsal dinner and casual, sort of."

"Oh."

"So, what's wrong with you, Barbara Ann? You got a tummyache or a spelling test?"

"I just feel yucky...."

"Yeah, I know the feeling," Noelle said, having had a rather unsettled stomach herself that morning.

"Do you want something to eat?" Noelle offered.

Barbara Ann shook her head no.

"Not even a Popsicle? I have cherry. It's your favorite color...."

"Okay. But don't tell Mom. I didn't eat any breakfast."

Noelle knew she wouldn't have to tell "Mom"—the red-stained lips would give their secret away. But she figured it was okay to indulge Barbara Ann since she wasn't feeling well.

Barbara Ann was halfway through her Popsicle and only just started on her questions about Prince Charming when a honking racket started up outside the apartment building.

Did motorcycles have horns? Noelle wondered.

She didn't want to look, so she sent Barbara Ann to the window.

"Wow!" Barbara Ann pronounced. "It's a really big long car."

"Is it black?" Noelle ventured, visualizing a hearse as a worst-case scenario.

"Nope. It's white."

"White!"

"Uh-huh . . . and some guy's waving at the apartment building while he's standing beside the big car honking the horn. I think he wants you to come down."

Noelle took a deep breath and closed her eyes. "Is he wearing a suit?" she asked hopefully.

"Uh-uh. He's got on jeans and a baseball cap. The cap's on his head the wrong way."

Backward—of course. Noelle opened her eyes. "He does have a shirt on, doesn't he?" she inquired, picking up her suitcase and purse before he woke everyone in the building, including the retired mailman.

"Uh-huh. It's pink."

"Pink?"

"Uh-huh. Pink. He's tall."

"I know."

"Is he a good kisser?"

"Barbara Ann!"

"Well, my cousin says—"

"Don't you listen to what your cousin says. You're entirely too young to know about kissing."

"Oh." Barbara Ann didn't sound all that convinced.

The racket continued as Noelle shooed Barbara Ann out into the hall with her bare Popsicle stick.

"I can't take this, Mom'll know," Barbara Ann said, handing Noelle the stick. "Will you tell me all about the wedding when you come back?"

"Yes," Noelle agreed, locking the apartment door.

"And show me the bride's bouquet, if you catch it?"

"I'm *not* catching it."

"But you might," Barbara Ann insisted.

Not if she could dodge it, Noelle vowed to herself.

"Bye!" Barbara Ann waved as Noelle went down the stairs.

She was going to kill Hunter when she was done with him. A slow...painful...embarrassing—

"Good morning," Hunter said brightly, holding open the trunk of the limo.

"Is this what you do? Are you a limo driver?" Noelle asked, as he placed her suitcase and the wedding gift in the trunk.

"Not right now. I used to, though. That's how I got the limo for the wedding. It wasn't rented for the weekend."

Used to. That probably meant Hunter was unemployed and explained why he was so anxious to take her to the wedding. It meant plenty of free meals.

And flowing champagne.

She groaned inwardly as he closed the trunk and went around to open the door for her. All she wanted was for the weekend to be over so she could get back to her nice, safe, sane life.

"Do you always eat Popsicles for breakfast?" Hunter asked, nodding at the stick in her hand as they pulled away.

"No, it's— Oh, never mind."

"Cherry, huh? My favorite flavor..."

She glared over at him.

"Red's my favorite color," he explained.

"Here, have it. It's all yours," she said, shoving the Popsicle at him. "Enjoy."

A seven-year-old. She was going home to her sister's wedding with a man who shared a seven-year-old's taste for cherry Popsicles.

It couldn't get any worse.

Barbara Ann sat in the window seat at her bedroom window and spied on Noelle and her Prince Charming. She thought she'd look a lot happier if she were Noelle. She began to imagine herself older and in a pretty red dress. To imagine she was the one being picked up to go to a fancy ball in a long white limo.

She was so caught up in her fantasy, she didn't even notice the limo pull away or hear her mother come into her bedroom.

"Where have you been, Barbara Ann? You didn't go bother Noelle, did you?" Barbara Ann's mother asked upon seeing her daughter's red lips.

"I only went to say goodbye. Did you see the guy who came to take her to the wedding? Cousin Missy

would call him a hunk. I bet he's a good kisser. Missy
says—''

"Barbara Ann!"

"Aw, Mom, I know about kissing," Barbara Ann
said, a worldly seven.

"Barbara Ann, you're *contagious*."

"Constageous? What's that?"

"The doctor just called and confirmed you have the
chicken pox."

That afternoon the sun came out from behind the
clouds to play hide-and-seek in Noelle's empty apartment. The splash of light traveled across the plush
peach carpet, up over the floral-print bedspread and
over to the open closet where it reflected off the clear
plastic bag covering the celery-green dress hanging
forlornly on the door.

The late-afternoon sun caught the bugle beads on
the cap sleeves of Sophie's wedding gown, shooting
off sparkly prisms of light as she turned to model it for
her mother.

"What do you think?" Sophie asked, uncharacteristically shy and unsure. Sophie and her mother not
only resembled each other physically, both were of the
same temperament. Headstrong and spoiled, Sophie
was having prewedding jitters.

Grace got up from the beige brocade chair in the
ornate dressing room of the bridal shop. She hugged
her daughter's shoulders from behind. "I think that
if you get stood up at the altar, there will be lots of
volunteers to take the groom's place. Besides what

man would have the nerve to stand up a redhead? We're not well known for our tempers for nothing.''

"Oh, Mother you don't think that—''

Grace, more petite than her daughter, pulled Sophie around to face her. "No, of course not, darling. You're going to be a beautiful bride. The wedding will be perfect. Trust me.''

"It will, won't it?'' Sophie said, her dark eyes brightening. "And you know what? I've got it all worked out with everyone so that Noelle catches the bridal bouquet!''

"I'm afraid, dear, that it's going to take more than a bridal bouquet to get your older sister to the altar,'' Grace said, with a weary sigh.

Sophie grinned, lifting a padded hanger from a hook on the wall and smiling at her mother. "You mean something like what Daddy did to get you to marry him.''

"How did you— Oh, you mean the kidnapping. Yes, a kidnapping might do the trick. Only I was a willing hostage. Something tells me Noelle would go kicking and screaming.''

Sophie began removing her wedding gown. "She is coming to the wedding, isn't she? Every time I've talked to her in the past six weeks, she sounded vague.''

"She's coming. She called this morning.''

"Is she bringing a date?''

"Well, to tell the truth, she did sound a little vague about that when I asked.''

2

———◆———

They settled into an uncomfortable silence on the drive out of Chicago. Since he had the urge to talk to *someone,* he began a mental conversation with Valerie.

"Well, Valerie, now what am I going to do? Noelle won't even talk to me."

"So you talk to her. You're the one who always puts words in my mouth."

"But this time I don't know what to say. You gotta help me out, here."

"Are you gonna get me out of this red bustier and into something decent?" Valerie reminded.

"Look, Superwoman doesn't complain about her outfit. Why can't you be more like her?"

"Because I'm a woman of the nineties. That's how you created me. You know. With a mind of my own."

"That was a mistake."

"What did you say?" Valerie demanded.

"I said, what kind of outfit did you have in mind? Not that I'm agreeing to anything, you understand."

"I'd settle for a sports bra and biker shorts," Valerie suggested. "At least I'd be comfortable."

"I'll think about it."

"And remember I like pink."

"Pink!"

"Pink."

"But you can't pummel people in pink."

"So make me more charming. I'll use my brain and my wiles instead of my fists."

"We'll talk about it later. Right now I've got to figure out what I'm going to say to Noelle."

"Talk to her about the wedding."

"You think?"

"Well, you've got to find out what your role is. Are you supposed to be a first date, a boyfriend, a lover, or a fiancé?"

"Good question."

"So ask it, dufus...."

Hunter cleared his throat and banished Valerie Valor from his mind as he decided how to phrase the question she had brought up. It would certainly break the ice.

"Uh, I was wondering."

Noelle turned to him.

"You've changed your mind," she said on a note of wistful hope.

"No, of course not." Why was she so anxious to be rid of him? Here he was, all primed for an adventure, and he'd hooked up with someone who seemed determined to avoid it and him at all costs. "Maybe you could explain something to me," he said, glancing over at her. "I'm curious to know why you bought me for this wedding, when apparently you don't want to go with me."

She didn't deny it. He watched her smooth her hand over the plush seat of the limo while she chose her words of reply.

"I didn't exactly mean to buy you," she said finally. There was so much room between them in the huge car that her voice almost echoed.

"I don't understand." Hunter eased the limo up to a stoplight just before the entry ramp onto the interstate.

"Well," she began a little hesitantly, twirling a strand of her long dark chestnut-colored hair. "Uh, as you may recall, the women bidding on the bachelors didn't know which bachelor in particular we were bidding on until we'd bought him."

"Oh, so you're saying that you're— You're saying that you're disappointed with the... with me."

"I wouldn't put it that way."

"Well, how would you put it, then?" The light changed and he headed through the intersection, having to slam on his brakes when someone ran a red light at the last second.

Hunter threw his arm out to brace Noelle from flying against the dash. Because of the distance between them, only his hand broke her slide.

"Are you okay?"

"Yeah, I'm okay. I don't believe the idiots who take such chances."

"Chances with other people's lives..."

Noelle nodded.

He eased the limo through the intersection and onto the entry ramp while she resettled herself on the seat.

"Who did you think you were bidding on when you bought me?" he asked, once he'd melded into the high-speed traffic on the inside lane.

"The guy in the gray business suit."

"You're kidding. He looked pretty boring to me."

"I was looking for boring."

"I could be boring."

Noelle shot a glance over at him. "Not even on a good day."

"What's wrong with having fun? It's a wedding, after all."

"Maybe you're right. Maybe I should throw caution to the wind and treat this as a weekend 'adventure'. No. This whole thing has been an ill-conceived idea. It'll teach me to never do something on impulse again."

"Don't you want to go to your sister's wedding?"

"Of course I do."

"You just didn't want to show up alone, right? Why? Because you're older than she is?"

Noelle shook her head no. "You're a guy. You'd never understand."

"Sure I would. My twin sister, Daphne—you met her, she was running the bachelor auction—she says I can read her mind."

"Can you read mine?"

"No, but then I don't know you that well. Maybe if we talked I could get to know you better and help you out here. You might as well enjoy the wedding since you're going."

Noelle stared out the limo window and then looked away. Another car passing them on the highway had gawking passengers trying to discern if someone famous was in the limo.

"Why did you have to bring this limo? Everyone will be looking at us."

"It was an ill-conceived idea. It'll teach me to never do something on impulse again," he offered, repeating her phrase.

It got a smile.

"So, are we lovers?"

That got a frown.

"I mean, what exactly are you planning to tell people about me? I have to know to play my part."

"Oh, no, you're an unemployed actor, aren't you? This is going to be a disaster, I just know it."

"Calm down. I'm not an unemployed actor. I'm only trying to help, here. Don't you agree we have to get our stories straight? Or do you really want me to tell everyone that you bought a date to bring you to the wedding?"

"No!"

"My point exactly. Not that I think there's anything wrong with it. It's a great adventure. That's why I insisted on Daphne letting me be in the auction."

"A great adventure," Noelle repeated on a groan. "You think this is going to be a great adventure—"

"You know what I mean. We can make this work."

"We can?"

"Sure. Just tell me how I can help."

Noelle was silent for a moment, considering.

"Okay. I came to the bachelor auction because I've been so busy with my career, I haven't had time for dating. I didn't want to go home for the wedding and face a lot of questions from relatives about why I wasn't married and having babies. I thought if I at least showed up with a man, they'd be inclined to think I was involved."

"Your career. I should know what it is that you do."

"I'm vice president of a bank. Chicago Fidelity Trust."

Hunter whistled, impressed. "I'd say you were a real handy person to know."

"I turn down more loans than I approve," she was quick to point out. That had been a great move, telling an unemployed person she was a bank vice-president.

"I'll bet you do."

Hunter marveled at the way she went from being a bit shy and insecure to being very in control and sure about her career. One thing was for certain, she was the prettiest bank vice president he'd ever met—and he'd met a lot of them when he'd been trying to finance his own comic book.

Her porcelain skin glowed and made him want to touch her. Her full pink lips were bait she didn't even know she had. Kissing them crossed his mind a lot. He was afraid behaving like a gentleman wasn't going to be easy.

"So, what kind of relationship did you have in mind?"

"What?"

"For the relatives."

"Something just short of a fiancé. I don't want them throwing me a shower, for heaven's sake. We've been dating a while and we're . . . friends."

"*Good* friends?"

"Okay, good friends. But I don't want you getting any ideas. This is only for the relatives' benefit. When it's over, it's over."

"But you might change your mind. I can be very charming."

"I'm sure. But I'm very busy. I don't have—"

"Time for romance. I know."

They drifted into silence again as the rolling green hills of the countryside flashed past.

Hunter reached to turn on the stereo for some Kenny G.

Within moments Noelle had drifted off to sleep, he saw when he glanced over as they passed the halfway mark on the drive to St. Louis.

Valerie was lounging on the hood of the limo, her long blond hair blowing in the breeze. "Now what, Valerie? My conversation was so stimulating I put her to sleep."

"Let her sleep," Valerie said, unconcerned. "She's tired. Probably had a rough week. She'll come around."

"But she said she's too busy for romance."

Valerie stood on the hood of the limo pretending to be a hood ornament; she really needed a sailing ship to do her justice. "No woman is too busy for romance. You've got to show her what she's missing. Turn on the old Hunter Ashton charm. Sweep Ms. Noelle Perry off her feet."

"But Daphne told me to behave."

"Daphne," Valerie snorted. "Daphne is just like Noelle. They both could do with a little more fun in their lives."

"Fun, huh? Okay, I'll see what I can do to put some fun in this weekend. Though I suspect I'm going to have to drag Ms. Perry kicking and screaming into it. Her smile is about as rusty as the gate hinge of a neglected garden."

"Then buy her something pink. That'll cheer her up."

"No. Red. Red's better."

Valerie sighed, resigned. She lay back down on the hood, draping herself provocatively. "Just as long as it isn't a bustier."

"Why not?"

Valerie smiled seductively. "Because only I can carry off a red bustier."

Hunter left Valerie to her ego while he thought about ways to make Noelle enjoy the wedding weekend. He liked to make people feel good—it made him feel good to make others feel good. He liked everyone to have a good time; it was just that lately he'd begun to notice that *he* wasn't. Transient good times weren't as satisfying as they once had been.

Even Valerie was getting cranky.

Noelle wasn't asleep any longer.

She'd woken up when Hunter had stopped for gas, a quart of milk and a handful of Twinkies. Still, she pretended to be asleep as they passed through the tall cornfields near the border of Missouri. In half an hour they'd be at her parents' house. She needed the time to collect her thoughts.

A wedding was sure to be fraught with chaos in her family, especially since—at the moment—her parents were in the money. If they hadn't been, they probably would have bought Sophie a ladder to elope.

If only Noelle could have begged off the wedding, claiming she was ill. At the moment her stomach could lay legitimate claim to queasiness.

But the excuse wouldn't work anyway, with her loony family. They'd probably just bring the wedding to her.

Her loony family...

Why did she have to be the only sane one of them?

If she ever decided to get married, she'd have to do it before the prospective groom met her family. She wondered how Sophie had managed to hold on to her fiancé after he'd met the family. It didn't bode well for Marky that he hadn't bolted, to date.

It could mean one of two things.

She was either getting a brother-in-law who was a saint, or, after their marriage, Noelle would still be the only sane one in the family.

With a name like Marky, she didn't hold out much hope for sainthood.

Not for the first time, she wondered if perhaps she hadn't been adopted. When she'd voiced that particular concern out loud, the whole family had laughed—said she was being silly.

Silly indeed.

She'd never been silly a day in her life.

Her thoughts drifted back to the impending wedding. It wasn't that she didn't wish her baby sister well. She did. Though, at eighteen, she wasn't sure Sophie knew enough about love—knew enough about anything—to make such a lifetime commitment.

Maybe she was just jealous. At twenty-eight, Noelle had begun to notice how much of the world was divided up into couples. It would be convenient to have a permanent escort, but to marry a man for convenience wasn't her speed.

For all her practicality, Noelle was a romantic at heart. But she didn't want just some smooth talker. She wanted a man of substance.

The right man for her would have to sweep her off her feet *and* penetrate her wall of defenses. The few men who'd even tried had gone down to crashing defeat.

She knew she wasn't easy.

Her standards were very high.

She peeked over at Hunter, who was completely relaxed behind the wheel of the car.

What would her parents think of him?

What would Sophie think?

Her relatives?

Old beaux?

She smiled. Hunter Ashton was an old beau's nightmare. Maybe this weekend wouldn't be so bad, after all. In reality it was just one weekend out of her life and when it was over, her life would go on as before.

* * *

"Well, now I've done it," Hunter said, looking over at Noelle.

"What?"

He pointed to the Welcome to Missouri sign as they started across the bridge from Illinois. "I've taken you over the state line."

The words were no sooner out of his mouth than the limo conked out and coasted to a halt.

"I think you may have spoken too soon," Noelle said, as they sat in the dead car in the middle of the bridge above the Mississippi River. They weren't causing a traffic jam because traffic was light on a Thursday afternoon. But it wouldn't be long before there was one if Hunter didn't get the limo started.

"Come on, baby, start," Hunter coaxed, as he kept trying the ignition switch to no avail. His patience gone, he swore as he got out of the car to lift the hood.

Great, Noelle thought. The limo probably hadn't been rented out because it was a clunker. And now they were stranded in the middle of a bridge with people gawking as they drove around them.

Hunter returned to the limo.

"What's the verdict?"

"I've checked under the hood and everything looks okay to me. If I had to hazard a guess, I'd say the electronic modulator is out."

"Which means?"

"We need a tow truck."

Not exactly the entrance Noelle had planned.

"Hey, Noellie..." someone called from a Toyota Tercel sedan that passed them. The Toyota pulled over in front of them and stopped and a guy got out.

Oh, no, Noelle groaned to herself. No one worse could have stopped. It was Freddie Barton, of all people.

An old beau. And an old lover. Her first.

One who'd dumped her when one of her father's businesses had gone under. Now that her father was back on top, Noelle supposed Freddie had changed his tune. She was good enough to talk to again.

She'd be polite, but only because they needed a ride.

"Friend of yours?" Hunter asked, watching Freddie approach.

Freddie was short and dark, and thought he was handsome. You could tell by the swagger. What he was was cute—in a pesky sort of way. He had brown puppy-dog eyes and a great head of slicked-back hair.

As far as she was concerned, Freddie had never happened. She'd almost convinced herself of that. Almost forgotten the back seat of his Chevy. Unfortunately the twinkle in Freddie's eye said it had happened, and he hadn't forgotten.

Only she was the one who'd have to deal with the skeletons crawling out of her closet to meet her on the way home.

"He was once," she muttered, hating to admit to her bad judgment.

"*Good* friend?" Hunter prompted.

She didn't answer him.

Hunter slid down the window of the limo. "You look like the cavalry to me, man."

"Sure thing. Why don't we load you up in my car and we'll call for a tow truck on my car phone while I run you over to Noellie's parents'. You're here for the wedding, aren't you, Noellie?"

"You know about the wedding?" she asked, surprised.

"Heck, I'm in it. I'm the groom's cousin."

She'd forgotten. The scenario worsened. Not only was she at the wedding with a pretend date, Freddie was going to be there, too. All weekend, if he was a member of the wedding party. Great, just great.

"Well, *Noellie,* whatcha wanna do?" Hunter asked, teasing her with his killer grin.

"What I want to do isn't legal in this state," she retorted.

"Noellie!"

"Murder, I meant," she said, shoving open her door before Freddie came around to do it.

When they were all standing by the limo's trunk, Noelle made introductions.

"Aren't you dressed kinda casual for a limo driver?" Freddie asked Hunter as he shook his hand.

For the first time, Noelle read what was on Hunter's pink T-shirt. The pink color was due to the T-shirt having been washed with something red. The color was as tacky as the message on the T-shirt. You've Been a Naughty Girl—Go to My Room.

"I'm not the limo driver. I'm Noellie's date. I borrowed the limo."

"Quit calling me Noellie," Noelle said between clenched teeth.

Hunter just grinned at her as he opened the trunk of the limo and began lifting out their stuff; his bag, her suitcase, the wedding gift....

"Where's my dress?" Noelle cried out when she realized that it wasn't in the trunk of the car.

"What dress? You didn't bring any dress with you when you came down from your apartment. Your hands were full with the gift and your suitcase and your Popsicle stick."

"Oh, no! I let Barbara Ann get me so rattled that I left my perfect dress hanging in my bedroom. No, it was you with your honking—that's what got me so rattled. You're the reason I—"

"Now, sugar pie, don't be upset. You don't want Freddie here to see us quarrel, do you? I'm sure we can find you another perfect dress right here in St. Louis. A nice red one."

"Uh, cars are starting to pile up, we'd better get this show on the road and a tow truck called," Freddie interjected.

Hunter slammed the trunk closed and followed Freddie to his car, carrying the luggage and the wedding gift. Bringing up the rear, Noelle wondered how she could ever have liked Freddie. Comparing Hunter and Freddie showed Hunter in a much better light.

Hunter was taller, cuter, had some charm, and somehow she didn't think money was all that important to him. Wow, that was a first—her preferring a man to whom money wasn't important. Money was everything to Freddie. He would never have offered to buy her an awful red dress.

A tear slid down her cheek. She couldn't believe she'd left her perfect dress behind. And worse, she couldn't believe that she would be arriving for Sophie's wedding with a bought date and an old beau.

It didn't bode well for the weekend.

Freddie made the call for a tow truck, then turned to Noelle who'd dived into the back seat so she wouldn't have to sit next to Freddie. "So, what does your date do, if he's not a limo driver?"

Hunter didn't take offense. She didn't know what Hunter did, but she wasn't going to let Freddie get away with being the jerk he was.

"Hunter does well. *Very well.*"

Hunter chuckled in the front seat.

"How about you, Noellie? I hear you're doing real well for yourself in Chicago," Freddie said, his eyes back on the road. "Your mama said you worked at a bank. You already a head teller or something?"

"She's vice president. Vice president of Fidelity Trust," Hunter informed him. "How about you, Freddie? What do you do?"

"I've built a Toyota dealership into a real profitable little business. This baby is one of my brand-new models. What do you think of it, Noellie?"

Noelle didn't want to burst his bubble, but the Toyota, while impressive, had looked more like an economy car next to the white limo Hunter drove—even if the limo was borrowed.

"How's Sophie holding up? Last time I talked to her she had prewedding jitters. I hope after all the plans Mom and Dad have made, she doesn't leave Marky waiting at the altar."

"Not a chance. Cousin Marky's a catch. He works for me as a mechanic."

"Are you going to be at the rehearsal?" Noelle asked, hoping against hope he wasn't.

"I wouldn't miss it. The rehearsal dinner afterward is at Damon's. I've been hungry for barbecue ribs and onion loaf all week. Well, here we are, folks," Freddie said as they pulled into the long, winding drive that led to her parents' new home.

When the car stopped, Hunter got out and held the back door open for Noelle. As she slipped out of the car, she noticed Freddie watching them and impulsively threw her arms around Hunter's neck. The kiss she laid on the surprised Hunter was as salacious as she could make it and Hunter returned it in kind until she was weak in the knees.

"Wowie, Miss Noellie. I guess we're much better good friends than I thought," Hunter whispered beneath his breath when she broke away.

She glared at him.

"Oh, that was for ol' Freddie's benefit, wasn't it?" he said, as if he hadn't known it all along.

Noelle had to repress the urge to kick him in the shin. It would have given away the truth to Freddie. Although after that kiss, she wasn't sure just what the truth really was. In any case, Hunter Ashton knew his way around a salacious kiss.

When she didn't answer, Hunter persisted. "What the hell did Freddie do to you, anyway?"

"He dumped me, okay?"

"Noelle!" A younger, shorter version of Noelle came running from the house to embrace Noelle.

Where Noelle was racehorse sleek, Sophie still had some of her baby fat. Noelle's brown hair was discreetly sexy while Sophie's riot of red curls was outrageous.

"Guess I'll be going," Freddie said.

Hunter opened his wallet and pulled out a C-note. "Here's for your trouble. Now, if you'll open the trunk, I'll get our things."

Sophie and Noelle were chattering as Freddie drove away leaving Hunter standing with his arms full. "This suitcase of yours weighs a ton. What'd you do—bring work with you?"

Noelle's guilty look told him she had.

"Don't be silly. Noelle's going to be busy having a great time this weekend. Oh, we haven't met, have we? I'm Sophie, Noelle's baby sister."

Hunter took her offered hand and kissed it. "Hunter Ashton," he said, then looked to Noelle and added, "Noelle's very good friend."

"Noelle!"

"We're here to celebrate one wedding—yours, Sophie. Don't put any ideas into Mom and Dad's head, promise?"

"Okay, I'll behave, but you know Mom and Dad.... Wait till they see what a dishy guy you showed up with. I bet Freddie is spitting nails. Why did Freddie bring you, anyway?"

"The limo broke down on the bridge and we had to call a tow truck. Freddie came along and..." Noelle shrugged.

"Limo—"

"I thought maybe you could use an extra," Hunter said, winking.

"Wow, where did you two meet?" Sophie asked, impressed.

Noelle and Hunter looked at each other.

As Noelle remained speechless, Hunter answered, "We met at a hotel."

"Noelle!"

"It was a . . . ah . . ." Noelle began trying to explain.

"It was a charity function my sister organized," Hunter supplied.

"Well, come on inside before it starts getting crazy around here. Mom and Dad think they're marrying off a princess or something. The wedding has grown from an intimate dinner for friends to something I don't even want to think about. I'll get too nervous."

"You're going to make a beautiful bride," Hunter offered, "Just relax and enjoy your special day."

"I like this beau of yours, Noelle," Sophie said, grinning. "Why don't you take him upstairs to your new bedroom, Noelle, so you can freshen up before Mom and Dad get back from the florist's. It's the bedroom on the left at the top of the stairs."

Hunter followed Noelle upstairs with their luggage. Once they were inside the room he set down the luggage and went to test out the bed. Bouncing on it, he pronounced it to his liking.

"Come on over here, Noellie, and join me," he coaxed.

"No. And stop calling me Noellie, I told you. We're in my bedroom to freshen up, not for you to get fresh."

"Guess we're not such good friends behind closed doors, huh?"

"We're not going to be behind closed doors together. I'm sure there must be an extra bedroom for you somewhere in this big house."

"Now, Noellie, how would that look?"

"Like you're a gentleman and I'm a proper lady."

"Proper ladies don't know how to kiss like you do. Where'd you learn how? You got some sort of secret past you want to confess?"

"I was only acting for Freddie's benefit and you know it."

"Want to do some acting for my benefit . . . ?"

She threw her brush at him.

3

━━━━➤◄━━━━

"But, Mother, I don't want—" Sophie broke off her complaint as Hunter and Noelle joined the family in the living room.

"Why hello, son." Noelle's father rose to his full six feet to offer his bear paw of a hand. "I'm Jack Perry." Noelle's father was a big imposing man with prematurely white hair. His dark brown eyes were as warm and friendly as his manner. "What's your handicap, son?"

"Excuse me?"

"Father's a golf nut," Noelle explained. "And don't get nervous, he calls everyone son."

Jack pulled the redhead beside him on the sofa to her feet and hugged her to him. "And this gorgeous lady is my wife, Grace."

"They're always necking. You'll get used to it," Noelle whispered, as Hunter took her mother's hand.

Noelle noticed how much her mother's taste in decor had changed since their last home. She'd changed from chrome-and-glass sleek to casual chic, by the look of the cushy white sofas with ruffled skirts fronting the oversize fireplace. Pickled wood floors and black-and-white photo prints were further evidence of her mother's change in taste.

"We're just having a little discussion here about a family custom Sophie's balking at," Jack said as they all settled on the sofas.

"I don't care what anyone says. I'm not agreeing to it. It's dumb," Sophie declared.

"It's a harmless family custom," Noelle said, trying to mediate.

"You wouldn't think so if it was you being kidnapped. I know you. You wouldn't have it."

"What are we talking about?" Puzzled, Hunter looked from one to another.

"They want to have me kidnapped at the wedding reception," Sophie complained, looking to someone outside the family for support.

"It sounds like a great adventure to me, Sophie. If you want, I'll even volunteer to be the one who comes to rescue you."

Sophie didn't brighten a watt. If anything, she looked even glummer.

"The groom has to be the one to rescue her, according to family custom," Noelle explained.

Hunter grinned. "Even better."

Jack planted a big kiss on Grace's cheek. "That's right. I rescued Grace—eventually we even made it back to the reception."

"But what if Marky won't pay the ransom to get me back? What if he gets cold feet or something?"

Grace reached over and patted Sophie's thigh. "Of course, Marky will pay to get you back. Don't talk such nonsense."

Sophie clearly wasn't convinced, for whatever reason.

"Come on, Sophie, we'll talk some more about this later," Jack coaxed. "Right now, I think we all should get acquainted with Noelle's new beau."

It was the part of coming home Noelle had been dreading ever since Hunter had got up at the bachelor auction to acknowledge he was the man she had bought. It would be just too embarrassing if anyone found out she'd had to buy a date for her baby sister's wedding.

"What do you do, son?"

"Father—"

"It's okay," Hunter assured her. "I do a little drawing...."

Yeah, unemployment, Noelle thought. He really should be in sales. He was certainly selling her family a bill of goods.

"Oh, an artist. How lovely," Grace said, her eyes approving. "I dabble at painting a little myself. Do you do portraits...still life...landscapes...?"

"What I do is more along the lines of fantasy...."

Noelle squirmed. Now was not the time for him to start being truthful.

Hunter looked at Sophie. "I draw a comic book," he said with a dismissive shrug. "Valerie Valor..."

"You're *him*. You're *that* Hunter Ashton!" Sophie cried, her dark eyes wide.

"'Fraid so."

When her parents and sister looked puzzled, Sophie went on to explain. "Valerie Valor, the Viking Princess of Venus—you know."

"Who?" Grace and Jack chorused.

"What!" Noelle looked at Hunter as if he'd grown three horns from the top of his head.

"Hunter's the guy who does the best superheroine comic book ever. Valerie Valor is so cool. She wears this red bustier and thigh-high boots while doing in the bad guys. All my friends just— Wait till they hear you're dating Hunter Ashton, Noelle! Why didn't you tell me?"

"Yes, *why* didn't you tell us?" Jack asked, suspicion in his eyes. "I thought Sophie said the two of you were—"

"It's my fault, sir," Hunter said, jumping in. "Obviously a bank vice-president isn't the comic-book-reading type. When I realized she didn't know what I did, I thought I'd keep it my secret for a while. It was refreshing not to have someone wanting me just because I was a celebrity of sorts. Noelle wanted me only for myself."

His shin wasn't handy so she ground her heel into his foot.

He swallowed his "Ouch!" almost inaudibly.

Grace nudged Jack and beamed at the smiling Hunter and blushing Noelle while Sophie went to answer the ringing telephone.

"You should have gone into sales, Hunter," Noelle muttered under her breath.

"I did," he whispered back, a cocky grin in his tone of voice. "You bought me, Noelle, remember?"

Sophie came running back into the room and threw herself at her father, sobbing.

"What's wrong, princess?" Jack asked, looking at Grace helplessly.

"My wedding is ruined!" Sophie cried.

"What are you talking about, Sophie? What's gone wrong?" Grace asked, rushing to console Sophie.

"I just...just talked to the singer for the band I—" she sniffed "—I hired for the wedding and... and..." She started crying again.

"What is it? What's wrong?" Noelle asked.

"They had a fight and broke up. Now I don't have music for my wedding," Sophie wailed.

"Don't cry, Sophie," Jack said, patting his daughter's head. "We'll think of something."

"Who's got a newspaper?" Hunter asked.

"The newspapers are in the basket there by the sofa," Grace said, pointing. "Why?"

"It's Thursday, there should be a listing of entertainment for the weekend, the names of local bands, where they might be playing."

"But I don't have time to look for another band," Sophie wailed. "I have a million things to take care of before the wedding."

"Don't worry, Noelle and I will take care of it," Hunter assured her, picking up the calendar section of the newspaper and scanning it.

"We will?" Noelle said, looking at him.

"Sure. Don't worry about the music. Noelle and I will find something for Saturday night, Sophie. Aha, here's what I was looking for. The Blue Shamrock is having open band auditions starting at two o'clock. Noelle and I will go check it out."

"But the rehearsal dinner is—"

"We'll be back in time," Hunter assured Grace.

Grabbing Noelle's arm, he ushered her outside.

"Do you really think we can—"

Hunter closed the door of the limo—which had been returned from the repair shop and was now running smoothly—and went around to the driver's side and got in, assuring her they'd find a band for Sophie's wedding. They drove in silence—a silence that was only punctuated by Noelle's directions on how to get to the Blue Shamrock. Hunter parked the limo and they went in.

Noelle was not impressed. The Blue Shamrock didn't look too promising. It was decorated in early rec room, with wood paneling and a gold-veined mirrored-tile wall behind the bar.

The band onstage was playing "Spanish Eyes" about one beat too slow and twenty years too late.

"I saw the limo outside, it must be Heartbreaker's," the burly, bold bartender said, taking their drink order.

"The limo is mine," Hunter explained. "What's a band like Heartbreaker doing here?"

"They're here to check out the drummer in Silver Moon, I heard."

The group onstage finished and a new band, carrying accordions and tubas, took their place. Soon oompah music filled the air.

"What do you think?" Hunter teased Noelle. "Do you think Sophie knows how to polka?"

"No. I sure hope the bands get better or we're wasting our time. We're never going to get a decent band at the last minute, Hunter."

"Oh, ye of little faith. I promised a band and I'll get one."

"I said a *decent* band, Hunter."

They endured the polka music played with more enthusiasm than skill. Even though Noelle didn't believe Hunter's promise to find a band, still, she found it very endearing that he was trying.

"Ah, here's something a little more contemporary," Hunter said when the polka band finally finished and new musicians took their place.

"You've got to be kidding."

"What? You don't think Sophie would like them?" Hunter pretended disbelief, his wiseass grin giving him away.

"I hardly think it's any girl's dream to have the band of an Elvis impersonator play at her wedding."

Hunter clutched at his heart as if she'd wounded him to the quick. "Don't be cruel, Miss Noelle."

"Hey, Heartbreaker's here. The bartender wasn't just kidding around. That's Blake Penny at the door," Noelle said, pointing.

Hunter looked around. "You're right. Order me another drink, will you? I'll be right back." With that, Hunter got up and left the table to walk over to where Blake Penny stood talking to the owner of the Blue Shamrock.

Well, Hunter wasn't shy, she'd give him that. And a lot more, if pressed, she thought, acknowledging the strong physical attraction between them. Hunter wasn't the serious kind of guy you made long-range plans with but he sure was a fun date. And a considerate one.

Not many hired dates would try to scare up a band at the last minute for a wedding.

As she watched the Elvis impersonator sing in a white studded jumpsuit, she wondered why all the Elvis impersonators played Elvis in his later years. She had the feeling an impersonator of a young, hunky Elvis would clean up.

Hunter returned to the table a few minutes later when the Elvis band was finished with its audition.

"Silver Moon is up next," he told Noelle. "I understand they're pretty good."

"Maybe we can hire them for the wedding, then," Noelle said, brightening. "I hate to go back home without a band to replace the one that canceled out on Sophie."

"Oh, we won't disappoint Sophie. She's going to have a wedding to remember. Everyone will be talking about it for a long time, I promise."

Noelle carefully studied Hunter. "I don't mean talking about a ridiculous band," she warned, just in case Hunter had any crazy ideas. So far they hadn't seen a band she'd even remotely consider. A boom box would be preferable.

Surprisingly the next sounds from the stage were fabulous. Silver Moon was a talented band. They played a medley that displayed their versatility.

"We've got to get them!"

Hunter smiled at the excitement in Noelle's voice. He'd like to see more of it. It was obvious to him that she exerted a great deal of effort clamping down on her natural enthusiasm. She kept a tight rein on herself. But every so often he glimpsed the unrestrained

Noelle . . . and he wanted her to come out and play—with him. This weekend he planned to see what he could do to coax her out.

"The drummer is really good. I can see why Heartbreaker is thinking about recruiting him," Hunter agreed.

They weren't the only ones applauding when Silver Moon finished.

"Go talk to them," Noelle urged as they were packing up their instruments to go offstage. "And try to keep their price reasonable. I don't want Mother and Father to go broke."

Hunter got up and went over to the stage just as Blake Penny did.

Noelle nervously watched the two men talking to the band members of Silver Moon. It seemed to take forever for Hunter to return to the table.

"Well?" she asked hopefully.

Hunter shook his head no.

"Why not?"

"They've got a gig. They're playing here on Saturday night."

"Oh."

Noelle frowned. "I told you we're not going to get a band. It's hopeless. Sophie's wedding is going to be ruined."

"There're still three more bands to audition," Hunter said, reasonably.

Noelle finished the drink she'd been nursing and glumly watched a new band take the stage. The musicians' dreadlocks and hip-hop clothes indicated they played rap.

"I think you need another drink," Hunter said, signaling the bartender. "You've got to have faith in me."

The band did a cover of a Snoop Doggy Dogg tune and Noelle rolled her eyes at Hunter. "I don't think my father would be able to two-step to this, do you, Hunter?"

"Maybe the next band," Hunter agreed.

The next band was rock and roll.

"Do you think teeth can rattle?" Hunter asked when they turned up their amps.

The last band was Three Jacks and a Queen. The jacks were in their eighties with the queen probably a young seventy-five.

"Got any more ideas?" Noelle asked Hunter, her tone of voice informing him that if he did, she didn't want to hear them.

"I guess it's the boom box, then. Sophie is going to be so disappointed. She really thought you could pull off coming up with a band."

Just then Blake Penny came up to their table. "Gotta leave, man," he said to Hunter.

"Blake, this is Noelle Perry. Noelle, this is Blake Penny," Hunter said.

"Uh, hi," Noelle said, tongue-tied. Unlike Hunter, she couldn't make friends with a celebrity at the drop of a hat.

"Perry?" Blake Penny repeated. "Is this pretty lady any relation to the bride?"

"Noelle is Sophie's sister, and my date for the wedding," Hunter answered.

"You ought to hang on to him," Blake said. "The man has good taste in bands and women. Well, I'll be seeing you." Blake Penny left them to have a final word with the drummer in Silver Moon. Noelle gazed at Hunter in puzzlement.

"How did he know Sophie's name?"

"I told him."

"Oh."

Hunter paid their bar tab and left a healthy tip. "Come on, we'd better get back," he said, looking at his watch. "The rehearsal is in an hour."

As they left the Blue Shamrock, Noelle persisted, "Why did you tell Blake Penny Sophie's name?"

Hunter held open the door of the limo. "It seemed like a good idea," he said, adding, "since Heartbreaker is going to be playing at Sophie's wedding."

"What?"

"Heartbreaker is going to play at your sister's wedding."

"That's impossible."

"Why?"

"Because first, Heartbreaker has a hit album out and must be booked, and even if they did have an open date, my parents could never afford—"

"I took care of it."

"But I can't let you—"

"Sure, you can. Don't worry. Blake Penny is a huge fan of Valerie Valor's. All it cost me is an autographed original strip."

"But that must be worth—"

"A wedding gig. Just say, 'Thank you, Hunter.'"

She reached up and did just that with another one of her surprising kisses. The kind she'd laid on him for Freddie's benefit when they'd first arrived. Only this time it was for his benefit.

"You're very welcome," he said, breaking off the kiss before he did something foolish.

When they arrived at the Perrys' home and told Sophie the news, she kissed him, too. About a hundred times in succession.

And then she was on the phone calling everyone.

He was everyone's hero before the wedding even began.

An hour later they all rode to the rehearsal in the white limo. On the way out, Jack Perry had grabbed a bottle of champagne from the fridge and was passing the bottle. While he and Grace continued their discussion with Sophie about the family custom of kidnapping the bride at the wedding reception, Noelle turned her thoughts to Hunter Ashton and Valerie Valor.

He spent his days with a cartoon heroine who ran around rescuing people, dressed in a red bustier and thigh-high boots. Hunter dealt in fantasy, all right.

He was a fantasy.

Her kind of fantasy man.

Suddenly she had the strongest desire to have an adventurous fling with Hunter, a fling that would last as long as the wedding weekend and no longer.

Who would know—what could it hurt—if for just one weekend she gave in to impulse? No one in the banking community would ever know. Her conservative-banker image would remain intact.

Hunter gave her a wink before leaning his head against the door and napping, tired, no doubt, from a sleepless night and the long drive.

Noelle continued to study him as he napped.

Hunter Ashton was as tempting as they came. Springs of blond hair curled in the vee of his dark polo shirt. On the drive from Chicago she'd noticed how the sun glinted on his bare arms, giving him an almost-golden glow. Making him look like a wicked angel.

How would it feel to run her hands over...? What no one knew or even suspected was how similar she was to the rest of her loony family—or would be, if she allowed herself to give in to her wild inclinations.

What was stopping her was her awareness of just the sort of trouble giving in to her desires could lead to. And unlike her parents and sister, she wasn't cut out to live in constant turmoil. She hadn't thrived on the continual upheaval the way the rest of the family had.

But maybe she had gone a little overboard in protecting herself from herself. The real reason she hadn't dated much was because the men who appealed to her in truth were a lot like Hunter Ashton.

She was drawn to men who were unconventional and who were effortlessly sexy.

Men who were uncontrollable.

Trouble.

Unsettling.

And unsafe.

But, hey, she wasn't making a lifetime commitment, here. This was just a weekend out of town. It would be like one of those vacation shipboard romances. They'd have some fun, part, and neither of them would be hurt by the experience.

A little fun never hurt anyone.

Hunter Ashton wasn't napping.

He was thinking.

And knew Noelle Perry would be surprised at his thoughts.

When he'd begun the trip to St. Louis with Noelle he'd thought of it as an adventure. He liked feeling a part of a family. Maybe Daphne was right. Maybe he did need to get out more. His usual method of operation was to bury himself in his projects and then have a week or two of what Daphne referred to as "wreck-reation" that involved a meaningless fling with a willing woman.

Maybe, at twenty-eight, he needed more stability in his life. His career was firmly established and money would never be a problem. But the way he was living wasn't very healthy—physically or emotionally.

This time, he was going to take it slow and see if it developed into something more than a slap and a tickle. Not that there was anything wrong with slap and tickle . . .

"What are you smiling at?" Noelle demanded to know, nudging his knee with her foot from where she sat across the seat.

He opened one eye.

"I was thinking about shopping for a red dress with you for the wedding. When do you think you'd have time for a little shopping spree?"

"I'm not buying red. And I'm not going with you. I can shop for my own clothes. I'm a grown-up girl, you know."

"I've noticed," he said, popping open his other baby blue and surveying her. "Size ten, right?"

"How do you—"

"My sister, Daphne is a size ten. I go shopping with her all the time. She thinks I have great taste."

She'd responded negatively to his proposal of a shopping spree out of habit. Actually, a shopping spree would be fun. A new experience. She'd never had a man shop with her or for her before.

"Okay," she agreed. "Maybe tomorrow morning when the stores open we can hit Plaza Frontenac or the Galleria."

"What time do the stores open?" Hunter asked, considering.

"Nine-thirty, ten . . ."

"I have a golf game."

"I should have known. Don't play him for money. And I should warn you he likes to look for golf balls when he plays, which means it will take you until at least three."

"Let's plan to shop at four. That will give me time to shower and we can catch a bite to eat before I have to go to the bachelor party, according to your father."

"There really is a bachelor party?"

"Your father arranged it."

Noelle just shook her head. Some weekend "fling" this was going to be. Hunter would have to schedule her in between *his* social engagements.

* * *

The minister kept looking at his watch.

Sophie kept looking at the door.

Jack and Grace kept looking at his other.

As did Hunter and Noelle.

The looks between Grace and Jack were looks of parental concern. Grace made mention of "all that potato salad."

The looks between Hunter and Noelle were inappropriate, considering the situation. Noelle knew it full well. They had a possible crisis on their hands. Marky was late for the wedding rehearsal. Not a good sign. Especially with what seemed to be a skittish bride. Sophie was nothing if not a volatile teenager. Her mother was right—there was "all that potato salad."

And all Noelle could think about was seducing Hunter as soon as possible, as often as possible.

Hunter, for his part, looked as though he was enjoying every aspect of the evening's prospects.

"We'll have to begin," the minister said, his words echoing in the massive empty church and focusing all thoughts on how to conduct a wedding rehearsal without the groom. "I can't wait any longer. I have another rehearsal scheduled in half an hour that I must get to. Someone will have to stand in for the—"

There was a crash of the heavy wooden entry door as it was shoved open, and a young man entered the church, running.

"Marky, where have you been?" Sophie demanded to know.

"At the hospital. Freddie fell off the loading dock and broke his leg. He's going to be all right, but we're going to have to find a replacement for him. Okay, let's get started."

"Is he always so pale?" Hunter asked Noelle, as they stood on the sidelines and watched the bridesmaids and groomsmen assemble and go through the trial run for Saturday's wedding.

"I shouldn't think so," Noelle answered, "but I can't say for sure, as I've never met him."

"It's a whirlwind courtship, then? That explains some of your sister's nervousness."

"Brides are always nervous."

"I thought that was grooms."

"What does a groom have to be nervous about? All he has to do is show up."

"Exactly."

Noelle shoved her elbow into his ribs.

"Will you quit beating me up? If I'd known how physical you were, I'd have demanded combat—"

"Shh..." Grace shushed them, as Marky and Sophie went through their vows.

"Okay, I think that about covers it," the minister said, wrapping up. "I'll see you all on Saturday. Don't forget the rings." With that, the portly man snapped his Bible shut and scurried down the aisle for the exit.

"Okay, everyone. It's barbecue ribs and onion loaf at Damon's on South Lindbergh. Drive carefully," Jack said, organizing the rehearsal dinner. "Oh, it's outside in the garden, don't forget."

"Can one hope that's a beer garden?" Hunter inquired.

"I do like your young man," Jack said, capturing Hunter in a bear hug. "We're going to ride to Damon's with Marky's parents, Noelle. We're still haggling over who's gonna cough up for the open bar and how open the bar is going to be. We'll see you there. And, Hunter, have a cold one waiting for me, okay?"

"Yes, sir." As they watched everyone pile into their cars and Sophie into Marky's clunker, Hunter stated the obvious. "I guess it's just you and me in the limo."

"Good, I've always wanted to see what it felt like to sit in the back of one."

"Noelle, they're expecting us to be at the rehearsal dinner—Jack's expecting his cold beer to be waiting for him.... Okay, okay, don't kick me. I get it. You want me to drive."

They ended up in the front seat together.

Noelle rationalized it was because she didn't want anyone to think there was anything strange about their relationship.

"Do me a favor, would you?" she asked when they were on the road."

"If you promise not to hit or kick me."

"I'm serious, Hunter. I want you to quit being so perfect. My father is going to get attached to you and ask me all kinds of questions when you don't show up my next trip back home."

"It makes me wonder what kind of men you've been bringing home."

"You're the first," she reluctantly admitted.

"No wonder they're so happy to see me."

"Just drive, Hunter."

"Yes, ma'am."

In the lush garden adjacent to the restaurant, a long table was set up with white balloons attached to each of the chairs. Several bottles of champagne stood on the table. A water fountain, in the center of the garden, lent a festive atmosphere to the evening. After the wedding party was seated, a waiter began serving barbecue ribs, coleslaw and baked beans.

Marky and Sophie seemed to have settled their differences.

Both sets of parents were beaming.

The wedding party was flirting and popping balloons once the meal was over.

A string quartet that had been playing in the restaurant, came into the garden to play a romantic ballad for the engaged couple and a special piece for Grace from Jack.

Despite Noelle's request, Hunter went on being perfect.

Just before the dinner broke up, Marky was called to the phone.

"Did you tell her?" a male voice demanded.

"Not yet," Marky said loudly into the phone, and then guiltily looked around. He was relieved that no one from the wedding party was in listening distance.

"You are going to tell her, aren't you?"

"Yes," Marky whispered.

"See that you do."

Marky flinched at the sound of the phone receiver being slammed down. He gently hung up his phone, and with a sigh, he turned and went back to join the wedding party.

4

—→·←—

"Who wants a piece of my caramel-pecan apple
pie?" Grace asked when she and Jack arrived home
just after Hunter and Noelle did. Sophie and Marky
had gone out on the town with the rest of the wedding
party.

"Not me, dear," Jack said. "I'll just have one of
your sticky sweet kisses to tide me over until morning." He pulled Grace into his arms and stole one.
"I'm going up to bed," he announced, upon releasing Grace. "Don't forget we've got a golf game in the
morning, son."

"I won't," Hunter promised.

"Count me out, too," Noelle said, unsuccessfully
trying to stifle a yawn. "All that food has made me
sleepy. I'm turning in early, too."

Grace looked at Hunter. "You aren't going to make
me eat alone, are you, dear?"

"You know, I might just have an inch of space left
for something sweet."

He followed Grace out to the greenhouse kitchen
and took a seat at the square oak table cluttered with
R.S.V.P. cards and mail.

Grace took the pie from the refrigerator and sliced generous pieces for both of them. Then she heated the slices in the microwave before adding scoops of French vanilla ice cream atop them.

She set the pieces of pie on the table and poured each of them a cold glass of milk before taking a seat at the table.

While Hunter savored the pie and ice cream, Grace sorted through the day's mail, adding a tardy wedding R.S.V.P. to the pile for the final count for the wedding-reception dinner.

"Great pie, Grace," Hunter said, as she slit open the tab from the credit-card company.

Grace frowned at the bottom line on her credit-card statement. "I'll sell you the recipe for twenty grand. Jack would stroke out if he knew how much money I've spent on this wedding. The potato salad alone—"

"Surely Jack knows how much," Hunter said, as Grace toyed with her slice of pie.

Grace shook her head no. "Jack's trouble is he can't say no—to me, to his daughter, his friends, himself. And he doesn't like to be bothered with mundane things. Unlike Noelle, keeping track of money bores him."

Hunter polished off the last bit of his pie. He licked his lips to show appreciation and got a smile from Grace. "So then you're the one who worries, is that it, Grace?"

Grace looked a little remorseful, then shook her head. "I'm afraid I'm not much better than Jack. I only worry when the statement comes at the end of the

month. I must admit, shopping is a great mood
booster. There's just something about buying that
gives you a little thrill, you know what I mean?''

Hunter had the distinct feeling he was talking to a
shopaholic. No wonder Noelle was so conservative.
Someone had to be responsible and she'd been elected
a long time ago by her family. Jack and Grace were
charming, but irresponsible. Sophie was, after all,
only a kid who thought the world revolved around
her—as most teenagers did.

He supposed in a way he'd shoved his twin sister,
Daphne, into that same role. More so since their parents had died in a boating accident when they were in
college.

Well, people could change. He was prepared to
demonstrate to Noelle that he was not some loony
cartoonist. He'd be a perfect gentleman all weekend.
There would be plenty of time when they were back in
Chicago for him to see if anything would come of this
humming attraction he'd felt between them right from
the start.

This weekend he'd concentrate on working on Jack
and Grace so he'd be invited back to visit. Winning
them over couldn't hurt his cause. And Sophie was
already on his side, having immediately been taken by
the fact of him being *the* Hunter Ashton.

Yes, being a perfect gentleman was just the ticket.

''Well, Grace, you be sure and let me know if you
need a loan. It'll be just between the two of us,'' he
said with a wink as he stood to go upstairs to collect
his stuff and put it in another bedroom.

"Don't tempt me," she said, waving him off and stacking the R.S.V.P. cards into tidy piles of twenty-five for a final tabulation.

"Who do you think you're kidding, Hunter?"

"You know, Valerie, most comic-book characters don't risk giving their creators grief." Hunter started up the stairs.

"Yeah, but *you* a perfect gentleman? I know you want Noelle bad." Valerie fell in step beside him.

"So do I, believe me. That's why I'm moving my stuff to an empty bedroom. That way I won't be tempted. Great plan, don't you think?"

"You're forgetting something—there's a flaw in your 'great' plan," Valerie argued, as Hunter continued upstairs to the second floor.

"What's that?" he asked, sticking his head in an open bedroom and turning on the light. "Oh yeah, now I remember."

The bedroom—like all the others he'd made a casual perusal of earlier in the day—was filled with wedding presents and decorations for the reception at the country club.

"It doesn't matter," he assured himself and Valerie. "We can share a bedroom without—"

"Sure, you can...."

"Valerie—"

"Yes?"

"I'm going shopping tomorrow with Noelle to find her something to wear to the wedding. I *was* planning to look around for a new outfit for you as well, while

I was at it. I thought I might even get Noelle's input. But since you seem bent on annoying me . . ."

"Okay, okay. I believe you can share a bedroom with Noelle and remain a perfect gentleman. What else would anyone expect from a man who allows himself to be sold at a bachelor auction?"

"It was for a good cause."

"Right."

"I can behave. In fact, I promised Daphne that I would."

"Right."

"I'm promising you right now. I will go knock on Noelle's bedroom door. And when she lets me in I will be a perfect gentleman."

"I believe you. And stay away from Victoria's Secret tomorrow. I want something sporty, nothing remotely like lingerie."

Hunter turned off the light and walked down the hall to Noelle's bedroom. Valerie believed him, so why didn't he believe himself? he wondered as he raised his hand to knock on her bedroom door.

"Come in," she called out.

He took a deep breath and went inside.

It was pitch-dark. She'd turned off the light and gone to bed already, if not to sleep. That would make it easier. He'd just get undressed in the dark, hug his edge of the bed and sleep like a baby till morning.

"Lock the door."

He was hearing things.

"Lock the door," Noelle repeated.

He did as she asked and reached to turn on the light.

"Don't turn on the light."

"O-kay." He lowered his hand to his side, waiting, desperately trying to adjust his eyes to seeing in the dark of the bedroom.

"Do you like me, Hunter?"

"Ah, sure." Why the hell was he so nervous? He turned in the direction of Noelle's voice and was just beginning to make out where she sat on the bed when she shoved back the sheet and got up.

"Do you like me enough, Hunter?" she asked, walking toward him wearing what sounded like satin and looked in the dark like boxer pajamas.

"Enough..." he repeated, clearing his throat.

"I like you, Hunter. I like you a real lot. Do you mind if I show you how much?"

"Um...n-no." He was dreaming. He'd fallen asleep eating pie at the kitchen table.

She reached out to place her hand on his cheek.

No. He wasn't asleep. He was awake. Fully awake. Bright-eyed and bushy-tailed, as a matter of fact. He could hear his own breathing in the silent, suddenly airless room.

Her thumb trailed over his lips.

He grabbed her hand, stilling it.

"You aren't going to chicken out on me, are you, Hunter? It's okay, you know. I know you prefer to deal with fantasy women. I'm not here to complicate your life. Or mine."

"What...what, ah... What are you here to do, Noelle?" He could see her now; his eyes had adjusted to the darkness of the bedroom. She wet her lips nervously.

"You aren't the only one weddings make horny, Hunter. So I thought, why not?"

"Why not, what—" He wanted to be sure. Jack Perry was a very big man. And even with her parents' bedroom being on the first level, below them . . .

"Have a weekend fling. No strings. We both go back to the city and our own lives. Admit it. It's what you've had on your mind, anyway."

"I'd made up my mind I was going to be a perfect gentleman on the way up the stairs. I thought that was what you wanted."

"I changed my mind." She turned her head, pressing her lips to the back of his hand. "Is that a problem?" she murmured, licking his thumb.

"Noelle, honey, you can do whatever you please."

She brushed her body against his erection straining behind the fly of his dress slacks.

"Oh, yes, please!" Hunter rasped. His thigh muscles tightened instinctively when he slammed his mouth against her lush lips. As she leaned into him fully, returning his kiss, eager and hot, he tightly embraced her and slid his own hands over her satin-clad bottom to urge her even closer against him.

While they continued to frantically kiss, Noelle tugged at Hunter's polo shirt. Freeing it from his slacks, she pulled it over his head with a sense of urgency, and ran her soft hands over the thick hair covering his chest.

Hunter then took her hands in his, stilling them, and captured her lips in a drugging kiss.

Then, with a groan, he released her. "Jeez, I love an aggressive woman."

"Why? 'Cause you're a lazy man?" she teased.

"Lazy? I'll show you 'lazy,' woman. Take off my pants and I'll show you—"

Her hand went for his belt buckle.

His went for the satin-covered buttons of her pajama top. Clearly he knew his way around a button better than she knew her way around a buckle. He lowered his head, his mouth covering the nipple of her exposed breast.

He felt her fingertips clench the waistband of his slacks. She shuddered, a small moan escaping her lips when he began to lave the smooth coolness of her breasts, warming them until the peaks tightened.

Losing rein on his passion, he thrust a hand beneath the hem of her boxer pajama bottom to cup her warm, moist heat. He squeezed and released until she cried out and began working at his belt buckle with renewed urgency. Unfastening it, she slid it from the loops and let it slip to the floor.

"Careful, you'd better let me take it from here," he said, reluctantly moving his hands to undo the button of his slacks and gingerly inch down the zipper.

"Hurry," she urged.

"Greedy little thing, aren't you, Miss Noellie."

"Don't—"

"I know, I know." He dropped the "Noellie" and his pants at the same time.

"Uh-oh, looks like we've got us a problem here," he said, looking back and forth between them.

"What are you talking about?"

It was hard to keep the grin from his voice. "Well, since we're both wearing boxer shorts...I'm confused."

"So am I. What are you talking about?"

"Who gets on top—"

She tucked her fingertips inside the waistband of her satin boxers and slid them down her hips to her feet and swiftly kicked them aside. A tight, daring smile played on her lips.

"Still confused?"

"I'm speechless."

"Good."

He shed his boxers in a heartbeat and for the next ten minutes they came together fast and furious. Her bites at his neck were followed by a nibbling forage of his jawline. When he lifted her astride him, her hands clutched his hair. Moving so that she was braced against the wall, they took what they wanted from each other.

Selfishly.

Deliciously.

Both of them buried their mouths against each other to keep their cries of ecstasy from summoning her father with shotgun in hand.

Wonderfully saturated, the two slid down the wall together in a limp, sweaty tangle. His legs had turned to jelly, but he'd managed to pull her on top of him to cushion her descent to the floor.

After a moment he felt her fingers at his lips.

"What?" he asked, kissing them.

"I just knew I would feel you grinning."

"That's because I always grin when I'm happy."

"Not bad for a start," she said with a laugh.

"*Start?*"

"Are you telling me that's it? I thought you were *the* Hunter Ashton."

"I draw 'super' characters. *I'm* not one."

"Coulda fooled me."

"You do know how to encourage a fellow," Hunter said, glancing down for signs of life.

"I can be more encouraging," Noelle said, sliding down the length of him until her head rested at his groin.

"I've changed my mind."

She looked up, stopping her "encouragement."

"No, don't stop. How much champagne did you drink tonight, anyway?"

"Just enough," she informed him saucily, as she went back to encouraging him.

He certainly wasn't going to argue with that. Not when the result felt so, ah . . . sinfully good.

He told himself he was going to let her encourage him to hell and back.

He told himself he could handle anything she could dish out.

He was up for her. He chuckled to himself.

And then he bit his lip, overcome by the exquisite sensation.

"Noelle, honey," he breathed on a strangled groan, his hands cupping her head.

When he caught his breath and his eyes fluttered open, he saw that she had her head propped up on her elbow as she watched him.

"I, ah . . ." he began. He couldn't believe he'd . . .

"Guess I was a little too encouraging, huh?"

She giggled.

He laughed.

She got the giggles.

And suddenly he was kissing her.

And suddenly nothing was funny anymore.

They broke apart, both startled by the spontaneous real emotion. True feelings were frighteningly intimate.

And all at once they were shy with each other.

She reached for her pajama top.

He faked a yawn. "Guess we better hit the sheets. I have to get up early to play golf with your father."

"Me, too," Noelle said, trying to make conversation to hide the awkwardness between them. "I mean, I need to get some sleep, too. I have to go with Sophie and Mother in the morning to check out the last-minute details for the wedding. And then you have to power-shop with me tomorrow afternoon."

Hunter eased his body up. "That's right. I have to buy you that red dress I promised you."

"You've got to rent a tuxedo tomorrow, too. I can't believe you let Mother talk you into filling in for Freddie in the wedding party. Only Freddie would wind up in the hospital with a broken leg two days before a wedding."

"You going to go sign his cast?"

"No, I'd be too tempted to break his other leg."

"I'll remember not to piss you off. If I'm not giving you what you paid for, you be sure and tell me."

The look on her face was stricken. He'd said the worst thing he could say. He hadn't meant it like that.

And worse, there was nothing he could say that would take it back. Any attempt to make it better would only make it worse.

She scooped up her boxer sorts, pulled them on and dived beneath the sheet on the bed. Her body language said it all, making him feel like an even worse jerk. She was curled in the fetal position, her back to his side of the bed.

He slept in the nude. Normally it didn't chill him. But as he lay beside her, hugging the edge of the bed, he was cold.

Sleep was impossible.

"A perfect gentleman, huh?" Valerie said, intruding on his brooding.

"Go away."

"Oh, no, this is too good."

"Don't rub it in."

"Why don't you apologize to her?" she asked.

"It'll only make it worse."

"You mean you don't have the guts, Hunter."

"Go away."

"You're not going to let her spend the weekend thinking that you didn't feel anything—that tonight was just a performance of your duties as a weekend escort."

"How do you know it wasn't? She seduced me, you know. I really did plan to be a perfect gentleman—whether you believe it or not, Valerie."

"I've been there when you've been performing, just going through the motions between projects. I've been there when the women really didn't mean anything. This was different. You actually felt something. And when you begin to feel something you run like hell back inside yourself. You're a coward, Hunter Ashton.''

"And you're pushing it, Valerie. I'm sure they must have erasers around here somewhere," he threatened.

"You can rub me out, Hunter, but you can't erase the mistake you're making with Noelle."

"I'm not making a mistake." He wrapped the sheet around him tighter. "Leave me alone. I need to get some sleep so I can beat Jack's pants off him in the morning."

"I'd let Jack win if I were you. Okay, I'll leave you alone, if that's what you really want. It won't help you go to sleep, though. You're going to stay awake. Your conscience is going to bug you."

"*You* are my conscience."

"Right. I forgot. As I was saying, if you were the superhero Noelle thought you were, you'd apologize to her right now."

"She's sleeping."

"And you're dreaming."

"Well, I'm not the superhero she thought I was, okay?"

"Tell me about it. And here I thought Peter Pan was growing up."

"Shut up, Tinker Bell."

She was an idiot.

Noelle lay quietly beside Hunter, not moving a muscle. She didn't want him to know she hadn't fallen asleep. She wanted him to think that she'd been able to seduce him without another thought. Wanted him to think his careless words hadn't stung her.

What had started out as a lighthearted romp had become dangerously intimate when they'd connected through shared laughter.

Who would have thought an act of desperation—buying a male for sale at a bachelor auction—would have brought her someone she could really *like?*

If she were looking for someone she could truly like—which she wasn't.

Hunter Ashton wasn't looking for a relationship any more than she was.

This was a weekend fling.

Hunter was a date, nothing more. And she planned to get her money's worth. Plumping her pillow, she settled in for some very good dreams.

"What do you think of Noelle's young man?" Grace asked when she'd joined Jack in their big pine four-poster bed.

"I'll tell you tomorrow after we play golf," Jack mumbled sleepily.

"I like him."

"But then you never were a very good judge of men," he said on a chuckle. "If you were, you'd have taken your parents' advice and married that lawyer you were dating when you met me. He had great prospects. I didn't even have a job."

"I didn't fall in love with the lawyer. I fell in love with you."

"Much to your parents' chagrin."

"But not to mine," Grace assured him, snuggling up close.

"Did Sophie come home yet?" he asked, nuzzling Grace's ear.

"Not yet. You've got to stop worrying about her, Jack. She's going to be a married woman."

"You're a married woman and I worry about you," he countered. "Now, are you going to tell me how much this wedding is costing us, or am I going to have to pry that out of you?"

"My lips are sealed," Grace said with a giggle.

"We'll just see about that."

"Jack!"

"Why don't you want me to talk to her?" Sophie demanded. "She wants to talk to me."

"We've been over this before, Sophie," Marky said, exasperation in his voice. "Polly is an old girlfriend. She is jealous of you and doesn't want us to get married."

"Why didn't you tell me about her?"

"Look," Marky said, running his hands over the steering wheel as they sat outside Sophie's house in his car. "Polly will only try to come between us. She's a head case. Just ignore the notes she's been sending you. I'll deal with her."

"Well, I don't like it."

"Neither do I, but there's nothing I can do about it for the moment. Once we're married she'll give up on trying to get me back."

Sophie looked at her ring in the moonlight that filtered into the car. "I love my ring."

"It isn't very big."

"I don't care."

"But I do. I want my wife to have—"

"It doesn't matter, Marky. We've been rich and we've been poor. My mom and dad never let money—"

"Rich is better," Marky declared.

"Kiss me good-night, Marky," she said, changing the subject. She knew there was no changing his mind once he made it up.

When the kiss ended, Sophie said dreamily, "Just think, Marky, in only one day I'm going to be Mrs. Marky Bergen." She pushed open the car door to go inside.

"Remember what I said. Stay away from Polly," Marky warned.

"All right, all right. I will."

5

The golf course at the country club where Sophie was to have her wedding reception the next night was one of the best in St. Louis. Old money had laid out the manicured grounds and new money kept them clipped and green. That and chemicals.

Something about the dead calm of the golf course unnerved Hunter. There wasn't a bird chirp, a scurrying chipmunk or the flitting color of a butterfly anywhere. The wildlife paid a handsome price for all the dark green carpeting of the sculptured grounds.

This was no Disneyesque perfect picture, but a chilling picture of environmental irresponsibility. A picture of something that looked pleasant, but wasn't. Maybe this was a subject for Valerie Valor to tackle in his next project.

"Does the comic-book business pay well, son?" Jack Perry asked, interrupting Hunter's thoughts as he stopped the golf cart at the second hole of the course.

Hunter smiled to himself. Jack Perry not only looked like a big bear, he was a protective papa bear with his family. He was giving Hunter the "Are your intentions honorable, young man?" speech. *Were* his intentions honorable? They had been when he'd started up to Jack's daughter's room last night.

But lust had overpowered his best intentions. The match hadn't even gone one round. The song went, "Turn out the lights, the party's over..." But at last night's "Turn out the lights," the party had only just begun.

"I do all right," Hunter said modestly, watching Jack slice a drive down the fairway way to the left of the green.

Hunter sliced a drive straight and true to the green, eliciting a frown from Jack. The frown brought to mind Noelle's advice to let her father win. What the heck, he'd vowed to be a good guest. By the end of the second-hole play, Jack took a score of par and Hunter was one under par.

Jack's spirits had improved tremendously. "Bad luck on that hole, son. But don't worry, you're catching on real well. You know I bet you'd be a good golfer if you took a few lessons with the club pro and applied yourself. Golf is a game of concentration."

Concentration. If that was the case, Hunter knew he might as well hang it up for the day. He couldn't have concentrated on anything but Jack's daughter, Noelle, if his life had depended upon it. Last night had been amazing.

The sex had been ... the best. But it wasn't the sex that had him unable to concentrate. It was Noelle. There was something about her that had gotten under his skin. He'd almost woken her first thing this morning. But he hadn't because she'd been hurt by his words when they'd gone to bed and he didn't know how to make it right.

"How is Noelle really doing in Chicago?" Jack questioned. "Is she happy with her job? I think she spends too much time working. She was always such a serious child. I hope you can lighten her up, show her life can be fun."

"I'm doing my best, sir."

"It's your turn to putt, son. Try to keep your shoulders straight. You'll find you have more control of your ball that way."

Hunter sent his ball within inches of the third hole.

"See, what did I tell you? Yes, sir. I think I may have found me a golfing buddy."

"What about Marky, sir?"

"Even I know *that's* not going to last."

Hunter couldn't say that he could argue with Jack. "Then, how come—"

"Sophie's eighteen. She's my baby and she's got her heart set on marrying the guy. What if I'm wrong? What if she never forgave me?"

"It's pretty tough being a father, I guess."

"You'll find out, son. You'll find out. Take my advice and have sons."

They finished the third hole and Hunter drove them in the cart to the dog-legged hole four.

Jack stepped up to the tee and sailed one wide into the woods. "Wait here," Jack said, indicating a wooden bench. "I'm going to look for my ball."

Hunter sat down on the bench knowing it would be a while, as Noelle had forewarned him about Jack's expeditions into the woods. Some people just had a thing about finding free golf balls. Even people who spent thousands of dollars to belong to a private club.

"Did you hear that, Hunter?" Valerie taunted, practicing her golf swing with one of his woods. "Guess whose sons ol' Jack wants you to have?"

"Don't you ever give it a rest? The project is over. I told you to take a vacation. Be a pal, Valerie, and take a hike."

"Don't be getting all holier-than-thou on me, Hunter. I caught you thinking about a new project this morning. Who never takes a vacation?"

"Okay, so you've got me there. But I'm not having sons. Even for Jack."

"Like I said—Peter Pan," Valerie said, tossing her long blond hair over her shoulder.

"And knock off the Peter Pan cracks, too."

"You know, Hunter, one of these days Daphne is going to get tired of taking care of you. She's going to find some nice doctor and—"

"Incorporate, I know."

"You should have talked to Noelle this morning. Now it's going to be awkward."

"No, it won't. I'll pretend nothing happened. It will give her an out. Maybe she won't even remember. She'd had a lot of champagne to drink at the rehearsal dinner."

"She'll remember."

"How do you know?"

"I'm a woman."

"No, you're not. You're a comic-book character. I created you. You think what I tell you to think."

"Right."

"Valerie—"

"Here comes Jack. Better not let him know you talk to yourself. He might have second thoughts about you fathering his grandsons." Valerie disappeared behind a tree.

"Look at all the balls I found, son," Jack said, emptying his bulging white shorts pockets. "Evidently I'm not the only one with a bad slice at this tee."

"I've been thinking, Jack. . . ."

"What is it, son?"

"Well, I was wondering— How did you know when you were ready to have Sophie and Noelle? Did you just wake up one day and want babies, or what?"

Jack chortled. "I woke up one day and Grace told me she was pregnant. That's how I knew."

"Oh."

"Never regretted it for a moment. Let me tell you a secret about marriage, son. When it's bad, nothing's worse. Got a cousin who married the wrong woman. And that's a real sorry mess. But when it's right, you're over the moon. Grace and I got lucky. We were young and stupid kids and there have been times when we haven't had a dime. But we've always had each other. Always. And you can't touch that."

"You do seem to be a happy man."

"I only wish for Sophie and Marky the kind of happiness Grace and I have had. Though I have my reservations about the groom. I wish the same thing for you and Noelle."

Hunter didn't have the heart to tell him he was wishing down an empty well. "How about Freddie

Barton? I hear he was a pretty strong contender for Noelle's hand back a ways."

Jack scowled. "That peckerwood! He nearly broke my Noelle's heart back in high school. He was only interested in my money and disappeared fast when I lost it. He's cut out of the same cloth as Marky, I'm afraid. Just hope to heaven I'm wrong about that boy."

Hunter nodded, not attempting any rebuttal. He held Marky in the same low esteem.

But it was none of his business.

If Sophie loved him, so be it. He'd put on his rented tuxedo and be the best man at the wedding.

Noelle hadn't heard Hunter leave to go play golf with her father. She wasn't aware that he wasn't still sleeping—far across the bed—until Sophie came in the room and began jumping up and down on the mattress insisting she get her lazy bones out of bed because they had dozens of things to do and Mother had a headache from obsessing over how much food to order for the reception since she was sure lots of guests were going to show up, even though they hadn't R.S.V.P.'d.

Sophie and Grace had already been to the photographer's to change the time for the shooting of bridal pictures. The next stop was the bakery where the final decision on the cake had to be made. Sophie insisted on having the cake gaudy with handmade sugar-dough flowers, each of which was priced separately—a fact that Noelle pointed out to her sister and her sister blatantly ignored.

Grace popped two more headache pills and agreed. Next, the florist's.

Noelle didn't take it as a good sign that the name of the florist's was Surprise! But everything went smoothly. For once, the three of them agreed on a simple wildflower arrangement that complemented the filmy pale pink dresses of the bridesmaids. The bridal bouquet was to be white roses and pink lilies.

The ordeal of the last-minute details out of the way, Grace insisted on going home to lie down. Although Noelle and Sophie had been planning to go out for lunch, they, too, opted to nap after first raiding the refrigerator.

"Sophie, why didn't you run away and elope?" Noelle asked, busily slicing fresh tomatoes for their BLT sandwiches. "Mom and Dad are going to go bankrupt paying for this wedding. All this planning for one day is a nightmare. No wonder mother has a headache. I'd never willingly go through all this. I can't believe you are. You're the one who started a picket march outside the third grade when they wouldn't let the girls go on the jungle gym. When did you go and get so traditional?"

Sophie shrugged, knifing some mayo out of a jar she took from the fridge. She spread the mayo on the slice of whole-wheat bread in her hand readying it for the bacon sizzling in the microwave.

"It's not my idea, I promise you."

"You mean it was Mother and Father's?"

"The big wedding is Marky's idea."

"*It is?*"

"He says the bigger the wedding, the more gifts—hopefully cash gifts. He wants to start his own business."

Noelle couldn't think of anything worse.

"What kind of business?" she asked, taking the bacon from the microwave when the ring signaled it was done.

"Promise you won't tell Father?"

"What is it?" Noelle asked, trying not to show her concern.

"Marky wants to start his own band. And I can be the singer."

Noelle bit her tongue to keep from saying what was on the tip of it. It would have made her sound too much as if she was Sophie's mother.

She'd always felt like Sophie's mother because of the ten-year age difference between them. When they were growing up she'd dressed Sophie up and played with her as though she was a baby doll. When Noelle was in high school, Sophie had tagged along wherever she could nag her sister into taking her. And when she couldn't—like when Noelle went out on dates—Sophie would sit on her bed and watch her big sister do her hair and makeup.

They hadn't shared boy stuff as they would have if they'd been closer in age, but they did have a bond that Noelle went out of her way to maintain. Sometimes that included keeping her mouth shut. She knew from memory that eighteen-year-olds didn't like advice, didn't listen to it and certainly didn't take it. No sense in wasting her breath and ruining their relationship.

"A band?"

"I know it sounds like a harebrained idea, Noelle. But it isn't, really. Marky is good. He's talented and all he needs is a chance. Don't you think it would be fun to sing with a band, didn't you ever want to do anything fun like that?"

Last night with Hunter flashed in her mind. "Sure. I've even done some kinda crazy things. But they don't always turn out the way you expect."

"I know that. But you have to try—or you'll never know."

There was something Noelle felt compelled to ask. Yes, she knew it was meddling. Yes, she knew Sophie was going to be annoyed. But she had to ask it, anyway.

"Sophie, we're sisters, right? You'd tell me if there was something wrong, wouldn't you?"

"What makes you think there's something wrong?" Sophie asked defensively, piling bacon high on her sandwich.

"I don't know. It's just this feeling I've got. You would tell me, wouldn't you?" She took a bite of her sandwich and chewed. "I mean, if there were something wrong..."

"Noelle..."

"Okay, okay."

"There's nothing wrong."

"Marky?"

"Yeah," Marky said belligerently. He leaned against the kitchen wall in the Perrys' home, cupping the receiver tightly as he listened.

"Did you tell her?" a female voice badgered him.

"The time hasn't been right," he said defensively.

"There isn't any more time. Tell her now," she ordered.

"I said I'd tell her," he whined.

"See that you do." Once again, Marky heard the now familiar slam of a phone receiver.

When Marky hung up the wall phone in the kitchen, Hunter turned and went to the stairs. He'd planned on getting a drink from the refrigerator when Marky's furtive, tense conversation had stopped him. He'd lingered just outside the door to eavesdrop.

The time wasn't right for what? Hunter wondered. Who was Marky supposed to tell what?

Hunter shook his head and banished his questions.

It was none of his business.

Still, the tone of Marky's voice bothered him. He'd seemed both scared and out of control.

Noelle took Hunter's lead and pretended nothing had happened between them. Perhaps he assumed that since she'd drunk so much champagne at the rehearsal dinner, she wouldn't remember.

She did.

All too well.

It had been heady pleasure. A rush. A sensual feast. Right up until the moment Hunter had ruined it.

Really, it wasn't his fault. After all, he'd only pointed out the truth. It was she who was at fault for forgetting he was only her bought and paid-for date.

It wasn't a mistake she'd make again. But now that she had a grip on how he saw things, she'd take what he offered and not build up false hopes.

She glanced over at him as he drove to the next shopping mall on the list. They'd spent over an hour combing the mall for a dress for her and a tuxedo for him. Finally they'd stumbled across a rental shop where Hunter found a tux—and he looked drop-dead handsome in it.

If she'd gone to the doctor with a case of the blahs, he'd be just the tonic the doctor would have ordered. What more could a woman need to instantly lift her spirits than a blond, blue-eyed charmer?

And rich to boot. Once Sophie had pointed out how famous Hunter was, she realized she'd misjudged him.

As they reached the Frontenac mall Noelle hoped that she would find something to wear to the wedding here and not have to spend the day hitting every single shopping center in St. Louis.

"Father was in a good mood," Noelle said, as Hunter parked her father's car and they walked toward the mall. "I guess you took my advice and let him win the golf game this morning. Or did he find a cache of golf balls in the woods?"

"Both."

"Let's try this shop first. They usually have something I like," Noelle suggested when they came to one of the more popular chain boutiques in the mall.

"No."

Noelle turned and looked at Hunter.

"No?"

"I've called ahead and made an appointment for us at Concepts."

"You did what?"

"My treat," he said, smiling expansively.

"Why?"

"So you let me pick out the outfit."

"Hunter, did anyone ever tell you you give good bribes?" Concepts was an exclusive designer shop she'd never even gone in because the air was too rarefied to breathe.

"And I need a favor from you," he added.

"What kind of favor?" she demanded suspiciously.

"I need you to help me pick something out before we leave. I see Concepts, it's over there." He held the big glass door open for her, then followed her in.

She felt like a sacrificial lamb as the saleslady with lacquered hair and nails approached her. The woman openly disapproved of Noelle's off-the-rack ribbed top and pleated shorts.

"May I help you?" the saleslady asked, her tone clearly conveying that Noelle was in the wrong store.

Just as Noelle was about to say something biting to the snotty salesclerk Hunter came up behind her.

"We have an appointment. I'm Hunter Ashton."

In a snap, the saleslady's attitude shifted from snotty to fawning. "Yes, Mr. Hunter. We have a room for you," the woman said, turning to lead the way.

"A room?" Noelle mouthed, glancing back over her shoulder at Hunter.

The dressing room had faux marble walls and thick beige carpeting. Hunter sat in the wing chair to the left of the wall mirror.

"What would you like to see?" the saleslady asked.

"We need a dress and a pair of shoes," Hunter informed her.

The saleslady glanced over at Noelle and then back at Hunter. "Size ten?"

"Yes, a ten," he answered a little too smugly, a little too possessively, Noelle thought. She felt like a harem girl.

"And will this be a formal occasion, sir?"

"Yes, it's a wedding reception."

The woman nodded. "Nothing white."

Noelle wasn't used to being part of the furniture. She didn't even let a date order for her at dinner, for heaven's sake. She was about to speak up when Hunter said, "Red, I think. We'll see whatever you have in red."

"Red."

Hunter nodded. "The sexier the better."

The saleslady glanced back over at Noelle, said nothing, then went to find something red, the sexier the better.

Noelle gave Hunter a look of censure.

"Isn't this fun?" he responded, refusing to be put down.

Noelle crossed her arms in front of her chest. "You do this a lot?"

Hunter shook his head no. "First time. But I kinda like it. I feel sorta like a—"

The door to the dressing room opened and the saleslady brought in two red dresses and held them up. One was a slinky flared-skirted dress with a sweetheart neckline.

Hunter shook his head no.

"Leave the other one," he told her, nodding at the red stretch-lace slip dress in an-above-the-knee length.

The saleslady did as he instructed.

Noelle continued to stand with her arms crossed in front of her, as she eyed the skimpy dress.

"It won't bite. Come on, be a sport and at least try it on, Noelle."

She'd have to take everything off to try on the dress and he knew it. And was enjoying it.

She uncrossed her arms and lifted the hanger from the hook where the saleslady had hung the dress. She held the provocative red garment against her body and looked at her reflection in the mirror. It wasn't a dress she herself would ever have imagined trying on, much less buying, much less wearing.

But she'd promised herself a weekend adventure. Now was not the time to chicken out—not completely, anyway.

She looked over at Hunter who was sprawled in the chair, lazily watching her. Daring her.

"And what will you be doing while I'm trying this on?" she asked him pointedly. It wasn't pitch-dark in the dressing room the way it had been in her room last night. The lights here were spotlight bright.

Hunter pushed himself up from the chair reluctantly and stood. "I'll see what's holding up the shoes I asked to see." Making good on his promise, he left the dressing room in search of them, closing the door behind him.

Noelle laid the dress on the chair Hunter had vacated, and quickly began slipping out of her clothes, planning to be in the red dress before he returned. Her shorts, top and front-clasp bra landed on the floor in a heap. When she fiddled with the spaghetti strap that got hung up on the hanger, a few choice nonconservative-banker phrases erupted.

Freeing it at last, she scrunched the dress in her hands and pulled it over her body. Oh, my. It looked like lingerie. Very expensive lingerie, mind you. There was nothing subtle about the dress. She kicked off her sandals. Better. Could she really wear a dress like this?

"Well, what do you think?" Hunter asked, coming back into the dressing room.

"It's red," she answered his reflection in the mirror.

His reflection held up a pair of red satin high heels with ankle-wrap ribbon ties.

"Oh, my," she said aloud, swallowing dryly.

"Come sit down and I'll put them on for you. They're perfect for this dress. You are going to look so hot. It's a good thing ol' Freddie Barton won't be at the wedding. He'd go home and hang himself."

Noelle smiled at his compliment and took a seat.

"How did you know the size?" she asked, when the one he slipped on fit her. "Do you have a foot fetish?"

"I overheard Sophie and your mother discussing storing her wedding dress and stuff for you in case you wanted it some day when you got married. They de-

cided against the shoes because she wears a five and
you wear two sizes bigger. Do these wraps tie in front
or in back?"

"In front, in bows."

"Good, it's easier that way." Several attempts later
Hunter had both shoes on her and tied in saucy bows.
"Okay, let's have a look." He stood and moved back
so she could go to the mirror.

Noelle rose and took a few cautious steps, making
sure she could walk at all in the precarious spike heels.
Confident that she could navigate without pitching
forward, she moved to study her reflection in the mirror.

"I don't know, Hunter," she said, looking in the
mirror at her image.

"You don't like it?" A note of disappointment
tinged his voice.

"It's not that, exactly." In truth, she found it all
rather exciting. The dress was indeed starting to grow
on her. In fact, it made her feel pretty sexy. "Don't
you think, though, that it's a little . . ."

"Hot? Yeah!"

"I don't know. . . ." She tugged at the dress where it
clung to her hips.

"Wait a minute. I know what's wrong." Hunter
moved to stand behind her, inching his fingertips beneath the stretchy red lace material.

"Hunter, what are you—"

"Your panties ruin the line of the dress," he answered, inching them down.

"Hunter!"

"See, look," he said, when he'd accomplished his mission.

He was right, she saw, stepping out of her panties and studying her reflection. *If* she wore the dress, she'd have to wear it with panty house and nothing else.

"What do you think?" he asked, coaxing.

"I bet it cost a small fortune. I can't let you..." she began hedging.

"Let me, please—"

"Don't you think you're going a little overboard trying to give me what I paid for?" she couldn't resist saying. It was so easy to get caught up in the fantasy that he was nothing more than a regular date. But regular dates didn't look like him—at least hers hadn't. And they didn't buy you designer dresses that looked like expensive lingerie. Her whole family would be shocked if she showed up in it.

"I deserve that," Hunter said. "But only because you took it the wrong way."

"How was I supposed to take it?"

"It wasn't what I meant. It came out all wrong. I'm the one who got lucky in this deal, Noelle."

He was a smooth talker. Real smooth.

"Let me buy you the dress to make up, please. I'll feel better."

She looked in the mirror at the dress one last time.

"You really think it looks okay?" Was she making a mistake? Oh, hell, what was the point of having an adventure if you played it safe?

"Let's take it."

"Right decision," Hunter agreed, pulling her into his arms to celebrate it with a kiss. His fingers tightened at her back as the kiss surged to an unsettling depth, taking her by surprise.

Noelle had to admit that Hunter was a special man. The kind of man who could make her the kind of woman no man before him had been able to. He sensed the part of her she kept hidden—even from herself.

He was coaxing every facet of her to come out and play with him. To come into the light from the shadows of repression.

He was the kind of man who wanted her to ask for what she wanted and to take pleasure in it.

The room was small.

The dress was hot.

The next thing she knew, the dress was off, tossed at the hanger in their haste.

Hunter walked her backward to the chair and settled her in it, kissing her senseless all the while. He moved back from her and rested on his knees. "Lordy, these shoes, Miss Noellie..." Hunter said, kissing her instep with baby kisses that tickled deliciously, that teased and promised to inch toward her ankle.

Noelle laughed, taking pleasure in the teasing...in Hunter's playful seduction. The shoes were indeed a piece of work. They had very little to do with walking, even less to do with comfort.

Feeling reckless and emboldened, she decided to try to beat Hunter at his own game. "Give me a clue, Hunter. Where do you want these fanciful, sinfully impractical shoes—around your neck or mine?"

"I thought you'd never ask, but since you have—" His grin was wicked as he lifted her knees and settled the red satin shoes around his shoulders.

"I was kidding!" Noelle squealed as he began kissing his way up her calf to her inner thigh in earnest, nipping and licking and growling.

"Hunter!" she cried out when he moved dangerously high on her inner thigh with his titillating kisses, his hand stroking lightly.

"Shush, woman," Hunter whispered. "Do you want to bring store security?"

"Oh, Hunter, you did lock the dressing-room door, didn't you?" Noelle reminded.

"Lock the door?" Hunter echoed, looking up at Noelle.

"But I thought you knew, it doesn't lock," he said on a quick breath, then had her screaming his name again.

"Hunter! Ah...ahhh...*Hunter!*"

6

——►◄——

"So Hunter, what did Noelle pick out for me?" Valerie asked, adjusting her red bustier.

"Go away, there are no girls allowed at a bachelor party."

"You forgot, didn't you?"

"Don't worry, I promised you a new outfit and you'll get it on the next project."

"I'm not wearing those red shoes, Hunter. You can forget it." Valerie stood in the doorway with her arms crossed.

Hunter flushed and returned to the poker table. He was down a hundred, but then his mind wasn't on the cards. Noelle was playing havoc with his concentration—no matter what he was doing.

"I hear you're replacing me as best man," Freddie said, tossing in his cards. He wasn't playing much better than Hunter.

"Rented the tuxedo today. How's your leg feeling?"

"Damn thing is uncomfortable as hell." He patted the leg in the cast propped up on a folding chair. "Doc says I have to have this cast on for six-to-eight weeks. I'm not looking forward to it, I'll tell you."

"You weren't looking backward, either, when you fell off the dock," Marky said to a chorus of laughter.

"You're fired, Marky."

"Again? Don't you think you should wait till you're out of the cast? Right now you need me to bring you coffee and drive you home."

"Okay, you're fired in six-to-eight weeks," Freddie grumbled without meaning it.

Hunter glanced at the fluorescent-orange lightweight cast on Freddie's leg. "That's some cast you've got there, Freddie. I hate to tell you, but it's going to clash with Noelle's dress, so don't stand by her, okay? The dress is really sexy. Too bad you won't be able to dance with her."

Freddie mumbled something else that he did mean.

"Pizza's here!" one of Marky's friends called out from the door.

Hunter groaned. Pizza, his ass.

He'd bet the pot it was a stripper. He was getting too old for this. That thought pulled him up short. Hell, he was only twenty-eight. Since when was he not interested in a woman taking off her clothes?

Daphne would be glad to know that maybe Peter Pan was growing up. That just maybe he'd found a grown-up woman, too.

Noelle was home alone.

Hunter and her father were at the bachelor party for Marky.

Sophie was at her own bachelorette party, which Noelle had begged off because of a headache.

And her mother had gone out for dinner with some friends.

Noelle went downstairs to rummage in the refrigerator for something to nibble on. Not feeling very inspired, she wound up settling for a toasted cheese sandwich and a cold glass of milk. She sat down and stared at the food. The whole evening she'd been unable to concentrate on anything. Anything but Hunter.

What had started out as a straightforward arrangement was getting increasingly complicated. Reading Hunter was difficult. Just when she had pegged him as a devil-may-care wastrel, he'd turned out to be rich and famous. That meant he was capable of discipline, that he was a responsible person.

But he sure did like to play—and he was good at it. Maybe she herself had gone overboard on leaving play out of her life. Work, while satisfying, was not a whole life.

Her problem was twofold when it came to Hunter.

One, was Hunter just having a good time, an adventure, with her? Was she reading more into what was happening than was really there? And two, if she wasn't, could she have a relationship with a man like Hunter? Could she adjust to his spontaneous, live-for-the-moment style of living? She hadn't much success at it as a child.

Still, it could be done. Her parents and Sophie seemed to thrive on it. Turmoil didn't seem to distress them the way it distressed her. In fact they flourished in that kind of chaos.

Even now, when she suspected her parents were flirting with bankruptcy again and Sophie was entering into a questionable marriage, she was the only one who was worried.

Sophie.

Only her sister would marry a boy because she wanted to sing in the band. Even at eighteen, Noelle hadn't been that young. At eighteen she'd been more concerned with her SATs than boys, and marriage had been the furthest thing from her mind.

But it was more than just the foolishness of her eighteen-year-old sister's decision making that bothered Noelle. There was something wrong. Something Sophie either didn't know, or wasn't telling her.

Had Sophie changed her mind but didn't have the guts to cancel at such a late hour? Maybe she didn't have the nerve to disappoint their parents—Noelle smiled—and leave her mother with "all that potato salad" she seemed so obsessed over.

At the bottom of everything was Sophie's wedding's effect on *her*. It was forcing her to think about marriage. Did she ever plan to marry? Why? Or why not?

It was a subject that she hadn't had the time or energy to give much thought to while climbing the corporate banking ladder. But she needed a personal life, too. And Hunter had shown her she desperately needed some fun in her life. She didn't need to worry about everything so much. Control was an illusion anyway, if you thought it through. Anything could and usually did happen over the course of a life, and it usually wasn't what you expected. It was time she took some risks.

And any way you looked at it—Hunter was a risk.

Noelle wiped up her crumbs and put her dish and glass in the sink. Tomorrow was a busy day, so she might as well go to bed early and get as much sleep as possible.

She saw Sophie had left the light on in her room when she left.

As she walked down the hall to her sister's room, she smiled, recalling another room—the dressing room at Concepts. It all seemed like some incredible dream. Had Hunter really taken her there? Had he really bought her that sexy red dress and shoes? Would she really have the nerve to wear them?

Nerve. She'd nearly lost it when Hunter had told her the dressing-room door didn't lock! Only later did he explain that he'd paid the saleslady to give them some time alone.

The thrill of danger had only been in her imagination. The look of censure on the saleslady's face as they left, however, had been real.

The woman needed to get a life, Noelle thought, and then laughed. Good advice that she herself should take.

When she reached to turn off the light in Sophie's room, her gaze was caught by another spectacular dress—a white one.

Sophie's wedding dress.

It was the first time she'd seen it. She crossed the room to where the dress hung on a door hook.

The dress suited an eighteen-year-old. It had Fairy Princess written all over it. White, beaded Alençon lace made up the fitted bodice. The neckline was off-the-shoulder tulle and the full skirt was a puff of tulle.

At the sight of it even a twenty-eight-year-old melted, despite her best defenses. Noelle reached out and touched the magical wedding dress.

On impulse, she lifted the hanger off the hook and went to the mirror on the wall, holding the dress up in front of her. She swayed as if she were dancing.

Caught up, she acted out of character and slipped the frothy dress from the padded hanger.

Dare she? she wondered, pausing. No one would know if she tried it on. She was four inches taller than Sophie, but the dress would fit otherwise, because she and her sister both wore the same size.

It was amazing what you could talk yourself into when you were alone and no one would know. Quickly, she slipped out of her clothes, shedding them in a pile on the floor. She stepped into the dress and gingerly zipped the long zipper up the back.

On her the dress was ankle-length instead of floor-length, but the image reflecting back at her was appealing. It occurred to her that she had tried on several new images since being with Hunter.

She wondered what Hunter would think if he could see her in the bridal gown? Did he ever think of marriage? Probably not. As a celebrity, he probably had women swooning over him all the time. Men seldom worried about balancing a career and a marriage. Seldom had to. It was women's work.

But if two people worked on it maybe they could create a marriage that would suit both of them as if it were tailor-made. She really was daydreaming. There probably couldn't be a worse candidate for marriage than someone like Hunter, who spent most of his time in the fantasy world of comics—a place where women saved the world wearing red bustiers and thigh-high suede boots.

A noise in the house startled her. Thinking quickly and identifying where exactly the noise had come from, she froze when she realized it was at the top of the stairs.

Someone had come home early!

It didn't matter who. Being caught in Sophie's wedding dress would be mortifying.

She had to get out of the dress fast.

But she couldn't move. The footsteps were already coming down the hall toward Sophie's bedroom. There wasn't time—and no way could she hide in the frothy confection.

Wait, Hunter wouldn't come to Sophie's room, she reasoned on a sigh of relief. That meant it was Sophie. Somehow she'd have to explain— No, wait. She heard footsteps, plural. It had to be her parents. But why would they...?

She turned to the open door and took a deep breath, trying not to let her nervousness show. It was no use. She felt like a little girl caught playing with her mother's makeup. She felt ridiculous.

But it wasn't her parents.

Fear replaced embarrassment when she saw the two big guys filling the doorway to Sophie's room.

"We want to talk to you, Sophie," the taller one said.

"I'm not—" she started to say, then clamped her lips shut.

"Come on. Don't give us any trouble, okay? Let's get out of here before someone comes home and someone winds up getting hurt," the younger one said, looking around to check the hall.

"Go?" Noelle backed away from them, trying to make herself a smaller target. In the bridal gown, she felt like a huge spider.

"Don't be alarmed. We're not going to hurt you. We're just going for a little ride. All we want to do is talk to you."

Don't be alarmed? He had to be kidding. She was shaking, she was so scared. Two strange men wanted her to go for a little ride and she shouldn't be alarmed? What if they were nut cases? She checked and didn't see a gun. That relieved her somewhat, but the two guys were still awfully big.

"What do you want?" she demanded, trying to sound a lot braver than she felt.

"We'll tell you what we want in the car. Quit stalling and come outside with us. If you cooperate, you'll see that everything will be fine."

"If you try to make me leave with you, I'll scream," she threatened.

"No, you won't," they assured her.

"Then at least let me change out of this," Noelle said, playing for time, praying for Hunter to show up early, after all. "If I leave this house in my wedding dress, I'll look ridiculous... and suspicious."

"It doesn't matter what you're wearing. No one is going to see you because it's dark outside. Listen to me. There isn't time to change. This has to be done quickly. Come with us and don't cause a scene," the younger man coaxed.

"Where are we going?"

They didn't answer her. The two looked enough alike to be brothers. And they seemed nervous, like this wasn't something they did all the time. Noelle didn't know whether to be relieved or worried about that.

"I'm not going anywhere with you," she said, finally trying to bluff her way out of whatever situation her sister had gotten herself into.

"We're leaving *now*. Shut up and do as we say or we'll have to. . ." The older guy started advancing toward her, forcing her bluff.

"What?" Noelle demanded.

"Escort you out," they chorused. The younger guy also approached and they did just that, each of them taking her arm and hustling her out of the room and into the hall.

"Let me go," Noelle cried, trying to pull free of their grip. The two men held her firmly and lifted her off her feet to get her down the stairs.

For one brief hysterical moment all she could think about was that there was going to be a headline on the cover of one of those awful tabloids and her captioned picture in Sophie's wedding dress. Her career in banking would be over.

It took some doing but they got her in the car. She found herself in the back seat of a seventies Chevy. It was one of those boat-size models so she, the dress and the younger guy fit. The bigger guy drove.

"Why are you doing this? Where are we going? What's going on?" Noelle was full of questions they were unwilling to answer.

All the driver said was, "You'll find out soon enough. You don't have to worry about us, we mean you no harm. There's just something that you have to know before you marry Marky."

The guys seemed sincere about no harm coming to her. And as they hadn't been brandishing a weapon or been menacing, she took a deep breath and tried to keep her anxiety down.

What was Sophie's prospective groom involved in? It could be anything from gambling to bank robbing. Oh, no, she hoped that wasn't what this was all about. Had Freddie mentioned to Marky that she was vice president of a bank? It came back to her that Marky worked as a mechanic for Freddie Barton in his car dealership.

A chop shop, she thought all at once. Maybe that was it. Maybe Freddie was involved up to his fluorescent-orange cast. Maybe that was why Freddie had a broken leg to begin with.

She tried to straighten the bridal gown in case she got out of this somehow and could return the dress to its hanger without evidence of it having been worn.

"How do the two of you know Marky?" she asked, attempting to make conversation.

"We don't know Marky," they informed her in unison.

"You've never heard his band...?" she prompted, searching for some connection.

"I heard his band was pretty good," the younger guy beside her said. "But I've never heard it myself. Have you, brother Ben?" Brother Ben didn't comment, just looked straight ahead.

Brother Ben. Did that mean they were brothers, or were they in some sort of religious cult? Did they want Marky to belong to the cult? Did Marky already belong to the cult? Was there even a cult? Her headache was even worse than it had been before.

This was definitely not her idea of a good adventure.

"So, are the two of you brothers?"

"Yeah," the guy in front said curtly. He'd seemed to be waiting for some signal to put the car in gear and drive away. Whatever it was, he got it. They started rolling.

"Why don't you just tell me what I need to know? Why do we have to go somewhere? Can't you tell me here and let me go back inside before someone sees me in this?"

At the end of the block the driver pulled the car over alongside a woman and stopped. What was this—a serial kidnapping?

When the young woman opened the car door to get in, Noelle could see she was about seven months pregnant. This was some strange gang that was kidnapping her.

"Did you tell her?" the woman asked the driver, once she'd closed the door and they were driving away.

"No, I thought you wanted to tell her."

"Oh, great. You've probably scared her half to death, Ben."

"Yeah, he has," Noelle piped in from the back seat.

The woman turned around and stared at Noelle in complete surprise. "Who are you?"

"What do you mean, who is she?" the guy beside Noelle retorted. "She's Marky's intended."

"No, she's not."

"Of course, she is," Ben said. "She's wearing the wedding dress, isn't she? Who else but the bride would be trying on her wedding dress the night before the wedding?"

"You tell me, Ben. I've seen Sophie and that ain't her."

Now all three of them were staring at Noelle, Ben in the rearview mirror as he drove.

"I'm not Sophie," Noelle said, stating the obvious.

"Then why are you wearing her wedding dress?" Ben asked.

"I don't have a good answer for that one," Noelle replied. "It was a dumb impulse, okay?"

"But *who* are you?" the woman demanded.

"I'm Sophie's sister, Noelle."

"Now what?" Ben demanded. "Do you want me to keep driving or should we take her back?"

"What are you planning to do, exchange her for Sophie? Don't be an idiot. Just drive, okay? Let me think. I can't believe I have brothers who can't even carry out a simple—"

"It was an easy mistake—she's in the wedding gown," the guy beside Noelle said defensively. "They're sisters, so they look alike. How were we to know?"

"Just be quiet and let me think," his sister said. People kept waving when they saw a bride in the back seat. Every time they stopped at a light Noelle hid her face. All she needed was for someone to recognize her.

Now that she knew the situation wasn't really threatening, she wanted to know what was going on.

"Why don't we just tell her?" Ben finally suggested.

"Yeah, she can tell Sophie."

"There doesn't seem to be any choice since you guys screwed everything up."

The woman turned around to look at Noelle. "I'm Polly Palmer."

"And she's pregnant," Ben added, accusingly.

"I'm sure she's noticed, Ben."

"Tell her who the father is," Ben urged.

"I'm getting to it, okay?" She looked Noelle straight in the eye and said what Noelle had the sinking feeling was coming. "Your sister, Sophie, is marrying my baby's father in the morning."

Noelle didn't know what to say.

So she didn't say anything. She was too stunned. How was she going to tell Sophie? *Should* she tell Sophie? And if she did, would Sophie blame her? Would Sophie ever forgive Noelle for ruining her wedding? *Would* it ruin the wedding? Or would Sophie marry Marky anyway? How much in love with Marky was Sophie?

All those questions ran through Noelle's mind.

All those and one more.

Was this woman telling the truth?

She had to ask. But how to put it?

"How—ah—I mean, are you sure the baby is Marky's?" she finally said.

"I'm sure. There isn't anyone else but Marky. I love him. And I know he loves me."

"So then why is he marrying my sister?"

"Because he's afraid."

"I don't understand," Noelle said, puzzled. Marky was afraid of Sophie? Sophie was about as threatening as a butterfly.

"Hey, here's a Taco Bell. Can we stop? I'm hungry," the brother seated beside Noelle said, pointing to the Mexican restaurant on the corner.

"Sam, now is not the time to—"

"Get him something to eat, you know he's hypoglycemic. Pull in the drive-through lane," his sister said protectively. "I could go for a taco salad, myself."

Ben did as his sister ordered. Polly didn't seem shy about getting her way. So why was she in her situation? Noelle decided there was more to the story.

"You said Marky was afraid. What does that have to do with his marrying my sister?"

"Sophie wants to get married to Marky because she thinks if she's married to him, it guarantees she will be the singer for his band."

"Are you saying Sophie is marrying Marky to be in a band? That that's the only reason?"

"Yeah, and the only reason Marky is marrying Sophie is because he loves me. Marky needs her. He's afraid the record contract he has lined up will fall through without her as the singer. He's afraid if he tells Sophie he doesn't want to get married, she'll quit the band.''

"What a mess." Noelle buried her head in her hands, while Ben placed an order for their food into the squawky speaker. He looked at Noelle. "Do you want something to eat?"

"No. Listen, if I promise to tell Sophie, will you let me out here? I can't get taco sauce all over Sophie's wedding dress. She'll kill me."

They let her out.

Once she was outside the car, she wondered about the wisdom of what she had just done. A woman in a wedding dress stood out like a sore thumb. And to top it off, she was barefoot. Sophie's shoes were too small, so she hadn't tried them on with the wedding dress.

But even worse, she didn't have a cent on her. No identification. Nothing.

She looked back to the Palmers' car, but they'd already gone through the pickup area and left with their food. There was only one thing for her to do. She would have to ask someone to lend her a quarter to call...who?

Only one name came to mind.

Hunter.

The night kept getting worse.

The trouble was there wasn't much foot traffic. Most people were in cars. And the few people she tried to borrow change from gave her a wide berth, thinking it was some kind of prank or setup.

Her head was pounding and her feet were dirty, but the wedding dress so far seemed to have held up, she noticed, as she waited at the stoplight, summoning the courage to go across the street to the bowling alley. It was going to take a lot of nerve to walk in there and beg for a quarter.

She looked like an abandoned bride.

This was definitely not turning out to be the sort of adventure she'd had in mind for the weekend.

When and if she got Sophie's dress back home safe and sound, she was never, ever, doing anything even remotely impulsive again. She simply didn't have the stomach or the nerves for it.

The light changed and she limped across the walkway, having stepped on a bit of gravel. When she crossed the bowling-alley parking lot she was careful not to brush the pristine white gown against any of the cars. When she got to the entrance of the bowling alley she paused to take a deep breath and calm her jittery nerves.

She had to think, to concentrate on one thing at a time. Otherwise, she'd be overwhelmed and do nothing.

First, the quarter for the phone call to Hunter. She closed her eyes and prayed he was still at Freddie Barton's. Freddie, of course, would have been the one to throw the bachelor party for Marky.

Steeling her resolve, she pushed open the heavy glass door to the bowling alley and went inside. She'd forgotten how noisy bowling alleys were. The crash of the balls into the pins and the camaraderie made up a steady din.

A middle-aged man stood at the desk renting bowling shoes. He had a kind face. Maybe he would lend her a quarter to make a phone call. Maybe he'd even let her do it without asking questions. She waited for the two teenage boys who were admiring an expensive bowling ball in the glass display case below the counter to leave, and then she walked up to the rental desk.

"Hello," he said with a straight face.

She nodded.

"Will that be a party of two bowling?" he asked, in a blasé tone. Not much seemed to surprise him, she thought.

"No. Ah, I'm not planning to bowl."

"I see."

"I've had, ah, I missed a connection and I was wondering if I could borrow a quarter to call for a ride?" She hoped she didn't faint—that was all she needed to make the evening complete. She willed herself to breathe evenly.

"There's no need to borrow a quarter, miss. I can dial the number for you, if you like," he offered, picking up the telephone on the desk.

"Um, do you have a phone book," she asked, feeling even more embarrassed.

"Sure, of course." He turned and lifted one from beneath the counter.

"Freddie ... please be listed," she murmured beneath her breath, as she flipped through the pages till she came to the Bs and then to Barton ... Frederick James.

It was listed!

She read the phone number off to the man and he dialed it for her.

She watched his face anxiously. "It's busy," he said, hanging up the phone.

She felt her shoulders slump in defeat.

"Tell you what, I noticed you've lost your shoes. Why don't you put these on so your feet don't get hurt, and I'll try the number again in a minute."

He handed her a pair of size-seven red-and-green bowling shoes.

How could she refuse when he was only being nice?

She accepted the shoes and sat down to put them on while the man took pity on her and bought her a soda.

"Let's try again," he said after handing her the drink. Noelle jumped up when the man smiled and said, "It's ringing."

She took the phone.

"Freddie? Is Hunter there? Could I talk to him, please?"

"Wait a minute, I think he was leaving a bit ago. Let me check."

Oh, please, she silently prayed.

"Noelle?"

It was Hunter!

"Yes, it's me, Hunter. I need to have you do me a favor. Would you mind terribly leaving the bachelor party and coming to pick me up at the Red Bird Bowling Alley? I'm sort of stranded here."

"Are you okay? You sound strange."

"I'm . . . I'm okay. Just pick me up. Right away."

"Where will you be waiting?"

"I'll be at the door. The bowling alley is at the corner of Hampton and Gravois. Don't worry, you won't miss me when you get here. I'll be the one in a wedding dress and bowling shoes."

7

Noelle finished her soda, thanked the nice man who'd got busy at the desk from a rush of customers, then went to wait by the door of the bowling alley to watch for Hunter. She endured a lot of curious glances and some outright stares as people came and went. It was a busy Friday date-night. If her mind hadn't been taken up with worry about what she was going to do about Polly Palmer's bombshell news, she'd have been truly mortified. As it was, she had more pressing problems than her strange attire.

Finally, after what seemed like hours, her knight in the white limo arrived. As he pulled up to the entrance, she stepped outside to meet him.

He parked the limo and got out.

She knew he was chewing the inside of his cheek to keep from laughing at the sight she must be. Still, he was unable to resist a wisecrack.

"Are you ready to go, or did you want to bowl a couple of games first?" he asked, eyeing her shoes.

She looked down at the shoes, then back up at him and glared.

"Guess not," Hunter said, opening the rear door of the limo to accommodate the bridal gown.

Noelle piled in, taking care every layer of the tulle skirt cleared the door before he closed it.

While Hunter walked around to his side of the car, she hastily removed the ugly bowling shoes and shoved them at him when he opened the driver's door. "Would you run these back inside for me and give the guy a dollar?"

Hunter took the shoes and did as she asked without giving her any further trouble.

While he was inside she tried to think of something plausible to tell him to explain why she was dressed as she was.

When Hunter returned to the car he glanced back at her. "Where to?"

"Home, and quickly."

"Are you running away from a groom? And more important, is he armed?"

"There is no groom," she answered through clenched teeth. "This is Sophie's wedding dress."

"I see."

Clearly, he didn't.

"Just drive and I'll explain it to you on the way, okay?"

Hunter put the limo in motion while Noelle cast about for a way to begin. "Did you ever do something impulsive when you were alone and thought no one would ever know?"

"You mean like smear your body with tuna fish and let the cat lick it off?"

She glanced up in the rearview mirror and saw that he was joking.

"I mean, like try on a wedding dress. . . ."

"Oh."

She waited, knowing he wouldn't let it drop at that. This was too good.

"Trying on the wedding dress, that's not so bad— we all give in to the occasional bad urge. Going to the bowling alley in it and renting shoes is kinda where you lose me. There seems to be some sort of gap there, when—"

"I didn't plan to.... Going to a bowling alley, going anywhere in Sophie's dress wasn't—" She gave up in frustration. "Just take me home."

"Do you think that's wise?"

"Where exactly do you think I should be going? I've got to get this dress home."

She saw Hunter glance at the dash.

"It's ten o'clock. I'm sure your parents are on their way home from dinner by now. You don't want them to—"

"No, of course not. But I don't know what else to do."

The night just kept getting worse. She started to cry.

"Oh, now, don't start doing that. Listen, I've got an idea. Why don't we find you something else to wear? Then I can drop you off at the bachelorette party so you can stall Sophie on the off chance the party was to break up early. While you're doing that, I'll find a way to sneak in the wedding dress."

"You'd do that for me?" she sniffed.

"Of course. I aim to please."

Right, part of the thousand-dollar bargain, Noelle thought glumly.

"Where am I going to find something to change into? The malls are all already closed."

"Let me think. We could try the supermarket, but all we'd find there are T-shirts and I don't think you want to go bar-hopping in just a T-shirt." He turned and checked just to be sure.

"I'd rather wear the wedding dress."

"Okay, okay. I know—we'll cruise the laundromats until we find someone who's left their clothes to dry."

"We can't do that!"

"Do you want to get the dress back home without anyone knowing, or not?"

"I guess...."

It took them a half hour, but they finally found a laundromat with the dryers circling and no one around. Hunter parked the limo and while Noelle played lookout leaning over the front seat by the horn, he went inside the laundromat and lifted some clothing for her.

He came back with it stuffed beneath his polo shirt, got in the car and tossed it back to her.

"These are guy's clothes," she complained, as Hunter pulled away.

"Beggars can't be choosers. I'll loan you my belt if the jeans don't fit."

She struggled out of the wedding dress, a task made easier by its off-the-shoulder style. She didn't need Hunter's belt. The jeans fit, if she didn't plan to breathe. She pulled on the dark tank top and tried to imagine the guy's clothes she was wearing as comfortable. In truth, she was as uncomfortable in a strange man's clothes as she'd been in the wedding dress. But she didn't say anything because Hunter was doing the best he could to help.

"Are you dressed?" Hunter asked from the front seat, slamming on the brakes as someone ran a red light.

"Yes, I'm dressed."

"Okay, then, we're off to find Sophie. Any ideas?"

Noelle thought for a moment. "I know. We can find her by the bus. They rented a bus to go bar-hopping since they would all be drinking. And they were going down to the Landing. We'll just cruise until we find the bus."

They took the bumpy ride down the cobblestone streets of Laclede's Landing, but there wasn't a parked bus to be seen.

"Maybe it did break up early," Noelle said with a sigh of resignation. "Wait—let's try Soulard. They might have gone to one of the bars there."

Ten minutes later they sighted the bus outside the most outrageously funky establishment in Soulard—one with a wildly colorful decorated hearse parked outside. Hunter let Noelle out so she could make sure Sophie's group was inside the Venice Café. In minutes she was waving him on from the doorway.

Taking his cue, Hunter drove away with the wedding dress in the back of the limo before anyone came outside and saw it.

He turned on the radio and hit Highway 55 as the quickest route back. It was a golden oldies station, and an old Motown hit of the Temptations came on. He was singing and grinning, still recalling how Noelle had looked in the wedding dress and bowling shoes. His blond creation appeared on the seat beside him.

"Don't start liking those bowling shoes too much, Hunter," Valerie said. "I'm not saving the world in bowling shoes, either. And I'm getting impatient to know what my new outfit is going to be."

"I guess you want combat boots, right?"

"Yeah, that'd be cool. It's what Madonna wore on Letterman. I could handle that." Valerie looked in the rearview mirror, applying blood-red lipstick.

"Well, I couldn't. Forget the combat boots," Hunter said, turning up the radio to drown out Valerie's pestering.

"How about some nice, tall, shiny black boots that come up to my knees?"

"Where'd you get that idea?"

"Must be the siren that made me think of them. You know, they're the kind state troopers wear."

Hunter heard it then and saw the flashing red lights. With a sinking feeling in the pit of his stomach, he knew he was the one being pulled over for speeding.

He slowed and followed the beam of light from the trooper's flashlight directing him to the shoulder of the highway behind a red sports car that had also gotten caught.

He waited impatiently as the trooper dealt with the guy in the sports car, making the driver take the breathalizer test. Hunter tried to recall how long it had been since he'd had a beer at the bachelor party.

He wasn't a heavy drinker, but he could have beer on his breath. All he needed was to be taken in and have Noelle have to come rescue him.

"Hello, officer," he said, when it was his turn.

"Good evening, sir. Are you aware that you were going sixty-nine miles per hour. That's over the speed limit."

"I was in a hurry, I guess," Hunter said by way of excuse.

"Could I see your driver's license, please."

Hunter complied.

The trooper took the license and went back to his squad car to check out Hunter.

In a few minutes he was back with his ticket book open. Three minutes later Hunter was on his way with a speeding ticket to pay. The delay hadn't been that long but it was probably long enough that he would run into Jack and Grace returning or returned home from dinner. They wouldn't be staying out late the night before the big day of their daughter's wedding.

How was he going to sneak the wedding dress past them?

"You could go in the back way," Valerie suggested, reappearing in the front seat next to him.

"But what if they're still up watching television or something?"

"Then you stash the dress until they go to sleep. Once they're asleep you can sneak it up to Sophie's room."

"Good thing you're not writing the comics," Hunter said, dismissing the idea.

"Why, what's wrong with my idea? I think it's a good idea." Her red lips formed a pout.

"It stinks. You'll have to think of something better than that. First of all, the dress is too unwieldy to stash anywhere without it being noticed. And second of all, even if I could stash it—what if Sophie came home before I had a chance to get it back to her room?"

"Then you'll have to disguise it."

"That's it!"

Hunter took the exit off the highway.

He kept his eyes open for a supermarket until he saw a National all lit up to signal it was open twenty-four hours to the public. He went in, bought a package of hefty green garbage bags and returned to the car. He slit the package open and slipped two bags over the wedding dress.

Sure enough, when he arrived at the Perrys', Noelle's parents were home already. Their car was parked in the drive. He left the wedding dress in the limo and loped up to the house to check out the lay of the land. It looked cool, he decided after a brief inspection of the entry hall and stairway. In the background he heard a shower running in Jack and Grace's bedroom.

Finally luck was with him.

He hurried back out to the limo and gathered up the garbage-bagged wedding dress. The plastic was dark green so you couldn't see what was inside the light but voluminous bundle. Easing it out of the back seat of the limo, he shoved the door closed with his foot.

The thud seemed to echo in the quiet night and he swore at his stupidity. Still, no one came to the door. He continued to have a clear path.

Getting the bundle through the front door proved no easy task, but he managed finally and breathed a sigh of relief. Starting up the stairs, he was stopped by a woman's voice.

"Oh, Hunter, it's you. I thought I heard a car door. What have you got there?" Grace asked as she came along the hall toward him.

"It's nothing, Grace. It's, ah, balloons for the reception-hall decor. Balloons, that's all."

The bundle tipped precariously.

"Here, let me help you with them—" Grace started forward.

"Oh, no. No, I'm fine—really." He got a better grip and began climbing the stairs.

Grace looked uncertain. "Well, if you're sure."

"I'm sure," he called back.

Hunter navigated the stairs and hurried down the hallway to Sophie's room where he saw the empty hanger Noelle had told him would be on the door hook. Quickly, he pulled the dress from the bags and shook it to fluff it out. Lifting it to the hanger took some doing since it was an off-the-shoulder bridal gown. He managed the feat once he found the little loops sewn inside the dress.

His mission successfully accomplished, he stood back and studied the gown. It looked pretty good to him. There were no rips or dirt stains. Sophie would never know her wedding gown had been bowling.

But he would.

A car pulled up out in front of the house and he heard Sophie and Noelle call out good-nights.

All of a sudden he was exhausted—so exhausted he almost forgot the green plastic bags he had to dash back for at the last minute.

* * *

"You'd think you were the nervous bride getting married in the morning instead of Sophie, the way you keep tossing and turning," Hunter complained from his side of the bed as Noelle plumped a pillow for what seemed like the fiftieth time.

He glanced at the digital clock on the dresser. "It's four o'clock in the morning. Don't you think it's time you got some sleep, Noelle? What are you worrying about? Sophie's wedding gown is back safe and sound. No one need ever know it hasn't been there all night."

"The wedding dress isn't worrying me any longer. I can't believe Mother almost caught you."

"Well, she didn't. So quit worrying and go to sleep. I'm exhausted and you should be, too."

She had to tell someone. She had to talk to someone. All night she'd tried to work out in her mind the best thing to do about Polly Palmer's news. There just didn't seem to be any easy answer. She was going to be wrong no matter what decision she made.

"Hunter?"

"What is it?"

"Can I trust you?"

"I told you I wasn't going to tell anyone about the wedding gown. What do I have to do to make you believe me?"

"This isn't about the wedding gown, Hunter. If you would listen to what I'm saying, you'd know that."

"Noelle, it's four in the morning. I don't know much of anything at four in the morning. If you want to tell me something, just say it. My mind is too foggy to guess what in the hell it is you're getting at."

"Oh, Hunter, I feel so stupid. I don't know what to do."

"Wait a minute, this is about *why* you were at a bowling alley in Sophie's wedding dress, isn't it?"

She nodded.

"I think I want to hear about this." Giving up on sleep for the foreseeable future, he sat straight up in bed and stacked pillows behind his back to brace himself.

Beginning was so embarrassing. She closed her eyes and plunged in. "Well, as you know, I was in Sophie's room. I'd gone to turn out the light. And I don't know why—maybe because I've never tried on a wedding dress, whatever—I gave in to the urge. I didn't think anyone would ever know. I was home all alone."

"No one will know," Hunter said, pulling her into his arms and comforting her. "It's our secret."

"Thank you," she sniffed.

He hugged her and patted her head as if she were a child that needed comforting.

"Anyway, that's when the Palmer brothers showed up."

"The Palmer brothers? Aren't they the guys on the box of cough drops?" Hunter said, trying to make her smile.

"They told me I had to come with them, that they had to show me something—that Sophie had to know something before she married Marky in the morning."

"Are you saying they *took* you—kidnapped you?"

"They insisted I come. And they wouldn't let me change out of the wedding gown. They thought they had Sophie."

"Then what happened?" Hunter asked, tension in his voice.

Noelle wiped at the tears on her cheeks. "After they got me in the car they assured me they weren't going to hurt me. They didn't. A woman got in the car then. Their sister, Polly."

"Polly and Marky, right?" Hunter said, leaping ahead of her.

"Yes. Polly's seven months pregnant, Hunter. She says the baby is Marky's."

"Is it?"

"I don't know—I don't know what to believe. I don't know what to do. What if I don't tell Sophie and it's true? What if I do tell her and it's not? What if she calls off the wedding at the last minute. There's all those hundreds of people, all that food, the presents.... Mother and Father will ..."

"You'll have to tell her, Noelle. You know that, don't you? I know it's a terrible position to be put in, but Sophie has to know. Do you want me to tell her for you?"

"You'd do that?"

"Hey, I'm the guy who bagged a wedding dress. I'd do anything." He almost said, "For you." He wasn't sure why he hadn't. Maybe he was as much of a chicken as Noelle when it came to showing real emotion. Sex was easy. Romance—now that was hard.

"No, I have to be the one to do it. It has to come from me. Even if she hates me for it."

"She won't hate you," Hunter assured her, kissing her forehead. "You worry too much."

"Wouldn't you hate me, if I told you the person you were in love with was—"

"I could never hate you."

"You're just being sweet, Hunter, 'cause you feel sorry for me."

"I've always been sweet, you just haven't noticed," he assured her. "Come on, now, let's get some sleep. First thing tomorrow morning is going to come soon enough. I'll wake you at seven and you can go have a talk with Sophie before your parents are up."

"I wish I didn't know, Hunter. It was all so exciting before. . . ."

"Come on, lie down here next to me," Hunter said, rearranging the pillows and sheet. "I'll hold you until you fall asleep."

"Jack, are you awake?"

"I am now."

"Can you believe you're going to be giving away our baby girl in the morning?"

"Not if I don't get some sleep."

"Jack?"

"What is it?"

"Do you think we have enough food? What if all those people who didn't R.S.V.P. show up?"

"There will be leftovers. There are always leftovers."

"How do you know that?"

"Because that's what I always get to eat."

"Why, Jack Perry, you take that back—"

"Make me...."

"Jack!"

"Well, you're the one who won't let me sleep."

"Jack?"

"What is it, Gracie, love?"

"It's going to be a beautiful wedding, isn't it?"

"It ought to be, it's costing enough."

"How do you know?" she asked worriedly.

"I know. Let's just say you owe me...."

Grace laughed—a satisfied laugh.

"It would never work, you know," Valerie said, kneeling beside the bed with her chin resting in her hands.

"Will you go away and let me get some sleep."

"Come on, Hunter, this is the best fantasy you've ever dreamed up. You and Miss Uptight Banker. It'll never work, I'm telling you." Valerie pushed her blond hair back from her face and gave him a defiant look.

"How do you know?" Hunter felt compelled to defend what he wanted to work. It was certainly a new feeling for him. Wanting a relationship to last longer than the fling of a few days or weeks. He didn't know what to make of it. Was it because he was getting older, or because he was growing up? "Maybe Noelle is exactly what I need," he insisted. "I need someone like Daphne to take care of me. Look after me when I'm working on a project. You know what a mess things get in then."

"Then hire an assistant," Valerie said, getting up and pacing, warming to her argument. "An assistant can organize your life for you if Daphne cuts you off. She won't, anyway. She's been threatening to for ages and she still cleans up your messes."

"I think she's serious lately. After all, I'm twenty-eight. And so is Daphne. She's going to want a family."

"So's Noelle. She's going to want a family, too. Her biological clock should start sounding louder to her pretty soon."

What if Noelle did want a family? Did he? Why hadn't he even considered it before now? He danced away from giving it too close an inspection. Denial worked well for him; why change now? "She's not going to want a family. She's not even going to want to get married. Look at her loony family. Noelle is a career person just like me. We could live together and—"

Valerie stopped pacing and gave Hunter a considering look. "She could take care of you. Sounds like such an attractive offer, Hunter. How could she refuse?"

Valerie was right. But not completely; not about how selfish he was. Okay, maybe he had been in the past, but he didn't feel that way anymore. "I'd take care of Noelle, too," he said, defending himself.

"You mean when you remembered she was there. You know how lost you get in your projects. No woman is going to put up with that. You're too self-absorbed, Hunter. You might as well face it. Like I said, it will never, ever work."

"I could change."

"Stop laughing, Valerie."

"It's not that funny," he continued. "People can change if they want to badly enough. They can."

"Come on, Hunter. You're trying to tell me you could give up what you love—give it all up for a woman? Who are you trying to kid? It's just sex."

"No, it's not! It's something more than that."

"What do you mean, 'something more'? Do you love her, Hunter?"

Did he? He sat straight up in bed.

"Hunter, you aren't answering me."

"I don't know. Maybe."

"All this may be a moot point anyway, Hunter," Valerie said, crossing her arms in front of her.

"Why?"

"I haven't heard Noelle tell you she loves you."

"Give me time, Valerie. I've only had two days with her."

"Hunter, you aren't thinking straight. You're tired and sleepy. Noelle is a banker. How would it look for her to show up with you on her arm—a cartoonist? Do you really think anyone in her business is going to take her seriously after that? The banking community is very stuffy. It's a small, closed circle. And image is everything in the banking world. She's worked hard to make it all the way to vice president. What makes you think she'd throw all that away for you?"

Hunter slumped back against the pillows. "Maybe you're right. Maybe it would never work. I guess I'm not thinking straight. I'm going to get some sleep."

"Good idea. Then I can get some, too."

But neither of them did for at least an hour, because Hunter kept wanting to wake Noelle and ask her to marry him, to find out if there was a chance she felt the same way he did. Sleep claimed him before he got up the courage to act on his impulsive urge.

Hunter Ashton was the sweetest, most wonderful man.

After Hunter had finally fallen asleep, she'd gotten up to go stand at the window, gazing out at the moonlight.

Hunter was perfect. Why had she been too stubborn to see that until now?

She didn't want the weekend to end . . . didn't want Hunter to go out of her life.

A bright light in the night sky caught her attention. She watched as a shooting star streaked across the inky dark.

And then she squeezed her eyes closed and made a wish.

"I wish I were marrying Hunter in the morning. I wish Hunter was in love with me."

8

Noelle sat curled up in a chair beside Sophie's bed watching her baby sister sleep. She'd watched her for the past half hour. It had been six-thirty when she'd first awoken and slipped down to Sophie's room. She wanted to talk to her before the wedding day craziness started.

She didn't really want to talk to her—she had to.

Hunter was right. She had to tell Sophie what she knew about Polly Palmer and Marky. Even if Sophie hated her for it.

While she waited for Sophie to wake up, allowing her the pleasant dreams she hoped her sister was having, Noelle glanced around Sophie's room. It was typical, she supposed, of the average teenager's room.

The wallpaper and bedspread were a pretty striped pattern she'd bet their mother had picked out. Juxtaposed with the wallpaper was a bright Beavis and Butthead poster. A stack of CDs was scattered on the floor next to a portable CD player and discarded clothing. A teddy bear rested in the window.

It wasn't the neat and tidy room Noelle had kept at Sophie's age, but then the two of them were quite different. Still, seeing her sister sleeping brought back all sorts of shared memories. She'd not known how lonely she was in Chicago. Work had kept her distracted from the fact that she actually did miss her loony family.

Missed her mother's power-shopping. Missed her father's grandiose ideas, even if he was one of the few people to ever invest in a fast-food franchise that failed. His new venture, a birdfood franchise, seemed to be holding its own. And she'd missed a lot of Sophie's teenage years.

Sophie—who, it seemed, had grander ideas than their father. A singer. A career path filled with risk and possible heartbreak. There were no guarantees for anyone who followed a creative path. But then Hunter had, and he seemed to have done all right. Besides, uncertainty and change didn't scare Sophie the way it did her.

The fog outside began to clear and sunlight filtered into the bedroom. Sophie stirred and Noelle hoped the sunlight was a sign that everything would turn out all right on her baby sister's wedding day.

When Sophie opened her eyes, Noelle said, "Good morning, sleepyhead. We need to talk."

Sophie rubbed her eyes and sat up. "I hate to tell you, but I know all about the birds and the bees and penises." She grinned, then yawned.

"This is serious, Sophie."

Sophie paled. "Has something happened to Mother or Father?"

"No. It's about Marky."

"Something's happened to Marky?" Sophie grabbed Noelle. "What is it?"

"Nothing's happened to Marky. It's not something like that. I'm sorry if I scared you. But I do have something to tell you that—"

"What is it?" Sophie dropped her hands and settled back on the bed. "You *are* going to be at the wedding. You didn't get called back to Chicago for work, did you? You wouldn't miss my wedding, Noelle?"

She had missed a lot of things for Sophie—proms, plays, Sophie cheering at football games as head cheerleader. Noelle knew, that instant, that it had mattered to Sophie. Sophie had missed her not being a part of the family and living in another city. From the age of eleven Sophie had for all intent grown up a lonely only child, Noelle saw for the first time.

And now she was going to ruin the one thing she was there for. She was going to ruin Sophie's wedding day—or at the very least, put a damper on it.

She glanced over at the wedding gown, and quickly looked away, returning her attention to Sophie.

"It's not about me, it's about Marky, remember. I have something I have to tell you that I found out only yesterday evening. I don't know any way to tell you other than to just say it straight out."

Sophie's hands were twisting in the pale pink sheet, her perfectly manicured nails, a flash of bright red matching the two spots of color in her cheeks. She stared at Noelle, waiting anxiously.

"Okay." Noelle took a deep breath. "Yesterday evening when you were at your bachelorette party, the Palmer brothers paid me a visit."

The name didn't register with Sophie.

"They said there was something you should know before you married Marky today. Sophie, their sister Polly is pregnant. The claim is that she's pregnant with Marky's baby."

Sophie didn't say anything at first.

Noelle moved to sit beside her on the bed. "Sophie, I'm so sorry. I'd give anything not to have had to tell you. But I couldn't keep it from you. I couldn't let you marry without knowing. Please don't hate me, Sophie."

"It's not true," Sophie vowed.

"What?" Noelle pulled away to look at Sophie. "Do you think I would make up a lie like that? Do you think I would want to hurt you?"

"Polly's not pregnant," Sophie insisted, her chin thrust in the air.

"She's pregnant, all right."

"How do you know?"

"Her brothers took me to her last night. They wanted to prove to you that she was pregnant. They knew you wouldn't believe it unless—" Noelle stopped. She didn't want to get into the fact that they'd thought they were showing Sophie the evidence of Polly's pregnancy.

"How pregnant?" Sophie demanded on a sniff, her eyes glassy with unshed tears.

Noelle couldn't gauge the source of emotion calling up Sophie's tears. Was it anger, fear, jealousy... ? Probably all of those emotions and more.

"I don't know for sure how pregnant she is, but she looked like she was about seven months. She's tall and maybe she's further along and not showing it."

"It's not Marky's baby—she's lying." It was a statement of hope. Noelle followed Sophie's gaze to the wedding dress hanging on the door.

For Sophie's sake she prayed the hopeful accusation was true. But in her gut she didn't believe it.

"She'd do anything to stop the wedding. I believe in Marky. She just wants him to get a job, any old job. He's a really good musician. I know the band is going to be a success. I know it, Noelle."

"What if she's telling the truth, Sophie?"

"I don't know. This isn't supposed to be happening," Sophie said, pouting, not liking being a grown-up at all. "The photographer, the cake, the music, the hall, the flowers, my dress, all the food... Everything is all set. Mother and Father have spent so much money. Oh, Noelle, what am I going to do?"

Noelle hugged her. "You're going to talk to Marky. The two of you have to work it out." She glanced up at the neon-pink clock on the wall. "Whatever you do, you'd better do it soon. The wedding starts in a few hours. I'll go down and see if Mother needs any help with breakfast and you can call Marky, okay?"

Sophie wiped her tears and nodded.

"You don't hate me, do you, Sophie?"

Sophie forced a smile and shook her head no. As Noelle left the room, she heard Sophie pick up the phone.

"What's taking Sophie so long to come down?" Grace asked, as everyone sat around the breakfast table.

"She was calling Marky," Noelle answered, pulling a carton of milk from the refrigerator and filling a glass pitcher with it.

"She's going to be seeing him in a few hours."

"I know, Mother, but she needed to talk to him about something."

"Oh, what?" Grace asked, turning, concern in her eyes.

"Something about the honeymoon, I think," Noelle lied, not wanting to worry her mother until it was time to worry. This could be a tempest in a teapot. Sophie could be right; Polly could be lying. If she was, Marky and Sophie could work it out. Love could conquer anything—or so she'd heard.

Noelle set the pitcher of milk on the table beside a big box of doughnuts. Half of the doughnuts in the box were jelly, so she knew her father had gone to fetch them. He adored jelly doughnuts and had the jelly belly to prove it.

"Dad, what do you think of Marky?" Noelle asked, coming around the table to give him a peck on the cheek.

Jack looked up from the newspaper. "He's not good enough for my baby."

"All fathers say that about their daughters, Jack," Grace said, pouring milk into her cup of steaming coffee.

"Yeah, what do you really think, Father?"

"He's okay, I guess. He's eighteen, hardly even a person yet. Too young to be getting married. He doesn't even have a regular job."

"Listen to that." Grace laughed. "You weren't any different when we got married. It worked out okay, don't you think?"

"I was mature," Jack said in defense.

"Right," Grace pretended to agree, rolling her eyes at Noelle.

"I saw that," Jack said from behind the newspaper.

Noelle grinned at her mother while pouring a glass of cold milk to go with the apple-fritter doughnut she'd selected. It was heavy and rich and maybe would weigh down the butterflies in her stomach.

Just as she lifted it to take a bite, Sophie came tearing down the stairs, heading for the front door.

"Wait, where are you going?" Grace called out.

"I have to see Marky."

"But—"

It was no good, Grace was talking to dead air as Sophie sprinted out the door.

"I can't believe—"

"It's okay, Mother. I'll help you with all the details. Don't worry, I'm sure Sophie won't be gone long."

"I know, dear, but Sophie and I have a hair appointment in an hour. I hope she remembers."

"She's not going to forget something that important, Mother. Come on, Father and I will help. Let's make a list while we finish breakfast so we don't forget anything."

"Your father's list is short. He only has two things to do."

"What's that?" he asked, putting down the newspaper and reaching for another jelly doughnut.

"You've got to write checks," Grace answered.

"I've already written enough checks," he grumbled.

Grace ignored his complaint and began counting them off. "We need a check for the pastor, one for the church, another for the soloist, the organist, and one for the florist."

Hunter came walking into the kitchen in the middle of Grace's listing of who was to be paid.

When Grace was done, Jack looked up at Hunter. "That's why you should have sons—they're cheaper to marry off."

"I'll remember that, Jack," Hunter said, grinning and taking a jelly doughnut.

Jack beamed at Noelle. "He likes jelly doughnuts," he said approvingly.

"I like living dangerously," Hunter said with a wink. He took a big bite of his doughnut and the jelly oozed out. "You just never know where the jelly is going to end up."

"Yes, you do," Grace mumbled. "It ends up on the newspaper sticking together the funny pages."

For some reason that tickled Hunter.

"What was that other thing I had to do, Grace?" Jack asked, pouring another cup of coffee into his mug.

"Birdseed. Did you remember to bring home the birdseed?"

"Birdseed?" Hunter looked puzzled.

"For throwing at the bride and groom. Uncooked rice kills the birds when they peck it from the ground after the wedding."

"Good idea, birdseed," Hunter agreed.

"The birdseed is in the garage," Jack said, pleased he'd remembered.

"Good, you and Hunter can wrap up the little lace bundles for throwing."

"We can?" the two men chorused.

"You can," Grace and Noelle chorused.

"You know that might not be a bad item to carry in my store..." Jack mused, as Hunter shot Noelle a questioning look.

Noelle shrugged her shoulders to tell him she didn't know how things were going with Sophie.

"Has anyone seen Sophie?" he asked.

"I talked to her this morning and then she went off to see Marky," Noelle explained.

"Oh."

"I just hope she remembers our hair appointment," Grace muttered.

"Everything is going to be fine, Mother," Noelle assured her, though she herself was still feeling queasy.

"That was Sophie," Noelle said, hanging up the telephone in the living room. "She met Mother at the beauty salon."

"Guess that means the wedding's still on," Hunter said, trying to tie one of the thin white ribbons around a lace-covered pinch of birdseed.

"Of course, the wedding's still on," Jack responded. "Don't even think such a thing. Grace would—"

"I think we've got enough of these," Noelle said, adding her lace packet to the basket. "Why don't you and Hunter go ahead and get your showers now so there is enough hot water for everyone. I'll clean up here."

"Good idea," Jack said, happy to be done with the tedious task. Jack pushed back his chair. "I picked up your tuxedo with mine, Hunter. You might want to try it on since you ordered it on such short notice. You never know what can go wrong at a wedding."

Hunter looked over at Noelle. Both issued a silent hope that a wrong-size tuxedo was the only mishap on Sophie's wedding day.

Hunter followed Jack to get his tuxedo from the master bedroom. When he returned with it hung over one finger, Noelle had cleaned up the birdseed and scraps of lace and ribbon on the dining-room table.

"Do you think everything is okay?" he asked, tipping her chin and looking into her worried eyes. "You don't, do you?"

"Sophie hasn't talked to Marky."

"Why not?"

"She hasn't been able to find him."

Jack Perry was in his tuxedo, the very image of a proud father. He sat at the desk in the master bedroom writing out checks. "I think I could do this in my sleep."

"What, dear?" Grace asked absently, deciding against the pearl earrings she'd planned to wear with her sophisticated designer suit. Sophie had picked out the suit and nagged Grace until she'd bitten the bullet and bought it. It was beautiful, and Sophie might be the only daughter who married. This might be her only chance to be the mother of the bride. Noelle didn't seem so inclined.

"Write checks," Jack replied. "How much do I make the one for the organist for again?"

"A hundred dollars," Grace said, sorting through her earrings for the pair she'd decided on for sentimental reasons. They were the pair she'd worn on her wedding day.

"You know, Grace, when this wedding is over, you may just have to get a job," Jack teased.

Grace gave Jack a look. "No swearing on Sophie's wedding day, dear." They'd agreed when they married that Grace would never work—and she'd kept her part of the bargain.

Jack closed his checkbook and got up. He moved to zip up the inch of zipper Grace had missed at the top of her dress. He buzzed a kiss on her cheek. "How'd I get so smart at such a young age to pick you for my bride?"

"I've got a secret to share with you, Jack," Grace said, turning and putting her arms around his neck. "I picked you."

Hunter sat stretched out on the bed. The tuxedo fit him perfectly, Noelle thought, as she came out of the shower with a towel wrapped around her. When she turned on the blow dryer to start drying her hair, Hunter turned up the volume on the television so he could hear the St. Louis Cardinals' home game against the Chicago Cubs.

"You know in this house you have to cheer for the St. Louis Cardinals," Noelle called over to him.

Hunter glanced over at Noelle. "Hey, I'm cheering for the towel," Hunter said, grinning lasciviously. "Do you think if I concentrate on it hard enough, it'll fall?"

"Not a chance," she said, laughing as she cautiously raised her arms to dry the top of her head.

Hunter's attention went back to the baseball game and Noelle dropped her false cheer. Where was Marky? Why hadn't he been home? Why couldn't Sophie find him on his wedding day? Was he with Polly? She couldn't stand it if Sophie got left at the altar. It didn't bear thinking about.

She concentrated instead on putting her hair up in a French twist when she had it almost dry. It took all her effort, knowing Sophie was down the hall getting dressed in her bridal gown.

The wedding gown that knew too much.

She was beginning to think the wedding gown had some sort of spell on it.

Now she was really getting fanciful—or was it hysterical? She wiped at the smear of lipstick her unsteady hand had made, repairing it. The lipstick was a matte red that matched the racy dress Hunter had bought for her. She was working on her nerve to put it on. It was the last thing she planned to do before she went to the wedding.

She still had her doubts about it and the matching red satin shoes with the ribbon-wrap bows. The shoes were as bright as the ones Dorothy had worn in *The Wizard of Oz*.

She put in the diamond studs her father and mother had given her for graduation, dusted on a hint of blush and stood back to see the effect of her handiwork.

"That smells good," Hunter said, getting up from the bed and coming to where she stood in front of the mirror applying perfume.

"Thank you. Are you all ready for the wedding?"

"I'm ready. Nervous, but ready."

"Why? Because you're in the wedding?"

"Could be."

"It's not like you're the groom or anything."

"Sometimes I wonder what that would feel like."

"Really? I thought only girls daydreamed about their weddings."

"Well, it's not like I've given it much thought—until just lately."

Had he meant what she thought he meant? Noelle wondered, her heart leaping with hope.

"How about you?" he coaxed.

Afraid, she purposely misunderstood him. "I've been planning my wedding since I was a little girl."

Hunter laughed. "No wonder you couldn't resist trying on Sophie's wedding dress."

"Yes, and look at the trouble that got me into. I guess I should take it as a warning that some things just aren't meant to be," she hinted.

"You don't believe in fate? That if two people are right for each other that they will find a way to be together?"

"Do you?" she asked, looking at his reflection.

"Yes, I do," he answered, holding her gaze in the mirror.

A half smile formed on her lips.

"I think all weddings are meant to be. You make your own happiness, Noelle. And if something isn't meant to be..."

Her half smile gave away her worry.

"How can I make it all better?" he asked, kissing the nape of her neck as he stood behind her. "There's only an hour till the wedding, so there isn't time to make love," he teased, making her smile full-blown. "And besides, I'd muss your hair. We can't have everyone talking about that hussy sister who looked like she'd just gotten—ah, out of bed."

"You don't have to try to make me feel better," Noelle replied, placing her hand on his cheek in a gentle caress that said more than she'd have given away if she weren't so worried.

"But I want to," he said, sincere.

"This is something you can't kiss and make better. We'll just have to wait until we get to the church to see what will happen. Maybe everything will be all right."

"I'll make it all right," Hunter promised. Not for nothing had he created a comic-book character who made everything all right.

"I'm going down to Sophie's room to see how she's doing," Noelle said, stepping from his embrace.

"Okay, I'll go pretend to cheer for the Cardinals in case your father has the room bugged."

When she got to the doorway of Sophie's room, she saw Sophie hang up the phone with a frown.

"You still haven't talked to Marky..." Noelle said, coming into the room.

"No. Either he's not home yet, or he's getting ready and not answering the phone." Sophie tugged at the bodice of the wedding gown and went to pick up her veil.

"What are you going to do?" Noelle crossed the room to help Sophie with her veil.

"I'm going to trust Marky."

The sisters looked at each other for a long moment. "You're going through with the marriage."

"Yes."

Noelle didn't say anything. She decided she'd already said enough. It was Sophie's life. Sophie's decision. And, she sincerely thought, Sophie's mistake.

"Girls, we need to hurry," Grace said, coming into the room as Noelle settled the fingertip veil on Sophie's head. The old-fashioned veil was a beautiful complement to the wedding gown.

"Noelle—you're not even dressed. I'll help Sophie, you go get dressed. Hurry, now."

"You look so beautiful I think I'm going to cry," Noelle heard her mother say as she left the room.

"Mother, don't cry—"

Hunter was still stretched out on the bed watching the baseball game on television.

"What's the score?" she asked, rummaging through her luggage for panty hose.

"It's all tied up."

"Don't tell me that. We'll never get Father to the wedding."

"It's a tape, Noelle."

"Oh." She found the panty hose and took them and the red dress into the bathroom to get dressed. There was no graceful way to put on panty hose.

She didn't look at herself in the mirror when she had the dress on. She'd lose her nerve. Taking a calming breath, she left the bathroom to get her shoes.

"Could you help me with these?" She stood before the bed, dangling the red shoes by their inch-wide ribbon ties. Hunter looked away from the game on television and up at her. The pupils of his blue eyes widened, softened.

He patted the bed beside him.

She sat down and handed him the shoes.

He pulled her foot onto his lap and slipped her foot into the red satin shoe. Then, after wrapping the red ribbon ties in an X across her foot, he circled her narrow ankle and tied a bow.

He repeated the process with the other shoe.

When he was done, she gazed up at him.

Between them was the memory of the dressing room at Concepts.

He lowered his head and kissed the inside of her ankle. "You sure we have to go to this wedding?" he asked. The glint in his eye coaxed her to play. To be impulsive.

Oh, and how she wanted to play.

But her parents would never forgive her if she missed the wedding.

Sophie needed her.

Sometimes you just had to be responsible.

"We could be late," Hunter said, kissing the inside of her knee.

"I can't—" She slid from Hunter's grasp.

"I know."

"Hunter?"

He looked over to where she stood at the window.

"Thank you."

"For what?"

"For this weekend. I don't know what I would have done without you here."

He got up and went to her, put his arms around her. "You would have done just fine, Noellie."

She sniffed.

"Don't cry, you'll ruin your makeup. It'll be wet and rub off on my tuxedo and people will point and say that hussy sister has been necking with that stranger from the big city."

Noelle smiled. "St. Louis *is* a big city, Hunter."

"You just go on believing that."

She punched his arm.

"Feel better?"

She nodded.

"Okay, then let's go. We don't want to be late. Well, *I* want to be late, but you being such a responsible person and all . . ."

He offered his arm and she took it.

The way she'd been taking the shoulder he'd offered all weekend.

When they got downstairs the rental limo was there for Jack, Grace and Sophie. Jack and Grace beamed with pride as they settled Sophie in the limo.

Hunter and Noelle waved them off and followed in the white limo.

The church was small. Their regular church had been unable to accommodate them because it was all booked up with spring weddings.

But the small church had a lot of charm and the minister was friendly, if a bit absentminded.

Only family and close friends had been invited to the wedding ceremony. The big shindig would be the reception that evening.

Hunter followed the black limo in front of them to the church and parked right behind it.

On the curb in front of the church waiting in his tuxedo was Marky.

Noelle didn't know whether to be happy or sad that Sophie wasn't going to be left standing at the altar.

9

The service was late getting started.

The guests were restless, murmuring among themselves and glancing back past the pews behind them to the lobby of the church expectantly.

A baby cried.

Someone coughed.

The groomsmen told awful wedding-night jokes among themselves. The groom was still absent from the altar group.

The heavy church door thudded as a late arrival came hurrying in and took a seat at the rear.

The murmuring grew louder as minutes ticked by and the organist didn't begin playing.

Everyone looked at each other curiously as an usher came up and escorted Hunter to the back of the church.

A hush settled over the crowd—a hush of worried anticipation.

It didn't look good, Hunter thought when he reached the lobby at the rear where everyone was gathered. The bridesmaids—six wide-eyed nervous girls in party dresses—stood off to one side. They were looking at the scene that greeted Hunter.

Sophie was in tears in her father's arms.

Jack was trying to console her.

Another young woman was clinging to the intended groom. A pregnant young woman. Polly.

Noelle was trying to calm her mother, while Grace looked completely flustered, unable to muster a solution to "all that potato salad."

"What's going on?" Hunter asked the question that had a pretty obvious answer: nothing was going on, most especially a wedding.

"I'm not getting married—" Sophie sobbed. "Marky's... He's...not marrying me. He belongs with the mother of his baby."

"Hunter, could you stay with Mother while I go up to the front of the church to announce the wedding has been called off?" Noelle pleaded.

"No."

"Well, then, could you announce it?"

"No."

"Hunter, I don't know what else to do."

"I do. Notice how easily 'I do' tripped off my lips, Noelle. Suddenly I'm not nervous at all."

"What are you talking about...?"

"I think fate has just come knocking, Noelle. What do you think?"

"You mean?"

"Why don't you trade dresses with Sophie?" Winking, he couldn't resist adding, "I think the dress will fit you."

"But—"

"Yes, it'll fit," Grace encouraged as Marky and Polly slipped out of the church. Grace clapped her hands together with excited relief. "We can have a wedding, after all."

"But—"

"Listen to your mother, Noelle," Jack said, still comforting Sophie. "Everything is in place. It would be a shame—"

"But—"

"Don't you love me, Noelle?" Hunter asked bravely.

All eyes were on her and Hunter was looking very vulnerable.

"I'll meet you at the altar," she agreed, and everyone smiled as the mood in the church lobby elevated.

Hunter hurried to rejoin the groomsmen waiting anxiously at the front of the church.

The organist began playing and the guests turned their attention to the back of the church once again with a collective sigh of relief.

The bridesmaids in their floaty pale pink dresses started down the center aisle that had been laid with a white runner. Pastel ribbons fluttered from their spring bouquets as they walked. The entire church was decorated with an assortment of fresh white flowers whose fragrance filled the air.

The guests smiled at the bridesmaids as they passed by the pews. One girl made a misstep and nearly fell, but then bridesmaids were always nervous. The girl giggled in embarrassment, then regained her composure. Finally all the bridesmaids had taken their places at the altar and it was time for the bride.

The organ was silent for a few minutes and people were starting to crane their necks to see what the holdup was at the back of the church. Just as a buzz of questioning started, the organist began again.

"Dum...dum...de...dum...   Dum...dum... de...dum..."

Jack Perry appeared with a flash of white tulle at his side and everyone relaxed. A few older women smiled in approval at the old-fashioned veil that covered the bride's face—even if the wedding gown was off-the-shoulder.

The pair began their slow walk down the center aisle, the bride clinging to her father's arm.

"Oh..."

"Oh, my..."

"Did you see...?"

"Look at that...!"

"Why do you suppose...?"

"It's scandalous, that's what it is...."

"Mommy, look at her shoes—aren't they pretty...?"

"Well, I never. I can't believe Grace would let her daughter wear such a thing...."

"I think they're cool. You should be able to wear whatever you want to your wedding. I'm wearing combat boots to mine...."

"Can I wear red shoes like those when I get married, Mommy?"

The bride was glad of the tulle veil that hid her face. She could feel it flushing with color at all the whispered comments she heard as she walked down the aisle, her red shoes plainly visible.

The comments continued as she made her way on her father's arm to the front of the church. Her father squeezed her hand in a show of support. The look on her mother's face as they passed her pew at the front of the church was one of complete astonishment.

A gasp went up from the guests when Hunter stepped forward to take the bride from her father—in their fascination with the bride's red shoes, no one had noticed the groom hadn't arrived.

What was going on?

"Hunter, what are you doing!" Valerie Valor asked, incredulous, tugging on his arm.

There was whispered concern sweeping the crowd as Jack Perry took his seat in the pew next to Grace and bent his head to speak with her.

"Hunter—" Valerie repeated urgently.

The minister cleared his throat to gain the guests' full attention before starting the service. His face had a sheen of perspiration and his gray hair was in slight disarray from the minor fender bender he'd been in on his way to the church—he wasn't seeing as well as he used to.

Still somewhat flustered, he leafed through his Bible nervously. Unable to find his notes, the minister glanced down at the floor around him—to no avail.

He looked at the couple in front of him and smiled reassuringly. Finally giving up on his notes, he cleared his throat a second time and began.

"Friends and family, we are all gathered today to join...ah...this lovely couple...in holy matrimony...."

"Hunter...don't tune me out, this is serious," Valerie said.

The minister pulled at his ear and then announced, "The happy couple will now recite the vows they've composed themselves.... Ahem..."

Hunter, who'd been looking at the veiled bride, spun his head to look at the minister.

The minister nodded, encouraging him to begin.

"Now what are you going to do, Hunter? How are you going to write yourself out of this one?" Valerie asked.

Hunter turned back to the bride and took her hand. It was shaking, but then so was his. He gave her hand a slight, reassuring squeeze, looked down at her red shoes and then back up at her and smiled.

"From the first time I heard your voice, I knew I would be yours. I knew it was good that we—I knew we were meant to share an adventure—life's adventure. I'm so happy that you chose me as the man for you. I promise to honor your choice and to be here for you, to be the man you need."

"I guess that's the best in the way of romance one could hope for," Valerie said grudgingly, "from a cartoonist."

"You took my breath away from the first time I saw you," the bride countered. "At the time I had a wedding on my mind and you said you loved weddings. I didn't know how much, but I'm glad I found such a romantic superhero."

The minister looked even more puzzled and the guests began to whisper again as the minister asked for the rings.

"Rings?" Valerie repeated. "Did I nod off? I don't recall you buying any rings." Valerie threw her arms in the air, giving up.

The groomsman who'd slipped over to best man came forward and bent his head toward Hunter, who whispered something. The groomsman nodded, handed Hunter the rings from his pocket and returned to his place.

"Oh, that's pathetic, Hunter— You're not really going to exchange..."

Hunter handed the minister the rings.

The minister looked down at the rings he'd dropped with a thud in his open Bible, and then back up at Hunter.

Hunter nodded for the minister to continue.

"You are," Valerie confirmed.

The minister held up the clunky college ring with the red-faceted stone. He handed it to Hunter. "Place the ring on her finger and repeat after me—'With this ring I thee wed.'"

Hunter took the bride's left hand and looked at her as he slipped the ring on her third finger where it wobbled as he repeated, "With this ring I thee wed."

"Is this a Kodak moment or what, Hunter? I bet the DeBeers diamond company is hiring a bit on you right this minute. You've single-handedly set fine jewelry back a century," Valerie said.

"And now the bride." The minister handed her the other college ring with a blue-faceted stone. "Repeat after me, 'With this ring I thee wed.'"

The bride shoved the ring on Hunter's finger as a tear slid down her cheek.

"A perfect fit. *Quel surprise*, eh, Hunter? Guess this was just meant to be," Valerie added.

The bride and groom turned to the minister expectantly.

"Oh. You, ah, I now pronounce you man and wife—I mean, husband and wife," the minister said, flustered. "And you may now kiss your bride."

"Hunter, do you know what you've done?" Valerie demanded. "This isn't a fantasy. You can't use your eraser to make it right."

Hunter lifted the bride's veil and a wave of shock rolled over the assemblage.

"It's not only not the same groom, it's not the same bride," a shocked woman behind Grace said.

The woman leaned forward and tapped Grace. "I thought your daughter was getting married."

"My daughter did get married," Grace informed the woman. "My older daughter."

Hunter had pulled Noelle into his arms. Her earlier tears from nerves had vanished. The kiss he bestowed on her went on... and on... and on...."

"Hunter this is a PG crowd," Valerie chastised.

The kiss was interrupted by the organ music, festive and loud.

"Da...da...di...da...da...da...da..."

Hunter wrapped Noelle's hand around his arm as they turned to face the crowd. He looked down at his college ring on her finger. "I'll get you some tape so it'll stay on," he promised.

"At least it matches my shoes," Noelle said, smiling at the red stone. Just before they returned down the aisle arm in arm, she clicked the heels of her red shoes together and said, "Hunter, I don't think we're in Kansas anymore."

While the guests remained seated, still in shock, Hunter hurried Noelle to the rear of the church.

"Now you've really gone and done it, Hunter. You've made a promise you're going to have to keep," Valerie declared, approving.

Before them, as if in slow motion, Noelle saw a glimpse of red. Sophie had stayed to watch the ceremony, even when it was supposed to have been her day. Even when Marky had told her Polly's baby was his.

How could Noelle be happy when she knew what Sophie had gone through minutes before Hunter had decided to make the substitution that would bail Sophie out.

On impulse, Noelle tossed the bridal bouquet at Sophie.

It sailed high into the air and traveled slowly to the pew where Sophie sat . . . and landed in the lap of the U.S. Navy pilot in white dress uniform sitting beside her.

The surprised pilot lifted the bouquet and turned to Sophie. His dark eyes looked into her blue ones. Seeming to suddenly remember he had the bridal bouquet, he handed it to Sophie, saying, "I believe this was meant for you."

Meanwhile Hunter grabbed a bunch of white flowers tied with satin ribbon to the last pew and handed them to Noelle as he hustled them to the waiting limo for a chance to continue that interrupted kiss.

PG just wasn't his style.

Sophie and the navy man stood with the others outside the church tossing birdseed at the limo as it drove off.

Wishing hard, she flung her tiny bundle of birdseed, and cried out, "Be happy!"

10

————◆————

Hunter escorted Noelle from the registration desk at one of St. Louis's ritziest hotels toward the elevator. They were on their way to the bridal suite Hunter had just wangled for a few hours.

"Think you're pretty hot stuff, don't you?" Noelle said.

The elevator doors closed on Hunter's wicked grin. "Well, I did perform a rescue today. That's something, don't you think?"

"A rescue, huh?"

"Yeah." Hunter put his finger on her nose. "I saved your mother's potato salad."

Noelle took his finger and kissed the tip of it.

"I don't play by the rules, as you may have noticed, my bride—witness the lack of a marriage license."

"Wait till my father thinks of that!"

"Don't worry. The main thing is we saved the potato salad when Sophie decided to call off the wedding."

"Poor Sophie."

"I don't know, she didn't look very unhappy at the reception in that red dress of yours, dancing with that guy in the white dress uniform."

"No, she didn't, did she? Makes me think that Polly was right. Sophie was marrying Marky to sing in his band."

"Sophie's going to be just fine. Your parents are going to be just fine about this eventually. And in a minute you and I are going to be just fine." Hunter scooped her up in a billow of white tulle just as the elevator doors swished open on the floor of the bridal suite.

Hunter kissed Noelle soundly as he kicked the door to the suite shut behind them. "I'll give you one thing, my beautiful bride. You give great adventure," he said, as he set her down. He smiled, glancing at her feet. "And you don't give bad shoe, either...."

"I think you're having way too much fun," Noelle retorted, sliding him a saucy look.

He stepped toward her, pulled her into an embrace and slipped his hand into the strapless crumb-catcher bodice of her wedding dress. "Bride, I have only just begun to have fun."

There was a knock at the door. A discreet knock.

They looked at each other, puzzled. With a great show of reluctance Hunter withdrew his hand from the "toy chest" and went to the door.

"Yes?" he said through the closed door.

"Room service, sir."

"But I didn't order anything—"

"Compliments, sir..."

Hunter looked at Noelle, shrugged, and opened the door.

The bellman handed Hunter a silver bucket with a bottle of iced champagne nestled in it. "Compliments of the hotel."

Hunter laughed. "Thanks." He took some money from his wallet and passed it to the bellman who nodded his thanks and pulled the door closed.

Hunter leaned back against the door. "Finally we're alone. Your sister isn't at the end of the hall, your parents aren't downstairs, the saleslady isn't hovering.... We're—"

"I'm hungry. Let's call room service."

"What?"

"How do you like marriage so far, Hunter?" Valerie taunted.

"I'm hungry," Noelle repeated.

"Didn't you eat at the reception?" Hunter asked, incredulous. "How can you be hungry?"

"I couldn't eat with all those people watching me."

Hunter crossed the room, set down the bucket of champagne and picked up the phone. He ordered up the chef's specialty with instructions to leave it outside the door.

"Happy?"

"Very."

"Let's have a toast to your happiness." Hunter opened the champagne with a pop.

"I *am* happy, Hunter," Noelle said, sighing with contentment. A girl would have to be a fool not to know that it didn't get any better than the bridal suite at the Ritz with Hunter Ashton.

"So you're admitting you're not really angry with me. That I make you happy. Happy enough to let me drink champagne from your slipper?" he asked, eyebrows wagging lasciviously. He paused after filling his champagne glass, waiting before filling hers.

"Hunter Ashton you are not going to drink champagne from Noelle's shoe—for one thing, they won't hold champagne," Valerie admonished.

"Maybe I should rephrase that—I meant to say lick champagne from your shoe," Hunter said to Noelle, considering Valerie's point.

"I don't think that's a good idea, Hunter."

"Besides she'd squish when she went back to the reception," Valerie said.

That would assume, Hunter thought, someone planned on going back to the reception.

He poured her a glass of champagne, unable to do battle and win with two women.

"To happy ever after," Hunter toasted, clinking his champagne glass with hers. "And to my removing the white lace garter from your thigh...I can assure you of that."

"Plan to keep it as a souvenir of battle, do you?"

"Battle?"

"There's no marriage license," she reminded him.

"And if there was?" he said, tossing her on the high, cushy bed.

The game was suddenly over.

They weren't playing anymore.

The groom knew it.

The bride knew it.

"Hunter—"

"Yes, or no...?"

"You're a romantic—"

"Fool, I know."

For a superhero, he looked really vulnerable.

"Well . . . ?" he prompted.

"Are you sure— How much champagne did you drink at the reception, Hunter?"

"Not *that* much."

"It's this dress—"

"What?"

"It wants me to be its bride. There must be some sort of curse on it. I put it on during a weak moment— That's what happens when you give in to impulse. Everything gets so crazy and . . ."

"Wonderful," he supplied.

"Noelle?"

"What?"

"It's not the dress."

"It's not?"

"It's the shoes."

"Then I'm taking them off."

His grin was decidedly wicked. "You'll get no argument from me."

"Hunter?"

"What?"

She crooked her finger for him to come closer and he complied. She reached up and loosened his tuxedo tie. "That was a yes, Hunter. Pay attention."

"Really?"

"As real as it gets, Hunter."

"Then let the honeymoon begin." He pulled her into an embrace for the tenderest kiss a wild man could give.

"Uh-uh, Hunter." She slipped out from under him. "I didn't really know it when I was getting married. I want to *really* know it when I'm having my honeymoon. We get the wedding license first thing Monday and then we *plan* the honeymoon. The license will make our wedding today legal."

Hunter stared at her from the bed. "Are you telling me yes *and* no?"

"Ah... You're starting to pay attention." She crooked her finger for him to come closer and he did. She reached up and retied his bow tie.

"You're serious. You really want to wait."

"Sandy beaches, moonlight, skinny-dipping."

"All right, we'll wait. Two weeks, max."

"Perfect."

Epilogue

➤◆➤

"**Y**ou know you aren't getting any work done," Valerie complained, picking up a dirty sock and making a face.

"I'm on vacation. Give me a break, I just got married two weeks ago and I haven't even been on my honeymoon yet. We did everything backwards from the splashy family wedding on Saturday night to the wedding licence on Monday."

"I know. That's why you've been so cranky."

"I'm *not* cranky."

"Right."

"*Daphne is cranky.*"

"Boy, is she ever. You're in deep doo-doo for not inviting her to your wedding."

"I can't help it. I didn't know I was going to get married."

"Well, you'd better introduce her to your wife soon before Daphne writes you out of the family. It's not like you have a lot of family to lose."

"I've already thought of that. Daphne is driving us to the airport today so we can fly off on our honeymoon."

"Clever boy, you've thought of everything, haven't you—except the new outfit you promised me."

"Oh, I've thought of that, too. I just haven't told you about it yet."

"So, tell me before I get too old to wear it!"

"Now who's cranky?"

"Hunter—"

"Okay, okay. What would you think of a pair of faded jeans and a tank top?"

"Jeans and a tank top? Where'd you ever come up with that?"

Hunter didn't answer. He smiled, recalling how sexy Noelle had looked silhouetted in the lighted doorway of the Venice Café wearing the jeans and tank top he'd lifted from the laundromat.

"I like it, Hunter. Good work. Maybe some kind of insignia for the tank top—think about it. Oh, and combat boots would go good with it. Yeah, that'd be perfect. You've got it, Hunter."

"No combat boots."

"Hunter, I'm not wearing those red shoes."

"I know."

"I'm certainly not wearing bowling shoes."

"I know."

"What, then?"

"Nothing. Well, maybe a little grape toenail polish would be a nice touch."

"Barefoot? Forget it, Hunter. The next step is pregnant. Superheroines do *not* get pregnant."

"No, no. I was thinking of teaching you a little martial arts—"

The doorbell rang, interrupting his mental dialogue with Valerie.

He turned down the air conditioner on his way to answer the door.

"Daphne, you're early."

"I knew I'd have to help you pack."

"Shows what you know," he informed her, slouching down in his chair in front of his drawing board, and scratching his chest. "I'm already packed. In case you didn't know it, Daphne, you don't need much gear for a honeymoon."

Daphne let his remark ride and came over to see what he'd been working on, accidentally knocking a pen off the drawing table and smearing India ink on the floor.

"I'll get it," Hunter volunteered, going to the kitchen to get a cloth to wipe up the ink. "Take a look at Valerie's new outfit and tell me what you think."

Daphne looked up from the piece of bristol board on the drawing table when Hunter returned to wipe up the ink.

"Well, at least she won't catch her death of cold in the wintertime," Daphne sniffed. "Why is it so cold in here?"

"It's hot in here."

"It is not." Daphne flipped her blond hair back and peered at Hunter. "Are you all right? Your eyes look a little glassy. Maybe you should let me take your temperature."

"Get away from me with that nurse stuff, Daphne. I'm perfectly fine." He scratched his arm. "I'm just excited to be going on my honeymoon. That's bound to raise any guy's temperature, don't you think?"

"I suppose. Why don't you let me take your temperature anyway."

"Back off," Hunter said, holding up two fingers in a sign of the vampire cross. "There's as much chance of me letting you do nurse things to me as there is of me finding a rare issue of the first comic to feature Superman."

"All right, all right, be stubborn, but you look kinda peaked to me."

"You're just mad because I packed all by myself. You nag me to grow up and then you get annoyed when I do."

"Did you remember to pack—"

"Yes. I packed my Speedo, my suntan lotion, megavitamins to keep up my strength—" he winked "—and condoms just to be safe," he ribbed.

"Hunter, really."

"Come on over and look at this brochure for where we're going. Doesn't it look great? A little sun and rum, and I'll be fine."

"I thought you said you felt all right."

"I do. I do. Will you quit with the nurse stuff."

"All right. Then tell me what my new sister-in-law is like."

Hunter smiled. "You're gonna love her."

"What makes you so sure?"

"Because she's just like you. She's practical, smart, and won't cut me any slack."

"I'm surprised you had the sense to marry her. She sounds too good to be true."

"You know you ought to have another one of those bachelor auctions. Maybe you could find a nice doctor—"

"There are no nice doctors. They all think they're—"

"It's Noelle," Hunter said, getting up to answer the doorbell. "Wait right here, you're going to love her," he promised, rubbing his eyes.

Hunter made the introductions and watched the two women he loved size each other up.

"Do you think Hunter looks peaked?" Daphne asked Noelle, deciding Noelle was indeed okay.

"Daphne, you think everyone looks peaked. Tell her to clock off duty as Nurse Daphne, Noelle," Hunter said, scratching his neck.

"What are you scratching?" Noelle approached Hunter for a closer inspection.

She began unbuttoning his shirt.

"Noelle, wait till we at least get to the islands to start celebrating our honeymoon!" He grinned over at Daphne and winked. "It's hell being so sexy my woman can't keep her hands off me. But what's a stud like me to do? I'm doomed to be her plaything."

Noelle felt Hunter's forehead with the back of her wrist and shook her head. "Daphne, I think you'd better get the thermometer. I was afraid of this as soon as I found out about Barbara Ann."

"Barbara Ann? There haven't been any other women, Noelle. I promise."

"I know. Barbara Ann is the little girl who lives in my apartment building."

Hunter looked completely puzzled as Daphne went to his bathroom to retrieve the thermometer from his medicine cabinet—a little too eagerly, he thought.

"How do you feel? Do you feel hot?" Noelle asked.

"Maybe a little," he admitted. "But it's nothing. I'm telling you—"

Daphne returned with the thermometer in hand. She shook it down to 98.6. "Okay, Hunter, open wide and then try to keep your mouth shut for a few minutes."

"You are going to have your hands full with him, you know, Noelle," Daphne warned. "He won't pick up after himself. He isn't house-trained at all. There probably isn't any male in the city of Chicago more spoiled rotten, and I'm afraid I'm responsible."

"Wait a minute, you can't talk about me like—"

"Mouth shut, Hunter," Daphne instructed.

He frowned at her, but followed her instructions, knowing Daphne now had an ally in Noelle. His life was going to be—

"He does have some good qualities," Noelle said, defending her husband.

Hunter smiled and nearly flipped out the thermometer.

Daphne caught it before it dropped to the floor. "Just as I thought, you have a temperature. You're not going anywhere but to bed."

"That's what honeymoons are, Daphne. You should try it sometime."

"No honeymoon trip, Hunter. You're going to bed now. You're sick," Daphne insisted.

"Sick? I can't be sick. I've waited two long weeks for... for... Noelle has been working overtime since we got married so we could take a honeymoon. I haven't hardly even seen her since we got married. I'm going—"

"She's right. You are sick," Noelle agreed.

"I would know if I was sick," Hunter argued. "So, okay, maybe I'm feeling a little hot and itchy, but—"

"Look at your chest." Noelle pointed.

Hunter looked down.

"You could play connect-the-dots," Daphne said.

"It's nothing. It's just some sort of rash or something." Hunter dismissed the red dots, rationalizing.

"It's some sort of rash, all right," Noelle agreed. "It's probably shingles."

"Shingles!"

Noelle turned to Daphne. "Barbara Ann, the little girl in my apartment building, came down with chicken pox just as I was leaving to go to St. Louis with Hunter for my sister's wedding."

"But that was two weeks ago," Hunter reasoned.

"Two weeks is the incubation period," Daphne informed him. "Noelle's right. Shingles is the adult version of chicken pox."

"Does this mean I can't—"

"That's right." Daphne read him off the recipe for recovery. It didn't involve sun, sandy beaches or rum on an island.

After she told Noelle what to do for Hunter, she left, as she hadn't had chicken pox as a child, either.

A half hour later Hunter was propped up in bed in a dark room wearing his Speedo with Noelle sitting beside him.

"How come *you* didn't get the shingles? You're the one who was exposed to Barbara Ann."

"Because I've already had the chicken pox, that's why."

"Read to me from the travel brochure," Hunter said, looking pitiful.

Noelle picked up the brochure and obliged. "'Rumbling surf, sailboats silhouetted against the sky, thatch-roofed bar, tables in the sand, wicked rum punch, snoozing in hammocks, turtles racing on the beach, swaying palm trees, thong bikinis...'"

"Come here," Hunter said, taking the travel brochure from her hand and pulling her toward him.

"I thought you were sick."

"Not that sick. Daphne didn't say anything about not having a honeymoon, she just said I had to stay at home and go to bed."

"I don't know, Hunter—"

"Just be gentle with me. You'll have to do most of the work because I'm sick, you know...."

Noelle chuckled. "Daphne was right. You are spoiled rotten."

Hunter moved his hand beneath her crop top.

"And fresh at the same time..."

"Noelle—"

"Um...what?"

"Put your bikini on and get the suntan oil while you're at it."

"Hunter Ashton, you're making me blush."

"Not yet, Noellie, but I will...."

* * *

"It's not funny." Valerie stomped her foot.

"I'm laughing."

"It's not funny, Hunter."

"I'm the cartoonist, I'll be the judge of what's funny."

Valerie glared at him. "I knew this would happen. I just knew it."

"Well, you're the one who wanted to have an adventure with Eric the Great. I told you that I didn't like the idea."

"Then you shouldn't have listened to me. You're the one who's got the pen. You're the one who's supposed to be in control."

"Right. Like I'm in control where any woman is concerned. Daphne and Noelle already plot against me all the time. And you, well, we both know I've never been able to control you."

"That's because you're not disciplined."

"If I were disciplined, I wouldn't be creative. And if I weren't creative, you wouldn't exist."

"Don't go getting all reasonable on me, Hunter. I'm not used to it. I think Noelle is beginning to—"

"If you want to blame someone, blame Noelle. She's the one who got carried away with the suntan lotion."

"I don't want to hear about it."

"I didn't want to hear about all the details with Eric the Great, either, Valerie, but I did. Face it, Valerie, you and I are like Daphne and me. We share a mind. Just like I always know what my twin is thinking, we always know what each other is thinking. We share everything. I want you to be happy, too."

"I knew this was going to happen when you wouldn't let me wear the combat boots. I knew it. As soon as I started going barefoot, I saw what it was going to lead to. I warned you, but no—"

"You're a wuss of a superheroine, Valerie. You don't see Noelle complaining. She goes to work, so you have to go to work, too."

"Noelle doesn't have to pummel people right after tossing her cookies every morning from morning sickness. All your wife has to do is go to her bank and do math."

Hunter chuckled. "Come on, Valerie. We both know math is hard. You've seen my checkbook."

"Funny, Hunter. You're a laugh riot."

"I know. That's why I make big bucks."

"I think it's time you started spending some of those big bucks on a new outfit for me. These jeans are beginning to get a little snug around the waist," Valerie said, tugging.

"Okay, if you promise to stop complaining, I'll give you a new outfit."

What kind of outfit?

"I don't know. I'll talk to Noelle about it tonight." He talked to Noelle about everything. It was wonderful, he was finding, sharing things with someone you loved. Waking up with them beside you.

"Does Noelle know what you've done?"

Hunter chuckled. "I think the morning sickness is a pretty good clue."

"I'm talking about the house," Valerie said, shooting him a pained look.

"No. She doesn't know. I want to surprise her."

"What are you waiting for?"

"The decorator."

"Noelle's not going to like that. She'll want to decorate the house herself. Gosh, don't you men know anything?"

"Eric's going to take exception to talk like that, Valerie. I'm only decorating one room as a surprise for Noelle when I bring her home from the hospital."

"You mean the nursery." Valerie smiled at the goosey look that word brought to his face.

He couldn't believe he was going to be a father. He couldn't believe anyone could be as happy as he was. It was the reason he'd gotten Valerie hitched. He thought the whole world should be as happy as he was.

"But she only just found out she was pregnant. You've got seven months yet to go before the baby is due. More if the baby is late."

Seven months of pampering Noelle. He was going to love it.

Daphne was amazed he'd even learned to pick up his own socks. Hell, *he* was amazed.

"I'm going to need all the time I can get," he assured Valerie. First I'm going to have to figure out what you do with a pregnant superheroine, and second, I'm going to need time to make up my mind whether to paint the nursery pink or blue."

"You might want to paint it half-and-half," Valerie offered with a grin.

"Why would I want to do that?"

"Think about it, Hunter. You...Daphne... There's a really good chance the baby could be twins."

"That's not funny, Valerie."

* * * * *

How I spent my summer holiday
by Morgan Brigham, age 29

Traci and I used to spend every summer together. But that was when we were kids, back when our biggest goal was to see who could stuff more spiders down whose back.

I honestly didn't expect to get stranded with her here today at the old cabin. But now I'm glad. Wow, she has changed! This night-alone-in-the-dark is starting to have definite possibilities...

But, of course, I'm not the kind to kiss and tell. And I have a more important mission in mind: I've got to convince her not to marry Dr Dull. She deserves so much more! She deserves someone who will treat her like an equal; someone who will challenge her, who will keep her life exciting—

Hey! That sounds like someone I know!

MARIE FERRARELLA

Traci on the Spot

About the author

Dearest person who has picked up this book,

All right, I admit it. I'm a cartoonaholic. Cartoons have always fit prominently into my life. I learned how to read by reading wonderful comic books. I progressed to 'Superman' (in every single publication that bore his name) and could have graduated in super heroes (ask me a question, any question, I dare you). By the time I got my master's degree in Shakespeare (yes, I read comic books through college), I could not only intelligently discuss the bard's plays, but I could also tell you all of the people who figured into Superman's life whose initials were L.L. Even now I feel my day is incomplete without opening the paper and reading the funnies. I love to smile, and if a laugh can be tucked into it, all the better.

That was why writing *Traci on the Spot* was such a kick for me. I could imagine writing a daily comic strip that reflected my life. (Hey, I can deal with pressure—I have two kids, a husband and a German shepherd who thinks she's a lap dog.) I hope Traci (and I) manage to entertain you for a little while.

With love and gratitude,

Marie Ferrarella

To all the writers
of the comics
and comic strips
that have fuelled my imagination,
brightened my day,
or made me laugh.
Thank you.

Prologue

➤◀

Morgan Brigham slowly set down his coffee cup on the kitchen table and stared at the comic strip in the center of his paper. It was nestled in among approximately twenty others that were spread out across two pages. But this was the only one he made a point of reading faithfully each morning at breakfast.

This was the only one that mirrored her life.

He read each panel twice, as if he couldn't trust his own eyes. But he could. It was there, in black-and-white.

Morgan folded the paper slowly, thoughtfully, his mind not on his task. So Traci was getting engaged.

The realization gnawed at the lining of his stomach. He hadn't a clue as to why.

He had even less of a clue why he did what he did next.

Abandoning his coffee, now cooling, and the newspaper, and ignoring the fact that this was going to make him late for the office, Morgan went to get a sheet of stationery from the den.

He didn't have much time.

Traci Richardson stared at the last frame she had just drawn. She ran her teeth thoughtfully over her lower lip. Debating, she glanced toward the creature sprawled out on the kitchen floor.

"What do you think, Jeremiah? Too blunt?"

The dog, part bloodhound, part mutt, idly looked up from his rawhide bone at the sound of his name. Jeremiah gave her a look that she felt free to interpret as ambivalent.

"Fine help you are. What if Daniel actually reads this and puts two and two together?"

Not that there was all that much chance that the man who had proposed to her, the very prosperous and busy Dr. Daniel Thane, would actually see the comic strip she drew for a living. Not unless the strip was taped to a bicuspid he was examining.

It wasn't that Daniel belittled the cartoon figure that had begun as a drawing on the bottom of a Christmas card to a childhood friend and evolved into a morning staple that held regular meetings with people over cereal and milk every day in thousands of houses across America. After all, *Traci on the Spot* could be viewed as her alter ego, which, at times, was exactly what she was.

Like now.

But lately, Daniel had gotten so busy he'd stopped reading anything but the morning headlines of the *Times*. His thriving practice had almost doubled in the past year and he was talking about taking on yet another partner.

Still, you never knew. Murphy's Law being what it was, he just might be feeling guilty and make a point of reading her strip.

"I don't want to hurt his feelings," Traci continued, using the dog she had saved from certain execution more than six years ago as a sounding board. She turned in the swivel chair to face the animal. "It's just that Traci is overwhelmed by Donald's proposal and, see, she thinks the ring is going to swallow her up." To prove her point, Traci held up the drawing for the dog to view.

This time, Jeremiah didn't even bother to lift his head.

He was probably used to the sound of her voice droning on in the background, she thought with a sigh.

The advantage of working out of her house was that she wasn't chained to a desk or a clock. She could come and go as she pleased, and if she felt like getting up in the middle of the night and working on a strip in her pajamas, there was no one to tell her not to. The downside was that there wasn't anyone to talk to, to use as a *real* sounding board for her ideas.

Oh, sure, she could always call into the office and talk to Matthew or Jill in the art department. But having to listen to a metallic voice offer her selections from a menu before she could get through to either of them took away some of the spontaneity from the situation.

And she was nothing if not spontaneous.

So why didn't she just jump at this chance to become Mrs. Daniel Thane?

Traci stared moodily at the small velvet box on the corner of her kitchen counter, where it had sat since Daniel had asked her to marry him last Sunday.

She blew out a breath and leaned back so far

in her chair it almost toppled over. Grabbing the edge of the drawing board, she steadied herself, but not before her pens went flying to the floor, a pointed rainbow scattering all over.

Out of the corner of her eye she saw that the sudden commotion had caught the dog's attention. Jeremiah came trotting over to investigate. And to sample.

Traci made a dive for the floor and got to the pens first. "Back. You don't help with the strip, you can't eat a pen."

Gathering them together, she deposited the pens back into the tray. And then studied the last frame again. The Traci character's query fit her quirky nature.

That settled it, she decided. It was going into the paper.

"Daniel isn't going to see it," she told the disinterested dog, more to convince herself than anything else. "He probably won't have time to see any of them."

But Daniel was going to suspect something eventually, she mused.

The very fact that she hadn't grabbed the ring from his hand and slid it onto her finger should have given him a clue that she had doubts about their union.

Traci sighed, dragging both hands through her hair. The blond strands curled around her fingers, momentarily straightening before springing back. What was the matter with her? Daniel Thane was a catch by any definition. A wonderful, kind, loving man who was a doctor, for heaven's sake. Okay, a dentist, but that was almost as good.

So what was her problem?

Her problem, if she were honest with herself, was that she wanted a combination. A mixture of Daniel's stability and kindness and Rory's charm. Rory Conway was an unemployed actor who had been in and out of her life before Daniel had ever entered it.

"Not unemployed," Rory had maintained with alacrity. "Just between jobs." He'd been between jobs for a long while. Longer than they had been together. Rory's main attribute, other than being tall, dark and deadly handsome, was that he could make a woman feel every inch a female in flaming capital letters, from the very tips of her frosted hair down to the edge of her pearl pink polished toes.

And he didn't have a nesting bone in his body.

But Daniel did. All of Daniel leaned toward nesting. Home, hearth, family, that was all he'd talked about this Sunday as she had sat there, holding the velvet box in her numbed fingers, waiting to be struck by that sunny ray of happiness. And waiting and waiting. Daniel said he wanted to take care of her, to fulfill her every whim. And he was even willing to let her think about it before she gave him her answer.

Guilt nibbled at her. She should be dancing up and down, not wavering like a weather vane in a gale. After all, she did love him. Who wouldn't?

But maybe, just maybe, she didn't love him enough.

Still, he was generous, loving and patient. "Can a man get any better than that?" Traci asked aloud.

Jeremiah, having denuded the rawhide bone of its tan color, moaned mournfully in reply.

She waved her hand at him and huffed. "What do you know?"

Pronouncing the strip completed, Traci scribbled her signature in the corner of the last frame and then sighed. Another week's work put to bed. Though she was completely scattered about everything else in her life, when it came to the strip, that was a different matter. There she adhered to schedules and deadlines as if her life, and not just her livelihood, depended on it. It was, at times, as if *Traci on the Spot* reflected her very soul.

"Beats lying on a couch one hour a week," she assured Jeremiah, who couldn't care less. He was settling in for a nice nap in the middle of a warm sunspot pooling on the tile floor.

Very carefully, she slid the strip into her portfolio along with the others she'd completed. That done, she glanced at the pile of mail on the counter. She'd been bringing it in steadily from the mailbox since Monday, but the stack had gotten no farther than her kitchen. She hadn't opened any of it. Most of the envelopes probably contained bills, anyway. Those she allowed to marinate.

The rest were undoubtedly ads and would only

go into the recycle bin. No hurry for that, either. But since she was finished with her work, she thought she might as well make a stab at cleaning, and sorting letters was the least heinous of the annoying chores that faced her.

Traci slid onto the kitchen stool and picked up a handful of mail. She began sorting, tossing envelopes into piles like a dealer at an Atlantic City gambling table.

"Bill, bill," she read, tossing, "ad, petition, pleas for contributions, catalog, bill." It was sad how the bills seemed to outnumber everything else. She shook her head as she continued tossing envelopes onto the uneven piles. "Letter."

Traci paused as she turned the long envelope over. The return address was embossed and in script. Morgan Brigham. Why would Morgan be writing to her? It wasn't Christmas.

Curious, Traci tore open the envelope and quickly scanned the short note inside.

Dear Traci,
I'm putting the summerhouse up for sale. Thought you might want to come up and see it one more time before it goes up on the block. Or make a bid on it yourself. If memory serves, you once said you wanted to buy it. Either way, let me know. My number's on the card.

Take care,
Morgan

P.S. Got a kick out of *Traci on the Spot* this week.

Traci folded the letter, then looked down at the card in her hand. He read her strip. She hadn't known that. A feeling of pride silently coaxed a smile to her lips. She always got that happy-shy reaction when she found out people read *Traci on the Spot*.

After a beat, the rest of his note seeped into her consciousness. He was selling the house.

The summerhouse. A faded white building with brick trim. Suddenly, memories flooded her mind.

Skinny-dipping in the lake when she was five until her mother and her aunt had ordered her and her cousin Adam out of the water. Morgan had told on them. She got even by putting a spider in his bed. He absolutely hated spiders.

Long, lazy afternoons that shone through bright green leaves and felt as if they would never end.

Morgan—his long, lanky body covered with red bumps—biting his lower lip as she applied globs of calamine lotion to his arms and back.

Other memories winked in and out of her mind like fireflies with a mission.

He was going to sell it. Or his parents were. Traci wondered why her mother hadn't told her anything about this. Julia Richardson still remained in touch with Eva Brigham. Friends for thirty years, they lunched together once a month. Talk of the sale must have come up. Why hadn't her mother said anything?

Probably because she'd been screening her

calls and avoiding her mother ever since she'd told her about the engagement ring on Sunday, she thought ruefully.

Traci looked at the far wall in the family room. Part of it was covered with framed photographs from the past. There was a large one of her and Morgan standing before the summerhouse. She couldn't remember which of their mothers had insisted on taking it. She only remembered that both she and Morgan had trouble standing still beside each other long enough for the shot to be taken.

Traci and Morgan. Morgan and Traci. Back then, it seemed their lives had been permanently intertwined. A bittersweet feeling of loss passed over her.

Picking up the card, Traci pulled the telephone over to her on the counter and tapped out the number on the keypad.

"Law Offices," a crisp voice announced after only one ring.

Either business was bad for the firm or someone was awfully efficient, she mused. Who woulda thunk it? Morgan Brigham, a criminal lawyer. "Mr. Morgan Brigham, please."

"Is he expecting this call?" the voice on the other end asked primly.

Traci wound her index finger around the cord as she rocked on the stool. "Absolutely."

It was obvious that the secretary was unconvinced and determined to remain an obstacle. "Whom shall I say is calling?"

She wanted to surprise him. "Why don't you let me tell him that?" Traci suggested stubbornly.

"Madam, this is highly irregular."

Traci wondered if Morgan knew how off-putting his receptionist was. Probably. "I'm nobody's madam, and trust me, he wants this call."

"Well, I—"

The woman abruptly stopped talking. There was the sound of a hand being passed over the receiver and then a muffled exchange of voices in the background. Cradling the receiver between her shoulder and ear, Traci wandered over to the coffeemaker and poured herself a mug. This was going to take a while.

"Hello?" The voice was deep, rich, like the black coffee in her mug.

Startled, Traci paused at the refrigerator, the door opened. "Morgan?"

"Yes?"

She didn't remember his voice being so resonant. It took her a second to collect her thoughts. "This is a voice from your past." Taking out the container of milk, she closed the door with her hip.

"Traci." It wasn't a question, but a statement.

She was a little disappointed that Morgan could guess so easily. It wasn't as if she called him all the time. Or ever.

Pouring, she watched the milk swirl into the darkness. "Yes, how did you know?"

He laughed and the sound seemed to surround her. "You're the only person out of my past who could give my secretary the beginnings of a migraine.''

Traci had no idea why that made her smile. ''You shouldn't hire such delicate help and you should definitely get yourself a more exciting past.''

Obviously, some things never changed, Morgan thought. Traci still had a convoluted way of looking at things. ''In order to do that, it would mean that I'd have to work on my present.''

Her grin grew. ''Yes, it would.''

''Still think you know it all, don't you?''

Was that a fond note in his voice or just her imagination? ''No, now I know I do. But let's not get into that. I'm holding your note in my hand.''

''I was beginning to think you weren't interested. I sent the note out last Friday.''

Traci looked at the stack of mail and then at the engagement ring box. She ran the tip of her finger along the lid, then pushed the box back.

''I've been busy.''

''So, does that mean you're interested in buying the old place?''

It might do her some good to get away for the day. To get away from the crowds and try to sort out not her mail but her thoughts. Which were in more of a jumbled mess than the stack on her counter.

''I don't know about buying it, but I'd certainly like to look around. When's a good time?''

She heard the rustling of paper, which she assumed was the pages of his calendar.

"How does tomorrow sound?" Morgan asked. "I don't have to be in court and there's nothing scheduled I can't push back. Can you get away?"

Tomorrow was Friday and, since she'd finished the strip, it stood wide open. Daniel wasn't due back from the convention until late Sunday night. Traci rustled papers of her own, though hers were only blank sheets on her drawing board. Funny how she could feel her competitive nature coming to the fore just at the sound of Morgan's voice.

"Looks like I can. Noon sound all right?"

He laughed softly. "Still like to sleep in?"

She did, but she didn't see the point in admitting it to him. Knowing him, he'd jump at the chance to make it sound slothful. "No, I just don't like driving in the dark and it's roughly a three-hour trip from where I live."

"All right, I'll meet you there at noon."

That settled, Traci was about to ring off, then stopped. "Morgan?"

"Yes?"

"Thanks for asking me."

Morgan shrugged it off. "Don't mention it. You spent as much time there as I did."

"More," she corrected. "You went away to school, remember?"

He was very quiet on the other end and she thought for a moment that he hadn't heard her. Then he answered, "I remember. So I'll see you at noon tomorrow."

"Bye."

Traci hung up and looked thoughtfully at the

telephone, wondering if she was making a mistake. An uneasiness skated through her, but she attributed it to the decision she had to make.

For a moment, she debated calling Daniel at his hotel and leaving a message for him that she was going to be away. But then she thought better of it. If he knew she was away, he might worry.

No, Daniel never worried. He knew she could take care of herself. He was good like that.

He was good in a lot of ways.

She should have her head examined for even vacillating, she thought, looking at the ring box again. Very carefully she opened it and looked down at the perfectly cut square diamond. It winked and blinked at her, catching the fluorescent light and playing ball with it.

She snapped the lid closed with a shiver.

"No doubt about it. It *does* grow." Putting the box down again, she got ready to take her cartoon strips to the office.

Early the next morning, Traci piled her sketchbook and her dog, along with a well-worn map she never quite got the hang of reading or folding, into her vintage Mustang and drove out of the city.

A sense of excitement and adventure telegraphed itself through her.

Jeremiah had sole possession of the back seat, patrolling the area with the air of a newly liberated king, moving from one window to the other.

Traci had opened each only far enough for him to stick out his nose and only part of his head.

She adjusted her rearview mirror, looking into the back seat as the road threaded onto the expressway. Jeremiah appeared to be one happy dog.

She wished it could be that easy for the rest of the world. "Unfortunately, it takes more than having your ears and tongue flapping in the wind," she said aloud to the dog.

Morning traffic slowly dissipated. It was a long, steady drive. She broke up the monotony by talking to the dog and singing along with the radio. The trip seemed to take longer than she remembered. But then, she'd never made it from the heart of New York City before.

Finally, she was on the last leg. Taking the narrow road off the beaten path, she looked around as she drove in what she hoped was a northeasterly direction. Things looked vaguely familiar, but that could have been wishful thinking on her part. She fervently hoped she wasn't on her way to the Canadian border.

Edginess began to waft through her again. She'd been feeling that way ever since Daniel had given her the ring. Up until that point, she'd been content enough just to float along. Although, at times, that tiny voice that advocated having a husband and children, the one that vaguely resembled her mother's voice, would get a little louder.

What was she doing here, anyway? she demanded silently. Granted, the scenery was tranquil and the ripe autumn colors made it look as if she had tripped and fallen headlong into nature's kaleidoscope. But that should have no bearing on her decision when it came to choosing a partner for life.

For life.

An involuntary shiver shimmied up and down her spine.

Stop it, Traci. He's going to make a great husband.

She knew he would. An excellent, loving husband. Traci thought of Daniel. Dr. Daniel Thane, a man whose blinding smile was the first thing you noticed about him, which was fortunate, given his occupation.

A blinding smile that seemed to lack heart.

Damn it, that wasn't fair. Daniel had heart. He had lots of heart. What he didn't have was chemistry, but so what? There was nothing wrong with being solid, dependable, trustworthy, and Daniel was all those things. He had all the qualities a woman looked for. Her mother loved him.

A feeling like a heavy, rain-soaked blanket fell over her soul. Her mother wasn't going to be married to him; *she* was. For better and for worse.

Forever.

How could one word be so unsettling?

What was the matter with her? She'd had flash and fire and been summarily burned by it when Rory decided to ride off into the sunset. Commitments frightened him the way they seemed to attract Daniel. Rory had abruptly left at the first sign that she wanted to become serious. That was where chemistry got you. With an empty bed and a bruised heart. Daniel wanted to fill her bed and take care of her heart. Forever.

That had to count for something. So he didn't curl her toes; she could live with that. Curled toes were hard to walk on, anyway.

Swerving quickly to avoid a squirrel that had darted out onto the road, she sighed. She wasn't convincing herself. Jeremiah yelped in protest as he tumbled to the side of the car.

"Sorry. You wouldn't want me to hit a squirrel, would you?" The half growl, half whimper behind her had her laughing. She could almost hear what the dog was thinking. "No, you wouldn't. They're too tough to eat."

Slowing down, Traci took a curve, then drove up the winding road slowly.

So what, she thought, picking up the thread of her own internal argument. So what if bells and banjos didn't fill the air when Daniel held her hand or kissed her? Electricity was for the utility company, and for teenagers fumbling in the back seat of a car, not for a grown woman. She would take stability over curled toes any day.

She just wished...

What? Traci thought impatiently, annoyed with the way she was vacillating. She just wished what? That she could feel the wind beneath her sails, to have the sky light up when a man kissed her?

Been there, done that. Gone nowhere.

She should be grateful that Daniel had happened. He'd turned love into a comfortable thing, something she'd just slipped into.

Like clean underwear in the morning.

Traci winced and forced herself to pay attention to the road before she really did hit something. Where *was* that house, anyway?

Traci halted the car abruptly as she stared at the fence up ahead. Was she lost? She didn't remember a fence on the property when her parents had driven up here. And she certainly didn't remember a No Trespassing sign being posted.

There was a tiny M. Brigham in the corner below the declaration.

No, she wasn't lost, Traci decided. The notice had obviously been put up by Morgan. Morgan Brigham had probably grown up to become a pompous ass and his waist had probably thickened while his hair had thinned. Growing up was the pits sometimes.

Traci got out of the car and approached the sign. She ran her hand along it. The last time she'd been here was—when?

Pausing, she linked events up in her mind, searching for a time frame. It had been right before she'd gone away to college. Once college had begun, there just hadn't been enough time to come out here anymore, even though she'd wanted to.

And then her parents had stopped reserving the house for the summer. There seemed to be no point to the time-sharing arrangement anymore.

Their only daughter had grown up and life had taken another road.

Away from here.

For a moment, Traci stood, debating with herself. Something was urging her to turn around and go back. The old adage about not going home again echoed in the corners of her mind. She was afraid that what she would see would shatter the idyllic time childhood had become for her in her mind.

"Coward," she mumbled under her breath.

Unlatching the gate, Traci pulled it open far enough to accommodate her car. Then she got back in and drove up the grassy road.

She could see the house.

Her pulse began to hammer as excitement spilled through her. Yes, that was definitely the house—a two-story, wood-frame building with a chimney that was dwarfed by the trees around it. Just beyond, she knew, was the dock and the lake where she'd learned how to swim. How to kayak. And how to dream.

Without realizing it, she pressed down on the accelerator just as she crossed the wooden bridge.

Traci zoomed over it the way she'd zoomed over so many things in the past few years. Suddenly, she desperately wanted to see the house.

Following the winding path, she traveled the rough, uneven gravel-paved road as far as she could, then pulled the car over to the side. After getting out, she locked it out of habit and went the rest of the way on foot. Jeremiah, eager to stretch his legs after being in the car for so long, fairly galloped down the path. Holding on to the leash, she all but flew behind him.

"C'mon, dog, I don't want to be dragged."

Traci was nearly in front of the door when she heard someone behind her. Alerted, Jeremiah began to bark. And cower.

Cartoonist found dead at house where she spent summers. Film at eleven.

Heart hammering in her throat, vying for space with a gasp, Traci swung around. Her hand was raised up in a pseudo self-defense movement she had absolutely no idea how to execute.

"Took you long enough."

Her mouth fell open. Her hand remained in the air only because it was frozen in place. This drop-dead gorgeous guy just couldn't be—

"Morgan?"

The dark green eyes narrowed within their handsome setting. "None other."

His mother was right, Morgan thought as he looked at Traci. Actually, she had understated the matter. She'd said that Traci had grown up to be a "pretty little thing." But she hadn't. Traci Richardson had grown up to be a drop-dead, teeth numbing knockout.

Remembering the strip he'd read today, Morgan glanced down at her left hand. He wasn't too late. Unlike her counterpart, there was no huge diamond winking and blinking on her hand. It was bare.

It was also turning an interesting shade of pink. Red, really. The leash was wrapped around her hand and it was obviously cutting off her circulation. The creature attached to the other end of the leather strap seemed bent on dragging Traci back down to her car.

The dog, for all its size, appeared to be cowering. Morgan couldn't help grinning at the sight as he breathed a little easier. He nodded toward the animal. "Some watchdog you have there."

Traci lifted her chin defensively and took umbrage for the dog. Actually, she thought that when it came to Morgan, she probably would have taken umbrage no matter what he'd said. Their relationship had always taken on antagonistic ramifications whenever they ventured past "hello." It was the nature of the beast, and now that she was older and could look back at her life with a more discerning eye, she had to admit that she rather liked it that way. She'd enjoyed the daily confrontations. They had kept her on her toes and kept her summers from being dull.

Traci glanced at her pet. "Jeremiah does the trick when I need him."

Jeremiah didn't look up to *any* sort of tricks, defensive or otherwise. What the dog did look like was downright sleepy. Even now, his big brown eyes were shutting.

"How?" Morgan asked. "By lying down on the intruder and smothering him to death?"

Blue eyes with flecks of gray narrowed into gleaming slits over the bridge of a very pert nose. "Want a demonstration?"

She'd do it, too, Morgan thought. She'd sic that four-footed monster on him. He wouldn't put anything past her. Morgan held up his hand and laughed. "No, I'll pass, thanks."

Vindicated, Traci loosened her hold on the leash. "Smart move." Eyes moving up and down the length and breadth of him, she sized up a person she'd once known as well as her own reflection. "It would be your first, I imagine."

Same old Traci. In a way, in an ever-changing world, that was almost comforting. Almost.

Morgan nodded. "Seeing as how I invited you up here to look around the old place, I'm inclined to agree with you. At least as far as today goes."

Ready to fire back, Traci opened her mouth, then shut it again. And laughed.

It was that same, skin-tingling, sexy, smoky laugh that he remembered. At the time, it seemed incongruous for a teenage girl to have a laugh like that. But it fit right in with the woman he saw before him. Traci had been a thin, bouncy, perky girl, and while he could still see that in the woman she'd become, there was something a hell of a lot more unsettling about the way she looked at him now than there had been then.

And even then, the sound and the occasional look had gotten to him, although Morgan would have willingly swallowed his own tongue before admitting it to her or anyone else.

"Well, I see you haven't changed any," Traci told him.

At least, she amended silently, his attitude hadn't. Looks-wise, well, that was a whole other story. Her mother had told her that he was good-looking, but mothers were obligated to say things like that about their best friends' sons. It was a rule that was written in stone somewhere or other.

Who would have thought that, for once, it was actually true?

In response, Morgan made an exaggerated show of looking down at himself, as if to check out what she was saying. In his opinion, he'd changed a hell of a lot, and they both knew it. He had a well-worn, banged-up set of weights housed in his garage that he had exercised with daily for the past eight years to prove it.

"I was a lot skinnier the last time you saw me. I've put on a few pounds."

And magnificently well, too, she thought. But if he expected her to admit that, he was going to be sadly disappointed.

"I noticed," she murmured. She suddenly jerked to attention as Jeremiah yanked hard on the leash. It felt as if her left hand had lengthened by a good inch. "Jeremiah, stop that."

To reinforce the command, Traci gave the leash

a good, solid tug. The dog responded by yanking even harder on his end.

Unprepared, Traci gasped, stumbled and then fell unceremoniously into Morgan's arms. The unexpected weight made him fall backward. Breaking her fall, he landed with a hard thud against some very hard upstate New York earth. The pain was temporarily muted by the fact that Traci, and every single curve she possessed, was on top of him.

Traci was more than vaguely aware that the contours melding with hers were infinitely pleasing. More than that, she felt a warm rush spreading fast and furious through every pulsing inch of her body, like a backdraft bent on eating its way through a building in record time.

The overwhelming sensation made her suck in her breath in surprise. If she hadn't known better, she would have said she was on fire.

And maybe, just maybe—in a very unnerving way—she was.

The slow, lazy smile that drifted across Morgan's lips, filtering down from his green eyes and settling in the dimple at the corner of his mouth told her that he was not unaware of what was happening here.

On the contrary, he seemed very, very aware that their bodies were fitting together like two missing pieces of a puzzle.

There was a catch in her throat she didn't like. A catch that *wasn't* there when she was in the same sort of position with Daniel. Of course, she'd never had the wind knocked out of her by Daniel, she argued with herself.

Maybe that was just the trouble.

She'd gotten softer than he remembered, Morgan thought, and yet she was firm. Ripe for the touch. He found himself wanting to gather some very vital, hands-on experience.

To placate himself, Morgan raised his hand to her hair and lightly combed his fingers through it. "I see you have your dog well trained."

Nope, she definitely didn't care for this feeling zipping through her. Traci scrambled up, purposely driving an elbow into his chest as she gained her feet.

"You frightened him," she accused, grabbing at the first defense she could think of. Lame at best, she admitted silently. But then, she wasn't feeling very witty at the moment. Just disoriented.

It took Morgan a moment to catch his breath. Her elbow, sharply applied to his solar plexus, had temporarily siphoned off his air. No doubt about it, he thought. Traci was still quick with her hands and her tongue. In an odd sort of way, that left him with a rather pleasant sensation.

The cards they exchanged at Christmas were basically the typical kind, saying very little, just keeping old lines open much the way occasionally flipping through a dusty family album kept old memories alive. But it didn't fill in any of the missing gaps that were occurring as time passed.

Morgan had learned more about her life from her strip than he had from the cards she'd sent him over the years. It gave him a window into her world that she didn't have into his, he thought. That, too, pleased him. He'd always liked being one up on her.

Drawing his feet to him, Morgan rose and dusted himself off. She looked a little frazzled, he noted. It was a good look on her.

He looked cute with his hair mussed, she mused, then immediately upbraided herself for it. And him for putting the thought into her head in the first place.

"Nothing broken?" she asked solicitously.

He was glad the storm that had been threatening hadn't hit yet. Otherwise, he would have found himself caked in mud. "No."

Traci shook her head. "Damn."

He had to look to see if she was serious. The Traci he remembered would have been. She was always bent on one-upmanship and getting the better of him. They had that in common, he mused. He would have said she was a she-devil if there hadn't been moments when a kinder nature had broken through.

But those moments were few and far between, more of an aberration than anything else. He told himself that he always breathed a little easier when he wasn't around her.

Still, Traci had fluttered along the perimeter of his mind all these years like a tune he couldn't get rid of but couldn't remember all the words to, either. That was Traci all over. Too annoying, too unsettling, to forget. Ever.

He realized he was staring at her and cleared his throat, mentally getting his bearings. "So, you want to see the house or not?"

There was an awkwardness between them, she realized. Beneath the light sparring, there was something she couldn't quite pinpoint. She wondered if time had done that to them or if there was another cause behind it.

"I'm here," she reminded him needlessly.

His eyes washed over her, taking full measure. Boy, but she had filled out. Her blond hair was still as unruly as ever, giving her a moppet look, but the moppet had a figure that made a man's mouth water and his hands grow suddenly restless. Like the rest of him.

"Yes, you certainly are." He took a deep breath and tried to place the scent that had been driving him crazy since she'd landed on top of him. "Sin?"

Traci stared at him, uncomprehending. "Excuse me?"

The surprised look on her face had him wondering if she thought he was propositioning her.

"The perfume you're wearing, is it Sin?"

It took her a minute to put the two pieces of information together. He was looking at her the way she wasn't accustomed to being looked at, not by him, at any rate.

"Oh, yes, it is." She hated this awkward feeling. To counteract it, she was purposely sarcastic. "Good nose. Is that part of your skills as a lawyer?"

He was probably going to hear a hell of a lot of lawyer jokes before this visit was over, he thought. "No, Cynthia favored it."

"Cynthia?" Traci frowned, rolling the name over her tongue. "Is there a Cynthia?"

Was there ever, but that, mercifully, was in his past. Every man was entitled to one Cynthia. One damn mistake in judgment. "There was."

Traci paused. There was a note of sadness in his voice, and something more. For a second, compassion filled her. And then she remembered. Compassion went out the window.

"Wasn't that the girl who used to hang on your arm, simpering all the time?"

She had hated Cynthia Fairling from the first moment she laid eyes on her. Morgan had brought her out the summer Traci was sixteen. The last summer he was here. Delicate, curvy and china-doll perfect, Cynthia had had Traci constructing dolls out of rolled tissues and sticking pins into them in her room. She hadn't realized then that she'd created the voodoo dolls out of jealousy. She did now.

"She didn't—" Morgan thought better of his protest. There was no point in denying the truth. "Well, maybe she did at that."

Maybe? "She most certainly did." Traci fluttered her lashes and hooked her arm around his. She almost hung from it as she pushed her chest forward, mimicking Cynthia to a tee. "Oh, Morgie, that's so clever."

Morgan had the good grace to wince at the imitation. "Ouch."

Traci sighed and shook her head in disapproval as she released him. "I can't believe you let anyone call you Morgie."

Morgan shrugged. "I was eighteen and she was a knockout."

Traci's frowned deepened. Men were so shallow, it was a wonder they survived as a race at all. "You were an idiot and she was out for your money."

He thought back to the way Cynthia had dumped him without warning when he had told her about his father's finances taking a sharp nosedive because of a series of bad investments. It had been a hell of a rude awakening for him on more than one level. He'd learned what it was like to go out and earn his own money quickly enough. It had taken him five years to get through his undergraduate studies, but the degree had meant more to him in the end.

And so had losing Cynthia. It was only at the end that he realized how narrow his escape had really been.

"You had that right." He laughed shortly. "She really was out for my money. How did you know?"

Traci rolled her eyes. "Oh, please, she was transparent."

Not to him. But he allowed Traci her moment of triumph. "Even to a sixteen year old?"

Traci let out a short, exasperated breath. "Even to a mushroom."

The dried, brown leaves crunched beneath the heels of his new boots as he led the way to the front door. "Doesn't say much for me, does it?"

"Nope."

For a second, she wanted to rub his nose in it. She could have told him what Cynthia was all about from the start, but he wouldn't have wanted to listen. He was completely besotted with her. Traci had been angry and hurt when all of his attention had gone to the pretentious little witch. But he'd learned the hard way and, in a way, Traci did feel bad for him.

After a beat, Traci relented. "I guess all men are a little blind when they're being played up to."

He stopped at the front door, his hand on the knob. She was sounding a little too highhanded for his taste. "And you're an expert on this?"

"I see things. I have to," she added deliberately, adding one more log to the fire that was about to catch.

Morgan nodded sagely, as if taking every word as gospel. "That would be the tremendous insight you have into life as a cartoonist, I take it."

She saw the way he was poking his tongue in his cheek. She could endure a lot, but she didn't like having her strip ridiculed. "Did you invite me out here to argue with you?"

She was right. There was just something about having her around that turned him into a competitive adolescent. Something he hadn't been for quite some time.

"No, I invited you to take a last look around. Truce?" To back up his words, Morgan put his hand out to her.

Jeremiah immediately began barking again. The fur on the animal's back stood up as straight as it could, given the shortness of his coat. Morgan wondered uneasily if the dog was all bark and no bite. He certainly hoped so, but since it was Traci's dog, he wasn't placing any bets yet.

"Truce."

Traci placed her hand into his. His handshake was firm, warm. But for some reason, she felt as if, somewhere, a bell was ringing, signaling the beginning of another round.

She glanced over her shoulder. "Jeremiah, quiet!" she ordered. The look she gave the dog was far more effective than her words. The dog lowered his head and looked almost contrite.

"Impressive."

Traci grinned in response. The years melted away and she looked fifteen again, he thought. There was mischief in her eyes.

He opened the door and she began to follow him inside. Morgan placed a restraining hand on her shoulder. He nodded behind her. "Is he coming in, too?"

An amused brow arched. Was he afraid of Jeremiah? "Don't worry, he's housebroken."

"I don't like the emphasis on the word *broken*."

Her smoky laugh surrounded him.

"Trust me." Traci glanced up at the sky. Since she had arrived, the dark clouds had moved in, blotting out the sun and any blue that had been noticeable. "Besides, it might rain any minute. I don't want him getting wet." Jeremiah smelled absolutely atrocious when he was wet, but she refrained from mentioning that.

"Maybe he'll shrink," Morgan commented.

She looked at Morgan in surprise. "You've gotten a sense of humor. Where did you find it?"

He graciously put up with her dig and countered. "I always had it. I had to, spending summers out here with you around."

She shrugged, finally walking into the house. "You never displayed it before."

Any other words faded away as she looked around the large front room. It was dusty and unused, and sad because of it. It was a place meant for laughter and long summer nights shared with friends and family. If she tried hard, she could almost see past summers spent here.

Waves of yesterday surrounded her as the scent of wood from the woodpile by the fireplace wafted to her. The house smelled dank and musty.

And wonderful for all that.

She'd forgotten how much she enjoyed coming here. How much she missed it.

It was yesterday again. And yet an eternity seemed to separate her from that carefree, mischievous girl she'd been.

Morgan stood by, silently letting her reacquaint

herself with the room. He'd journeyed down his own memory lane earlier. It was odd how sentimental you could get about a place that hadn't meant anything to you at the time.

"It hasn't changed much," she commented slowly, the words drifting from her lips.

Even the old television set in the corner was there. With rabbit ears, she thought fondly. Reception had always been miserably poor. It had been her main complaint about vacationing here. Tired of her complaints, her mother had urged her to use her imagination to entertain herself rather than an electronic baby-sitter. Traci had complied by finding new ways to get under Morgan's skin.

"Not down here," Morgan agreed. He began leading the way out of the room, uneasily keeping one eye on the dog. Jeremiah was investigating the multicolored throw rug in front of the fireplace, sniffing so hard he looked as if he were going to absorb the material through his nose. "They redid the bedrooms a few years back. And the attic seems more crammed—"

Traci looked at Morgan sharply. "The bedrooms? My room? They redecorated my room?"

The possessive note surprised him, but then it shouldn't have, he thought. She was always possessive about things she laid her hands on. They spent an entire summer arguing over who got to use the kayak. She usually won.

"Technically, it wasn't your room, it was—"

"My room, Counselor," Traci interjected. "It was always my room in the summer." She was already heading for the stairs, eager to see it. "I don't care what it was the rest of the time. Can I see it?"

"Sure. This way." Hurrying, Morgan got in front of her. Jeremiah, he noted gratefully, had decided to rest on top of the rug he had all but inhaled. He felt along the wall for the light switch. "I had the electricity turned on so I could show the house to its best advantage."

Quickening her step, she passed Morgan and reached the stairs first. She laid a hand on the banister, Columbus claiming the new land for the queen. "You don't have to show me."

He raised his hand, making a show of backing off. "Sorry, habit."

Foot planted on the first step, Traci turned and looked at him, amused. "You're a tour guide on the side?"

"No, I'm used to being polite." The staircase was steep and narrow. It wasn't meant to accommodate two. He joined her, anyway, standing stubbornly on the first step. The fit was tight. "Something you probably are unfamiliar with."

There it was again, that tingling sensation as if a thousand fireflies were holding a convention along her skin. It came when he was brushed up against her. Traci struggled hard to ignore it. "When it comes to you, yes."

He looked down into her face and marveled at the blueness of her eyes. Had they always been that intense? "Does it give you pleasure, bickering with me every chance you get?"

"Infinite pleasure." It wasn't easy, remembering the train of her thought. The tracks were leading toward some very unfamiliar ground. "And
this is the first chance I've gotten in years,
remember?"

"Yeah." The word stretched out as the smile
took hold of his lips and spread. "Maybe we
should have done this more often."

She didn't care for the arrhythmic beating of
her heart.

"You're the one who went off to college with
Cynthia," she said the name in a singsong tone,
"and got too busy to come back to the lake."
That sounded too much like an accusation, she
thought, but it was too late to take it back. Any
protest would have him thinking things that
weren't true.

With a huff, she pushed past Morgan and
walked up the stairs ahead of him.

"You weren't far behind," he countered.
"Valedictorian."

Surprised, she turned and looked at him again.
"I never wrote you that."

"Didn't have to." He urged her on with a motion of his hand. He was in no hurry to have his
systems scrambled again. "My mother made sure
I got word." He didn't add that, at times, he prodded his mother for information in what he told
himself was just idle curiosity.

"Mothers." The single word spoke volumes.
"They can be a network all their own."

"Yeah, they can." At the landing, he followed

her down the hall to her room. It was the last one in a row and the first to get the morning light.

Morgan allowed her to open the door, seeing as how she thought of the room as her own. "Speaking of which, does she ever take offense?"

Traci stopped just short of the threshold. "Who?"

"Your mother."

Turning around, she looked at him, perplexed. "Take offense to what?"

Morgan remembered a recent cartoon that had been less than flattering. "At the way you portray her sometimes in the strip."

Traci waved that aside. "That's not my mother. That's a composite."

That might be what she told others, but he knew better. And he knew her mother, or had. "Is that what you tell her?"

Traci couldn't help the grin that slipped out. "Yeah."

Morgan nodded solemnly, but his eyes were glinting. "And she buys it?"

"Pretty much." Traci grew serious. "Besides, it's all in fun and the traits are exaggerated."

Morgan folded his arms before him as he leaned against the wall, studying her. He could always tell when she was lying. "But it is your life."

"Hey, writers always draw on what they know." She played the words back in her head when he grinned at her. "No pun intended."

He felt as if he'd been watching her life for the past three years. For the most part, it had been amusing. Like Traci. But now, something serious was about to take place. Something he'd found himself not quite ready or willing to accept. "So, are congratulations in order?"

He'd acquired an unnerving way of skipping around conversations since she'd last spoken to him. "What do you mean?"

"Your engagement. To the doctor."

"Dentist," she corrected. "And I'm not."

"Oh?" he asked a tad too innocently. "I thought he gave you a ring."

She wondered if he had picked that up from the strip, or if her mother had told his. "He did. I just haven't given him an answer yet."

That was interesting, he thought. Very interesting. "I see."

She had no idea what he thought he "saw," but she knew what she wanted to see. Her room.

"I doubt it." Turning her back on him, Traci opened the door and stepped into the small guest room.

3

"You got rid of the bureau."

Traci went straight toward the new piece of furniture that stood in its stead and looked at it as if it were an intruder. If she tried hard, she could visualize the old one—a honey-colored triplechested bureau that gave the room a crammed, homey quality. Coupled with her double bed, it had turned the place into her own tiny kingdom when she had been growing up. The new bureau was sleeker and took up far less space.

She hated it on principle.

Morgan followed her into the room and shrugged casually. "It was old."

That was the beauty of it, but she doubted if Morgan could understand. Sighing over the loss, Traci ran her fingertip along the dark wood.

"It had a dent in it, right here." She rested her finger on the uppermost corner closest to him. "Where you chipped your tooth."

He remembered the incident vividly. His manhood had been shaken that day. Thin and wiry, two years younger, Traci had easily gotten the best of him. He'd persuaded his parents to buy him his first set of weights that autumn.

"Where *you* chipped my front tooth," he corrected. He knocked against the side in a rapid tattoo. "Somehow, my parents didn't think refurbishing the bureau was a high priority." The bureau was fairly falling apart when they had finally gotten rid of it.

Traci shifted her attention from the bureau to Morgan. She'd completely forgotten about his chipped tooth until this moment.

"Let me see," she said suddenly, catching him off guard.

As he stared at her, Traci placed her thumb on the edge of his chin and pulled down lightly with the familiarity of a maiden aunt or annoying sibling. Or the girl he had partially grown up with.

She nodded at the gleaming white crown. If she hadn't known which one was chipped, she wouldn't have been able to guess which was the false tooth.

"Nice job."

Morgan pulled his head back. "In case you haven't noticed, I'm not a thoroughbred whose teeth you can check out."

The choice of words tickled her. "Thoroughbred?" Traci echoed. "If I was passing out labels, I would have said an old firehouse plug."

She crossed to the bed. By the way it sagged slightly in the middle she could tell it was the same one she'd slept on all those hot summer nights. If Morgan hadn't been in the room, she would have jumped on it for old times' sake.

"Firehouse plug?" He laughed. Who talked like that anymore? "You're dating yourself."

She glanced at him, bemused at the way he was watching her. Was he expecting her to do something weird? "I'm dating my research."

With Traci, it was always difficult to tell if she was being flippant or sincere. He had a fifty-fifty chance of guessing right. "Is that how you met?"

The view from her window was as stirring as she remembered. But the lake looked as if it was going to be blotted out at any minute by the dark clouds that were rolling over it with the intensity of an oncoming express train.

"Who?" she asked, preoccupied.

"You and the dentist?"

She turned around slowly and looked at Morgan. It took her a moment to make sense of his words. She couldn't read his expression. What was he up to?

"No, and his name is Daniel. I meant I was giving a date *to* my research." She touched the curtains. They were the same. Light, filmy. They suited the room, and now, ultimately, her. They hadn't when she was younger. She'd been a tomboy through and through when they'd first begun to take their vacations here and had jeered at the curtains and blue eyelet comforter. "I'm watching old cartoons—"

He could see her, Morgan thought. Sitting curled up on the sofa with a bowl of popcorn in her lap, fascinated by silly little animated characters doing absurd, impossible things in the space of seven minutes. It was a scene directly out of his past, one he'd ridiculed countless times.

Now it just made him feel oddly nostalgic.

"Aren't you afraid they're above you?"

She purposely ignored him. Idly, she opened the nightstand drawer. A spider skittered away, vainly seeking sanctuary. She shut the drawer again. Traci didn't know what she expected to find, maybe a memento from years gone by...

"To see what made some of them special and gave them longevity," she finished, her teeth clenched. "You are as irritating as ever."

He laughed at the expression on her face. His answer held no malice. "Right back at you."

"'Right back at you'?" she repeated incredulously. "A Harvard graduate and that's the best you can do?" Traci shook her head. "Boy, they must have really lowered their standards for you."

They both knew that he'd been an honor student in high school. His studiousness was one of the things she'd used as ammunition when she teased him.

"It was Yale," he corrected patiently, "and the standards were quite high." His eyes washed over her. He wondered if this Daniel character knew what he was letting himself in for. And if he deserved her. "It seems that every time I'm with you, I regress."

She couldn't resist reaching up and mussing his too-perfect hair. "Or loosen up."

Morgan ran both hands through his hair, attempting to smooth it back down. "Trust me, no one wants to be that loose."

Made no difference to her. "Have it your own way. You don't know what you're missing."

Traci ran her hand over the new bureau again. It felt too sleek to her, too benign and devoid of character. The old one had had nicks and scrapes awarded by time all over its surface. Some of the nicks, of course, had been awarded by her.

She smiled to herself, remembering, feeling the room's ambience. For a moment, Traci closed her eyes, letting it all return to her. She'd been five when they had started coming out here. Or maybe even four, she wasn't sure.

Standing in her old bedroom now, feeling the years all melting away, it was as if nothing had really changed. But of course it had. She'd grown up and so had Morgan. An awful lot.

He watched the way her lashes, so much darker than her hair, swept along the swell of her cheeks, resting there like silken kittens reposing on a satiny cushion.

And wouldn't she laugh if he voiced that thought aloud, he thought to himself. Traci was far too earthy to stand still for sentiments like that.

"What are you doing?" he asked.

Her eyes remained closed. "Remembering." And then they fluttered open and she turned them on him. "Whatever happened to her?"

"Who?" Morgan was thoroughly convinced that there were short circuits throughout the entire surface of her brain. How else could she possibly think her disjointed statements made any sense?

"Miss Shallow of 1985." When Morgan still didn't seem to comprehend, Traci batted her lashes at him coquettishly. "Cynthia."

He really didn't feel like discussing Cynthia any further. She was a mistake he wanted to leave buried in his past. A mistake that had made him hesitant to put his heart up on the block again.

"She found someone else. With more money." He stood with his hand on the knob, impatience creasing his brow. "Are you done in here?"

He wasn't impatient with her, Traci thought, but with the subject. It didn't take a rocket scientist to see that.

"Not yet." She paused. Though she didn't often admit it, even to herself, there was a small, soft spot in her heart when it came to Morgan. After all, he was rather like the big brother she'd never had and, while they might fight constantly, she didn't like the idea of anyone else hurting him, no matter what she might profess verbally to the contrary.

Traci placed her hand on his arm. It felt hard to the touch. She ran the tip of her tongue along her upper lip before she managed to force the words out. "I'm sorry."

She was, he thought. He could see it in her eyes. The last thing in the world he wanted was pity, especially hers. That wasn't what they were all about, he and Traci. It added a dimension he didn't want.

"About what?" he asked a little too innocently. "You've got so much to be sorry about, you're going to have to narrow that down a little for me."

She stiffened, dropping her hand. That's what she got for being nice to Morgan. "I was going to say about Cynthia, but—"

He relented. There was no point in closing off this new avenue between them. It just might lead somewhere. "You were?"

Too late to take her words back now, she thought. "Yes." The admission came grudgingly.

Morgan studied her face, trying to ascertain a reason for this change in attitude. He failed.

"Why?"

She shrugged. She'd never cared for having to explain herself. And feelings were a great deal harder to explain than anything else. "I don't like seeing people get hurt."

That might be true enough, but he wasn't "people." He was Morgan. Someone she had taken delight in teasing and torturing. She was throwing away a perfect opportunity to crow and say "I told you so" in every way available to her. It wasn't like her.

"I would have thought the idea would have made you overjoyed, seeing it was me."

For a moment, she stood and looked at him, seeing both the boy she'd known and the man she merely assumed she knew. Maybe they both deserved the truth. Although they both probably wouldn't understand. Men rarely did. She'd learned that one the hard way.

"No, I can rag on you all I want, but that doesn't mean I want to see your heart pierced with a lance. She really didn't deserve you, you know." Traci bit her lip. The last sentence had just slipped out.

His eyes narrowed. She couldn't have surprised him more than if she'd announced that she was harboring a secret crush on him all these years.

"Are you being nice or is there a hidden barb in there that I'm missing?"

She let out a long sigh. *Cast ye pearls before swine...* "I'm being nice," she snapped. And then her sense of humor returned. "Don't blink or you'll miss it."

Something small and warm stirred within him. "I won't."

Ushering her out of the room, Morgan closed the door behind them. Even so, he could hear the wind picking up, mourning low like a choir beginning to rehearse a rousing spiritual. He hoped the storm would hold off until the night.

"Want some coffee?" he offered. "I just put some up before you arrived."

"I'd love some. There's a real chill in the air." Almost reflexively, she ran her hands up and down her arms. The thin sweater she was wearing wasn't nearly warm enough to ward off the cool turn of the weather. "It was always so hot whenever we were out here."

He followed her down the stairs, enjoying the gentle sway of her hips. She had certainly filled out since he last saw her. Something about being a late bloomer stuck in his mind. It was a phrase his mother liked to use. He'd never understood it until now.

"That's because you just spent summers here," he reminded her.

Traci stopped at the landing and turned toward him. "Did you ever come out any other time?" It had never occurred to her that he might have.

He nodded. "A couple." The look in her eyes told him she wanted details, so he stopped to consider. "Once for Thanksgiving. And then once over the Christmas holidays." That time he remembered more vividly. It was actually the last time he'd been here, until this month. "Mother and Dad were in Europe that year.'' A thin, humorless smile curved his mouth. ''One final hurrah before tightening their belts.''

Once in the kitchen, Traci crossed to the cupboard where the dishes had always been kept. It surprised her to find only a few pieces left. But then, of course there wouldn't be many. No one stayed here anymore.

She took down two mugs, rinsed them out and then set them on the counter beside the coffeemaker.

''And you were here alone?''

He might have known she'd probe. ''No, not quite alone.''

''Oh.'' Something in his voice had alerted her. ''Cynthia?'' She knew the answer to that would be yes before he said anything. She just didn't know why it bothered her so much.

It was easier answering Traci with his back to her. ''Yes. That was when I asked her to marry me.''

''You actually—'' She hadn't known that it had gone that far. Maybe because she'd refused to think about Morgan and Cynthia together in any more intimate a situation than sitting beside each other on the dock. Traci realized that her mouth had dropped open. ''Well, your bad taste was your business, I guess. I take it she turned you down.''

That must have stung. Compassion stirred again within her.

He took two spoons out of the drawer and then

shoved it closed a little harder than he intended. Feelings long dead resurfaced and did a little war dance within him.

"Not at first." Morgan turned around. "At first she said yes. It was when she was planning our life together in very lavish terms that I told her about Dad and what the stock market had done to his investments."

Traci knew that the Brighams' financial woes had begun in October. That left a gap of two months.

"You hadn't told her until then?"

He slowly shook his head. Morgan remembered rehearsing in the mirror the way he would break the news to Cynthia. Stupid way for a man to behave. He'd never felt that unsure of himself again. "It wasn't something you wanted to take out an ad about."

She didn't understand. "But this was the kind of thing you would share with someone you were close to."

Morgan shrugged again. In typical blunt fashion, Traci had gotten to the crux of it. "Maybe that was the trouble. Maybe I was never really that close to her." He sighed, remembering the way moonlight caught in Cynthia's hair. Hell of a criterion to pick a bride by. "Just dazzled and wildly enamored."

Enamored? "God, I haven't heard anyone talk like that since—" Traci's mouth curved. "The last time I was here with you."

Morgan's story only confirmed her own argu-

ment that she should be overjoyed at finding
someone as steady, as dependable and loving, as
Daniel. Look what being head over heels got you.
Nothing but disappointment.

There, that settled it. She'd made up her mind.

But her heart...

Morgan took no offense at her words. Lifting
the coffeepot, he took it off the hot plate and
brought it over to the table.

"Still take it with a ton of cream?" he asked,
pouring the dark liquid into her mug. He placed
the carton of cream in front of her.

He took his black. Had he bought this especially for her? The thoughtfulness behind the
small action surprised and pleased her.

Traci nodded. "And sugar."

Morgan filled his own mug, then set the pot
down. He still had a few packets of sugar in his
pocket from when he'd gotten a container of coffee at the diner. Digging them out, he tossed the
white packets on the table beside her mug.

"This is all I have. I forgot about the way you
liked to rot your teeth."

She tore open one envelope, then another.
White crystals rained into the mug. "Hey, I still
have all of mine."

He shook out one for himself. "Mine didn't
rot," he reminded her. "It was punched out."

"Not technically," she was quick to retaliate.
"I hit you in the stomach. *You* were the one who
hit your mouth on the bureau."

She remembered how frightened she'd been

when she'd seen all that blood. Morgan had been teasing her and she'd only meant to get him out of her room, not maim him. He'd surprised her when he'd taken the blame and told his parents that he'd tripped on the scatter rug in her room. She'd never been able to figure out why he had passed up that perfect opportunity to get back at her. It was almost chivalrous.

Maybe that tiny, warm spot in her heart for him had been created that day.

Mug cupped in his hands, Morgan regarded her quietly. "You would have made a hell of a lawyer, you know that?"

Since he was one himself, she took it as a compliment. And returned it in kind. Remembering the incident had her feeling rather magnanimous toward him. "You were the one who kept me sharp."

"I take no credit for that. You were born sharp. With a sharp tongue to match. Hell, you were probably born talking."

He was one to throw rocks. She lifted her chin slightly. "I'm not the one who could talk the ears off a brass monkey."

"No," he admitted agreeably, then his eyes crinkled with a smile. "But you're the one who could make the monkey run off, holding his ears and screaming."

Just like old times. Traci grinned at Morgan over the rim of her mug. A cozy feeling nestled in her chest. "Nice to know nothing's changed."

There he had to disagree. Again. A whole

world had changed since they had sat here like this the last time. "But it has. We're older. Reasonably successful—"

"Not to hear your mother talk about it."

He knew what she meant. His mother heralded every win in court as if he had just single-handedly preserved justice. "Or yours."

The wind was definitely getting louder. She took another sip of her coffee. The extra shot of warmth fortified her. "I guess they have a one-upmanship of their own going on."

There, at least, they were in agreement. But it was a friendly sort of thing between their mothers. Not like between them. He thought of the way they had taken an instant dislike to each other, much to their parents' dismay. "I think we really disappointed them."

She set her mug down and leaned forward. Even in the fading light, his eyes were intensely green, she mused. "How so?"

She was so close, he felt an overwhelming urge to touch his mouth to hers. The thought startled him. Morgan stared down into his almost empty mug. "I think they saw us winding up together."

Traci laughed, grateful she wasn't drinking at the time. She would have choked. She sincerely doubted that her mother had ever thought of the two of them as a couple. Julia Richardson was far more perceptive than that.

"Not if they were looking."

Fragments of a dozen different memories

flashed through his mind. "I guess that does sound pretty crazy."

She didn't quite like the way he said that. "Yeah, thinking I'd settle for you."

There it was again, that superior tone of hers. *That* hadn't changed in more than twenty years. "I was thinking of it the other way around."

She sniffed and looked away. "You would."

His eyes narrowed. For a second, he was fifteen again. And she was thirteen. An annoying, bratty, know-it-all thirteen. "Yes, I would."

This time when she leaned across the table, her eyes were flashing. "What makes you think I'd want to be with you?"

He rose in his chair, inch for inch. "What makes you think I'd want to be with you?"

She waved her hand carelessly at him. "Nothing, except that for once you'd have shown more taste than to go mooning after a money-grasping Barbie doll."

All right, since she'd chosen to go down this path again, he'd call the shots. "And you've done better with your dentist?"

He surprised her. It wasn't like him to fight dirty. That was her domain. "You leave Daniel out of this. You don't know anything about him."

Bull's-eye. He'd gotten to her, he thought with a touch of smugness. He savored the tiny victory. "Word gets around. Your mother told my mother."

That didn't make any sense. Anything her

mother would have said would have been rose-colored. "My mother adores Daniel."

That might very well be true. When Morgan had called his mother last Friday, as soon as he'd read the cartoon, he'd been told that the man was practically sterling. But Morgan had also read between the platitudes.

"From the description I got, your intended is as lackluster as liver."

Traci rose to her feet so quickly the chair almost fell over. She grabbed for it before it could crash to the side. Incensed, she came to Daniel's rescue. "He is not. He's an exciting, vibrant man."

Morgan wondered if Traci was trying to convince him, or herself. In either case, she wasn't succeeding. He could see it in her eyes. "So, why are you having doubts?"

Everything about her body language reminded him of a soldier preparing for battle.

"I am not having doubts," she lied.

The higher her voice rose, the lower, calmer, his became. "Then why aren't you wearing his ring?" A knowing smile took over. "Afraid a squirrel will mug you out here?"

She said the first thing that popped into her head. "It's too big for me to wear." She realized her mistake the moment the words were out.

He looked at her knowingly. She thought she saw compassion in his eyes and could have spit. "Yes, I read the strip this morning."

Flattery took a back seat to indignation for

Daniel. "I told you, everything there is an exaggeration. I take liberties with things," she insisted with more passion than she intended. "Otherwise, they're not funny."

He'd forgotten how magnificent anger made her. Or maybe he'd never really noticed. He did now. "You know what's funny? You settling for comfortable and complacent."

Was he comparing Daniel to himself? She wasn't sure, but she took a stab at it, anyway. "Comfortable and complacent doesn't give me a headache, and what would you know about what I want in a man?" His presumption galled her.

"Educated guess," he answered calmly. "You'd want someone to send your temperature soaring, to keep you on your toes." He hadn't meant to use her own description of him. That had been an accident. He hoped she was too fired up to notice.

"Shows how much you know. Daniel is mentally stimulating enough, thank you." She dragged a hand through her hair. "Look, maybe this wasn't such a good idea, coming up here again, I—" She fairly jumped at the loud crack that shook the heavens and the house. Her eyes widened. "What was that?"

He'd instinctively placed his hand on her shoulder. The way she stiffened had him dropping it immediately. "Thunder." Morgan glanced toward the living room. "From the looks of it, your dog isn't too keen on that, either."

Traci turned to look behind her. From where

she stood she could see Jeremiah slipping under the rug he'd just been lying on. Argument forgotten, Traci hurried over to the dog.

"Poor baby." She sank down on her knees beside the animal. "It's all right, Jeremiah, just noise. Nothing else."

She wasn't aware that Morgan was right behind her until he spoke. "You'd think he'd be used to noise, being your dog. You still talk to anything with ears?"

It didn't sound like an insult, so she smiled. "Yeah."

Morgan folded his legs under him as he sat down on the floor beside her. "Here." He handed her a fresh mug of coffee. "Sorry, out of sugar."

Traci took it from him. "I'll just dip my finger in."

"That should spice it up," he commented dryly.

Sipping, Traci stroked the animal's fur slowly, knowing the repetitive action would soothe him. The coffee didn't taste half-bad, even without sugar.

She raised her eyes to his. "Thanks."

Morgan shrugged. "No sense in throwing out a good pot of coffee."

Had he always had this core of shyness? she wondered. "Very prudent. Did you get economical after your father lost all that money?"

"I had to. Suddenly things I always thought I couldn't live without were expendable." It had made him take stock of what was really important to him.

She cocked her head, her fingers still tangled in Jeremiah's fur. "Like Cynthia?"

"Yeah."

She saw something flicker in his eyes. For once, she didn't want to return to old ground. "Sorry, low blow."

He lifted a shoulder and let it drop carelessly, unfazed. "I'm used to it with you."

"Very gracious of you." She hesitated. For a moment she actually wanted to tell him about Rory. She hadn't the faintest idea why.

Thunder rolled again. Jeremiah emitted a low moan. Time to get things moving. "I'd better take a walk out back before the storm hits."

He rose to his feet. "That might not be such a bad idea," he agreed. "This storm might not come for hours," he mused, "but then again—"

"It might be here in five minutes," she concluded. In which case, she'd better get on the road. She wanted to get back to the city before any storm of consequence hit.

Morgan took her hand in his and pulled her to her feet. Her body slid against his, igniting a very pleasant sensation.

"You know," she murmured, "if it wasn't you, I would have said that was a choreographed move."

"And if it was anyone but you," he countered, "I would have said you went along with it willingly."

"Good thing we know each other."

"Good thing," he echoed, following her out the back door.

But he couldn't help wondering if they did.

Traci pulled the sleeves of her sweater down to cover her arms, hunching her shoulders slightly against the wind. The incline from the house to the dock below felt steeper than she remembered. She took smaller steps. Age had taken away some of her bravado and made her more careful. So had the fear of falling in front of Morgan and making a fool of herself.

The weather didn't help. It was more suited for a homecoming to a dark, gloomy castle on a lonely cliff than a warm summerhouse nestled beside a lake.

It had been a long time since anything had been tied here, she mused as she looked along the dock. Morgan's father had owned a small motorboat, but she had favored the kayak he'd left for her and Morgan to use. There had been room for two, but she usually got to it first and was on the lake before Morgan was up. They fought about the kayak a lot.

And once, she remembered, sitting down on the edge of the dock, the kayak had been more than just the source of conflict. It had caused Morgan to be a hero. He'd saved her from an ignoble, watery end. The kayak had capsized, something she'd been completely convinced that it couldn't do, and she hadn't been able to right it, or get out. Her feet had somehow gotten stuck inside. Morgan had been the only one on the dock at the time. She'd abandoned him there. He'd seen the kayak go over and he'd jumped in, swimming out to her rescue.

Morgan hadn't let her forget about that one for a long time.

Traci braced her hands on either side of her. The dock felt rough to the touch. Needed work, she mused. The whole house did, really. But it was well worth the effort in her opinion. She hated to think of it as belonging to someone else.

Traci lifted her chin, letting the wind rake spiky, ghostly fingers over her face. Her hair was whipping around her head like curly blond snakes. She looked, Morgan thought, like an illustration for unharnessed mischief.

Or a temptress.

"It's a lot more beautiful than I remember." She nodded toward the lake. On the other side was a pristine, three-story white house. It appeared closer to her than she recalled. Her mouth curved. "And maybe a little smaller."

There was something almost soft about her, Morgan noted. A dimension she probably wanted to keep under wraps.

"And darker." Rain was only minutes away, if that long.

"That, too." She looked up at the angry sky. It was as if a huge, dark comforter was being slipped over them. "It looks like it's going to be a mean one."

He laughed shortly to himself. "Reminds me a little of you."

The comment caught her by surprise. "I was never mean." Morgan arched a brow at the protest. "All right," she relented slightly. She could see how he might have misinterpreted her actions over the years. "But not *mean*-mean."

Leave it to Traci to be obscure about something so straightforward and simple. "That terminology might fit right into a long-running children's program where the guy is forever changing his shoes to sneakers and back again, but I'm not sure I follow the distinction here.''

Traci blew out a breath. It was lost in the wind. ''I was just being a kid—''

He shook his head at her explanation. ''Not like any kid I ever knew.''

It was getting really chilly and she shivered. Morgan curbed the urge to put his arm around her. She'd probably bite it off, just like a fox gnawing off its own foot to be free of a trap.

Traci squared her shoulders. The wind ran right up her back. ''I'll take that as a compliment.''

He put a pin to her bubble. ''It wasn't intended as one.''

''Never mind.'' She sniffed, hiding her grin. ''Too late.''

Funny how he was amused by the very thing that would have sent him up a wall a decade ago. ''With you, it was too late from the first moment.''

''If you mean you were a dead duck from the minute our parents introduced us, you were smarter back then than I gave you credit for.''

He opened his mouth to answer, then thought better of it. It was futile to battle it out verbally with her. Morgan knew by experience that one way or another, Traci would always come out on top. It was the warrior instinct in her.

The description made him smile.

''What?''

He shook his head. ''Never mind.''

Jeremiah, safely ensconced in the house, howled his displeasure about being left behind. Morgan looked behind him and saw the dog through the screen door. Jeremiah was hardly more than a dark shadow. A dark shadow that was trying to paw through the mesh and get out, he noted.

"Where did you ever find him?" As Traci began to answer, Morgan stopped her. "No, let me guess. He's a stray."

Jeremiah didn't look like a mutt that had lived on the street. "How did you know?"

That was easy. Morgan's short laugh was swallowed up by the wind. "You're the type to take in strays."

Something about the set of his mouth as he said that alerted her. "Is this leading up to another crack about Daniel?"

"Hardly." *Touchy, touchy.* He had to have struck a nerve earlier, Morgan thought. Maybe she really was having strong doubts about marrying this dentist of hers, just as he'd suggested.

He looked up at the sky and thought about getting back. But there was something oddly nice about sitting out here with her. He didn't know which was more invigorating, Traci or the wind. "A successful dentist who has two practices in New York City can't be considered a stray by any stretch of the imagination."

She turned toward him, pulling her legs up against her body for warmth and wrapping her arms around them. "How do you know so much about him?'' Before he could say anything, she had her answer. ''My mother, right?''

He nodded, completing the thought. ''Your mother relates information to my mother who, in turn, feels honor bound to pass it on to me, as if I would be missing something if I didn't know.'' The look on his face told Traci what he thought of *that* idea. ''I think she hopes that our sense of competition will have me running to the nearest altar.''

Traci rocked back, studying him. A smile played on her lips. ''Little good that'll do you alone.''

''She was hoping I'd bring someone with me,'' he said dryly.

''So, why don't you?'' She would have expected someone like Morgan to have already been married five years and working on his second child. ''You're young, reasonably attractive,'' she paused, catching her tongue between her teeth, ''and some women even like lawyers—''

He looked away. The water was getting choppier on the lake, like a bathtub where a child was conducting a battle with toy ships. It was going to be a big one when it hit, he thought.

''Thanks for the crumbs, but the truth is that I haven't found anyone.''

How hard could that be? She stared at him incredulously. ''My God, Morgan, you found Cynthia. Anyone else could only be a step up.''

''Maybe.'' He shrugged. ''But I've been too busy to step anywhere—up or down.''

His words stirred a memory. "That was always your excuse."

He looked at her, surprised.

"If you hadn't hidden behind your schoolwork, you wouldn't have been such ripe prey for someone like Cynthia."

Morgan didn't see the connection, but then, he didn't have Traci's convoluted way of thinking, either. "What's that supposed to mean?"

For a supposedly smart man, Morgan could be very dumb sometimes. Traci recited the answer in a singsong voice, as if she was trying to get the concept across to a child. "You lacked experience and were an easy target for a shark."

He had a strange, bemused expression on his face.

"What's the matter?"

He leaned closer so his words weren't blown away before they reached her. "I just had a sudden vision of this turning up in your strip." The look in her eyes didn't lay his suspicions to rest. "It won't, will it?"

She looked at Morgan innocently. Now that he mentioned it...

"No, why should it? This is your life, remember? Not mine."

That didn't assure him. She sounded much too innocent. "Yes, but somehow the edges have gotten blurred since I've been talking to you about it." The Traci in the strip had a best friend named Velma with whom she dissected practically ev-

erything. He could just see himself being dissected by the two.

Traci raised her hand as if making a solemn
promise. Mentally, she crossed her fingers. All
was fair in love, war and comic strips.

"Don't worry, I'll leave you out of it. Although
the thought of drawing a shark with Cynthia's
face does have its appeal."

He could see where it might for her, and if he
were being completely honest, the thought appealed to him, as well. With one stipulation.

"Well, if she does turn up, I'd appreciate it if
you draw her nibbling away at someone else."
The last thing in the world he wanted was to open
the morning paper and look at a caricature of himself mooning at a sharklike Cynthia.

"Rory," Traci muttered to herself. Someone
like Cynthia should have feasted on someone like
Rory. They deserved each other.

"Who?"

Traci looked at him in surprise. She hadn't realized that she'd said the name out loud. "Hmm?"

Morgan moved closer to her. He had no desire
to shout. "You said a name."

Funny, how with all this wind she could still
smell his cologne. She had no idea what it was,
only that she liked it. Maybe a tad too much.

"No, I didn't," she protested staunchly.

He knew she had. "Roy?" he guessed. It had
sounded something like that.

She'd be damned if she was going to play
twenty questions about her past. She might want

him to bare his soul, but hers was staying right
where it was, hidden. No one else knew about
Rory and it was going to stay that way. She had
better things to do than publicize her own stupidity. It was far more entertaining to tease Morgan
about his.

Pity filled her eyes. "Approaching thirty and
losing your hearing already. What a shame."

He was about to say something about the wind
being responsible when a large splotch of rain hit
Traci directly in the face. Even larger drops followed in rapid succession, falling harder and
faster.

Morgan rose to his feet at the same time she
jumped to hers. "Yikes," she cried. "These drops
are as big as swimming pools."

Without thinking, Morgan grabbed her hand
and they ran up the hill toward the house.

"'Yikes'?" he echoed. "Who the hell says
yikes these days? You've been watching too
many cartoons."

"Never too many." She laughed as they made
it through the back door. And just in time. Suddenly, sheets of rain began falling.

Jeremiah, agitated and distressed by the
weather, almost managed to knock Morgan down
as they hurried in. Morgan grabbed for the door-
jamb and shifted out of the way just in time.

Running a hand through his hair to shake off
the rain, Morgan glared at the dog. "Can't you
train this animal?"

She managed to maintain a straight face for almost a minute. "Not a problem. Jeremiah," she said, looking sternly at the dog. "Knock him down. See?" Traci turned a sunny smile on Morgan. "He almost did it."

When was he ever going to learn? "Do you ever get serious?"

Traci pushed her hair out of her face in the careless manner of a woman who was content with her looks in any situation.

"Not if I can help it. It doesn't pay. Too depressing."

She'd always been just a little too crazy for his tastes. "You know, there is a happy medium between Kafka and Jocko the Clown."

"Tell me when you find it." She looked down and saw that there was a small puddle forming on the floor where she stood. She'd gotten wetter than she thought in that short run. "You have any more towels around here, or do I just stand dripping on your floor?"

"Sorry, this is all I have. I wasn't expecting a storm." His eyes washed over her as he passed her the lone towel. "Although, maybe I should have been."

She fluttered her eyes at him the way she'd done when she'd imitated Cynthia. "You say the sweetest things." Traci rubbed the towel through her hair quickly, then offered it back to him.

Morgan took it, vaguely aware that her scent was clinging to it. It became more potent when he brought the towel closer. Disturbed, he dropped it on the back of his chair.

Something moved through him, restless and unsettled when he looked at her.

He had to be crazy to be having these feelings about her. She was just as competitive, just as irritating, as ever. And she was about to be engaged. Any way he looked at it, the package was not inviting.

Or wasn't supposed to be.

Avoiding her eyes, Morgan crossed to the window. "Not exactly the greatest weather for a reunion." The trees directly outside the window were bending to and fro, like stately dancers doing stretching exercises before their performance. "You'd think the weather bureau could be right once in a while."

Traci stroked Jeremiah's head, then moved beside Morgan. It was really beginning to look foul out there. Her first weekend off in months and it had to turn into this.

She shrugged philosophically. "What? And spoil a perfect record? Not hardly. Think it's easy always being wrong?" she quipped.

He turned to look at her. She was back on the floor, stroking that wimp of a dog of hers. "I don't know. Is it?"

"Oh, low blow." She grinned, and somehow the storm stepped back a few feet away from them. "I like that. You're beginning to show promise."

The look in her eyes warmed him.

The crack of thunder made Traci jump back to her feet. "I think it's time to take this show on

the road before there isn't a road to take it on.''
But even as she said it, Traci found herself not
wanting to leave just yet. As if, once she walked
out the door, she'd be closing a chapter of her life
forever.

It was a silly thought, but she couldn't shake
it.

''You might be right,'' Morgan agreed and then
grinned at her. ''I guess there has to be a first
time for everything.''

''Just because I said I liked that low blow
doesn't mean you should get carried away. A little
sarcasm is a good thing, but there is such a thing
as overkill.''

''You ought to know,'' he murmured. There
was humor in her eyes and he was drawn to it.

Every inclination directed her toward the door
and the road beyond. She was right in wanting to
leave before the road became impassable. And yet
something—she wasn't sure just what—was telling her to linger a little longer. Linger despite
common sense and a whining dog to the contrary.

She supposed there was no harm in giving in
for a couple more minutes. Traci pretended to
look around for her purse, stalling.

''You never told me—why are your parents
selling the house now?''

She would have thought that was something
they would have done during that low period
they'd experienced, not now, when, according to
her mother, everything was going so well for

them. Jim Brigham's company had not only regained its former ground but grown beyond it.

Morgan paused, looking for the right words to
frame his answer. "They want to be free to travel
around in, to put it my mother's way, 'the sunset
of their years.'" He shrugged, looking around as
if he hadn't done so a dozen times already before
she'd arrived. "My guess is that the house was
beginning to need too many things—"

"Like good storm windows?" There was a definite chill in the air that seemed to be coming
from outside despite the fact that everything appeared to be locked up tight.

He'd noticed the draft earlier; he nodded. "And
other things." He was warming to his explanation. "They were beginning to think of it as a
burden, so they asked me to sell it for them."

She could guess at the practical reasons behind
it, but she wasn't all that crazy about practicality.
No matter how much Daniel swore by it, she
thought suddenly. The unexpected thought unnerved her.

"Seems a shame to let it go."

He studied her closely. "Why? It's falling
apart."

She sniffed her contempt of his view. "You
would only see that."

Morgan set his jaw hard and folded his arms
before him. "What do you see?"

Her expression softened as if she were looking
beyond the walls. "Memories."

Habit as ingrained as breathing had him challenging her. "I don't need a building to see that. Memories are in your head and your heart and, occasionally, in an album."

Her eyes widened as she looked at him. "Why, Morgan, that's positively poetic."

Morgan knew better than to take her comment at face value. He waited for a punch line. She wasn't about to disappoint him.

"Limited," she added airily, "but poetic."

He knew he could count on Traci. "Okay, I'll bite. Why limited?"

She glanced toward the fireplace in the living room and wished for a fire. It only reminded her that she really should be leaving.

"Because if we followed your way of thinking, no one would have ever bothered with preserving historic landmarks."

He couldn't help laughing at the comparison. "This house is hardly a historic landmark."

The man was hopeless. "No, not to the world. But to those of us who spent a lot of time here..." She stopped and looked at him. "You don't feel anything, do you?"

"Confused," he volunteered. "Does that count?"

Traci laughed as she hit his chest playfully with the flat of her hand. "No, that doesn't—"

The next thing she knew, Jeremiah was up and growling at Morgan as fiercely as if he'd just uncovered an entire battalion of enemy soldiers—or cats.

Traci made a grab for the dog's collar a second

before he reared at Morgan. Teeth snapped with a menacing finality.

Morgan took a step back uneasily. "What's his problem?"

"I guess Jeremiah thought we were fighting and he was coming to my rescue."

Those teeth really did look large close up. And lethal. So much for thinking the dog a wimp. "Better tether him if you and Daniel ever argue."

Traci stroked Jeremiah until the dog calmed down again. With a tentative yawn, he lay down at her feet. "We don't argue."

Morgan laughed out loud and Traci looked at him accusingly.

"Oh, come on, Traci. This is me. I know you. You'd argue with God."

She stuck by her statement. It was the truth. "Daniel and I don't argue."

As she said them, her own words made her think. Why *didn't* they argue? Normal people argued. She more than most, although she wasn't about to admit that point to Morgan.

He looked at her closely. "You're really serious." True concern nudged him on. And maybe just a little bit of hope. "Traci, I was only kidding earlier, but maybe you should really think about this. He obviously can't be the one for you. You need passion in your life, zest. The kind of man who can make you argue. A man who can periodically take you and shake you up—and you him."

Realizing he was saying a hell of a lot more

than he intended to, Morgan abruptly stopped talking.

He wasn't telling her anything she hadn't thought herself, in the wee hours of the morning when the world was its blackest and doubts loomed their largest. The fact that she agreed, however, wouldn't have stopped her from taking umbrage at his words.

What stopped her was the look in Morgan's eyes. He wasn't baiting her, wasn't trying to arouse her ire. He was serious.

As if he cared.

The way she had cared when she had thought of Morgan throwing away his life on someone like Cynthia. It gave her pause and momentarily took away her tongue.

When she found it, she spoke quietly. "He's a good man, Morgan."

Morgan wasn't quite sure exactly how he had gotten in so close to her, he only knew that, somehow, they were standing almost toe-to-toe and the distance was rapidly shrinking, even though neither one of them was moving a muscle.

"So's the pope. You're not marrying him."

A half smile curved her full mouth. "No, he didn't ask."

Her answer told him more than she realized. "So, you are marrying Daniel?"

She thought that one over carefully. Slowly, she nodded. "I think so."

Morgan resisted believing her. Because he didn't think that in her heart she believed herself.

"That doesn't sound like the Traci I know. The one who runs headlong into things without thinking."

No, it didn't. She forced a smile to her lips. "Maybe I've grown up."

He remained unconvinced. "I don't think so. Not you. Not like this."

She lifted her chin, suddenly feeling very uneasy, as if the ground beneath her feet were liquefying. But that was impossible. That happened only during an earthquake, and they didn't get earthquakes out here.

Only storms.

Like the one swirling around her now.

"What would you know about it?" she challenged, digging for some of her customary bravado. "You haven't seen me in, what, eight years?"

"Nine," he corrected softly.

Very lightly, he feathered his fingers along her face. He couldn't seem to help himself. Nor could he help this feeling that was taking hold of him against his will.

It *was* against his will, wasn't it?

"And I know." He smiled into her eyes, quieting her protest, as if anything earthly actually could. "I read your strip."

"I already told you, Morgan. All that's exaggerated." The words were supposed to be shouted. But they merely dripped from her lips like a faucet that wasn't quite turned off.

"Yes, I know." His face, his lips, drew closer. "But so are you."

Something was twisting inside her stomach. "Morgan?" she whispered.

"Hmm?" She seemed to be all around him, invading his senses like a virus.

She ran the tip of her tongue over her parched lips. "You're standing too close."

He cupped her cheek. "No, I'm not. I can't kiss you from across the room."

"Oh." Slowly, she nodded her head, as if in a trance. And maybe, just maybe, she was in one. Otherwise, she'd be running for her life. Because what she was feeling was scaring her. "Good reason." Her throat had never felt so dry in her whole life. As dry as the world outside the window was wet.

And then his lips touched hers and the world outside might as well have existed on another planet.

Because she certainly did.

5

She heard them.

She actually heard them. Bells. Banjos. And maybe even a sousaphone thrown in for good measure. They were all there, an entire symphony full of them. Along with music she couldn't place and a rush of fire that threatened to consume everything in its path.

Her, first of all.

She'd seen the kiss coming. But what she hadn't foreseen was what could come after. Nothing could have prepared her for that.

Caught completely off guard, Traci had no defenses against the feeling that swept over her with the speed of a flame eating its way up a narrow line of gunpowder. And because her head was spinning around like a carousel at warp speed, she had no desire to offer any, either.

Breathless, intoxicated, Traci allowed herself to be taken away by the feeling. To savor it, to revel in it. Most of all, to be awed by it.

It was almost like when Rory kissed her. Almost but not quite.

This was different.

Better.

Her fingers tightened on Morgan's shoulders as she rose on her toes to surrender completely to the sensation. It was absolutely incredible.

Traci?

Her name throbbed in Morgan's mind as bewildering, demanding sensations throbbed in other parts of his body.

This was *Traci?*

How a woman who had been as irritating as scratchy long winter underwear for more than a decade of his life, who was damn irritating *now*, could possibly inspire this rush he was feeling—

this bone melting, mind numbing reaction that made him want to plunge himself into the kiss, into her, and never come up for air—was completely beyond him.

He couldn't begin to fathom it.

Traci?

Naw, couldn't be.

And yet, here she was, in his arms, sealed to his mouth, sucking out life forces from him with a speed that had Morgan reeling. And wanting more. A hell of a lot more.

The very thought that he wanted to make love with her sobered him even as it threatened to send him over the edge.

Shaken, dazed and more confused than he'd possibly ever been in his life, Morgan drew away from her. But as if some part of him refused to let go, he found himself still holding on to her arms.

Morgan's eyes narrowed as he studied her face. Yes, it was Traci. No doubt about it. What was in doubt, though, was his sanity. So much the more because part of him, against all odds, had suspected this all along.

Traci swallowed. It didn't help. Her throat felt dry, scratchy. She was aware of everything around her. She could have even sworn that she could feel her hair growing.

"Were you trying to prove a point?" The question came out in a low whisper. Anything louder and she knew her voice would crack. Or even give out completely. And when had it gotten so damn hot in here? She blew out a breath. Her bangs fluttered against her damp forehead.

Pulses throughout Morgan's body scrambled to reclaim positions. He cleared his throat. "I don't know, was I?"

If he had been, it was completely lost on him. As were his bearings and, just possibly, his name, rank and serial number.

Very slowly, the world came back into focus for Traci. This was ridiculous. She couldn't be having this kind of a reaction to Morgan. Not *Morgan*. They were friendly enemies, competitors, maybe even fond of each other, but nothing more.

But if that was true, how the hell had he managed to evoke this wild, erotic tune that was even now still ricocheting in her brain?

"What's the matter?" he asked. She had an odd expression on her face. Did she feel as disoriented as he did? It would help if she did. Not a hell of a whole lot, but some.

Traci slowly shook her head before answering, trying to buy herself a little more time.

"Nothing," she mumbled. Then her eyes looked up at him, wide with wonder. She had to say it. "You never kissed me before."

He would have, he thought, if he'd known that kissing her could pack such a wallop. But admitting it would put him at a disadvantage. "It never came up."

She could only stare at him incredulously, willing her knees back among the functioning. "And it did now?"

He had to make light of it. If he didn't, she'd see right through him—down to the shaken mess that was passing as his soul at the moment.

"We were standing close, your lips were there." He shrugged, at a loss as to where to go from here. "I don't know, maybe I was struck temporarily insane."

It seemed as good an explanation as any, at least to him. Why else would he have kissed her? It wasn't as if he was actually attracted to her. Sure, she was pretty, gorgeous, even, in the right light, but he *knew* her. Knew what she was like. How could he be attracted to a woman who had once put red ants into his sandwich?

And yet, hadn't he, in some small, imperceptible way, been attracted to her all along? Hadn't he wondered, in the back of his mind, what it would be like to kiss her?

Well, now he knew. And it blew out all the stops.

There was something more there, Traci thought. She could see it in his face. Or maybe she was just hoping there was more—to placate herself and her still erratically fluttering pulse.

"Is that your best defense, Counselor?"

"That's my best explanation," he clarified. And then, because he believed in telling the truth, or at least some measure of it, he relented. "It's either that, or call you a witch."

She didn't knew whether to be annoyed or amused. "So this is my fault now, is it?"

"Not so much a fault as—" He stopped as a thought struck him. "Do you kiss Donald this way?"

"Daniel," Traci corrected. Donald was the name of her cartoon suitor. *Traci's* cartoon suitor, she amended, annoyed at herself for the slip. Annoyance shifted to a more likely target. "And that's none of your business."

Maybe, but he thought it was. And he did have a point to make. "Okay, but if you do kiss him like that, and he's still as bland as he sounds, I'd check the man for a pulse—or, barring that, antennae."

Now he had really lost her. "What?"

Morgan hated admitting any more than he already had, but he supposed he had to. "Nothing human could have withstood that and not felt his socks getting short-circuited."

Indignation and confusion slowly slipped away, replaced with a glimmer of a satisfied smile. So he *had* felt something. Hopefully, more than she had, although she wasn't certain how that was humanly possible. "Is that a compliment?"

She looked like a cat that had fallen headfirst into a vat of cream. He refused to give her an ounce more. "That's an observation."

She knew it was more than that, but for both their sakes she played along and nodded. A fresh crack of thunder and Jeremiah's accompanying wail only served as a distant backdrop to the scenario going on before her. Her mouth still felt as if it was throbbing. And the rest of her was vibrating like a tuning fork.

Traci knew she had to leave. Now, before something unforeseeable happened. Something she would undoubtedly live to regret.

She nodded again, dumbly, like a windup toy with one trick. That Morgan had managed to disorient her to this extent really annoyed her. "I guess you're not so bad yourself."

The cast-off comment had him smiling. If she admitted to smoke, there most certainly was fire. "Gosh, can you spare that?"

Traci blew out a breath. It was still far too shaky for her liking. "Just barely. Well, like I said, I'd better be going."

She was backing up, away from Morgan. Away from what she'd just experienced, even though a very large part of her wanted to move forward, to explore this new, uncharted region a little more.

Wanted to feel a little more.

To feel more. Traci almost mocked herself. She'd been that route and knew the danger that laid therein. All sensation, no substance.

But that had been Rory and this...

This was Morgan, for heaven's sake. She's seen him naked, albeit years ago, but still, there was no mystery here—except, maybe, that she would have never dreamed in a million years...

Nope, never.

She groped for her purse. Time for Cinderella to rush home while she still had a pumpkin to work with. Traci clapped her hands and Jeremiah came at her call. She picked up his leash, wrapping it firmly around her hand. If nothing else, it served as insulation against Morgan.

Only then did she look at him again. "It's been an experience, Morgan. One we'll have to do again—in about another nine or ten years. But right now, I have a storm to beat." She found she had to force cheeriness into her voice.

He didn't want her leaving and he definitely didn't like the idea of her leaving in this kind of weather. It was particularly nasty outside. "Ordinarily, I'd say my money was on you when it came to beating anything." He glanced out the window. "But it looks pretty bad out there, Traci."

For some reason, she found the serious note in his voice unsettling. She liked it better when they were sparring. She felt equipped to handle that, not this shaky vulnerability he'd managed to uncover.

"Don't worry, I'll be fine." *As soon as my double vision goes away,* she thought, giving her head one more shake.

She glanced at Morgan over her shoulder as she opened the door. *It had to have been a fluke.* Maybe she was coming down with something. That had to be it. Otherwise, she'd have to think that she and Morgan...

No, she didn't have to think that. Not ever. Besides, it was too late for something like that. She had her commitment before her and it was to Daniel.

"I'll see you around," she told him, raising her voice above the wind. Traci gave the leash a slight tug. "Let's go, Jeremiah."

The dog resisted crossing the threshold. He barked twice at the brooding, darkened sky.

Morgan wondered what sort of perverse psychology he could use on Traci to make her stay. Nothing came to mind and he knew that asking her to wait out the storm would never work.

He nodded toward her pet. "He has more sense than you do."

Morgan was standing way too close again, she thought. Driving in the storm would be a comfort by comparison. At least that didn't involve scrambling pulses and confused thoughts.

"Lovely parting shot, Morgan," she quipped. "You should put them all in a book and give them out as gifts for Christmas. Well, see you." Her voice was way too high, but nerves were causing that.

Thousands of little nerves, scattered throughout her body like ants whose hill had just been demolished by an overeager anteater.

Traci almost fled to her car.

She should have parked closer, she thought, annoyed with herself. She should have also left earlier—for a lot of reasons. But that was a moot point now.

The wind lashed at her hair, whipping it around her head and reducing it to a soggy, springy mass of curls within seconds. Muttering under her breath, Traci opened the car door and herded Jeremiah in, then rounded the hood and got in on the driver's side. She jammed the key into the ignition, pushing wet bangs out of her eyes.

She held her breath as she drove. The downpour was pretty intense, but it was too late to turn back. She refused to return with her tail between her legs because of the storm. Not when she would bet her soul that Morgan was standing in the doorway, waiting for her to come back. Waiting to smugly say, "I told you so."

Or worse yet, to kiss her again and watch the reaction on her face.

What had happened back there, anyway? Why the sudden combustion? It was as if something had just been lying in wait all these years, lying in wait for the right moment.

This wasn't getting her anywhere.

A bolt of lightning creased the sky like a crooked javelin hurled by an angry Norse god. It temporarily threw the world into daylight and then back into numbing darkness again.

Jeremiah was not happy about it.

"Hush," she chided. "We'll be home in time to watch reruns of 'Lassie.' They have to be playing on some channel." The thought of curling up on her sofa, basking in the warm glow cast from the television set, comforted her.

It was a hell of a lot more comforting than attempting to drive through the English Channel, which was what this was beginning to feel like, she thought. She pressed her lips together, concentrating.

Visibility went from poor to almost nonexistent in an alarming few minutes, even though the windshield wipers were doing double time. They no sooner pushed the rain aside than another deluge fell to take up the space, completely blotting out her view of the road. And no matter what she did with the heater and the defrost switches, her windows insisted on fogging up. The situation was almost impossible.

Desperate, Traci rolled down the window on the driver's side, cracking the other for balance. Rain came into the car, lashing at her face. But at least she could see. What there was to see.

Craning her neck, Traci peered through the open window. She squinted, trying to make out the road that rain and encroaching darkness were bent on obscuring.

Holding her breath, Traci drove slower than she'd ever driven in her life. The wind continued to pick up, howling. Jeremiah joined in the competition.

It got on her nerves. "I hope you don't intend to do that all the way home. I'm fresh out of aspirin." And patience, she added silently.

She should have remained in the house with Morgan, she told herself. She realized that her jaw was clenched, as clenched as her fingers were on the steering wheel. Focusing, she tried to ease up on both. But the tension in her shoulders persisted.

And there was something more. The wind had initially masked it, but now the sound grew louder. Water. Rushing water. It took her a second to make the connection. The gully beneath the bridge had filled with water. That meant she had to be getting close to it.

Damn it, where was the bridge? Why couldn't she see it? It had to be here somewhere.

Traci craned her neck farther, searching for the small wooden structure. Crossing it earlier, she'd thought that time had made the bridge almost rickety. Not that it had ever been all that strong to begin with. And in this weather it would have to be—

Gone.

Fear seemed to manually force her heart into her throat where it remained, stuck, as Traci realized that she was now directly over where the bridge should have been.

And there was nothing there.

The edges of her front tires were touching nothing. The headache that had been threatening to engulf her ever since she left the house made an appearance, full bodied and strong. It pounded over her temples and forehead like a scorned, irate lover as Traci frantically threw the car into reverse, trying to keep the car from plunging straight into the gully.

She overcompensated, turning the steering wheel too far to the left, and the car went speeding backward, making contact with a tree.

Shrieking, Traci slammed on her brakes, but it

was after the fact. The collision was already in motion. Metal against wood.

It felt as if something vital had been jarred loose in her body as she hit her forehead against the steering wheel. The last thing she heard was Jeremiah's mournful cry.

And then there was an inky blackness dropping over her, too heavy to resist.

Her eyelids weighed a ton. Each one. It took her several vain attempts to pry open her eyes. Each time she tried, she found she couldn't lift them. It was as if they were nailed down.

Traci thought she heard a voice. Someone was talking to her, but she couldn't place who it was or what was being said. And there were shadows moving, drifting here and there. Some belonged to the voice. Others didn't.

Each time she was sure she'd opened her eyes and looked, she discovered that she hadn't.

It was frustrating as hell.

Traci moaned, trying to turn, to sit up, confident that if she did, her eyes would open.

She began to make things out more clearly. There were hands holding her down. Gentle hands. Strong hands. She struggled against them and lost that fight, too. There seemed to be no energy flowing through her. Nothing. No blood.

Blood.

Jeremiah.

Oh, God, she'd killed Jeremiah. She'd heard his pitiful moan just before she—what?

Where was she? Traci twisted again, but the same two hands were holding her down. They were pressing on her arms. She fought, struggled, tried to speak, and still her eyes refused to budge.

Was it a dream? Was she dead?

It was a lot drier where she was.

Heaven?

In the distance somewhere, she heard the crackle of something. Fire?

Was she in hell? She groaned in fear.

"Damn it, even when you're unconscious, you're a problem."

Morgan, that was Morgan's voice. Was he dead, too? No, she'd left him in the house. Him and his lips.

With supreme effort, Traci concentrated on the sound of his voice, on surfacing out of this cottony netherworld she was trapped in.

Inch by inch, she made it to the top. Her eyes finally flew open and focused on Morgan. He was looming over her, almost larger than life. And he was holding her down. Touching her. Never mind that it was only her arms. She could feel it all along her body.

This had to stop.

"Get your hands off me," she breathed.

Grasping at indignation and hoping it would give her the shot of adrenaline she needed, Traci bolted upright. A second later, she became one with the pain that rushed up to greet her. Her head felt like an egg that had been cracked open against the side of a pan.

Instinctively, her hand went to her head. There was a bandage there.

"What the—?"

Morgan grabbed her wrist and firmly held on to it. "Leave that alone," he ordered. "You hit your head on the steering wheel and cut your forehead." When he saw that she was actually going to listen to him, he released her wrist. "Although I didn't think anything as hard as that could be cut by anything less than the sharp edge of a diamond."

Everything felt as if it were submerged in her mind, mired in thick chicken soup. She looked around. She was back in the house. On the sofa. Before the fireplace. But that was impossible.

"How did I get here?"

The color was returning to her cheeks. That was a good sign. She'd given him one hell of a scare back there. When he had found her slumped over the steering wheel, he'd thought she was dead. It had taken him a moment to quell and manage the panic that had shot through him. "I brought you back here."

She drew her brows together and found that it hurt. "You?"

He lifted a shoulder and then let it drop carelessly. "Sir Lancelot was busy."

It still didn't make any sense to her. She'd left him in the house. How could he have known she was in an accident? And why was he all wet?

"Why—? How—?"

Since neither one of them was going anywhere,

Morgan sat down on the edge of the sofa beside her.

"The 'why' is because I didn't think leaving you out in the rain was such a good idea. And the 'how' is that I carried you." His mouth curved. Now that she was conscious, he could allow himself that luxury. "You weigh less than I thought."

Traci tried to assimilate what he was telling her, feeding it into her brain above the pounding pain. She held her head, afraid that if she didn't, it would fall off.

"But I left you in here," she began, hoping that saying the words aloud would somehow help her make sense out of her scattered thoughts. It didn't. She couldn't seem to get them in order.

Watching her car disappear into the rain had given him a very uneasy feeling. Morgan had waited five minutes, maybe six, before finally getting into his own car and following her. He'd arrived just in time to watch her car travel backward into the tree. Racing from his car to hers had been the longest and worst minute of his life.

"I'm ambulatory in case you haven't noticed." He might as well tell her the whole truth. "I was worried and decided to go out looking for you. Lucky thing for you I did. We're marooned out here, at least for the duration of the storm. My distributor cap decided to play dead just as I got to the lovely mess that used to be your car."

The reason for the car's sudden shuddering and then sputtering halt had registered in his mind only after the fact. Nothing had registered at the time except that her car was crashing right before his eyes. And that she was in it.

Traci winced as the memory returned. "My car—it's bad?"

"Only if you want to drive it. As an accordion it still has possibilities." He became serious. It could have very well gone a different way. "You're damn lucky to be alive."

She was almost afraid to ask. But she had to know. "Jeremiah—?"

He'd dragged the dumb mutt along with him in his wake. It hadn't been easy but he wasn't about to abandon the mangy animal in the storm.

"Smells like hell wet," he informed her gently. "Can't you smell him?"

She took a deep breath and then visibly calmed down. "Now I can." Her eyes turned to his and she mustered a smile, despite the pain that was splitting her head in half. "Thanks."

Morgan made light of her gratitude. Accepting it was more difficult than he thought.

"Don't mention it. It was selfish, anyway." He saw her brows draw together. "Your mother would have killed me if I let anything happen to you."

"Can't have that happening," she murmured. She was vaguely aware that Jeremiah had moved closer to her. Hand dangling over the side of the sofa, Traci managed to lightly run her fingers over his wet coat. It was a comforting gesture.

Almost as comforting as having Morgan sitting beside her.

If someone had ever attempted to tell him that Traci had a vulnerable side, Morgan would have laughed him out of the room. But there was no other word that could describe the way she looked lying there on the sofa, her eyes half-closed, the bandage taped to her forehead. He had this over-whelming urge to take care of her. An urge he knew would irritate her if she suspected it.

He'd felt this way about her only once before, he remembered. The time he'd saved her when she was drowning. But all that had happened so fast, he hadn't had time to dwell on it.

He did now.

A strange, bittersweet feeling drifted through him. He never realized how frail she looked. Morgan took Traci's hand between his. It felt small and cold. "How do you feel?"

Much too much. It was as if something was opening inside of her. Opening like a flower to the sun after a long rainy period. Opening and being drawn to Morgan. It had to be the result of the trauma to her head, she thought. There was no other explanation for it. She wasn't going to let there be another explanation for it.

"I'm all right," she murmured. "A little woozy, but under the circumstances, I guess that's allowed."

She felt a great deal more than that, but with luck, it would pass. Her mother liked to brag that the women in the Richardson family were made of stern, pioneer stock. Right now, she felt like a pioneer woman a cow had stepped on.

He wasn't quite certain he believed her protest. "I tried to call for an ambulance, but the phone isn't working. The storm must have knocked out the lines."

All this and heaven, too. "I don't need an ambulance," Traci said with the first ounce of feeling he'd heard since she'd opened her eyes. It made him feel a little better about her condition. "I just have to lie here for a few minutes, that's all."

He nodded. Right now, that seemed to be the only thing they could do, anyway. Morgan looked down at her. The sofa was turning dark from the water it was leeching from her clothes.

"You're going to have to get out of those wet things." Advice he should follow himself, he thought. His own were sticking to him and felt clammy along his body.

"You know, if it was anyone but you saying this, I would have said that you had an ulterior motive."

The idea had already crossed his mind—more than once—but now wasn't the time to tell her. Probably never was more like it.

"Well, it is me," Morgan said a little too briskly, "and I do. I don't want you to get sick on me. I didn't carry you all the way back here just to have you come down with pneumonia."

He'd told her that before, but his words seemed to suddenly fall into place. He had actually carried her back. In the storm. The vision was hopelessly romantic. And yet she refused to accept it as such. She couldn't be having romantic notions. Not about Morgan. And she engaged, for heaven's sake. Or almost engaged. She'd made up her mind to tell Daniel yes.

Hadn't she?

Traci tried to prop herself up on her elbows, but the effort was too much for her. Weakly, she sank down against the sofa.

"You carried me all the way?" It had to be, what, at least a mile from the bridge to the house? Maybe two. She wasn't any good at gauging distances and she wasn't very good at gauging what was going on inside her right now, either. She didn't know what to say.

Morgan maintained a stony expression. "I thought of dragging you by one foot, but then you would have gotten mud in your hair and I would have never heard the end of it."

The answer made her smile. "I guess a little of me has rubbed off on you over the years."

He shivered in response, then deadpanned, "Horrible, isn't it? I'm seeing about having it surgically removed. In the meantime, we've got to get you into some dry clothes."

He'd saved her life once, maybe twice if she stretched it, and they'd known each other forever, but there was a place to draw the line and it was here.

"Not 'we,' Morgan. This isn't a joint project." This time she managed to get herself into a sitting position. But not without a price. Pins and needles attacked her from all angles, all aimed at the bump on her head. "Ow." Her hand automatically flew to her forehead. The lump beneath the bandage felt as if it were the size of a melon. "Oh, heck, maybe it is a joint project, after all."

Right now, she didn't feel as if she could even stand by herself.

"Be still my beating heart."

His tone was softer than she thought it would be. Traci looked at him, wondering what he was thinking and if what had happened just before she'd left was somehow coloring everything for Morgan. It certainly was for her, even though she was steeped in pain and clutching on to denial with both hands.

Much as the idea of peeling her clothes off for her appealed to him, Morgan knew that in his present state of mind, it was tantamount to playing with fire.

"I think you can manage, given time," he assured her. But what to put on was the problem. "I don't suppose you brought a change of clothes with you?"

She began to shake her head and then stopped. "No." She breathed the word out heavily. "Why should I?"

It had only been a shot in the dark. "Good point, but then, you've never conformed to the norm. Nothing wearable in the car at all?"

Morgan was thinking along the lines of a cast-off sweatshirt or sweatpants Traci might have tossed into the car after a workout at her health club. Traci had always been gung ho for physical fitness and liked exercising with people around. He preferred working out in solitude in his own garage.

Traci sighed. "Not unless I feel like wearing

spark plugs and trying out for Ms. Toolbelt of 1997.''

"You wouldn't win," he commented. "You don't have the injectors for it."

She wondered if that was a veiled comment about her chest. She'd always been small, or, as she preferred thinking of it, "athletically built." The idea that she was wondering if he was thinking about her bra size at all told her that she'd gotten more shaken up in the accident than she'd thought.

"And what's that supposed to mean?"

"Nothing." He rose to his feet. What he needed, he thought, was some distance between them so he could sort out these very odd feelings he was having. "It just sounded like some inane thing you'd say to me." He squared his shoulders. "I've got a flannel shirt upstairs. I guess that'll have to do."

She didn't understand. Her mind kept drifting. Had he always been this good looking? "Do? Do for what?"

"For you to change into," he said patiently, slowly, as if he were speaking to someone whose brain had been dropped in a blender. "Until your clothes dry. I can hang them out here by the fire." He nodded toward the fireplace.

She stared at the empty, dark hearth. "There isn't one."

"I'll make it."

In all the years she'd been coming here, they hadn't once used the fireplace. She'd always wondered what it would look like with a big, roaring fire blazing in it. "Do you know how?"

She really did think of him as inept, didn't she? "Yes, I know how." He began to back out of the room. "Now let me go get that shirt for you. You see if you can conserve your energy for a while— by not talking."

She wanted to get up and show him that she was fine. But her stubborn streak went only so far. Her energy deserted her and she sank back against the sofa. Damp or not, the cushions felt good beneath her. "Knew you were going to say that."

He laughed. "If you didn't, then I really would be worried that you hit your head too hard." Morgan paused, looking at her, then crossed back to the sofa. He looked down into her eyes.

Traci felt as if she were lying on a science lab table, about to be dissected. She tried to look indignant. "What are you doing?"

Very carefully, Morgan looked from one eye to the other. "Checking the size of your pupils."

Somewhere in the back of her mind, Traci recalled mismatched pupils were a sign that a person had a concussion. "Why, Morgan, you say the sexiest things."

He wondered how incapacitated she'd have to be before she stopped talking. "I want to see if they're both the same size."

She waved him back. "You've been watching too many medical programs."

"Maybe, but you'd be surprised what you can

pick up." Satisfied, he backed away again. "You're okay." Then he grinned. "Or as okay as you can be."

"Thank you, Dr. Brigham. Does the AMA know you're practicing without a license?"

"Only on guinea pigs," he retorted as he left the room.

She opened her mouth to answer his retort and found that she couldn't think of a damn thing. She was too tired to be irritated by it.

He had rescued her.

That made it twice in her life, she thought absently. Twice that she was indebted to him. Who would have ever thought that her personal Sir Lancelot was a man she was destined to fight with every time they were in the same room together?

Well, maybe not every time, she mused. Ever so slightly, she skimmed her fingertips over her lips.

Bemused and still very much confused, she sighed. The chill, thanks to her wet clothes, was definitely seeping into her bones. Without thinking, she reached for the crochet afghan that had always lain across the top of the sofa.

But her hand came in contact with only upholstery. Traci looked, even as she remembered that the bright blue-and-gold afghan was now in her parents' den, spread across the sofa there.

She closed her eyes and shivered again. She was just drifting asleep when a hand on her shoulder shook her awake again.

Damn, if she did have a head injury, he

couldn't let her fall asleep. He had to keep her up a few hours. This particular piece of insight came from the same program she'd just ridiculed, but he had no doubt that it was accurate.

Morgan shook her shoulder again, less gently. "Here, take this."

She pried her eyes open. This time was a lot easier than the last had been, but it was still annoyingly painful.

Morgan was standing before her, a glass of water in one hand and a couple of aspirins in the palm of his other. A blue-and-white flannel work shirt was slung over one forearm.

"What's this?" she murmured, bracing herself as she sat up. Though it was cold, she could feel a light sheen of perspiration forming along her forehead and beneath the bandage.

"Aspirin. I figure you probably have one hell of a headache." He sat down carefully beside Traci and offered the pills to her.

Without thinking, she leaned her shoulder against him as she took the aspirins and then the glass of water. "I do." She swallowed, then looked at him as she returned the glass. "Thanks. Is it my imagination, or have you gotten more thoughtful?"

He took the glass from her, placing it on the scarred coffee table. Morgan debated putting his arm around her, purely for reasons of comfort, and then decided not to. No sense testing new ground at the moment.

"Neither. I've always been thoughtful. You just never noticed."

"Thoughtful," Traci repeated slowly. The word evoked scenes in her mind that were completely to the contrary. "Was that when you glued together my sheets with bubble gum, or when you—"

He knew she could go on forever if he let her. "That was only in retaliation for things you did. I never started any of it on my own." He waited for her to deny it, even though it was true. When she didn't say anything, he smiled. "Got you, don't I?"

For the moment, she was forced to concede. "Until I can come back with an answer. That smack to my forehead has made things a little fuzzy." She saw the look that entered his eyes and it touched her. "Don't look so concerned, I was just speaking figuratively." She pointed to the shirt on his arm. "Is that what I'm supposed to wear?"

Morgan nodded, passing the shirt to her. Traci held it up against herself. It looked like an abbreviated nightshirt. She could remember a time when they were almost the same height, but in the past fifteen years, he had outdistanced her by a foot.

Traci laughed, some of her steadiness returning. "How chic. Our mothers would have a heart attack."

He didn't know about hers, but his would have probably been overjoyed, and hoping for more.

But then, his mom had belonged to a commune or something like that in her late teens and he'd been convinced that there was something a little unorthodox about her.

"Our mothers are highly practical women who know the value of warm clothes and dry feet." He gestured toward the bathroom. "Get changed."

"Right." She rose to her feet and the room followed. At an angle. "Whoa." Traci felt behind her for the sofa and found Morgan instead. She landed in his lap. "Nice catch."

He shook his head. Everything was a joke with her. Or an argument. He wondered if there was any middle ground. "I keep in shape. Are you all right? Do you want to lie down some more? I can take you up to your room," he offered.

She didn't like being fussed over. "I'm fine." With renewed determination, she stood again. "Just let me get my sea legs."

This time, he rose with her. Just in case. "We're on land, Traci."

The man was a stickler for precision, she thought. A little like Daniel. Except different. Very different. "Then just let me get my land legs." Traci exhaled, leaning against him without meaning to. Realizing that she was, she straightened and then took a deep, cleansing breath. "Better. All right, let me change into this little number before my sanity returns."

He watched her leave the room, knowing that

to offer any more help would be leaving himself open to another duel of words.

"Small chance of that," he commented. "It hasn't made an appearance in all the years I've known you."

She looked at him over her shoulder, a grin playing along her lips. "Flatterer."

She was going to be okay, he thought.

When she returned to the living room, Morgan was busy stoking the fire. To her amazement, he had a healthy-sized blaze going in the hearth, just like the one she'd fantasized about in her imagination.

Barefoot, she padded over to Morgan and, standing behind him, she let the warm glow from the fireplace graze her skin. As the only source of warmth in the room, it felt wonderful.

Or almost the only source of warmth in the room, she amended, looking down at the back of Morgan's head.

He sensed her entrance as soon as she walked into the room. For once, she wasn't talking, but he knew she was there just the same.

Morgan could feel nerve endings coming to attention all along his body, especially when she carelessly brushed her bare leg against his arm a moment before she crouched down beside him. To keep himself sane, he began mentally cataloging her vices.

He didn't get very far, even though he told himself there was a host to choose from.

Traci tried not to dwell on how romantic it all seemed.

"So, you really do know how to make a fire. And all these years, I thought of you as a klutz." She spread her hands out before the fire, palms up, letting the heat glaze over them. "It feels better already."

Morgan rose, moving away from her. Staying too close was only inviting the kind of trouble he wasn't prepared to deal with.

He looked toward the window. There was nothing to look at. For all intents and purposes, they might as well have been the last two people in the world.

Now there was a sobering thought. He felt her eyes on him and nodded toward the window. "The storm's getting worse."

She came to stand beside him, suddenly feeling very isolated. "That means we're stuck here for the night?"

He thought of the two disabled cars and the phone that didn't work. "Looks that way."

She blew out a breath, hoping he wouldn't notice how nervous the thought made her. "Lovely."

Something nudged at him. He refused to recognize it as jealousy because then he'd know that he had really gone over the deep end. "Daniel waiting for you?"

"Daniel's at a convention," she said absently. It looked like the end of the world out there. Just how isolated were they out here? When she'd spent summers here, the town had been little less than a handful of stores and a garage. She hoped it had built up since then. "He won't be back until Sunday night." She turned to look at Morgan. "What are we going to do for food?" Except for a granola bar in the car, she hadn't eaten since early this morning.

"I brought some up with me this morning."

She looked at him curiously.

"I was planning to stay the weekend."

Relieved, Traci followed him to the kitchen and watched as Morgan opened the refrigerator to show her it wasn't empty. There were several items on the glass racks and there was a bottle of wine on the top shelf.

Traci turned amused eyes toward Morgan. "Were you planning on spending it drunk?"

"No." He shut the door again, then leaned his back against it, studying her. "I thought of toasting the old place one last time. With you if you wanted to. Alone if you didn't."

"Very thoughtful." She grinned. "There's that word again."

Morgan turned to look at her. He was making her feel very uneasy, looking at her that way. She suddenly wished she'd thought to comb her hair or maybe put on a fresh layer of lipstick. She probably looked like something the cat dragged in.

So what? This was Morgan, remember?

That was just the trouble, she did remember. All the way back to the front door and the kiss that had subversively changed her feelings about a lot of things.

She gestured toward the refrigerator. ''Well, bring it out.'' Traci looked down at the flannel shirt that skimmed the middle of her thighs. ''I'm as ready as I'll ever be, I guess.''

For what? The question came from nowhere and he knew the sort of answer he wanted to give. He'd never seen his work shirt look so good before, he mused. On her it wasn't just a comfortable yard of material. It was sensuously enticing. He watched the way the hem moved back and forth along her soft skin and it made him envious of a bolt of cloth.

He shoved his hands into his pockets before he did something stupid, like drag her into his arms and kiss her again. ''Don't you think that you should have something to eat first?''

Eating, right. What was she thinking? She knew exactly what she was thinking—of making love with Morgan. Of seeing if those bells, banjos and whatnots would show up again.

''When did you get this mothering nature?''

Here he was, mentally stripping away the flannel shirt from her body inch by torturous inch, and there she was, calling him maternal. He should have his head examined.

Morgan pulled open the refrigerator door. ''Fine, suit yourself—''

She hadn't meant to insult him. Heaven help her, she actually liked the fact that he worried about her. What was the matter with her?

"Something to eat would be nice," she answered airily. "What do you have?"

He opened the refrigerator again to show her. "Eggs, bread. Ham." There was some mayonnaise in the pantry as well as a children's breakfast cereal that he had never managed to outgrow.

She nodded, hardly hearing. "Sounds good. I'll do the honors."

He took out a frying pan and placed it on the stove. "You cook?"

She took the handle of the pan and moved it to another burner. "There is no end to my talents, Morgan." Taking out the carton of eggs, she shut the door with her hip. The edge of the work shirt hiked up on her thigh. "How do you like them?"

You don't want to know. It took a moment before he could tear his eyes away from her legs. The last time he'd seen them that exposed, they'd been toothpicks. They certainly weren't now. "Whatever's easy."

She had to get past this sizzling feeling in her veins, Traci told herself. This was Morgan. Morgan, not a hunk centerfold of the month.

But it might have been. He certainly looked good enough to be one.

"Easy it is."

Expertly, she cracked four eggs against the side of the skillet and deposited them one at a time into the pan. Eggs were her specialty. Actually, eggs were the only thing she could make with confidence, but she wasn't about to tell him that.

When she popped four slices of toast into a

very dusty looking toaster, the fluorescent lights overhead began to wink.

"Uh-oh, something tells me I'd better make this quick." The thought of being stranded here in the dark was less than pleasing. "You have candles?"

Morgan was already opening the drawers housed beneath the counter. There were three in a row. The first two were empty, except for a few dead insects. "That's what I'm looking for."

The last drawer yielded only one candle. A further search of the kitchen didn't add to the booty. Morgan laid the candlestick on the table. "I've got a flashlight in my car. You stay here, I'll go get it."

The idea of being left behind didn't appeal to her. Neither did the idea of having Morgan go off alone. Not when the weather resembled something Noah must have experienced as he loaded two of everything onto the ark. What if Morgan couldn't find his way back?

"How long will you be gone?"

He detected a nervous note in her voice and interpreted it his own way. "Don't worry, I'm not about to hitchhike into town and leave you." He wondered if there was any sense in putting his jacket on. It was still soaked. "I doubt that anyone is going to be out in this."

She frowned. Was it her, or had the wind gotten louder? "I wasn't thinking of your leaving me. I was worried that you might get lost." She thought of calling him a few choice things for even thinking of going out in this, but knew it was futile. He was as stubborn as she was when it came to taking advice. "Take the dog with you," she added suddenly.

Morgan walked into the living room. Jeremiah was stretched out before the hearth, a living throw rug. "Why, so he can bite me? I'd rather do this alone, thanks."

She sighed, her fears multiplying. Well, if he wanted to go out in this, that was his choice.

Traci turned on her heel and returned to the kitchen. "You're as stubborn as you ever were."

"Thanks." His voice drifted back to her.

In the kitchen, she braced her shoulders as she heard the front door slam shut. It took her precisely two seconds to make up her mind. Shoving the skillet onto the side of the stove, she raced to the door, unmindful of the fact that, except for the nightshirt, she was barefoot up to the neck. Throwing open the door, she was all set to run after him.

Her body slammed into his. Morgan was still standing on the front porch.

Amusement whispered over his features as his eyes washed over her. "You always run out barefoot into a storm like that?"

The creep. He knew why she'd gone running out like this. Words tumbled out after one another without thought. "Only when I'm running after an idiot. You're not going to find the car. It's pitch-black out and you'll get lost. You've got the sense of direction of a dead frog."

He placed a hand over his heart. "I'm touched." And he was, although he wasn't about to say it. Not yet. Not until he understood what was happening here.

"I don't want to have to explain this to your mother," she muttered, utilizing the excuse he'd given her earlier. "Hard as it is to believe, she's attached to you." As was she, Traci added silently.

He glanced back at the inclement weather. His sense of direction was a good deal keener than she speculated, but he didn't think he could find the cars easily.

"Hard as it is to believe," Morgan echoed, "you actually make sense. I might lose my way in this." He sighed, ushering her back inside. "I guess we're just going to have to stay around the fireplace if the lights go out."

Just as the door closed behind them, the lights went out. She turned, her head brushing against his chest. "You were saying?"

"Fireplace it is." Taking her arm, he guided her back into the living room. "What about the eggs?"

"Fortunately, they're ready. I'll go get them." Leaving his side, she shivered.

He thought of putting his arm around her, then decided against it. In her present condition, she might just bite it off.

"I think there are still a couple of blankets in the hall closet," he remembered. "I'll get them."

"Thanks."

He paused, watching as she walked off to the kitchen. The light from the fireplace wrapped itself around her silhouette and did very strange things to the condition of his gut.

Morgan blinked and forced himself to fetch the blankets.

7

Traci pushed aside her empty plate on the hearth. Because of the damp chill throughout the house, she and Morgan had opted to eat on the floor before the fireplace.

Jeremiah came instantly to attention. He trotted

over to the plate and began licking it, obviously picking up some of the flavor of the scrambled eggs. She'd left some toast behind for him to dispose of as well, even though, for lack of anything better, Morgan had given the dog a ham sandwich.

"I guess it beats having a dishwasher," Morgan commented, setting his own plate down beside hers on the floor.

"No matter how good his food is, or how full he gets, I've found that Jeremiah always likes what I'm eating better." She shifted so that she could face Morgan. It wasn't that easy a maneuver, given her present outfit. "You wouldn't have any popcorn around, would you?"

Morgan looked at the dog, then at Traci. "I guess foraging must run in the family." Tension and scrambled eggs had been enough to fill him up. "You're still hungry?"

She frowned at her plate, now completely cleaned. Jeremiah was working on the flowery design. "This wasn't exactly a gourmet seven-course meal we just had."

On the floor, Morgan leaned his back against the sofa. "I'm full."

She sniffed. As if that was supposed to make a difference. "You probably had lunch. Besides, I thought making popcorn would give us something to do. There's no radio or TV and it's only six o'clock."

He looked at his wristwatch, angling the face

so that he could get enough light to read it. "More like seven."

Seven. She could remember when her evenings didn't even start until nine.

"Boy, time sure flies when you're having fun." Content to let Jeremiah amuse himself with the plates, she settled back beside Morgan. If it was actually close to seven, that meant she was missing a chunk of time. Her eyes narrowed. "How long was I out when you brought me back?"

Fear had blanketed him when he hadn't been able to rouse her. "Long enough to make me worry."

Pulling on the hem of the shirt, she shifted around further and stared at him in surprise. "Were you? Really? Worried about me?"

The thought evoked a warm, shimmery feeling throughout her body that Traci wasn't certain if she wanted to savor or push aside. For now, she merely explored it. It did feel nice.

He didn't want her making too much of his admission and using it to his disadvantage. "Traci, I would have worried about a complete stranger I dragged out of a wreck. I am human, you know."

Stupid to think he'd actually meant something by it. Her smile faded as she turned her face from him. "Sorry, didn't mean to tread on your humanity."

He noted the hurt in her voice. It was slight, but he was certain it was there. For once, he hadn't meant to wound her pride.

"Besides," he went on, "we do go back a long way and I do care about you—I guess."

Renewed interest entered Traci's eyes when she looked at him. "You guess?"

For the life of him, he couldn't read the look on her face. "Sure, the same way I care about your mother and father. And Mr. McGillis." How stupid could he get, pulling that out of the air? he upbraided himself.

So much for thinking that he was trying to tell her something. "Mr. McGillis?"

"My mailman."

"Oh."

She looked toward the kitchen. The rooms were arranged so that they all fed into one another, all appearing to share common ground. There was enough light for her to wash the dishes if she was so inclined. At the moment that didn't seem like such a bad idea. She needed some distance between them.

But when she began to rise, she found that there wasn't a ladylike way to manage it.

She tugged at the hem of his shirt again, exasperated. "You know, this isn't the easiest trick, keeping this down to acceptable lengths."

He had to stop looking at her legs, he admonished himself. Out loud, he was the essence of nonchalance. "I've seen you naked before."

"I was six, you were eight."

He shrugged, allowing his eyes to elaborately slip over her body. Was it his imagination, or was it getting increasingly harder to maintain his poise? "Not much difference."

Traci clenched her teeth together and tugged at the hem again, beginning to rise. "Thanks."

"Don't mention it." He noted the losing battle she was waging. "You pull on that any harder, and it's going to tear."

She let out a loud sigh and sank back down. The hell with the dishes. "This is payback time, isn't it?"

He hadn't the slightest clue was she was driving at. "Payback?"

"For the time I stole your clothes when you were skinny-dipping."

She'd yanked them from the bushes where he'd had everything spread out and had run, laughing, into the house. Morgan had finally entered an hour later, holding two branches around himself. One had turned out to be poison oak. Guilt ridden, Traci had stayed up, helping him apply salve to the blisters that were accessible until his parents and hers had returned from the party next door.

That had been the first time he'd witnessed any compassion in her. And just possibly the only time, until today when he had told her about Cynthia.

"If you mean that I arranged the storm, the bridge washing out and the tree being in a place where you would back up into it, you're giving me just a little more credit than I deserve."

He was being deliberately obtuse. "I mean the clothes."

It wasn't easy keeping the smile from his lips, but he managed. "Check my closet. There's nothing there."

She didn't have to look to know it was empty. That wasn't the point.

"But you're wearing dry pants." She dared him to deny that he had completely changed his clothes before coming down with the shirt he'd given her. "I distinctly remember that they were wet when you went upstairs."

"I only had one extra pair." He'd packed for a weekend, not for an entire month. "I put it up to a vote and decided that your legs could stand the exposure better than mine could."

"A vote?" she echoed, confused. "Who voted?"

"Me," he answered innocently. "And since possession is nine-tenths of the law, I figure that tipped the scale in my favor." Affably, he unnotched his belt and slipped the tongue from the buckle. "Of course, if you really want me to take them off—"

Her hand flew out to stop him. "No!" Traci shook her head vehemently, then moaned. The playful exchange stopped.

Morgan leaned forward, feeling damn helpless. "Bad?"

Traci bit her lower lip. She hadn't meant to let the sound escape, but the pain had caught her by surprise. "I wouldn't even wish this on you."

"You're getting me really worried, Traci." Morgan rose, looking toward the door. The storm hadn't let up, but there were worse things than braving a storm. "Look, maybe it's not my distributor cap. Maybe it's something else. If I can fool around with the engine—"

Startled, Traci was up on her knees. He couldn't be serious. "In a monsoon?"

Annoyance at his own helplessness added a sharp edge to his answer. "Do you have any better ideas?"

"Yes." When he looked at her expectantly, her mouth softened into an inviting smile. "Just sit down and talk to me."

"I don't see how—"

She wrapped her fingers around his hand and tugged him back down. "You wouldn't, but fortunately you don't have to."

Her smile chased away some of the tension he was feeling—or at least, the tension related to worry. The tension that was related to the sexual disquietude weaving back and forth between them only intensified.

"The sound of your voice makes me feel better." She wondered if she was going to regret admitting that. Probably. "I guess it must all be part of that blow to the head."

"Must be." Relenting, he got comfortable and then surprised them both by slipping his arm around her shoulders. "Still cold?"

She shivered, but this time it wasn't from the chill. Anticipation rippled through her. Traci tried vainly to relax.

"Not anymore." Nerves played leapfrog within

her and she hadn't a viable explanation as to why. "That's a nice fire," she whispered, wishing she wasn't feeling so incredibly fidgety.

"Thanks."

He stared into the flames. He felt it was safer than looking at her. Or allowing himself to smell her hair, or think how soft her body might feel beneath his shirt.

The glow from the hearth did a decent job of lighting the room. Shadows reached out along the walls and ceiling in vague, undefined shapes.

Rather like the feelings that were racing through him, he mused.

"It's kind of eerie, though," he commented.

She stared at the shadows, at the way the light played with them. There was a time she would have seen monsters in every shape. But she'd come a long way from that little girl.

Or so she liked to think.

"Oh, I don't know," she mused loftily. "With the right kind of mind-set, you might even call this romantic." Too late, she realized her mistake. Traci looked at Morgan. She didn't want him misunderstanding. "With the right person, I mean."

"Absolutely," he agreed softly. "With the right person."

His eyes were on hers and she could feel his touch, though he hadn't moved an iota since placing his arm around her. Her nerves were growing at a disproportionate rate. "Not the two of us," she felt compelled to say.

Desire, strong and urgent, was making an unexpected appearance and it was all he could do to keep from kissing her. "Are you that sure?"

"Of course I'm sure." Her voice broke and she cleared her throat.

What the hell was the matter with her? She'd come up here to sort out her feelings about Daniel, not pick up new ones about Morgan. But she couldn't think when he was looking at her like that. Like someone she didn't know. Like someone she wanted to know.

Traci looked away. "Oh, you mean what happened earlier. Well, that was your fault."

He didn't think he'd ever seen her nervous before. "I don't think the word *fault* is the right one in this case."

She continued staring into the flames. Her nerves refused to settle down. "Well, whatever you want to call it, it was an aberration." Gathering her courage to her, she turned to look at him, her eyes daring him to dispute her words. "Like Halley's comet falling."

Satisfaction lit his eyes and curved his mouth. "Felt that way to you, too, did it?"

This conversation wasn't going the way she wanted it to. She pulled away from him. "I'm going to get some wine."

Morgan watched in fascination as Traci rose to her feet. For once, he forgot to be a gentleman. Damn, but she had turned out to be a beautiful figure of a woman.

"Why?" he called after her.

"Because you're out of popcorn." She disappeared into the kitchen.

Morgan heard the refrigerator door being opened and then slammed shut. He looked at the dog who, finished scavenging, was curled up on the far side of the hearth. "She's gotten harder to follow, hasn't she?"

Jeremiah didn't bother lifting his head. He opened his eyes and looked with disinterest at Morgan for a moment before his lids slid shut again.

Traci entered the room, the bottle tucked under her arm and two mugs plus the corkscrew he'd brought with him in her hands. Kneeling down, she folded her legs under her before offering the mugs to Morgan.

"We're going to have to toast each other with these. I can't find any glasses." She placed the bottle between them.

"Glasses." Morgan shook his head at his oversight. Somehow, drinking out of mugs just wasn't the same. "I knew I forgot something."

"You forgot extra clothes," she accused. Glasses didn't matter. Dignity, however, did. Holding the hem of the shirt down again, she rearranged her legs.

He caught a glimmer of her thigh where the shirt had risen. He couldn't find it in his heart to regret the oversight on his part. "Sue me."

The lawyer's answer to everything, she mused. "Don't tempt me."

He grinned at her just before he sank the tip of the corkscrew into the cork. "Ditto."

He thought she blushed, but it might just have been the light from the fire washing over her face. Still, he had his doubts. Morgan twisted the corkscrew in and then pulled.

Traci kept her eyes fixed on the mug as he poured, afraid to look at him. Was he telling her that he was being tempted by her? Or was this just his attempt at wry wit?

She didn't know and she was afraid to speculate.

Morgan filled Traci's mug halfway, then poured a like amount into his own. He lifted his mug toward her and the fireplace. "To the house."

She touched the side of her mug to his. "And to memories."

Their eyes held for a long moment before she brought her mug to her lips.

The wine aroused her sensations, just as the look on his face aroused her. She needed something else to concentrate on.

Traci took another long sip, then studied her mug. "Not bad."

The warmth the liquid spread over her limbs was pleasing. For a moment, it nudged aside the other warmth that was zipping erratically through her, popping up and down like beads of water on a hot skillet.

Desperate to drown it out completely, Traci

drank the rest of her wine, then presented the mug to Morgan for a refill.

"Go easy," he warned, pouring.

She didn't need him telling her how to behave. And she didn't need him looking at her like that, either. Least of all, she didn't need him kissing her.

Or did she?

She raised her chin. "You think I don't know when to stop?"

None of his business how much she downed. "Sorry, don't know what came over me to suggest that."

Morgan set the bottle down on the stone hearth before them, then savored his own drink. Somehow, he'd lost his taste for it. He looked at her, watching the way the flames caressed her face. Wishing he could do the same.

"So, you're really getting married to this Daniel guy?"

She was already starting to feel the effects of the first mug as she began to make short work of the second. Her head was spinning, but that didn't change anything. She still felt an uneasiness inside of her. And a new hunger she didn't know what to do with.

"Yup, I'm really getting married to this Daniel guy," she snapped.

That wine tasted awfully good. She had had no idea she was this thirsty. Draining the mug, Traci reached for the bottle.

"Traci, I don't think you should be drinking this much."

"Much?" she repeated, struggling not to slur the word. "You think this is much? You, sir, have no idea what much is."

Did she have a problem with alcohol? He tended to doubt it, but it might have slipped by both their parents' detection. Very deliberately, Morgan placed his hand on the bottle and took it from her. "You don't do this all the time, do you?"

She pressed her lips together. Did he think she was some kind of wino? She didn't even know why she was doing this now. Maybe because what she was feeling was easier to tolerate when the wine blurred the edges from it.

Holding the mug in both hands, she sighed. "I can't remember the last time I had a glass of wine."

He moved the bottle behind him. "Maybe that's because your mind's getting foggy again."

"Nope, it's clear as glass," she declared, taking another long sip. And then his question about her marrying Daniel came echoing back at her, as if she hadn't answered it at all. But she had, hadn't she?

She wasn't sure. Testing her tongue, she voiced her thoughts aloud. Maybe if she heard them, she would believe them. "You know, Daniel's very nice."

Morgan studied her expression. Inebriated or

not, she was trying to say something that wouldn't come out. "But?"

Traci blinked, looking at him. "But what?"

He shook his head. When she raised the mug to her lips, he placed his hand over her wrist, guiding it back down to her side. He wanted her to finish what she was trying to tell him.

"No, you have a 'but.'"

She glanced down. It took her a moment to focus her eyes. Her mouth spread in a wide smile as laughter threatened to bubble up in her chest. "Yes, I do. It makes sitting easier."

He laughed, then shook his head. She raised her eyes to his face questioningly. The lady, he thought, was on her way to being smashed.

"In your sentence," he prodded. "You had a 'but' in your sentence."

She thought for a moment, remembered and then opted for denial. "No, I didn't."

Morgan saw the defensiveness kick in as if it were a physical thing. "Be honest, Traci."

For a moment, she sobered. Loyalty to Daniel warred with her true feelings. "Do I have to?"

His voice softened as he moved closer to her. "Makes things easier."

If he only knew. "Not from where I'm sitting." She sighed again, leaning back, not completely aware that she was leaning into Morgan, as well. She thought of Daniel. Sweet, patient Daniel. He deserved someone who could love him the way he should be loved, not by half measures. "He's everything a woman could want."

That was a party line, Morgan knew, not her true feelings. The small kernel of jealousy he'd felt earlier fell through the cracks and disappeared.

"But?" he prodded gently.

She looked at him and bit her lip. The truth came before she could lock it away. Someone had to know. "He doesn't make the bells and the banjos play for me." *Like you do.*

He thought he understood, but he wasn't quite sure. "And having an orchestra around is important to you?"

"Yes."

Reaching around him, she secured the bottle and wrapped her fingers around its neck. Traci drew it to her and poured a little more of the rose-colored liquid into her mug. But instead of drinking it, she stared into the container, as if seeing things there that would quell her troubled soul.

"There's no music without one. No chemistry. No fire." She raised her eyes to his. "There's even chemistry when I look at you and you're not as good-looking as Daniel is."

She really was getting smashed, he thought. Gingerly, he took the mug away from her, surprised at how easily she surrendered it. "Thanks."

"No," she said, not wanting him to get the wrong idea. "You're cute. Maybe you're even gorgeous, but your nose is a little crooked."

She really was pretty adorable this way, he

mused. If he wasn't careful, he'd let himself get carried away. "You broke it, remember?"

Yes, she remembered. Remembered swinging the door into his face. But it had been an accident. She hadn't known Morgan was behind her. And he hadn't stopped walking in time.

"You were always such a klutz." Traci smiled fondly. Her eyes narrowed as she took further inventory of his face. "And your mouth's a little too full."

As if to give it a stamp of approval despite that fact, she leaned over and kissed him. Surprising the hell out of him.

As he reached for her, she moved her head back. She gave it a smart nod. "But it does taste good." She ran her tongue over her lower lip, sampling. "You been drinking?"

"Just a little." He didn't want to laugh at her, but it wasn't easy. "Traci, I think that you've had a little too much."

"No, I haven't." She looked around for her mug. It was here somewhere. She remembered holding it, or at least she thought she did. "I'm still trying to make the bells and the banjos go away."

She was rambling, but he humored her. "I thought you said you wanted them."

"With Daniel." Her eyes looked into his. Didn't he understand? "Not with you."

He wondered if his mouth was hanging open. It sure felt that way. "With me?"

She nodded, then blinked hard because there

were two of him. She waited until the images merged. They did, but only partially. "Stop moving around so much. You're vibrating."

Yes, he probably was at that, he thought. Morgan took her hands into his. A thousand thoughts ran through his mind, like field mice scurrying for high ground during a flash flood. He had to have misheard her.

"You hear those bells and banjos with me?"

"I think so." Right now, she wasn't certain of anything. "Only one way to make sure." Taking his face between her hands, she kissed him. Hard. As if everything depended on it.

He didn't mean to kiss her back, knew that if nothing else, he was taking advantage of the situation. And of her. She was obviously feeling no pain right now and he should be stepping back.

But it was more than he could resist. She was more than he could resist.

At least for a moment.

Her mouth was so eager, so giving, and her body so soft against his. He felt his own head reeling as he deepened the kiss, meeting her more than halfway and getting lost in the process so that he couldn't begin to find his way back.

He wanted to make love with her. To strip away the games they'd both been playing all these years and all day. He wanted her the way he'd never wanted any other woman. His hands felt as if they were trembling as he reached for the button at her throat and began to push it through the tiny hole.

Beneath his fingers, he could feel the swell of her breasts as she caught her breath.

This was wrong. He couldn't do this, not when she was so intoxicated. What if it was only the wine talking and not her?

Digging deep for strength, Morgan took hold of her arms and held her back.

"See?" she asked huskily. "Bells and banjos. Can't you hear them?"

He did, he thought. He really did. She was scrambling his brain.

Traci didn't wait for his answer. She clutched at his shirt. "Make them stop, Morgan. I can't have them playing when I'm kissing you. They're supposed to play when I'm kissing Daniel." And then she suddenly paled. Dropping her hands in her lap, Traci began to sway. "Oooh, boy. Suddenly, I don't feel so well."

Was she going to be sick? "Small wonder. I think you'd better get some sleep before I have to pour you into bed." He rose, ready to guide her up the stairs.

But Traci remained where she was. The world was too dark to venture into. She liked it right here, by the fire. And him.

"No, it's dark up there."

Morgan squatted down beside her. "Would you rather sleep down here?"

"Yes." She turned her eyes to his. "With you."

"Um, Traci, it's not that I'm not flattered, but

I really don't think that's such a good idea right now.''

But she didn't appear to hear him. Traci was already curling up beside the fire, drawing the blanket around her.

"You can sleep over there and I can sleep here." Traci sighed, getting comfortable. "By the fire. That makes sense, doesn't it?"

Resigned, Morgan smoothed out the other blanket he'd found for them. He thought of sleeping on the sofa, but somehow, it didn't seem right, not with Traci taking the floor. He debated moving her onto the couch, but one look at her had him giving up that idea. She seemed to be completely settled in.

"Whatever you say." This whole visit didn't make sense, but he wasn't about to get into that.

A thought snuck up on her as her eyes were drifting shut. "Morgan?"

He'd just laid down. "Now what?"

"You won't go anywhere, I mean, in the middle of the night, will you?"

The floor was decidedly uncomfortable. He looked toward the sofa, tempted. "Only if I have to.''

She didn't like the sound of that. Upset, Traci sat up. The room was reeling, but she held her ground. "What?"

Why was she getting so panicky? "You know, 'have to.' The call of nature," he added when she didn't seem to understand.

"Oh." Relieved, Traci lay back down. "That's okay. Just as long as you don't leave."

"I won't," he promised.

She was asleep before he uttered the last syllable, leaving Morgan to lay awake and stare at the shadows on the ceiling, wondering what the hell he was going to do about this turn of events.

8

Daylight came in with combat boots, stomping around on the hardwood floor like a battalion of marines during basic training maneuvers.

Or was that just Morgan moving around?

Feeling more dead than alive, Traci opened

what she was certain were bloodshot eyes. She was the unhappy owner of a mouth that felt like a bale of cotton.

The light hurt and she automatically shut her eyes down to tiny slits. Only belatedly did she realize that the sun had to be up. Which meant that the storm had to have abated.

But all Traci could think of was that she wished this miserable throbbing would cease.

Sitting up, she held her head and then paused a moment to take in her surroundings. She felt utterly disoriented. She was on the floor, beside a fireplace. The scene had a vaguely familiar feel to it.

Morgan was crouching in front of the fireplace, holding what looked to be a battered, covered pot over the fire.

Focusing hurt.

Traci shut her eyes completely. The moan was involuntary. She could almost literally feel Morgan's eyes on her.

"What did you do to me last night?" Even talking hurt. This was bad. "There are about a thousand little men playing the *Anvil Chorus* in my head."

He didn't envy her the "day after." He'd been there once or twice himself. The only cure was time. And maybe coffee. He was doing his best about that.

"My responsibility ended when I took the bottle away from you." He stared impatiently at the pot he was holding. Damn, this was taking longer than he'd anticipated. He thought that the water would be hot by the time she woke up. "Sorry I can't offer you coffee yet, but the power's still out."

With effort, she turned her head toward the window. "The rain's stopped."

The storm had blown over a little after midnight. He'd gone out at first light to check things out and then hiked over to their cars. "I guess maybe He changed His mind about ending the world via flood again."

She didn't hear him. Traci's attention had meandered back to something Morgan had said previously.

"What did you mean, you can't offer me coffee yet?" Right now, she'd kill for just a little of the dark bracing liquid.

"I've been out to the cars." He nodded toward the door. "I picked up some odds and ends to bring back. Your purse, what looks like a portfolio, my flashlight and some instant coffee."

She would have commented on the portfolio and his thoughtfulness if the coffee hadn't been of eminent importance to her at the moment. "Where did you get instant coffee?"

He gave the pot another shake, as if that would somehow speed up the process. "As it happens, I had some in my car."

She dragged her hand through her hair, trying to make sense out of what she was hearing. Her hair hurt. If she concentrated, she could feel every follicle. "You carry instant coffee around in your car?"

"It came in my morning mail. A free sample." Morgan looked over his shoulder at the packet he'd dropped on the coffee table beside her purse. "I tossed my mail into the car, thinking I'd look at it later. I forgot about the sample until I went to get the flashlight." He looked at the dog that was sitting beside him. Jeremiah's head was resting regally on outstretched paws. "Took your dog out for a walk while I was at it. You know, he's not half-bad once he settles down."

"I guess the same could be said for you." He had taken her dog out for a walk. And brought back her purse and portfolio. Was this really Morgan? She tried to muster a smile and realized that it hurt the corners of her mouth. Everything felt as if it had been disassembled and then passed through a wringer. She'd never been hung over before, and as far as she was concerned, she didn't see the attraction drinking held if this was what you felt like the next morning.

Her eyes narrowed slightly as she watched him. "What are you doing?"

He grinned at her. "Heating water for your coffee. It's not going to taste very good," he warned, "but at least it'll be hot."

Very gingerly, she got up and crossed to the coffee table. She picked up the small green-and-red packet and turned it over in her hand. The pulsating in her head abated enough for her to be able to read the instructions on the back.

"There's only enough here for one cup." She looked at Morgan. "You're letting me have it?"

He shrugged carelessly. "I figured you need it more than I do."

Moving slowly back to the hearth, she reclaimed her position on the blanket on the floor. "Very chivalrous of you. Your list of good qualities is growing."

A half smile curved his mouth. "So you mentioned last night."

Last night. What else had she said to him last night? Traci tried to remember, but it was all a hazy, vague fog. Snippets drifted through her mind. She prayed she hadn't made a fool of herself.

She glanced toward him. Was thát a smug expression on his face? "About last night..."

A well-shaped, dark brow arched in her direction. "Yes?"

She couldn't bluff her way through this. There was nothing else to do but admit the truth. "I don't remember it."

Morgan slowly turned his head to look at her. This had definite possibilities.

Surprise and disbelief entered his eyes. "You mean you really don't remember what amounts to the greatest night in my life?"

Oh, no, what had she done? Fear skittered through her like tiny spiders sliding along a glass-top table.

"No, I—" Traci braced herself for the worst.

Or thought she did. "What happened?" she whispered nervously.

Morgan sat back on his heels. "What didn't?" Admiration filtered through his voice. "I had no idea you were that agile. And with a head injury, too." His eyes skimmed over her, lingering on her long legs. It wasn't difficult adding enthusiasm, not when she looked as tempting as a hot cross bun that had just emerged from the oven. "Why didn't you ever tell me you could bend that way?"

She opened her eyes so wide, her headache intensified another notch. The cottony taste in her mouth threatened to choke her. "What way?"

The smile that slid over his face was sensual enough to have her pulse jumping. "You know."

That was just it, she didn't know. Exactly. But she was afraid that she could make a calculated guess.

Agitated, she rose up to her knees, her hand on his shoulder. "Listen, Morgan, I was under the influence—"

He pretended to be willing to accept that explanation. "If that's the case, maybe I can scrounge up some more around here. I'd hate to think last night was a fluke—"

A fluke. What a funny term for having her life flushed down the toilet. She had to make him understand that it was a mistake. Making love with him—and she was sure that was what he meant—had been a mistake. She couldn't be making love with him when she was almost engaged to Daniel. How had everything gotten so out of hand?

"Whatever happened—I didn't mean for it to happen. I mean—you've got to forget about it." Nerves and throbbing temples made uttering a coherent sentence an unattainable dream. Her mind was running back and forth, unable to get a toehold on anything logical.

He shook his head, his expression solemn. "I doubt I can. Not in a million years."

He fought to hide a grin. Traci looked as if she was going to come unglued right in front of him.

"And if there's a baby—" Morgan began speculatively.

"A baby?"

Her knees gave way and she sank down on the blanket again. She hadn't even thought about that. Traci covered her mouth to smother the squeak of horror bubbling in her throat.

He took her reaction in stride, patiently explaining the situation to her.

"We didn't use any protection. Your purse was still in the car and I didn't think to bring any. Who knew this was going to happen?" No longer hidden, his grin was wider than a Cheshire cat's. "You know, this puts a whole new light on our relationship."

Traci fell over to one side, almost prostrate, on the blanket. She buried her head in the pillow. "There is no relationship. At least, not that way. I think I'm going to be sick."

Morgan set the pot to one side on the hearth

and looked at her. "Why? Is making love with me that repulsive a thought to you?"

With supreme effort, she dragged herself up into a sitting position once more. She really didn't want to hurt his feelings, especially since he was being so nice. But this was an awful mess she had found herself in. She tried to make him understand.

"No, no, it's not. But, Morgan, this wasn't supposed to happen." It had all seemed so simple yesterday morning. How could it have gotten so fouled up in less than twenty-four hours? "I was supposed to come up here, look around, have a few pleasant memories and try to figure out what to do with that engagement ring that's sitting on my kitchen counter." She moaned as she looked at Morgan. "I wasn't supposed to make love with you." Hanging her head, she felt almost desperate. And then she slanted a look at him. "Was it really that good?"

Morgan played it out a little further as he sat down beside her. "There's only one word for it, Traci. Indescribable."

She felt like tearing out her hair. "Then why can't I remember?"

"I don't know." And then the solemn look on his face melted into a wide smile again. "Maybe it's because you passed out."

She couldn't believe what he was admitting to her. Never in a million years would she have thought that Morgan was the kind of man who would force himself on a woman.

"You took advantage of me?"

How could she even think that, no matter how scrambled her brain was? "I covered you."

That wasn't an answer. He was deliberately avoiding her question. "With what," she demanded, incensed, "your body?"

"With a blanket." He tugged at the end of it, catching her off balance. Traci fell over, then scrambled back up to her knees. When she opened her mouth to protest, he told her the truth. "Nothing happened, Traci."

"Nothing?" Her eyes narrowed as she looked at him intently. She'd know if he were lying, she thought. Wouldn't she?

Very calmly, he shook his head. "Nothing."

She thought hard, trying to will last night back in her mind. Only a tiny slice materialized. "But I remember a kiss." She was positive about that. A kiss. A long, warm, lingering kiss.

Caught, Morgan shrugged. "Well, yes, that did happen. But nothing else," he assured her. He thought it best not to point out that she had been the one to kiss him. She probably wouldn't believe him, anyway.

There was still a smidgen of suspicion in her eyes and it annoyed him. She should have known better than to doubt him about something like that. But then, maybe they really didn't know each other any more at that.

"I wasn't about to take advantage of a completely inebriated woman, Traci. If I make love to someone, I expect her to have a clear mind and to remember something beyond the *Anvil Chorus* the next day.''

''Then we didn't—?''

Not that it didn't cross his mind and play havoc with his desire, but he wasn't about to tell her that. ''No, we didn't.''

Incensed, Traci grabbed the pillow and walloped him with it. ''You brute!''

Morgan threw his hands up to ward off the assault, then scrambled up to his feet, nearly upsetting the covered pot behind him. Jeremiah danced out of his way, barking and adding to the commotion.

He stared at her, completely at a loss. ''Because I didn't?''

Disgusted, she threw aside the pillow and glared at him. ''Because you lied to me.''

Peace restored, he reached for the pot. ''I was just having a little fun at your expense. You must know what that's like.'' Jeremiah barked at them again. ''Careful,'' Morgan warned, picking up the coffee sample packet, ''my new friend doesn't seem to like you beating me.''

Frowning, she rose to her feet. ''Traitor,'' she snapped the accusation at Jeremiah, who whined in response.

It took Traci a minute to calm down. They hadn't made love. It was all a joke. Thank God.

Yeah, thank God.

Everything was all right. So why was she feeling so let down instead of—?

Aspirins, she needed aspirins. And coffee. Hot

coffee, poured straight into her veins. Maybe then she could think straight again.

She looked at Morgan. ''Is the water ready yet?''

''Just.'' He took the mug out of the sink and rinsed it once, then poured the hot water into it. Ripping open the packet of flavored coffee, he added that to the water, then stirred. He brought it back to Traci.

She took the mug in both hands, grateful for something to change the subject. Chagrined, she could still feel her face burning.

Traci took a long sip of coffee, then winced. Nothing would taste good to her right now, she thought. But like Morgan said, it was hot and it was the only thing she had available. She drained the rest of the coffee, then shivered involuntarily. ''I think I need a toothbrush.''

Morgan took the mug from her, setting it aside on the coffee table. He couldn't help wondering if her violent reaction earlier had been a matter of the lady protesting too much, or if the thought of making love with him had been that repugnant to her. Making love with her wasn't repugnant to him. As a matter of fact, as he sat here near her, the idea was growing on him by the minute.

He wondered what she would say if he told her?

''Mine's upstairs,'' he told her. ''Feel free to use it.''

The less they shared, the better. ''No thanks, you've put yourself out for me enough as it is.''

She ran her tongue over her lower lip, trying to gather her thoughts together. "So, where do we stand?"

He gave her the rundown he'd already been through himself. "The power and the phone are still out, as is the bridge—" The water in the gully was lower this morning and it was only a matter of time before it dissipated altogether, provided it didn't rain again.

She could have sworn that her father had once taken a different route to get here. "Isn't there a long way around out of here?"

He'd taken it several times. "Yes, but it requires a car and we don't seem to have one that's running at the moment." He'd tried to turn his engine over with no luck when he'd gone out for the flashlight. "I thought I'd come back, check on you and then see what I could do with the cars."

He'd never struck her as particularly handy. Changing a light bulb in a ceiling fixture had been a challenge for him when they were younger. When had this transformation happened? "You know how to fix cars?"

"Just a few basic things. I had a client a while back, a mechanic accused of robbing a gas station." Morgan played it down, although he had learned a great deal from Scott. "He couldn't pay me. So I took it out in trade." Morgan shrugged the matter away. "He taught me how to do a few things."

Another man would have just had the mechanic fixing things on his car for him. That Morgan had tried to learn how to do it himself showed Traci a side of him she hadn't thought existed. "Did you win the case?"

Morgan rose, taking her mug with him. "Of course I won."

Traci followed him into the kitchen. "That wasn't a foregone conclusion, was it?"

He didn't mean to make it sound as if he were bragging. "No, but he wouldn't have been able to teach me very much behind bars, now could he?"

He looked at her over his shoulder. She was standing in the doorway, his shirt still swaying gently along her thighs as it settled into place. He felt that same odd tightening in his gut. Best to leave temptation out of the equation. He'd already seen her reaction to having him as a lover.

"Your clothes are dry, by the way, if you want to put them on. Although I have to admit that I rather hate giving up the view."

She felt a warm blush slipping all along her body. He was having fun at her expense again, she thought. Turning on her bare heel, she left for the bathroom to get dressed. "Yeah, right."

"Actually," he said quietly to himself, "it is."

Traci had occupied herself for most of the day by making sketches and plotting further dilemmas for her alter ego to encounter. Toward the end of the afternoon, a new character began taking shape beneath her pencil. A chiseled, strapping repairman who bore a striking resemblance to Morgan.

When she lingered over where his rolled-up shirtsleeves tightened along his biceps, Traci knew she had to take a break.

Morgan had been out of the house for the better part of the afternoon. She knew most of it had been spent working on his car. He'd been right about hers. It was a mangled mess, its bumper crushed up against a tree. It was hard for her to visualize herself in it.

Harder still to visualize Morgan pulling her out of it, then carrying her back here.

But he had.

Very romantic, she thought despite herself. This wasn't helping.

She needed something to contrast his actions with, something to remind her that this was Morgan she was having these feelings about, not some latter-day Lancelot.

Rising, she woke up Jeremiah, who raised his head to watch her go out the front door in search of Morgan. After a moment, he trotted out behind her.

She didn't have far to look.

Morgan was sitting on the front steps of the porch, running a rock over the edge of an ax.

Curious, Traci sat down beside him. The dog planted himself directly behind them. The wood under her jeans was still slightly damp from the rain, but she ignored it.

Traci nodded toward the ax. "What are you doing?"

He'd been trying to talk himself out of these

strange feelings he was having about her all afternoon. It didn't help, having her sit here next to him, smelling sweet and exotic. Stirring him. Didn't that damn perfume of hers ever wear off?

"Sharpening an ax," he answered shortly. "What does it look like I'm doing?"

"Sharpening an ax," she parroted. Traci watched Morgan as his hand moved rhythmically back and forth along the dull blade. "Should I be pushing furniture against the door?"

He spared her a glance. "This isn't *The Shining*. And I'm not Jack Nicholson," Morgan told her glibly, looking back at his work. One slip and he was going to be very unhappy that she had distracted him.

He wasn't particularly overjoyed she was doing it as it was.

Very slowly, she was beginning to feel at ease with him again. Funny how that seemed to be ebbing and receding this weekend. "Very good. You picked up on that."

"I picked up on a lot of things, spending summers around you." There, he thought, that seemed to do the trick. If it didn't, they were going to have to rough it tonight. He had nothing else available to sharpen the ax with.

Morgan rose from the step and headed to the side of the house. "We need firewood for tonight and we're almost all out."

It took her a moment to comprehend. When she did, she was quick to rise to her feet and follow him. "Do I get to watch you chop wood?"

She'd probably feel called upon to narrate the activity, blow by blow, he thought, irritated.

"If you're that bored." Setting a chunk of wood on the stump, Morgan swung down hard. The wood cleaved neatly in half.

Traci watched as Morgan's muscles flexed and relaxed. Just like the character she'd drawn. She tried not to dwell on the comparison.

"Ohh, how primal," she quipped, her eyes lit with amusement. "This must be what Swiss Family Robinson felt like."

He set another chunk of wood on the stump and swung down hard. This time, he mentally tacked a face on the wood. A male face. "That was fiction and they were marooned on an uninhabited island, not in upstate New York."

He seemed particularly short with her. She wondered if it had anything to do with her reaction to what had taken place last night, or rather what she had *thought* had taken place last night.

"You do know how to take the fun out of things, don't you?"

"I try." The sound of ax meeting wood reverberated in the late-afternoon air. He glanced at her as he picked up another piece. "How's your head?"

She'd forgotten about the headache. And the lump beneath the bandage seemed to be shrinking. "Much better, thanks. I think I'll live."

Gritting his teeth, Morgan swung down harder than before. The two pieces flew wildly out. "Daniel will be happy to hear that."

He'd almost spat out Daniel's name. "That's a very disparaging tone," she observed.

Morgan shrugged, then swung. He felt his shoulder muscles protesting. He wasn't accustomed to physical labor in any great amounts. "It's your life."

"Yes, it is." Because she had to do something, she began gathering up the pieces he'd split. "I don't owe you any explanations."

"I'm not asking for any." With a grunt, he swung again. As the pieces fell on either side of the stump, Morgan looked at her. "All right, I am. Why are you throwing away your life on—"

"On what?" she challenged, throwing the two new pieces into the pile against the side of the house. "A successful, kind man?"

"On someone who doesn't make the bells and the banjos play for you," Morgan corrected.

She turned on her heels like someone in a trance. "Who told you that?"

"You did." Another two pieces flew to the ground. "Last night."

She refused to look at him. "That was the wine talking."

He knew better than that. And so did she. "That was the wine *letting* you talk."

She blew out a breath. "All right, if you must know, there was someone before Daniel." She didn't notice the way Morgan's shoulders stiffened. "It didn't last very long. His name was Rory and he was very dynamic, very sexy." She glared at Morgan, her mouth set hard. "The kind of man who could make your toes curl."

Morgan positioned another chunk. "I sincerely doubt that."

"All right, the kind of man who made *my* toes curl." She winced at the sound of the ax meeting wood. "He was exciting and, yes, he made bells and banjos play in my head. He was also a cheating womanizer who left me for someone who could further his career. He was an actor."

Morgan couldn't visualize a man who would willingly turn his back on Traci. "Well, that explains it. He wasn't real."

"Oh, he was real, all right." She tossed the last two pieces on top of the others. "Too real. He left an image in my head that refused to be shut out. Except when—" She stopped.

Morgan stopped swinging. "When—?" he prodded.

She'd said too much already. If he expected her to stand here singing his accolades, he was going to be disappointed.

"Nothing. I'm going inside to see if I can do something creative with ham and eggs. You go on chopping wood." She paused on the steps. "Think the power will be back on tomorrow?"

"At least the phone. That way we can call someone from the town to come get us and our defunct cars." He raised his eyes to hers. "And you can call Daniel."

"Yes, I can," she answered firmly, marching up the stairs again.

She slammed the door in her wake.

"If there was snow on the roof," he commented to Jeremiah, "we would have had an avalanche just then." He rolled the thought over in his head. "I think I would have taken my time before I dug her out."

Jeremiah barked his agreement.

"This is very nice," Morgan commented, taking his seat at the table.

They were eating in the kitchen instead of the living room. There were two candles on the table. They were mismatched, one higher than the other and of a different color, but it didn't matter. Somehow, it seemed right.

"I found a second candle in the attic when I went exploring earlier," she told him. "It had rolled under the old love seat your mother left behind."

"That belonged to your mother," he corrected. They were having cold ham and more scrambled eggs. Traci had cooked them over the fire in the hearth and felt very smug about it.

But she scowled now. "I don't remember ever seeing that at home."

There was a reason for that. "That was because your parents bought that their first summer here." He remembered how his father and hers had struggled, getting the love seat out of the van and up the front steps while their mothers had coached them from the sidelines.

Traci looked ruefully at the mugs filled with

water. Not much of a meal, she mused. "I'm sorry there's no wine tonight."

He smiled, remembering last night. "So am I."

She meant because she'd finished his whole bottle. She had a feeling he meant something else. She looked down at her mug. "At least there's plenty of water."

Outside, it had begun raining again. This time, the sound was gently lulling.

Morgan raised his mug to the sound. "Amen to that."

It sounded, she thought, lifting the mug to her lips, vaguely like a prophesy.

YES, I GAVE DONALD BACK HIS RING. I'M A FREE WOMAN AGAIN AND THIS TIME I INTEND TO STAY THAT WAY.

BUT THAT VCR REPAIRMAN WAS KIND OF CUTE....

9

They lingered over dinner as long as they could, but eventually it was over. The leftovers were awarded to Jeremiah, who disposed of them within a blink of an eye and then lay down to doze by the fire. There weren't many dishes to wash and they were quickly done and put away. There was nothing left to do except to sit by the fire and wait for dawn and, hopefully, restored phone lines.

The evening stretched out endlessly before them. It reminded Traci a little of the first evenings she had spent here with her parents, when she'd bemoaned the lack of a television set and whined that there was nothing to do. But then at least there were other people to talk with and listen to.

There was nothing to do now, either. Except to listen to the beating of her own heart and be acutely aware of the man sitting beside her.

As if to deny his presence, or at least block it out, Traci pulled over her portfolio and took out her sketch pad. Maybe if she got a little more work done, the evening would melt away.

She couldn't think straight.

Exasperated, after a few minutes she set the sketch pad aside on the coffee table. She could feel him looking at her. When she raised her eyes, it was to look directly into his.

Morgan had contented himself with merely watching her; he hadn't said a word. It was his impression that she was only going through the motions. He read between the lines and made his own interpretations.

And came to the same conclusion he had earlier. She was nervous. Something was going on between them and it was barreling toward a showdown, and soon.

It couldn't be soon enough for him. He'd never cared for waiting.

Morgan nodded at the portfolio as she shoved the last of the papers back into it. "I looked over your sketches earlier. While you were in the kitchen."

"Oh?" Belatedly, she remembered her latest sketches. Had he seen himself in the muscular VCR repairman? Traci braced herself for a smug comment.

If he were given to ego, Morgan would have said that the half-finished sketch of the man entering her apartment looked like it was a takeoff on him. But ego wasn't his problem.

She and the feelings she generated were. And he meant to do something about that.

"They look like they have possibilities." Then, because he felt stuck for anything else to say, he added, "I read *Traci on the Spot* every morning before I leave for work."

She really couldn't visualize him taking the time to read a comic strip, at least not one without some sort of political satire attached to it. "Why?"

He had a feeling that she thought he was putting her on. He wasn't. "It helps me see that there's still humor in the world." Due to the nature of the crimes he was forced to face on an almost daily basis, finding humor was of vital importance to him. "And it gives me a little insight into what's going on in your life," he added.

She wouldn't have thought he cared about what was happening in her life. "Does that matter?"

He shrugged casually. He didn't want to admit too much, not when she hadn't said anything yet about her feelings. Otherwise, the balance would be completely off. "Well, we're friends. Kind of."

Yes, they were, she thought. Maybe they really had been all along. Feeling magnanimous, she decided to let him in on a secret. "You're the reason the strip exists, you know."

He didn't see the connection. "Me?"

"Yes." Eager, warming to her subject, Traci moved closer to him. "Don't you remember? I used to draw a little figure on the bottom of my Christmas envelopes, waving goodbye."

"That's right." He did remember that—a tiny, quick little sketch that bore only a slight resemblance to the familiar figure that graced his breakfast table every morning.

"You said it would be interesting to see what she was capable of doing besides waving. So I took it a step further—"

That was putting it mildly. He hadn't thought of Traci as capable of modesty. But then, he hadn't thought she was capable of burning his socks off with a single kiss, either.

"A very big step. You've got calendars and T-shirts and Christmas cards—"

The way he was rattling off the litany surprised her. "How do you know that?"

He laughed shortly. "Hard not to when it's staring you in the face everywhere you go."

Traci knew better. He wasn't getting off that easily. "Not if you don't go where they're sold."

She had him there. He had been following the development of her creation with more than just passing interest. "I suppose not."

Traci tucked her feet under her on the sofa, settling in like a squatter. "So you have all this insight into me and I don't really have any into you." She cocked her head, her eyes holding his. "Don't you think you should reciprocate?"

"No." He didn't like talking about himself. His job, his career choice, was to listen and to plead other people's causes, not his own.

"C'mon, tell me something about you." His reticence reminded her of the old Morgan. She tugged on his shirtsleeve. "How did you go from a skinny guy to a muscular backwoodsman who practices law on the side?" Her own words evoked a girlhood image in her mind. "Hey, that sounds a little like Lincoln." She considered that. "Except he wasn't so muscular."

Only she would reach for a comparison that far off. He thought for a moment. "I guess you're partly to blame for that."

Traci blinked, surprised. "Me?" She'd never made any suggestions to him, not ones that were constructive at any rate.

"Yes." He grinned as he saw the confusion in her eyes. She really did have a hand in his decision, though he hadn't realized it consciously until now. "I figured arguing with you every summer put me in fighting condition to plead cases before juries."

Was it her imagination, or did he look even better by firelight? The golden glow from the hearth bathed his skin in deep, tanned hues. Just looking at him had her stomach muscles tightening until they were taut, like the head of a drum.

She was more interested in the other aspect. "And the backwoodsman part?"

That was even simpler to trace. "I started working out the fall right after you knocked out my tooth."

Traci frowned. "I thought we settled all that yesterday. You knocked out your own tooth."

Morgan wasn't about to concede that so easily. "Which I wouldn't have done if you hadn't punched me in the stomach," he reminded her.

She grinned, amused. "You're right, you were destined to become a lawyer." She paused, her eyes skimming along the ridges of muscles that were firm and hard, even though they were relaxed. "So these are mine, huh?"

He wasn't quite sure what she was driving at. "What?"

Lightly, she ran the tip of her finger along his biceps. "Well, you just said you wouldn't have started working out if it wasn't for me, so I guess that makes me partially responsible for them. Translated, that makes them mine."

He laughed as he shook his head in wonder. "I've never met anyone who thinks the way you do. Do you realize that your thought process is so scrambled that it seems to work almost sideways?" That was the best description for it he could come up with.

The light in his eyes warmed her. As did his smile. If she were a cat, she thought, she'd be purring right now. "That's what makes me unique."

He inclined his head. "If you say so." Morgan paused. She didn't shift her gaze. "You're staring."

She was, she realized. Caught, she averted her eyes and looked into the fire. "Sorry, just thinking."

He'd embarrassed her, he thought. Curiosity aroused, he prodded. "About?"

No way was she about to tell him that she was wondering how those arms would feel around her just now. He could torture her and she wouldn't admit it. At least, not without his giving up a piece of himself first.

Traci waved her hand vaguely. "Just that I can't wait for tomorrow, when this nightmare is finally over."

Her choice of words didn't exactly please him. Morgan studied her face. "This has been a nightmare for you?"

Instead of answering, she asked, "Do you like being stranded like this?"

His eyes skimmed lightly over her face. "That depends on who I'm stranded with."

He couldn't be thinking what she thought he

was thinking. Nervously, she cleared her throat. "My point exactly. You probably can't wait to get back to the city." Holding her breath, she watched his face for a reaction.

"Oh, I think I can wait."

When he looked at her like that, she could almost feel his touch. Her breath caught in her throat, refusing to budge. "You mean you don't like your work?"

He smiled slowly as he began to toy with a button on her shirt. "I like my work very much, but I wasn't thinking about that just now."

Breathe, Traci, breathe. She forced oxygen into her lungs—and felt light-headed. "What were you thinking about?"

The smile had worked its way into his eyes. And her soul. "Guess."

She'd never been a coward before. But she was afraid to guess. Afraid of being wrong and looking foolish. "Morgan, you're beginning to scare me."

This was something new, a Traci who wasn't sure of herself. "Why, Traci?" he asked softly, his breath whispering along the planes of her face. "Why am I beginning to scare you?"

She wet her lips. They seemed to dry instantly. "Well, maybe because I'm having the same kinds of thoughts that you are—and I shouldn't be. I mean, this is us. You and me." And it was so improbable.

Wasn't it?

"Yes." He pressed a soft, small kiss to her temple, instantly melting her. "It is."

It was hard to talk when her tongue refused to move. "We're not supposed to feel—understand?" She couldn't make it come out any clearer than that. She felt completely inept.

"Probably, but right now, I am." Very lightly, he feathered kisses along her forehead, even around the bandage. He felt rather than heard Traci moan. "I'm feeling a whole host of things that are confusing the hell out of me."

At least he was being honest. But then, this was Morgan. He would always be honest. That much she knew about him. It meant a lot.

"Like?"

"Like wondering what it would be like to kiss you again." Deliberately, he avoided her mouth as he wove the wreath of kisses along her face. He was driving them both crazy. "Wondering what it would be like to hold you against me and feel your heart beating." His hands slid down along her arms, his eyes holding her prisoner. "Wondering what it would be like to make love with you."

She really wished he hadn't said that. It sliced apart the last of her resistance.

"You, too, huh?"

He felt as if he were looking into her soul and it was a mirror of his own. "Meaning you've thought about it, too?"

She couldn't give him that. It was too much. "No, I've tried not to think about it."

He grinned, his mouth grazing the side of her temple again. She could feel his smile seeping into her skin. "There's that sideways thinking again."

Deftly, he worked his way down to the next button, removing it from the hole even more slowly than he had the first one.

She felt herself sinking into an almost drugged state. Drugged and energized at the same time. How was that possible? "Crops up every time you're around." Every word was an effort for her.

"I doubt that." She probably thought like that all the time, he mused. He was beginning to get accustomed to it. And like it.

"Don't." When he stopped, his fingers releasing the button he'd been teasing out of its hole, Traci placed her hands over his and guided him back to what he was doing. "I meant 'don't doubt it,' not 'don't do it.'"

Two buttons were released. His fingers tugged on a third. "Then you want me to?"

She didn't ask what. She didn't have to. She merely nodded.

"That's good. That's very good." Because if she'd asked him to stop, he wasn't certain he could, not without sacrificing a chunk of himself in the process.

Very slowly, he removed the rest of the buttons from their holes. All the while, his gaze was fixed on hers. He saw the excitement leap to her eyes as his fingers skimmed along the outline of her breast. It fed his own.

"You know, if you were wearing my shirt, this would go a lot faster."

"You don't like fast." It wasn't a guess. She *knew*. "If you did, you would have had this off me by now."

She was right. He smiled as he slid the material down her bare shoulders, anointing each first with a kiss. "Complaining?"

"Noticing." Nerves jumping, she bit her lip. "Being afraid."

He didn't want her to be afraid, not of this. Not of him. "Of what?"

She took a deep breath and let it out. "That I'll get enough courage to make you stop." His hands stilled for a moment. "Or that you will stop."

Only Traci. His thumb teased the clasp at her back. "Can't have it both ways, Traci."

The bra slipped away from her breasts like a queen's servant bowing his way out of a room. Her skin tingled as the cool air came in contact with it. Traci fell into his arms, pressing herself against him, her mouth sealing to his.

"Yes, I can," she breathed. "Don't tell me what I can do."

"Wouldn't dream of it," Morgan murmured against her mouth. She was a constant source of surprise to him. A mystery box that defied opening.

But he was bent on trying.

His hands were hot upon her body, hotter than any flame could ever be, she thought. Excitement leapt so high within her that it made her dizzy.

And everywhere he touched her, everywhere he brushed against her, was singed. Pulses were vibrating all along her body, anticipation within her mounted with every pass of his fingers, every movement of his hands.

Every promise he silently made her.

Eager to bring her flesh to his, Traci began taking off his shirt. She felt several buttons loosen as she mimicked his actions.

And in between, they kissed. Kissed so that both were completely numb, operating on automatic pilot and needs that were far greater than any sense of order or logic could ever be.

She wanted him. She wanted him more than she'd ever wanted anyone before. More, she knew, than she would ever want anyone again.

Except for him.

Guilt rose, distant, but hoary, to torment her. She struggled against it.

"We shouldn't be doing this," she breathed against his mouth.

She didn't mean it, he thought. But what if she did? "Want me to stop?"

No! She fairly whimpered. The very thought of his stopping now weakened her knees. "If you do, I'll be forced to kill you."

The laugh in his throat was deep, sensual. Almost primal. "Wouldn't want that."

She stopped a moment, her lips blurred from racing along his face, and looked at him. "No, but I do want you. Am I crazy?"

"Probably," he guessed, framing her face so

that he could kiss her again. "But so am I." He couldn't get enough, never enough. The more he kissed her, the more he wanted to kiss her. The more he felt her body rub along his, the more he wanted that body. "Traci, you turn everything inside out, including me."

He wasn't the only one. "There's a lot of that going around," she murmured.

Nude, with their clothes tangled in a hopeless heap, Traci and Morgan reveled in an exploration of tastes, textures and contours.

Nothing was left untouched. Most especially not their hearts.

Morgan gathered her close to him, his mouth drawing in sustenance from hers. And while he sealed his lips, his very soul, to her, his hands took possession of what already had been declared his.

It humbled him. She was soft to the touch. Soft and giving and incredibly silken. She seemed to pour through his hands like a precious life force. The image of that laughing-eyed girl melted away in the heat of the passion generated by the ripe woman who twisted so urgently beneath his hands.

Needs pounded against him. Morgan wanted to rush, to claim what he knew was waiting there for him. But he forced himself to take it slow, to give her every bit of her due.

And to imprint this night indelibly on both their minds.

For he wasn't about to let her return to Donald

or Daniel or whatever the hell his name was, with her heart intact. Not after tonight. Not after he'd had her like this. And not after she'd had him.

Drunk, she was completely drunk, Traci realized. Far more drunk than she'd been on the wine last night. Drunk and empowered at the same time.

Whatever he was doing to her was making her feel as if she were having an out-of-body experience. She delighted in his expertise on a dual level, both joining him and yet standing back and taking a reckoning of what was happening to her. To them. She wasn't a novice, but this was an entirely new level of pleasure for her.

Morgan? This was Morgan? When had he learned to be all things to her? To make her want to sob in sheer ecstasy even as she scrambled to grab a little more of the pleasure he was doling out to her so freely.

Had she somehow missed all the signs? Or was this something he'd acquired of late? From Cynthia?

Jealousy reared and then disappeared in the same instant. It didn't matter what had come before. All that mattered was this moment, now.

With him.

Traci grasped his shoulder, tempted to bite down hard as his mouth seared her breast. She twisted and turned, eager to absorb more, as he trailed his lips along her body, grazing, teasing.

He was making things happen to her she'd

never thought possible. Anticipation rippled through her like a lightning bolt creasing the sky. She didn't know if she could take much more of this.

"Where in the world did you learn to do that?" she gasped. Morgan raised himself back up to her level. She wasn't sure if she could move anymore.

"Instinct." He smiled into her eyes. "Pure instinct."

If there was a quip for this, she wasn't capable of mustering it, not now. All she could do was raise her head slightly as she knotted her arms around his neck. With the last bit of energy she had, Traci brought his face down to hers.

"There's something to be said for that," she whispered just before she kissed him. Draining him. Draining herself.

And then he was over her, claiming her the way her body begged to be claimed. The way he'd wanted to from the moment he'd seen her standing outside the house on Friday.

Slipping into her, Morgan could feel her heart hammering hard against his chest. Very slowly, he began to move. She moaned, then joined in, mimicking him. The intensity grew as journey's end approached.

The rhythm they achieved was echoed by the pounding of both their hearts. They rode out the storm they had created until it crested. Exhausted, they slid down the mountainside together, still locked in an embrace.

It seemed an eternity before his head finally

cleared. Morgan turned his face toward hers and looked down. He was just barely balancing his weight, trying not to crush her beneath him, although the temptation was there. He wouldn't mind being sealed to her for all time.

"That was you, wasn't it?"

She let out a long, contented sigh, her eyes still closed. "I think so."

"Maybe I'd better check." He shifted a little. "Any distinguishing moles or scars?"

It took her a moment to gather enough breath to answer. "Just the tire marks over my body that you left behind when you ran over it just now." Traci opened her eyes and looked up at him in unabashed awe. "Morgan, you do have hidden talents."

He nibbled on her lower lip. "Just takes the right person to bring them out."

And that would be her, she thought, secretly hugging the comment to her. "That *is* a compliment."

The time for games was over. At least for now. "Yes, I know." Shifting, Morgan lay back on the floor. He tucked his arm around her shoulders and nestled her against him. "Next time, we have to try it on a bed."

"Next time?" She didn't know whether to laugh or to cry. Or what to make of either reaction.

"Next time," he repeated firmly.

Hope skipped through her. "Then this isn't a one-night stand?"

He wasn't that kind of a man. He never had been. "Not in my book."

Guilt rose again, insistent and annoying. "I'm supposed to be engaged."

He wasn't about to let her wheedle out of this. She cared about him. He knew that, had felt that. There were no more secrets, not after tonight. "No, you were thinking about whether or not to be engaged. And I think you came to a decision."

"I did?" She tried to sound flippant, but couldn't quite manage to carry it off.

He shifted her so that she was over him. "Let me refresh your memory."

"Oh." Startled, she realized what she'd just felt beneath her. A grin burst out, lighting her eyes. "Okay."

10

Hazy with sleep and the rosy contentment that came from a night of lovemaking, Morgan reached for Traci before he even opened his eyes.

His hand came in contact with her hair. The vague thought drifted across his mind that she must have slid down to waist level on the pallet they'd formed out of blankets on the floor.

He didn't remember her hair feeling so coarse. Or being so short.

When she growled, his eyes flew open. Morgan sucked in his breath before the image looming over him stabilized into a mass of fur, hot breath and dripping tongue. It was Jeremiah.

The sound of Traci's laughter surrounded him. This would be her idea of a joke. Sitting up, Morgan uttered a good-humored oath as he dragged his hand through his tousled hair. He was feeling too good to be annoyed.

"You're up."

Traci had thrown on her clothes and was sitting cross-legged on the floor not far from him, sketching. She'd felt inspired this morning. Things were finally coming together for her. It showed in her work.

"Uh-huh." She glanced at her watch. "I've been up for about half an hour." She nodded toward the kitchen. "The phone's working."

Suspicions began to nudge at him. He studied her profile. "How would you know that?"

Traci put the finishing touches on the middle panel. She liked to complete each before going on to the next. This one was shaping up rather well, even if she did say so herself.

"I made a call." Her answer was distracted as she plotted the next frame.

Why was there this odd, unsettled feeling in the pit of his stomach? As if he were waiting to find out if he was going to be wheeled into the operating room, or released from the hospital with a clean bill of health?

"Oh?" He tried to sound disinterested. But he wasn't. He was very interested in whom she had placed the call to. "To a garage in town?"

"No, to Daniel in his hotel in Connecticut." Two figures began to take shape in the last panel. She smiled. She had a feeling that Mike the VCR repairman was going to be a new regular in *Traci on the Spot*. "I told him I had to see him once he got back."

So it was business as usual. And last night had meant nothing. Morgan's jaw hardened. He glanced down at the sheet that was haphazardly sprawled out over his lower extremities, just barely covering the essentials.

"Do you think you should be telling me this while I'm lying here, naked?" He looked around. Damn, where were his clothes, anyway? The dog had probably buried them. He wouldn't put it past the mutt. After all, it was her dog.

"I don't know, should I?" Calling Daniel at the hotel had been one of the hardest calls she'd ever made. And the worst was yet ahead. But it had to be done. Her voice grew quiet. "I told him we had to talk about getting engaged."

"Then you are?" He had to hear her say it, say that last night hadn't meant anything to her. Say that she was marrying Daniel, anyway. Then maybe this sinking feeling would leave.

"No, we're not." She set the sketch pad aside

and looked at Morgan. Why was he so surprised? Didn't he realize that she couldn't have made love with him if her heart belonged to someone else? "I want to tell him in person that I can't be engaged to him and emotionally involved with—" Morgan was looking at her so expectantly she just couldn't bring herself to say it. "Well, I just can't get engaged, that's all."

He moved closer to her. He needed to hear the words. "Why?"

He was going to make this difficult, wasn't he? Why wasn't she surprised? Traci blew out a breath. She might as well recite her reasons.

"Because you showed me that the bells and the banjos are too important to me to leave out. That, ultimately, I won't be happy without them." Traci looked at his face and saw Morgan for perhaps the first time. Her heart skipped a little beat. Damn, that was the face of the man she wanted. The man she loved. But she probably couldn't get him, last night notwithstanding. "That they still do exist for me and that I shouldn't sell out before I find them."

Morgan frowned. "I think you've lost me here. Didn't you just say that you'd found them?" *With me,* he added silently.

"Yes, that's what I said." Traci discovered that her patience this morning was very short and raw. "But that was with you."

He didn't see the problem. "And—?"

She hated having to spell out everything like this. "Well, you don't want a relationship." She slanted a look at him and prayed that it didn't appear as hopeful as she felt. "Do you?"

She was a puzzlement, there was no disputing that. "What made you think I didn't?"

She laughed shortly. "Ten years of coming up here each summer for openers."

He took this slowly, one step at a time. Love wasn't ordinarily something you jumped into, although he certainly seemed to have. Somewhere in the middle of the night, it had hit him. And he rather liked the impact. He was in love with Traci and was willing to allow that maybe a part of him in some small way always had been.

Otherwise, why would he have felt so compelled to orchestrate all this?

"I grant you that the twelve-year-old boy I was didn't want any sort of a relationship—on any level—with the ten-year-old girl you were. But that's in the past. The distant past," he emphasized. "Last night is still palpitating."

Nervous, she ran the tip of her tongue along her lips. She saw desire bloom in his eyes and it thrilled her. And gave her hope. "And you think last night is the basis for starting something?"

Was she being deliberately dense, or couldn't she see? He laughed. "Lady, haven't you noticed? It's already started. The train has left the station and you're in the head car."

Pressing her lips together, she managed to hold back her smile. "Who's the engineer?"

Arranging the sheet over himself, he sat back. "Guess."

She didn't have to. This was just like him. Never mind that she was beginning to really like what was just like him. "Why don't I get to be engineer?"

Just like old times, he thought fondly. But with one hell of a difference. "'Cause you're a girl and it was my idea."

Traci sniffed and pretended to look away disdainfully. "Sexist."

His mouth curved as he grabbed her and pulled her to him. She tumbled against him willingly. "Only when it comes to the things that count— like you."

She gloried in the feel of his body beside her. "I count?"

Morgan could only shake his head. "If you haven't figured that one out yet, you're not as bright as I always thought you were."

He lowered his mouth to hers, but she pushed him back. "You always thought I was bright?" This was certainly news to her.

Why did she look so surprised? "Sure."

He was just saying that to get on her good side now. "You never said anything."

"Of course I didn't," he admitted. "It was against the code."

Warm wisps of desire floated through her as he ran his hand along her arm. "What code?"

He pressed a kiss to her throat. "The male supremacist code."

He was making it awfully difficult to think. "And since when were you a supremacist?"

Morgan stopped and raised his head to look at her. "You mean you didn't notice?"

"No." She almost laughed the answer in his face.

He feigned disappointment. "Damn, I must have been doing something wrong."

Love softened her expression. "No, Morgan, I think you were doing everything right."

He rose, the sheet pooling to the floor at his feet. Damn, but he was a magnificent specimen of manhood, she thought. And as unselfconscious about it as the day he was born.

Morgan took her hand in his and turned toward the stairs. "Why don't we go upstairs to your bedroom where we can discuss this further?"

Traci let herself be led off willingly, but she glanced at the phone as they passed. "Before we call the towing service?"

He was gently tugging her up the stairs. "Way before."

Humor and desire vied for the same space. "Don't you want to be rescued?"

"No." Morgan's hand tightened around hers. "Not particularly."

She could feel her heart begin to race. "You know what?"

At the landing Morgan turned to look at her. He hadn't known it was possible to want someone so much. And he had a feeling he hadn't even begun to scratch the surface. "What?"

"Neither do I."

He took her into his arms, unable to wait. His

mouth found hers and did incredible things to the composition of her body, turning it to hot liquid. It melted in the heat coming from his hard, lean body.

"Knew we'd find common ground if we looked hard enough." Taking her hand again, Morgan guided her to her room.

"Morgan?"

He looked at her. Was she hesitating? No, he didn't think so. "Hmm?"

Doubts and anticipations nibbled at her. "Do you think it'll work between us?" She'd never wanted anything to succeed so much in her life.

The woman talked way too much. "Damned if I know." He began unbuttoning her shirt, just as slowly as he had last night. "But I think it's worth a shot."

She could feel her breath catching in her throat. "How long?"

"The first hundred years ought to do it." The shirt hung open at her sides. He noticed with satisfaction that she hadn't bothered putting on her bra. He rather liked this style. Morgan slid his hands beneath her blouse, cupping her breasts. "After that, you get your walking papers."

She raised her chin, her eyes dancing. "No, you get yours."

He pretended to take that into consideration. "We'll work out the fine print later."

Traci laughed. "Deal. You know, I think I *am* going to buy this house from your parents, after all."

"Sorry, it's not for sale."

Her eyes narrowed. "But you said—"

Morgan smiled at her. "I lied."

She didn't understand. It didn't make any sense. "Why?"

"Because I picked up the paper last week and read *Traci on the Spot*. Suddenly, I knew I had to see you before you became officially engaged."

"Why?" she pressed.

It was the same question he'd asked himself. Over and over again. "That I didn't know." He drew her even closer. "Until now. I guess, subconsciously, maybe I always knew that you and I were meant to be." He grinned. "Either that, or I was a hell of a masochist."

It was hard carrying on a sensible conversation with a nude man. Not when she wanted him so much. Anticipation was growing to phenomenal proportions within her. Traci glanced meaningfully toward her bed.

"About those negotiations…?"

He laughed. It was going to be a damn good life. And they were going to make their mothers very happy women. "Ready when you are."

Traci laced her arms around his neck and pressed her body against his. "I'm always ready—when it comes to you."

"I'm very glad to hear that." He picked her up into his arms. Turning to enter the room, he saw that the dog was about to follow them. "Sorry, dog. These negotiations are going to be held in private.'' With the heel of his foot, Morgan closed the door behind him.

With what seemed to pass for a loud sigh, Jeremiah laid down before the bedroom, settling in as if he sensed that it was going to be a long time before the door was opened again.

* * * * *

If you've enjoyed this story,
look out for new novels
from Marie Ferrarella
in July and August 1998.

Maureen's Do's and Don'ts for the perfect _pretend_ honeymoon:

DO:

1. Agree to sleep in separate beds, even if they're only yards apart.

2. Cuddle up to that handsome 'groom'—for the photographers, of course!

3. Admire his sexy smile—looking isn't a crime, is it?

DON'T

4. Get lost in soul-stirring kisses.

5. Wish this trip would never end.

6. Fall in love!

DIANE PERSHING

First Date: Honeymoon

About the author

I cannot remember a time when I didn't have my nose buried in a book. As a child, I would cheat the bedtime curfew by snuggling under the covers with my teddy bear, a torch and a forbidden (read 'grown-up') novel. My mum warned me that I would ruin my eyes, but so far, they still work.

First Date: Honeymoon combines several of my favourite pastimes with the 'if onlys' and 'what ifs' that thrash about in my mind: two completely incompatible people thrown together; a free spirit versus a control freak; the gypsy in my soul; an enduring love of London and Venice; and an absolute *adoration* of fine food. Heaven, sheer heaven.

I live in Los Angeles, but I'm not the least affected, promise. My two children, Morgan Rose and Ben, are both in college, and I enjoy a fun career as a voice-over performer. I'm blessed by a second career as a writer, having published several romance novels in the past three years. This is my first for Mills & Boon®, and I want to thank them for letting me vent my sense of humour. Hey, I'm easy; if you laugh at my jokes, I'm yours forever.

Diane Pershing

To my foreign advisors, Stu, Brenda, Aunt Pearl,
Ettore, Luana and Federico—and to
Jill Marie Landis for a plot twist. Thanks.

"**H**i, Carla! Great day, huh?" Mo waved at the dark-skinned woman behind the counter.

"Afternoon, Mo. In a hurry, I see. For a change." This last was said sardonically, and Mo grinned at the woman as she dashed past, heading for the post-office boxes. Row upon row of small locked compartments lined the walls. When Mo got to number 747, she dug around in her oversize purse.

"Now, where did I put that key?" she muttered to herself, kneeling as she heaved the huge bag from over her shoulder and plopped it onto the marble floor. She had promised herself she would put the key in *one* place so she'd always know where to find it. And she had. But she couldn't remember where that one place was.

Sighing, she began to unload the purse's contents onto the floor, trying not to get in the way of other box holders at this busy San Francisco post office. Wallet, sunglasses, half a bagel, pink baseball cap, a small notebook with Barney on the cover, scrunchies and ribbons and rubber bands.

These were followed by a checkbook with a distressingly low balance, a cotton wraparound skirt to put over her shorts for her interview later, a small stuffed panda with a missing ear that she'd promised her nephew she'd

repair, gas receipts, gum, a half-empty box of
Good & Plenty, a dented can of cat food that her mother
had asked her to return to the market. Finally, at the
bottom of the bag, in a package of striped birthday candles, she found her round gold post-office box key.

"Aha!" Mo said in triumph. After putting the key
ring over her pinkie and hurriedly stuffing everything
else back into the purse, she stood up and slung the bag
over her shoulder.

Mo opened her mailbox and removed several mail-
order catalogs, which she jammed into her purse for later
perusing. She'd been hoping for some positive responses
to the résumés she'd sent out—she'd been out of work
for a month—but the only other object in the box was
a thick, oversize envelope. She tore it open, extracted
and unfolded several sheets of paper.

What seemed to be a booklet of tickets dropped to the
ground. She bent over to retrieve them. Airline tickets,
she saw as she straightened up. Round-trip, first-class
tickets. To Europe.

Mo felt her heart accelerate as she clutched the booklet in her hand. Europe—the dream, daily and nightly,
since she could remember.

Quickly, she skimmed the papers. It seemed to be
some sort of itinerary, with the departure from San Francisco scheduled for the following evening, a Sunday. Her
eyes scanned the first sheet, then the second. Two weeks.
Five cities. Ending up in—could it be?—Budapest! On,
of all days, June eighteenth!

Hugging the itinerary and the tickets to her chest, Mo
closed her eyes, her rapid heartbeat thumping loudly in
her ears. Was it possible? Was this a sign? No, beyond
a sign. A miracle?

Reason nibbled at her whirling brain. She tried to ignore it, but it kept pecking at her like an insistent bird; reason had a way of doing that. With great reluctance, Mo opened her eyes and forced herself to look more closely at exactly what it was she was holding.

First she read the name on the envelope.

Matthew Vining.

Then the names on the itinerary and tickets.

Mr. and Mrs. Matthew Vining.

Mo sighed loudly. It was no miracle at all.

"Of course," she muttered, her high mood plummeting like the sawed-off upper branch of a redwood tree.

Matthew Vining, the drop-dead gorgeous restaurant reviewer and host of the syndicated radio show "Dining With Vining," had the post-office box next to hers; she'd received his mail by mistake a couple of other times. So then, that's what this was, a mistake. Not a sign, and certainly not a miracle.

Oh, well, she thought. Oh, well. It had been nice to get this close, anyway, even if only for a couple of moments.

She stuffed the papers back into the envelope and was about to hand it to someone behind the service window, when a thought struck her.

Tomorrow. The trip was for the very next day. What if Matthew Vining didn't get to the post office in time? What if something last-minute happened and he didn't collect his tickets? That would be terrible. To ruin an incredible, fantastic trip like that because the post office messed up.

His show originated at KCAW, she knew that, and KCAW's studios were just around the corner. Mo would do a good deed; she would deliver the tickets in person. In any case, it was the proper thing to do, as she'd thoughtlessly ripped open the envelope without first checking who it was addressed to.

Suffused with the spirit of noble generosity, Mo shoved the envelope into the black hole she called a purse, waved a quick goodbye to Carla and dashed out the door.

Matthew Vining was not happy. In fact, he was extremely annoyed. He stood in the reception area of radio station KCAW, staring at his fiancée. His fists were clenched with tension and his frown was deep.

"I'm not sure I understand, Kay," he said tightly.

"I'm sorry," Kay said, "but this is the right thing to do."

"You're calling off our engagement? You're canceling the wedding? And the honeymoon?"

"Yes," Kay replied in her usual measured, reasonable way. "It simply won't work. We don't love each other."

"But how can you do this? I mean, it's tomorrow." They were momentarily alone—the receptionist was on a break and things always quieted down at lunchtime— but Matt matched Kay's even tone. They never raised their voices to each other. "What will happen?"

"As I'm the one causing the problem, I'll take care of all the details."

"Yes, but—" He groped for something to say, anything that might salvage this impossible turn of events. "We get along so well."

"Do we?"

"Of course we do. We're so compatible. We read the same magazines, like the same films...." Not to mention the fact that Kay was an organized person, and not given to emotional outbursts. Two very good reasons why he'd been attracted to her in the first place. "You're exactly the kind of wife I want."

She stared at him, her normally placid expression overlaid with a hint of—what? Sadness. Even regret. "There's a difference between the kind of wife you want and the woman you want for your wife," she said gently. "It's not enough, Matthew. I thought it would be, but it's not."

His heartbeat sped up with panic. "But what about the book? I mean, I have a contract to write a book about my honeymoon." He kept the volume down, but he actually felt like shouting right about now. "Everything's set—hotel reservations, photographers, the cable TV–show contract. How the hell will I be able to write the book now?"

Kay's expression lost its sadness; in its place was a bitter little smile. "I was right."

She removed the diamond ring from the third finger of her left hand and dropped it into his suit pocket, making sure to pat the wrinkles out after she did. Then she gazed into his eyes one last time, nodded and said, "Have a nice career, Matt." With that, she walked out the double glass doors of the reception area.

Matt stood staring after her for what seemed like hours, but was probably no more than half a minute. His hands remained in fists at his side and his heart thudded insistently. He was shocked. Shocked speechless. Not, interestingly, at the thought of losing Kay, although that was bad enough. No, it was more that he could almost hear the walls of his carefully built career tumbling down around him, and that thought was unbearable.

A phone rang four times, then someone from one of the offices must have picked it up because the ringing stopped. Over the speakers, Matt could hear the voices of the talk-radio show that was on the air live. A woman was whining about her husband and the host was soothing her with the usual psychobabble pabulum. As though from a distance, Matt wondered when his thought process would get in gear again and when he would move from his frozen position.

Then the reception area's double doors burst open and a small bombshell came blasting through.

"Oh, goody," she said. "You're here."

"Huh?"

She was young, mid-twenties, he guessed. With the part of him that wasn't still reeling from Kay's announcement, Matt observed that the newcomer had a wild mane of red-gold hair, its thick curls reaching halfway down her back.

"I have something for you, Mr. Vining," said the young woman, setting an enormous purse on the beige carpet and kneeling beside it. She proceeded to unload the most amazing clutter he'd ever seen. Books and food and clothing and a can of cat food.

"Excuse me," Matt said. "I don't think you ought to—"

She interrupted him with a triumphant "I know where it is!," and produced a thick envelope from a side pocket. "This was put in my post-office box by accident. It belongs to you."

Still on her knees, she hugged the envelope to her chest and gazed up at him. She had the most incredibly large blue eyes, the color of cornflowers. At the moment, they were brimming with tears. With the back of her hand, she swiped at the moisture impatiently and, even though her luscious lower lip trembled, managed a shaky smile. Her teeth were small and straight and very white.

"Sorry," she said. "I didn't mean to get all teary there."

Again, Matt did and said nothing. She rose, brushed off her knees and handed the crumpled envelope to him. She wasn't tall, he noted, but her body was perfectly proportioned with drop-dead curves. Slowly, he took the envelope but kept staring at her.

"I'm a little emotional," she said. "You see, I thought my *nagyanya* had sent a sign, but I guess she didn't."

"*Nagyanya?*" Matt managed to say. He peered into the envelope, barely registering its contents, then stuffed the whole thing into his inside suit pocket and shifted his attention to his visitor. He had the feeling he'd been dropped into someone else's dream. "Sign?"

She nodded. "My grandmother. She's gone now, but she lived with us when I was little. Anyway, Great-grandma, that's *Nagyanya's* mother, she had a hot affair with a Gypsy while her husband was off fighting in some war and that's why *Nagyanya* had the sight. She used to tell me stories and read the tarot cards, and one day she said, '*Kis macska,* in your twenty-eighth year…'"

She stopped and laughed. "Sorry. When I try to imitate my grandmother, I wind up sounding like Zsa Zsa Gabor underwater. Anyhow," she went on in her natural voice, a melodic, clear tone, the words tumbling over one another like a fast-moving stream over pebbles, "*Nagyanya* said that in my twenty-eighth year I would meet a man with silver eyes on the banks of the Danube, and he would be my love for life. She was real clear about the silver eyes and the Danube." Breaking off her enthusiastic recital, she wrinkled her nose sheepishly. "Kind of silly, huh."

"Kind of," he agreed. Matt was usually not at a loss

for words, but this woman was reducing him to speech-lessness, much as Kay had moments before.

She wore what seemed to be a magenta halter top under a see-through polka-dot-patterned blouse, tied at the waist. Her lime-green shorts—not tight, but not loose either—revealed long, shapely legs. On her feet were leather sandals with straps that wound halfway up her calf. One of those free-spirit types; there were more colors in her outfit than in any Impressionist painting Matt had ever seen.

"Would you care to sit down?" Not sure just why he'd said that, he motioned to one of the beige tweed couches that were set about the large room at various angles.

"Oh, no thanks. I have to get going."

Just then, the door opened and a silvered-haired man hurried through, nodding briskly. "Matt."

"Tim," Matt answered. After the station manager disappeared behind the door leading to the offices and studios, Matt turned to the woman. "But what were you saying about something being a sign?"

"Oh, yes. Well—" she cocked a hip against the edge of the receptionist's unoccupied desk "—I'm twenty-seven, which means I'm in my twenty-eighth year, right? And as they say, time's a-fleeting. I've been trying to save enough money to go to Europe, but, well, Tom—he's my brother, well, one of my brothers—he needed a second car. I mean, with all the kids, you know, it's not fair. Anyway, I lent him the money, and he'll pay me back, he always does, my family's real good about that. But, I guess not before my birthday."

"Which is?"

"In two weeks." She spread her hands. "Get it? In two weeks I begin my twenty-ninth year, and when I opened my mailbox and saw the tickets, and that the last stop on the trip is Budapest—home of the Danube—on my birthday, well, I mean, how could I *not* think it was a sign that the silver-eyed man was, maybe, more than a, you know, bedtime story?''

She grinned, the rosy color of her lips unaided by lipstick, Matt noticed.

''You see?'' she said, then shrugged. ''Oh, well. I guess it's silly to get your hopes too high, especially at a free trip that comes out of nowhere. Listen, have a nice time, you and Mrs. Vining. I really have to get a move on.''

She pushed herself away from the desk and was half-way toward the door, when Matt said, ''Wait.''

She stopped and turned to him, her eyebrows raised in inquiry.

''Your, uh, purse.''

''Oh.'' She put her hand over her mouth. ''I'm sorry. I'm not usually this forgetful. Well, actually, I am.'' She was on her knees, throwing everything back into the bag before he could offer to help. Standing up again, she slung the purse strap over her shoulder—Matt thought the bag might weigh nearly as much as she did—and said sheepishly, ''It seems like I've been working all my life at being more organized, but it hasn't happened yet. I'm considering prayer.''

''It can't hurt, I suppose,'' he said distractedly.

''Well, goodbye again.'' She headed back toward the door.

''Wait,'' he said one more time, and she turned again, her hand on the knob. ''Who are you?''

Her hand flew to her mouth once more. ''Oh, I'm sorry. I know who you are, of course. Matthew Vining.

I've seen your picture on the back of the bus, you know, advertising your show—''

Matt winced. He'd hated that campaign; he'd felt like a sleazy tabloid subject instead of a serious culinary expert.

''And my mom listens religiously to your program,'' she rattled on. ''She likes to fantasize that she's actually eating all that fancy food you talk about, so I feel like I know you. I'm Mo.''

''Mo?''

''Maureen, actually. Czerny. That's C-Z-E-R-N-Y.''

''Well, Maureen—''

''Mo, please.''

''All right. Mo.''

''And are you Matthew or Matt?''

''Either,'' he said, preoccupied with something entirely different from names.

His brain had begun to function again. An idea was forming rapidly and furiously in there, and a list of requirements to make the idea work was forming right along with it. Tunneling his fingers through his hair, he walked over to the desk, thought a moment more, nodded to himself, then half sat on the edge, near the very spot occupied by this Maureen woman moments earlier.

He looked up and met her openly curious gaze. ''Would you mind answering a couple of questions?'' he asked.

''Questions?'' She cocked her head to one side. ''What kind of questions?''

''Such as, are you employed?''

''Not at the moment.''

''What is your career?''

''Uh, not much of anything, really. A little of this and a little of that.''

"Are you encumbered? Husband? Children?"

"Nope."

"Do you have a reference or two that I could call? Um, let's see. Good health and a good constitution, and a minimum of allergies?"

"Hold it just a minute," Mo said, looking perplexed. "Am I being considered for something weird here? What's going on?"

Suddenly, the double doors opened with a bang, and a crowd of returning employees came through, chattering and laughing. The noise and bustle was as annoying as it was unexpected.

Matt pushed himself away from the desk and walked over to Mo. "Come on," he said. "Let's get out of here."

"Excuse me?"

"I would like to buy you a cup of coffee. All right?"

Puzzlement wrinkled her forehead as she pointed her thumb at the door. "Well, but... Uh, I have to go. A job interview. I mean, I need to change into a skirt and—"

"Give me twenty minutes." He grasped her gently by the elbow and smiled at her. "Please. A half hour, tops. Maybe you won't need to go on that interview."

2

It was the smile that did it, Mo thought as they hurried along the sunny, bustling North Beach street. There'd been nothing, zip, not a hint of warmth from Matt Vining until then. What he'd done was mostly frown and stare at her, stoney-faced, from the moment she'd entered the reception area. She'd thought him cold, even arrogant.

Oh, sure, his looks were incredible. Rugged, really, with his jet-black hair, longish and styled by an expert, the olive skin, the richly dark brown eyes under thick, fierce eyebrows. His picture on the bus hadn't done justice to his slightly crooked, masculine nose, the high cheekbones and the way his mouth formed into a stern, we-are-not-amused line.

He was quite tall and well-built and, she imagined, had to come from money; he seemed so at home in his perfectly tailored navy pin-striped suit and soft gray shirt and tie that were clearly not sale items at a discount department store. But Mo had never been a fan of great-looking men, or wealthy men, or famous men. No, she usually went for more offbeat, oddball guys. Matt Vining was definitely not her type.

And then he'd taken her arm and turned that amazing smile on her. Boy, what that change in the angle of his mouth did to his face! Lifted it, lightened it. Warmed him up, made him human, accessible. Younger, too. The smile was slow and kind of lazy...and very, very sexy. It made her think of hot nights and rumpled bedsheets.

So, here she was with Matt Vining in one of San Francisco's hundreds of coffeehouses. In the background, Paul Simon sang softly about being crazy as Matt settled Mo into a ladder-back wooden chair at a small corner table, away from the rest of the customers.

"Hungry?" he asked her.

As a matter of fact, Mo hadn't eaten breakfast that morning. "I could use a doughnut, I guess."

"And how does a caffè latte sound?"

"Whatever name you give it," she said, "just make it hot with lots of cream."

He turned that charming smile on her again and went over to the counter. Like the way he talked, he moved with easy, graceful assurance, as though he knew where he was going and also knew he would be accepted when he got there. You couldn't buy that, Mo thought, and it would be hard to learn. The man had self-confidence and class. Pure and simple.

The diametric opposite of her and her family. The Czernys and the O'Tooles were from good, hardworking peasant stock, unpretentious and down-to-earth, with a little music and magic thrown in. Not a speck of class in any of them—and she was crazy about the whole clan.

She dragged her concentration back to the matter at hand. Why had she been invited here? A job offer? Maybe to house-sit or care for his pets, or maybe even his kids, if he had some. What did Matt Vining want of her?

And why was she ready to say yes, whatever it was?

That one brought her up short. Cut it out, she told herself, turning her attention to the nearby window and gazing out on the passing parade. He was a married man. It was perfectly permissible, she told herself, to be *slightly* turned on by someone who belonged to someone else, as long as she kept it to herself.

"Brioche, scone or biscotti?"

Mo whipped her head around. Matt stood by the table, a plateful of foreign-looking goodies in his hand. She stared at them, then at him. "You pick it."

"The bitter-chocolate biscotti, I think," he said, taking a couple of long crescent-shaped cookies from the plate and setting them on napkins in front of her. Then he returned the plate to the counter and brought back their coffees. Lowering himself onto the chair opposite hers, he took a sip, then nodded. "This place really knows how to make coffee," he said, his rich baritone registering approval. "Their beans are shipped in from Antigua."

"That's nice."

Mo tasted her coffee. It was good, she supposed, but hey, coffee was coffee. She took a bite of her biscotti. It was certainly tasty, but she preferred apple fritters from Winchell's. She didn't say so, though. After all, she was in the presence of a famous Food Expert.

Matt took another sip of his coffee then set the cup down. "So."

"So," she agreed, and waited for him to continue.

When he didn't right away, she wondered why. Suddenly, she was struck with the thought that underneath his smooth exterior, Matt Vining was actually uncomfortable. Mr. Smooth with an attack of nerves?

"What did you want to talk to me about?" she asked brightly, hoping to help things along.

Propping an elbow on the back of his chair, he leaned back and gazed at her for a few moments before giving her a tentative half smile. "I have a little proposition for you."

Mo froze in place, then closed her eyes and counted to ten. Not him, not Matt Vining. Since puberty, she'd been the target of lewd comments and indecent suggestions from way too many males of the species. One of whom was obviously sitting across from her right now.

And her antennae hadn't been working, because she certainly hadn't seen it coming.

Mo lifted her purse strap from the back of her chair and stood. "I'm not interested," she said.

"But you haven't heard my proposition yet."

Slinging the bag over her shoulder, she rested her knuckles on a hip. "You have a new way of saying 'Let's go to bed'?"

Matt seemed startled, then his face creased into a broad grin. Shaking his head, he chuckled. "Sit down. Please. That's not what I meant at all."

"Wasn't it?"

"Scout's honor," he said wryly. "Please, sit down."

Mo did, although at the edge of her chair, ready to take off at a millisecond's notice.

"Look," he said, "this is…business, really. Nothing to do with, well, sex. No," Matt said, more firmly now. "Nothing to do with that."

Oh, Mo thought, aware that she was actually disappointed by his vehemence. Talk about double standards. Protesting when she thought the man was coming on to her, and then feeling let down when he didn't.

Okay, she admitted to herself, okay, so she was a little attracted to him. But only a little. It had been a long time for her. Call her crazy, but men whose soulful brown eyes made her think of thick rugs in front of crackling fireplaces tended to get her blood flowing.

Behave, she told herself. Put a leash on the fantasies.

Moving away from the edge of her chair, she sat up straight and folded her hands on the table. Business, he'd claimed, and business he'd get. "All right," she said reasonably. "Let's hear your proposition."

"It's a little complicated, but the bottom line is..." He paused, then shrugged and said simply, "I need a wife."

"You need a—? But don't you already have one?"

"I would have had one tomorrow. I mean..." He paused again and frowned, then went on crisply, "I was supposed to get married tomorrow and take off on the honeymoon tomorrow night."

"Yes?"

"But just before you came to the station, my, uh, fiancée..."

Matt swallowed. Something in him rebelled against completing the sentence, *My fiancée dumped me*. Instead, he came out with, "My fiancée and I decided to call it a day."

Liar, he thought. Kay had been the one to break it off, but for some reason, he'd been unwilling to say that to Mo. Pride, he supposed. It wasn't easy being rejected, or announcing the fact. Or maybe he was trying to avoid being the recipient of one of those pitying looks that women always gave at these moments.

He might as well have told the truth. Mo's expression was imbued with soft, gentle compassion. "I'm so sorry," she said. "You must feel awful."

He waved it away. "Don't. It's all right. Really. But the thing is, it puts me in a bind. I have this contract for a new book—"

"Good!" she interrupted. "Writing a book will help you forget your pain."

Clearly, she didn't understand. "What I mean is—"

He was interrupted once again, this time by the looming presence of a large woman—her sensible walking shoes, cotton skirt, sunglasses and camera hanging from her neck practically screamed, "Tourist!"—who tapped Mo on the shoulder.

"Excuse me?" the woman said with a thick Southern accent.

"Yes?" Mo said.

The woman was joined by what seemed to be the husband and two teenagers, one of whom was pushing a stroller containing a young child with strawberry-jam smears all around his mouth. The family introduced themselves as the Salingers from Savannah, then Mrs. Salinger produced a city map of San Francisco and showed it to Mo. "We're tryin' to find out where they have those seals, you know, the ones that sit on those rocks and visit with each other?"

"Oh," Mo said with delight. "You mean up at the tip of Golden Gate Park, near Point Lobos. It's not real close—we're on the Bay side. Here, let me show you."

For the next ten minutes, Mo and the family—who pulled up chairs to the small table at Mo's invitation—discussed directions to various venues on BART, where to find the best clothing bargains, the spiciest and most authentic Chinese food, how to get the ferry to Tiburón and the best routes to the Redwoods and the wine country. Matt was asked to contribute, but, except for ideas on which restaurants to frequent, left all the advice-giving to Mo. Mo admired the lady's bracelet, the lady admired Mo's blouse, and all had a generally friendly, person-to-person good ol' time.

Except for Matt. All he could think about was if he was making a major mistake. Was there possibly some other option he could come up with? Surely there was *someone* else…wasn't there? He mentally flipped through his address book, desperately searching for a name that would announce its suitability, but for the life of him, he couldn't think of one woman he knew well enough to ask, or he could imagine tolerating for too long.

No, it would have to be this gregarious, emotional Maureen Czerny…if she went for it. Desperate times, he told himself, called for outrageous measures.

He wished they'd all stop talking. Apart from the fact that, despite his small amount of fame, he never felt comfortable being accosted by strangers, he really needed to get Mo's attention back to their discussion. The seconds were ticking away. It was deadline time.

Still, one, nonanxious part of his mind admitted to a reluctant admiration of Mo and her lively personality. She was a people person, with a kind of glow about her that made others light up, as though in her reflection.

He knew he appeared more standoffish. He'd been a shy child, not unloved but often ignored, and had moved around a lot in his younger life. Later, as a scholarship student at several exclusive schools, he'd come in contact with social snobbery and had developed calluses in the area of interpersonal relationships.

He heaved an inward sigh of relief when the Salingers bid warm goodbyes to Mo, polite nods to him, and exited. The family waved one more time through the storefront window. Then Mo turned to him. "Nice people, weren't they?"

"Salt of the earth," he agreed. "Now, about—"

"Your book!" she said enthusiastically. "I bet it'll be terrific."

"If it gets written." He pulled his chair in closer and

leaned his elbows on the table. "I have quite a lot riding on it. My career, to be exact. I'm trying to expand out of the purely local market, to become more, well, nationally well-known."

"Really?"

He nodded. "The book is to be a guide to romantic eating places and hotels. I'm to review five of the best restaurants in Europe—"

"That sounds like fun," Mo interjected with enthusiasm.

"Yes, but the book's slant—the selling point—is that it's about my honeymoon trip. You see? It will include all kinds of other information for newlyweds—you know, after-hour clubs, unusual shops, jewelry stores. Romantic views, private picnic spots. Out-of-the-way, uh, alcoves for, well, doing what you do on a honeymoon."

A faint blush made Mo's cheeks pink, and she picked up her biscotti. "I see." She took a bite and chewed thoughtfully.

Matt leaned in a little more. "Maybe you don't. There are supposed to be pictures of me and my bride. The book jacket will say something like, 'Matt Vining and his wife show all the ways to celebrate just-married romance on the most romantic continent in the world.'"

He stopped and met her clear, blue-eyed gaze. "The problem is, there *is* no book…if I go on my honeymoon alone. So, I need a wife. Well, a pretend wife. You, I hope."

Mo seemed about to take another bite of her biscotti when his offer registered. Frowning, she stared at him, chewing on one corner of her bottom lip instead of the cookie, which she returned to the napkin. He could see her taking in what he'd said and working it over in that active little mind of hers.

Matt watched Mo's face for her reaction. At least she didn't seem about to get up and leave, for which he was profoundly grateful, so he pressed home his advantage. "You need to get to the Danube by—when?"

"The day before my birthday," she said slowly. "The eighteenth."

"Perhaps your grandmother did send you a sign," he said, not believing it for a minute, but willing to make use of whatever was at hand. "And now you can take advantage of it, make it happen."

Wondering if he was pushing too hard, Matt made himself sit back in his chair. "There'll be a photographer in each city, and a certain amount of, well, fuss made over me and my bride, but I'll try to keep it to a minimum. Of course, there won't be an actual wedding picture because there won't be an actual wedding, but I'll come up with something later, after the trip is over and the book is written. Something about a divorce or an illness." He smiled self-consciously. "I'm making up a lot of this as we go along, but it will work out, you have my word."

"I see."

He waited for something more from her, but she sat, for once, unmoving. He thought of suggesting a percentage of the royalties, but decided not to get too carried away, not just yet. If she needed persuading, maybe he would throw that in. Again, he tried to gauge her reaction, but all he could tell was that he'd stunned her.

He plowed ahead with as much conviction as he could muster. "Frankly, it makes sense to me. You'll get to go all over Europe, fulfill a childhood prediction, and—" he gave her what he hoped was a relaxed, ingratiating smile "—dining alone is depressing. Say you'll do it."

She chewed the other corner of her bottom lip. "Why me?"

The question took him by surprise, but he decided to state the truth. "I'm really not sure, except it has something to do with you being there at the moment I needed you. I would ask someone else, if there were someone else to ask. But I don't have many female friends, and not a lot of people can just pick up and leave with one day's notice. When you came into the station, well, it seemed…" He shrugged.

"Like it was meant to be." Mo finished Matt's sentence, nodding slowly as the full impact of what he was offering hit her. "And the silver-eyed man…"

She let that sentence trail off dreamily in her head. Then she shivered. *Nagyanya* had come through, after all. Mo could feel all kinds of tingling excitement building up in her nerve endings and gathering in her chest. She wanted to sing, to shout, to shower Matt's face with grateful kisses.

But not yet, reason cautioned. Not quite yet.

"So, you'll do it?"

Matt's voice broke into her reverie and she blinked and met his gaze. He was still trying to hide it, but she could tell he was anxious about this, more anxious than he wanted to let on. She imagined he was just heartbroken, and was having an I'll-tough-it-out type of male reaction. Poor man.

"How would we work the money?" she asked. "I'd have to pay my way. I'd insist on that. Afterward, I mean, when I get a job. In installments. I wouldn't feel right otherwise."

"Don't even think of it," he said abruptly.

"But—"

"You're doing me a great favor and the publisher is paying for the whole thing."

"But I—"

"Not another word. Please. Consider it a closed subject."

He was back to the arrogant Matt, the one in control, and part of her wanted to keep on arguing with him just to see if she could get a rise out of him.

But there were other, more pressing details to clear up. Shrugging, she said, "Well, okay. If the publishers are paying."

"So," Matt said. "Can we consider this settled?"

She didn't answer, too busy trying to gather her chaotic thoughts. When making plans, Mo often forgot one or two crucial things. She wanted this time to be different.

"Let's see," she said. "I have no job, so I wouldn't have to give notice." Concentrating hard, she counted off on her fingers. "I could ask Mom to feed the parrot and the duck, but she can't stand the snake. Maybe one of my nephews would do that. I have a passport—it's never been used, but it's up-to-date. I've been prepared for years."

His eyebrows arched in surprise, then he nodded. "Well, good. You'll need a smaller purse and comfortable shoes."

"Will I?"

"We'll be walking a lot."

"Goody. I love to walk." Her forehead wrinkled. "If I go, that is. Let me see, what else?"

She gazed directly at him for a moment, and considered what she knew about him. Not a lot, really; they were strangers. But she could usually tell about people right away, and she knew instinctively she'd be safe with him.

She closed her eyes and let her mind drift. Now was not the time to be her usual impetuous self; this kind of thing shouldn't be decided too quickly.

Matt drummed his fingers on the table. *Please,* he said silently. *Do this.* He waited for her answer, wondering what was going on in that hopscotching brain. He'd just decided that Mo had gone into some kind of trance in the middle of the coffeehouse, when she opened her eyes again. He was treated to yet another of her quicksilver mood changes. Her eyes shone brightly with tears brimming behind her lower lashes.

"This is like something out of a dream," she said softly.

"The trip?"

"The envelope in my mailbox, the offer, the conversation, all of it."

"Do you cry a lot?"

"Sometimes. Yes. When I'm moved, I guess. Don't you?"

"No." He felt his back teeth clenching. He really needed an answer, but he had a feeling that no one ever made Mo's mind up for her. "Are there any questions I can answer?" he said, swallowing his impatience. "Anything I can do to help you decide?"

She steepled her fingers and rested them against her mouth. "If I go—"

"Yes?"

"We'd need to set some ground rules."

"Certainly."

She seemed to be struggling with embarrassment. That face of hers registered everything, Matt thought. You would never have to wonder what she was thinking—it was all out there.

Finally, Mo lowered her hands, lifted her beautifully rounded chin and met his gaze straight on, her large blue eyes wide and serious. "I'm willing to pretend to be your wife, in public. But pretend is all. I expect the relationship to be platonic. I mean, separate bedrooms. Okay?"

"Of course," Matt said stiffly. "I thought that was understood. We're booked into the honeymoon suite at all the hotels. There'll always be a sitting room and a bedroom. I'll sleep on the couch. There will be no problem, I assure you."

It was a perfectly reasonable request, Matt thought silently, and one he would have no trouble honoring. No, Mo might have a buoyant personality and a body to die for, but she was the furthest thing from the serene, capable kind of woman he usually found attractive. They'd just met, but it seemed to him that Mo talked too fast, was scatterbrained and disorganized, and had mood swings that could be written up in medical journals. In other words, his own worst nightmare.

Hands off? Gladly. It would make the trip easier, less fraught with tension.

Why, Mo might even be an asset, he thought generously. Unlike him, she was an unmistakable romantic, with her easy tears and silly tales of silver-eyed men on riverbanks. She obviously liked to talk to people and people liked to talk to her; he could turn that intrusive habit into an advantage. Yes. He would take care of the nuts and bolts of the book—the dining, the accommodations—but it would take someone both gregarious and sentimental, someone like Mo, to sniff out the unconventional, interesting places he would need to fill in the pages.

One might even say that running into her this way was good luck.

A sign, she would say.

"Matt? Hello, Matt?"

Damn. Mo had been speaking, and he'd been off wool-gathering. "Yes?"

"I'll do it."

A moment passed before he said, in an easy and relaxed manner, "Good. I'm pleased."

But deep down inside, in that subterranean, subliminal place where both demons and passions reside—a place not heard from for many years—he could just make out a little voice saying, "Yippee!"

3

Matt paced the area near the international departures gate. For the fifteenth time in as many minutes, he tried to tamp down the nervous excitement he was experiencing while waiting for Mo. Excitement wasn't really the word; it was more a mix of dread, exhilaration and terror, all of which were more volatile emotions than he was used to feeling. But feel them he did.

Asking a complete stranger to pose as his wife! Was he nuts? And why did she have to be late? Twenty minutes, so far. But then, somehow, he knew that she always ran just a little behind schedule. She would forget something and go back for it and then decide she'd forgotten something else—the lights, the oven, her head.

He checked his watch one more time. He had the boarding passes in his hand. The photographer was here; Matt had fed him a lame excuse for Mo's not being with him, something about a last goodbye to her family. She wouldn't do this to him, would she? Not show up?

And then she was there, running toward him, her huge purse knocking against her. He offered a silent prayer of thanks.

Mo wore some sort of filmy, flowery long dress; flopping about her face was a large hat, which she held tight to her head with one hand as she made her way through the crowd that milled around. As she lifted that hand to wave to him, her purse dropped to the floor with a clunk, spilling some of its contents on the floor.

Mo skidded to a stop, bent down to retrieve her purse, and her hat fell off her head. A man in a brightly colored native robe tripped over her, but managed to retain his balance. Apologizing, he helped her load everything back into her purse, then assisted her in standing up, and was rewarded with one of her sunshine smiles. Grabbing her bag in one hand and her hat in the other, she came hurrying up to Matt.

"Hi," she said, out of breath, her cheeks rosy, her large blue eyes alight with excitement. "Sorry. I tried to get here on time, but there was a hassle with the key— my friend Laura is going to house-sit and I had to show her how to hold the snake and then she got kind of weird about it, but it's all right. And I'd forgotten to buy kitty litter."

"You have a cat, too?"

"No, it died. But the parrot likes kitty litter on the bottom of her cage instead of newspapers. And then there was the cleaners, the only nice dress I own, they had to rush it because I had to bring it with me. I mean, I figured I should have one nice dress with me, don't you think, even though it's old? Plus, I put my passport in a really special, secret place," she went rattling on, "but I forgot where and then I found it, guess where?"

"Where?"

"It was in the freezer! That way, if there's a fire, it's safe. The trouble was, some grape juice had spilled on it and it was pretty sticky so I had to wash it off. Then I put it in the microwave but I got scared it would burn so I finished the job with my hair dryer. I looked everywhere for that thing, even under the fish tank. Not the hair dryer, the passport.''

"Do you live in a zoo, by any chance?"

She laughed, then bit down on her bottom lip with small, white teeth.

"This her, Mr. Vining?" the photographer interrupted from behind him.

"Yes," Matt answered, snapped back to the practical world. "We just have time. Where do you want us?" he asked, turning toward the man.

The photographer, cynical-looking and middle-aged, with an unlit cigarette dangling from one side of his mouth, began taking shots even as he indicated the large Arrivals and Departures monitors against one wall. "Stand there," he said, clicking away, "with your arm around the bride. Better dump the purse, Mrs. Vining. And maybe the hat, too."

"Mrs. Vining?" Mo said. "Oh, that's me." She laughed again, more of a nervous giggle, and took her place next to Matt, stowing her purse and hat on the floor behind her. "Don't worry," she said, fluffing her gold-red curls. "I have a smaller bag inside this one. And comfortable shoes, too, like you told me."

"Good," he said.

Matt was a man to whom conversation came fairly easily; he liked words and knew how to use them. But Mo had this strange effect on him. With her, he found himself reduced to stunned, one- and two-syllable responses.

Could he have found anyone more wildly different from Kay? he wondered. No, probably not. Closing his eyes, he prayed silently, asking for strength to endure all the chatter, the noise, the *chaos* that seemed to follow Mo wherever she went.

The photographer positioned them, fiddled with his lenses and snapped some more pictures. Matt put his arm around Mo's slender shoulders, but lightly, impersonally. He had to keep this in perspective, he told himself, even as his nostrils detected her powdery, light flower fragrance, mixed with something lemony. It was an amazingly pleasant smell, earthy and otherworldly at the same time, and he breathed deeply, finding himself relaxing just a bit.

"You could hug her a little tighter," the photographer said, "maybe pull her to you. Didn't you two just get married?"

Married. Matt heard the word and remembered.

"Here, put this on," he said to Mo, reaching into his pocket and withdrawing a plain ring. "It had to be adjusted for size," he explained for the photographer's sake.

Mo didn't understand at first, but when Matt slipped the ring on the third finger of her left hand, she got it immediately. She stared at the thin gold band, amazed at how strange it felt to be wearing a wedding band. The ring was loose, but only slightly.

She glanced up at Matt at the same moment he looked down at her; their gazes locked, and she caught her breath. Oh, he had to have the most *soulful* eyes she'd ever seen on any living thing that wasn't a dog or a horse. A person could drown in those warm chocolate eyes, she thought, gladly, gratefully drown and not regret it.

"Thank you," she whispered, swept up with emotion. "It's a very nice ring."

"It goes along with the title of Mrs., I think," he said dryly. "And so does a look of bliss."

She grinned at him. He grinned back. *Click, click, click* went the camera.

"Good one," said the photographer. "How about a kiss?"

Mo watched as Matt bent toward her ever so slightly. But something stopped him. He remembered—she could see the thought take shape in his brain and reflect in his expression—that the two of them had an agreement, one she'd insisted on. There was to be nothing physical between them. Pretend only.

It would be difficult to pretend to kiss.

"How's this?" Matt pulled her closer so that her head was nestled in the crook of his arm, her cheek resting against his chest. He wore a lightweight sports coat, and its fine wool was soft against her skin. She heard his heartbeat, steady but on the rapid side. Like hers, she imagined. Closing her eyes, she cuddled up even more. So the picture would look authentic.

"Yeah, another good one." With several more clicks and a whirring sound, it was done.

Matt released her so abruptly she almost lost her balance. "I'm afraid that's all we have time for," he told the photographer. "We have some paperwork to take care of. Thanks."

Any intimacy between them—real or imagined—was broken off the instant he let her go. Mo shook her head to clear it. What had she been doing? Playacting, for sure, but then? Indulging in fantasy. For a change. Well, that would have to stop. She would rein in her wayward imagination, especially as Matt was back to his former self now—efficient, removed and all business.

Fine, she thought. In fact, good. It was time to get this show on the road. Ten thousand miles away, the silver-eyed man awaited!

* * *

When they were finally aboard the plane, in the air, ensconced in the plump luxury of first-class seats, Matt felt a little more inner tension slip away. They were here, they were on their way. It was real. He allowed himself a silent ''Hallelujah!''

A loud sigh from Mo drew his attention to her just as she leaned back and closed her eyes. ''Tired?'' he asked.

''Really pooped. I haven't slept since yesterday. You?''

''Not a wink.''

Her eyes snapped open and she turned to face him. ''You had all that wedding stuff to deal with. What did you do? I mean, what did you tell people?'' She grimaced self-consciously. ''I'm sorry. It's none of my business, I know, so you can tell me to shut up—''

''It's all right,'' he said. ''Kay, my ex-fiancée, took care of it all. She's very efficient. And it wasn't going to be a large wedding. Just a few friends and family.''

''Still…'' She paused meaningfully. ''This must be a difficult day for you.''

Matt considered how to respond to that. He wasn't really sure just what kind of repercussions his aborted wedding was having. In all the rush, he'd barely thought about it. The truth was, he'd barely thought about Kay— which probably didn't speak well for the depth of his feelings for her. So why *had* he asked her to marry him?

His career was going well. In the three years of its existence, the radio show had built a nice following in San Francisco, not an easy town to break in as a food expert, there being a glut of the species already. He wrote regular columns for some midsize newspapers. A hired public relations firm had been pushing his name, there was the book and a cable TV contract in the works. He was getting there, but he wanted more.

All his life, he'd been driven, first to turn himself into someone to respect, then to get an education, then to make a name, to be known, to be someone. But focusing on those things so much had taken a toll. Recently, he'd found himself missing something that had no name. That was why he'd wanted to marry; he'd thought Kay would slide into his life without a ripple and alleviate the loneliness.

That *did* sound pathetic.

Not only did he not care for that particular insight, Matt didn't think he really wanted to trade intimacies with Mo. Still, she deserved some sort of response to the tentative feeler she'd put out about his state of mind.

"Yes, the day has been difficult," he said evenly, "but, if you don't mind, I'd rather not talk about it."

"Of course." She was all compassion and understanding. "But I'm here, Matt, I want you to know that. I know I talk a lot—"

He felt the corner of his mouth quirk up. "I hadn't noticed."

"But, believe it or not, I also know how to listen. Everyone tells me all kinds of stuff. You can too."

What a sweet smile she had. He found her declaration comforting. Touching, really. "Thank you."

Just then, a yawn seemed to take Mo by surprise and she covered her mouth as she yawned again. "Sorry. I'm really beat."

"Can you sleep on a plane?" he asked her.

"I'm not sure. I haven't flown a lot—and then only on short hops. How long will this take?"

"Ten hours. And when we get there, it'll be noon tomorrow."

"Noon. In London." She crossed her hands over her heart. "Oh, gosh, I really can't believe this is happening to me."

Her enthusiasm made Matt's mood lighten even more. Maybe it wasn't such a crazy thing he'd done, after all.

The flight attendant offered them pillows, blankets, fancy nuts and drinks. Feeling like a kid in a free toy store, Mo took two of everything and turned to Matt, laughter bubbling up inside. "So, this is first class. I like it. It's just like on the commercials. You're probably used to it, huh."

Matt closed his eyes. "Hmm."

He really did look exhausted, she thought. There were shadows under his eyes. She hadn't noticed them earlier, she'd been so self-absorbed with her new adventure. Poor man. This was to have been his wedding day. He must be so sad, and covering it up so well. He'd made it clear he wouldn't discuss it. That's how it was with some people. Not her, of course. Mo liked to get everything out in the open as soon as possible, so it didn't fester and explode later.

She studied Matt's profile as he lay with eyes closed. Short thick black lashes shadowed his cheek. His nose had that bump that was quite appealing. And she had the most insane urge to run her fingertips over his cheek where the hint of a new growth of black beard appeared just beneath his olive skin.

Another of those nervous giggles rose in the back of her throat. She was so tired, yet so keyed up, she was practically on the edge of hysteria. She needed to splash some cool water on her cheeks.

"I'll be right back," she whispered, rose from her seat and went into the lavatory.

After she locked the door behind her, she scrubbed

her face and rinsed out her mouth. Then she stared into the mirror; there were shadows under her eyes, too, but there was a glow about her that even she could see.

"Thank you, *Nagyanya*," she whispered, and as she did, memories came pouring back. Soft, wrinkled, old skin. The smell of glycerin and rosewater hand cream, and the lime Life Savers her grandmother had loved so. Small bright eyes, large bosom and large arms, great for hugging.

Nagyanya had been one of the only people in the whole family that could get Mo to sit still, but always gently, with patience and love. During Mo's childhood, the old woman's stories, half English, half Hungarian, had held her enthralled for hours.

In the mirror, Mo watched her reflection as she flattened her palms against her flushed cheeks. *Nagyanya* had taught her to dream. But this wasn't a dream. She was here and it was real.

So was the attraction she felt toward Matt, the one that had started yesterday. It had gotten a grip on her libido and her head, and hadn't let up in the least. Through all the running and calls and planning last evening and this morning, she'd had Matt Vining with her the whole time, like an inner-ear hum that wouldn't go away.

But why? Mo was supposed to be with someone else—a man with silver eyes. She simply couldn't dismiss her grandmother's prediction. To ignore the sheer *coincidence* of how she had gotten on this plane and where she was heading, well, that would be the height of arrogance, wouldn't it?

So, Mo figured the silver-eyed man, not a brown-eyed food expert with a broken heart, was where her destiny lay. And she'd better keep that uppermost in her mind.

That thought, she wasn't really surprised to discover, caused a little twist of disappointment in the area of her heart.

When she returned to her seat, she found that Matt was not only wide-awake, but had chosen their dinner from several selections; he hoped she didn't mind.

"Fine with me," she said, helping herself to another handful of nuts. "I'm starving."

"You might want to save your appetite."

"My mother always used to say that. But I'm more of a nibbler. I pick a little all through the day." She shrugged and took some more nuts. Why did first-class snacks taste so much better than coach? A higher-grade nut? "It's how my system works, I guess."

A frown appeared between Matt's eyebrows. He disapproved of her eating habits, she supposed. Hmm. She shrugged mentally as she swallowed the last mouthful. Really, she was too tired to care. Her eyelids fluttered closed, and she nodded off.

Matt tried to sleep, too, but his five-minute catnap had taken the edge off. Instead, he read over some notes for his book, glancing occasionally at Mo. She slept, as she did everything else, with energy. She mumbled. She changed positions often. At one point, her head found its way to his shoulder and he let it stay there. Her hair smelled as though she washed it with springtime.

He woke her up as dinner was being served. She seemed groggy, and he told her food was just the thing to fix that. The flight attendant brought them each a glass of chilled white wine—quite decent, really—which Matt sipped appreciatively and Mo declined.

"I'm not much of a drinker," she said. "Just Coke and the occasional beer."

The appetizer was stuffed mushrooms with an interesting hint of sage. More than decent, Matt thought, rolling a forkful around in his mouth. Especially for airline food.

Mo took a bite, looked at it as though she'd just tasted castor oil and put the mushroom back on the plate.

"I guess I'm not very hungry," she said.

"Too many nuts?"

"Maybe. And I'm not a big mushroom fan. Something about the color. Also they're so…slimy."

"Wait till you taste truffles. You'll change your mind." It might be fun, he thought, to introduce her untutored taste buds to new food textures.

When the main course was served, Mo took a forkful, frowned and put down her utensil. "Oh. This is fish."

"That's what *poisson gribiche* is."

"I don't care for fish. Never have."

Mo couldn't help noticing that the frown between Matt's eyes grew more pronounced when she declared her aversion to slithery things that lived in the water. Yes, she had specific food likes and dislikes, but didn't everyone? He was simply hitting on a lot of dislikes at one meal.

"Perhaps," Matt said with a hint of arrogance, "you've never had fish cooked properly."

"Mom used to roll it in bread crumbs and fry it and pour ketchup all over it to get me to eat it, but fish is fish."

"Have you had it in *sauce matelote?* Cayenne pepper and wine? Or scallops *mousseline,* made with hollandaise and whipping cream?" He smiled mysteriously, his nostrils flaring slightly. "Have you ever sampled a lightly buttered fillet of sole so fresh it slides down your throat without chewing?"

Listening to Matt's rich baritone, watching his mouth

as he spoke was…well, it was downright sensual. "I still don't like fish, but I sure like the way you talk about it."

He seemed startled by her statement. "It's my field."

"It sure is. Listen, Matt, believe it or not, I like a lot of food, but—I confess—it's mostly junk food. I've always loved it, probably always will."

That frown again. "All those fats and chemicals. It's so bad for you."

Mo was definitely getting irritated. Matt's judgmental attitude was bringing out her combative side. She was the youngest of eight, and had learned to deal with authority by refusing to honor it. Mo was a doormat for no one.

"I can read health columns, too," she said with a touch of what her father used to call snippiness. "Hey, is this going to be a problem? I mean, you didn't mention that having the same food preferences as yours was a requirement for this trip."

"No, but I am going to be reviewing several four-star restaurants."

"Yes, *you* will be doing that. Does that mean *I* have to review them, too?"

Really, she thought, the man did have a streak of pomposity. She wouldn't stand for being treated as though she were some pesky schoolchild. No way she would put up with that for the next two weeks, and Matt needed to know it now.

"Well," she challenged. "Do I?"

One jet black eyebrow was raised, then he nodded slowly. "You're right and I apologize. Of course you don't have to share my taste buds, but—" now he nodded more confidently "—your entire palate will change on this trip, I promise you. You'll even learn to like fish, especially in Paris.''

"I wouldn't count on it.''

4

There were more photographs taken at the airport when they arrived in England, then a taxi ride from Heathrow through overindustrialized countryside. Eventually, they drove along a broad street filled with all kinds of famous sights, including Buckingham Palace, then to their hotel, a large stone edifice near Covent Garden. Humming "Wouldn't It Be Loverly?" all the way up the "lift," Mo followed the bellman into the suite—and oh, was it wonderful! Victorian, mostly, lots of antiques, Turkish carpets, painted flowers on the wallpaper and fresh ones in vases all around the room. An enormous fruit basket and champagne in an ice bucket sat on a side table, awaiting the newlyweds.

Mo whirled around the room, inspecting everything, the maroon-velvet settee, the spacious, lace-curtained windows with a view of the Thames, across which spanned Waterloo Bridge. Waterloo Bridge! The very name conjured up graceful women in Empire dresses, and ships appearing out of the fog, and men in full battle dress, wearing tricorn hats.

Sighing with contentment, Mo pushed open a pair of ornate double doors to the bedroom. It too was darling and fussy, made up of frills and flowers and lots more lace. It even had a four-poster bed hung with rich tapestries.

"Oh," she said. "Isn't this all too incredible?"

Matt, right behind her, scratched his head. As Mo inspected the "loo," he glanced at the double bed, then back at the small settee in the sitting room. How, he wondered, would he unfold his long legs on that?

Mo pirouetted back into the room. "I love it all! I'm going to change, then I'm heading right out to see the sights. Coming?"

"Actually, it would be better if you napped first." Matt went into the walk-in closet and unzipped his hanging bag so he could unpack. "I've done a lot of traveling, and I find if you sleep the minute you get off the plane, you're not bothered by the time change and jet lag."

"Sleep?" Mo appeared in the closet's doorway, her head cocked to one side. "When I just got here?"

"I recommend it, most strongly. Remember, I've done this a lot."

Mo shrugged. "Sorry, I'm too keyed up. But please, you do that—sleep yourself silly. I'm taking off."

Leaning against the doorway, Matt draped his arms over his chest and watched her as she tore through the luggage the bellman had set on a wooden chest at the foot of the bed. Her clothes seemed to have been packed with some semblance of order, but by the time she withdrew shoes, a pair of jeans and a striped cotton sweater from the bowels of the suitcase, its contents looked like the aftermath of a rummage sale.

She ran into the bathroom to change and he stared at the closed door, pondering.

Matt liked order. Maybe, he admitted, to a degree that was beyond reasonable.

Still, the way to get order, he'd found, was always to be in charge.

Obviously, no one was ever in charge of Mo.

"All right," he found himself saying to the closed door, "let's make this deal. I'll join you now if you agree to nap before dinner."

Mo poked her head out and said, "You don't have to."

"I want to."

"You got it."

"The dinner plans have changed, by the way," he told her. "Our reservations were for tomorrow night, but there's some royal fuss or something then, so it has to be tonight."

"Royal fuss?" She came out of the bathroom, tucking her sweater into her jeans.

"Some princess of something or other. They're taking over the entire Arbuthnot Restaurant."

"Oh, is that how it's pronounced? I think I read the name somewhere—an old Lord Peter mystery or something. Well, good, it'll be fun. Coming?"

She turned to the mirror over a finely carved chest of drawers and gathered her hair onto the top of her head, then did things with pins and clips so that it stayed up there. Matt was always fascinated by the way women did that, taking all that wildness and taming it. In Mo's case, of course, it was more a matter of keeping it at bay.

But he couldn't help noticing the way the movement of her arms pulled her sweater tight over her rib cage, so that he was treated to the sight of her small waist flaring out to shapely, jeans-clad hips and derriere. He was reminded, just for a moment, of a painting he'd seen as an adolescent of a woman in front of a mirror, pinning up her hair, and the way his then-undisciplined, hormone-driven body had reacted to the sight, right in the middle of a museum.

"Matt?" Mo's eyes met his in the mirror. "Are you okay?"

Shaking his head to clear it, he sternly ordered his body to behave. "Just a little light-headed, I guess, from traveling. I'll be ready in a couple of minutes."

As he headed off to change clothes, Mo said, "Tell me something. Are we supposed to keep up this newlywed stuff for the whole trip?"

He paused in the dressing-room doorway. "What do you mean?"

"You know, in the lobby, on the street... I mean, do we have to hold hands and look into each other's eyes and sigh? That kind of thing?"

Matt was aware that somewhere inside he was actually disturbed—hurt?—by her question. Apparently, she would prefer no physical contact with him at all. "I would say not. Only if we're posing for pictures, or need to seem married for the purposes of getting information for the book. Okay with you?"

He kept his tone deliberately neutral, and when she answered with a hearty, "Great," he frowned and yanked at the zipper of his suitcase a bit harder than necessary.

Mo was in heaven. Just walking down the street and hearing all the various accents from passersby—high-class, low-class, Pakistani, Jamaican. Just gazing at the buildings, the old mixed with the new, the seedy and the grand, the slums and the castles. All of it, sheer heaven.

Back in the States, Mo's two favorite pastimes were watching travelogues on TV and browsing through the travel sections of bookstores, so she knew quite a lot about what they were seeing. But actually to be here, in the flesh, well, it was past words.

As they exited their hotel Mo said, "I love to walk. It's the best way to really see a city, don't you think? So, today, I'd like to walk, and walk some more, until I pass out, hopefully near the hotel."

She could see Matt bite back a cautioning reply. Then he shrugged. "Okay, this is your call."

As Mo and Matt crossed the crowded piazza of Covent Garden, bustling with the summer's first tourists, she was an enthusiastic audience for the sidewalk entertainers—singers, musicians, jugglers, mime artists—who performed for passersby. She and Matt wound their way through a warren of boutiques and colorful street stalls and on into the Market Building—a huge, skylight-covered mall with lots of shops.

Several blocks north on Neal Street Mo exclaimed happily over the odd things for sale, everything from apricot tea, harmonicas and vintage bomber jackets, to halogen desk lamps, shoes with heels lower than toes and Afghan tribal jewelry. She picked out a few trinkets for various family members, paid for them with pounds and pence then shoved everything back into her oversize purse, which she had neglected to leave in the hotel room.

She and Matt walked, as she'd requested, then walked some more. They visited St. Paul's Church, known as the actors' church because of all the theaters in the parish, and strolled past The Strand to the Victoria Embankment Gardens—where the homeless and the tourists seemed to coexist—and stood at the edge of the Thames River.

"Cleopatra's Needle," Mo said, pointing to the sixty-foot pink granite obelisk ahead. She turned to Matt and beamed at him. "I've been hearing about this my whole life. *Nagyanya* told all of us about it. She came over from Hungary via London, and worked at the fruit markets in this area till she got on a ship to America. This was the one thing she remembered, above all. How this large, pink, kind of silly thing rises into the heavens."

He responded to Mo's story with that rare, unexpected smile of his, the one that turned his eyes warm in an instant.

There, she said silently. There's the real Matt, the one underneath his take-charge, autocratic exterior.

She liked him, she was amazed to realize. Funny, they had nothing in common and he could be kind of off-putting, but she liked him.

And as for that class-A body—well, she had to admit it, because she tried never to lie to herself, that the man was definitely sexy. In fact, Mo was still attracted to him big time.

But, sometimes she irritated him, it was obvious. And vice versa. The two of them were like male and female sandpaper, rubbing each other the wrong way. Which could be kind of interesting, as far as being attracted went.

No, she warned herself. *No.*

Even if the two of them got past their incompatibility, Matt had just been dumped by his fiancée, and there was no way Mo was going to be a rebound lover.

Even if he wanted her.

Which he didn't seem to.

Which was fine because Mo could hardly wait for her first glimpse of that silver-eyed man by the Danube.

Stifling a yawn, Matt watched as Mo tore the pins and clips out of her hair and tossed them onto the dresser.

"I think I'll hop in the shower," she said. "I feel really grungy. Unless you want to first?"

"No, I'll wait till after we nap." Matt picked up the phone and requested a wake-up call in two hours. He could hear the sound of running water from the bath, then Mo's voice singing something about steam or cream, he couldn't really make it out. He was past exhaustion and wondered where in hell the woman found all her energy.

According to his calculations, it had been forty-four hours without any significant sleep for either of them; he was feeling as though all the juices had been sucked out of him, and Mo was vocalizing like a diva about to make her debut at the Met.

He grabbed his briefcase and sat on an armchair so he could look over the itinerary. Instead, he set the paperwork aside, rubbed his eyes, then closed them.

And again heard Mo in the shower, now singing a mournful-sounding love song, and he pictured her soaping herself. He groaned. Amazing how easily he filled in the image from what little he knew.

That outfit the first day had given him a view of her legs, and everything she'd worn since had impressed the outline of her body in his mind. The woman had an honest-to-God hourglass figure, voluptuous breasts, a perfectly indented waist, rounded hips and amazingly long legs for someone so short. A pinup fantasy, slightly in miniature.

He smiled. He would never utter that thought out loud. Mo didn't appear the type to find being compared to a centerfold a compliment. Of course, you could never tell with women; some would like it, some would not. They seemed to get upset over the oddest things.

He liked quiet, competent, conservatively dressed, *tall*

women. Mo was none of those adjectives, not one. So why did all these semi-pornographic pictures keep popping into his head?

Matt moved over to the settee and lay down. His head was at an awkward angle and his feet hung over the edge, but he was so tired, he would have found a cave floor acceptable. He closed his eyes and was just about to drift off, when he heard, "Sorry you have to sleep on that thing."

He raised heavy lids to see Mo standing in the doorway of the sitting room, a Japanese kimono wrapped around her as she towel-dried her newly washed thick curls. The expression on her face was sympathetic.

He shrugged. "I offered."

"Maybe you could call housekeeping and get a roll-away bed or something. Or sleep on the floor—that carpet is as thick as a lot of sleeping bags I've seen. Do you ever go camping?"

"Not for years. I'll manage."

"All right." Leaning against the door frame, she emitted a long sigh. "Gosh, it just hit. All my bones have turned to jelly."

"It's jet lag." He refrained from saying, I told you so. "You'll feel better later."

"I'm counting on it." Keeping a hip against the door frame, she went back to toweling her hair. "So, what kind of restaurant are we going to?"

"Indian. One of the best in the world, I hear. I'm looking forward to it."

"Curry and stuff, huh. I've never had Indian food."

Lowering his lids again, he smiled. "It's a little more than just curry."

"You're the expert. Well, sweet dreams."

"I've left a wake-up call."

"Good. I need about twenty minutes to get ready."

"If that's so," he said, opening one eye to look at her, "you're the first woman I've known that does."

She favored him with a huge grin. "Okay. Twenty-five."

She turned away from him and, continuing to rub her hair, gently closed the door that separated their rooms. What flashed into his mind was Mo tossing the towel aside and dropping her robe to the floor, offering him a fine, full view of her tapering back and firm, rounded buttocks.

"Great," Matt muttered, attempting to turn on his side. As fatigued as he was, he could actually feel his body stirring. *No*, he thought. *Cut that out.*

Still, as he drifted off to sleep, it crossed his mind to wonder if, just maybe, Mo would be interested in changing the terms of their agreement....

5

Dinner began well enough. The restaurant was decorated in softly draping curtains of bright colors, with brass-accented, intricately carved fixtures. Quiet sitar music joined the tinkling of bells and the smell of nutmeg, saffron, anise and other spices, to create a most authentic Indian atmosphere.

Mo looked enchanting in one of her flowing, filmy concoctions that was sheer without being revealing, that seemed free-floating but clung to the outline of her body as she walked on high-heeled sandals. The dress had been her mother's, she'd told him.

She wore her hair partly up and partly down, with lots of curling red-gold wisps framing her face. She wasn't wearing a bra, Matt observed, swallowing as he did, and very little makeup. She didn't need either.

As a food critic, Matt had informed her, he usually sampled a variety of dishes, so he quickly focused his attention on the menu's careful selection of delicacies, then made some notes in a small journal. Meanwhile, Mo loaded up on the *na'an* and *poori* bread—subtly flavored with garlic and black onion seeds—and chattered happily after each mouthful.

"I was reading about that little pub we passed, on Rose Street? The Lamb and Flag? It used to be called the Bucket of Blood.'' She shivered. ''Isn't that awful? I mean, who would want to have a drink at a place called the Bucket of Blood? It was named that because they held all these boxing matches there. Do you like boxing?''

''Actually, I do.''

''Really? So does my dad. I hate it.'' She took a bite of bread and chewed it. ''This is delicious.''

In between bites, she took a few sips of wine. One of her sleeves sank into a plate of cucumber, onion and tomato relish and she winced, then rubbed at the stain with water from her glass. When the mulligatawny soup was served, she put a spoonful to her mouth, declared it too spicy and dug into the bread again.

The main courses were a superb *padsheh z'affran murgh,* or saffron chicken, and an excellent *hyderbadi korma,* lamb curry with yogurt. Matt studied the composition of the food on the plate, closed his eyes and sniffed at the hot, spicy aromas rising in front of him and nodded. So far, so good. More than good. Excellent. He began to eat, slowly savoring each mouthful. Cilantro, cumin, a touch of cinnamon. Yes, definitely first-class.

He glanced over at Mo to see her staring at him, her mouth slightly open and a dazed look in her eyes. When she realized he was looking at her, her cheeks flushed and she dropped her gaze to her plate.

''Everything okay?'' he asked.

''Just fine.''

Matt went back to his dinner. He was already composing a sentence about the *tori ka dal,* a zucchini dish, when Mo sighed and pushed her plate away.

''Gosh, I'm just too full,'' she said.

"You can't be serious. Please, one taste. This Pesha-wari chickpeas is the best I've had, even in Bombay."

"You've been to Bombay?"

"Two years ago. Please try it."

She gathered a bit of food on the edge of her fork and put it gingerly into her mouth. Then she made a small face. "It's…not my kind of thing," she pronounced, putting the fork down. "Sorry."

Matt felt inordinately let down by her reaction, and it must have shown because she said anxiously, "What's wrong?"

"It's just that Kay and I— Never mind."

Mo put her hand over Matt's. His skin warmed under her gentle touch.

"I'm sorry," she said. "I've been insensitive. You must be missing Kay a lot."

He thought about that for a moment, then replied truthfully, "Actually, it's not that. It's just, well, we both enjoyed dining. Kay was, still is, of course, a master chef. It's her career."

"Oh, I see." Mo withdrew her hand and picked up another piece of bread. "You were colleagues, then."

"Yes. It was something we had in common."

The only thing, really, Matt amended silently. Still, he used to enjoy his and Kay's spirited discussions over dinner. Of course, there had been all those silences in between….

He preferred conversation to introspection. "So, tell me about your career."

"I told you. I don't have one, not really."

"Not even a wish?"

She shook her head. "I've always worked, since high school, but not at one thing. I've been, let me see—" she counted off on her fingers "—a waitress, camp counselor, cosmetics demonstrator, school-bus driver, restaurant hostess, berry picker, bagel maker, door-to-door knife sharpener's assistant. And in between, I work at temp agencies. My typing isn't the greatest, but I'm good on the phone.''

"Good Lord."

''Yeah, a pretty long list, huh? Oh, and I also go to school. I have two years of community college and a bunch of credits in whatever interests me, which would never add up to a degree unless they have a Bachelor of Dabbling.''

"But, don't you want to finish college?"

"Nope. Or, anyway, not yet. Lots of time."

That bothered him, although why, he wasn't quite sure. He broke off a piece of bread and chewed it absently.

"I wonder if this was a mistake."

Matt looked up at Mo. He'd been wool-gathering again. "Excuse me?"

"You and me, here, the whole thing."

"A mistake? I don't think so. It's more of an adjustment, I suppose. What brought that on?"

"Well, you're sort of in mourning, and I'm not the right kind of person for this whole food thing, and besides, well, you're— No, never mind."

"I'm what?"

She waved away his question. "No, I don't want to get into this."

"Don't want to get into what?" He set his fork down firmly. "I hate it when people don't finish sentences. Please, I insist."

She spread her hands. "The fact is, I'm kind of impetuous and emotional and you're kind of, well, daunting to be with, I guess. Not very relaxed. Except, of course, when you're—'' Again she stopped abruptly.

"Except when I'm what?"

"When you're eating," she said with an embarrassed laugh. "That's why I was staring at you before. I mean, when you lift your fork, you close your eyes and go into slow motion. You practically swoon when you put food into your mouth. You roll it around in there, I can almost see you basking in every little bit as it hits your taste buds. It's like…''

She paused, then blushed a rosy pink.

"It's sensual?" he said with a small smile.

"That would be the word, yes."

"I learned a long time ago that the aim of eating is not to devour food, but to cherish it. They do say eating is one of the most sensual experiences there is."

"Yeah, well, for whoever 'they' are, and for you, I guess it is."

"It could be for you, too. I'm afraid all that bread dulled your appetite."

Mo closed her eyes for a moment and seemed to be either counting or gathering her thoughts. Was she annoyed with him? he wondered. What had he said?

Opening her eyes, she propped her elbows on the table and glared at him. The sleeve that wasn't soiled drifted into a dish of sweet mango chutney.

"Uh, your dress," Matt said, pointing.

Mo looked down, grimaced and lifted the fabric out of the sauce. She swiped at it with a napkin. "Honestly, you can't take me anywhere. Everything I own has some kind of stain on it. I'm hopeless."

She was a whirlwind, moving here, prancing there, never still, never deliberate. He wouldn't be surprised if her entire wardrobe spoke of every meal she'd ever eaten, every place she'd visited.

She was also adorable, a word he didn't ever remember using in his life. But she was. Absolutely adorable. Also genuine, vibrant and eminently huggable.

He verbalized none of these thoughts because Mo was definitely irritated with him. "Have I offended you?"

She looked up from dabbing at her dress. "Not really. I was about to, well, set the record straight." She put the napkin back down. "In case you can't tell, I don't share the same interests you do. I mean, maybe some of them, but not this one. I don't have this same...*passion* you do about food. I guess I'm mostly indifferent to it. It fuels my body, and once in a while I get a sugar craving or a need for something hot and greasy, so I go find a McDonald's or a Dunkin' Donuts, and indulge myself."

He shuddered. "How can you?"

"You're intolerant, you know that?"

"You're angry."

"More like aggravated. I don't really want to sit here and apologize for the way I am. I mean, am I going to have to spend the rest of the trip doing that?"

He studied her with a frown. "I didn't mean to give that impression, Mo. It's just that I so love what I do, I guess I'm having a hard time believing anyone can be indifferent to food."

Mo took another few moments to ponder just how to respond. Patience was required here, to get her point across, and patience wasn't her strong suit. "Okay," she said finally. "Do you like rap music?"

"Not particularly. But then, I don't know very much about it."

"Well, what would you say if I told you I have a hard time believing anyone can be indifferent to rap music?"

"Are you really comparing them? Fine food and—" he gestured vaguely "—street songs?"

"They're both sensual experiences, aren't they? There are creative, interesting rap songs and stuff that's just so-so. Like food. But both food and music appeal to the senses. One's taste, and the other's hearing."

"I suppose so."

"So, what if I asked you to go to a rap concert with me? And not just go, but really enjoy it? In fact, insist that you *love* it."

He looked at her with disbelief. "Rap music?"

"Hey, it's an interest of mine, sometimes even a passion. What's the matter, are you a snob?"

"I don't know. Am I?"

"Sounds kind of like it." Pausing, she grinned sheepishly. "I'm sorry. I'm being too hard on you."

He shook his head at her apology; from the furrow between his eyebrows, it was obvious that he was considering what she'd said. Then that face-shifting smile of his altered his expression from distanced to accessible. It's effect was like warm brandy on a frosty night.

"You're not the first person who's called me on that, you know." He nodded slowly. "All right, I'll try to be less intolerant. The next time I get on my high horse, feel free to let me know."

She stared at him. "Really?"

"Yes."

All her annoyance with him dissolved in an instant. "Wow, that's really terrific of you."

He chuckled. "I'm glad you find something about me terrific."

"Oh, I do. In fact, I—" Mo bit her lip before she

could wax eloquent on just how terrific she found him.
Nope. That was one sentence that would remain unfinished.

"In fact," she said instead, "well, I'm having a wonderful time."

"Good. Now, here's what I suggest. I'll try to lighten up about the food, if you promise not to take me to a rap concert. Deal?"

"Deal."

"And I really can't talk you into one bite of this *kofta?*"

"The truth is, the smell reminds me of something that I don't think I'll mention, not at the dinner table. My stomach is shuddering at the thought. I guess Indian food is all a little too exotic for my tastes."

They finished the rest of the meal companionably. Mo even had a taste of the *kheer,* declaring it kind of like rice pudding. When he told her it was rice pudding, she wrinkled her nose and laughed. "So, why don't they call it that?"

Afterward, they decided to take a stroll and talk some more. The evening was pleasant and cool. It had rained briefly while they'd been inside the restaurant, and they walked along the slick, shiny streets of Soho, along Shaftsbury Avenue, with its many theaters and cinemas.

Mo told Matt about her family—her mom and dad, who ran a corner convenience store, her seven brothers, five sisters-in-law, all her nephews and nieces. She told him how great it was to have a large, loving family—and how awful it was to have a large, loving family.

"We have a hot line. Something happens to one, everyone else knows about it within ten minutes. A divorce, losing a job, a hangnail, everyone knows everything. Before I came on this trip, I had about forty phone calls, lots of advice, clucking, travel tips, warnings about taking along toilet paper. I mean, you would have thought I was going into space.'' She sighed. ''I love them to death, but sometimes I'd like to snap my fingers and make them all go away.''

Matt shook his head. ''I have no idea what that's like. None.''

''Were you an only child?''

''Most of the time.''

''Excuse me?''

''My mother had a hobby called marriage,'' he said sardonically. ''She did it on six separate occasions. We moved a lot. Sometimes I had stepbrothers and -sisters, but never for long.''

Mo didn't answer for a little bit. ''That must have been tough,'' she said finally.

''It was interesting, for sure. We got to travel a lot. I've lived in three different countries, and by the end of the sixth grade, I'd been to seven different schools.''

''You may call it interesting, but I call it a difficult way to grow up.''

It had been difficult, often painful. But Matt was unused to talking much about his past, even though, as she'd said, Mo knew how to listen. Still, something squirmed inside; he hadn't opened up the Pandora's box of his childhood in a long time. And he was reluctant to do so now. It seemed...needy, somehow.

He changed the subject. ''Are you tired yet?''

''You bet.''

''After a good night's sleep, we'll be back to normal by tomorrow. Why don't we head to the hotel? I need to make some phone calls to the States and scribble some notes for the book. I want to record my impressions of the meal while it's fresh in my mind.''

"Oh," she said. "Well, then, I guess I'll see you later. I'm going to check out the city at night.''

"We can go anywhere you want tomorrow. Besides, you can't travel around London alone after dark. It can be quite dangerous.''

"Sorry. I really want to see the Thames by moonlight." She whirled around with her arms up in the air. "I've always loved water, especially rivers, which is one of the reasons *Nagyanya* made her prediction about the Danube. Maybe in another life, I was a water sprite.''

She whirled away again. Matt caught up to her and put his hands on her shoulders to make her stop.

"Water sprite? Listen, you simply cannot do this. You cannot go traipsing about alone in a strange city at night.''

"Excuse me, but I *can* do that. I *will* be doing that. Right now, as a matter of fact.''

And with that, she marched off down the street, determination in her every stride. Matt watched her go, watched her hail a cab and get into it. He forced himself to stay where he was. No way was he going to run after her. No way.

A soft knocking made Matt rise, throw on his robe and make his way to the door of the suite. It was Mo, looking sleepy and apologetic. "Sorry," she whispered, "I forgot to take my key and I didn't know if I should ask the man at the front desk for another because we're supposed to be newlyweds and how would it look?''

He scratched his head and yawned. "It's all right," he said, stepping aside and letting Mo walk into the room. He closed the door and watched her walk toward the bedroom.

"I was in this little pub," she said, still talking softly in deference to the lateness of the hour. "It'll be good for your book. They have a thing called a newlywed corner, and everyone who passes by toasts them and buys them drinks. There's white ribbons and stuff all over it. Kind of corny, but cute. See you in the morning."

She floated into the bedroom and closed the door behind her. Matt lay back down on the settee and closed his eyes. A few moments later, he heard a soft knocking again.

"Matt?"

"Hmm?"

He opened his eyes to see Mo standing in the living-room doorway. She wore that silky kimono again, the one that silhouetted her luscious shape. His body responded immediately, as though it were on automatic pilot. He groaned silently at how she affected him.

"Thank you," she said softly.

"For what?"

"For the best day I've ever had in my life."

She looked down for a moment, then up at him again. He couldn't really see those large eyes of hers, but he had the feeling they were slightly moist, which wasn't really a surprise.

"And I owe you an apology," she said. "You were right. I shouldn't have gone off by myself like that."

Alarmed, he sat up, rubbing his hand over his face. "What happened? Are you okay?"

"Yes, I'm fine. I danced a little and had some of that awful warm ale, and then I slipped on some water on the floor—I'm always doing that—and there was this guy who caught me. He was pretty pushy. Kind of a biker type. He came on kind of hard, and I said no, very firmly, but he didn't want to hear it. I even showed him my ring—" she held up her hand, the gold band glinted in the moonlight "—but he didn't seem to care. Finally, this other guy with this wonderful cockney accent, Mick, his name was, came to my rescue. They didn't get physical or anything, but they did have some words. I think I learned how to curse in cockney."

Matt wanted to know what cockney cursing sounded like, but Mo kept up her usual river of words.

"It turned out that Mick was a cabdriver and he drove me back here. I was out of English money, but he took dollars. He was really nice. He has eight kids and one of them is named Maureen, like me... So, I'm okay. Anyhow," she said with a yawn, "like I said, you were right. I won't go out at night without you again."

She turned and went back into her room, shutting the door behind her. Feeling as though he'd just witnessed a film scene played at warp speed, Matt stared at the closed doors for a moment longer before trying to curl onto his side without too much of his rear hanging over the edge of the couch. Tomorrow, he would definitely ask for a cot, make up some kind of excuse—work, illness, whatever.

He was beyond tired; he was blithering with weariness. While Mo was out, he had not closed his eyes once because of worry over her safety; now that she was back, he was relieved, but most certainly not relaxed. He was puzzled by his reaction to her. He was not by nature someone who worried about others...or obsessed about them, either. That would mean people, relationships, connection had become important to him. And he'd shut down that part of himself long ago.

He wished Mo wouldn't take up room in his head like this, wished she liked fine cuisine, wished she were less of a free spirit and...wished he weren't attracted to her.

But he was. Damn. Pure lust, for sure. What else could it be?

The question kept him awake for a while longer.

6

With the living arrangements as they were, it was difficult to forget that Mo was around. The two of them had separate sleeping quarters, but there was one closet and one bath and they kept bumping into each other. Matt nodded to her the following morning as Mo was exiting the bath and he was entering. The room was filled with steam mixed with Mo's own personal aroma—baby powder, was it? Lemon? It surrounded him. It sank into his pores, invaded his head and made him dizzy. Also set off his libido and his imagination to the extent that, forgoing his usual hot shower, he took a cold one instead.

They breakfasted in the hotel's stately, high-ceilinged dining room, Mo's usual bright, chipper self reflected in her choice of a cheerful red minidress with a ruffle around the V-neck. This drew attention—his, anyway—to her more than ample endowments.

Announcing that she was starving, Mo dug into a huge English breakfast of eggs, fried potatoes, scones and marmalade. She turned down the kippers, of course. Matt, still full from the previous evening's meal, made do with a piece of toast and a cup of coffee, while Mo ate and talked, took a bite and talked some more of their plans for the day, of the reading she'd done on this city and all the others, of conversations she'd had the previous evening in the pub.

Matt watched her, fascinated by all the activity. It wasn't that Mo was a messy eater, exactly, more that she used food the way she used her life—voraciously, quickly and with a definite lack of tidiness. He watched as she licked the butter off a scone, then extended the tip of her tongue to the corner of her mouth, to catch a dollop of marmalade. His body tightened with desire at the sight; he wanted to lick it off for her.

This was becoming absurd, Matt thought. He was reacting like some randy sailor on leave. At some point, soon, he would have to do something about this impossible state of affairs. Or non-affairs, he amended.

He got his chance later in the day, after a boat trip along the Thames and more sight-seeing, before a scheduled stop at Regent's Park. The early-summer roses were in bloom, beds and beds of them, and Mo was exclaiming over the glorious colors, the sweetly pungent, individual smell emitted by each bush, when a small, thin man wearing plaid pants and a slouch hat came up to them.

"Mr. Vining?" The man spoke in a high-pitched, Northern English voice. "Simon Starkey's the name. I'm the picture taker."

Matt shook the photographer's hand, then introduced him to Mo. "Darling, this is Simon," he told her, putting his arm around her shoulders in a friendly, just-married-and-still-possessive manner.

"Hi, Simon," she said.

"Shall we pose here?" Matt asked the photographer, pulling Mo closer, and stroking her flesh softly, savoring the smooth feel of her under the pads of his fingers. The

skin of her bare upper arm was warm from the sunshine.
"With the rosebushes as a backdrop?"

"Don't need to pose at all, guv. I'll just tag along and
snap away."

"Oh, then can we go to the zoo?" Mo said excitedly.
"The area where all the birds are? I saw a whole TV
show on it."

"Good idea, Mrs. V."

Simon ran around them, his camera clicking away, as
Mo and Matt made their way through the park to the
London Zoo, a lovely, animal-friendly place where
moats separated the onlookers from its residents' habi-
tats. No bars and cages; Mo liked that. She also liked
the feel of Matt's arm around her, and was in no particular hurry to ask him to remove it.

They passed various animal exhibits until they arrived
at Snowdon's Aviary. Row upon row of mesh cages
were filled with thousands of chattering tenants. They
were able to actually enter one of the huge, oddly shaped
structures, one that reached taller than the tallest tree.
Bits of blue sky were visible through the netting and
towering branches. Mo gazed up with amazement at the
fluttering wings of all the brightly colored creatures.

"Wow," she said, laughing with sheer delight. "Bird-
land, for sure."

"Right-o," Simon said as he took another picture.
"Now, how's about standing in front of that bush there,
the one with all the yellow flowers?"

"Shall we, my lady?" Matt said, and Mo angled her
head up at him, ready to say, Certainly, my lord, when
the expression on his face froze her for the moment. She
caught him focusing on her mouth, his dark eyes even
darker with some deep emotion.

He wanted her. He was trying to mask the intensity,

making an attempt at being casual and charming—and most of all, in control—but he wanted her. Even though his facial movements were subtle, she was reminded suddenly of a stallion sizing up a broodmare.

Mo swallowed nervously as something deep and primitive inside her responded to him. She wasn't sure what to do next, especially as she could feel her cheeks heating up, more than just her cheeks, actually. ''Uh, I think he wants us over there,'' she said finally.

Matt nodded and, still holding her to him, aimed them toward the bush. They turned to face the photographer and Mo smiled self-consciously at Simon, but could feel Matt eyeing her instead of gazing straight ahead. The air was most definitely sizzling, and not with bird chatter.

''How about a kiss?'' suggested Simon, obviously unaware of the unspoken sensual tension beneath the surface. Mo swallowed again and slowly turned her head to meet Matt's gaze.

He almost stopped breathing, that was the effect the woman had on him. Here she was, fitting perfectly into the crook of his arm; Matt imagined there would be a good fit between them whatever the activity. Her eyes, huge and questioning, were a glorious blue. Her copper and gold hair flew wildly around her face in the soft summer breeze.

With his free hand, he reached down to push a strand of hair off her forehead. Then he brushed his fingertips over her forehead, her eyelids—so soft!—and her cheeks.

More. He wanted more.

He ran his thumb across her chin, then over that incredible bottom lip of hers. He actually did stop breathing then, with the sheer pleasure of touching her.

''What...what are you doing?'' Mo whispered.

"You still have a little marmalade there."

"Do I?"

He bent over and licked the corner of her mouth. "That's better."

"Oh." The word came out in a sigh.

Good God! Matt thought with shock, what was he doing? *Licking* a woman in public, in the middle of a zoo, in the middle of London, in the middle of the day!

Yes, as a matter of fact, that was exactly what he was doing. And what's more, he didn't give a damn who saw it.

Now his fingertips traced down the line of her neck, across her collarbone, and around the fringe of ruffles on her dress, barely touching the gentle swell of her cleavage and the dip between her two perfect breasts.

"Do I have marmalade there, too?"

"Unfortunately, no."

Part of his brain wondered why Mo wasn't protesting, but he wasn't going to bring it up. Birds swooped and chirped overhead, and somewhere nearby a child laughed. Matt had to kiss her. Had to. Propriety be damned.

Her mouth was trembling as he did; or was it his? Her lips were full and gentle and oh so enticing. He almost sighed aloud when he felt her ease closer to him, as though she too wanted more. Yes, yes, he wanted to shout. This was what they both wanted.

But not here, in the middle of a zoo.

Breaking the kiss, Matt smiled down at her. Mo gazed back up at him through dazed, half-lidded eyes, her breath coming lightly and rapidly through her parted lips.

"Did you get your picture?" Matt's voice was hoarse as he spoke to the photographer.

"How 'bout one more?"

Thank you, God. "Gladly," he said.

This time he couldn't pull off gentle. He commandeered her mouth and her tongue like a warrior claiming newly conquered territory. And she returned his enthusiasm by opening to him with an intensity that matched his own. Tongues and lips dueled and tasted and stroked; the inside of her mouth tasted like moist fire.

Mo had no time to think, no time to say or do anything. She was being swept up in a whirlwind of delicious, dizzying sensations and wondered vaguely if she would faint from the excitement. She had no idea how long they clung to each other, but eventually she heard Simon say, "Hey, guv, best come up for air."

This intrusion into the magic was enough to snap Mo back to reality. What was she doing? What was she allowing to be done to her? Her body was tingling, humming, crying out for more of the magic of Matt's mouth. Lord, the man could kiss! And Lord, she'd responded to his kisses as though she'd been starving for them her whole life!

None too gently, she untangled her arms from their clinch and eased Matt away from her. "Uh, I think the picture taking is over." She was unable to meet his eyes.

Simon sauntered up to them, nodding and grinning. "I got a bunch of good ones." He touched the brim of his hat. "It's been a pleasure, Mr. and Mrs. V. Enjoy your honeymoon." He snickered. "Although, it's obvious you already are."

Both Mo and Matt watched him stroll away. Two chartreuse parrots squawked loudly at each other and hopped onto a higher branch.

"Well," Mo said brightly, gazing up and around, everywhere but at Matt. "This is quite a place, isn't it?"

Matt placed a hand on her shoulder. Just that slight touch made her nerve endings flutter. "Mo," he began. "We've started something—"

"No." She shook his hand off and forced herself to glance up at him. "Please, don't. I don't want to be a substitute for Kay."

He seemed genuinely surprised. "You're kidding."

"No, I—"

She never got to finish her sentence because at that moment a jet-black bird dive-bombed between them, causing Mo and Matt to step back from each other. Then the creature flew up toward a branch, changed direction, swooped down near Matt's head, rose again and...

"Oh dear," Mo said. She couldn't believe what the bird had just done to the entire front of Matt's shirt. Covering her mouth with her hand, Mo bit her lips together so the laughter bubbling up inside her wouldn't escape.

In the space of a few seconds, Matt's expression went from startled, to offended, and finally to really annoyed. He reached into a back pocket for a handkerchief, and swiped at his shoulder and chest. Then his gaze met Mo's; he narrowed his eyes, as though daring her not to laugh.

But she did, she couldn't help it. Peals and peals of laughter, even though she tried hard not to. Eventually, Matt's mouth twitched a little on one side, then the other, and soon he too was laughing, a wonderful, rich roar of a laugh. The first she'd ever heard from him.

They collapsed against each other for a moment, catching their breath. Then Matt said, "I think it's time to escape this place, before I receive another token of appreciation."

They made their way back toward Regent's Park in

what seemed to be companionable silence. After a moment, Matt said, "We haven't finished our conversation yet."

"Sure we have."

"Mo, please, allow me to assure you that you aren't— you couldn't be—a substitute for anyone, most especially not Kay."

"Hah. That's what they all say."

"They all say you're not a substitute for Kay?"

"No, no, you know what I mean. Men. When they want you, they assure you they're over their girlfriend or their wife, or whatever, and then you believe them, but all they really want is to get in your pants and then they break your heart."

"Has this happened to you a lot?"

"Once is enough, believe me."

She knew she sounded more emphatic than she felt; the truth was, she was scared. That little necking session back there in the aviary had really thrown her, tossed her into space, really. Matt's kisses had affected her like no other man's kisses ever had. Right now, it seemed pretty important that Mo discourage any further moves in that direction.

She stopped near an empty park bench and turned to face him, her arms crossed over her chest. "Listen, what is this, Monday?"

"Tuesday."

"Okay, Tuesday. Two days ago, you got unengaged—"

"Three days ago." Matt looked at the handkerchief he was still holding in his hand, scowled briefly and tossed it in a nearby garbage pail.

Mo bit back a grin. She needed to be serious now, but he looked so cute when his dignity was threatened.

"Okay," she said reasonably, sitting down on the bench and gazing up at him. "Three days ago, your wedding was called off and you were forced to ask a perfect stranger to go on your honeymoon with you. See? I was supposed to be Kay, but I'm not—"

"You can say that again." He sank onto the bench next to her.

"So, you're probably filled with all kinds of anger, not to mention resentment for being cheated out of, well, what usually happens on a honeymoon, you know what I mean. So, I'm not trying to sound like a shrink or anything, but I think you're just a little too close to the situation to be objective and to know if I'm a substitute or a fantasy or what I am."

"You are most definitely a fantasy," he said, draping his arm casually over the back of the bench, just near her shoulders.

"Seriously, if you take a minute to think about it, you'll agree with me."

"I am serious, and for once in my life, I don't want to think. I wonder—" his finger made circles on the sensitive skin of her arm, and she jumped at the contact "—if you'd be interested in renegotiating our agreement, the part about platonic only?"

She shivered with sensation, then shrugged his hand away. "Hey, come on."

"Is that how you feel about me? Platonic?" He lifted her hand to his cheek and rubbed it over his recently shaved skin. Her palm burned and she heard herself sigh. Those meltingly brown eyes of his drew her into their depths until she wondered wildly if he was some sort of sorcerer.

"Well, uh, I—"

"Are you really going to say," he went on in a voice

that would have pulled down the covers on any bed in the world, "that I'm the only one feeling this attraction between us?"

Mo tried never to lie, really she did. But how would it sound if she said, yes, she was attracted, that she'd barely thought of anything else since they'd left the States? If you were an upright, unhypocritical type of person, what could you do with an admission like that except act on it? And she wasn't ready for that. No, really, she wasn't. So she equivocated.

"Time out."

She removed her hand from his and studied her lap. Then she let her words out in a rush. "You're a good-looking man, and a really fine kisser, I mean really fine, but all I want from you is friendship."

A moment passed, then Matt said dryly, "You may have observed that friendship is not what I'm feeling at the moment."

She allowed her gaze to wander down his body; he wore neatly pressed jeans that day, and it was impossible not to notice his rather prominent arousal. It was also impossible not to notice the thrill that rushed through her veins at the sight.

Irritated with herself for her reaction, she rose from the bench and began walking again. "Men," she muttered.

Matt followed. "Excuse me?"

"I said, all you men are so—" she threw her hands in the air "—filled with testosterone."

He had the audacity to find that funny. Grinning, he challenged, "And women don't get lusty?"

"Well, sure we do, but..." She stopped in her tracks and faced him, hands on hips. She had to set boundaries, and now. "Listen, I have a great idea. How about I leave you?"

"Go back to the hotel?"

"No, leave England. I could take my ticket and just go on to Hungary, to the Danube. That's why I came on this trip, anyway, right? Remember? The silver-eyed man? That way, you can do research for your book without having me in your hair."

Her hand flew to her mouth. "Oh, no, I'm sorry. That's right, I can't do that—I agreed to be your wife, I mean, your pretend wife." She grabbed some of her hair and clutched it between two fists. "Oh! You have me so crazy I don't know what I'm saying. But this whole—" she threw her hands in the air again "—sex discussion has got to stop!"

Matt stiffened as Mo's words sent a deep shaft of disappointment through him. What was happening here? How had he allowed this woman to affect him this way? And he'd never behaved so outrageously in public before. Not to mention that he was practically *begging* Mo to go to bed with him, something he'd also never done in his life.

Matt didn't think of himself as a vain man, but, frankly, on those occasions when he evinced interest in a woman, he wasn't used to being turned down, especially when he sensed the lady was just as attracted to him as he was to her. Which this lady was, he knew, even if she kept taking contrary action.

But why was he surprised that Mo never did the expected thing? Or that she caused him to act completely out of character? Didn't he get it yet? This woman was totally, completely unique, one of a kind, unheard of by mankind up to this moment. And she was his traveling companion.

For better or for worse.

Looking off into the distance, Matt made himself take a moment to calm down and gather his pride. Also to allow his body to get back to being unclenched—all over. Enough of acting the besotted, love-crazed suitor. He didn't even believe in the emotion, so why give it any credence? Finally, he nodded, knowing what he had to do and almost welcoming the decision, even with the disappointment, not to mention discomfort, it would surely bring.

"You're not in my hair," he said. Then, more resolutely, "Mo, all I really want to do is write a great book, one that will further my reputation and career. It's all I've ever cared about, to be truthful. As for you and me, well, I'm a grown-up and can certainly control my libidinal impulses. You might even be right about me not being over Kay yet. Yes." He nodded firmly. "Friends. We'll be friends. You have my word. Shall we shake on it?"

After an initial look of wariness, Mo offered up a tentative smile. "You did it again," she said wonderingly.

"Did what again?"

"Heard me. You listened, you thought it over, and took it like a champ. That's a really, well, admirable quality, you know that?"

He returned her smile. "One you value in a friend?"

"Better believe it." She put her hand in his and shook it firmly. "Friends."

7

They took one of the ferries across the English Channel the next day, to Calais. Matt couldn't help smiling as he watched Mo leaning on the railing; she was like an excited child as she stood with her head thrown back and her eyes closed, letting the ocean's salt spray bathe her face. After a while, she opened her eyes again and grinned at him, wiping her damp skin with the sleeve of her oversize peasant blouse.

"Can I thank you again for this trip?" she said.

"Sure."

"*Merci,* which is one of three French words I know. But, tell me, isn't this the slow way to France? I mean there's the new Chunnel, and all. Why did you choose the old-fashioned route?"

"That was Kay. She said, on a honeymoon, people should take their time and always choose the most romantic way to travel."

"Oh."

Mo gave him a look of warm understanding then went back to studying the view, the wind blowing her hair all around her and the sun glinting on its red-gold strands, making them seem like thin wires of living copper.

Friends. He'd kept the word and the concept of

"hands off" uppermost in his mind since agreeing to it yesterday. It wasn't easy.

Seagulls swooped and cawed loudly overhead. Mo seemed fascinated by their movements. Everything interested her; all the pleasure she took from just being alive glowed on her face. Reluctantly, Matt made himself stop looking at her and gazed instead at the fluffy white clouds over the channel and the waves sent up by the boat. Ruthlessly, he shut down any admiration he might be feeling toward Mo's hair, or the way the wind pressed the fabric of her clothing against the outline of that provocative body of hers.

She wanted friendship? She'd get friendship. Paris, France, the world-renowned City of Love, was about to receive two pretend honeymooners, two could-be-but-unfortunately-not lovers, instead of the real thing.

Mo adored Paris. After checking into the hotel, a large, rambling building that used to be the chateau of some count or duke three hundred years before, she and Matt went out to engage in her favorite activity—walking.

They strolled along the broad boulevards, past park benches where men puffed on cigarettes and argued in that beautiful language of theirs, and couples kissed in corners. They walked through gardens and under bridges, smelling the dampness from the Seine and the subtle scent of flowering chestnut trees.

Eventually, Mo requested something sinfully sweet instead of lunch, so they stopped for pastries at one of the city's hundreds of little cafés. This one, with tiny, marble-topped tables tumbling onto the crowded sidewalk, was near the base of the massive Arc de Triomphe. She told Matt that he could order for her, but to remember that she didn't require anything too fancy, just something sweet and greasy. Like Winchell's apple fritters.

He smiled and, in perfect French, requested *Mille-feuilles aux fruits rouges,* which turned out to be layers of thin puff pastry and fresh raspberries and strawberries. For himself, he ordered sweet biscuits and a glass of wine.

Mo's salivary glands started working overtime from the moment the dessert was set on the table until she finished every creamy crumb of it. Then she sat back and sighed. "That was heaven. Much better than Winchell's. Is this considered an A-type place?"

Matt finished making a notation in his notebook. "On a scale of fair to excellent, it's very good."

"Only very good? You mean, something could taste even better than this? No way, Matt."

He favored her with that knowing little smile that she had come to think of as his I'm-the-expert grin, and which she now found kind of dear instead of off-putting.

"There is a *pâtisserie,*" he said, "in a tiny town in the south of France that, legend has it, was founded by angels. Their pastry is the lightest, their cream the freshest, their fruits and sorbets the closest thing to heaven I have ever tasted. That is where 'excellent' is."

Leaning an elbow on the table, Mo rested her cheek in her hand and gazed at him. He looked yummy today, for a change, in a rust-colored cotton sweater with the sleeves pushed up, and a pair of brown slacks and brown loafers. His arms were corded with muscle, though not overly so. The sweater was slightly scoop-necked, and dark chest curls were visible above the neckline. He was shaved and tanned and, with that slightly broken nose, unbearably attractive.

Even as she found parts of her body humming while

she studied him, she wondered idly how his clothes always stayed so neat. Except, of course, at the London Zoo, when the bird had used him for target practice. She smiled at the memory, but shared none of these musings with him.

Instead, she asked, "With all this eating you do, why aren't you fat?"

He shrugged. "Metabolism. Plus, I don't eat like this all the time, and I work out at a gym."

"Really? I don't see you in sweats, somehow." Little tiny shorts, maybe, she amended silently. And nothing else.

"Why don't you?"

"Why don't I what?"

"See me in sweats?"

It was her turn to shrug as she tried to mask her embarrassment over her sudden mental pictures. After finding a little more pastry on her fork, she said, "I don't know. You're such an aristocrat."

"Me?" He chuckled. "Not even close. My mother was an underage cocktail waitress when she met my father. Husbands two and four were more financially comfortable than the others, and I guess I learned a little about clothing and manners from them. But I went all through school on scholarships. And I worked construction jobs during the summers. Sorry," he said ruefully. "There's not an aristocrat on any branch of the family tree."

Mo's mouth dropped open. "Wow, I can't believe this. I had you pegged as old money. Yacht clubs and debutantes and stuff. So then, how'd you get into this whole food thing?"

Sitting back in his chair, he said thoughtfully, "My mother's husband number four—Henri Chartier—was

French. His family ran a little place in Cherbourg, four or five tables only, and he cooked only what he wanted each night. There were always lines around the block.''

The look on his face grew more introspective, even tender. ''I had some of the best times of my life in that kitchen. The smells, the warmth of the oven, the laughter, the scarred old wooden cutting board and the huge white sink. The absolute delight they took from feeding people. After a while, I knew it was something I would be involved with forever. Even when my mother went on to husband number five,'' he added sardonically.

Mo felt a small wrenching in her heart at this revealing bit of Matt's history. She wondered if he was even aware he'd found something in that kitchen he must have been missing all his life. Biting her lip, she fought down a sudden urge to cry for a little boy desperate for nurturing.

She played with her napkin for a few moments until the threat of tears was past. Then she said softly, ''I find this totally fascinating.''

''Do you?''

''And you're fascinating.''

''Am I?'' He seemed surprised but amused.

''Yes. You're so...different from the way you appear.''

''You're not.'' His grin was wry. ''You register everything you're feeling, right on your face. Just now, you were sad, although I don't know why.''

He hadn't a clue, had he? Mo thought. No wonder he seemed distant so much of the time; he was distanced from himself, most of all.

She waved away the moment with an embarrassed laugh. ''It was nothing, a passing thought. So—'' she quickly changed gears ''—I'm easily readable, huh?

Shoot. And I've always wanted to be mysterious. The fascinating woman in the corner that everyone wonders about—'' she arched one eyebrow dramatically ''—but no one really knows.''

He shook his head, chuckling. "Sorry. You're about as subtle as a billboard."

"How boring."

"Never that. On the other hand…" He paused, his expression more serious now. "You are sweet. And kind." Seeming to choose his words carefully, he went on, "And real. And…quite, quite lovely."

This last sentence was spoken softly, and it made her shiver with pleasure. Looking down at her plate, Mo said, "Thank you," in a voice that sounded a little wobbly, even to her, and traced the table's marble pattern with her finger.

After a while, Matt covered her hand with his and squeezed. "Come," he said. "The city awaits."

They strolled along more of the stately, tree-lined Avenue des Champs-Elysées, a little over a mile to the Place de la Concorde, a large square filled with flower beds and trees.

In a small section of the Jardin de Tuileries, a lovely park nearby, a street puppet show made Mo laugh, especially when she looked at the rosy-cheeked children surrounding the makeshift stage, their eyes wide and trusting. It was so comfortable being with Matt this way, without all that sexual tension in the air.

In fact, Matt seemed almost lighthearted today, and certainly less guarded. She watched as he walked over to a flower seller, picked out a rose and, bowing, presented Mo with it. She curtsied back and they grinned at each other. She sure liked the way his face creased up when he was happy, and the way his dark eyes got lighter somehow, becoming almost a dark amber.

Yes, this friends thing was good, Mo thought. Really good. She was glad he'd thought it over and decided she was right—the two of them did not belong together as lovers. He was probably even feeling silly about how hard he'd come on to her the day before.

He had stopped touching her at the slightest provocation, and studying her when he thought she wasn't noticing. Good. Obviously, Matt was over whatever he'd thought he was feeling.

She was sure pleased he'd had a change of heart, pleased he'd heard her.

Really she was.

The restaurant setting was certainly a major winner, perched as it was on a hill just across from—Mo could hardly believe it!—the Eiffel Tower. The view was of twin sandstone pavilions, the Palais de Chaillot, Matt had told her, which had a series of descending gardens and pools all the way down to the river. It took your breath away, she thought. Like something out of a fairy tale.

As the night was clear and only slightly chilly, they ate on the outside flagstone terrace, at a lovely umbrella table. White-coated waiters moved around them in near silence, and from the other tables came the sound of murmured conversation and soft laughter, and the smell of garlic and French cigarettes.

London had been great, but they all spoke English there. Being in France was a real foreign feeling. Exotic. And terribly exciting.

Mo wanted to be a good sport, so she promised herself

that during dinner, she would try at least to taste everything Matt offered her.

They started with wine, and after it was poured, Matt
spoke softly to the waiter in his perfect French. When
Mo asked him to translate, he told her, with a sheepish
grin, that he'd asked him to hold the bread till the food
was served. She decided to respond to this none-too-
subtle hint by laughing it off.

Reading from the parchment menu, Matt translated
some of the first-course dishes for her, and she got to
choose between sautéed duck liver and beans, warm potatoes with gelatinous pig's feet, fresh sardines marinated in thyme, jellied spider crab and eggplant caviar
in tomato sauce. *Yippee,* she thought silently.

In all honesty, none of them sounded appetizing, but
she went for the duck liver because there was no way
he was getting her to eat fish and she hated purple vegetables. The wine was pretty good, though, and she had
a couple of spoonfuls of the duck. The beans were a
little too spicy.

Matt ordered fillets of fresh marinated mackerel on a
bed of "rosemary-infused tomato coulis," whatever that
was, grilled pigeon and a roast rack of lamb sliced ta-
bleside. Also another, different bottle of wine. It was a
good thing he wasn't paying for all this, Mo thought,
because this meal would cost your basic arm and leg.

Still, it was all quite elegant, and Mo was glad she'd
worn her black minidress with the beaded straps; it was
pretty old, but still serviceable. Also that she'd brought
along a shawl, after Matt had absolutely insisted on it.

He was in a perfectly tailored charcoal-gray suit with
a soft yellow shirt and a silver tie. She almost sighed
out loud. The way the man carried himself, well, for sure
there had been some aristocracy—maybe even royalty—

in his bloodline. Or maybe in a previous life, if you bought into that kind of thing. Whatever, he looked good enough to, well, eat.

However, she reminded herself, he wasn't on her particular food plan. She was reserved for the silver-eyed man. A wave of guilt swept over her; she'd practically forgotten him altogether. It was best to bring him to the forefront of her mind and shove Matt to the back, where he belonged.

Mo had the lamb, which was too pink and needed salt, and refused both the fish and most especially the bird. Cute little pigeons? No way. She had her bread, though, and it was really good. Somewhere halfway through the meal, when Matt stopped asking her to "just taste," Mo breathed a sigh of relief. She'd tried, really she had.

The photographer showed up, and took all kinds of pictures of Mo and Matt laughing and holding hands and feeding each other bites of food at the table. Matt actually tried to sneak a forkful of fish into her mouth without her knowing, but she got a whiff and actually spit it out. After blushing profusely and apologizing to the waiter, she glared at Matt as she gulped down some water. Matt apologized, but soon both he and the French photographer were laughing and she joined them.

The nice part about the picture session was that this time they were able to avoid all that fuss with pretending to be passionate. Good, Mo thought, tamping down another, slightly disappointed voice that informed her that she had kind of *enjoyed* all that pretending to be passionate.

At one point, when the waiter leaned over and asked, in thickly accented English, if everything was okay, Mo smiled sweetly and said, *"Oui."*

To Matt, however, she confessed that French cooking

just wasn't her thing, except, of course, for that warm,
crusty bread. Heaven. Poor Matt shook his head in wonder, but seemed to accept it with good grace.

They'd begun the meal at twilight, and by the time
dessert was served it was completely dark. There were
clouds over the moon and only a sprinkling of visible
stars. In the distance, light came from the palace and the
Eiffel Tower; the flickering candles at the tables provided a soft glow closer in. It was quite romantic, Mo
thought, and kind of a shame they had to waste it. Being
that she and Matt were only friends.

Dessert was, of course, more than okay, although her
favorite so far had been the pastry that afternoon. They
had a chilled peach soup, which was not sweet enough
for her, and a bitter chocolate sorbet topped with hazel-
nut cream sauce. Mo tasted both, but preferred the sorbet, only without the sauce.

"Whew, I'm full," she said when the dishes were
taken away.

"We're not quite done."

"Isn't the end of a meal the dessert? Oh, you mean
coffee."

"No," Matt said, smiling.

Just then the waiter brought a platter of cheeses and
apple slices, with small, sharp silver knives and new
plates. And of course, another bottle of wine.

"What kind of cheese is this?" Mo asked Matt warily.

"There are four different varieties of *bleu*."

"You mean, there's more than one kind of blue
cheese?"

"Several."

"Huh. Well, whatever. I'll have some apple."

The slices were good, tart and sweet at the same time.

She chewed one final bite, swallowed, then sat back in her chair. "So. Is the meal done now?"

"Coffee with brandy, and then we're done."

"Silly *moi*. Of course. But I think I'll skip the brandy. And I want you to know that I'm in love with Paris...in spite of the food. You're being really patient tonight, putting up with my low-life taste."

Shaking his head, Matt laughed good-naturedly. "You certainly do have your likes and dislikes. But you gave it a try, and that's all anyone could expect." Raising his wineglass, he said, "To Paris...in spite of the food."

Mo could drink to that. She could drink to a lot of things, actually. Had, all evening, as a matter of fact, and was now definitely tipsy. The meal had lasted about four hours and they'd polished off quite a lot of wine. She raised her long-stemmed glass to Matt and considered what to say.

Here's to sexy men in dark suits.

Here's to men named Matthew who tempt her something awful, in spite of her resolve.

No, to both. Not cool, in the least. All right then, what? "Here's to post office boxes," she said finally, then giggled and took one more sip.

"To post office boxes. And...friendship."

She glanced up at him, but in her current inebriated state, couldn't tell if that pause was ironic or not. "Yes," she agreed. "Good ol' friendship."

"And, my good ol' friend, I think we'd better get you back to the hotel."

A half hour later, as she and Matt stood side by side in the elevator, Mo noticed a couple of exquisitely dressed women giving Matt an appraising glance. Then one whispered slyly in the ear of the other, both of them laughing softly afterward.

Matt turned that slow, sexy smile on the two women, and Mo felt red-hot jealousy rise up and bite her. She wanted to shout at them, to raise her hand so they could see her ring, then maybe even raise a different finger to them. Hands off, she wanted to say. He was hers.

But of course, he wasn't.

She was being irrational; she knew that. Probably the wine. She'd had her chance and she'd said no. If Matt wanted to flirt with other women, maybe even to do more than flirt, well, it was nothing to her. Nothing.

The elevator opened at their floor, and Mo scowled surreptitiously at both women as she and Matt stepped out onto the thickly carpeted hallway. On their way to their room, Mo tripped once and Matt caught her around the waist. "Careful."

"Shoes wobbly," she said.

"Too much wine."

"That too."

"Are you going to be all right?"

"Sure."

The honeymoon suite had two separate entrances, one to the living room and one to the bedroom. Matt paused outside the latter. He used his key to open Mo's door and gently pushed her inside.

"Sleep well," he said.

"Where're you going?"

"I think I'll have a nightcap in the bar. I'd ask you to join me, but it seems to me you need your sleep more."

Are you going to meet someone there? she almost blurted out, but managed to bite her bottom lip before the words could escape. Obviously, he didn't want her with him. He wanted to put the moves on one of those simpering French "ladies" from the elevator. They'd probably passed notes and room keys to each other when Mo wasn't looking. She envied all French women, with their Chanel suits and their subtle perfume and the way they growled in the back of their throats when they spoke their language.

"Good night, Mo," Matt said. "Tomorrow we'll go to the islands right in the middle of the city. You'll enjoy it." He smiled again and closed the door.

She plopped herself down on the bed and frowned, assessing her condition. A little light-headed, she decided, but not sick. From the wine, anyway. The green-eyed monster was another thing, though.

A long, cool glass of water helped. Also washing her face and brushing her teeth, after which she crawled into the deliciously soft-yet-firm bed and pulled the down comforter over her. Faint accordion music from somewhere reached her ears. She stared at the ceiling, all carved curlicues and fat cherubs, while shadows from the lighted terrace made strange shifting patterns.

Somehow, as she remembered thinking back at the restaurant, it seemed such a shame not to take advantage of this romantic French atmosphere. Yes, a definite shame to waste a bed like this, a suite like this, a night like this, sleeping alone.

Hmm. If she wanted to, Mo thought, she could crawl into Matt's bed and surprise him when he returned to his room....

No, no. No! She'd worked too hard to establish this friend thing. Besides, he didn't want her with him anymore that evening. She could take a hint as well as the next person.

She wondered if Matt would be sleeping alone that night. The idea brought a sudden painful lump to her throat, but she knew if she thought about that, she might get really crazy. The inside of her head was whirling now, so she closed her eyes. After a while, she slept.

And dreamed of pastries and angels and men with eyes that went from silver to brown and back to silver again.

8

————▶◀————

"I look awful," Mo said the next morning, removing large sunglasses and squinting as she sat down across from Matt. "I know it."

Matt had chosen the hotel's outdoor patio for breakfast. He had been waiting for Mo, at a table shaded by lime trees, for the past hour. "Not awful," he said, pushing a large cup of hot black coffee toward her, "just a little less cheerful than usual. Most people who drank as much as you did last night would look a lot worse the next day, believe me."

"Is that supposed to make me feel better?" Leaning her forehead on her hand, she shoveled several spoonfuls of sugar into her cup and stirred. "Besides," she said, after raising her cup to her mouth and taking a sip, "you drank as much as I did."

"The family hollow leg—we're famous for it. Also, with all the wining and dining I do, I've had to learn to pace myself."

"Well, I haven't. Right now, I don't care if I ever see another glass of anything vaguely alcoholic again."

"But you look so cute when you're hungover," he said with a laugh. She did, too. Her hair was pulled back in a high ponytail. There were still sleep lines across her cheeks and her eyelids were morning-heavy and without a trace of makeup.

Mo scowled. "I hate being called cute. And I wish I were five foot ten."

"Sorry." Matt bit back another smile. On this trip he'd seen her in various emotional states—warm, moved, irritated, joyful, turned on and flustered—but this was the first time he'd seen her grouchy. He found her in this mood, as he did in all of them, utterly adorable. He would continue to keep that thought to himself, however. If she hated "cute," "adorable" would make her come after him with a knife.

Drawing the cover off a silver tray, he said, "*Voila!* Croissants. Strawberry jam. Great for what ails you. They'll fix you right up."

"Plying me with bread again, are you?" She reached for one of the flaky crescent rolls and smeared jam all over the top.

"It seems to work."

After a few bites, some of the grumpy tension seemed to go out of Mo's body. With a contented sigh, she said, "I feel better already. I think there is definitely a God. And, when I taste a croissant, I believe his first language was French."

Resilient soul that she was, the food and coffee made Mo snap right to, and in short order, Matt and she were walking along the tree-lined quays of the Seine. The day was warm, the sky blue, and the streets filled with all the scenes of daily life in Paris: men in green uniforms sweeping excess water into the sewers with twig brooms; distracted drivers careening around narrow corners. Chess players, lovers. Matt saw and enjoyed all of this, as though for the first time.

"You know what?" he said, his heart light with an emotion close to happiness.

"What?"

"I'm having fun."

Mo glanced over at him. "Well, sure. So am I."

"No, what I mean is—" No, he thought, don't say it. He shrugged. "Nothing. It's not important."

She stopped and faced him, her arms crossed over her chest. "What did you say about people who don't finish sentences? I'm not moving till I hear it."

Matt felt awkward now, but he scratched his head and gave it a try. "It's just that, I usually travel alone. And this trip wasn't supposed to be anything more than research. It was a career move, really."

"I thought it was to be your honeymoon. Yours and Kay's."

"That, too." He frowned. "I owe Kay an apology when we get back."

"For what exactly? If you don't mind my asking."

"No, it's all right. For…" He searched for the words. What he was experiencing was difficult to pin down; he was in the realm of emotions here, and he wasn't well versed in that territory. But Mo was easy to talk to, and safe somehow.

"For not taking her feelings into account," he said finally. "For treating something as important as a honeymoon as, well, as business. I think she tried to tell me that when she called off the wedding."

"I see. But, the trip…I mean, haven't you been to all these places before? And isn't it still business?"

"Of course, but being with you makes it unlike the other times. I mean," he went on, "you've never been here before and I guess I'm seeing things through your eyes. You're fun to travel with."

He hadn't allowed himself a lot of fun. Work, not relationships, had ruled his adult life. But not at the present. Something about the way Mo experienced the world—head-on and with enthusiasm—was contagious. He wasn't sure when his priorities had changed, but now the trip was about giving Mo a wonderful time and watching her face while she did.

"Anyhow," he said, "it's you that makes the difference."

"Really?" Mo gave a little embarrassed shrug at his compliments. "Well, I'm happier than a pig in slop. Now that I've finally gotten myself across the Atlantic, I know I'll be back. Often, if I can swing it. But for now, it's good that one of us has traveled a lot before, so we don't wind up lost all the time."

"If you'll keep on supplying the enthusiasm, I'll supply the experience."

"I guess we make a pretty good combination, huh."

He met her gaze deliberately. "Yes," he said quietly, "a pretty good combination."

He watched her face as both of their last comments still hung in the air. Mo's eyes were wide-awake now, and softly vulnerable. She and Matt stood there, in the middle of a busy Paris street, with people walking and jostling on either side of them, but he felt as though they were in their own private world.

This sense of closeness and connection to her made his heart lurch. It was more than simply sexual attraction, although that was always there. But just *what* it was, he had no idea. He wanted to say something, but he didn't know what.

Instead, he took her hand, and she didn't draw it away. It was small and smooth and cool in his palm. He laced their fingers together and smiled. "Friends can hold hands, can't they?"

"I...guess so," she said slowly.

"You know, this friendship concept is all right."

For a quick second he thought he saw disappointment on her face at his use of the words *friend* and *friendship*. But, no, he'd probably imagined it, he decided in the next moment, because she favored him with one of her sunny smiles and said, "Absolutely. Friendship. The best."

They spent the rest of the day walking around the Ile de la Cité and Ile Saint-Louis, the two islands at the heart of Paris. As Matt pointed out the monuments—the Eiffel Tower, the Grand Palais, the Louvre—Mo pointed out the people. He smiled along with her at the poignant sight of an extremely wrinkled elderly woman with a very young child sitting in her lap, both of them fishing in the river. They stopped and watched an argument between a bearded man carrying a birdcage and a hefty woman brandishing a long baguette, the spittle flying as both screamed at the top of their lungs.

When a midget in a beret and a silver eye patch slyly offered postcards of nineteenth-century pornography, Mo insisted on looking through the selection, then glanced up at Matt with raised eyebrows. "Boy, things haven't changed much, have they?"

"Let me see," he said, reaching for them.

"Nope." Mo handed the postcards back to the little man with the eye patch, blushing slightly as she said, *"Merci."* Then she grabbed Matt's arm. "Too corrupting. Come along."

When they passed the magnificent Notre-Dame Cathedral and Matt was in lecture mode on all the Gothic carvings, Mo spied two nuns near the curb, licking ice-cream cones. "I want what they have," she said, pointing.

"A religious life?"

She giggled. "Ice cream."

"Your wish is my command."

They took a taxi to Berthillion, the home, he informed her, of the best in the world. Once there, they had to wait in line for a while. Finally, an extremely surly woman in a pink apron looked at them with one raised eyebrow. *"Oui?"*

Mo said, "Chocolate."

"Chocolat."

"No, wait," Matt interrupted, then turned to Mo. "Look, the thing about this place is that it's different. They make their ice cream from all kinds of fruits, whatever's in season. They're famous for it."

"That's nice. But I still want chocolate."

"Un moment, madame," he said to the lady who was now tapping her fingernails on the counter impatiently. "Mo, please. Trust me. It's delicious. Think of it—ice cream made from rhubarb, black currants, figs, kumquats."

She crossed her arms over her chest, as though declaring war. "Sorry. I want chocolate and nothing you're saying is making me change my mind."

"Were you like this as a child?"

"You know, Matt, it's really not okay to try to force people to eat things they don't want."

He glared at her, then relaxed. He was doing it again, wasn't he? Still—

"All right," he said. "We'll get two cones. One chocolate, and one fresh melon. One taste, that's all I ask. Are we agreed?"

"You are the pushiest man..." She shrugged. "Okay,

as long as you don't take my rejection personally. This has nothing to do with you.''

"Promise."

Matt didn't know why he was pressing so hard—and yes, he was taking it personally, he knew it—but it just seemed important to him that she find *something* he recommended worthwhile.

When the cones were served, and they'd left the shop, Mo held the melon-flavored one in her hand, looked at it as though it had horns, then gave the ice cream a small swipe with her tongue. The look of surprise on her face, followed by a grin and a thumbs-up gesture, let him know the treat passed muster. He felt his chest filling with pride, although he wasn't quite sure why. About time, he thought silently.

"You're right, I'm wrong," Mo said graciously. "It's really good."

She went to work on the cone with her usual gusto, but after several nibbles, the scoop of ice cream fell to the ground. "Oh, no," Mo said, bending down with her napkin to scoop it up.

"I'll get you another one," he said, kneeling beside her to help.

"It's my own fault. I'm always in a hurry." She mopped at the mess. "It's why I trip all the time and drop things and get stains on everything. I don't take enough time." She raised her head and gazed at him, the look on her face one of such sweet, sorrowful self-reproach he wanted to grab her and kiss her till she stopped chastising herself, and then kiss her some more.

Instead, he went into the shop for more napkins, wondering how the hell he was expected to have such a lively, laugh-filled day with someone like Mo, and not want her.

Friendship was all well and good, but he wished someone would tell that to his body.

At breakfast on their last day in Paris, Mo looked up from her third croissant and said, "What do you think about me taking over? For today, I mean."

"Excuse me?" Matt set down his coffee cup.

She folded her elbows on the table and gazed at him earnestly. "Most people on a honeymoon can't afford all this—" she made a vague waving gesture with her hand "—four-star dining and class-A surroundings, now, can they?"

"I suppose not."

"So, if you'll translate, we can talk to a bunch of people and find some fun affordable places for your book and check them out."

Matt considered her suggestion, then nodded slowly. "You're right. I should have thought of that, and I'm the expert." More and more, he appreciated her resourceful mind. "I'm game. Where do we start?"

Mo's plan involved them talking to the hotel maids, then to a young, long-haired waiter, who conferred with a chef's assistant and a potato peeler. A Vietnamese busboy and a Jamaican pot scrubber joined in the conversation.

Away from the hotel, Mo and Matt chatted with various couples at sidewalk cafés—all of them young and not particularly affluent. Rather, Mo did the chatting and Matt translated her ebullience as well as he could. After a few of these conversations, he was amazed to find himself loosening up, actually exchanging some spirited comments with several of the people—strangers all, but pleasant strangers. Soon he and Mo had a list of small, offbeat restaurants and after-hours clubs.

On this final day in Paris, Matt agreed to put away his need to lead in an orderly fashion and let Mo call the shots. Hers was a world of improvisation.

They walked and took taxis all over the city, Mo stopping whenever the mood struck her and insisting they investigate some small shop or walk down an alleyway that "called" to her. At each eating place, Mo assessed the atmosphere, Matt the menu and the smells emanating from the kitchen, always getting only a couple of notes scribbled in his book before Mo grabbed his hand and announced it was time to move on.

Late in the afternoon, they wound up at a small outdoor bistro on the Left Bank, located in a secret garden between two eighteenth-century mansions. There, too full for a proper meal, they sat at an umbrella table and nibbled hors d'oeuvres and drank wine. They made up stories about the history of the two buildings and, as they had all day, laughed a lot.

As the sun began to set and the sky changed from bright to midnight blue, a sudden flash of lightning illuminated the dark garden.

"Oh," Mo said. "Look!"

"At what?" He couldn't take his eyes off her.

"It's raining. I love rain."

She got up from her chair, stepped out from under the umbrella and put her face up to the sky.

Matt stared, aware that right then, he wanted to do nothing but savor the moment. To dine in Paris, cooled by the rain, watching Mo lifting her face to the sky, it was exhilarating. She was so special—so alive! He wanted to join her, to pick her up and twirl her around. Her skin, her hair, the shining gaiety in her eyes, she called out to his senses as though he were under a spell.

Still, it was raining. He grabbed her hand and made her sit down. "You'll get soaked."

"It was only a light sprinkle."

But the sprinkles had done their work. The front of her blouse was dampened and clung to her. Her nipples stood out beneath the damp fabric, impossible to ignore.

Not that he wanted to. He swallowed a sudden infusion of saliva. If she expected him to ignore her, he was in deep trouble here. Or she was.

As Mo brushed out her hair with a hairbrush from her purse, she said, "Time to hit the nightspots."

The dark, smoke-filled basement club was filled with bodies writhing on the dance floor and superloud music pouring from the speakers. Mo found herself keeping time to the music from the moment they walked in the place.

"This is perfect," she said. "All of it. I don't understand any of the lyrics, but who cares, right?" She grabbed Matt's hand. "Dance with me?"

"Shouldn't we get a table first?"

"Nope."

He hesitated a moment more, and Mo thought that maybe he didn't like to dance. Or couldn't.

"Unless you'd rather not," she added.

A small smile played around his sensuous lips. "Oh, I'd rather. Most definitely."

The drums and bass were cranked way up, the beat pulsed through Mo's bloodstream. She loved to dance, loved to let go. Matt probably didn't let go on the dance floor.

But he surprised her. The man could move, really move, with an abandon she hadn't seen in him yet. Except when they'd kissed in the zoo.

The beat was hot and Mo felt in total sync with Matt, whirling, swaying, keeping time without speaking, coming together and parting, all kinds of unspoken messages dangling in the air between them. A fine sheen of perspiration glowed all over his face, and his dark eyes were lit with an inner fire, when they weren't closed in what seemed an expression of bliss.

Then the driving music changed to something slow and dreamy. As though they'd been choreographed, she and Matt came together, him pulling her into his arms, lifting her hands to his shoulders and wrapping his own around her waist. Without thinking, she rested her head against his chest. His shirt was silk, and her cheek rubbed against the soft fabric as they danced.

Neither of them spoke for a while. His heartbeat thrummed in her ear. She felt magical, warmed, cared for.

And turned on. Oh, yes, most definitely turned on. The way they moved together on that wooden floor, each somehow knowing what the other would do before they did it, with matching rhythms. It was, Mo thought dreamily, like really good sex.

"Oh," she said.

"What?" Matt murmured in her ear.

She glanced up at him, couldn't meet his eyes, and rested her cheek on his chest again. "I was just thinking about what a good dancer you are."

"Surprised?"

"Yes, as a matter of fact."

"Good."

She glanced up at him again. "Why 'good'?"

"I like to think you don't know everything about me."

"Well, I don't, of course."

"Good."

What did he mean? she wondered, and then for a while she stopped caring. She lost herself in sensation. The hard planes of Matt's body and the smell of him— the remnants of his lime-scented after-shave, the very maleness of him. The perspiring bodies around them, the faint sweet smell of cigarettes. The pulse of the music, a woman's voice sighing in what had to be the sexiest language in the world.

Matt was feeling it, too; she knew it. His arm tightened around her even more. As he pressed into her, she was aware of his arousal against her stomach, and something about that felt wonderful.

And...not quite right.

She pulled away. "I think we have enough for the book, right? I think we should go back to the hotel."

His lids lowered and a half smile played on one corner of his mouth. "Sounds good to me."

He leaned toward her, his mouth very close, too close. He was going to kiss her.

She placed her hand against his chest. "I can go myself if you'd like to stay here. I mean, if you're not tired, the way I am."

Mo was being evasive again, and she hated that. But if this went on any longer, they'd wind up in bed, no avoiding it, and something deep in her still didn't feel right about that. She tried to remember why, but she was having trouble. Something about a man with silver eyes...and her romantic destiny. However, that inner warning voice was pretty faint at the moment. She was almost ready not to listen to it, she was so swept up in the essence of this man. Almost.

"Matt, I'm sorry. I need to be alone."

"Alone?"

"Yes. We have a pretty early departure in the morning, don't we? So, I need to get some sleep."

"Alone," he repeated.

She swallowed. She hated not dealing with this now, but she couldn't think with Matt around. "Yes. Alone."

His expression turned thunderous. That frown of his could probably stop an army from advancing. "Fine," he said, pulling away abruptly. "But you're not going back alone. Not at night."

"But—"

"Don't even think it. Come on."

The scowl on his face was pretty awesome. She figured the best thing she could do was to go along.

She would lock the door between their rooms that night.

Not that she was afraid of what Matt might do.

It was her own actions she was uncertain about.

9

"**M**any *bambini* stay," the manager apologized with appropriate bowing and raising of regretful eyebrows. "Every *letto*, bed, taken. Many *famiglie* with *bambini, si?*"

Mo and Matt were in Venice, in the lobby of a wonderful hotel with a balcony overlooking the canal. And there seemed to be a problem with the booking. A big problem.

She and Matt had been polite but strained since the night before in Paris and on the plane today. She felt uncomfortable, and he was his old detached self.

Mo had been listening for the past few minutes as the manager, in a mixture of broken English and Italian, translated by Matt, explained that there had been terrible water damage in the honeymoon suite, making it unfit for habitation. Only one other room was available, with one bed, but *grazie a Dio* a double bed.

"Miscusi signore, potrebbe raccomandarmi un altro hotel?" Matt said.

"What?" Mo said. "What did you just say?"

"I asked him to recommend another hotel."

"No, no, Signor Vining, Venezia e' al completo, e' la stagione estiva!"

"What did he say?"

"He said the town's all full."

She was surprised to feel a small rush of excitement at the thought of being forced to share a room with Matt that evening, but she immediately crossed her arms to try to dampen that rush. "Ask him about another room."

"He already said there isn't one."

"Yes, but there has to be something—a maid's room, a linen closet, something."

Matt stared at her for a moment, then turned back to the manager, a short, balding man with a huge mustache. Another torrent of Italian, complete with hand gestures and raised eyebrows, followed. After several back-and-forth exchanges, Matt turned to her, shaking his head and obviously trying not to smile.

"What?" she said again.

"I asked is there a maid's room. He replied, 'Excuse me, sir, why do you need another room? Is it not a honeymoon for you and your new wife?' and I said, 'Yes, but I need a room to work in. I'm writing a book.' Then he said that was a very sad thing, to be writing a book on your honeymoon."

The manager was gazing at her with great sorrow, shaking his head and rolling his eyes. *"Americani,"* he said sadly. *"Cosi buffoni."*

Mo didn't need a translation for that one.

The little man let fly with another flood of words. *"Una nuova moglie, e anche cosi' bella. Se non to dispiace il mio dire, una moglie di cui ogni uomo sarebbe orgoglioso, e mol tial trisarebbero daccordo—bellissima!"*

"Grazie."

"What?" Mo asked.

"He complimented me on my choice of wives."

"There was more."

"You're beautiful, he said. I should be grateful to have you. I believe I was being lectured on the dangers of ignoring a new wife."

She narrowed her lids. "You're enjoying this, aren't you?"

Matt shrugged, but the gleam of laughter in his eyes was hard to miss. She much preferred it to his earlier coolness. "Hey, I'm doing the best I can here."

"How about a cot?"

He leaned an elbow casually against the marble reception desk. "Many families, he said, remember? Many *bambini,* so no extra beds. Besides, what would I use as an excuse?"

"I don't know," she said, throwing her hands up in the air. "You're the writer, make something up."

"Sorry. I only write about food. Fiction isn't my strong suit."

"You did fine with the book story."

"It was all I had in my arsenal."

"Well, then, tell him I'm sick. Or I have my— Oh, forget it. I don't know."

Mo chewed her bottom lip and stared up at the ceiling, hoping for inspiration. Since that first night in Paris, when she'd had too much wine and realized she was jealous, since the last night in Paris, when they'd danced and she realized her attraction to him was getting stronger and stronger, since, well, all along, really—this scene had been coming. There was somehow a sense of inevitability about the whole thing. As though it was fated. She could feel it closing in on her, like ocean waves too strong to fight.

At least, up to now, she'd been able to swim away. They'd been in separate rooms, or in public, when the subject of that chemistry between them had come up.

Now, short of throwing a tantrum and walking out of here with her bags, she would be sharing not just a room, but a bed, a very private bed, with the gentleman this very night. And the next. And the next.

He couldn't have planned this, could he? The whole thing was too corny, too shifty, too *manipulative,* for someone like Matt. Still, to be sure, she turned and glared at him accusingly.

At the moment, he would win a poker tournament for all the expression he wore on his face. Noncommittal to the max. "So," Matt said. "What do you want to do?"

She chewed her lip again while she considered, then said, "I don't know. I'm going for a walk."

"But—"

She waved her hands at him. "Why don't you work on your book, okay? I'll be back later. I gotta get out of here."

He stared at her as though trying to figure her out. Then, frowning, he glanced down at their luggage, still gathered on the floor in front of the desk. "Well, I do need to put in a couple of hours on my notes. I haven't been keeping up with them."

"Gee, how awful," she said sarcastically. "Too much fun, I suppose."

He allowed a small crack of a smile. "Something like that. But, look, don't go off just yet. Venice is filled with lots of alleyways and streets with no signs and that go nowhere. You'll get lost. If you wait till I'm finished—"

"I'm a big girl. I'll manage."

"Mo, really—"

"Matt, really," she said, imitating his tone of voice.

He got it then, and cut off his lecture abruptly. Removing his elbow from the desk, he stood up straight.

"Mo, believe it or not, I'm sorry it's working out this way, but I didn't plan it."

She emitted a sigh and nodded. "I know," she said grudgingly. "But that doesn't mean I'm happy about it."

A spasm of hurt crossed his face quickly, replaced immediately by that familiar closed-off look. "Am I that difficult to take?"

"Of course not. You're too *easy* to take. That's the problem." She covered her mouth with her hand then, wishing the words hadn't sprung out of her quite that way. She'd been responding to that fleeting glimpse of hurt feelings, instead of monitoring her speech. For a change.

"Forget I said that."

His sudden grin was wide and smug. "Yes, ma'am."

All compassion for him vanished in an instant. "I'm out of here."

As she turned to go, he grabbed her arm. "Wait. At least, will you take this?" He snatched up a street map from the desk, where the manager was avidly trying to follow the conversation. He handed her the map. "Maybe this will help."

"Sure," she replied, managing to leave out the fact that she was hopeless with maps and had never had anything even approaching a sense of direction. A person was born with that one or a person wasn't. Still, she always found her way back. Eventually.

Grabbing her purse and stuffing the map inside, Mo walked to the front door, then turned back one more time. "Oh, yeah, is the big dinner tonight?"

"No, tomorrow."

"Good."

"But I know a place for this evening—"

"Of course you do," she interrupted him. "But

please, pretty please, make it small. And casual. With simple, easy-to-digest food.'' Patting her stomach, she added, "It can't take too much more."

"What? The original junk-food queen is having tummy problems?"

"I guess it's time to pass the crown to someone else."

He nodded. "All right. I'll take care of it."

"Thanks," she said with a small forgiving smile. She wasn't used to feeling angry, and, really, how could she be angry at Matt? It was the situation that was bothering her, not him.

Matt smiled back at her, and the manager, beaming at the two of them, said something flowery and emotional. Then he kissed his fingertips and released the kiss into the air.

Mo eyed Matt warily, almost afraid to hear what had just been said.

He deadpanned, "Signor Mazzeo assures us it's normal for newlyweds to fight. We'll make up later, in our small, cozy room. Venice is a magic place—" he paused "—for lovers."

Matt's brown-eyed gaze was warmly amused and filled with promise, and at that moment, Mo knew she was in trouble.

The deep, deep kind.

Matt looked at his watch again, then glanced out the room's one small window. The view was of a narrow alleyway, but if you craned your neck you could see part of the street in front of the hotel. No Mo. She'd been gone nearly three hours. Night was closing in. Where the hell was she?

With a curse of disgust, Matt grabbed a jacket and, leaving his notes scattered all over the small table, tore

down the three flights of stairs. Once out the hotel's front
door, he gazed all around him. He could choose one of
five directions to go in; Venice was like that. With hands
on hips, he peered down each street for any sign of her.
Damnit, he thought, he didn't even know if Mo had the
name of the hotel written down. He should have insisted—

"*Buona sera, signorina,*" said a man's voice nearby,
and someone who sounded exactly like Mo replied,
"*Buona sera, signore.*" Matt turned around to see Mo
coming out of an alleyway, scooting past the leering man
who had spoken to her. Although several bundles were
in her arms, she was managing to nibble on an ice-cream
cone.

As she came toward Matt, he observed her outfit: all
her hair was tucked up under a baseball cap and she
wore a short, swingy green skirt and matching T-shirt
and sandals. Which was strange, because when she'd left
she'd been wearing jeans and a blouse and sneakers.

"Hi," she said, crunching on some more of her cone
and coming to a stop a couple of feet in front of him.

"Hello." He made it casual, easy; he was damned if
he was going to tell her he'd been worried.

"You were right. I got hopelessly lost. And I slipped
when this guy who owns a jewelry store was watering
his plants. I fell pretty hard—" She showed him a
scraped elbow, then took another swipe at the ice cream.
"And I got all soaked, but everyone was so nice to me.
I gave them the jeans and got beads for my mom and
some other stuff for my nephews and this outfit." She
twirled around, the skirt lifting and ballooning slightly
as she did. "Like it?"

He swallowed. Her long, shapely legs could make a

blind man weep. "Very nice. Are you sure you're all right?"

"Tip-top. But my watch is ruined. What time is it?"

"Seven. How did you get back? Did you use the map?"

"It got soaked, too. Not that I had the least idea how to read it." She shrugged and licked at the last of the ice cream. "I asked people."

"But you don't speak the language."

Grinning, she shifted a couple of packages to the other arm. "Yeah, I didn't understand a word, but some of the gestures were kind of ballpark, directions-wise, and well, here I am."

"Let me take those." He reached for one of the bags but she stepped away, as though not wanting to place herself within touching distance.

"No, it's okay, I'll just put them in the room. You probably want to eat dinner, huh?"

"It appears you already have."

"Just a little appetizer-type gelato." She tossed the rest of the cone into a trash container. "I'll take this stuff upstairs, then I'll be right down."

Matt sat at a little outdoor table and ordered a *martini bianco* while he waited. He still felt a little tense. Mo's mood, on the other hand, had seemed relaxed, if somewhat impersonal.

He drummed his fingers on the table. What had she decided to do about the room? he wondered. Whatever she did decide, it was up to her, and that was all there was to it. He'd made his interest in her known more than a couple of times. He was willing and available; she couldn't have missed that message. Any more on his part and he would appear—and be—a fool.

He nodded to himself, his position clear. He would no longer pursue her. If Mo wanted him, she'd have to make the first move.

10

When she came down, Matt still couldn't figure out her state of mind. The two of them headed off while Mo chattered happily about everything she'd seen that day.

"Shops and cafés and homes, and these wonderful cobblestoned streets. Everybody has flowers, geraniums mostly, in boxes under their windows. There are lots of trees and bushes, but no grass, you know? It's funny. And everywhere you go, there's the water. Stop for a minute," she said as they passed a small clothing store, its owner closing up for the day.

"Buona sera," said the store owner.

"Buona sera," Mo said with a smile, perused the window for a moment, then turned to Matt. She put her hand on his arm, then withdrew it quickly. "What do you smell?"

"The ocean."

"Okay, what *don't* you smell?"

"Is this a trick question?"

"Gasoline. There's no gas smell. You're not allowed to have cars or buses or trucks here, right? So there's no city smell, like we're used to in San Francisco. All you get is this kind of faint stale-fish odor that you have near an ocean. And the humidity has a...damp smell to it, too. And listen."

She paused, then whispered, "See how quiet it is? There's all that non-noise of traffic, so you hear people laughing and talking, and birds chirping, and water lapping against the sides of the canals. But it's quiet. Because there're no cars."

Closing his eyes, Matt made himself listen. She was right. The city of Venice *was* quiet, and it was refreshing. He'd been here five or six times before, and had never really noticed the smells and sounds. Now he couldn't help noticing them, thanks to Mo. She really was extraordinarily perceptive.

They walked some more. Mo went on talking, but he noticed a strained quality; it was as though she was afraid of there being too much silence between them, and was babbling to fill the emptiness.

"I can't count how many bridges I crossed. I mean, there are so many bridges! And the alleyways are so narrow, sometimes you have to practically turn sideways to pass someone."

"Did you get pinched?"

She snorted. "Better believe it. And each time I turned around to give the guy a piece of my mind, I could never tell who it was. It's a stupid tradition."

"But a very old one."

"Yeah, well. Old is not necessarily good. Oh, look!"

She pointed. In the distance was San Marco Square. Mo ran ahead of him, toward the enormous plaza, her arms stretched out like a child pretending to fly. All around her, pigeons scattered and flew into the darkening night sky. Mo twirled and laughed, then turned to face him and laughed again.

"I've seen this place in so many movies! The huge church and all the tables here and there and all the people. It's just like I thought it would look, only better!"

He nodded, feeling some of her enthusiasm shooting into his bloodstream. Yes, Saint Mark's was special. Tonight, the square was illuminated by the soft amber lights on the huge cathedral, reflecting off the other buildings and cobblestones and the faces of diners at the many cafés, giving the whole scene the appearance of being made of gold.

Mo got to choose the café, as Matt was of the opinion that all the food in the square was decent. She picked the one right in the center of the action. As they sat down, she couldn't stop smiling and looking around her. Venice. She was in Venice!

Music came from four different orchestras playing four different kinds of music and alternating sets so as not to interfere with each other or the diners' ears. At any moment they might hear jazz, then American pop standards, then Vivaldi, and all the sounds bounced off the walls of the surrounding buildings, creating a natural stereophonic effect.

It was another magical night on this perfect trip, Mo thought. Except, of course, for that slight tension in the air. She and Matt had unfinished business—the room situation—but both seemed reluctant to deal with finishing it. He had been unusually quiet, while she'd been hopping and skipping and prattling for dear life.

Boy, it was hard not to deal with something that wouldn't go away, no matter how hard you tried to make it do just that. Take that afternoon, on her journey through the streets of this city that she'd been reading and dreaming about all her life. Even as she oohed and aahed over what she was seeing and smelling and hearing, a lot of her head for a lot of the afternoon had been taken up with fantasies, steamy, X-rated stuff, about the night to come. And each time she invented one, she would berate herself for allowing her imagination to go off in that direction.

But fantasies were one thing, reality was something different. You didn't have to go to bed with a person just because you were sharing a room. Did you? Unless, of course, that was what you wanted to do anyway. Did she want to?

There was something more niggling at her, something real important—about another layer of feelings—yet when she tried to focus on what that was, it whisked away like a feather caught in a back draft.

At any rate, she and Matt were due for some sort of showdown. Okay, a discussion at least. But...not yet. Coward, she called herself silently. You got it, she answered.

"Excuse me?" Mo realized that Matt had been speaking to her and she'd been off in la-la land. "What did you say?"

"I said we're meeting the photographer for pictures tonight, after dinner."

"Oh, where?"

"Well, when she and I spoke earlier, she suggested a night gondola ride. She's setting it up now."

"Oh." An instant fantasy flashed through Mo's mind—she and Matt sitting side by side in the moonlight, his arm around hers in the cozy darkness. The air is warm as they pass under a bridge. Shadows, then darkness. His hand finds its way to her—

"I've arranged for us to meet her at ten," Matt said, "a short walk from here."

"Who?" She was in a daze and had to snap out of it. Now. "Oh, yes, the pictures. For the book."

"I assume that's all right," he said politely.

"Of course."

So, an hour later, Mo found herself in what—once again—felt like a scene from a movie. The graceful gondola and the olive-skinned Italian man at the helm. The dark sky and the moon. The sound of lapping water rustling through it all. The man and the woman trying not to be attracted to each other.

The photographer, Angelina, was shorter, younger and rounder than Mo, with enormous gold hoop earrings dangling past her shoulders. She was also a little on the hyper side. Mo kept wanting to giggle as Angelina danced around, arranging her lights and directing her subjects in various dramatic poses, as though she were Fellini.

Finally, Mo and Matt settled themselves on the cushioned bench at one end of the gondola, while Angelina encouraged them to snuggle up ever closer. Mo leaned her head against Matt's chest and felt his arm come around her shoulders, but lightly, as though not ready to commit to actual touching. The flash went off several times, interspersed with *"Fantastico!"* and *"Bello!"* from the photographer.

When she insisted the newlyweds kiss, Mo said "I don't think so tonight," at the same time Matt said, "We already have a lot of those."

They looked at each other and smiled self-consciously. Neither of them wanted any physical intimacy, it was obvious. Mo felt a small dart of hurt, but told herself to cut it out. Matt was behaving, being a good sport. A gentleman.

After the picture-taking session was over, and they'd said their goodbyes to Angelina, Mo assumed they were done. She was in the act of pushing herself up from the seat, when the oarsman pushed them off from the dock instead.

She sat back down with a thump. "Oof."

"You all right?" Matt said.

"Sure, but why are we moving?"

"Probably because we're on the water in a seagoing vessel," he said dryly.

"No, no, I mean, I didn't know we were actually going on a nighttime gondola ride."

Matt spoke to the gondolier, who answered with a languid shrug and a rush of words. Matt turned back to Mo. "He says we paid for his time, we might as well get our money's worth."

They were away from the dock now, moving slowly through the canal. The soft splashing of the water as they glided along was gentle, lulling. It felt wonderful.

"But I'm not sure—" She stopped.

"You're not sure of what?"

His question lingered in the air for a couple of heartbeats. It was, after all, the problem in a nutshell.

"Not sure if I want to go on a gondola ride," she said finally, in a voice that sounded, even to her ears, petulant.

"Then we tell him to turn around," Matt said stiffly. "You call it."

Sighing, she eased herself back till she was staring up at the night sky. The more time she took to think about what she wanted to do, the farther away from the dock they drew. Eventually, they turned into another canal, a wider, darker one, far away now from the lights. Mo's mind drifted with the gondola's movement.

The moon was three-quarters full, the sky cloudless. Stars shone above, looking the way stars looked all over the world, and Mo understood then that she had avoided dealing decisively with the room situation all day because she already knew what she wanted to do, deep down in the inner recesses of her soul. She wanted Matt. Craved him. It was that simple, really.

Wasn't it? Shouldn't it be?

Matt sat straight, rigid even, next to her, staring ahead. She gazed at his profile—stern and classic, the planes of his face harsh in the faint light of the moon and the occasional street lamp along the canal. He was making no moves toward her, was in fact being specifically neutral.

Propping herself up on one elbow, Mo laid a gentle hand on his arm. He jumped slightly and turned to face her.

"It's a beautiful night, isn't it?" she said.

He said nothing.

"It would be a shame to waste this ride." She brought her face closer; his eyes glowed like banked coals.

"Are we wasting this ride?" he asked.

"So far." Tentatively, her hand found its way around his neck and she brushed her fingers lightly against the nape. "What do you think?"

"About what?"

He wasn't making this easy for her, was he? And Mo wasn't real skilled at seduction. Oh, well, you never know till you try it, she counseled herself silently.

"What do you think about giving your, uh, pretend wife a real kiss?"

His indrawn breath was the only reaction he showed her. "I think it sounds just fine."

Leaning closer to her reclining body, he said, his voice hoarse, "More than fine. It sounds like heaven."

He covered her mouth with his, cupping one cheek in his hand as he did. At the moment of connection, she heard a low moan. She wasn't sure if it was from her or from him. Closing her eyes, she let the sensation of him wash through her.

His mouth was soft, yet insistent. He stroked her face with his fingertips, then caught her chin and angled her head slightly and kissed her again, more deeply this time. His mouth did wondrous, delicious things to hers. She was being savored, appreciated, *tasted*, on many levels by a connoisseur. She was in the hands of an expert, and the contrast between this supersensual Matt and the one she'd met only a few days ago was, again, mind-boggling.

Heat raced through her bloodstream and brought warmth to her cheeks, but there was no thought; she turned into a quivering mass of sensations. He turned her head again, changing the angle of his mouth on hers, and this time his tongue burst through with a strong, moist surge. The fire that shot through her veins surprised her with its sudden intensity. Her tongue met his and she felt the movement of his hand over her shoulders and toward the front of her shirt.

Hold it, she thought. Wait. Things were heating up a little faster than she was prepared for. Especially as there was a gondolier practically right over their heads.

"Matt," Mo said softly, breaking off the kiss.

"What?" He turned his attention to her ear, making her quiver some more.

"We have a witness."

"He's probably used to it."

"I'm not."

"Then how about if I tell him to head back?" He kissed her neck, then all along her collarbone, sending small shivers up and down her spine and to the tips of her breasts. "So we can get to our room quickly," he added in a whisper.

Muscles clenched deep inside and she exhaled loudly, and audibly. "Yes," she said.

Matt lifted his head and gazed at her through passion-glazed eyes. "You're sure you want to do this," he said in a self-assured way that let her know he didn't really expect an answer—her body's response to him had been answer enough.

But, why, oh, why had he asked her? After half a beat, she said, "Sure I'm sure."

Her slight hesitation made some of the glaze leave his eyes. "Mo…"

"Yes."

"I'm—we're—about to pass all reasonable behavior, and I want you to be *very* sure. One hundred percent sure, as a matter of fact."

She played with the collar of his shirt. "Would you accept ninety-eight percent?"

Sitting up, Matt raked his hair with trembling fingers. "God almighty. For once, couldn't you have lied?"

"Okay. One hundred percent."

He muttered a succinct curse, wiped his face with his hand, then studied her as though she were a new kind of puzzle. "All right. What is the other two percent about?"

"Stuff rattling around in my head." She couldn't seem to meet his gaze. "Like, I still wonder if I'm a substitute for Kay."

He heaved a sigh of exasperation. "Mo, Mo, Mo," he said, shaking his head. "What in the hell am I going to do with you?" He grabbed her by the shoulders. "Listen and listen carefully. That Kay theory is nonsense, utter nonsense. This—you and me—has nothing to do with anything but the moonlight and an undeniable attraction that we both feel, and you are just as caught up in it as I am. Don't say you're not.''

"I won't," she said quickly. "Promise."

He nodded and gentled his hold on her shoulders, absently massaging the material of her shirt. Then he ran one of his thumbs across her lower lip and offered her a sexy now-where-were-we? half smile. "Does that take care of the stuff in your head?"

"Well, there's the silver-eyed man, which is why I came here in the first place. I'm supposed to be on my way to meet him."

"Nonsense," he said again, a little more sharply than before. "Do you honestly believe anyone can tell the future? And even if you do, what does this fire between us have to do with someone you haven't even met yet? Are you saving yourself for him? For some fantasy man?"

"No, no, of course not."

She felt foolish and very young at that moment, not at all womanly. Except for her body's reaction to Matt— there was nothing childish about that. She told herself to cut out all this silliness.

"I'm sorry," she said. "Forget I said anything. I'm a grown-up and we both know what's happening here. It's not like I'm a starry-eyed eighteen-year-old or anything." She was babbling, but she couldn't seem to stop herself. "I mean, it's not like either of us is expecting anything, you know, like commitment or love or anything like that—"

"Hold it," he interrupted.

"But—"

"Who said anything about love?"

"Not me," she said quickly. "Not me, I didn't."

Why, why, *why* had she used that word? Mo wondered, seeing that black furrow forming on Matt's face, the one that preceded one of his emotional shutdowns. And *where* had that word come from?

Matt sat up, his back ramrod straight. At his withdrawal, something deflated inside Mo. Don't go away, she wanted to say.

But what had she been expecting? Words assuring her that what they had together was more than just a physical thing? That it was somehow special? Different?

An act of—admit it, now—of love?

Lowering her head, she concentrated on her hands, folded in her lap. Matt spoke to the gondolier, and they reversed direction.

Neither of them said anything for a while. Mo couldn't help feeling wrong, somehow, uncomfortable in her skin. What was he thinking? He was angry, for sure. Well, of course he was. Who could blame him? Just what was going on here?

Love? Did she love him?

But…she'd never even considered it. She'd found him attractive, sexy, amusing, intelligent and good company, especially when he wasn't distanced or controlling. She felt affection and friendship for him, and sometimes when he looked at her a certain way, something funny and fluttery happened in the region of her heart.

But love?

She certainly hadn't been aware of anything like that. But then, her stupid head was always betraying her, either by encouraging her to leap blindly into strange new situations or neglecting to inform her that something pretty important was percolating. Obviously, in the area of self-awareness, she was about as clueless as you could get.

After a while, she put a hand on his arm. "Matt, I'm sorry."

"For what?"

"I'm not sure. For making something simple into something, well, complicated."

He stared out at the night, his jaw clenching and unclenching several times before he said, "The thing is, I don't believe in love. It's a foreign concept. Sorry, but there it is."

"But you were engaged to be married."

"If you remember my history and my mother's many husbands, you'll understand why I don't connect marriage and lasting love. The lessons we learn in childhood have a way of staying around permanently."

"Oh."

"I was career-oriented and so was Kay. We had some good times and things in common. I've never expected anything else from a relationship. Mostly, I guess, we each had…empty moments in our lives. I thought it could work. It seemed a good idea at the time."

He said this distractedly, without emotion, except for that underlying coldness. Some more time passed during which the only sound was the steady swish of the oar in the softly rippling water.

"God," Mo said finally. "That's so sad."

"Please, I don't need your pity."

"No, I mean, that's not a reason to marry."

"I don't think there's any reason to marry, really, unless there are children involved." His chuckle lacked any trace of humor. "Remember where I come from. Most marriages I see are a farce. It seems to me that love doesn't last."

"That kind of talk is even sadder than marrying someone to fill up space."

"So, you believe in all that romantic claptrap—the house, the kids, growing old together."

"I've seen it work, so I guess I do. Someday, at least."

"Well, I don't. Anyway, I am what I am, and I don't really want to sit here and philosophize on the nature of love and life. Okay?"

He looked out on the water and shook his head again. The rest of the ride passed in silence. When they pulled up to the dock, Matt helped her out of the gondola, then walked with her, his hands firmly in his pockets, back to the hotel.

They climbed the stairs slowly. At the door, Matt looked at her and said, "Sleep well."

"Where are you going?"

"If you think I'm spending the night with you in that room, you're crazy. I'll see you in the morning."

11

Matt's thoughts kept pace with his furious strides as he headed into the nighttime streets of Venice; his mind invented and discarded images as quickly as paper through a shredder.

Earlier, Mo had talked about seeing San Marco Square in the movies. Wasn't the whole evening like something out of a film? The one where the man walks through a foreign city at midnight, his hands in his pockets, his shoulders hunched, frustrated as all get out, and not a little confused, while a lovely woman sits in a hotel room, ambivalent, and also not a little confused, and looking sexy as hell while she does?

Well, if it wasn't a scene from a movie, it should have been.

Just where was he to sleep tonight? Maybe he could find a small *pensione,* a local YMCA, if they had them in Italy—he'd never needed to know before.

Even a park bench.

Because he was through playing his role in this farce; his and Mo's prospects, sexually speaking, were finished, done, terminated. One more time, one more pail of cold water had been thrown on his raging hormones. It had to be some kind of record.

Most of the small bed-and-breakfast places he passed

were full, others were dark. He knocked on one door that showed a light in a downstairs room, but someone had fallen asleep in front of the TV and they were *cosi' mortificati,* so sorry, there was nothing available.

As Matt turned a corner, one of Venice's ubiquitous cats meowed loudly and brushed up against his shin. He told it to scram in a harsh voice.

No. Absolutely no. He was not about to go back to that room and imitate another familiar scene from film-dom—the one where the man and woman share a bed, each of them spending a sleepless night with their backs to each other, maybe even one of them under the sheet, the other above it, to prevent temptation from taking over. Not when, once again, Matt had been driven al-most senseless with desire that ended up going nowhere.

The door of a small bar was ajar as he passed it, so he went in and ordered a large Campari and soda at the bar. But the sounds of people, of clinking glasses and conversation and laughter, made him feel lonely more than anything, so he left after quickly tossing down the drink.

What a way to spend a honeymoon—even a phony one! The honeymoon from hell, that's what it was.

He stopped and stared at a park bench. It looked hard. And wet. And cold. A youngish couple, their arms around each other as they laughed softly, passed him. The woman's perfume drifted across his nostrils; it was strong, too strong, not like the scent Mo wore. He always meant to ask her just how you got lemon and roses to blend that way.

Not that he cared.

Mo. Maureen Flynn Czerny—he'd seen her full name on her passport. Maureen Flynn Czerny believed in love.

Love.

Of all the juvenile…irritating…fantasy-filled concepts. Absurd.

Several more *pensiones* later, Matt had to give in to the obvious. There was no room at the inn, except for his own. Well, fine, the night was nearly over. He would march into the room, get some blankets and sleep on the floor, as far from the bed as possible. Mo and he had two more nights in Venice before going on to Prague, and he would find other accommodations first thing in the morning.

When he reached the hotel, he eyed the lobby's couch briefly before shaking his head ruefully and heading upstairs. At the room, Matt opened the door quietly. He didn't want to wake Mo up—he absolutely refused to deal with the woman again that night. The interior was fairly dark, lit only by a faint stream of moonlight coming in from the terrace. In the far corner was the bed, piled with bedclothes, under which Mo slept the sleep of the untroubled.

He made his way to the bathroom in the dark, closing the door before he turned on the light. Washing up, he tried to ignore the familiar aroma of Mo's perfume in the small space. He looked through the mess of bottles and tubes and tissues that was on her side of the sink for a bottle of perfume, but there wasn't one.

Leaning on the sink, he stared into the mirror. His dark beard shadowed his jawline, his hair was tousled, his eyes were bloodshot. He really was tired. That was the truth.

And he wished like hell that Mo's scent didn't permeate every room she inhabited, even when she was no longer in it.

He removed his clothes, but kept on his T-shirt and briefs. Leaving the bathroom door open a little for light, he felt around in the closet for an extra blanket. There were none. Yawning, he eyed the generous mound of linens on the bed, with Mo under them. Maybe just one sheet and one pillow.

Quietly, he went over to the bed and pulled gently at the top cover. Mo didn't stir. He pulled at it a little more, half expecting a groan of protest. But instead of protesting, the lump collapsed.

Matt ripped the covers off the bed. There was no one there.

His heart began to beat more rapidly. Had the foolish, idiotic woman gone off again, into the night, unprotected? Good God, did she never learn?

"Matt?"

He jumped at the sound of his name whispered in the shadowed darkness. Gazing toward the balcony, he saw a murky silver moon with clouds covering it like gauze. And beneath the moon, against the terrace railing, was Mo. Her face was in shadow, but her hair stood out from her head like a soft nimbus, and her body underneath a filmy long nightgown was perfectly outlined by the moon's light. The curve of her breast, the swell of her hips, those long, perfectly shaped legs. Drawing in a breath, he couldn't stop himself from staring.

And then she ran toward him, her arms outstretched, and as though on automatic pilot, he gathered her to him. He reminded himself that he was still furious. With her? The situation? Who the hell knew? It didn't matter because his body didn't seem to care about his state of mind.

"Matt," she said, pulling his face down and planting quick kisses all over it. "Matt, I'm sorry. Did I act like a tease? Leading you on, and all? I hate that, I'm not like that."

Her lips left tiny jolts of electricity in their wake. "No, no," he managed to say. "I knew you weren't teasing."

"I'd like to take the evening back to the moment when I asked you to kiss me, and forget about what happened afterward. No more words." She placed her small hands on the sides of his face and gazed up at him. Her eyes were huge in the moonlight, her face pale. "Can we?"

"Oh, Mo," he whispered.

"Come," she said softly.

"Where?"

"Here." She grabbed his hand and led him over to the bed. With her other hand, she swept away the pile of bedclothes, leaving clean bare sheets and nothing more. Then she lay down and reached her arms up to him. "Come."

He gazed at her luscious form, lying prone on the white sheets. He'd been down this road once before earlier tonight, and he didn't think he could take another rise and fall, metaphorically and physically. He thought about saying something sardonic like, "Are you sure this time?" or "Even without love?," but couldn't seem to form the words.

Because even as a part of him whispered a warning not to trust what was happening and called him all kinds of fool, he knew, deep inside, that this time Mo wouldn't stop for anything. She wanted him as much as he wanted her, if that was possible.

He sat on the edge of the bed, his attention drawn to the rosy brown nipples showing under the gauze of her nightgown. He felt almost dizzy. Gathering her hands in his, he brought them to his chest and pressed her palms to his heated skin. His heart thudded rapidly; in fact, his

DIANE PERSHING   133

entire body was shuddering now, and he wondered briefly if he was coming down with some kind of exotic fever. Why else would a woman—no, this woman—affect him so deeply?

"Dammit," he said. "Do you see what you do to me?"

Mo wanted to cry all of a sudden, at the intensity of the moment, and at the emotion jammed up in the back of her throat. Lord, Matt's face was just too unbearably masculine, those strong cheekbones shadowed and sexy in the moonlight, those nearly black eyes alive with banked passion, but still darkly mysterious.

"Yes," she said, because she saw what she did to him. His body was shaking; he was on the edge of tumbling off a cliff, taking her with him.

And when he swept her up in his arms and buried his face in her neck and groaned as though he'd been waiting for her for two hundred years, she knew that she'd have to toss away those few lingering doubts, or watch them burned to ashes in the fire to come.

Grabbing both her wrists, Matt pulled her arms upward, so they rested on the pillow above her head. Then he kissed her, hard, devouring her mouth, crushing her head against the pillow. His actions verged on being violent, and Mo felt a quick tremor of excited fear. But immediately afterward, she watched him get hold of himself and put brakes on the surging need he was so obviously experiencing—as was she.

With utmost gentleness, Matt released her wrists to slowly undress her. After removing his own clothes, he reached into his pants pocket and withdrew a silver foil packet.

Finally, with a look on his face that was as tender and

unguarded as any she'd seen, he bent over and kissed her.

But gently, this time, even though she could sense the effort it was costing him. For the first few moments, Mo felt a little shy. But, as though a silent signal had been given, she and Matt quickly abandoned the slow, almost tentative touches, and were soon caught up in a maelstrom of sensations.

His mouth made magical forays on every part of her, making her nipples harden, her flesh come alive, and the woman's place between her legs and up into her womb, cry with eagerness to be touched, to be loved, to be possessed.

He played her like a skilled guitarist—stroking, plucking, setting up a rhythm that she could do nothing but follow and lose herself in. The rhythm increased and she followed that, too, and then he was poised over her.

She opened for him and made him welcome, and he plunged into her with one powerful surge. He filled her up, and she felt as though she was welcoming something new and something familiar at the same time. As if a part of her that Mo hadn't known was missing was suddenly returned to her, and she cried for joy.

Matt froze his thrusting movement even though she felt him still hard, still pulsing. Balancing himself on one elbow, he caught up some of her tears on a fingertip. "Oh, Mo. Have I hurt you?"

"No, no, no. Sorry." She sniffled. "This is just… incredible and, well, I'm so emotional."

Wrapping her up in his arms, he hugged her to him, and she could hear his breath still coming out in quick desperate spurts. She hugged him tightly. The man kept astonishing her. If she'd thought him in the least bit stodgy or formal or distanced, tonight he was proving her very, very wrong.

She moved her hips to let him know that even though she was crying, he didn't have to stop doing what he was doing. He picked up on her cue instantly. Emitting a loud groan, Matt took up where he'd left off, with firm strokes of hard, potent, insistent male magic. Her hips and inner muscles responded, and then it was impossible to tell who was setting the rhythm and who was following.

As the jolt of her climax ripped through her, Matt checked his movement for a brief moment. Then, with a cry as ancient as days, he released his life force into her. They trembled and quaked and gasped until Mo had no more energy left to do anything but lie in Matt's arms.

Even with her brain fogged-up with an afterglow unlike anything she'd ever experienced, it was still functioning enough to know that yes, she loved him. Was in love with him. Amazing, really amazing, as amazing as the skill and sheer *intensity* Matt had brought to their coupling.

No way could that have happened, with all that *passion* and, well, *rapture,* without love.

On her part, anyway. What Matt felt, she had no way of knowing, and after their discussion earlier that evening, she imagined he wouldn't welcome her own revelation. Which was kind of sad, but not hopeless, was it?

The wise course would be to say nothing to him about her discovery. Nothing at all. She rarely did the wise thing, but this time, she had to.

After a while, Matt withdrew from her and, turning her so her back was to him, pulled her close. He cupped her breasts in his hands and expelled warm breath onto her neck.

"Well, now," he murmured in her ear, "this is more what a honeymoon is supposed to be like." And with the next breath, she could tell he was asleep.

She did not join him immediately. Dazed and sated and exhausted, she allowed herself a brief moment to wonder just what he'd meant by that last remark.

And then she decided not to read anything into it. Snuggling herself even closer to his long, lean frame, Mo joined Matt in dreamland.

12

They made love again sometime in the middle of the night, and again as dawn broke in the sky. Matt couldn't seem to get enough of her. His passion for her astonished him, as did the way she seeped into him on all levels when their bodies were joined. He could feel those walls of privacy he kept around himself becoming thinner with each hour spent in Mo's arms. He wasn't quite sure what to do without the walls; this was uncharted territory, and he felt apprehensive about what would happen next.

They were awakened by a soft knock on the door announcing breakfast. Soon, Matt and Mo were sitting up in bed, sipping cappuccinos and munching on *ciambelles,* soft, warm doughnuts coated with sugar. Mo declared these actually better than Winchell's glazed buttermilk.

She seemed slightly subdued this morning, although a slightly subdued Mo would appear energetic on anyone else. He thought about asking her if she had any regrets or if the night had been as unique, as special for her as it had been for him. But every time he framed the question in his mind, it sounded too damned vulnerable. Or, at least, he decided, too serious for such a fine morning.

Instead, he held her close and licked scattered sugar crystals from around her mouth. ''We can spend the rest of the day like this," he murmured, "or we can do what I'd planned."

"Mmm, that feels good. What had you planned?"

"Lunch at Treviso, a visit to Murano—where they make all the Venetian glass—then a nap before the big official dinner tonight at Ristorante Ettore, a Vivaldi concert afterward, and a lot of walking and sight-seeing in between."

"Good heavens. It sounds like a lot for one day. Aren't you just the tiniest bit exhausted? I am."

"You mean I've accomplished the impossible—worn you out? If I could crow, I would."

She slapped his cheek lightly. "Men. Always bragging about their prowess."

"If the shoe fits."

"It fits fine, as do a lot of things, and I think we'll drop the subject, thank you, before I turn into a blushing fool." She sat up straight and fluffed up her pillows before leaning back against them. "Oh, except about shoes—I'd love to buy a pair of those soft leather sandals for my sister-in-law. She's pregnant again and her feet are killing her."

"Done. How many nephews and nieces do you have?"

"Let me see. Twelve...no, thirteen. Number fourteen on the way."

"Seriously?"

"Yeah. Family picnics can get kind of crowded. And yes, we always have tacky old fried chicken and potato salad."

"I happen to like fried chicken," he said, "if it's dipped in milk, rolled in rice flakes and fried in sesame oil."

"Wow, that sounds terrific."

How would he react, Matt wondered, to such a huge crowd of relatives? Would he feel invaded? Or would having all that affection and caring and connection fill a hole he'd been carrying around his entire life? It was a sobering yet happy thought and it surprised him with how right it felt.

He turned onto his side and, resting his head on his hand, gazed at her, all soft, round, morning-after femininity. Yes, last night had been a new experience for him, a giving and receiving, a meshing of all his senses that he'd never known before. An emotion startlingly close to joy rose in his throat.

"You've been busy buying presents for your family and I'd like to buy something for you," he said impetuously. "Something very expensive."

"Gee, well, thanks, but it's not necessary."

He stroked the soft skin from her wrist to her elbow. "What would you like?"

"Mmm, not a thing, I mean it."

"But—"

She pressed her fingers over his mouth. "Matt, no gifts," she said more firmly. "This trip is gift enough. And that's the end of the discussion."

She threw back the covers and leaped out of bed. "Last one in the shower has to wash the other's toes."

They spent too much time and too much hot water, but it was a shower to remember. Afterward, very clean and dressed in cool summer clothing for the humid Italian day, they descended the stairs, their arms entwined around each other, and entered the lobby. Signor Mazzeo was on duty at the desk and, upon seeing them, the round man smiled broadly and bid them *Buongiorno*. He then told Matt that there had been a cancellation for the upcoming two nights and would they care to move to a beautiful suite?

Matt translated the manager's offer for Mo, and she looked up at him and tilted her head. "Whatever you'd like, Matt."

"No. I want you to decide."

"Really? Then, I guess you can tell him that I like where we are just fine. In fact, I'm kind of sentimental about that cute little room."

She wrinkled her nose and he gazed down on her shiny, freshly scrubbed face, with that mischievous smile lurking behind her luminous eyes, and he knew he had never felt so lighthearted and carefree in his life. He also knew he was going to kiss her, right there in front of God and the world, and he didn't care who saw.

He did just that, kissed Mo soundly and thoroughly, restraining himself from putting his hands anywhere but on her back and shoulders. Finally, and with great reluctance, Matt tore his mouth away from the kiss and gazed at her. "Any regrets?" he whispered, not sure he wanted to hear the answer. "About last night?"

She kept her eyes on his for a long moment, as though she was looking for messages there. Then she shook her head and offered a small, incredibly sweet smile. "Not a one."

"Whew. Good." He hadn't known he was holding his breath until she answered. He squeezed her shoulders and raised his head to find that he and Mo had an audience, the friendly faces of people who had stopped whatever they were doing to beam their approval. Two Japanese tourists, a gray-haired maid, a boy wheeling a breakfast cart, a workman wearing a tool-filled canvas apron. And Signor Mazzeo, whose expression of warm approval said he took credit for the whole thing. And perhaps, Matt thought, he had the right to do just that.

"Abbiate una piacevole giornata," the manager called out to them, then repeated it in English. "Enjoy the beautiful day."

Matt took Mo's hand and walked with her into the bright sunshine of late morning. Stopping as they hit the street, both of them lifted their faces to the sky, while their hands tightened in unspoken agreement that it was, indeed, a beautiful day.

After they'd walked a while, soaking up the ancient, magical, mystical city, Matt said, "I meant what I said before. About the gift. I would have bought you something and surprised you with it, except I'm not really sure what would please you."

Her cheeks grew rosy. "I think you know that very well."

Chuckling, he threw an arm around her shoulders and hugged her to his chest. "Our tastes are rather different, in case you hadn't noticed. I thought a piece of jewelry, or artwork."

Halting, she disengaged herself from his embrace and stared at him. "But why?"

"So I can watch your face when you pick it out. And, on a less altruistic note, so you'll always remember me and Venice and this time together."

"Is it over already?" She looked alarmed.

"No, no, I didn't mean it to sound like that." He hugged her to him again and kissed the top of her head. They walked on some more, past a shabby but defiantly pink palazzo. "I guess I'm kind of...off-kilter this morning, and things are coming out, well, dramatically."

"Yeah, I'm a little off-kilter, too." She gazed up at him and smiled again, a little shyly, he thought. "Thank you, Matt, you've done plenty already. But you know what? If you really want to watch my face, why don't I go with you and supervise while you buy *yourself* something."

He stopped and stared at her. "What would I want to buy myself?"

"Clothing, I think. Don't get me wrong, you have wonderful taste, very elegant. But I'd like to see you in something casual. You know, a little less formal."

"I'm not sure they sell shirts with palm trees here in Venice," he said dryly.

"If we looked hard enough, we could probably find one, but, no, I had something else in mind. A lightweight summer suit, I think, like Humphrey Bogart wore in *Casablanca.*"

"I wouldn't even know where to start looking."

"I would."

And so Mo accosted every passing man who wore clothing she admired, and with Matt as translator, got several names of local tailors. When one name was mentioned three times, she smiled triumphantly and said, "Apparently, it's Signor Riccobono. On Via Luana. Goody, we'll put it in the book."

A short water-taxi ride later, Mo found herself in the rear of a small shop, sitting cross-legged on a pile of fabric bolts, while Matt was measured and then fitted for a scrumptious off-white linen suit. She loved watching him in his briefs and T-shirt, loved checking out his arms and chest and legs. He was brown and lean and oh-so-nicely muscled, all over. Especially his buns; the man could have posed for an abs-and-glutes-machine ad. And he'd been hers for an entire night. Lucky, lucky her. She actually sighed aloud, then met Matt's startled glance at her and grinned.

Springing up from the pile of fabrics, Mo played the part of the clucking wife, telling Signor Riccobono a little tighter there, a little more pleat there, then walked slowly around Matt as though she were a designer studying one of her models.

Finally, when the suit was all measured and pinned and draping beautifully over Matt's form, she grabbed a white Borsalino hat from one of the shelves and placed it on his head, tilting it so it dropped rakishly over one eye.

She clapped her hands. "Bravo. Yes, oh, yes. You should be named Giancarlo or Jean-Paul. So continental, so chic, so sexy." She fanned her face with her fingertips exaggeratedly. "Be still my heart."

Matt laughed. "That good, huh? Maybe I should have dressed like this from the beginning. You'd have started panting the moment we got on the plane."

"I *was* panting from the moment we got on the plane."

"Could've fooled me."

"Good. I wanted to."

Arrangements were made to ship the new suit to Budapest, then they went off to a late lunch. They sat in mottled shade on a tree-filled patio and drank mineral water and wine. Mo was starving, for real food, not sweets, for once.

First, they had *bruschetta*—just-picked tomatoes, olive oil with fresh garlic and basil, grilled on thick slices of bread. The taste of the tomatoes was like nothing Mo had ever experienced; closing her eyes, she felt adrift in their sweetness.

"I think I'm starting to get it," she said, then licked some oil from the corners of her mouth.

"If you keep doing that with your tongue, I'll be

forced to take you behind one of those bushes.'' When she giggled, Matt said, ''You're starting to get what?''

''This taste thing. There are three or four sensations, one after the other. It's...enticing, isn't it, the way the garlic flirts with your mouth.''

A slow, pleased look creased his face and he nodded. ''Yes, you're starting to get it.''

The pasta with pesto sauce that followed made her want to cry with how scrumptious it was. She wondered briefly if all senses were heightened the morning after a night like the one she and Matt had just had. Probably, she thought with contentment. And why not just give in and enjoy?

''You know, we always talk about my being a food critic, but we hardly ever discuss you, your career.''

''How many times do I have to say it? I don't have a 'career.'''

That furrow between his eyebrows made an appearance. ''It seems a waste somehow. You're so intelligent and have so much energy. If I'd been your father, I would have insisted that you finish college and come up with a goal and work toward it.''

''Yes, well, but you're not my father, are you?'' She was feeling defensive now. Someone as driven as Matt would have a real hard time understanding a life-style like hers.

''Besides—'' she decided to try for lightness ''—if you ever meet my dad, you'll understand how silly that is. You know that play, *You Can't Take It With You?* My dad's the guy in the basement who keeps inventing new fireworks and blowing the place up. Except my dad, he's always down there creating the next big-selling kitchen gadget. None of them ever work real well, except once he came up with a way to vacuum the seeds out of watermelon. Then someone invented seedless watermelon.''

The furrow deepened. ''But don't you miss having a purpose?''

''I have a purpose. To see what's around the next corner.''

''That sounds so...''

''Immature? Aimless? Unsettled?''

He had the grace to look chagrined. ''You've heard those words before.''

''Yeah, and it used to bother me, still does, I guess. It's just that—and you may not be able to understand this—I'm not sure *settled* is such a good thing to be. I change my mind about that a lot. In the meantime, I support myself and have fun. I learn a little bit about the things that interest me, and I meet some wonderful people, and when I think of all the years ahead of me to have more fun and learn more and meet more people, I feel, well, excited. And, you know, I think—I hope— that's an okay way to be. For now, anyway.''

She could see him mulling that over, deciding if he found what she said acceptable. At that moment, Matt was most definitely in his autocratic mode. Really, it was such an ingrained part of him, he would probably always have the tendency.

But he couldn't fool her. She knew what was underneath. It didn't take a genius to see that Matt was a passionate man who'd come to value goals and order because he'd had none as a child, and he squashed down his emotions because no one had ever taken care of him. She felt her eyes filling at the thought of all that need going untended. She looked down at her plate so Matt couldn't see how that sudden insight had moved her.

A soft breeze came up from the canal and made the

leaves overhead rustle. Matt gazed at her for the longest time before shaking his head. "I've never come across anyone like you before."

"And you hope you never will again."

"I'm not sure about that anymore."

A half smile accompanied his answer and Mo said, "Ah-ha, progress. Okay, then let's stop talking about careers and stuff. I mean, here we are, in Venice, for heaven's sake. Who'd have thought it, just—let me see—seven days ago?"

"Eight," he corrected. "Do you know the best time to be here? In February, for the carnival. Everyone dresses in costumes and masks, and there's dancing in the street and a parade. It's a pretty wild time."

"Oh, Matt, it sounds wonderful."

"Maybe we can come back here then."

She looked up at him. He'd said that easily, almost as an afterthought. But was he talking about a future? With her? She shouldn't really read anything more into a casually dropped comment like that, but oh, she wanted to. Maybe the silver-eyed man wasn't her destiny. Maybe Matt was. A little flower of hope started to bud inside her chest. It sprang from the fact that she was in love with him, and the feeling grew by the hour.

Maybe, in time, he could learn to love her. Maybe.

Even though the very mention of the word made him turn colder than a glacier.

13

As Matt followed Mo out of the airport into the terminal, he sensed the change in his mood, from lightness to a grayer, grimmer reality. Too bad, he thought. Prague was a fascinating city, but Matt had been fighting a feeling of—what? gloom—since they'd had their last glimpse of Venice. He really hadn't wanted to leave.

Three incredible days. In that ancient city on the water, he and Mo had had three days in which he'd allowed himself to let go, to get caught up in a mind-melting, body-burning affair. No, not an affair, a romance. It was the only word for it. Romance.

Three days with Mo in a city which cheerfully offered nothing to do except walk, sip coffee, window-shop and ride in a gondola. As he'd written in his notes, when in Venice, one walked, one breathed, one thought, one dreamed.

And, in his case, one made love. With Mo. Often. Astonishing bouts of lovemaking. Afternoon delights in their small room, while the gauze curtains billowed in the breeze from the canal and the sun cast shadows on their naked bodies. More lovemaking in the middle of the night and the early morning. He had taken to it like a parched man at the sight of a waterfall. It had been paradise. The city had worked its spell on him, no doubt about it.

And now it was over.

Ah, well, he thought as he and Mo made their way to a taxi stand at the airport, they would return to Venice together one day.

They? Return together? One day?

Wait a minute, he said to himself. Hold it just one minute.

"Matt? Why are we stopping?"

"Huh? Oh, sorry, I was thinking, uh, about the book."

They walked on, but Matt's mind kept up a furious diatribe. He'd been future-planning with Mo. How could he even allow himself thoughts like that? It must have been a holdover from all the passion and sense of freedom and, yes, sheer happiness, he'd felt in Venice.

All well and good, but Venice was in the past tense.

He had a few more days of travel, a book to write, a career to get on with. It was entertaining, and physically satisfying, having Mo as his travel partner, but there was no way the two of them could survive—together—one day after this trip was over. No way in the world.

The taxi ride took about forty-five minutes, and Mo, with her usual wide-awake verve, kept looking around and commenting about what she saw out the window—groves and groves of trees and fields with women in kerchiefs bent over, tending crops. Once in Prague, they passed stately buildings with soot- and smog-blackened facades, churches with Gothic spires and tall stained-glass windows, clanging trams and small, square automobiles, and houses painted all the colors of the rainbow.

He'd booked them into a hotel in the heart of Wenceslas Square in the New Town section. The building was both run-down and elegant. The honeymoon suite was roomy, with a faded, turn-of-the-century feel to it— delicate furniture with silk-brocade upholstery.

Mo shoved her suitcase into the walk-in closet, then inspected the room, touching everything. "Boy, it's amazing how each city has a completely different character from the one before, huh. Ready to go walking?"

Matt smiled. Mo's delight factor, wherever they were, still operated on all cylinders. "I'm ready."

Taking her hand and tucking it in the crook of his arm, he escorted her down the hall to the antique cage elevator. A few moments later, they were on the streets of Prague.

There were a lot of people and a lot of trees. Also narrow, winding, cobblestoned streets that went up and down hills almost as steep as those in San Francisco. Young people with backpacks and well-dressed women and men strolled by.

"It's a happy city, isn't it?" she said. "People are laughing and talking. How often have you been here?"

"Just once, years ago when the country was still called Czechoslovakia. I've never been to Budapest, by the way."

"Really? Well, good, it'll be one place we can discover together. Until the silver-eyed man shows up, of course," she added lightly.

He stiffened. Had she said that to evoke some kind of jealous response from him?

No, a look at her face told him she'd tossed it off as a joke.

Not that Matt even remotely believed in her *nagyanya's* predictions, but something about Mo's reference to her fantasy future lover made him a little...edgy.

Was he jealous? Absurd, he told himself as they

walked along. It was fatigue. He pushed any other thoughts away as unworthy.

Mo thumbed through a travel book she'd produced from her huge purse. "What shall we see first? The Prague Castle? The Charles Bridge? Oh, look, the Loreto Museum, it has all kinds of fun stuff. Let's go there first."

By late afternoon, Mo and Matt ambled across the Charles Bridge to Old Town Hall, to meet with the photographer. Matt watched Mo's face as they approached the world-famous astronomical clock tower, rising hundreds of feet into the air.

"Wow," she said softly. "Double wow."

"It's something, isn't it?" Matt said.

"Incredible."

Tall and graceful and golden, the huge, intricate clock showed the movements of the sun and moon through the twelve signs of the zodiac.

"Matt, why is the sun going around the earth?"

"The clock's been here since 1490, and they hadn't gotten the news yet that it works the other way around." He slung an arm over her shoulder. "It's almost four—watch what happens on the hour."

Mo watched, feeling like a child waiting for a magic show. As four o'clock struck, she got it. Bells clanged, trapdoors opened and wooden statuettes emerged. Death struck the bells; the Apostles marched past him; a rooster crowed, all in an elaborate mechanical dance.

"It's like a little morality play, huh," she said. "Death is warning about the passage of time, and the rooster is signaling life, and all the other guys telling us to behave along the way."

"That about covers it. They say the clock maker was

blinded by some of the town's big shots, to prevent him from repeating his triumph anywhere else.''

"Boy, they really knew how to take care of competition in those days."

He chuckled. "He got them back by plunging his hands into the clock workings, which pretty effectively ended his life—and the clock's too, for a while."

"Yuck."

Out of the corner of her eye, Mo noticed the approach of a tall, very thin man with the saddest face she'd ever seen. In a bass, deeply accented voice, the newcomer said, "Mr. and Mrs. Vining? I am Janusc Kapek. I am here to take the picture."

Mo bit back a smile. The man looked and sounded as if he were informing them of a recent death. He led them around the square, snapping pictures in front of various monuments at a stately pace. When Janusc requested the usual newlywed shot, Mo turned to Matt and clasped her arms around his waist.

She whispered, "This is the first honeymoon picture we've posed for since we've, uh, had carnal knowledge of each other."

"Well, now, I suppose it is. Let's do it up right."

She threw her arms around his neck, then planted her mouth on his. He responded instantly, ferociously, till the two of them were wrapped up in each other and oblivious to everything around them.

Eventually, a low whistle from somewhere made them break the kiss. Dizzy, Mo looked around and remembered where they were. Feeling the heat on her cheeks, she smiled weakly at Janusc.

"A-OK, Mr. and Mrs.," said the photographer solemnly. "I got many good photographs."

As he walked away, Mo glanced up at Matt. It registered then. Something was wrong, had been wrong with Matt's manner all day. Mo's senses had been heightened by their physical intimacy. She was plugged into Matt now in a way that was almost scary; she could feel the slightest change in his mood.

That kiss—it hadn't been in the least bit playful. There had almost been a kind of desperation in it. As though he'd been trying to blot out something dark.

"Matt? Is anything wrong?"

He shook his head. "No. It's just that—it would be nice if a man and woman could sustain the kind of high we had in Venice forever, wouldn't it? But everyone has to come down sometime."

Oh. Was Matt telling her this nice little fairy tale the two of them had been enacting was about to come to an end? Her spirits started to plummet, but she caught herself before they hit bottom.

No, no. Just because Matt said something, or was even feeling something, temporarily, didn't make it so—she had to remember that. She, personally, was not ready to end anything. "I know what will fix that letdown feeling," she said. "Something sweet and disgusting to eat." She smiled at him and took his hand. As they walked away from the square, Mo looked back one more time. "You know what? I think that clock is my favorite sight so far on this trip. I'll always remember it. Something about how it's kept on going all these years, and how beautiful it is."

Which was a funny way to feel, she added silently. Because under that clock, when she and Matt had kissed, she'd felt a different clock ticking, as if they were running out of time.

They sat at the Europa Café with cups of coffee and cream cakes in front of them. Resting her elbow on the table, Mo gazed around the room. The café's interior had remained untouched since its completion in 1912, and the atmosphere of down-at-heel grandeur included a down-at-heel string quartet, playing on a small stage in the corner.

"I feel like I'm in the middle of one of those old black-and-white movies," Mo said. "You know, where all the women wear those slinky gowns and no bra and painted-on eyebrows, and platinum blond hair in tight waves. And all the men dress in white tie and tails every night and everyone is just too too bored? Except I don't own a slinky gown and you're not wearing a tux."

"I didn't bring it with me."

"You actually have one, don't you? Of course you do. And I'll bet it looks great." She cocked her head as she looked at him. "I guess you're the first man I've ever met who actually owns a tux."

"Two, as a matter of fact."

"Why two, for heaven's sake?"

"It was a whim. I couldn't decide between two different styles, and I'd just signed the contract for the radio show and wanted to celebrate."

"So, you celebrated by buying two tuxedos? Weird."

"And four vests. What would you have done?"

Resting her chin in her hand, she thought about it. "Bought presents for everyone I know. Got myself a new car, maybe, or at least a better used one—mine is addicted to gas and is ready for a museum. Let me see. Oh, yes, I would most definitely have hopped on a plane to Europe."

"My two tuxedos were considerably less expensive than all that."

"It does seem that way. I guess it's a good thing I

never have extra money. I'd spend it. Never can seem to hold on to the stuff.''

"Really?"

"You probably balance your checkbook every month. I open a new account every year—it's easier that way."

He shook his head. "We are so different, you and I. And I admit it, there are things about you I'll never understand."

"Or approve of, huh."

He didn't answer. Instead, he turned in his chair to watch the musicians. Mo studied that classic, brooding profile of his. He was back to judging her again, wasn't he?

But she didn't feel the need to defend herself. She understood now that he went into his judgmental mode when he was hiding from himself, fighting his feelings. Feelings for her? She seriously hoped so. Because he did have them, strong ones—the warmth in his eyes, the touches he gave her, the looks he snuck when he thought she wasn't looking, even the small spurts of jealousy. She hadn't imagined any of that.

However, that didn't mean he would do anything about those feelings. Would he confront them? she wondered. Or let them drain away, like water down a sink?

Maybe she was inventing the whole thing because she wanted him to be feeling all these things. Who knew?

That evening, they attended a Mozart concert in a gorgeous old opera hall—all gold and mosaics and crystal—followed by a late supper at a basement restaurant that descended several stories beneath Old Town Square.

It was a dimly lit medieval stone vault with rough-hewn wooden tables, with a mixed crowd of both Czech and foreign customers. They dined on what Matt told her were traditional dishes of hearty potato soup and beef broth with dumplings. Mo found herself straining to keep the conversation going, and wound up talking too much to fill the silence.

Back at their room, she took a bath in the large old-fashioned claw-footed porcelain tub, and thought about the day. It was time to talk to Matt. Exactly what she would say, she wasn't sure. But things were festering again, and needed airing out.

Wrapping a huge towel around herself, she entered the bedroom. Matt was propped up in bed, making notes.

"I'm not real familiar with Mozart," she said, "or most classical music. Maybe when we get back to San Francisco, I'll take a class."

He glanced up at her, his eyes darkening as he took in her costume, or lack of it. He put his notebook down and held out his arms.

Hmm, Mo thought. Maybe they wouldn't talk, after all.

"You trying to say something, Meester Vinink?"

"I think you started the sentence already. Come here. Now."

"With that kind of masterful invitation, how can a girl resist?"

He pulled her onto the bed, shoved aside her towel and covered her with his body. Soon she was too caught up in the heat to even think about talking things out.

His lovemaking was, as always, inventive and tender, but there was a subtle difference this time. It was serious, almost somber, with no lightness about it in the least. Part of Matt was removed from the act, observing it instead of being totally involved, the way he'd been in Venice.

It scared her. He was pulling away, withdrawing into his shell. And it most definitely was not her imagination.

"Matt?" Mo said afterward, on her side but still enveloped in his arms.

He didn't answer. She angled her head around. He was fast asleep.

She told herself it was natural to pull away. No one could keep up the kind of intensity they'd shared in Italy. Or maybe they'd been together too much and he was feeling tied down. Had she turned into one of those clingy, dependent women because of all the excitement he aroused in her, because of how her emotions were involved?

All right, then, she thought, snuggling back into him in her favorite sleeping position. Dependency she could do something about. If Matt was feeling smothered, she'd take care of that tomorrow.

Matt stared at his toothbrush, shaking his head as he tried to wake up. He was alone in their huge, ornate suite. Mo had risen early, and had been all dressed and ready to leave when he opened his eyes. She'd announced brightly that she was taking off because she needed to be alone to do her exploring thing, and she knew he needed to work on his book.

"See you later," she'd said, and she'd swept out of the room with her usual flurry and bustle.

They'd been here less than twenty hours, and already it looked as if a small tornado had hit her side of the sink. He wondered what it would be like to live with her. Maybe this was one of those compromise areas his married friends talked about, where as long as Mo respected his space, he would have to respect hers. If, of course, they lived together.

Live together? With Mo? What was he thinking?

Matt gripped the sides of the sink and stared into the mirror. Did he actually want to live with Mo? Not only would she be a constant challenge, he'd never lived with a woman before, had never shared dishes, towels, bookcases. He had no idea what that would be like. He and Kay had looked at apartments and figured they'd deal with moving when they returned from their honeymoon. This was an area he knew nothing about.

"Live with Mo?" he said aloud to the bleary-eyed, unshaven man in the mirror. "Together?"

14

Mo threw open the door of the suite. "I did it. I ate carp."

"Carp?"

"Fish. It was terrific. You're always hassling me because I don't eat fish, so I did. Without knowing it. And oh boy, was it good."

She plopped herself down on a gilt-edged chair with spindly legs. Her face glowed with color. She wore one of those pants things that was really a skirt. It was short, too short, Matt thought. Her sleeveless top seemed too skimpy to him, too formfitting. Although he supposed any kind of shirt would look that way on her.

Hold it, he said to himself. Not only was he being a grouch, he was feeling possessive again. He didn't like this mood, didn't like *feeling* any of these things.

"It sounds like you had a great time," he said.

"I did a bunch of exploring, for the book. There's this place that serves blue margaritas, and a vegetarian plate called the Gringo." She pulled her purse onto her lap and started unloading everything onto the floor. "I wrote it all down here somewhere. There was a Cajun restaurant, too, isn't that weird? There was even a sports bar, and I realized I was being a snob—you know, like only Westerners eat Cajun and have sports bars. After all, they might not speak the same language, but people still follow their favorite teams all over the world, and everybody has to eat.''

She found a crumpled piece of paper, glanced at it, then shoved it back into one of the pockets of her purse. ''Now, where did I put that? Oh, and I went to a beer hall, in this kind of arcade right near Old Town Square—lots of wood and those long, long tables...you know, where everyone eats together? And I had a dark beer and some salami and ham. Did you know that Budweiser is a Czech beer? Then they brought out the carp, only they didn't tell me it was carp and it was delicious. Deep-fried and crunchy. Served with this warm potato salad. And the whole thing was only about eight dollars American. So you can put it in the book, you know, for an inexpensive, atmospheric place. Ah-ha. There it is.''

She brought out a torn piece of paper with scribbling on it and handed it to him. It was the top part of a dry-cleaners ticket for a place in San Francisco.

''Won't you need this?'' Matt asked.

''No, they know me.'' Getting up from her chair, Mo beamed a broad smile at him. ''Matt, you have to come with me. Are you done with your writing? I mean, I don't want to interrupt you or anything.''

Was he done with his writing? What writing? How could he tell her he'd done almost no work on the book? That the day had been filled with mood swings he'd never experienced before. That instead of writing, he'd stared out the window, then gone out for a while, bought her a gift, then suffered all kinds of doubt as to whether or not she'd like it. He'd returned to the room with a lumpy sandwich from a corner shop, and had been at his post at the window ever since, waiting for her to return.

He rose from his chair, determined to shake this

strange, uncharacteristic, downright unfocused state of mind. "Sure, I'll go with you. Where to?"

"It's a hotel."

"But we already have a hotel."

"Not like this one."

As they entered the modest reception area, Mo whispered, "It's owned by nuns, can you believe it? And you don't have to be a nun to stay here, but it helps. Smoking, drinking and staying out after 1:00 a.m. are strictly forbidden."

The building was square and old and not particularly distinctive, at least on that floor. However, Mo told him, in the fifties, it had once housed the secret police.

She led Matt down a flight of stairs and pointed at a row of closed steel doors. "They used to be prison cells, still are, with cots and bars on the windows and everything."

"People stay there?" Matt asked in astonishment.

"Yes. Can you imagine? The nuns have painted them this kind of pink color, but they're still really gloomy."

"Dear God."

She pointed to one of the cells. "P6, that's where President Havel was jailed for a while. It's the most popular room in the place."

Mo took him down one more flight of stairs, one that opened onto a long tunnel. They walked along a chilled, dark underground corridor for several yards until they reached an indentation that led into a cavelike room. Matt could just stand up in the grotto, which he realized was real rock. Its walls dripped with moisture.

"What do you think?" Mo whispered. "Creepy, huh."

Matt was not fond of closed, dark places, and he

didn't care for this one at all. He shivered. "Creepy is the word."

"There used to be skeletons here, one of the sisters told me, from the old days when they tortured people. But not anymore. We hope," she added with a giggle.

Matt started to tell Mo he'd like to leave, but instead, he let out a huge sneeze.

"Bless you," Mo said. "It's soggy down here, huh. You can put this in the book under 'Ex-prison facilities, for that honeymoon with a twist.'"

"Or under 'Places to catch cold so you can have an excuse to stay in bed.'"

"Are you catching cold?"

"I think so." He stepped into a shallow puddle, then shook his foot, annoyed. "I'm sorry, Mo. I'm not feeling adventurous today."

"Scratch one cave exploration."

By the time they got to the restaurant Matt was to review that night, Mo could tell he wasn't well. His skin was pale under his tan, and clammy. And he was as gruff as a bear deprived of hibernating room. This behavior was not unknown to her. One of her brothers was like this; when Patrick got sick, he felt insulted that his body had failed him, and was a cranky, miserable patient.

The restaurant, located in *Stare mesto,* Prague's historic old city, was elegant Art Deco, all polished wood, etched glass and dark marble. Mo and Matt were seated at a window with a view of the Vltava River and Prague Castle, the huge medieval collection of buildings that sat high above the town. Mo wished there were time to go there, but it would have to wait till she returned here. And she would be back, she knew that.

Matt was silent throughout most of the meal. He

seemed to need all his concentration to do his job. Part of her, she was ashamed to admit, felt relieved that he was sick. It might explain some of the last two days' dark mood.

They started with tomato soup, followed by some sort of snail-liver dish the place was famous for. Snail livers? Mo declined to taste it, or the hare salad that followed, which was pronounced by Matt to be decent but not exceptional.

On the other hand, the bread was brown and thickly sliced, very different from French and Italian bread, and she had no trouble eating several slices, slathered with sweet butter.

Mo really worked to cheer Matt up; making her brother laugh had often been an effective way to get him out of his doldrums. She told a couple of terrible jokes, but—like map reading—telling jokes had never been a strength of hers. She usually ruined the punch line.

The entrées were tiny Icelandic shrimp baked with mushrooms, wild boar stew and venison fillets broiled in butter. She actually ate some of all three dishes, telling herself she only had to take a couple of bites and swallow. Matt would be pleased.

For all her sacrifice, he barely seemed to notice. He looked at his food, ate some, made some notes. Period.

Eventually, his mood affected hers and she poked dispiritedly at some of the side dishes—rice and honey, stewed sour cherries, caramelized fennel and roasted potatoes. "These aren't bad," she said to Matt. "Or are they?"

"Not bad, yes."

Oh, dear, Mo thought. Matt, sick, was worse than her brother had ever been. Even the dessert, profiteroles drenched in chocolate sauce, which Mo praised lavishly, declaring she was being corrupted, did nothing to raise his spirits. She decided to stop trying. He was allowed, after all, to be in a bad mood.

The whole meal was too damned heavy, Matt decided, too busy. Besides, he didn't have much of an appetite, which was not a good thing in a food critic. He would have to bend over backward to offer a fair assessment of this restaurant.

On top of that, he was nervous, dammit, because he wanted to present Mo with her gift and he wasn't sure how she would take it. Summoning up whatever fortitude he had left, he signaled the headwaiter to bring the package he'd dropped off earlier. When it arrived, Matt placed it on the table in front of Mo. "Here."

"What's this?"

"Happy Birthday."

"But it's not for two days."

"I know, but I thought while we're in Prague…"

He watched as she tore at the paper around the package with eagerness. "I don't know," he went on. "I just wanted to buy you something and you said I wasn't to buy you anything, but, you know, if it was a birthday gift, well, I assumed you wouldn't refuse."

Why was he babbling this way? He was sounding just like Mo, complete with run-on sentences and all kinds of "you knows" and "wells."

She gasped when she saw the music box—a beautiful miniature of the astronomical clock, complete with statues striking the hour.

"Oh, Matt," she said with tears in her eyes. "Oh, Matt, this is beautiful. Thank you so much."

"You really like it?"

"Like it? I love it."

He exhaled a sigh of relief. "So, then, you're not going to turn it down, even though it is a gift."

"Are you kidding?" she said with a large grin. "Try to take it away from me."

Her smile warmed him momentarily, but then he felt himself sagging. By the time they got to the room, his energy was nonexistent, his headache was pounding and he wanted to bite someone's head off.

With his face still wet from washing it, he threw open the bathroom door and glared at Mo. "Can't you even keep the bathroom clean?"

Mo was unzipping her dress, and he saw her jump at the irritation in his voice. Then she came over to the door, and he could see hurt and anger warring on her face.

"I'm sorry," she said. "I try, really I do. But things just—" she shrugged "—get away from me. I start to clean up, and then something fascinates me, and I get all caught up in that, and then there's no time to go back and make it neat."

Sweeping past him into the bathroom, she pushed all her bottles into one corner, then wiped around the counter with a tissue. "All I've been able to do, over the years, is train myself to keep my mess separate. I haven't touched your stuff, have I? I mean, I've never actually traveled with a man before, not on a trip, so I, well, I'm doing my best." She met his gaze defiantly in the mirror, then bit her lip and looked down. "And I'm running on at the mouth, for a change. Sorry."

He felt ashamed, utterly ashamed. "No, I'm sorry. I shouldn't have said anything. I'm feeling awful, and I'm taking it out on you."

"But you're right."

"No, no. It's okay. Really."

She turned around and faced him, leaning back against the sink and looking up at him with those enormous blue eyes that seemed to ask for a sign of some affection from him. "My gift is beautiful," she said softly, "no matter how you're feeling. It's the best birthday present I've ever had."

What he wanted to do was put his arms around her and bury his head in her soft neck and apologize some more.

But no, he told himself, she would catch his cold. It was better if he made no physical contact with her at all.

"Good," he said, grabbing the towel and wiping his face. "I'm glad."

At another time, Mo thought, it might have been fun to take the night train from Prague to Budapest. But, with these up-and-down bunk beds, and with Matt taking the prize for worst patient in the history of the universe, it wasn't, she decided, the high point of her honeymoon.

She punched in her pillow, which felt as though it were filled with sand and pebbles. This ride wasn't what she'd expected from all she'd heard about intercontinental railroads and watching old Hitchcock movies. This was supposed to be a first-class sleeper, but it was pretty tiny and not at all classy. There was no helpful porter, no drinking water, no dining car, and not even any food machines. And she was practicing self-control rather than utilize the bathroom, which had never heard the word *hygienic*.

Some honeymoon, she thought again.

Stop that, she reminded herself. She wasn't really on an actual honeymoon, even if, up to a couple of days ago, she and Matt had given a pretty good imitation of one.

At any rate, the honeymoon was over. Matt was avoiding her, and she knew deep in her heart it had only a little to do with how sick he felt.

It was a good thing she hadn't told him she loved him, considering how she was pretty sure he wouldn't be real receptive to hearing the news. Even if his feelings for her were as strong as hers were for him, he was fighting them like crazy. And she didn't really want to do battle, not when it came to loving someone.

Still, tomorrow she would be in Budapest, a city she'd been hearing about her whole life. Budapest and the Danube. Mo thought of *Nagyanya* and her predictions. Silliness, of course. After all, who had silver eyes? Gray, maybe, but silver? Ridiculous.

As the train made its way through the countryside, Mo drifted into sleep, keeping one ear out for Matt, should he need her.

Which, of course, even if he did, he'd never admit.

Trains rocking back and forth were supposed to be soothing, but this one was annoying as hell. Matt wished it would stop—his head was killing him. And he was having these strange half thoughts and dreams.

About love.

Love. The word wouldn't stop echoing in his head. Had he ever felt love? he asked himself. For anyone? He must have loved his mother, at least when he was little. Didn't all children love their mothers?

He changed his position. The bed was as small as a child's camp cot. How the hell were people supposed to sleep on these things?

His thoughts drifted. Friends? He had a few. Women? Several in his past. But had he loved?

No, he hadn't felt that particular emotion—if it really existed—for any of them.

He turned over, mopped his forehead with the edge of the coarse cotton sheet and grumbled. He would *not* ask Mo, one more time, for a Kleenex or an aspirin, or mineral water, all of which she packed in that absurd suitcase/purse of hers. He'd been managing alone all his life, dammit, and he could manage to get through a stupid cold without Mo.

But, of course, Mo was why he was thinking about love. He kept pushing the thought away, but it kept coming back with the inevitability of a boomerang. Love.

He wished the word had never been invented.

15

➤━━━◀

The Budapest station was enormous, with skylights set in very high ceilings. They arrived there at seven in the morning, and for the first time on their trip, Mo put herself in charge of getting them to the hotel. Matt was in bad need of a bed and some sleep—and a doctor, although he refused that suggestion emphatically.

She was pretty sure the taxi driver took the long way around, and she usually wouldn't put up with that, but with all their luggage and a large, sniffling, unhappy man by her side, she figured it wasn't the time to argue about it.

Budapest—actually two cities, Buda and Pest—was a very busy place. Lots of people and cars, charming historical buildings, as soot-covered as Prague's, but not as many. They seemed more uniform somehow, and higher, with tons of windows.

Their hotel was another winner, a great old place which had apparently once been an actual palace. The people who waited on them actually wore uniforms with shiny buttons and epaulets. And the lobby was all brass and chandeliers and Oriental rugs and huge sofas on which were seated all kinds of people in suits with portable phones in their ears. Just like San Francisco.

Their room was the largest one they'd had so far.

Maybe a prince's quarters in the old days, Mo thought. The bed was fitted with thick, feather-filled linens. And the view was spectacular, out over the Danube—the Danube!—and some of the bridges that spanned it, joining the castles of Buda to the market town named Pest.

Mo ordered Matt into the bed and he actually did just that. When she felt his head, it was cooler than it had been on the train, but was still bathed in perspiration.

She called room service and managed to explain she wanted some tea and orange juice sent up, then she tucked his blankets around him and sat on the edge of the mattress. "My dad has a cure for a cold. You down echinacea and goldenseal from the health-food store, a pint of orange juice, two shots of brandy. Then you bundle up like an Eskimo, get under the covers and sleep. One night like that and you sweat it out."

"If you don't die of suffocation. I'll pass. Look, why don't you take off? I hate you seeing me like this."

Biting back a grin, Mo held up her hands to indicate that she was through fussing. A picture formed then, of how Matt must have looked as a little boy, all adorable and furious because he felt helpless and hated it. Her heart went out to him in a mixture of maternal, and definitely not maternal, emotion.

"Well, then, if you're okay, I'll sightsee while you sleep." She kissed his forehead, then smoothed back some of his thick black hair that had stuck to the damp skin. "Get some rest, okay? I love you."

It came out of her mouth just like that.

Automatically. As though she'd said it a hundred times before.

She'd kissed him, then said what she'd been trying not to say for days. Just a simple "I love you."

Not since the night in the gondola had anyone mentioned the *L* word. Usually, Mo blurted out her feelings as they occurred to her, bypassing the judgment part of her head in the process. Holding this one back must have been too much strain.

At any rate, it was out there now.

She held herself still, barely breathing, as she watched Matt's face go from surprise, to something like tenderness, to panic.

The panic was the last thing she saw before he closed his eyes.

His mouth formed two stern lines. He said nothing. Nothing at all. Not one word of reply to the famous three little words.

The son of a bitch.

Slinging her purse over her shoulder, Mo ran out of the room and down the stairs. They were on the twentieth floor, so she got a good workout. When she threw open a door that she thought was to the lobby, she found herself on the mezzanine instead. Before her was a huge breakfast spread—meats and cheeses and breads and fresh fruit and cereals and yogurt. She should have been starving, as they'd last eaten early the evening before, but she'd lost her appetite.

What a surprise. You tell a man you love him and his immediate reaction is to pretend he doesn't hear you, well, you'll probably never want to eat again.

She walked out of the hotel at a fast clip, aware that she was pissed off and probably feeling a bunch of other stuff, too. But after the initial spurt of anger, now she had this incredible blank mind that didn't want to dwell on it. Rejection was like that sometimes. You delayed feeling it as long as you could because it really hurt.

She turned off a main street and found herself in a quiet residential neighborhood. The scent of garlic and onions wafted from a kitchen window. A woman with a brightly colored kerchief tied around her head swept the sidewalk with a homemade broom.

At a small park, men played chess in the shade while a small dog darted through the chestnut trees. She passed huge apartment buildings with courtyards that boasted fruit trees and flower gardens, and where jars of pickled vegetables sat on the sunny window ledges.

At another time she would be rejoicing to be here in the land of her ancestors; she would be exploring, taking it all in with bright curiosity. Instead, she hardly saw any of it. She walked, her mind switched off, disconnected and numb, for what felt like hours. At one point, her stomach rumbled in protest as she passed a line outside a small shop. People were exiting, licking ice-cream cones. Her stomach rumbled again.

Her purse was hurting her shoulder—she should have left it behind, but there'd been no time to unpack it and she'd been in a hurry to escape from Matt. Switching the bag to the other side, she joined the line. She got herself a cinnamon-flavored scoop and thought about how she would tell Matt she'd actually ordered an offbeat ice cream and how proud of her he would be.

And then she remembered that Matt didn't love her; or, at least, had pointedly refused to discuss the subject. The jerk. Being sick didn't mean you got to be unkind. She swallowed down the stab of pain in the back of her throat with soothing ice cream.

Later, much later, it seemed to her, she wound up walking along the banks of the Danube, passing one of the bridges she'd seen from the hotel window. On one side of her was the gray, swiftly moving water; on the other was a huge city street filled with trolley cars, buses and automobiles, and beyond that, a thriving shopping district. She noted both a bagel place and a fast-food restaurant. She smiled sadly at the sight—she couldn't even summon up any enthusiasm for some french fries.

Hugging her arms to her chest, Mo faced the river and stared at a castle in the distance. Castles and palaces and monuments and statues. Museums, parks, theaters, fine restaurants. Planes and boats and trains. What a lot she and Matt had packed into this trip.

This ''honeymoon'' trip.

The hurt, dark and salty, rose again in the back of her throat. Tears flooded her eyes. Darn it, why did she always have to cry? She reached into her purse for some Kleenex. Did she have any left after last night on the train? She was pretty sure she had a little travel pack somewhere in there.

Mo set the bag down on the concrete sidewalk and started to unload everything in it. Socks, matchbooks and ashtrays, a bottle of water, part of a muffin, a paper fan, a plastic rain kerchief. Stuff and more stuff.

Somewhere behind her, she sensed a presence, but before she could turn around, her purse had been snatched up and a teenage kid was running off with it.

''Hey!'' she called out.

Someone else shouted a word she didn't know and then she saw a man with dark sunglasses and a mustache take off in pursuit of the thief. Mo was about to go after both of them, when, twenty yards ahead, the second man attacked the kid who'd lifted her purse. There was a brief scuffle, then the thief ran away, and the man with the sunglasses and mustache trotted back to her with her purse in his hand and a huge grin on his swarthy face.

As he got closer, she noted the dark, curly hair and the printed bandanna worn across his forehead. He wore a torn T-shirt and jeans and seemed to be about her age.

Not too tall, but kind of cute. His impudent grin reminded her of Kevin Kline. She liked her purse's rescuer immediately.

Gypsies were Hungary's largest minority, and Mo was pretty sure one of those fascinating people was standing in front of her right this minute.

With a nod of his head and that charming smile, her hero offered her purse to her, saying something she couldn't understand.

She accepted the bag and slung it over her shoulder again, saying, *"Koszonom szepen,"* which meant thank you. It was one of the ten or so phrases *Nagyanya* had taught her.

More excited sentences tumbled from the man's mouth, but, laughing, Mo shook her head. *"Nem, nem,"* she said. "No, no. I don't speak Hungarian."

He switched to another language and she wondered if it was Romany, the international language of Gypsies. Not that she understood that one any better. Again, she shook her head sadly. "Sorry. No."

He looked disappointed, but in the next moment brightened up. Holding his finger in the air to indicate she should wait a minute, he went over to a small wooden cart by the side of the road. She hadn't noticed it before. It was crudely made and painted white. There were bunches of flowers on the cart, some in paper, some in vases. They weren't particularly fresh, but they were colorful.

Mo figured the cart belonged to the man. He perused his collection, then chose a bunch of mixed blooms—daffodils and daisies and a couple of tall, white blossoms that Mo didn't know the name of. Coming toward her again, he bowed from the waist and presented her with the bouquet.

She nodded, saying, *"Koszonom szepen"* again and taking the flowers from him. They stood looking at each other for a silent minute. Then he did a little soft-shoe step and she did one back, and they both laughed.

The man began to hum a song that had a waltz rhythm, then he swayed to the beat. How wonderful, Mo thought, her body moving automatically in time to the music. Just what she needed to brighten her day. A dancing man on the banks of the Danube.

Singing now in a loud, robust voice, the flower seller held out his arms to indicate she should join him. She didn't even have to think about it; after all, why not? Why not put away all thoughts of the grumpy man lying in bed back in the hotel, and give herself up to a little moment of gaiety?

As she drifted closer to the flower seller, he pushed his sunglasses up onto the top of his head and, laughing, reached for her.

Mo stopped dead in her tracks, her hands against his chest. She stared. Hard.

His eyes. They were…gray? No, not gray.

Grabbing him by the shoulders, Mo pulled him around so that he was facing the sun, and stared again into his eyes. No doubt about it. The very same color of the tea set that sat on her mother's sideboard at home. After it had been polished to gleaming.

16

Matt lowered himself onto the bench and rubbed his face with his hand. Why was he here? How big a fool would he seem to Mo, if he ever found her? She could be anywhere in the city, anywhere at all, probably slipping on a puddle or kicking up some kind of turmoil, from which she would extricate herself, somehow, intact. She certainly didn't need him to rescue her, or to even lay eyes on him, probably.

Two hours earlier, he'd been lying in the hotel bed, restless and feverish. He was pretty sure that all he had was a cold, but it seemed to drain his energy. He kept drifting in and out of sleep, but he remembered indulging in pop psychology by wondering if his illness was more emotional than physical. Was his body reflecting the war raging in his head? Did that kind of thing really happen? Whatever the answer, he had still felt pretty bad.

Suddenly, he sat up straight in bed, a sense of panic overtaking him. Mo had told him she loved him! And like some prizewinning idiot, he'd been so thrown by her admission, he'd clammed up. By the time he'd recovered his wits enough to say something—anything—she'd hightailed it out the door.

But where had she gone? Mo. He had to find Mo.

He'd risen from bed, thrown on some pants and a shirt and had gone out looking for her. No luck. So here he was, on a bench near the Danube, at a loss for what to do next. His gaze swept the gray, fast-moving river, the picturesque hills on the opposite shore, and finally rested on the sight of something in the distance, half a football field away. Two people. Mo?

And who was that with her? A dark-haired man near a flower cart? Matt half rose from his bench, thinking he would make his way over there and— Then what? What would he say to her? What was he prepared to say?

He sank back down, his gaze fixed on the scene farther down the riverbank. Mo and the stranger seemed to be laughing and having a great old time. Then they both began swaying and laughing some more; Matt felt his back teeth clench at the sight.

Then the stranger held out his arms to Mo and, still swaying, she walked toward him. But she stopped. Even at this distance, Matt could tell she was startled by something. He watched as she turned the stranger into the sun and stared into his eyes.

No, Matt thought. Not his eyes.

But yes, Mo gazed, astonished, into the stranger's eyes and no one had to tell Matt what color they were.

He felt as though someone had gut-punched him, as though all the oxygen had been whisked out of him. He slumped against the seat and held his head in his hands. So this was how it felt. To finally want something badly and at the point of admitting it to yourself, have it snatched away from you. His heart hurt. He'd heard the expression all his life, but he'd never known what it meant. But this was how pain felt, this was the cost of caring deeply about someone.

The cost of loving. There, he'd said it. To himself, anyway. And about two hours too late.

He forced himself to get up from the bench and, walking in the opposite direction of Mo and the stranger, made his way back to the hotel.

He was under the covers when Mo returned an hour later. What had she been doing all that time? He couldn't bear the direction of his thoughts. Through half-closed lids he noted that she seemed subdued. She came to the bed and stood over him, but he didn't look at her.

"Matt?" he heard her say.

"Hmm?"

He felt the mattress sag as she sat next to him and put her hand on his forehead. "You're cooler now. How do you feel?"

He shrugged. Again, he had no words, none at all.

"I found out that Budapest is famous for Turkish baths. They have this real ornate setup at the Hotel Gellert a couple of blocks away, and I went there to check it out." She spoke quickly but without her usual animation, which sounded strange to him. She'd been to a hotel? He hated that.

"Maybe it would be good for you to go there," she went on. "It's huge, lots of pools and steam rooms, and the ladies who give massages could be weight lifters. We could put it in the book. What do you think? Would you like to go?"

He shook his head and murmured, "Just sleep."

"All right. We need to cancel the restaurant tonight."

"No. I have to go," he mumbled. "Don't have a choice. It's not till ten, so I'll be better by then."

He heard her sigh softly. "Okay. Go to sleep then."

"Where are you going?"

He wondered if his fear showed in his voice, but he

was able to relax a little when she said, "Nowhere. I'll be right here."

And then he sought the oblivion of sleep.

The restaurant was located on the riverbank, just across the Margaret Bridge. Mo and Matt were seated on the upper outdoor terrace; colorfully costumed folk dancers performed on the level below. The waiters and waitresses wore traditional Hungarian peasant clothing. Mo liked the place because it was the least formal of all the official restaurants they'd eaten in on the trip.

Staring around the room at soft lighting and flickering candles on the tables, Mo felt strangely calm, and more than a little sad. Her grandmother had only got part of the prediction right. The flower seller might have had the right color eyes, but nothing else had been right. Her pulse had remained steady, there'd been no sizzling connection between them. The silver-eyed man wasn't the one for her.

Nor was Matt, apparently. Her anger at him had completely dried up as she'd watched him sleep away the rest of the afternoon. Instead, there had come a gentle sadness, which she wasn't used to feeling, and an inner stillness, which was most definitely uncharted territory.

When Matt woke up, he was even more remote than before. As they'd dressed for the evening—him in his new white suit, which, sick or not, looked deliciously continental on him; it was as though he were occupying a different planet. The two of them had barely talked on the way here. Mo wondered how a trip that had started out in such high spirits could finish on such a downer.

She also wondered if she'd ever smile again. She sure didn't feel like it tonight.

"I wonder where the photographer is," Matt said, looking around the restaurant. "He's meeting us here."

Mo shrugged and took a sip of wine. "Beats me."

He turned his attention back to her, gazed at her for a moment, then frowned. Uh-oh, she thought. What's the matter now?

"I need to ask you a favor," Matt said.

"A favor? What?"

"One of the side effects of a cold is stuffed nasal passages, which affects your sense of smell, which affects your sense of taste. So, I can't taste anything."

"Wow. Major problem, I guess."

"So, will you describe the tastes to me? As best you can?"

"Really? You trust me?"

"Yes, Mo. I guess I do."

Paprika, Hungary's famous red powder ground from peppers, seemed to permeate a lot of the dishes. First there was *babgulyas,* a hearty bean soup and *halaszle,* a fish soup. Mo described the first as thick and peppery, and the second as way too fishy. Matt made notes in his book.

For the main courses there were chicken paprikash with pasta dumplings; *toltott kaposzta*—whole cabbage leaves stuffed with rice, meat and spices; a combination platter including roast goose leg, goose cracklings and goose liver; and something called Szinbad's Favorite— pork stuffed with chicken liver, rolled in bacon and served in a paprika and mushroom sauce.

"Uh, this one," Mo said, chewing thoughtfully, "the chicken, it kind of hits the roof of your mouth like one of those red-hots, you know those little candies? Mixed with chicken soup."

"Red-hots and chicken soup," Matt repeated as he wrote it down.

"And this goose—well, it's kind of like well-done chicken, only saltier and tougher, you know, like a leather vest."

"Salty leather vest."

"This pork thing, it's got enough flavors to last a lifetime, but I really can't come up with the words. Spicy, I guess, and sweet and kind of greasy. Like bacon and goop."

Matt looked up from his notes and considered her. "Maybe we'd better forget it."

"Sorry. I don't know spice names and all that subtle stuff you do."

"Why should you? It's not your field."

She felt herself stiffening. Matt might be under the weather, but she wouldn't stand still for a barbed comment about her lack of direction. "I don't have a field, remember?"

"Yes, you do." He smiled, but it was more bitter-sweet than amused. "Your field is life, Mo, and the living of it. I envy you."

"Excuse me? You what?"

"I wish, part of me wishes, that is," he amended, "that I was more like you."

"You do?" Where had this come from? she wondered.

"Yes. Listen, Mo, I need to—"

Whatever Matt was about to say was thwarted by a Gypsy violinist who had been entertaining the other diners and who now swept up to their table. Short and stocky, nearly bald, and dressed in all his embroidered finery, he favored them with a broad, gold-toothed grin.

With a flourish of his bow, he began to play a very sad, very romantic melody.

Mo's attention was drawn to the musician; something about his song reflected an ache deep in her soul. Her head moved in time to the music. The Gypsy's bow moved smoothly over the strings, and she watched his hands for a while. When she caught a glimpse of the watch on his wrist, she noticed that it said eleven-fifty. In ten minutes, she would be twenty-eight. So what? Shaking her head, she smiled cheerlessly to herself.

"What are you thinking about?" Matt asked.

She glanced over at him and shrugged. "My upcoming birthday."

"Birthday?" said the violinist. He stopped his recital right in the middle, made a loud announcement in flowery Hungarian and began to play the Happy Birthday song.

Mo blushed as all the other diners joined in, with expansive smiles on their faces, in a language that was vaguely familiar from years spent on the lap of a woman she'd loved very much. Mo wished she could be happy about being born, but this evening it wasn't up there on her gratitude list.

After everyone had applauded, and Mo was wiping one lone tear from the corner of her eye, Matt said, "Mo?"

Now the violinist was joined by a dramatic-looking, dark-haired woman with large earrings and bangle bracelets; she began to sing an even more mournful song than the previous one, a wistful melody filled with suffering. Mo stared at the singer. Woman to woman. The singer obviously knew just what Mo was feeling.

Matt felt his jaw tightening. He was starting to get irritated. No, in truth, he was starting to panic. He went for it one more time. "Listen, Mo, I need to talk to you, to tell you something."

"I'll accept Happy Birthday."

"No, I mean it. There's something upsetting…no, difficult for me to say."

Turning toward him, she put her hand over her heart and looked at him anxiously. "What? You're scaring me."

"I didn't mean to." He was doing this all wrong. Where was Matthew Vining, glib radio personality, when he was really needed? "It's about what you said today."

"Today?"

"Earlier, in the room."

"You mean, about my dad's cure for a cold?"

"No, after that." Damn, this was hard.

"Is this Twenty Questions or something?"

"No. Dammit, about when you told me you loved me."

He saw her go very still. She could have been a statue except for the blinking of her eyelashes.

"What I want to say… I mean, the thing is—" He put his hand over hers and squeezed. She *had* to listen to him. "Mo. Please, don't go off with him."

"Don't go off with who?"

"That man. The one with silver eyes. I mean, he's a flower seller. Which, don't get me wrong, is probably a perfectly honorable living, but you don't know him. Mo, you don't even speak the same language—"

"How do you know about the flower seller?"

"I saw the two of you today."

"You followed me? But why?"

"That's not important. What is important, crucial, really, is that you understand that— The thing is— Dammit, Mo, I couldn't bear it if you left me.''

"But I wasn't going—'' As his last words registered, she stopped talking. She stared wide-eyed at him, a statue again, and for one of the few times in her life, Matt imagined, speechless. The music played on, but their gazes remained locked for many heartbeats.

"Are you going to say anything?'' he asked her, really worried now.

She shook her head slowly and seemed to come awake. "You're doing just fine.''

The violinist and the singer must have sensed the drama going on at their table because the two of them moved in even closer, one on each side of the table, and began another heartrending lament.

Mo glanced at each of the musicians, smiled quickly, then turned her attention back to Matt. Keeping one hand under his, she leaned on the table, rested her chin on her other hand and gazed at him with a small, encouraging smile. "So. You were saying?''

"I haven't cried since I was a little boy and I had to give away my puppy because my mother's new husband was allergic to animals, but I feel as though I could cry right now at the thought of losing you.''

Mo let out a gasp, unbearably moved. She clutched Matt's hand even harder as her own eyes filled. "Oh, God, that's so sad,'' she said, then burst into tears herself.

The dark-haired singer, seeing all the weeping at the table, crossed her hands over her heart and turned up the throbbing emotion in her song.

Through the haze of her tears, Mo watched Matt's shimmering eyes gazing at her. At this moment, he was the direct opposite of distanced, and all because he feared losing her. Her heart took off, on the wing, out of sight. It was glorious.

She gazed into Matt's soulful, brimming eyes and started to speak. Just then, the singer's bracelets caught the light from the candle, the reflection making Matt's tears shimmer. Which made his eyes shimmer. Which made his eyes...

Silver.

That brought another gasp, then more sobbing from Mo, a river of salt water, all the way down her cheek and onto her neck. Matt picked up a napkin and dabbed under her lids and around her collarbone. "You are so lovely," he said as though bewitched.

"But—" Mo's throat closed up.

"What?" he said. "Tell me what you want to say."

She sniffled a little bit more, grabbed the napkin and blew into it. "Oh, Matt."

"Yes."

"Your eyes—they're silver."

"Excuse me?"

"I mean, with the candle and the tears, they're silver. Get it? Here we are on the banks of the Danube, moments before my twenty-ninth year is about to start, and you are a man with silver eyes. Tell me now how absurd my *nagyanya* was."

She saw the light dawn on Matt's face. His expression of awe made him seem years younger, totally lacking in cynicism, as though he'd witnessed a miracle. He took the edge of the tablecloth and wiped some mascara from under her lower lids.

"Can't take you anywhere," he said in a voice as warm and adoring as she could have hoped for in any of her fantasies.

They sat and smiled stupid smiles at each other, totally

oblivious to the quiet murmur of the other diners, the sounds of violin and song, the quick breeze fluttering the candlelight at all the tables. Somewhere far away a clock sounded. Twelve slow strokes signaled the hour of midnight.

"Happy Birthday," Matt whispered. "And, in case you can't tell, I love you. It hurts how much I love you."

"I'm going to cry again."

He kissed her hand and held it tightly. "Weep away. I can handle it. And I want to apologize for snapping at you. You didn't deserve it. You're wonderful."

"So are you," she said, sniffling.

As though on cue, they both rose at the same time and leaned over the table. He framed her face with his hands, and they kissed.

"Ahem," Mo heard, then "Ahem" again. Reluctantly, she and Matt separated.

A paunchy man in an ill-fitting gray suit stood next to them, mopping his forehead with a large white handkerchief. "I am so sorry," he said. "My car, it is a disaster. I am late. Please forgive me."

"For what?" Mo asked.

"I am the photographer." He looked from one to the other. "I am to take pictures." When she and Matt continued to stare blankly at him, he said, "I am, am I not, talking to Mr. and Mrs. Matthew Vining?"

Matt turned to Mo and winked, then faced the photographer again, with a poker face. "Not really," he said, "but we're getting there."

Epilogue

As they were going through Customs at San Francisco International Airport, Matt watched while Mo explained to the Customs inspector, very sweetly, what all her purchases were and who they were for and how much they cost, even though she couldn't seem to find the receipts and how she knew they were here somewhere, if he would just be patient while she looked through her purse, until the official gazed at the heavens, muttered something under his breath and let her through without a penalty.

Mo slung her huge purse onto the cart Matt had rented, and, arm in arm, they came through the Arrivals gate just in time for homecoming pictures. As the photographer, a slim young man in a loud polka-dot shirt, danced around them, directing them in various poses, Matt said to Mo, "You know, I think I've figured you out."

"Let me in on it, so we'll both know."

"You seem scattered and mercurial, but underneath, I suspect, you're a rock."

She threw her arms around his neck. "And you, beneath that controlling, orderly exterior beats the heart of a marshmallow."

"Marshmallow?"

"Marshmallow."

"Well, this marshmallow loves you."

"And this rock loves you." Their kiss drew exclamations of approval from the photographer, who asked for another one.

"First," Matt said to Mo, pulling her body even more tightly to his, "I propose we travel some more together, dine a lot and make love all the time."

"Sounds like a plan."

"You could even have a field of expertise."

"We starting on that again?"

"No, listen. You could be a travel expert. You have all the makings of a great one, trust me. You could be a guest on my show...or we could have a show together!"

Mo leaned back and eyed him dubiously. Why did she suddenly feel as though they'd changed places? "Uh, Matt, aren't you getting a little carried away?"

"No. Listen. 'Dining With Vining' could be changed to 'The Matt and Mo Show.'"

"Excuse me?" she said, raising one eyebrow sardonically.

"Okay," Matt said graciously, "'The Mo and Matt Show.'"

Grinning, Mo shook her head. The man of her dreams was right here, right now, not silver-eyed on the Danube, but brown-eyed and in America. And dear, sweet *Nagyanya* had made it all happen. *Koszonom szepen,* she whispered silently to her grandmother. Thank you.

Aloud, she said, "Nah. You can have top billing, just as long as I can have you." She stood on tiptoe to kiss him soundly. "'The Matt and Mo Show' it is."

*   *   *   *   *

If you've enjoyed *Summer Loving*,
then be sure to take a look at some of our other titles.
Our Temptation® series is known for this kind
of fun-filled and sexy stories.
Check out our special BLAZE
titles—they're red hot!

Turn the page for a sneak preview of

SCANDALIZED!

by

Lori Foster

Scandalized!

Lori Foster

Out of sheer necessity, he pulled the car off the main street and onto a small dirt road that led to a dead end. When Tony was younger, he and his brother had come here to make out with girls. In those days there was a wide cornfield, but it had been replaced by a small park with a street lamp. Obviously things had changed, but the premise was the same. Isolation.

Despite the fact that he was sweating, he left the car running, for it was a cold night in early November. He killed the lights, though, giving himself some illusionary concealment. When he turned to face her, he already had his mouth open to start his argument, but he was brought up short by the picture she presented.

Moonlight poured over her, revealing the sheen of

dark hair, the shape of her ears, her high arched brows. Her eyelashes left long feathery shadows on her cheeks and shielded her eyes from his gaze. Her hands were folded in her lap. She appeared somehow very unsure of herself...vulnerable. It wasn't a look he was used to, not from her. She lifted her gaze to his face, and once again he felt that deep frustration.

It wasn't that Olivia was beautiful. She was by far the most elegant woman he'd ever known, but she wasn't classically beautiful. He had dated more attractive women, made love to them, had long-standing affairs with them that had left him numb. But Olivia was the only woman whose personality, intelligence and disposition were attractive enough to entice him into asking her to carry his child. That was something. More than something, actually, when you figured it was usually looks that drew a man first, and the other, more important features of a woman that kept him drawn.

When he remained quiet, she said, "I know what I'm asking seems absurd. After all, you could have any woman you want, and after knowing you for so long, it's obvious you don't particularly want me. That's okay, because up until you mentioned your plan, I hadn't really thought about wanting you, either.

"But you see, I've made my career everything." Her hands twisted in her lap and her voice shook. "Just as you don't want any involvements now, neither do I. That's why the idea seems so perfect. I haven't taken the time or the effort to get to know very many men, and almost never on an intimate level. These days, only an idiot would indulge in casual sex. But starting a relationship isn't something I want, either. So I thought, maybe we could both get what we wanted."

Tony searched her face, feeling dumbfounded. Surely she wasn't suggesting what he thought she was. "I want a baby. What is it you want, Olivia?"

She turned her head away from him and looked out the window. Sounding so unlike herself, she whispered in a small voice, "I want a wild, hot, never-to-be-forgotten affair. For two weeks. If during that time I conceive, the baby will become yours, and we'll go on with the rest of your plans. If I don't conceive, I'll be on my way and you can find another woman who, hopefully, will prove more fertile. You won't owe me a thing.

* * *

Temptation® turns up the heat in BLAZE.
Look out for Scandalized!
by Lori Foster, available in July 1998

MILLS & BOON®

Penny Jordan

COLLECTOR'S EDITION

Look out for the Penny Jordan Collector's Edition—a
selection of her most popular stories, published in
beautifully designed volumes for you
to collect and cherish.

Starting with *You Owe Me* and *Lovers Touch* in June 1998,
there are two books every month for ten months, so
you can build your very own personal set of Penny's
finest romances.

Available from WH Smith, John Menzies, Tesco,
Asda, Martins, Volume One and all good
paperback stockists at £3.10 each.

**Mail-in for free gifts
—see books for details**

LAURA VAN WORMER

❧⟡❧

Just for the Summer

Nothing prepares Mary Liz for the summer she spends in
the moneyed town of East Hampton, Long Island. From
the death of one of their own, Mary Liz realises that these
stunningly beautiful people have some of the ugliest
agendas in the world.

*"Van Wormer,…has the glamorama Hampton's scene down to
a T. (Just for the Summer is) as voyeuristic as it is fun."*
—Kirkus Reviews

1-55166-439-9
AVAILABLE NOW IN PAPERBACK

EMILIE RICHARDS

RUNAWAY

Runaway is the first of an intriguing trilogy.

Krista Jensen is desperate. Desperate enough to pose as a young
prostitute and walk the narrow alley ways of New Orleans.
So it's with relief that Krista finds herself a protector in
the form of Jess Cantrell. Grateful for his help,
she isn't sure she can trust him.

Trusting the wrong man could prove fatal.

1-55166-398-8
AVAILABLE NOW IN PAPERBACK

They were only watching...

ERICA SPINDLER

Shocking Pink

A chilling psychological suspense from the critically acclaimed author of *Fortune, Forbidden Fruit* and *Red*.

Spindler delivers *"a high adventure of love's triumph over twisted obsession."*

—Publishers Weekly

MIRA®

1-55166-415-1
AVAILABLE FROM JULY 1998